Charles Dickens' Best Stories

Charles Dickens' Best Stories

EDITED AND WITH AN INTRODUCTION
BY MORTON DAUWEN ZABEL

Hanover House, Garden City, New York

Contents

Introduction

INTRODUCTION

by Morton Dauwen Zabel

I

The world knows Dickens as the author of fifteen novels, of which a larger number are still read or remembered by the general public of modern readers than is the case with any other English novelist. He is also known universally for one shorter tale, *A Christmas Carol*, which has been, ever since its first appearance more than a century ago, in 1843, the unrivaled parable, favorite, and classic among English tales of Christmas. What is less well known or largely forgotten among his readers today is that Dickens was much more than a writer of novels. During the almost forty years of his career as an author he was continuously occupied as a journalist, editor, writer of sketches and stories for popular newspapers and magazines, of essays, editorials, and travel reports, of plays and entertainments, and of an enormous quantity of letters—in addition to all of which he rounded out his life as a hugely successful performer of readings from his works in England and America. Few careers in literature have been as densely and variously crowded. His energy—which was further involved in complex and taxing family affairs, in public causes and projects, and in the incessant demands of his enormous popular fame—was unresting from the beginning of his life to its end. Even today, ninety years after his death in 1870, a large part of his correspondence and miscellaneous writing has never appeared in book form. The standard collections of his fiction usually fill some twenty or twenty-two volumes. At least half again that number would be needed to hold even the part of his correspondence and minor writings that survives.

Many novelists have written shorter tales in the intervals of their longer books, and some of them—from Hawthorne, Turgenev, Tolstoy, and Flaubert to James, Joyce, and Hemingway—have not only expressed their genius quite as fully in the briefer forms as in their full-length novels but have made radical and original contributions to the art of the short story. It happens that none of these men were Englishmen. The tale and short story lagged in England as literary forms during the century in which they were seriously developed in America, France, and Russia. This is perhaps one reason why Dickens's tales occupy a minor place among his works. But a better reason is that it was in his novels that his genius expressed itself in its fullest strength of vision and invention. His genius was of a kind that required the full scale of the novel—and of the novel in its most expansive, all-inclusive, and comprehensive dimensions—to realize itself adequately. The scale of his imagination was immense. It accommodated itself only incidentally or marginally to lesser occasions. And since the practical conditions that shaped his life and dictated his industry required him to begin a new novel almost as soon as—and sometimes before—he had finished an old one, he was seldom allowed to rest or devote himself seriously to the shorter forms of narrative in the intervals between his longer books. Not until the last decade of his life did he begin to space these more widely. (In his first ten years as a writer he produced six full-scale novels; in his second, five; in his third, three; in his last five years a single unfinished book.) Considering the size, scope, and invention of his novels it is astonishing that he had the energy to produce his huge quantity of miscellaneous work; but large in bulk though this is, the fame of the novels has been such, from 1837 to the present day, that they have inevitably towered over everything else he wrote.

The inference is encouraged that his shorter tales are at best by-products or marginalia of his greater productions. This is true to an extent, but with certain qualifications. Dickens did not cultivate the short tale as an art form with rules and values of its own. He had no theory of the *conte* or *nouvelle* such as was shaping itself in France or among French-influenced foreign writers in his century. He took the short story very much as he found it: it was what had come down to him from the past—a newspaper sketch, a journalistic feature or filler, a bit of popular folklore, a "character," a fireside or Christmas tale, a holiday entertainment. He was to have no important influence on the future art of the story or tale. Yet it is always necessary to know an author, and especially a literary master, complete, and to see him in all the manifestations—however miscellaneous or marginal—of his creative powers. And since so large a part of Dickens's life was involved in journalism and popular entertainment, it becomes a matter of importance to see what these lifelong activities counted for in his achievement, and what they did to shape and direct his imaginative genius.

It is a fact of major importance that Dickens's novels derive closely from, and were strongly conditioned by, his career as a writer of serials or weekly and monthly publications. Their content—plots, situations, characters—as much as their form, was to a large degree dictated by the practical conditions under which they were written. Dickens, who was certainly an artist, was no art-writer or art-novelist. That type of craftsman, who was to become elevated to a heroic or sacerdotal rank in nineteenth-century France, scarcely existed in mid-Victorian England. We may take Jane Austen as the great example of the English novelist earlier in that century who wrote as far as it is possible to write in complete independence of practical or journalistic literary conditions, and there were other isolated cases—Peacock, for one—of the fiction writer who held himself aloof from the demands and pressures of the vast emerging reading public. Half a century after Dickens began his career the aesthetic novelist put in his appearance in England, following the approved French models of his type. But the great mass of Victorian fiction, its cruder as well as its greater manifestations, was based on popular taste, popular preference, the claims of the general reader. Scott had appealed to that standard; so, whatever their greater sophistication or intellectual ambition, did Thackeray, Trollope, George Eliot, and even, we are surprised to discover, the more recalcitrant or rebellious novelists of a later day, Meredith, Hardy, George Moore. Contemptuous though some of these may have been of the common reader, and stubbornly though they may have tried to improve his standards, none of them entirely disdained him. Most of these writers serialized their novels (when they could) in magazines of wide circulation; some of them condescended to cut, censor, or modify their pages in the interests of popular approval. The reading public—monster, tyrant, or despot though it might seem—was always there to hold the whip-hand over the writer. If the reader disapproved of what he was given, he stopped buying it. If he grew bored, he stopped reading. If his prejudices were offended, he howled his protest and the author or editor, unless he was a man of exceptional courage, dropped the offending article like a ticking bomb. Meredith trimmed his earlier books to avoid these risks; Thackeray, as editor of the *Cornhill Magazine*, broke off the serialization of Ruskin's *Unto This Last* when it brought the wrath of his subscribers down on his head; Hardy obediently excised the more scandalous or outspoken passages in his novels to make them acceptable to magazines. Dickens, greatest of the purveyors of popular entertainment to the Victorian public, watched his monthly sales figures with perpetual anxiety, and when the readers of *Martin Chuzzlewit* gave signs that they were becoming bored with an English story they found themselves reading once too often, he was quick to use his recent experiences on his first trip to the United States in 1842 and to send Martin and Mark Tapley off on their American adventures in order to entice the public with something novel. Popular writers in the twentieth century labor under these same risks, but we have come to expect the serious artist to ignore them. Perhaps no writer in any age does so entirely; in the nineteenth century and in England, almost no writer did.

This state of affairs is usually taken to be damaging to literature. It curbs, inhibits, and trips up the writer and his art; and when the writer rises in rebellion against it, he indicts the public as his first and strongest enemy. That public, the solid mass of bourgeois taste and prejudice, was a formidable force in the Victorian age. In France it provided the moral and aesthetic rebels with a powerful antagonist and the villain of their creed as artists. Dickens stood in a divided and ambiguous relation to it; in fact his ambivalence of attitude toward his readers is a central factor in his genius and creation. He hung on the public's demands; he kept his fingers on its pulse; his monthly sales figures were a continuous harassment and obsession of his working life. But he also wrote—in spite of his sentimental and psychological relations with the great mass of his readers—in constant resistance to their prejudices. As a critic of vested interests and institutions he worked against the grain—his own grain as well as the public's grain, the massive strength of the bourgeois tyrant. He was in more ways than one that typical creature of his age, the divided man: divided within himself but also divided between his necessary identification of himself with the mass society of his time and his own stubborn identity as an artist, rebel, and resister of convention. In this fact lies an essential clue to his role in his century, and to his peculiar achievement in art.

When an author writes under such conditions, he is obviously never going to be a self-defined, self-determined, or self-sufficient artist. He will be no Jane Austen, Flaubert, Pater, or Henry James. He will be a very much more mixed up and confused creator, and when his powers of mind and will are weak he will be worsted by his situation. But if he has the genius to survive it, he may gain something for what he loses. His books may not be self-contained units; they may jerk from climax to climax to hold the attention of their weekly or monthly serial-readers; they may be forced to break up into episodes, side issues, sub-plots, digressions, and irrelevancies to keep their public diverted. But they will also be obliged to keep themselves continuously alerted to new sources of interest, new ways of invention, topics of current interest which may enrich their substance and the substance of fiction generally. They may fail radically when it comes to purifying, concentrating, or cleansing the art of fiction of its dregs, adulterations, and sentimentalities. But they may add something of importance to its life, its vitality, its historical meaning. In doing so they are likely to invigorate the energy on which the craft of fiction counts for its survival and its future.

Dickens's great European counterpart on this score, as on many others, is Balzac. Like Balzac, he wrote for a public avid for excitement and eager to see its life portrayed in terms of vigorous, thrilling drama. Like Balzac, he brought a serious critical mind to the portrayal of his century, but he carried into this project everything the public expected of him—melodrama, sentimentality, thrills, theatrical effects, romantic glamour, lurid highlights, sinister mystery, and heavily underscored moral meaning. Like Balzac, too, he kept himself continuously on the alert for whatever his age offered in the way of excitement or novelty to enliven his stories. He may not have gone to Balzac's lengths in drawing on such contemporary novelties or notions as phrenology, spiritism, scientific fads and theories, or the machinations of high finance. But whatever fell into his hand in the way of new ideas, sensational events, or social phenomena sooner or later went into his books—the modern police-detective, the roaring monster of the modern railway, the modern financial swindler, *nouveau riche* social climbing, mesmerism, hypnotism, the modern factory system, trade unionism, class warfare. All these play their roles in his novels, and with them he combined everything he had inherited from the past in the way of drama and melodrama, Gothic mystery, domestic sentiment, folk humor, and romance. The result was a vast mixture of old and new, convention and novelty, the expected and the unexpected. At the same time that he summed up the past history of the English novel, he forecast its future explorations. Like Balzac's, his work forms a great divide or watershed in modern fiction. Past and future join in the excitement, disorder, and conflict of the age he took it as his special task to portray in his books.

Dickens's shorter tales are products of the same conditions that produced his novels. And since the short tale has always served the novelist as an opportunity for bringing his central themes or ideas into focus, we find it serving this purpose in the great mass of Dickens's work. He wrote around a hundred pieces that may, in one sense or another, be defined as stories, and they form, taken in their entirety, a remarkable inventory of his larger creation. Moreover, they gave him opportunities to employ certain themes and devices which the realism of his novels did not permit. Thus it is in his shorter stories that we find him writing his tales of ghosts and specters, of fantasy and the supernatural, his experiments in exotic or occult themes, his parables and allegories. It is true that all these elements figure in one form or another in his longer novels. In his short stories they become explicit, overt, intentional. The stories may be said to define or isolate the germs and sources of his greater achievements. They frame and outline his progress as a creative artist. They also offer many moments of charm and significance to readers who want to experience the world and genius of Dickens in their full dimensions. Hardly a page of them is without its authentic Dickensian quality, and perhaps none of them could possibly be mistaken for the work of anyone but Dickens.

II

A writer's beginnings frequently offer the most interesting facts about him, and there are few beginnings in literature more exhilarating than those of the young Dickens. Born in 1812, he was only a few years over twenty when, putting the troubles of his childhood and youth behind him and determining to free himself from his family's misfortunes and the wage slavery of parliamentary reporting, he made his first forays into literature as a writer of sketches of London life for the *Morning Chronicle* in 1834. They were so successful that he soon extended them to the *Evening Chronicle*, then to *Bell's Life in London and Sporting Chronicle* and two other periodicals, found that he had made a name for himself by these journalistic exercises, and in 1836 saw his first book published at the age of twenty-four under the title *Sketches by Boz*. (Like other popular journalists and illustrators of the time, he wrote under a whimsical pseudonym. "Boz," as Dickens explained, was the nickname used in his family for his young brother Augustus, "whom I had dubbed Moses in honor of the Vicar of Wakefield; which, being facetiously pronounced through the nose became Boses, and, being shortened, became Boz. 'Boz' was a very familiar household word to me long before I became an author; and so I came to adopt it." It clung to him for informal and convivial purposes throughout his life.)

The young Dickens who took his first flight into authorship under this name is a greatly appealing figure. He comes to us out of the obscurity of lower middle-class English life bursting with the charm, humor, and ebullience of his early manhood, already a well-known companion, *bon vivant*, and young man-about-London—a typical and decidedly Dickensian young hero for his future books. He shows all the capacity for life, friendship, curiosity, and human sympathy that he put into his *Sketches*. He has launched himself on the world and on London, resolved to make his conquest of them and find a place for himself in the crowded scene of his age. Behind him lay a troubled childhood and youth—his family's fall from respectability; his father's irresponsibility, debts, and imprisonment in the Marshalsea Prison; his schooling broken off after the short days of happiness at Chatham; the breakup of the family home; the anguished weeks he spent in the cellars of Warren's blacking factory when his parents put him to work in their clumsy effort to make his small wages contribute to the family's desperate financial situation; the dread of poverty and disgrace these experiences left with him. The memory of these humiliations was never to be forgotten by Dickens. It haunts and overshadows his future life and recurs repeatedly in the ordeals to which he subjects his heroes.

By dint of a stubborn resolution he has for the moment put his troubles behind him. He has learned shorthand, made himself an efficient reporter, trained himself to write, and broken into the London world of newspaper offices, theaters, family homes, and youthful merrymaking. He has given free rein to his natural gifts for friendship, conviviality, and fun. Most important of all, he has begun to exercise his spontaneous powers of curiosity and imagination. Before him lies the spectacle of London and England at the threshold of a new age—a world expressly inviting his exploration and conquest. He comes into the teeming life of the capital with a provincial boy's envy and astonishment. He was not a Londoner by birth; he had been born at Landport, Portsea, in Hampshire, while his father was stationed there as a clerk in the Navy Pay Office. The most impressionable years of his boyhood had been spent at Chatham, near Rochester, where his father was later stationed and where he spent the only happy period of his childhood—so happy that when, years later, he was a rich and famous author, able to set up a country home for himself, he returned to the old scene and bought the house at nearby Gad's Hill which his father had once pointed out to him as a suitable establishment for a successful man. When he rejoined his family in London at the age of twelve he found them slipping swiftly from the precarious standing in respectable society to which they had ascended from their servant-class origins and overtaken by bankruptcy and disgrace. Already at that early age Dickens saw London as a dangerous maelstrom of poverty and riches, good fortune and bad. Now, having become a young man, he determined to brave its perils and survive in it. He is that typical youth of the nineteenth-century novel—the boy out to succeed; and while he is still far too English and innocent to fit into the shoes of Stendhal's or Balzac's calculating heroes, he is their English counterpart. The world lies before him, and he means to conquer it, with nothing but his own gifts and ambition to help him.

The *Sketches by Boz* are the perfectly appropriate prelude to Dickens's achievement. They gave him an opportunity expressly designed for defining his ground and staking out his territory as a novelist. They form a conspectus of his world and indicate one of the radical traits of his genius. For it will soon become a central fact of Dickens's fiction that it attempts to be comprehensive and all-embracing in its portrayal of its age. He is not one of the novelists who focuses the microscope of his imagination on a single concentrated organism of life—a village, a county, a given province, or a chosen segment of society. He is poles removed from Jane Austen at one end of his century and from Hardy at the other. He belongs to a quite different and perhaps more typical order of nineteenth-century literature. Already at twenty-two his mind is stirring with a sense that a new age is in the making, a new world about to come into being. The instinct of history possesses him. Modest, miscellaneous, homely, and humdrum though most of the episodes that make up the *Sketches* are—and though they almost entirely confine themselves to the scene that is to become the special domain of Dickens's imagination, London itself—they suggest an organism stirring with signs of a larger life, ominously pregnant of change and disorder, and waiting for the hour of history to strike.

This may not be the impression one gains of the *Sketches* if one reads them one by one, or in a small selection. Their scenes of street life, home life, boardinghouses, theaters, law courts, Christmas feasts, skylarkings and junketings, "young gentlemen" and "young couples" may appear too modest for such larger claims. They are consciously random, droll, picturesque, domestic, bourgeois, miscellaneous. The Dickens who wrote them is still the child of an older order, the Regency England of his boyhood to which he will presently pay his tribute in *Pickwick* and to which he was to look back, from the stormier scene of his middle years, as to an England of simpler life and happier traditions, still unclouded by the evils that are soon to shut down on it as the ambitious, industrial, smoke-blackened and strife-ridden Victorian age moves forward on its headlong course. Yet the *Sketches* are not entirely simple and picturesque; they take note of other signs than those of domestic complacency and social stability. Criminals, prisons, beggars, drunkards, slum life, the stupidity of courts and the lethargy of lawmakers, the stirrings of ambition and the germs of evil and conflict, are also parts of the picture. Dickens is consciously charting the social, moral, and political conditions that will shape the drama of his most powerful future novels. The seeds of strife, injustice, and revolution are already being gathered for their later "sowing and reaping."

Dickens was never to abandon the scheme and scale laid down for his future work in the *Sketches*. They form not only his literary apprenticeship but his moral and historical point of departure. His next book and first work of unmistakable genius, the *Pickwick Papers*, will become, within its framework of the adventures of Mr. Pickwick and his fellow members of the Pickwick Club, a kind of roving survey or picaresque inventory of England and English life—a drama which begins in innocence and gradually tumbles into the snares and pitfalls of malice, greed, and danger. His work as editor and journalist will lead Dickens to project during the following decades other fictional miscellanies of English life and character—*Master Humphrey's Clock* and *The Uncommercial Traveller*. His editorial writings of the eighteen-fifties and -sixties in his two magazines, *Household Words* and *All the Year Round*, will oblige him to tackle the scene around him from innumerable angles. His novels based on a hero's adventures, descendants of the old picaresque line of storytelling—*Oliver Twist, Nicholas Nickleby, Barnaby Rudge, Martin Chuzzlewit, David Copperfield*, and *Great Expectations*—will canvass English and modern life through all its gradations, variety, class divisions, heights and depths. And when he comes to write his greatest dramas of social conflict and evil—*Dombey and Son, Bleak House, Little Dorrit, Our Mutual Friend*—Dickens will fasten on these conditions of latent unrest, hostility, alienation, and incipient revolution as his clues to the modern condition of life and the perils of the ominous future.

III

Presently, however, another institution invites his attention—the English Christmas—and it inspires the best-known and most popular of his shorter tales. During the eighteen-forties Dickens wrote his five longer *Christmas* "books"—*A Christmas Carol*, *The Chimes*, *The Cricket on the Hearth*, *The Battle of Life*, and *The Haunted Man*. And during the next two decades he wrote an annual feature for his magazines *Household Words* and *All the Year Round* in the form of a Christmas tale or entertainment—the twenty-one shorter pieces collected as his *Christmas Stories*. These include not only his most popular holiday tales but also his most celebrated writings in another and related vein, the ghost story.

Ghosts and Christmas have traditionally gone hand in hand in European tale-telling. In England their companionship is venerable: it goes back to folklore, old wives' tales, the lore of taverns, cloisters, wayside inns, and country houses. Their conjunction, old as it is, is on the face of it an incongruous one. Christmas is proverbially the season of peace, jollity, harmony, good feeling, and benevolence. Ghosts are symptoms of something else—discomfort, disturbance, mystery, the bad conscience and the uneasy. Dickens was entirely true to character in perpetuating their combination. He followed an established custom; he supplied an expected Christmas dish. Christmas was of all holidays his own favorite, the high season of his year, and the special occasion for the jubilations, merrymakings, and family entertainments he reveled in and of which he soon made himself a master conjurer. His Christmases in his London homes or at Gad's Hill were the festive climaxes of the year for his family and friends. We read, in his biography, of mammoth feasts, lavish charades, and extravagant outlays of expense and gift-giving. His feeling for Christmas in its religious meaning may have been slight or conventional, but his delight in its human significance was profound and incurable. Queen Victoria had recently brought the rites and ceremonies of the German Christmas into English life; the holiday had become newly festive, a symptom of the bourgeois domestic harmony dear to Victorian life, and Dickens was quick to make himself its celebrant and poet. He was by nature exactly fitted for the laureateship of the English Christmas, which has always been one of his first titles to popularity. The Christmas episodes form a kind of climax of cheer and brightness in the *Sketches by Boz*; the Christmas scene at Dingley Dell is one of the most delightful and immortal passages in the *Pickwick Papers*. Even today it is impossible to celebrate Christmas in the English-speaking world without thinking of the aura and atmosphere Dickens wove around the season.

Ghosts were an equally characteristic part of his emotional and imaginative furniture. They came to him as an element of his literary inheritance, partly out of common folklore and convention but also out of the Gothic tales that rivaled the picaresque story in his literary ancestry. Like writers of far more sophisticated minds—Hawthorne, Hardy, and Henry James—he could not resist the appeal of specters, hallucinations, and supernatural visitants. But they were also a necessary element of his imagination, messengers from the darker regions of the mind and soul who in one form or another haunt his books from first to last. His Christmas stories present them in their dual Dickensian character—as elements of folklore but also as symptoms of the secret life of character and conscience which is to become a haunting presence in his novels.

There is a large population of ghosts, revenants, and specters in Dickens's longer novels. But in the novels, where he writes as a realist, these must be given the form and shape of actual men and women. Yet there is always something weird and unnatural about them. Fagin, in *Oliver Twist*, is never quite a real man. His appearance is fiendish and spectral; he never appears in broad daylight but creeps and slinks through an atmosphere of filthy darkness; he hovers like an evil omen over the thugs and apprentices who inhabit his thieves' kitchen; when he and Monks peer through the window at the sleeping Oliver, they materialize like the horrid shapes of a nightmare; his touch is clammy and vise-like; he lurks like a fiend or devil in the streets and dens of his murky world. Quilp in *The Old Curiosity Shop* is another ogre of whom one is never quite sure whether he is man or brute, human being or monster. When Jonas Chuzzlewit's crimes begin to haunt him they take the shape of all but visible presences, driving him to his destruction and providing the plot of *Martin Chuzzlewit* with scenes of fury-haunted guilt that were to give a reader like Dostoevsky some of his clues to the conscience-stricken drama of "the possessed." The ill-fated houses of Dickens's novels are invariably stalked by the invisible presences of fate, secret crime, and evil conscience—Mr. Dombey's gloomy mansion in London; Mr. Tulkinghorn's eerie house in Lincoln's Inn Fields, where "foreshortened Allegory" points his warning finger from the ceiling; Chesney Wold in *Bleak House*, whose dripping Ghost's Walk echoes with the tread of the doom of the Dedlocks; Mrs. Clennam's hateful house in *Little Dorrit*, where the creak of an evil past and its stifled lives is made audible in the rotting timbers; Miss Havisham's Satis House in *Great Expectations*, with Miss Havisham herself in her rotting bridal gown a living revenant from the dead past; the opium den, ghostly cathedral, and gatehouse in *Edwin Drood* which combine to set a scene in which murder, secret vice, and a demon-driven villain join with the brightest colors of the English Christmas to create one of Dickens's most powerful dramas of crime and mystery. And this is to name only a few of the scenes and characters in Dickens which hover between the real world and the unreal—links between the living and the dead, the human and the unearthly.

Dickens's ghost stories of Christmas all take place in the borderland that divides these two domains of his imagination. But here he is not obliged to follow the dictates of realism: his ghosts now become actual, visible presences. Some of them are amiable, like the dwarves and elfin creatures of the bells in *The Chimes*—gnomes or sprites that step straight out of Victorian Christmas pictures, or benevolent fairies out of the old Christmas pantomimes. But the best of them are murky, discomforting specters who issue from a darker region—from the vindictive soul, the tormented conscience, the dead past that refuses to lie buried, the spirit that feeds on a hatred of life. Marley's ghost and the three Christmas specters in *A Christmas Carol* are typical of what they represent. They are haunters of the guilt-ridden mind of the man who is possessed by a fear of life or love and has become a hater of happiness; and Scrooge is Dickens's classic portrait of the "haunted man" out of whose guilty conscience such specters issue.

Almost all the stories Dickens wrote for or about Christmas have a common theme—the breaking down of hatred, fear, or hostility, and the release of the mortified spirit into the harmony that comes through love and forgiveness. Whether the tales actually introduce the Christmas season and its beneficent influence or not, this is their running lesson. In other words, they are written as fables or exempla. They epitomize in concise terms the theme that informs his larger novels and that constitutes one of the basic ideas of his moral and humanistic philosophy. The love, reconciliation, or surrender to the forces of harmony and justice at which most of his longer novels arrive in their closing chapters are here written out, plain and explicit, in the final sentence. This is the method of fables from time immemorial.

They are conceived in a didactic formula, and we listen to them with a divided mind. This is indeed the way things should be; this is no doubt the truth as we would like it to be; but the fact remains that this is the way truth seldom manifests itself or the way life usually works out. Therefore a fable, to be effective, has to be told in such a way that it forces us to suspend our disbelief. We are made to pause and hear a word of counsel, sage advice, or homely wisdom before returning to the confusion and betrayals of life as it is. Dickens took the Christmas season as such a moment of pause in the hectic distractions of the year—an occasion for idealizing the ability of men to put their greeds, lusts, and selfishness away and give thought to the possibility of love and happiness. His villains and evildoers go through the traditional paces of the transformation scene in a Christmas pantomime. Vice is transformed into virtue; fond or selfish delusions are dispelled; love and harmony are triumphant; and Tiny Tim's "God bless Us, Every One!" invariably brings down the curtain.

This didacticism is, of course, an essential part of Dickens's character. His Christmas stories merely gave him a chance to express it openly, and to make a seasonal toast on its behalf. By using the apparatus of the folk fable or the ghost story he was able to concentrate a moral theme that runs through his novels and that constitutes their essential teaching. But neither his novels nor his tales would have survived out of the countless numbers of such Victorian moral tracts had they contained nothing but the crude stuff of moral righteousness and complacency. What is true of Dickens's novels is true of his shorter tales: their argument is weighted in favor of virtue; rewards and punishments are meted out according to the rules of conventional justice; but the serious truth in them, the force that holds our attention, is likely to be the force of evil and human perversity rather than that of goodness and simple virtue.

It is Scrooge in his cantankerous meanness whom we remember from *A Christmas Carol*, not the Scrooge who miraculously becomes a benevolent, gift-bringing Father Christmas. It is Doctor Jeddler in the arrogance of his flaunting cynicism who lingers in the memory from *The Battle of Life*, rather than the man who is converted by the loss of his favorite daughter—"one little unit in the great absurd account"—to the "love, deep-anchored, [which] is the portion of all human creatures." It is Tackleton, the ogrish toy-merchant in *The Cricket on the Hearth*, living on children all his life while remaining their implacable enemy, despising his toys and fashioning hideous scare-makers out of them, who gives bite to this "fairy tale of home," rather than the Tackleton whose disappointment over the marriage of his betrothed, May Fielding, to Edward Plummer converts him into a "hearty, kind, and happy man." It may be an evidence of modern perversity that sees the evil in Dickens as more convincing than his good. It may be because his exponents of virtue are so often encumbered with Victorian smugness and sanctimony that we tend to discredit them. And we can easily overlook the genuinely valid goodness he often portrays in his heroes or representatives of decency— they are by no means all vapid or sanctimonious. Yet there is no question that Dickens's vision of wrong and evil issued from profound sources in his emotional and imaginative make-up, and that his depiction of these forces challenged him in a way that the simpler formulas of virtue never could. Writing in a tradition so steeped in the sentimentalities of domestic and bourgeois complacency, his instinct of perversity and evil came to his rescue as a realist and writer of tragic vision. Though he tried to show, in his work as a whole, that humanity is linked and harmonized by the bonds of love and devotion, the final effect of his work is that mankind is more profoundly united by the forces of fear, guilt, and retributive justice, and that it is these forces that search out the truth that finally tests and liberates the essential virtue in man.

They became an increasing prepossession of Dickens as he advanced into his novels of the eighteen-fifties and -sixties; and now his shorter tales have the effect of being holidays from the somber dramas of *Bleak House, Hard Times, Little Dorrit*, and *Our Mutual Friend*. The modern reader may be inclined to minimize the fact that his pictures of domestic and common life, his interludes of humor and lightheartedness, remain an essential part of Dickens, survivals of the high spirits that made *Pickwick* a masterpiece of comedy and that provide a leaven of wit or sentiment to lighten even the darkest of his social dramas. His "dark novels" continue to be enlivened by vestiges of the old comic invention, absurdity, and outlandish humor that had created Sam Weller, Alfred Jingle, Dick Swiveller, the Crummles caravan, and Sairey Gamp in his first decade. His pictures of Victorian home life, however idealized, form a necessary part of his record of his age. So in his later holiday tales he could revert to the spell of his early humor in a story like "The Holly-Tree" or "Somebody's Luggage," or write a story of pathetic misfortune and reassuring sympathy in "Mrs. Lirriper's Lodgings." He never entirely lost his faith in the regenerative powers of the human spirit. Vexed, sinister, or bedeviled though he saw his fellow men to be, and threatening the passions of greed, power, and ruthlessness in the world around him, he clung to his confidence that the good instinct at the heart of humanity would survive and reassert itself as the hope of the future. Rebirth, resurrection, and moral victory are written into the conclusions of *Little Dorrit, A Tale of Two Cities*, and *Great Expectations*. If it is a rebirth or victory humbled by a knowledge of the cruelties of life or the stiff lessons of humility and abnegation, it is none the less convincing for that. Moral and spiritual success had never been facile achievements for Dickens's heroes and heroines. Now they are won only at the price of sacrifice, self-humbling, and self-knowledge, and it is that price that makes seriously and psychologically effective the dramas of Arthur Clennam, Sydney Carton, Pip, Bella Wilfer, and Eugene Wrayburn.

But the devil of perversity and human corruption keeps on erupting in these later years, sometimes springing out of the weakness of the human heart, sometimes out of the social or corporate forces of a predatory age. The pathetic story of "Doctor Marigold," steeped in the dyes of the deepest Dickensian sentiment, alternates with a tale like "Hunted Down," in which appears a hypocrite so consummate that he plots a scheme of insuring the life of another man and then attempting to poison him, with the result that he finds his crime foiled and destroys himself. Here Dickens resorted less to the conventions of his sentimental imagination than to the phenomena of modern crime. His Julius Slinkton is closely modeled on the criminal career of Thomas Griffiths Wainewright, the artist-poisoner who became for Dickens (as for Wilde several decades later) a fascinating example of criminality developing into an art. In "George Silverman's Explanation" we get a drama of class hostility in which Lady Fareway's frustrated passion for power wreaks itself on the intelligent decency of her victim, George, whose guardian, the offensive religionist Hawkyard, gave Dickens another occasion for indicting the moral sanctimony that had always been one of his strongest detestations. Such tales are obviously a part of the general indictment Dickens leveled in all his later novels against the forces of power, aggression, and hypocrisy he saw working in the society of his time. On occasion he defined those forces in the symbolic form that becomes one of his signs of artistic growth and maturity. The railway in "Mugby Junction" connects with the engine of destruction it had already been in *Dombey and Son*. The "Police-Detective" is a symptom of the evil that ramifies society, as he had already been in *Bleak House*. With such forces of danger, darkness, and sinister portent abroad in the world, it is only in his moments of detached or retrospective vision that Dickens recalls the long distance humanity has traveled from its original innocence, and it is only on such occasions of fitful lucidity that he can recapture that memory of childish ecstasy in a brief glimpse of innocent beauty like "A Child's Dream of a Star."

IV

His tales and sketches, taken even in a selection of their best examples such as the present volume offers, do much to help us define the kind of novelist Dickens was and to explain his meaning not only in his own century but in the twentieth, which has found itself obliged to assimilate his work to its own experience and art.

For well over a hundred years his books have been recognized as classics of English history and folklore—galleries of characters who have become a part of the legend of the race of which Dickens made himself, from his earliest years, the popular spokesman and laureate. They have contributed a greater number of human types to common memory and hearsay than any works but Shakespeare's—more, perhaps, than the works of even the greatest European novelists and dramatists. In his own age Dickens competed both with novelists who wrote for the great public audience and with those of a more sophisticated, intellectual, and philosophic kind. It can readily be argued that some of his rivals—Thackeray, Trollope, George Eliot, as well as predecessors like Jane Austen and Scott or followers like

Meredith, Hardy, and Henry James—surpassed him as artists, moralists, psychologists, satirists, or historians, or as writers who brought the intellectual history of their age into closer and more productive combination with their skill in drama and historical vision. Some were certainly purer and more consistent artists (Jane Austen, Henry James); some were more astute satirists and critics of society (Thackeray, Trollope, Meredith); Scott had a far richer historical material and instinct to draw on; George Eliot and Hardy had more serious minds and a more ambitious intellectual and moral vision. Two wrote books which by any definition have raised the novel to a higher level of artistic truth and insight than has yet been reached elsewhere in English fiction. In none of these capacities—aesthetic, historical, philosophic—was Dickens their equal or a writer of their conscious and original gifts. Yet in their scope of experience, in their inventive and dramatic range, and in their comprehensiveness of human and moral vision, his books may be said to surpass those of any of his English contemporaries, and perhaps any of his English successors, down to the present day. He is the English novelist who most invites and justifies comparison with the Europeans who established the scale and capacity of modern fiction at its greatest.

These claims for Dickens—obviously the statements of someone with a strong, if far from exclusive, prejudice in his favor—are doubtless debatable; in any case they have been debated by every critic of the English novel of the past hundred years. But they are statements that any return to the subject or memory of Dickens's books inspires. Today, after more than eighty years of progress in the art and sophistication of modern fiction, and after a considerable period of distinct abeyance in the reading and esteem of Dickens's works, he has been reclaimed by even the most astute modern criticism as one of the dominant figures of modern literature. He comes to us, with our present-day education on the art and destiny of the novel, as one of the most mixed and heterogeneous of writers. His elements still require sorting and discrimination; he is of all the major novelists of his age the most uneven, mixed, erratic, indeterminate, impure. It is always necessary to see him as an example of the artist riddled, vexed, and bedeviled by the age he lived in and by the complex mind and emotions he brought to its rendering. There have, during the past century and more, existed attitudes toward Dickens of every conceivable type—enthusiastic, infatuated, massively affectionate, skeptical, rigorously discriminatory, contemptuous, and even hostile. The one thing that has never altogether happened to him, as it has to some of his most illustrious contemporaries, is to become unread. He is one of the centers and sources of vitality in modern literature and criticism. Barely has one decade decided to dismiss him than the next revives him. It is possible that no other great novelist has had a more fluctuating critical reputation; it is certain that none has had a steadier popularity or a more persistent fame.

These are signs of his vitality, and one of them lies in the fact that neither his readers nor his critics are able to arrive at a simple or settled judgment on him. It is possible to do this with lesser or greater artists than Dickens was. The lesser are easier to define; the greater define and impose themselves. In artists of consistent mastery like Jane Austen, Turgenev, or Flaubert, the elements exist under so continuous a control, so self-defined and balanced a taste, that opinion on their merits has been almost consistent from their first appearance. In masters of high visionary or philosophic powers—Stendhal, Tolstoy, Dostoevsky, James, Melville, Proust—the case is inevitably more complicated, yet these too impress their genius in inescapable terms. It is possible to quarrel with them, differ with them, even resist them, but there is no ignoring the force of their intellects or imaginations, the scope of their vision and intelligence.

It was a particular feature of the nineteenth century, the age in which the modern novel came into its full powers and prestige, that it made its novelists ambitious to comprehend the wholeness of life and experience. A new world was consciously in the making. History was in a phase of convulsion. The inherited values of the past were in dispute, and those of the future were shrouded in doubt and enigma. The mere physical existence of men and nations was undergoing a process of systematic renovation. Society and science were in a state of continuous revolution. It is, of course, always possible for the artist to seize this condition in some oblique or partial aspect, to fix it under the microscope of his art in the form of a selected fragment. Much of the finest art of the past hundred years has done so: it has isolated the clue to man's existence in concentrated form—a lyric poem, a short story, a novel that treats some limited, fragmentary, self-defined phase of life that may be made to stand for the whole. But there is another and, in modern fiction, a more characteristic way of attacking the problem—the way of comprehension, inclusiveness, totality. This has been the way of the master novelists of the past century and a half—Balzac, Zola, Tolstoy, Dostoevsky, Proust, Joyce, Faulkner. In these the large and complex dimensions of their age have been matched by an equivalent largeness and massiveness of purpose. They saw that an epic phase of human history was in the making, and they resolved to attack it with a no less enormous courage. It is they who have established the modern novel as an epic novel—the form of modern writing best suited to taking over the ancient tradition of the epic and to doing what the classic epics did: to contain the whole scope and meaning of life in a single, exhaustive vision of human destiny.

Dickens is notable, and perhaps alone, among English novelists in belonging to their company. He had his English predecessors in this ambition—Defoe, Fielding, Scott. He had his contemporary rivals and followers—Thackeray, Trollope, Kipling, and Wells. But he remains the Englishman who best stands up to the test of being matched with the authentic epic-makers of modern fiction, and certainly the one who has been recognized for this capacity by the Europeans who have shown a similar purpose—Balzac, Hugo, Dostoevsky, and Proust.

An epic undertaking is more easily assumed than achieved. The word itself—like that other term that obsesses modern art and criticism, "myth"—has come to suggest an evasion rather than a mastery of the specific commitment and responsibility of literature. Yet there is no question that the events of the past century have forced literature to measure itself up to the two great traditions represented by the epic and the myth. Both these traditions descend from a primary function of art and imagination: to seize the life of man in terms of its historical and moral unity, its singleness of destiny, its archetypal forms of action, purpose, and meaning.

When an age is stable, settled, sure of itself and satisfied in its mode of life and thought, these traditions tend to lapse or weaken. Literature, like thought, then becomes rational, formal, self-contained. But when the conditions of an age are the opposite of stable—when life and history show themselves to be in a process of change, disruption, or confusion—reason seems no longer capable of subduing existence to design or idea. Some other means must be found for interpreting it and giving meaning to it. The nineteenth century prided itself on having found such means in its great guiding ideals—the ideas of progress, of reform, of evolution and perfectibility. But as the great century wore on these principles—the inspiration of optimists, progressivists, idealists, prophets of enlightenment and political or scientific faith—fell under the increasing suspicion of men of realistic or critical insight. Ideals, in fact, became the villains of the modern social and historical drama—deluders, disguisers of hypocrisy, betrayers of human fact and necessity, enemies of truth; and a whole phalanx of late nineteenth-century critics—Turgenev, Ibsen, Flaubert, Butler, Shaw, Zola, Mann—became their indicters and condemners. It became the ambition of such men to rescue their century from the delusions of abstraction, idealism, and moral hypocrisy.

To describe the Dickens of popular legend—the genial humorist, the sentimentalist, the celebrator of domestic happiness, the poet of middle-class life—as an ancestor of these men would be an abuse of argument; but of course that Dickens has long ago been dispelled and a much more serious and interesting writer has taken his place. None of his really perceptive critics, from Taine and Gissing to Shaw, T. S. Eliot, Humphry House, George Orwell, Edmund Wilson, and Sylvère Monod, has allowed the simplified Dickens of the earlier

legend to pre-empt the truer Dickens who wrote the books. That
Dickens, if we read him attentively, was not a simple man, artist, or
thinker. He was a man profoundly and inextricably involved in the
age in which he lived, its hopes and promise but also its confusions,
distractions, and desperations. His inheritance of the old English
idealistic values, his personal hope, ambition, and high spirits, were
shackled by vexations that plagued his life and mind progressively
as he advanced into his mature manhood and into the full claims of
the art he practiced. Even *Pickwick*, written in the full tide of his early
ebullience, has its vision of treachery and evil. *Oliver Twist* plunges
straight into the darkness of crime, violence, and human corruption.
The high-spirited youth who set out with a vigorous confidence to
make a success of himself in his age was from the beginning afflicted
by a sense of the traps and snares set for the unwary or the innocent
in life. A share of this feeling derived from the conventions of good
and evil he inherited. But as he advanced into his closer study of the
forces at work around him, and as his own complex nature applied itself to understanding them, he came to see the modern world and
human life as a whole. He was profoundly baffled by the duplicity,
alienation, and perversions at its root—perversions which no hopes
of his own, optimism about the future, or faith in simple virtue could
disguise from him.

It was the best of times, it was the worst of times, it was
the age of wisdom, it was the age of foolishness, it was the epoch
of belief, it was the epoch of incredulity, it was the season of
Light, it was the season of Darkness, it was the spring of hope, it
was the winter of despair, we had everything before us, we had
nothing before us, we were all going direct to Heaven, we were
all going direct the other way—

When he described the old regime in France before the onset of the
Revolution in the well-known opening lines of *A Tale of Two Cities*,
some twenty-five years after his beginnings in authorship, Dickens
summed up his experience of nineteenth-century man himself, and
immediately admitted it: ". . . in short, the period was so far like the
present period, that some of its noisiest authorities insisted on its
being received, for good or for evil, in the superlative degree of comparison only." And it became a habit and obsession of Dickens to
see all men sharing a common destiny in this condition of confusion
and self-division: to see them, in spite of their hostilities and estrange-
ments, as moving unconsciously toward a single doom from which no
subterfuge or ignorance could exempt them. John Forster, his friend
and biographer, once pointed out (in a passage of his *Life* singled out
by T. S. Eliot in his essay on "Wilkie Collins and Dickens") that

On the coincidences, resemblances and surprises of life Dickens liked especially to dwell . . . The world, he would say, was so much smaller than we thought it; we were all so connected by fate without knowing it; people supposed to be far apart were so constantly elbowing each other; and tomorrow bore so close a resemblance to nothing half so much as to yesterday.

To envisage the life of mankind under this ideal of unity is one thing. To see the world in which men live as profoundly threatened and baffled by the confusions and perversities of human nature is another. To reconcile these two visions without falsifying the facts of experience on the one hand or the spiritual capacities of humanity on the other is still a third. It was Dickens's ruling passion as a novelist to achieve all three of these aims—to bring into a single vision his sense of life's unity, his honesty as a realist, and his intuition of the common destiny that makes men morally responsible both for their ideals and for the truths of experience which present themselves in the form of suffering and evil. It is in his painful and stubborn progress toward this destination that we trace his maturity as a novelist, and it is by the growth of that purpose in his books that he establishes his claim to a validly epic comprehension of life and history.

The claim is most fully realized in his large-scale novels of modern life, but the substance of insight and reality that gives body to those complex, highly ramifying pictures of his age may also be traced in his lesser tales and writings. The fresh-eyed observer who wrote the *Sketchs by Boz*, the sentimental allegorist who wrote the Christmas stories, the tireless investigator of contemporary life who wrote the scores of minor tales and essays, is the same writer who combined all his findings in his major novels and made of these some of the most comprehensive records of modern life and history that the nineteenth century produced. They are comprehensive in their abstract design and intention, but they are also so in a way that is far more important to the artist in fiction—in their particularity, their detail of invention and observation, their fidelity to the facts of reality from which no conventions of sentiment, melodrama, or fantasy exempt the novelist. To bring idealism, convention, and artifice into effective combination with the actualities of experience is the special responsibility of the authentic epic; and it is the union of these elements that defines the vision that animates Dickens's creation.

While we read him from page to page we may forget the presence of this vision. We are diverted by his wit and absurdity, his comic and dramatic invention, his inexhaustible high spirits or responses to the spectacle of life. Or we are held by his enchanter's spell as he conjures his specters of sin and evil, dread or mystery, the ghostly presences that haunt the brain and heart. When his ideal of life expresses itself openly, it may do so in terms of a sentimental wish-fulfillment which modern realism rejects. But Dickens was the kind of writer who never succeeds in reducing himself to the single effect, the pure insight, or the perfect and self-contained forms of art. He comes to us in the vexed and complicated terms of his own character, and in the equally distracted vitality of the century in which he lived. But the vision that sustained and guided him is always there, waiting to declare itself behind the riddles, confusions, and defeats which his honesty forced him to recognize as the condition of life as it is. When it finally emerges from the great panorama of his books, we see it, feel the force and necessity of it, and recognize it as one of the most inspired portrayals of the life of man in modern literature.

Morton Dauwen Zabel

Prelude: The Opening Scene

Dickens's first book, *Sketches by Boz*, was published in two volumes in 1836, followed by a second series in 1837. These were the sketches and stories of London life that formed Dickens's literary apprenticeship and his introduction to the world as a writer. He began them with a sketch called "Mrs. Joseph Porter" in *The Monthly Magazine* (known as *The Old Monthly*) for January 1834; the first sketch to which he attached his pen name, "Boz," was the second part of "The Boarding-House" in the same magazine for August 1834. Most of the sketches, however, were written for *The Morning Chronicle* in 1834–36 and for *The Evening Chronicle* during 1835–36, with various others appearing in *Bell's Life in London and Sporting Chronicle* in 1835–36, in *The Carlton Chronicle of Politics, Literature, Science and Art* in 1836, and in *The Library of Fiction or Family Story-Teller* in 1836. When the *Sketches by Boz* were collected in book form in their two series in 1836–37, they were illustrated by George Cruikshank, the first of Dickens's illustrators, with some pictures added by "Phiz" (Hablot Knight Browne), who was to illustrate most of his books between 1837 and 1860.

As now printed in most editions of Dickens, the *Sketches by Boz* fall into four divisions: seven under the title "Our Parish"; twenty-five under the heading "Scenes"; twelve under the heading "Characters"; and twelve under the title of "Tales." To these are added three supplementary series of later sketches: "Sketches of Young Gentlemen," "Sketches of Young Couples," and "The Mudfrog and Other Sketches."

The following selection of eleven sketches gives a short sampling of these *Sketches* and is designed here to set the scene and show the stage of Dickens's exploration of the world around him when he began his career as a writer, and to introduce the England and the London that were to remain the background of all his future works. "The Streets—Morning" was first printed in *The Evening Chronicle* for July 21, 1835; "The Streets—Night" in *Bell's Life in London* for January 17, 1836; "Shops and their Tenants" in *The Morning Chronicle*, October 10, 1834; "Scotland Yard" in *The Morning Chronicle*, October 4, 1836; "London Recreations" in *The Evening Chronicle*, March 17, 1835; "The River" in *The Evening Chronicle*, June 6, 1835; "Omnibuses" in *The Morning Chronicle*, September 26, 1834; "Gin-Shops" in *The Evening Chronicle*, February 7, 1835; "Criminal Courts" (under the title "The Old Bailey") in *The Morning Chronicle*, October 23, 1834; and "A Christmas Dinner" (as "Christmas Festivities") in *Bell's Life in London and Sporting Chronicle* for December 27, 1835.

The Streets—Morning

The appearance presented by the streets of London an hour before sunrise, on a summer's morning, is most striking even to the few whose unfortunate pursuits of pleasure, or scarcely less unfortunate pursuits of business, cause them to be well acquainted with the scene. There is an air of cold, solitary desolation about the noiseless streets which we are accustomed to see thronged at other times by a busy, eager crowd, and over the quiet, closely-shut buildings, which throughout the day are swarming with life and bustle, that is very impressive.

The last drunken man, who shall find his way home before sunlight, has just staggered heavily along, roaring out the burden of the drinking song of the previous night: the last houseless vagrant whom penury and police have left in the streets, has coiled up his chilly limbs in some paved corner, to dream of food and warmth. The drunken, the dissipated, and the wretched have disappeared; the more sober and orderly part of the population have not yet awakened to the labours of the day, and the stillness of death is over the streets; its very hue seems to be imparted to them, cold and lifeless as they look in the grey, sombre light of daybreak. The coach-stands in the larger thoroughfares are deserted; the night-houses are closed; and the chosen promenades of profligate misery are empty.

An occasional policeman may alone be seen at the street corners, listlessly gazing on the deserted prospect before him; and now and then a rakish-looking cat runs stealthily across the road and descends his own area with as much caution and slyness—bounding first on the water-butt, then on the dust-hole, and then alighting on the flag-stones—as if he were conscious that his character depended on his gallantry of the preceding night escaping public observation. A partially opened bedroom-window here and there, bespeaks the heat of the weather, and the uneasy slumbers of its occupant; and the dim scanty flicker of the rushlight, through the window-blind, denotes the chamber of watching or sickness. With these few exceptions, the streets present no signs of life, nor the houses of habitation.

An hour wears away; the spires of the churches and roofs of the principal buildings are faintly tinged with the light of the rising sun;

and the streets, by almost imperceptible degrees, begin to resume their bustle and animation. Market-carts roll slowly along: the sleepy waggoner impatiently urging on his tired horses, or vainly endeavouring to awaken the boy, who, luxuriously stretched on the top of the fruit-baskets, forgets, in happy oblivion, his long-cherished curiosity to behold the wonders of London.

Rough, sleepy-looking animals of strange appearance, something between ostlers and hackney-coachmen, begin to take down the shutters of early public-houses; and little deal tables, with the ordinary preparations for a street breakfast, make their appearance at the customary stations. Numbers of men and women (principally the latter), carrying upon their heads heavy baskets of fruit, toil down the park side of Piccadilly, on their way to Covent Garden, and, following each other in rapid succession, form a long straggling line from thence to the turn of the road at Knightsbridge.

Here and there, a bricklayer's labourer, with the day's dinner tied up in a handkerchief, walks briskly to his work, and occasionally a little knot of three or four schoolboys on a stolen bathing expedition rattle merrily over the pavement, their boisterous mirth contrasting forcibly with the demeanour of the little sweep, who, having knocked and rung till his arm aches, and being interdicted by a merciful legislature from endangering his lungs by calling out, sits patiently down on the door-step, until the housemaid may happen to awake.

Covent Garden market, and the avenues leading to it, are thronged with carts of all sorts, sizes, and descriptions, from the heavy lumbering waggon, with its four stout horses, to the jingling costermonger's cart, with its consumptive donkey. The pavement is already strewed with decayed cabbage-leaves, broken hay-bands, and all the indescribable litter of a vegetable market; men are shouting, carts backing, horses neighing, boys fighting, basket-women talking, piemen expatiating on the excellence of their pastry, and donkeys braying these and a hundred other sounds form a compound discordant enough to a Londoner's ears, and remarkably disagreeable to those of country gentlemen who are sleeping at the Hummums for the first time.

Another hour passes away, and the day begins in good earnest. The servant of all work, who, under the plea of sleeping very soundly, has utterly disregarded "Missis's" ringing for half an hour previously, is warned by Master (whom Missis has sent up in his drapery to the landing-place for that purpose), that it's half-past six, whereupon she awakes all of a sudden, with well-feigned astonishment, and goes down-stairs very sulkily, wishing, while she strikes a light, that the principle of spontaneous combustion would extend itself to coals and kitchen range. When the fire is lighted, she opens the street-door to take in the milk, when, by the most singular coincidence in the world, she discovers that the servant next door has just taken in her milk too, and that Mr. Todd's young man over the way is, by an equally extraordinary chance, taking down his master's shutters. The inevitable consequence is, that she just steps, milk-jug in hand, as far as next door, just to say "good morning" to Betsy Clark, and that Mr. Todd's young man just steps over the way to say "good morning" to both of 'em; and as the aforesaid Mr. Todd's young man is almost as good-looking and fascinating as the baker himself, the conversation quickly becomes very interesting, and probably would become more so, if Betsy Clark's Missis, who always will be a-followin' her about, didn't give an angry tap at her bedroom window, on which Mr. Todd's young man tries to whistle coolly, as he goes back to his shop much faster than he came from it; and the two girls run back to their respective places, and shut their street-doors with surprising soft-ness, each of them poking their heads out of the front parlour window, a minute afterwards, however, ostensibly with the view of looking at the mail which just then passes by, but really for the purpose of catching another glimpse of Mr. Todd's young man, who being fond of mails, but more of females, takes a short look at the mails, and a long look at the girls, much to the satisfaction of all parties con-cerned.

The mail itself goes on to the coach-office in due course, and the passengers who are going out by the early coach, stare with astonish-ment at the passengers who are coming in by the early coach, who look blue and dismal, and are evidently under the influence of that odd feeling produced by travelling, which makes the events of yes-terday morning seem as if they had happened at least six months ago, and induces people to wonder with considerable gravity whether the friends and relations they took leave of a fortnight before, have altered much since they have left them. The coach-office is all alive and the coaches which are just going out, are surrounded by the usual crowd of Jews and nondescripts, who seem to consider, Heaven knows why, that it is quite impossible any man can mount a coach without requir-ing at least sixpennyworth of oranges, a penknife, a pocket-book, a last year's annual, a pencil-case, a piece of sponge, and a small series of caricatures.

Half an hour more, and the sun darts his bright rays cheerfully down the still half-empty streets, and shines with sufficient force to rouse the dismal laziness of the apprentice, who pauses every other minute from his task of sweeping out the shop and watering the pave-ment in front of it, to tell another apprentice similarly employed, how hot it will be to-day, or to stand with his right hand shading his eyes, and his left resting on the broom, gazing at the "Wonder," or the "Tally-ho," or the "Nimrod," or some other fast coach, till it is out of sight, when he re-enters the shop, envying the passengers on the outside of the fast coach, and thinking of the old red brick house "down in the country," where he went to school: the miseries of the milk and water, and thick bread and scrapings, fading into nothing before the pleasant recollection of the green field the boys used to play in, and the green pond he was caned for presuming to fall into, and other schoolboy associations.

Cabs, with trunks and band-boxes between the drivers' legs and outside the apron, rattle briskly up and down the streets on their way to the coach-offices or steam-packet wharfs; and the cab-drivers and hackney-coachmen who are on the stand polish up the ornamental part of their dingy vehicles—the former wondering how people can prefer "them wild beast cariwans of homnibuses, to a riglar cab with a fast trotter," and the latter admiring how people can trust their necks into one of "them crazy cabs, when they can have a 'spectable 'ackney cotche with a pair of 'orses as von't run away with no vun;" a consolation unquestionably founded on fact, seeing that a hackney-coach horse never was known to run at all, "except," as the smart cabman in front of the rank observes, "except one, and *he* run back-'ards."

The shops are now completely opened, and apprentices and shopmen are busily engaged in cleaning and decking the windows for the day. The bakers' shops in town are filled with servants and children waiting for the drawing of the first batch of rolls—an operation which was performed a full hour ago in the suburbs: for the early clerk population of Somers and Camden Towns, Islington, and Pentonville, are fast pouring into the city, or directing their steps towards Chancery Lane and the Inns of Court. Middle-aged men, whose salaries have by no means increased in the same proportion as their families, plod steadily along, apparently with no object in view but the counting-house; knowing by sight almost everybody they meet or overtake, for they have seen them every morning (Sundays excepted) during the last twenty years, but speaking to no one. If they do happen to overtake a personal acquaintance, they just exchange a hurried salutation, and keep walking on, either by his side or in front of him, as his rate of walking may chance to be. As to stopping to shake hands, or to take the friend's arm, they seem to think that as it is not included in their salary, they have no right to do it. Small office lads in large hats, who are made men before they are boys, hurry along in pairs, with their first coat carefully brushed, and the white trousers of last Sunday plentifully besmeared with dust and ink. It evidently requires a considerable mental struggle to avoid investing part of the day's dinner-money in the purchase of the stale tarts so temptingly exposed in dusty tins at the pastry-cooks' doors; but a consciousness of their own importance and the receipt of seven shillings a week, with the prospect of an early rise to eight, comes to their aid, and they accordingly put their hats a little more on one side, and look under the bonnets of all the milliners' and staymakers' apprentices they meet—poor girls!—the hardest worked, the worst paid, and too often, the worst used class of the community.

Eleven o'clock, and a new set of people fill the streets. The goods in the shop-windows are invitingly arranged; the shopmen in their white neckerchiefs and spruce coats, look as if they couldn't clean a window if their lives depended on it; the carts have disappeared from Covent Garden; the waggoners have returned, and the coster-mongers repaired to their ordinary "beats" in the suburbs; clerks are at their offices, and gigs, cabs, omnibuses, and saddle-horses, are conveying their masters to the same destination. The streets are thronged with a vast concourse of people, gay and shabby, rich and poor, idle and industrious; and we come to the heat, bustle, and activity of Noon.

The Streets—Night

But the streets of London, to be beheld in the very height of their glory, should be seen on a dark, dull, murky winter's night, when there is just enough damp gently stealing down to make the pavement greasy, without cleansing it of any of its impurities; and when the heavy lazy mist, which hangs over every object, makes the gas-lamps look brighter, and the brilliantly-lighted shops more splendid, from the contrast they present to the darkness around. All the people who are at home on such a night as this, seem disposed to make themselves as snug and comfortable as possible; and the passengers in the streets have excellent reason to envy the fortunate individuals who are seated by their own firesides.

In the larger and better kind of streets, dining parlour curtains are closely drawn, kitchen fires blaze brightly up, and savoury steams of hot dinners salute the nostrils of the hungry wayfarer, as he plods wearily by the area railings. In the suburbs, the muffin boy rings his way down the little street, much more slowly than he is wont to do; for Mrs. Macklin, of No. 4, has no sooner opened her little street-door, and screamed out "Muffins!" with all her might, than Mrs. Walker, at No. 5, puts her head out of the parlour-window, and screams "Muffins!" too; and Mrs. Walker has scarcely got the words out of her lips, than Mrs. Peplow, over the way, lets loose Master Peplow, who darts down the street, with a velocity which nothing but buttered muffins in perspective could possibly inspire, and drags the boy back by main force, whereupon Mrs. Macklin and Mrs. Walker, just to save the boy trouble, and to say a few neighbourly words to Mrs. Peplow at the same time, run over the way and buy their muffins at Mrs. Peplow's door, when it appears from the voluntary statement of Mrs. Walker, that her "kittle's jist a-biling, and the cups and sarsers ready laid," and that, as it was such a wretched night out o' doors, she'd made up her mind to have a nice hot comfortable cup o' tea —a determination at which, by the most singular coincidence, the other two ladies had simultaneously arrived.

After a little conversation about the wretchedness of the weather and the merits of tea, with a digression relative to the viciousness of boys as a rule, and the amiability of Master Peplow as an exception, Mrs. Walker sees her husband coming down the street; and as he must want his tea, poor man, after his dirty walk from the Docks, she instantly runs across, muffins in hand, and Mrs. Macklin does the same, and after a few words to Mrs. Walker, they all pop into their little houses, and slam their little street-doors, which are not opened again for the remainder of the evening, except to the nine o'clock "beer," who comes round with a lantern in front of his tray, and says, as he lends Mrs. Walker "Yesterday's 'Tiser," that he's blessed if he can hardly hold the pot, much less feel the paper, for it's one of the bitterest nights he ever felt, 'cept the night when the man was frozen to death in the Brick-field.

After a little prophetic conversation with the policeman at the street-corner, touching a probable change in the weather, and the setting-in of a hard frost, the nine o'clock beer returns to his master's house, and employs himself for the remainder of the evening, in assiduously stirring the taproom fire, and deferentially taking part in the conversation of the worthies assembled round it.

The streets in the vicinity of the Marsh Gate and Victoria Theatre present an appearance of dirt and discomfort on such a night, which the groups who lounge about them in no degree tend to diminish. Even the little block-tin temple sacred to baked potatoes, surmounted by a splendid design in variegated lamps, looks less gay than usual; and as to the kidney-pie stand, its glory has quite departed. The candle in the transparent lamp, manufactured of oil-paper, embellished with "characters," has been blown out fifty times, so the kidney-pie merchant, tired with running backwards and forwards to the next wine-vaults, to get a light, has given up the idea of illumination in despair, and the only signs of his "whereabout," are the bright sparks, of which a long irregular train is whirled down the street every time he opens his portable oven to hand a hot kidney-pie to a customer.

Flat-fish, oyster, and fruit vendors linger hopelessly in the kennel, in vain endeavouring to attract customers; and the ragged boys who usually disport themselves about the streets, stand crouched in little knots in some projecting doorway, or under the canvas blind of a cheesemonger's, where great flaring gas-lights, unshaded by any glass, display huge piles of bright red and pale yellow cheeses, mingled with little fivepenny dabs of dingy bacon, various tubs of weekly Dorset, and cloudy rolls of "best fresh."

Here they amuse themselves with theatrical converse, arising out of their last half-price visit to the Victoria gallery, admire the terrific combat, which is nightly encored, and expatiate on the inimitable manner in which Bill Thompson can "come the double monkey," or go through the mysterious involutions of a sailor's hornpipe.

It is nearly eleven o'clock, and the cold thin rain which has been drizzling so long, is beginning to pour down in good earnest; the baked-potato man has departed—the kidney-pie man has just walked away with his warehouse on his arm—the cheesemonger has drawn in his blind, and the boys have dispersed. The constant clicking of pattens on the slippy and uneven pavement, and the rustling of umbrellas, as the wind blows against the shop-windows, bear testimony to the inclemency of the night; and the policeman, with his oilskin cape buttoned closely round him, seems as he holds his hat on his head, and turns round to avoid the gust of wind and rain which drives against him at the street-corner, to be very far from congratulating himself on the prospect before him.

The little chandler's shop with the cracked bell behind the door, whose melancholy tinkling has been regulated by the demand for quarterns of sugar and half-ounces of coffee, is shutting up. The crowds which have been passing to and fro during the whole day, are rapidly dwindling away; and the noise of shouting and quarrelling which issues from the public-houses, is almost the only sound that breaks the melancholy stillness of night.

There was another, but it has ceased. That wretched woman with the infant in her arms, round whose meagre form the remnant of her own scanty shawl is carefully wrapped, has been attempting to sing some popular ballad, in the hope of wringing a few pence from the compassionate passer-by. A brutal laugh at her weak voice is all she has gained. The tears fall thick and fast down her own pale face; the child is cold and hungry, and its half-stifled wailing adds to the misery of its wretched mother, as she moans aloud, and sinks despairingly down, on a cold damp door-step.

Singing! How few of those who pass such a miserable creature as this, think of the anguish of heart, the sinking of soul and spirit, which the very effort of singing produces. Bitter mockery! Disease, neglect, and starvation, faintly articulating the words of the joyish ditty, that has enlivened your hours of feasting and merriment, God knows how often! It is no subject of jeering. The weak tremulous voice tells a fearful tale of want and famishing; and the feeble singer of this roaring song may turn away, only to die of cold and hunger.

One o'clock! Parties returning from the different theatres foot it through the muddy streets; cabs, hackney-coaches, carriages, and theatre omnibuses, roll swiftly by; watermen with dim dirty lanterns in their hands, and large brass plates upon their breasts, who have been shouting and rushing about for the last two hours, retire to their watering-houses, to solace themselves with the creature comforts of pipes and purl; the half-price pit and box frequenters of the theatres throng to the different houses of refreshment; and chops, kidneys, rabbits, oysters, stout, cigars, and "goes" innumerable, are served up amidst a noise and confusion of smoking, running, knife-clattering, and waiter-chattering, perfectly indescribable.

The more musical portion of the play-going community betake themselves to some harmonic meeting. As a matter of curiosity let us follow them thither for a few moments.

In a lofty room of spacious dimensions, are seated some eighty or a hundred guests knocking little pewter measures on the tables, and hammering away, with the handles of their knives, as if they were so many trunk-makers. They are applauding a glee, which has just been executed by the three "professional gentlemen" at the top of the centre table, one of whom is in the chair—the little pompous man with the bald head just emerging from the collar of his green coat. The others are seated on either side of him—the stout man with the small voice, and the thin-faced dark man in black. The little man in the chair is a most amusing personage,—*such* condescending grandeur, and *such* a voice!

"Bass!" as the young gentleman near us with the blue stock forcibly remarks to his companion, "bass! I b'lieve you; he can go down lower than any man: so low sometimes that you can't hear him." And so he does. To hear him growling away, gradually lower and lower down, till he can't get back again, is the most delightful thing in the world, and it is quite impossible to witness unmoved the impressive solemnity with which he pours forth his soul in "My 'art's in the 'ighlands," or "The brave old Hoak." The stout man is also addicted to sentimentality, and warbles, "Fly, fly from the world, my Bessy, with me," or some such song, with lady-like sweetness, and in the most seductive tones imaginable.

"Pray give your orders, gen'l'm'n—pray give your orders,"—says the pale-faced man with the red head; and demands for "goes" of gin and "goes" of brandy, and pints of stout, and cigars of peculiar mildness, are vociferously made from all parts of the room. The "professional gentlemen" are in the very height of their glory, and bestow condescending nods, or even a word or two of recognition, on the better-known frequenters of the room, in the most bland and patronising manner possible.

That little round-faced man, with the small brown surtout, white stockings and shoes, is in the comic line; the mixed air of self-denial, and mental consciousness of his own powers, with which he acknowledges the call of the chair, is particularly gratifying. "Gen'l'men," says the little pompous man, accompanying the word with a knock of the president's hammer on the table—"Gen'l'men, allow me to claim your attention—our friend, Mr. Smuggins, will oblige."—"Bravo!" shout the company; and Smuggins, after a considerable quantity of coughing by way of symphony, and a most facetious sniff or two, which afford general delight, sings a comic song, with a fal-de-ral—tol-de-ral chorus at the end of every verse, much longer than the verse itself. It is received with unbounded applause, and after some aspiring genius has volunteered a recitation, and failed dismally therein, the little pompous man gives another knock, and says "Gen'l'men, we will attempt a glee, if you please." This announcement calls forth tumultuous applause, and more energetic spirits express the unqualified approbation it affords them, by knocking one or two stout glasses off their legs—a humorous device; but one which frequently occasions some slight altercation when the form of paying the damage is proposed to be gone through by the waiter.

Scenes like these are continued until three or four o'clock in the morning; and even when they close, fresh ones open to the inquisitive novice. But as a description of all of them, however slight, would require a volume, the contents of which, however instructive, would be by no means pleasing, we make our bow, and drop the curtain.

Shops and Their Tenants

~~~~~~

What inexhaustible food for speculation do the streets of London afford! We never were able to agree with Sterne in pitying the man who could travel from Dan to Beersheba, and say that all was barren; we have not the slightest commiseration for the man who can take up his hat and stick, and walk from Covent Garden to St. Paul's Churchyard, and back into the bargain, without deriving some amusement

—we had almost said instruction—from his perambulation. And yet there are such beings: we meet them every day. Large black stocks and light waistcoats, jet canes and discontented countenances, are the characteristics of the race; other people brush quickly by you, steadily plodding on to business, or cheerfully running after pleasure. These men linger listlessly past, looking as happy and animated as a police-man on duty. Nothing seems to make an impression on their minds: nothing short of being knocked down by a porter, or run over by a cab, will disturb their equanimity. You will meet them on a fine day in any of the leading thoroughfares: peep through the window of a west-end cigar shop in the evening, if you can manage to get a glimpse between the blue curtains which intercept the vulgar gaze, and you see them in their only enjoyment of existence. There they are lounging about, on round tubs and pipe boxes, in all the dignity of whiskers and gilt watch-guards; whispering soft nothings to the young lady in amber, with the large ear-rings, who, as she sits behind the counter in a blaze of adoration and gas-light, is the admiration of all the female servants in the neighbourhood, and the envy of every milliner's ap-prentice within two miles round.

One of our principal amusements is to watch the gradual progress—the rise or fall—of particular shops. We have formed an intimate ac-quaintance with several, in different parts of town, and are perfectly acquainted with their whole history. We could name off-hand, twenty at least, which we are quite sure have paid no taxes for the last six years. They are never inhabited for more than two months consecu-tively, and, we verily believe, have witnessed every retail trade in the directory.

There is one, whose history is a sample of the rest, in whose fate we have taken especial interest, having had the pleasure of knowing it ever since it has been a shop. It is on the Surrey side of the water—a little distance beyond the Marsh Gate. It was originally a substantial, good-looking private house enough; the landlord got into difficulties, the house got into Chancery, the tenant went away, and the house went to ruin. At this period our acquaintance with it commenced; the paint was all worn off; the windows were broken, the area was green with neglect and the overflowings of the water-butt; the butt itself was without a lid, and the street-door was the very picture of misery. The chief pastime of the children in the vicinity had been to assemble in a body on the steps, and to take it in turn to knock loud double knocks at the door, to the great satisfaction of the neighbours generally, and especially of the nervous old lady next door but one. Numerous com-plaints were made, and several small basins of water discharged over the offenders, but without effect. In this state of things, the marine-store dealer at the corner of the street, in the most obliging manner took the knocker off, and sold it: and the unfortunate house looked more wretched than ever.

We deserted our friend for a few weeks. What was our surprise, on our return, to find no trace of its existence! In its place was a handsome shop, fast approaching to a state of completion, and on the shutters were large bills, informing the public that it would shortly be opened with "an extensive stock of linen-drapery and haberdashery." It opened in due course; there was the name of the proprietor "and Co." in gilt letters, almost too dazzling to look at. Such ribbons and shawls! and two such elegant young men behind the counter, each in a clean collar and white neckcloth, like the lover in a farce. As to the proprietor, he did nothing but walk up and down the shop, and hand seats to the ladies, and hold important conversations with the handsomest of the young men, who was shrewdly suspected by the neighbours to be the "Co." We saw all this with sorrow; we felt a fatal presentiment that the shop was doomed—and so it was. Its decay was slow, but sure. Tickets gradually appeared in the windows; then rolls of flannel, with labels on them, were stuck outside the door; then a bill was pasted on the street-door, intimating that the first floor was to let *un*furnished; then one of the young men disappeared altogether, and the other took to a black neckerchief, and the proprietor took to drinking. The shop became dirty, broken panes of glass remained unmended, and the stock disappeared piecemeal. At last the company's man came to cut off the water, and then the linen-draper cut off himself, leaving the landlord his compliments and the key.

The next occupant was a fancy stationer. The shop was more modestly painted than before, still it was neat; but somehow we always thought, as we passed, that it looked like a poor and struggling concern. We wished the man well, but we trembled for his success. He was a widower evidently, and had employment elsewhere, for he passed us every morning on his road to the city. The business was carried on by his eldest daughter. Poor girl! she needed no assistance. We occasionally caught a glimpse of two or three children, in mourning like herself, as they sat in the little parlour behind the shop; and we never passed at night without seeing the eldest girl at work, either for them, or in making some elegant little trifle for sale. We often thought, as her pale face looked more sad and pensive in the dim candle-light, that if those thoughtless females who interfere with the miserable market of poor creatures such as these knew but one-half of the misery they suffer, and the bitter privations they endure, in their honourable attempts to earn a scanty subsistence, they would, perhaps, resign even opportunities for the gratification of vanity, and an immodest love of self-display, rather than drive them to a last dreadful resource, which it would shock the delicate feelings of these *charitable* ladies to hear named.

But we are forgetting the shop. Well, we continued to watch it, and every day showed too clearly the increasing poverty of its inmates. The children were clean, it is true, but their clothes were threadbare and shabby; no tenant had been procured for the upper part of the house, from the letting of which, a portion of the means of paying the rent was to have been derived, and a slow, wasting consumption prevented the eldest girl from continuing her exertions. Quarter-day arrived. The landlord had suffered from the extravagance of his last tenant, and he had no compassion for the struggles of his successor; he put in an execution. As we passed one morning, the broker's men were removing the little furniture there was in the house, and a newly-posted bill informed us it was again "To Let." What became of the last tenant we never could learn; we believe the girl is past all suffering, and beyond all sorrow. God help her! We hope she is.

We were somewhat curious to ascertain what would be the next stage—for that the place had no chance of succeeding now, was perfectly clear. The bill was soon taken down, and some alterations were being made in the interior of the shop. We were in a fever of expectation; we exhausted conjecture—we imagined all possible trades, none of which were perfectly reconcilable with our idea of the gradual decay of the tenement. It opened, and we wondered why we had not guessed at the real state of the case before. The shop—not a large one at the best of times—had been converted into two: one was a bonnet-shape maker's, the other was opened by a tobacconist, who also dealt in walking-sticks and Sunday newspapers; the two were separated by a thin partition, covered with tawdry striped paper.

The tobacconist remained in possession longer than any tenant within our recollection. He was a red-faced, impudent, good-for-nothing dog, evidently accustomed to take things as they came, and to make the best of a bad job. He sold as many cigars as he could and smoked the rest. He occupied the shop as long as he could make peace with the landlord, and when he could no longer live in quiet, he very coolly locked the door, and bolted himself. From this period, the two little dens have undergone innumerable changes. The tobacconist was succeeded by a theatrical hair-dresser, who ornamented the window with a great variety of "characters," and terrific combats. The bonnet-shape maker gave place to a green-grocer, and the histrionic barber was succeeded, in his turn, by a tailor. So numerous have been the changes, that we have of late done little more than mark the peculiar but certain indications of a house being poorly inhabited. It has been progressing by almost imperceptible degrees. The occupiers of the shops have gradually given up room after room, until they have only reserved the little parlour for themselves. First there appeared a brass plate on the private door, with "Ladies' School" legibly engraved thereon; shortly afterwards we observed a second brass plate, then a bell, and then another bell.

When we paused in front of our old friend, and observed these signs of poverty, which are not to be mistaken, we thought as we turned away, that the house had attained its lowest pitch of degradation. We were wrong. When we last passed it, a "dairy" was established in the area, and a party of melancholy-looking fowls were amusing themselves by running in at the front door, and out at the back one.

Scotland Yard

Scotland Yard is a small—a very small—tract of land, bounded on one side by the river Thames, on the other by the gardens of Northumberland House: abutting at one end on the bottom of Northumberland Street, at the other on the back of Whitehall Place. When this territory was first accidentally discovered by a country gentleman who lost his way in the Strand, some years ago, the original settlers were found to be a tailor, a publican, two eating-house keepers, and a fruit-pie maker; and it was also found to contain a race of strong and bulky men, who repaired to the wharfs in Scotland Yard regularly every morning, about five or six o'clock, to fill heavy waggons with coal, with which they proceeded to distant places up the country, and supplied the inhabitants with fuel. When they had emptied their waggons, they again returned for a fresh supply; and this trade was continued throughout the year.

As the settlers derived their subsistence from ministering to the wants of these primitive traders, the articles exposed for sale, and the places where they were sold, bore strong outward marks of being expressly adapted to their tastes and wishes. The tailor displayed in his window a Lilliputian pair of leather gaiters, and a diminutive round frock, while each doorpost was appropriately garnished with a model of a coal-sack. The two eating-house keepers exhibited joints of a magnitude, and puddings of a solidity, which coalheavers alone could appreciate; and the fruit-pie maker displayed on his well-scrubbed window-board large white compositions of flour and dripping, ornamented with pink stains, giving rich promise of the fruit within, which made their huge mouths water, as they lingered past.

But the choicest spot in all Scotland Yard was the old public-house in the corner. Here, in a dark wainscoted room of ancient appearance, cheered by the glow of a mighty fire, and decorated with an enormous clock, whereof the face was white, and the figures black, sat the lusty of the river, as they shouted out some sturdy chorus, or roared forth volumes of smoke, which wreathed heavily above their heads, and involved the room in a thick dark cloud. From this apartment might their voices be heard on a winter's night, penetrating to the very bank of the river, as they shouted out some sturdy chorus, or roared forth the burden of a popular song; dwelling upon the last few words with a strength and length of emphasis which made the very roof tremble above them.

Here, too, would they tell old legends of what the Thames was in ancient times, when the Patent Shot Manufactory wasn't built, and Waterloo Bridge had never been thought of; and then they would shake their heads with portentous looks, to the deep edification of the rising generation of heavers, who crowded round them, and wondered where all this would end; whereat the tailor would take his pipe solemnly from his mouth, and say, how that he hoped it might end well, but he very much doubted whether it would or not, and couldn't rightly tell what to make of it—a mysterious expression of opinion, delivered with a semi-prophetic air, which never failed to elicit the fullest concurrence of the assembled company; and so they would go on drinking and wondering till ten o'clock came, and with it the tailor's wife to fetch him home, when the little party broke up, to meet again in the same room, and say and do precisely the same things, on the following evening at the same hour.

About this time the barges that came up the river began to bring vague rumours to Scotland Yard of somebody in the city having been heard to say, that the Lord Mayor had threatened in so many words to pull down the old London Bridge, and build up a new one. At first these rumours were disregarded as idle tales, wholly destitute of foundation, for nobody in Scotland Yard doubted that if the Lord Mayor contemplated any such dark design, he would just be clapped up in the Tower for a week or two, and then killed off for high treason.

By degrees, however, the reports grew stronger, and more frequent, and at last a barge, laden with numerous chaldrons of the best Wallsend, brought up the positive intelligence that several of the arches of the old bridge were stopped, and that preparations were actually in progress for constructing the new one. What an excitement was visible in the old tap-room on that memorable night! Each man looked into his neighbour's face, pale with alarm and astonishment, and read therein an echo of the sentiments which filled his own breast. The oldest heaver present proved to demonstration, that the moment the piers were removed, all the water in the Thames would run clean off, and leave a dry gully in its place. What was to become of the coal-barges—of the trade of Scotland Yard—of the very existence of its population? The tailor shook his head more sagely than usual, and grimly pointing to a knife on the table, bid them wait and see what happened. He said nothing—not he; but if the Lord Mayor didn't fall a victim to popular indignation, why he would be rather astonished; that was all.

They did wait; barge after barge arrived, and still no tidings of the assassination of the Lord Mayor. The first stone was laid: it was done by a Duke—the King's brother. Years passed away, and the bridge was opened by the King himself. In course of time the piers were removed; and when the people in Scotland Yard got up next morning in the confident expectation of being able to step over to Pedlar's Acre without wetting the soles of their shoes, they found to their unspeakable astonishment that the water was just where it used to be.

A result so different from that which they had anticipated from this first improvement, produced its full effect upon the inhabitants of Scotland Yard. One of the eating-house keepers began to court public opinion, and to look for customers among a new class of people. He covered his little dining-tables with white cloths, and got a painter's apprentice to inscribe something about hot joints from twelve to two, in one of the little panes of his shop-window. Improvement began to march with rapid strides to the very threshold of Scotland Yard. A new market sprung up at Hungerford, and the Police Commissioners established their office in Whitehall Place. The traffic in Scotland Yard increased; fresh Members were added to the House of Commons, the Metropolitan Representatives found it a near cut, and many other foot passengers followed their example.

We marked the advance of civilisation, and beheld it with a sigh. The eating-house keeper who manfully resisted the innovation of table-cloths, was losing ground every day, as his opponent gained it, and a deadly feud sprung up between them. The genteel one no longer took his evening's pint in Scotland Yard, but drank gin and water at a "parlour" in Parliament Street. The fruit-pie maker still continued to visit the old room, but he took to smoking cigars, and began to call himself a pastrycook, and to read the papers. The old heavers still assembled round the ancient fireplace, but their talk was mournful: and the loud song and the joyous shout were heard no more.

And what is Scotland Yard now? How have its old customs changed; and how has the ancient simplicity of its inhabitants faded away! The old tottering public-house is converted into a spacious and lofty "wine-vaults;" gold leaf has been used in the construction of the letters which emblazon its exterior, and the poet's art has been called into requisition, to intimate that if you drink a certain description of ale, you must hold fast by the rail. The tailor exhibits in his window the pattern of a foreign-looking brown surtout, with silk buttons, a fur collar, and fur cuffs. He wears a stripe down the outside of each leg of his trousers: and we have detected his assistants (for he has assistants now) in the act of sitting on the shop-board in the same uniform.

At the other end of the little row of houses a bootmaker has established himself in a brick box, with the additional innovation of a first floor; and here he exposes for sale, boots—real Wellington boots—an article which a few years ago, none of the original inhabitants had ever seen or heard of. It was but the other day, that a dressmaker opened another little box in the middle of the row; and when we thought that the spirit of change could produce no alteration beyond that, a jeweller appeared, and not content with exposing gilt rings and copper bracelets out of number, put up an announcement, which still sticks in his window, that "ladies' ears may be pierced within." The dressmaker employs a young lady who wears pockets in her apron; and the tailor informs the public that gentlemen may have their own materials made up.

Amidst all this change, and restlessness, and innovation, there remains but one old man, who seems to mourn the downfall of this ancient place. He holds no converse with human kind, but, seated on a wooden bench at the angle of the wall which fronts the crossing from Whitehall Place, watches in silence the gambols of his sleek and well-fed dogs. He is the presiding genius of Scotland Yard. Years and years have rolled over his head; but in fine weather or in foul, hot or cold, wet or dry, hail, rain, or snow, he is still in his accustomed spot. Misery and want are depicted in his countenance; his form is bent by age, his head is grey with length of trial, but there he sits from day to day, brooding over the past; and thither he will continue to drag his feeble limbs, until his eyes have closed upon Scotland Yard, and upon the world together.

A few years hence, and the antiquary of another generation looking into some mouldy record of the strife and passions that agitated the world in these times, may glance his eye over the pages we have just filled: and not all his knowledge of the history of the past, not all his black-letter lore, or his skill in book-collecting, not all the dry studies of a long life, or the dusty volumes that have cost him a fortune, may help him to the whereabouts, either of Scotland Yard or of anyone of the landmarks we have mentioned in describing it.

London Recreations

The wish of persons in the humbler classes of life, to ape the manners and customs of those whom fortune has placed above them, is often the subject of remark, and not unfrequently of complaint. The inclination may, and no doubt does, exist to a great extent, among the small gentility—the would-be aristocrats—of the middle classes. Tradesmen and clerks, with fashionable novel-reading families, and circulating-library-subscribing daughters, get up small assemblies in humble imitation of Almack's, and promenade the dingy "large room" of some second-rate hotel with as much complacency as the enviable few who are privileged to exhibit their magnificence in that exclusive haunt of fashion and foolery. Aspiring young ladies, who read flaming accounts of some "fancy fair in high life," suddenly grow desperately charitable; visions of admiration and matrimony float before their eyes; some wonderfully meritorious institution, which, by the strangest accident in the world, has never been heard of before, is discovered to be in a languishing condition: Thomson's great room, or Johnson's nursery-ground, is forthwith engaged, and the aforesaid young ladies, from mere charity, exhibit themselves for three days, from twelve to four, for the small charge of one shilling per head! With the exception of these classes of society, however, and a few weak and insignificant persons, we do not think the attempt at imitation to which we have alluded, prevails in any great degree. The different character of the recreations of different classes, has often afforded us amusement; and we have chosen it for the subject of our present sketch, in the hope that it may possess some amusement for our readers.

If the regular City man, who leaves Lloyd's at five o'clock, and drives home to Hackney, Clapton, Stamford Hill, or elsewhere, can be said to have any daily recreation beyond his dinner, it is his garden. He never does anything to it with his own hands; but he takes great pride in it notwithstanding; and if you are desirous of paying your addresses to the youngest daughter, be sure to be in raptures with every flower and shrub it contains. If your poverty of expression compel you to make any distinction between the two, we would certainly recommend your bestowing more admiration on his garden than his wine. He always takes a walk round it, before he starts for town in the morning, and is particularly anxious that the fish-pond should be kept specially neat. If you call on him on Sunday in summertime, about an hour before dinner, you will find him sitting in an arm-chair, on the lawn behind the house, with a straw hat on, reading a Sunday paper. A short distance from him you will most likely observe a handsome paroquet in a large brass-wire cage; ten to one but the two eldest girls are loitering in one of the side walks accompanied by a couple of young gentlemen, who are holding parasols over them—of course only to keep the sun off—while the younger children, with the under nursery-maid, are strolling listlessly about in the shade. Beyond these occasions, his delight in his garden appears to arise more from the consciousness of possession than actual enjoyment of it. When he drives you down to dinner on a week-day, he is rather fatigued with the occupations of the morning, and tolerably cross into the bargain; but when the cloth is removed, and he has drunk three or four glasses of his favourite port, he orders the French windows of his dining-room (which of course look into the garden) to be opened, and throwing a silk handkerchief over his head, and leaning back in his armchair, descants at considerable length upon its beauty, and the cost of maintaining it. This is to impress you—who are a young friend of the family—with a due sense of the excellence of the garden, and the wealth of its owner; and when he has exhausted the subject, he goes to sleep.

There is another and a very different class of men, whose recreation is their garden. An individual of this class resides some short distance from town—say in the Hampstead Road, or the Kilburn Road, or any other road where the houses are small and neat, and have little slips of back garden. He and his wife—who is as clean and compact a little body as himself—have occupied the same house ever since he retired from business twenty years ago. They have no family. They once had a son, who died at about five years old. The child's portrait hangs over the mantelpiece in the best sitting-room, and a little cart he used to draw about is carefully preserved as a relic.

In fine weather the old gentleman is almost constantly in the garden; and when it is too wet to go into it, he will look out of the window at it, by the hour together. He has always something to do there, and you will see him digging, and sweeping, and cutting, and planting, with manifest delight. In spring-time, there is no end to the sowing of seeds, and sticking little bits of wood over them, with labels, which look like epitaphs to their memory; and in the evening, when the sun has gone down, the perseverance with which he lugs a great watering-pot about is perfectly astonishing. The only other recreation he has is the newspaper, which he peruses every day, from beginning to end, generally reading the most interesting pieces of intelligence to his wife during breakfast. The old lady is very fond of flowers, as the hyacinth-glasses in the parlour-window, and geranium-pots in the little front court, testify. She takes great pride in the garden too: and when one of the four fruit-trees produces rather a larger gooseberry than usual, it is carefully preserved under a wine-glass on the sideboard, for the edification of visitors, who are duly informed that Mr. So-and-so planted the tree which produced it, with his own hands. On a summer's evening, when the large watering-pot has been filled and emptied some fourteen times, and the old couple have quite exhausted themselves by trotting about, you will see them sitting happily together in the little summer-house, enjoying the calm and peace of the twilight, and watching the shadows as they fall upon the garden, and gradually growing thicker and more sombre, obscure the tints of their gayest flowers—no bad emblem of the years that have silently rolled over their heads, deadening in their course the brightest hues of early hopes and feelings which have long since faded away. These are their only recreations, and they require no more. They have within themselves the materials of comfort and content; and the only anxiety of each is to die before the other.

This is no ideal sketch. There *used* to be many old people of this description; their numbers may have diminished, and may decrease still more. Whether the course female education has taken of late days —whether the pursuit of giddy frivolities, and empty nothings, has tended to unfit women for that quiet domestic life, in which they show far more beautifully than in the most crowded assembly, is a question we should feel little gratification in discussing: we hope not.

Let us turn now to another portion of the London population, whose recreations present about as strong a contrast as can well be conceived—we mean the Sunday pleasurers; and let us beg our readers to imagine themselves stationed by our side in some well-known rural "Tea-gardens."

The heat is intense this afternoon, and the people, of whom there are additional parties arriving every moment, look as warm as the tables which have been recently painted, and have the appearance of being red-hot. What a dust and noise! Men and women—boys and girls— sweethearts and married people—babies in arms, and children in chaises—pipes and shrimps—cigars and periwinkles—tea and tobacco. Gentlemen in alarming waistcoats, and steel watch-guards, promenading about, three abreast, with surprising dignity (or as the gentleman in the next box facetiously observes, "cutting it uncommon fat!")— ladies, with great, long, white pocket-handkerchiefs like small table-cloths in their hands, chasing one another on the grass in the most playful and interesting manner, with the view of attracting the attention of the aforesaid gentlemen—husbands in perspective ordering bottles of ginger-beer for the objects of their affections, with a lavish disregard of expense; and the said objects washing down huge

quantities of "shrimps" and "winkles," with an equal disregard of their
own bodily health and subsequent comfort—boys, with great silk hats
just balanced on the top of their heads, smoking cigars, and trying to
look as if they liked them—gentlemen in pink shirts and blue waistcoats, occasionally upsetting either themselves, or somebody else, with
their own canes.

Some of the finery of these people provokes a smile, but they are
all clean, and happy, and disposed to be good-natured and sociable.
Those two motherly-looking women in the smart pelisses, who are
chatting so confidentially, inserting a "ma'am" at every fourth word,
scraped an acquaintance about a quarter of an hour ago: it originated
in admiration of the little boy who belongs to one of them—that
diminutive specimen of mortality in the three-cornered pink satin hat
with black feathers. The two men in the blue coats and drab trousers,
who are walking up and down, smoking their pipes, are their husbands.
The party in the opposite box are a pretty fair specimen of the generality of the visitors. These are the father and mother, and old grandmother: a young man and woman, and an individual addressed by
the euphonious title of "Uncle Bill," who is evidently the wit of the
party. They have some half-dozen children with them, but it is scarcely
necessary to notice the fact, for that is a matter of course here. Every
woman in "the gardens," who has been married for any length of time,
must have had twins on two or three occasions; it is impossible to
account for the extent of juvenile population in any other way.

Observe the inexpressible delight of the old grandmother, at Uncle
Bill's splendid joke of "tea for four: bread-and-butter for forty;" and
the loud explosion of mirth which follows his wafering a paper "pigtail" on the waiter's collar. The young man is evidently "keeping
company" with Uncle Bill's niece: and Uncle Bill's hints—such as
"Don't forget me at the dinner, you know," "I shall look out for the
cake, Sally," "I'll be godfather to your first—wager it's a boy," and so
forth, are equally embarrassing to the young people, and delightful to
the elder ones. As to the old grandmother, she is in perfect ecstasies,
and does nothing but laugh herself into fits of coughing, until they
have finished the "gin-and-water warm with," of which Uncle Bill
ordered "glasses round" after tea, "just to keep the night air out, and
do it up comfortable and riglar arter sich an as-tonishing hot day!"

It is getting dark, and the people begin to move. The field leading
to town is quite full of them; the little hand-chaises are dragged wearily
along, the children are tired, and amuse themselves and the company
generally by crying, or resort to the much more pleasant expedient of
going to sleep—the mothers begin to wish they were at home again—
sweethearts grow more sentimental than ever, as the time for parting
arrives—the gardens look mournful enough, by the light of the two

lanterns which hang against the trees for the convenience of smokers—and the waiters who have been running about incessantly for the last six hours, think they feel a little tired, as they count their glasses and their gains.

The River

"Are you fond of the water?" is a question very frequently asked in hot summer weather, by amphibious-looking young men. "Very," is the general reply. "An't you?"—"Hardly ever off it," is the response, accompanied by sundry adjectives, expressive of the speaker's heartfelt admiration of that element. Now, with all respect for the opinion of society in general, and cutter clubs in particular, we humbly suggest that some of the most painful reminiscences in the mind of every individual who has occasionally disported himself on the Thames, must be connected with his aquatic recreations. Who ever heard of a successful water-party?—or to put the question in a still more intelligible form, who ever saw one? We have been on water excursions out of number, but we solemnly declare that we cannot call to mind one single occasion of the kind, which was not marked by more miseries than any one would suppose could be reasonably crowded into the space of some eight or nine hours. Something has always gone wrong. Either the cork of the salad-dressing has come out, or the most anxiously expected member of the party has not come out, or the most disagreeable man in company would come out, or a child or two have fallen into the water, or the gentleman who undertook to steer has endangered everybody's life all the way, or the gentlemen who volunteered to row have been "out of practice," and performed very alarming evolutions, putting their oars down into the water and not being able to get them up again, or taking terrific pulls without putting them in at all; in either case, pitching over on the backs of their heads with startling violence, and exhibiting the soles of their pumps to the "sitters" in the boat, in a very humiliating manner.

We grant that the banks of the Thames are very beautiful at Richmond and Twickenham, and other distant havens, often sought though seldom reached; but from the "Red-us" back to Blackfriars Bridge, the scene is wonderfully changed. The Penitentiary is a noble

building, no doubt, and the sportive youths who "go in" at that particular part of the river, on a summer's evening, may be all very well in
perspective; but when you are obliged to keep in shore coming home,
and the young ladies will colour up, and look perseveringly the other
way, while the married dittoes cough slightly, and stare very hard at
the water, you feel awkward—especially if you happen to have been
attempting the most distant approach to sentimentality, for an hour or
two previously.

Although experience and suffering have produced in our minds the
result we have just stated, we are by no means blind to a proper sense
of the fun which a looker-on may extract from the amateurs of boating.
What can be more amusing than Searle's yard on a fine Sunday morning? It's a Richmond tide, and some dozen boats are preparing for the
reception of the parties who have engaged them. Two or three fellows
in great rough trousers and Guernsey shirts, are getting them ready
by easy stages; now coming down the yard with a pair of sculls and a
cushion—then having a chat with the "jack," who, like all his tribe,
seems to be wholly incapable of doing anything but lounging about—
then going back again, and returning with a rudder-line and a stretcher
—then solacing themselves with another chat—and then wondering,
with their hands in their capacious pockets, "where them gentlemen's
got to as ordered the six." One of these, the head man, with the legs of
his trousers carefully tucked up at the bottom, to admit the water, we
presume—for it is an element in which he is infinitely more at home
than on land—is quite a character, and shares with the defunct oyster-
swallower the celebrated name of "Dando." Watch him, as taking a
few minutes' respite from his toils, he negligently seats himself on the
edge of a boat, and fans his broad bushy chest with a cap scarcely half
so furry. Look at his magnificent, though reddish whiskers, and mark
the somewhat native humour with which he "chaffs" the boys and
'prentices, or cunningly gammons the gen'lm'n into the gift of a glass
of gin, of which we verily believe he swallows in one day as much as
any six ordinary men, without ever being one atom the worse for it.

But the party arrives, and Dando, relieved from his state of un-
certainty, starts up into activity. They approach in full aquatic
costume, with round blue jackets, striped shirts, and caps of all sizes
and patterns, from the velvet skull-cap of French manufacture, to the
easy head-dress familiar to the students of the old spelling-books, as
having, on the authority of the portrait, formed part of the costume of
the Reverend Mr. Dilworth.

This is the most amusing time to observe a regular Sunday water-
party. There has evidently been up to this period no inconsiderable
degree of boasting on everybody's part relative to his knowledge of
navigation; the sight of the water rapidly cools their courage, and the
air of self-denial with which each of them insists on somebody else's

taking an oar, is perfectly delightful. At length, after a great deal of changing and fidgeting, consequent upon the election of a stroke-oar: the inability of one gentleman to pull on this side, of another to pull on that, and of a third to pull at all, the boat's crew are seated. "Shove her off!" cries the coxswain, who looks as easy and comfortable as if he were steering in the Bay of Biscay. The order is obeyed; the boat is immediately turned completely round, and proceeds towards Westminster Bridge, amidst such a splashing and struggling as never was seen before, except when the Royal George went down. "Back wa'ater, sir," shouts Dando, "Back wa'ater, you sir, aft;" upon which everybody thinking he must be the individual referred to, they all back water, and back comes the boat, stern first, to the spot whence it started. "Back water, you sir, aft; pull round, you sir, for'ad, can't you?" shouts Dando in a frenzy of excitement. "Pull round, Tom, can't you?" re-echoes one of the party. "Tom an't for'ad," replies another. "Yes, he is," cries a third; and the unfortunate young man, at the imminent risk of breaking a blood-vessel, pulls and pulls until the head of the boat fairly lies in the direction of Vauxhall Bridge. "That's right—now pull all on you!" shouts Dando again, adding, in an under-tone, to somebody by him, "Blowed if hever I see sich a set of muffs!" and away jogs the boat in a zigzag direction, every one of the six oars dipping into the water at a different time; and the yard is once more clear, until the arrival of the next party.

A well-contested rowing-match on the Thames is a very lively and interesting scene. The water is studded with boats of all sorts, kinds, and descriptions; places in the coal-barges at the different wharfs are let to crowds of spectators, beer and tobacco flow freely about; men, women, and children wait for the start in breathless expectation; cutters of six and eight oars glide gently up and down, waiting to accompany their *protégés* during the race; bands of music add to the animation, if not to the harmony of the scene; groups of watermen are assembled at the different stairs, discussing the merits of the respective candidates; and the prize wherry, which is rowed slowly about by a pair of sculls, is an object of general interest.

Two o'clock strikes, and everybody looks anxiously in the direction of the bridge through which the candidates for the prize will come— half-past two, and the general attention which has been preserved so long begins to flag, when suddenly a gun is heard, and a noise of distant hurra'ing along each bank of the river—every head is bent forward—the noise draws nearer and nearer—the boats which have been waiting at the bridge start briskly up the river, and a well-manned galley shoots through the arch, the sitters cheering on the boats behind them, which are not yet visible.

"Here they are," is the general cry—and through darts the first boat, the men in her, stripped to the skin, and exerting every muscle to preserve the advantage they have gained—four other boats follow close astern; there are not two boats' length between them—the shouting is tremendous, and the interest intense. "Go, on Pink"—"Give it her, Red"—"Sulliwin for ever"—"Bravo! George"—"Now, Tom, now—now—now—why don't your partner stretch out?"—"Two pots to a pint on Yellow," &c., &c. Every little public-house fires its gun, and hoists its flag; and the men who win the heat, come in, amidst a splashing and shouting, and banging and confusion, which no one can imagine who has not witnessed it, and of which any description would convey a very faint idea.

One of the most amusing places we know, is the steam-wharf of the London Bridge, or St. Katharine's Dock Company, on a Saturday morning in summer, when the Gravesend and Margate steamers are usually crowded to excess; and as we have just taken a glance at the river above bridge, we hope our readers will not object to accompany us on board a Gravesend packet.

Coaches are every moment setting down at the entrance to the wharf, and the stare of bewildered astonishment with which the "fares" resign themselves and their luggage into the hands of the porters, who seize all the packages at once as a matter of course, and run away with them, heaven knows where, is laughable in the extreme. A Margate boat lies alongside the wharf, the Gravesend boat (which starts first) lies alongside that again; and as a temporary communication is formed between the two, by means of a plank and hand-rail, the natural confusion of the scene is by no means diminished.

"Gravesend?" inquires a stout father of a stout family, who follow him, under the guidance of their mother, and a servant, at the no small risk of two or three of them being left behind in the confusion. "Gravesend?"

"Pass on, if you please, sir," replies the attendant—"other boat, sir."

Hereupon the stout father, being rather mystified, and the stout mother rather distracted by maternal anxiety, the whole party deposit themselves in the Margate boat, and after having congratulated himself on having secured very comfortable seats, the stout father sallies to the chimney to look for his luggage, which he has a faint recollection of having given some man, something, to take somewhere. No luggage, however, bearing the most remote resemblance to his own, in shape or form, is to be discovered; on which the stout father calls very loudly for an officer, to whom he states the case, in the presence of another father of another family—a little thin man—who entirely concurs with him (the stout father) in thinking that it's high time something was done with these steam companies, and that as the Corporation Bill failed to do it, something else must; for really people's property is not to be sacrificed in this way; and that if the luggage isn't restored without delay, he will take care it shall be put in the papers, for the public is not to be the victim of these great monopolies. To this, the officer, in his turn, replies, that that company, ever since it has been St. Kat'rine's Dock Company, has protected life and property; that if it had been the London Bridge Wharf Company, indeed, he shouldn't have wondered, seeing that the morality of that company (they being the opposition) can't be answered for, by no one; but as it is, he's convinced there must be some mistake, and he wouldn't mind making a solemn oath afore a magistrate that the gentleman'll find his luggage afore he gets to Margate.

Here the stout father, thinking he is making a capital point, replies, that as it happens, he is not going to Margate at all, and that "Passenger to Gravesend" was on the luggage, in letters of full two inches long; on which the officer rapidly explains the mistake, and the stout mother and the stout children, and the servant, are hurried with all possible despatch on board the Gravesend boat, which they reach just in time to discover that their luggage is there, and that their comfortable seats are not. Then the bell, which is the signal for the Gravesend boat starting, begins to ring most furiously: and people keep time to the bell, by running in and out of our boat at a double-quick pace. The bell stops; the boat starts: people who have been taking leave of their friends on board, are carried away against their will; and people who have been taking leave of their friends on shore, find that they have performed a very needless ceremony, in consequence of their not being carried away at all. The regular passengers, who have season tickets, go below to breakfast; people who have purchased morning papers, compose themselves to read them; and people who have not been down the river before, think that both the shipping and the water look a great deal better at a distance.

When we get down about as far as Blackwall, and begin to move at a quicker rate, the spirits of the passengers appear to rise in proportion. Old women who have brought large wicker hand-baskets with them, set seriously to work at the demolition of heavy sandwiches, and pass round a wine-glass, which is frequently replenished from a flat bottle like a stomach-warmer, with considerable glee: handing it first to the gentleman in the foraging-cap, who plays the harp—partly as an expression of satisfaction with his previous exertions, and partly to induce him to play "Dumbledumbdeary," for "Alick" to dance to; which being done, Alick, who is a damp earthy child in red worsted socks, takes certain small jumps upon the deck, to the unspeakable satisfaction of his family circle. Girls who have brought the first volume of some new novel in their reticule, become extremely plaintive, and expatiate to Mr. Brown, or young Mr. O'Brien, who has been looking over them, on the blueness of the sky, and brightness of the water; on which Mr. Brown or Mr. O'Brien, as the case may be, remarks in a low voice that he has been quite insensible of late to the beauties of nature—that his whole thoughts and wishes have centred in one object alone—whereupon the young lady looks up, and failing in her attempt to appear unconscious, looks down again; and turns over the next leaf with great difficulty, in order to afford opportunity for a lengthened pressure of the hand.

Telescopes, sandwiches, and glasses of brandy-and-water cold without, begin to be in great requisition; and bashful men who have been looking down the hatchway at the engine, find, to their great relief, a subject on which they can converse with one another—and a copious one too—Steam.

"Wonderful thing steam, sir." "Ah! (a deep-drawn sigh) it is indeed, sir." "Great power, sir." "Immense—immense!" "Great deal done by steam, sir." "Ah! (another sigh at the immensity of the subject, and a knowing shake of the head) you may say that, sir." "Still in its infancy, they say, sir." Novel remarks of this kind, are generally the commencement of a conversation which is prolonged until the conclusion of the trip, and, perhaps, lays the foundation of a speaking acquaintance between half-a-dozen gentlemen, who, having their families at Gravesend, take season tickets for the boat, and dine on board regularly every afternoon.

Early Coaches

We have often wondered how many months' incessant travelling in a post-chaise it would take to kill a man; and wondering by analogy, we should very much like to know how many months of constant travelling in a succession of early coaches, an unfortunate mortal could endure. Breaking a man alive upon the wheel, would be nothing to breaking his rest, his peace, his heart—everything but his fast—upon four; and the punishment of Ixion (the only practical person, by-the-bye, who has discovered the secret of the perpetual motion) would sink into utter insignificance before the one we have suggested. If we had been a powerful churchman in those good times when blood was shed as freely as water, and men were mowed down like grass, in the sacred cause of religion, we would have lain by very quietly till we got hold of some especially obstinate miscreant, who positively refused to be converted to our faith, and then we would have booked him for an inside place in a small coach, which travelled day and night: and securing the remainder of the places for stout men with a slight tendency to coughing and spitting, we would have started him forth on his last travels; leaving him mercilessly to all the tortures which the waiters, landlords, coachmen, guards, boots, chambermaids, and other familiars on his line of road, might think proper to inflict.

Who has not experienced the miseries inevitably consequent upon a summons to undertake a hasty journey? You receive an intimation from your place of business—wherever that may be, or whatever you may be—that it will be necessary to leave town without delay. You and your family are forthwith thrown into a state of tremendous excitement; an express is immediately dispatched to the washer-woman's; everybody is in a bustle; and you, yourself, with a feeling of dignity which you cannot altogether conceal, sally forth to the booking-office to secure your place. Here a painful consciousness of your own unimportance first rushes on your mind—the people are as cool and collected as if nobody were going out of town, or as if a journey of a hundred odd miles were a mere nothing. You enter a mouldy-looking room, ornamented with large posting-bills; the greater part of the place enclosed behind a huge lumbering rough counter, and fitted up with recesses that look like the dens of the smaller animals in a travelling menagerie, without the bars. Some half-dozen people are "booking" brown-paper parcels, which one of the clerks flings into the aforesaid recesses with an air of recklessness which you, remembering the new carpet-bag you bought in the morning, feel considerably annoyed at; porters, looking like so many Atlases, keep rushing in and out, with large packages on their shoulders; and while you are waiting to make the necessary inquiries, you wonder what on earth the booking-office clerks can have been before they were booking-office clerks; one of them with his pen behind his ear, and his hands behind him, is standing in front of the fire, like a full-length portrait of Napoleon; the other with his hat half off his head, enters the passengers' names in the books with a coolness which is inexpressibly provoking; and the villain whistles—actually whistles—while a man asks him what the fare is outside, all the way to Holyhead!—in frosty weather, too! They are clearly an isolated race, evidently possessing no sympathies or feelings in common with the rest of mankind. Your turn comes at last, and having paid the fare, you tremblingly inquire—"What time will it be necessary for me to be here in the morning?"—"Six o'clock," replies the whistler, carelessly pitching the sovereign you have just parted with, into a wooden bowl on the desk. "Rather before than arter," adds the man with the semi-roasted unmentionables, with just as much ease and complacency as if the whole world got out of bed at five. You turn into the street,

ruminating as you bend your steps homewards on the extent to which
men become hardened in cruelty by custom.

If there be one thing in existence more miserable than another, it
most unquestionably is the being compelled to rise by candle-light. If
you ever doubted the fact, you are painfully convinced of your error,
on the morning of your departure. You left strict orders, overnight, to
be called at half-past four, and you have done nothing all night but
doze for five minutes at a time, and start up suddenly from a terrific
dream of a large church-clock with the small hand running round,
with astonishing rapidity, to every figure on the dial-plate. At last,
completely exhausted, you fall gradually into a refreshing sleep—your
thoughts grow confused—the stage-coaches, which have been "going
off" before your eyes all night, become less and less distinct, until they
go off altogether; one moment you are driving with all the skill and
smartness of an experienced whip—the next you are exhibiting à la
Ducrow, on the off-leader; anon you are closely muffled up, inside, and
have just recognised in the person of the guard an old schoolfellow,
whose funeral, even in your dream, you remember to have attended
eighteen years ago. At last you fall into a state of complete oblivion,
from which you are aroused, as if into a new state of existence, by a
singular illusion. You are apprenticed to a trunk-maker; how, or why,
or when, or wherefore, you don't take the trouble to inquire; but
there you are, pasting the lining in the lid of a portmanteau. Con-
found that other apprentice in the back shop, how he is hammering!—
rap, rap, rap—what an industrious fellow he must be! you have heard
him at work for half an hour past, and he has been hammering incessantly the whole time. Rap, rap, rap, again—he's talking now—
what's that he said? Five o'clock! You make a violent exertion, and
start up in bed. The vision is at once dispelled; the trunk-maker's shop
is your own bedroom, and the other apprentice your shivering servant,
who has been vainly endeavouring to wake you for the last quarter of
an hour, at the imminent risk of breaking either his own knuckles or
the panels of the door.

You proceed to dress yourself, with all possible dispatch. The flaring
flat candle with the long snuff gives light enough to show that the
things you want are not where they ought to be, and you undergo a
trifling delay in consequence of having carefully packed up one of
your boots in your overanxiety of the preceding night. You soon complete your toilet, however, for you are not particular on such an
occasion, and you shaved yesterday evening; so mounting your Peter-
sham great-coat, and green travelling shawl, and grasping your carpet-
bag in your right hand, you walk lightly downstairs, lest you should
awaken any of the family, and after pausing in the common sitting-
room for one moment, just to have a cup of coffee (the said common
sitting-room looking remarkably comfortable, with everything out of

its place, and strewed with the crumbs of last night's supper), you
undo the chain and bolts of the street-door, and find yourself fairly in
the street.

A thaw, by all that is miserable! The frost is completely broken up.
You look down the long perspective of Oxford Street, the gas-lights
mournfully reflected on the wet pavement, and can discern no speck
in the road to encourage the belief that there is a cab or a coach to
be had—the very coachmen have gone home in despair. The cold
sleet is drizzling down with that gentle regularity, which betokens a
duration of four-and-twenty hours at least; the damp hangs upon the
house-tops and lamp-posts, and clings to you like an invisible cloak.
The water is "coming in" in every area, the pipes have burst, the water-
butts are running over; the kennels seem to be doing matches against
time, pump-handles descend of their own accord, horses in market-
carts fall down, and there's no one to help them up again, policemen
look as if they had been carefully sprinkled with powdered glass; here
and there a milk-woman trudges slowly along, with a bit of list round
each foot to keep her from slipping; boys who "don't sleep in the
house," and are not allowed much sleep out of it, can't wake their
masters by thundering at the shop-door, and cry with the cold—the
compound of ice, snow, and water on the pavement, is a couple of
inches thick—nobody ventures to walk fast to keep himself warm, and
nobody could succeed in keeping himself warm if he did.

It strikes a quarter past five as you trudge down Waterloo Place on
your way to the Golden Cross, and you discover, for the first time, that
you were called about an hour too early. You have not time to go
back; there is no place open to go into, and you have, therefore, no
resource but to go forward, which you do, feeling remarkably satisfied
with yourself, and everything about you. You arrive at the office, and
look wistfully up the yard for the Birmingham High-flier, which, for
aught you can see, may have flown away altogether, for no preparations
appear to be on foot for the departure of any vehicle in the shape of a
coach. You wander into the booking-office, which with the gas-lights
and blazing fire, looks quite comfortable by contrast—that is to say, if
any place *can* look comfortable at half-past five on a winter's morning.
There stands the identical bookkeeper in the same position as if he
had not moved since you saw him yesterday. As he informs you, that
the coach is up the yard, and will be brought round in about a quarter
of an hour, you leave your bag, and repair to "The Tap"—not with
any absurd idea of warming yourself, because you feel such a result
to be utterly hopeless, but for the purpose of procuring some hot
brandy-and-water, which you do,—when the kettle boils! an event
which occurs exactly two minutes and a half before the time fixed for
the starting of the coach.

The first stroke of six peals from St. Martin's church steeple just as you take the first sip of the boiling liquid. You find yourself at the booking-office in two seconds, and the tap-waiter finds himself much comforted by your brandy-and-water, in about the same period. The coach is out; the horses are in, and the guard and two or three porters are stowing the luggage away, and running up the steps of the booking-office, and down the steps of the booking-office, with breathless rapidity. The place, which a few minutes ago was so still and quiet, is now all bustle; the early vendors of the morning papers have arrived, and you are assailed on all sides with shouts of "*Times*, gen'lm'n, *Times*," "Here's *Chron—Chron—Chron*," "*Herald*, ma'am," "Highly interesting murder, gen'lm'n," "Curious case o' breach o' promise, ladies." The inside passengers are already in their dens, and the outsides, with the exception of yourself, are pacing up and down the pavement to keep themselves warm; they consist of two young men with very long hair, to which the sleet has communicated the appearance of crystallised rats' tails; one thin young woman cold and peevish, one old gentleman ditto ditto, and something in a cloak and cap, intended to represent a military officer; every member of the party, with a large stiff shawl over his chin, looking exactly as if he were playing a set of Pan's pipes.

"Take off the cloths, Bob," says the coachman, who now appears for the first time, in a rough blue great-coat, of which the buttons behind are so far apart, that you can't see them both at the same time. "Now, gen'lm'n," cries the guard, with the waybill in his hand. "Five minutes behind time already!" Up jump the passengers—the two young men smoking like lime-kilns, and the old gentleman grumbling audibly. The thin young woman is got upon the roof, by dint of a great deal of pulling, and pushing, and helping and trouble, and she repays it by expressing her solemn conviction that she will never be able to get down again.

"All right," sings out the guard at last, jumping up as the coach starts, and blowing his horn directly afterwards, in proof of the soundness of his wind. "Let 'em go, Harry, give 'em their heads," cries the coachman—and off we start as briskly as if the morning were "all right," as well as the coach: and looking forward as anxiously to the termination of our journey, as we fear our readers will have done, long since, to the conclusion of our paper.

Omnibuses

~~~~~~

It is very generally allowed that public conveyances afford an extensive field for amusement and observation. Of all the public conveyances that have been constructed since the days of the Ark—we think that is the earliest on record—to the present time, commend us to an omnibus. A long stage is not to be despised, but there you have only six insides, and the chances are, that the same people go all the way with you—there is no change, no variety. Besides, after the first twelve hours or so, people get cross and sleepy, and when you have seen a man in his nightcap, you lose all respect for him; at least, that is the case with us. Then on smooth roads people frequently get prosy, and tell long stories, and even those who don't talk, may have very unpleasant predilections. We once travelled four hundred miles, inside a stage-coach, with a stout man, who had a glass of rum-and-water, warm, handed in at the window at every place where we changed horses. This was decidedly unpleasant. We have also travelled occasionally, with a small boy of a pale aspect, with light hair, and no perceptible neck, coming up to town from school under the protection of the guard, and directed to be left at the Cross Keys till called for. This is, perhaps, even worse than rum-and-water in a close atmosphere. Then there is the whole train of evils consequent on a change of the coachman; and the misery of the discovery—which the guard is sure to make the moment you begin to doze—that he wants a brown-paper parcel, which he distinctly remembers to have deposited under the seat on which you are reposing. A great deal of bustle and groping takes place, and when you are thoroughly awakened, and severely cramped, by holding your legs up by an almost supernatural exertion, while he is looking behind them, it suddenly occurs to him that he put it in the fore-boot. Bang goes the door; the parcel is immediately found; off starts the coach again; and the guard plays the key-bugle as loud as he can play it, as if in mockery of your wretchedness.

Now, you meet with none of these afflictions in an omnibus; sameness there can never be. The passengers change as often in the course of one journey as the figures in a kaleidoscope, and though not so glittering, are far more amusing. We believe there is no instance on record, of a man's having gone to sleep in one of these vehicles. As to long stories, would any man venture to tell a long story in an omnibus? and even if he did, where would be the harm? nobody could possibly hear what he was talking about. Again; children, though occasionally, are not often to be found in an omnibus; and even when they are, if the vehicle be full, as is generally the case, somebody sits upon them, and we are unconscious of their presence. Yes, after mature reflection, and considerable experience, we are decidedly of opinion that of all known vehicles, from the glass-coach in which we were taken to be christened, to that sombre caravan in which we must one day make our last earthly journey, there is nothing like an omnibus.

We will back the machine in which we make our daily peregrination from the top of Oxford Street to the city, against any "buss" on the road, whether it be for the gaudiness of its exterior, the perfect simplicity of its interior, or the native coolness of its cad. This young gentleman is a singular instance of self-devotion; his somewhat intemperate zeal on behalf of his employers is constantly getting him into trouble, and occasionally into the house of correction. He is no sooner emancipated, however, than he resumes the duties of his profession with unabated ardour. His principal distinction is his activity. His great boast is, "that he can chuck an old gen'lm'n into the buss, shut him in, and rattle off, afore he knows where it's a-going to"—a feat which he frequently performs, to the infinite amusement of every one but the old gentleman concerned, who, somehow or other, never can see the joke of the thing.

We are not aware that it has ever been precisely ascertained, how many passengers our omnibus will contain. The impression on the cad's mind evidently is, that it is amply sufficient for the accommodation of any number of persons that can be enticed into it. "Any room?" cries a very hot pedestrian. "Plenty o' room, sir," replies the conductor, gradually opening the door, and not disclosing the real state of the case until the wretched man is on the steps. "Where?" inquires the entrapped individual, with an attempt to back out again. "Either side, sir," rejoins the cad, shoving him in, and slamming the door. "All right, Bill." Retreat is impossible; the new-comer rolls about, till he falls down somewhere, and there he stops.

As we get into the city a little before ten, four or five of our party are regular passengers. We always take them up at the same places, and they generally occupy the same seats; they are always dressed in the same manner, and invariably discuss the same topics—the increasing rapidity of cabs, and the disregard of moral obligations evinced by omnibus men. There is a little testy old man, with a powdered head, who always sits on the right-hand side of the door as you enter, with his hands folded on the top of his umbrella. He is extremely impatient, and sits there for the purpose of keeping a sharp eye on the cad, with whom he generally holds a running dialogue. He is very officious in helping people in and out, and always volunteers to give the cad a poke with his umbrella, when any one wants to alight. He usually recommends ladies to have sixpence ready, to prevent delay; and if anybody puts a window down, that he can reach, he immediately puts it up again.

"Now, what are you stopping for?" says the little man every morning, the moment there is the slightest indication of "pulling up" at the corner of Regent Street, when some such dialogue as the following takes place between him and the cad:

"What are you stopping for?"

Here the cad whistles, and affects not to hear the question.

"I say [a poke], what are you stopping for?"

"For passengers, sir. Ba—nk.—Ty."

"I know you're stopping for passengers; but you've no business to do so. *Why* are you stopping?"

"Vy, sir, that's a difficult question. I think it is because we perfer stopping here to going on."

"Now mind," exclaims the little old man, with great vehemence, "I'll pull you up to-morrow; I've often threatened to do it; now I will."

"Thankee, sir," replies the cad, touching his hat with a mock expression of gratitude;—"werry much obliged to you indeed, sir." Here the old gentleman gets very red in the face, and seems highly exasperated.

The stout gentleman in the white neckcloth, at the other end of the vehicle, looks very prophetic, and says that something must shortly be done with these fellows, or there's no saying where all this will end; and the shabby-genteel man with the green bag, expresses his entire concurrence in the opinion, as he has done regularly every morning for the last six months.

A second omnibus now comes up, and stops immediately behind us. Another old gentleman elevates his cane in the air, and runs with all his might towards our omnibus; we watch his progress with great interest; the door is opened to receive him, he suddenly disappears—he has been spirited away by the opposition. Hereupon the driver of the opposition taunts our people with his having "regularly done 'em out of that old swell," and the voice of the "old swell" is heard, vainly protesting against this unlawful detention. We rattle off, the other omnibus rattles after us, and every time we stop to take up a passenger, they stop to take him too; sometimes we get him; sometimes they get him; but whoever don't get him, say they ought to have had him, and the cads of the respective vehicles abuse one another accordingly.

As we arrive in the vicinity of Lincoln's Inn Fields, Bedford Row, and other legal haunts, we drop a great many of our original passengers, and take up fresh ones, who meet with a very sulky reception. It is rather remarkable, that the people already in an omnibus always look at newcomers, as if they entertained some undefined idea that they have no business to come in at all. We are quite persuaded the little old man has some notion of this kind, and that he considers their entry as a sort of negative impertinence.

Conversation is now entirely dropped; each person gazes vacantly through the window in front of him, and everybody thinks that his opposite neighbour is staring at him. If one man gets out at Shoe Lane, and another at the corner of Farringdon Street, the little old gentleman grumbles, and suggests to the latter, that if he had got out at Shoe Lane too, he would have saved them the delay of another stoppage; whereupon the young men laugh again, and the old gentleman looks very solemn, and says nothing more till he gets to the Bank, when he trots off as fast as he can, leaving us to do the same, and to wish, as we walk away, that we could impart to others any portion of the amusement we have gained for ourselves.

Gin-Shops

It is a remarkable circumstance, that different trades appear to partake of the disease to which elephants and dogs are especially liable, and to run stark, staring, raving mad, periodically. The great distinction between the animals and the trades is, that the former run mad with a certain degree of propriety—they are very regular in their irregularities. We know the period at which the emergency will arise, and provide against it accordingly. If an elephant run mad, we are all ready for him—kill or cure—pills or bullets, calomel in conserve of roses, or lead in a musket-barrel. If a dog happen to look unpleasantly warm in the summer months, and to trot about the shady side of the streets with a quarter of a yard of tongue hanging out of his mouth, a thick leather muzzle, which has been previously prepared in compliance with the thoughtful injunctions of the Legislature, is instantly clapped over his head, by way of making him cooler, and he either looks remarkably unhappy for the next six weeks, or becomes legally insane, and goes mad, as it were, by Act of Parliament. But these trades are as eccentric as comets; nay, worse, for no one can calculate on the recurrence of the strange appearances which betoken the disease. Moreover, the contagion is general, and the quickness with which it diffuses itself, almost incredible.

We will cite two or three cases in illustration of our meaning. Six or eight years ago, the epidemic began to display itself among the linen-drapers and haberdashers. The primary symptoms were an inordinate love of plate glass, and a passion for gas-lights and gilding. The disease gradually progressed, and at last attained a fearful height. Quiet dusty old shops in different parts of town, were pulled down; spacious premises with stuccoed fronts and gold letters, were erected instead; floors were covered with Turkey carpets; roofs supported by massive pillars; doors knocked into windows, a dozen squares of glass into one; one shopman into a dozen; and there is no knowing what would have been done, if it had not been fortunately discovered, just in time, that the Commissioners of Bankruptcy were as competent to decide such cases as the Commissioners of Lunacy, and that a little confinement and gentle examination did wonders. The disease abated. It died away. A year or two of comparative tranquillity ensued. Suddenly it burst out again amongst the chemists; the symptoms were the same, with the addition of a strong desire to stick the royal arms over the shop-door, and a great rage for mahogany, varnish, and expensive floor-cloth. Then the hosiers were infected, and began to pull down their shop-fronts with frantic recklessness. The mania again died away, and the public began to congratulate themselves on its entire disappearance, when it burst forth with tenfold violence among the publicans, and keepers of "wine vaults." From that moment it has spread among them with unprecedented rapidity, exhibiting a concatenation of all the previous symptoms; onward it has rushed to every part of town, knocking down all the old public-houses, and depositing splendid mansions, stone balustrades, rosewood fittings, immense lamps, and illuminated clocks, at the corner of every street.

The extensive scale on which these places are established, and the ostentatious manner in which the business of even the smallest among them is divided into branches, is amusing. A handsome plate of ground glass in one door directs you "To the Counting-house;" another to the "Bottle Department;" a third to the "Wholesale Department;" a fourth to "The Wine Promenade;" and so forth, until we are in daily expectation of meeting with a "Brandy Bell," or a "Whiskey Entrance." Then, ingenuity is exhausted in devising attractive titles for the different descriptions of gin; and the dram-drinking portion of the community as they gaze upon the gigantic black and white announcements, which are only to be equalled in size by the figures beneath them, are left in a state of pleasing hesitation between "The Cream of the Valley," "The Out and Out," "The No Mistake," "The Good for Mixing," "The Real Knock-me-down,"

"The Celebrated Butter Gin," "The Regular Flare-up," and a dozen
other, equally inviting and wholesome *liqueurs*. Although places of
this description are to be met with in every second street, they are
invariably numerous and splendid in precise proportion to the dirt
and poverty of the surrounding neighbourhood. The gin-shops in and
near Drury Lane, Holborn, St. Giles's, Covent Garden, and Clare
Market, are the handsomest in London. There is more of filth and
squalid misery near those great thoroughfares than in any part of this
mighty city.

We will endeavour to sketch the bar of a large gin-shop, and its
ordinary customers, for the edification of such of our readers as may
not have had opportunities of observing such scenes; and on the
chance of finding one well suited to our purpose, we will make for
Drury Lane, through the narrow streets and dirty courts which divide
it from Oxford Street, and that classical spot adjoining the brewery at
the bottom of Tottenham Court Road, best known to the initiated as
the "Rookery."

The filthy and miserable appearance of this part of London can
hardly be imagined by those (and there are many such) who have not
witnessed it. Wretched houses with broken windows patched with rags
and paper: every room let out to a different family, and in many instances to two or even three—fruit and "sweet-stuff" manufacturers in
the cellars, barbers and red-herring vendors in the front parlours, cob-
blers in the back; a bird-fancier in the first floor, three families on the
second, starvation in the attics, Irishmen in the passage, a "musician"
in the front kitchen, and a charwoman and five hungry children in the
back one—filth everywhere—a gutter before the houses and a drain
behind—clothes drying and slops emptying, from the windows; girls
of fourteen or fifteen, with matted hair, walking about barefoot, and
in white great-coats, almost their only covering; boys of all ages, in
coats of all sizes and no coats at all; men and women, in every variety
of scanty and dirty apparel, lounging, scolding, drinking, smoking,
squabbling, fighting, and swearing.

You turn the corner. What a change! All is light and brilliancy. The
hum of many voices issues from that splendid gin-shop which forms
the commencement of the two streets opposite; and the gay building
with the fantastically ornamented parapet, the illuminated clock, the
plate-glass windows surrounded by stucco rosettes, and its profusion of
gas-lights in richly-gilt burners, is perfectly dazzling when contrasted
with the darkness and dirt we have just left. The interior is even gayer
than the exterior. A bar of French-polished mahogany, elegantly
carved, extends the whole width of the place; and there are two side-
aisles of great casks, painted green and gold, enclosed within a light
brass rail, and bearing such inscriptions as "Old Tom, 549;" "Young
Tom, 360;" "Samson, 1421"—the figures agreeing, we presume, with

"gallons," understand. Beyond the bar is a lofty and spacious saloon, full of the same enticing vessels, with a gallery running round it, equally well furnished. On the counter, in addition to the usual spirit apparatus, are two or three little baskets of cakes and biscuits, which are carefully secured at the top with wicker-work, to prevent their contents being unlawfully abstracted. Behind it are two showily-dressed damsels with large necklaces, dispensing the spirits and "compounds." They are assisted by the ostensible proprietor of the concern, a stout coarse fellow in a fur cap, put on very much on one side to give him a knowing air, and to display his sandy whiskers to the best advantage.

The two old washerwomen, who are seated on the little bench to the left of the bar, are rather overcome by the headdresses and haughty demeanour of the young ladies who officiate. They receive their half-quartern of gin and peppermint, with considerable deference, prefacing a request for "one of them soft biscuits," with a "Jist be good enough, ma'am." They are quite astonished at the impudent air of the young fellow in a brown coat and bright buttons, who, ushering in his two companions, and walking up to the bar in as careless a manner as if he had been used to green and gold ornaments all his life, winks at one of the young ladies with singular coolness, and calls for a "kervorten and a three-out-glass," just as if the place were his own. "Gin for you, sir?" says the young lady when she has drawn it: carefully looking every way but the right one, to show that the wink had no effect upon her. "For me, Mary, my dear," replies the gentleman in brown. "My name an't Mary as it happens," says the young girl, rather relaxing as she delivers the change. "Well, if it an't, it ought to be," responds the irresistible one; "all the Marys as ever I see, was handsome gals." Here the young lady, not precisely remembering how blushes are managed in such cases, abruptly ends the flirtation by addressing the female in the faded feathers who has just entered, and who, after stating explicitly, to prevent any subsequent misunderstanding, that "this gentleman pays," calls for "a glass of port wine and a bit of sugar."

Those two old men who came in "just to have a drain," finished their third quartern a few seconds ago; they have made themselves crying drunk; and the fat comfortable-looking elderly women, who had "a glass of rum-srub" each, having chimed in with their complaints on the hardness of the times, one of the women has agreed to stand a glass round, jocularly observing that "grief never mended no broken bones, and as good people's wery scarce, what I says is, make the most on 'em, and that's all about it!" a sentiment which appears to afford unlimited satisfaction to those who have nothing to pay.

It is growing late, and the throng of men, women, and children, who have been constantly going in and out, dwindles down to two or three occasional stragglers—cold, wretched-looking creatures, in the last stage of emaciation and disease. The knot of Irish labourers at the lower end of the place, who have been alternately shaking hands with, and threatening the life of each other, for the last hour, become furious in their disputes, and finding it impossible to silence one man, who is particularly anxious to adjust the difference, they resort to the expedient of knocking him down and jumping on him afterwards. The man in the fur cap, and the potboy rush out; a scene of riot and confusion ensues; half the Irishmen get shut out, and the other half get shut in; the potboy is knocked among the tubs in no time; the landlord hits everybody, and everybody hits the landlord; the barmaids scream; the police come in; the rest is a confused mixture of arms, legs, staves, torn coats, shouting, and struggling. Some of the party are borne off to the station-house, and the remainder slink home to beat their wives for complaining, and kick the children for daring to be hungry.

We have sketched this subject very slightly, not only because our limits compel us to do so, but because, if it were pursued farther, it would be painful and repulsive. Well-disposed gentlemen, and charitable ladies, would alike turn with coldness and disgust from a description of the drunken besotted men, and wretched broken-down miserable women, who form no inconsiderable portion of the frequenters of these haunts; forgetting, in the pleasant consciousness of their own rectitude, the poverty of the one, and the temptation of the other. Gin-drinking is a great vice in England, but wretchedness and dirt are a greater; and until you improve the homes of the poor, or persuade a half-famished wretch not to seek relief in the temporary oblivion of his own misery, with the pittance which, divided among his family, would furnish a morsel of bread for each, gin-shops will increase in number and splendour. If Temperance Societies would suggest an antidote against hunger, filth, and foul air, or could establish dispensaries for the gratuitous distribution of bottles of Lethe-water, gin-palaces would be numbered among the things that were.

Criminal Courts

We shall never forget the mingled feelings of awe and respect with which we used to gaze on the exterior of Newgate in our schoolboy days. How dreadful its rough heavy walls, and low massive doors, appeared to us—the latter looking as if they were made for the express purpose of letting people in, and never letting them out again. Then the fetters over the debtors' door, which we used to think were a *bonâ fide* set of irons, just hung up there for convenience sake, ready to be taken down at a moment's notice, and riveted on the limbs of some refractory felon! We were never tired of wondering how the hackney-coachmen on the opposite stand could cut jokes in the presence of such horrors, and drink pots of half-and-half so near the last drop.

Often have we strayed here, in sessions time, to catch a glimpse of the whipping-place, and that dark building on one side of the yard, in which is kept the gibbet with all its dreadful apparatus, and on the door of which we half expected to see a brass plate, with the inscription "Mr. Ketch;" for we never imagined that the distinguished functionary could by possibility live anywhere else! The days of these childish dreams have passed away, and with them many other boyish ideas of a gayer nature. But we still retain so much of our original feeling, that to this hour we never pass the building without something like a shudder.

What London pedestrian is there who has not, at some time or other, cast a hurried glance through the wicket at which prisoners are admitted into this gloomy mansion, and surveyed the few objects he could discern, with an indescribable feeling of curiosity? The thick door, plated with iron and mounted with spikes, just low enough to enable you to see, leaning over them, an ill-looking fellow in a broad-brimmed hat, Belcher handkerchief and top-boots: with a brown coat, something between a great-coat and a "sporting" jacket, on his back, and an immense key in his left hand. Perhaps you are lucky enough to pass, just as the gate is being opened; then, you see on the other side of the lodge, another gate, the image of its predecessor, and two or three more turnkeys, who look like multiplications of the first one, seated round a fire which just lights up the whitewashed apartment sufficiently to enable you to catch a hasty glimpse of these different objects. We have a great respect for Mrs. Fry, but she certainly ought to have written more romances than Mrs. Radcliffe.

We were walking leisurely down the Old Bailey, some time ago, when, as we passed this identical gate, it was opened by the officiating turnkey. We turned quickly round, as a matter of course, and saw two persons descending the steps. We could not help stopping and observing them.

They were an elderly woman, of decent appearance, though evidently poor, and a boy of about fourteen or fifteen. The woman was crying bitterly; she carried a small bundle in her hand, and the boy followed at a short distance behind her. Their little history was obvious. The boy was her son, to whose early comfort she had perhaps sacrificed her own—for whose sake she had borne misery without repining, and poverty without a murmur—looking steadily forward to the times when he who had so long witnessed her struggles for himself might be enabled to make some exertions for their joint support. He had formed dissolute connexions; idleness had led to crime; and he had been committed to take his trial for some petty theft. He had been long in prison, and, after receiving some trifling additional punishment, had been ordered to be discharged that morning. It was his first offence, and his poor old mother, still hoping to reclaim him, had been waiting at the gate to implore him to return home.

We cannot forget the boy; he descended the steps with a dogged look, shaking his head with an air of bravado and obstinate determination. They walked a few paces, and paused. The woman put her hand upon his shoulder in an agony of entreaty, and the boy sullenly raised his head as if in refusal. It was a brilliant morning, and every object looked fresh and happy in the broad, gay sunlight; he gazed round him for a few moments, bewildered with the brightness of the scene, for it was long since he had beheld anything save the gloomy walls of a prison. Perhaps the wretchedness of his mother made some impression on the boy's heart; perhaps some undefined recollection of the time when he was a happy child, and she his only friend and best companion, crowded on him—he burst into tears; and covering his face with one hand, and hurriedly placing the other in his mother's, walked away with her.

Curiosity has occasionally led us into both Courts at the Old Bailey. Nothing is so likely to strike the person who enters them for the first time, as the calm indifference with which the proceedings are conducted; every trial seems a mere matter of business. There is a great deal of form, but no compassion; considerable interest, but no sympathy. Take the Old Court for example. There sit the Judges, with whose great dignity everybody is acquainted, and of whom therefore we need say no more. Then, there is the Lord Mayor in the centre, looking as cool as a Lord Mayor *can* look, with an immense *bouquet* before him, and habited in all the splendour of his office. Then, there are the Sheriffs, who are almost as dignified as the Lord Mayor himself; and the Barristers, who are quite dignified enough in their own opinion; and the spectators, who having paid for their admission, look upon the whole scene as if it were got up especially for their amusement. Look upon the whole group in the body of the Court—some wholly engrossed in the morning papers, others carelessly conversing in low whispers, and others, again, quietly dozing away an hour—and you can scarcely believe that the result of the trial is a matter of life or death to one wretched being present. But turn your eyes to the dock; watch the prisoner attentively for a few moments; and the fact is before you, in all its painful reality. Mark how restlessly he has been engaged for the last ten minutes, in forming all sorts of fantastic figures with the herbs which are strewed upon the ledge before him; observe the ashy paleness of his face when a particular witness appears, and how he changes his position and wipes his clammy forehead and feverish hands, when the case for the prosecution is closed, as if it were a relief to him to feel that the jury knew the worst.

The defence is concluded; the judge proceeds to sum up the evidence; and the prisoner watches the countenances of the jury, as a dying man, clinging to life to the very last, vainly looks in the face of his physician for a slight ray of hope. They turn round to consult; you can almost hear the man's heart beat, as he bites the stalk of rosemary, with a desperate effort to appear composed. They resume their places —a dead silence prevails as the foreman delivers in the verdict— "Guilty!" A shriek bursts from a female in the gallery; the prisoner casts one look at the quarter from whence the noise proceeded; and is immediately hurried from the dock by the gaoler. The clerk directs one of the officers of the Court to "take the woman out," and fresh business is proceeded with, as if nothing had occurred.

No imaginary contrast to a case like this, could be complete as that which is constantly presented in the New Court, the gravity of which is frequently disturbed in no small degree, by the cunning and pertinacity of juvenile offenders. A boy of thirteen is tried, say for picking the pocket of some subject of her Majesty, and the offence is about as clearly proved as an offence can be. He is called upon for his defence, and contents himself with a little declamation about the jurymen and his country—asserts that all the witnesses have committed perjury, and hints that the police force generally have entered into a conspiracy "again" him. However probable this statement may be, it fails to convince the Court, and some such scene as the following then takes place:

Court: Have you any witnesses to speak to your character, boy?

Boy: Yes, my Lord; fifteen gen'lm'n is a vaten outside, and vos a vaten all day yesterday, vich they told me the night afore my trial vos a comin' on.

Court: Inquire for these witnesses.

Here, a stout beadle runs out, and vociferates for the witnesses at the very top of his voice; for you hear his cry grow fainter and fainter as he descends the steps into the court-yard below. After an absence of five minutes, he returns, very warm and hoarse, and informs the Court of what it knew perfectly well before—namely, that there are no such witnesses in attendance. Hereupon, the boy sets up a most awful howling; screws the lower part of the palms of his hands into the corners of his eyes; and endeavours to look the picture of injured innocence. The jury at once find him "guilty," and his endeavours to squeeze out a tear or two are redoubled. The governor of the gaol then states, in reply to an inquiry from the bench, that the prisoner has been under his care twice before. This the urchin resolutely denies in some such terms as—"S'elp me, gen'lm'n, I never vos in trouble afore—indeed, my Lord, I never vos. It's all a howen to my having a twin brother, vich has wrongfully got into trouble, and vich is so exactly like me, that no vun ever knows the difference atween us."

This representation, like the defence, fails in producing the desired effect, and the boy is sentenced, perhaps, to seven years' transportation. Finding it impossible to excite compassion, he gives vent to his feelings in an imprecation bearing reference to the eyes of "old big vig!" and as he declines to take the trouble of walking from the dock, is forthwith carried out, congratulating himself on having succeeded in giving everybody as much trouble as possible.

A Christmas Dinner

Christmas time! That man must be a misanthrope indeed, in whose breast something like a jovial feeling is not roused—in whose mind some pleasant associations are not awakened—by the recurrence of Christmas. There are people who will tell you that Christmas is not to them what it used to be; that each succeeding Christmas has found some cherished hope, or happy prospect, of the year before, dimmed or passed away; that the present only serves to remind them of reduced circumstances and straitened incomes—of the feasts they once bestowed on hollow friends, and of the cold looks that meet them now, in adversity and misfortune. Never heed such dismal reminiscences. There are few men who have lived long enough in the world, who cannot call up such thoughts any day in the year. Then do not select the merriest of the three hundred and sixty-five, for your doleful recollections, but draw your chair nearer the blazing fire—fill the glass and send round the song—and if your room be smaller than it was a dozen years ago, or if your glass be filled with reeking punch, instead of sparkling wine, put a good face on the matter, and empty it offhand, and fill another, and troll off the old ditty you used to sing, and thank God it's no worse. Look on the merry faces of your children (if you have any) as they sit round the fire. One little seat may be empty; one slight form that gladdened the father's heart, and roused the mother's pride to look upon, may not be there. Dwell not upon the past; think not that one short year ago, the fair child now resolving into dust, sat before you, with the bloom of health upon its cheek, and the gaiety of infancy in its joyous eye. Reflect upon your present blessings—of which every man has many—not on your past misfortunes, of which all men have some. Fill your glass again, with a merry face and contented heart. Our life on it, but your Christmas shall be merry, and your new year a happy one!

Who can be insensible to the outpourings of good feeling, and the honest interchange of affectionate attachment, which abound at this season of the year? A Christmas family-party! We know nothing in nature more delightful! There seems a magic in the very name of Christmas. Petty jealousies and discords are forgotten; social feelings are awakened, in bosoms to which they have long been strangers; father and son, or brother and sister, who have met and passed with averted gaze, or a look of cold recognition, for months before, proffer and return the cordial embrace, and bury their past animosities in their present happiness. Kindly hearts that have yearned towards each other, but have been withheld by false notions of pride and self-dignity, are again reunited, and all is kindness and benevolence! Would that Christmas lasted the whole year through (as it ought), and that the prejudices and passions which deform our better nature, were never called into action among those to whom they should ever be strangers!

The Christmas family-party that we mean, is not a mere assemblage of relations, got up at a week or two's notice, originating this year, having no family precedent in the last, and not likely to be repeated in the next. No. It is an annual gathering of all the accessible members of the family, young or old, rich or poor; and all the children look forward to it, for two months beforehand, in a fever of anticipation. Formerly, it was held at grandpapa's; but grandpapa getting old, and grandmamma getting old too, and rather infirm, they have given up house-keeping, and domesticated themselves with uncle George; so the party always takes place at uncle George's house, but grandmamma sends in most of the good things, and grandpapa always *will* toddle down, all the way to Newgate Market, to buy the turkey, which he engages a porter to bring home behind him in triumph, always insisting on the man's being rewarded with a glass of spirits, over and above his hire, to drink "a merry Christmas and a happy new year" to aunt George. As to grandmamma, she is very secret and mysterious for two or three days beforehand, but not sufficiently so to prevent rumours getting afloat that she has purchased a beautiful new cap with pink ribbons for each of the servants, together with sundry books, and pen-knives, and pencil-cases, for the younger branches; to say nothing of divers secret additions to the order originally given by aunt

George at the pastrycook's, such as another dozen of mince-pies for the dinner, and a large plum-cake for the children.

On Christmas Eve, grandmamma is always in excellent spirits, and after employing all the children, during the day, in stoning the plums, and all that, insists, regularly every year, on uncle George coming down into the kitchen, taking off his coat, and stirring the pudding for half an hour or so, which uncle George good-humouredly does, to the vociferous delight of the children and servants. The evening concludes with a glorious game of blindmans's buff, in an early stage of which grandpapa takes great care to be caught, in order that he may have an opportunity of displaying his dexterity.

On the following morning, the old couple, with as many of the children as the pew will hold, go to church in great state: leaving aunt George at home dusting decanters and filling casters, and uncle George carrying bottles into the dining-parlour, and calling for cork-screws, and getting into everybody's way.

When the church-party return to lunch, grandpapa produces a small sprig of mistletoe from his pocket, and tempts the boys to kiss their little cousins under it—a proceeding which affords both the boys and the old gentleman unlimited satisfaction, but which rather outrages grandmamma's ideas of decorum, until grandpapa says that when he was just thirteen years and three months old, *he* kissed grandmamma under a mistletoe too, on which the children clap their hands, and laugh very heartily, as do aunt George and uncle George; and grand-mamma looks pleased, and says, with a benevolent smile, that grand-papa was an impudent young dog, on which the children laugh very heartily again, and grandpapa more heartily than any of them.

But all these diversions are nothing to the subsequent excitement when grandmamma in a high cap, and slate-coloured silk gown; and grandpapa with a beautifully plaited shirt-frill, and white neckerchief; seat themselves on one side of the drawing-room fire, with uncle George's children and little cousins innumerable, seated in the front, waiting the arrival of the expected visitors. Suddenly a hackney-coach is heard to stop, and uncle George, who has been looking out the window, exclaims, "Here's Jane!" on which the children rush to the door, and helter-skelter downstairs; and uncle Robert and aunt Jane, and the dear little baby, and the nurse, and the whole party, are ushered upstairs amidst tumultuous shouts of "Oh, my!" from the children, and frequently repeated warnings not to hurt baby from the nurse. And grandpapa takes the child, and grandmamma kisses her daughter, and the confusion of this first entry has scarcely subsided, when some other aunts and uncles with more cousins arrive, and the grown-up cousins flirt with each other, and so do the little cousins too, for that matter, and nothing is to be heard but a confused din of talking, laughing, and merriment.

A hesitating double knock at the street-door, heard during a momentary pause in the conversation, excites a general inquiry of "Who's that?" and two or three children, who have been standing at the window, announce in a low voice, that it's "poor aunt Margaret." Upon which, aunt George leaves the room to welcome the new-comer; and grandmamma draws herself up, rather stiff and stately; for Margaret married a poor man without her consent, and poverty not being a sufficiently weighty punishment for her offence, has been discarded by her friends, and debarred the society of her dearest relatives. But Christmas has come round, and the unkind feelings that have struggled against better dispositions during the year, have melted away before its genial influence, like half-formed ice beneath the morning sun. It is not difficult in a moment of angry feeling for a parent to denounce a disobedient child; but to banish her at a period of general good-will and hilarity, from the hearth round which she has sat on so many anniversaries of the same day, expanding by slow degrees from infancy to girlhood, and then bursting, almost imperceptibly, into a woman, is widely different. The air of conscious rectitude, and cold forgiveness, which the old lady has assumed, sits ill upon her; and when the poor girl is led in by her sister, pale in looks and broken in hope—not from poverty, for that she could bear, but from the consciousness of undeserved neglect, and unmerited unkindness—it is easy to see how much of it is assumed. A momentary pause succeeds; the girl breaks suddenly from her sister and throws herself, sobbing, on her mother's neck. The father steps hastily forward, and takes her husband's hand. Friends crowd round to offer their hearty congratulations, and happiness and harmony again prevail.

As to the dinner, it's perfectly delightful—nothing goes wrong, and everybody is in the very best of spirits, and disposed to please and be pleased. Grandpapa relates a circumstantial account of the purchase of the turkey, with a slight digression relative to the purchase of previous turkeys, on former Christmas-days, which grandmamma corroborates in the minutest particular. Uncle George tells stories, and carves poultry, and takes wine, and jokes with the children at the side-table, and winks at the cousins that are making love, or being made love to, and exhilarates everybody with his good humour and hospitality; and when, at last, a stout servant staggers in with a gigantic pudding, with a sprig of holly in the top, there is such a laughing, and shouting, and clapping of little chubby hands, and kicking up of fat dumpy legs, as can only be equalled by the applause with which the astonishing feat of pouring lighted brandy into mince-pies is received by the younger visitors. Then the dessert!—and the wine!—and the fun! Such beautiful speeches, and *such* songs, from aunt Margaret's husband, who turns out to be such a nice man, and *so* attentive to grandmamma! Even grandpapa not only sings his annual song with unprecedented vigour, but on being honoured with an unanimous *encore*, according to annual custom, actually comes out with a new one which nobody but grandmamma ever heard before; and a young scape-grace of a cousin, who has been in some disgrace with the old people, for certain heinous sins of omission and commission—neglecting to call, and persisting in drinking Burton Ale—astonishes everybody into convulsions of laughter by volunteering the most extraordinary comic songs that ever were heard. And thus the evening passes, in a strain of rational good-will and cheerfulness, doing more to awaken the sympathies of every member of the party in behalf of his neighbour, and to perpetuate their good feeling during the ensuing year, than half the homilies that have ever been written, by half the Divines that have ever lived.

All of the selections in Part 1 are from SKETCHES BY BOZ, *1836*

Christmas and Its Ghosts

The "Christmas book" was an early Victorian holiday institution, and during the decade of the 1840's Dickens, then at the height of his early fame, wrote five of these books and published them in small-volume form as gift books for the Christmas season. The first of them, *A Christmas Carol*, immediately became and has always remained his most famous tale of this kind, but the four others were equally successful in their day. One of them, *The Cricket on the Hearth*, is a characteristic Dickensian and Victorian "fairy tale of home"; and the titles of two of the others—*The Battle of Life* and *The Haunted Man*—suggest cardinal motifs not only in Dickens's shorter stories but in his long novels. The books were charmingly illustrated, in typical Victorian style, by such illustrators of the 1840's as John Leech, who drew the celebrated pictures for *A Christmas Carol*; John Tenniel, later to become famous as the illustrator of Lewis Carroll's *Alice's Adventures in Wonderland* and *Through the Looking-Glass*; Landseer, Maclise, and Stanfield.

A Christmas Carol was issued in December 1843 and *The Chimes* in December 1844, both by Chapman and Hall of London. *The Cricket on the Hearth* followed in December 1845, *The Battle of Life* in December 1846, and *The Haunted Man* in December 1848, these three being published by Dickens's new publishers at that time, Bradbury and Evans of London. The five tales later made up the volume called *Christmas Books* in Dickens's collected works, and usually appear under that title in all modern editions.

A Christmas Carol

~~~~~~

STAVE I *MARLEY'S GHOST*

Marley was dead, to begin with. There is no doubt whatever about
that. The register of his burial was signed by the clergyman, the clerk,
the undertaker, and the chief mourner. Scrooge signed it. And
Scrooge's name was good upon 'Change for anything he chose to
put his hand to.

Old Marley was as dead as a door-nail.

Mind! I don't mean to say that I know, of my own knowledge, what
there is particularly dead about a door-nail. I might have been
inclined, myself, to regard a coffin-nail as the deadest piece of iron-
mongery in the trade. But the wisdom of our ancestors is in the
simile; and my unhallowed hands shall not disturb it, or the Country's
done for. You will therefore permit me to repeat, emphatically, that
Marley was as dead as a door-nail.

Scrooge knew he was dead? Of course he did. How could it be
otherwise? Scrooge and he were partners for I don't know how
many years. Scrooge was his sole executor, his sole administrator, his
sole assign, his sole residuary legatee, his sole friend, and sole mourner.
And even Scrooge was not so dreadfully cut up by the sad event,
but that he was an excellent man of business on the very day of the
funeral, and solemnised it with an undoubted bargain.

The mention of Marley's funeral brings me back to the point I
started from. There is no doubt that Marley was dead. This must be
distinctly understood, or nothing wonderful can come of the story I
am going to relate. If we were not perfectly convinced that Hamlet's
Father died before the play began, there would be nothing more
remarkable in his taking a stroll at night, in an easterly wind, upon
his own ramparts, than there would be in any other middle-aged
gentleman rashly turning out after dark in a breezy spot—say Saint
Paul's Churchyard for instance—literally to astonish his son's weak
mind.

Scrooge never painted out Old Marley's name. There it stood,
years afterwards, above the warehouse door: Scrooge and Marley. The

firm was known as Scrooge and Marley. Sometimes people new to business called Scrooge Scrooge, and sometimes Marley, but he answered to both names. It was all the same to him.

Oh! but he was a tight-fisted hand at the grindstone. Scrooge! a squeezing, wrenching, grasping, scraping, clutching, covetous, old sinner! Hard and sharp as flint, from which no steel had ever struck out generous fire; secret, and self-contained, and solitary as an oyster. The cold within him froze his old features, nipped his pointed nose, shrivelled his cheek, stiffened his gait; made his eyes red, his thin lips blue; and spoke out shrewdly in his grating voice. A frosty rime was on his head, and on his eyebrows, and his wiry chin. He carried his dog-days, and didn't thaw it one degree at Christmas.

External heat and cold had little influence on Scrooge. No warmth could warm, no wintry weather chill him. No wind that blew was bitterer than he, no falling snow was more intent upon its purpose, no pelting rain less open to entreaty. Foul weather didn't know where to have him. The heaviest rain, and snow, and hail, and sleet, could boast of the advantage over him in only one respect. They often "came down" handsomely, and Scrooge never did.

Nobody ever stopped him in the street to say, with gladsome looks, "My dear Scrooge, how are you? When will you come to see me?" No beggars implored him to bestow a trifle, no children asked him what it was o'clock, no man or woman ever once in all his life inquired the way to such and such a place, of Scrooge. Even the blind men's dogs appeared to know him; and when they saw him coming on, would tug their owners into doorways and up courts; and then would wag their tails as though they said, "No eye at all is better than an evil eye, dark master!"

But what did Scrooge care! It was the very thing he liked. To edge his way along the crowded paths of life, warning all human sympathy to keep its distance, was what the knowing ones call "nuts" to Scrooge.

Once upon a time—of all the good days in the year, on Christmas Eve—old Scrooge sat busy in his counting-house. It was cold, bleak, biting weather: foggy withal: and he could hear the people in the court outside, go wheezing up and down, beating their hands upon their breasts, and stamping their feet upon the pavement stones to warm them. The city clocks had only just gone three, but it was quite dark already—it had not been light all day—and candles were flaring in the windows of the neighbouring offices, like ruddy smears upon the palpable brown air. The fog came pouring in at every chink and keyhole, and was so dense without, that although the court was of the narrowest, the houses opposite were mere phantoms. To see the dingy cloud come drooping down, obscuring everything, one might have thought that Nature lived hard by, and was brewing on a large scale.

The door of Scrooge's counting-house was open that he might keep his eye upon his clerk, who in a dismal little cell beyond, a sort of Tank, was copying letters. Scrooge had a very small fire, but the clerk's fire was so very much smaller that it looked like one coal. But he couldn't replenish it, for Scrooge kept the coalbox in his own room; and so surely as the clerk came in with the shovel, the master predicted that it would be necessary for them to part. Wherefore the clerk put on his white comforter, and tried to warm himself at the candle; in which effort, not being a man of a strong imagination, he failed.

"A merry Christmas, uncle! God save you!" cried a cheerful voice. It was the voice of Scrooge's nephew, who came upon him so quickly that this was the first intimation he had of his approach.

"Bah!" said Scrooge, "Humbug!"

He had so heated himself with rapid walking in the fog and frost, this nephew of Scrooge's, that he was all in a glow; his face was ruddy and handsome; his eyes sparkled, and his breath smoked again.

"Christmas a humbug, uncle!" said Scrooge's nephew. "You don't mean that, I am sure."

"I do," said Scrooge. "Merry Christmas! What right have you to be merry? What reason have you to be merry? You're poor enough."

"Come, then," returned the nephew gaily. "What right have you to be dismal? What reason have you to be morose? You're rich enough."

Scrooge having no better answer ready on the spur of the moment said, "Bah!" again; and followed it up with "Humbug."

"Don't be cross, uncle!" said the nephew.

"What else can I be," returned the uncle, "when I live in such a world of fools as this? Merry Christmas! Out upon merry Christmas! What's Christmas time to you but a time for paying bills without money; a time for finding yourself a year older, but not an hour richer; a time for balancing your books and having every item in 'em through a round dozen of months presented dead against you? If I could work my will," said Scrooge indignantly, "every idiot who goes about with 'Merry Christmas' on his lips should be boiled with his own pudding, and buried with a stake of holly through his heart. He should!"

"Uncle!" pleaded the nephew.

"Nephew!" returned the uncle, sternly, "keep Christmas in your own way, and let me keep it in mine."

"Keep it!" repeated Scrooge's nephew. "But you don't keep it."

"Let me leave it alone, then," said Scrooge. "Much good may it do you! Much good it has ever done you!"

"There are many things from which I might have derived good, by which I have not profited, I dare say," returned the nephew. "Christmas among the rest. But I am sure I have always thought of Christmas time, when it has come round—apart from the veneration due to its sacred name and origin, if anything belonging to it can be apart from that—as a good time; a kind, forgiving, charitable, pleasant time; the only time I know of, in the long calendar of the year, when men and women seem by one consent to open their shut-up hearts freely, and to think of people below them as if they really were fellow-passengers to the grave, and not another race of creatures bound on other journeys. And therefore, uncle, though it has never put a scrap of gold or silver in my pocket, I believe that it *has* done me good, and *will* do me good; and I say, God bless it!"

The clerk in the Tank involuntarily applauded. Becoming immediately sensible of the impropriety, he poked the fire, and extinguished the last frail spark for ever.

"Let me hear another sound from *you*," said Scrooge, "and you'll keep your Christmas by losing your situation! You're quite a powerful speaker, sir," he added, turning to his nephew. "I wonder you don't go into Parliament."

"Don't be angry, uncle. Come! Dine with us to-morrow."

Scrooge said that he would see him—yes, indeed he did. He went the whole length of the expression, and said that he would see him in that extremity first.

"But why?" cried Scrooge's nephew. "Why?"

"Why did you get married?" said Scrooge.

"Because I fell in love."

"Because you fell in love!" growled Scrooge, as if that were the only one thing in the world more ridiculous than a merry Christmas. "Good afternoon!"

"Nay, uncle, but you never came to see me before that happened. Why give it as a reason for not coming now?"

"Good afternoon," said Scrooge.

"I want nothing from you; I ask nothing of you; why cannot we be friends?"

"Good afternoon," said Scrooge.

"I am sorry, with all my heart, to find you so resolute. We have never had any quarrel, to which I have been a party. But I have made the trial in homage to Christmas, and I'll keep my Christmas humour to the last. So A Merry Christmas, uncle!"

"Good afternoon!" said Scrooge.

"And A Happy New Year!"

"Good afternoon!" said Scrooge.

His nephew left the room without an angry word, notwithstanding. He stopped at the outer door to bestow the greetings of the season on the clerk, who, cold as he was, was warmer than Scrooge; for he returned them cordially.

"There's another fellow," muttered Scrooge; who overheard him:

"my clerk, with fifteen shillings a week, and a wife and family, talking about a merry Christmas. I'll retire to Bedlam."

This lunatic, in letting Scrooge's nephew out, had let two other people in. They were portly gentlemen, pleasant to behold, and now stood, with their hats off, in Scrooge's office. They had books and papers in their hands, and bowed to him.

"Scrooge and Marley's, I believe," said one of the gentlemen, referring to his list. "Have I the pleasure of addressing Mr. Scrooge, or Mr. Marley?"

"Mr. Marley has been dead these seven years," Scrooge replied. "He died seven years ago, this very night."

"We have no doubt his liberality is well represented by his surviving partner," said the gentleman, presenting his credentials.

It certainly was; for they had been two kindred spirits. At the ominous word "liberality," Scrooge frowned, and shook his head, and handed the credentials back.

"At this festive season of the year, Mr. Scrooge," said the gentleman, taking up a pen, "it is more than usually desirable that we should make some slight provision for the Poor and destitute, who suffer greatly at the present time. Many thousands are in want of common necessaries; hundreds of thousands are in want of common comforts, sir."

"Are there no prisons?" asked Scrooge.

"Plenty of prisons," said the gentleman, laying down the pen again.

"And the Union workhouses?" demanded Scrooge. "Are they still in operation?"

"They are. Still," returned the gentleman, "I wish I could say they were not."

"The Treadmill and the Poor Law are in full vigour, then?" said Scrooge.

"Both very busy, sir."

"Oh! I was afraid, from what you said at first, that something had occurred to stop them in their useful course," said Scrooge. "I'm very glad to hear it."

"Under the impression that they scarcely furnish Christian cheer of mind or body to the multitude," returned the gentleman, "a few of us are endeavouring to raise a fund to buy the Poor some meat and drink, and means of warmth. We choose this time because it is a time, of all others, when Want is keenly felt, and Abundance rejoices. What shall I put you down for?"

"Nothing!" Scrooge replied.

"You wish to be anonymous?"

"I wish to be left alone," said Scrooge. "Since you ask me what I wish, gentlemen, that is my answer. I don't make merry myself at

Christmas and I can't afford to make idle people merry. I help to
support the establishments I have mentioned—they cost enough; and
those who are badly off must go there."

"Many can't go there; and many would rather die."

"If they would rather die," said Scrooge, "they had better do it, and
decrease the surplus population. Besides—excuse me—I don't know
that."

"But you might know it," observed the gentleman.

"It's not my business," Scrooge returned. "It's enough for a man
to understand his own business, and not to interfere with other
people's. Mine occupies me constantly. Good afternoon, gentlemen!"

Seeing clearly that it would be useless to pursue their point, the
gentlemen withdrew. Scrooge resumed his labours with an improved
opinion of himself, and in a more facetious temper than was usual
with him.

Meanwhile the fog and darkness thickened so, that people ran about
with flaring links, proffering their services to go before horses in carriages, and conduct them on their way. The ancient tower of a church,
whose gruff old bell was always peeping slily down at Scrooge out of a
gothic window in the wall, became invisible, and struck the hours
and quarters in the clouds, with tremulous vibrations afterwards as if
its teeth were chattering in its frozen head up there. The cold became
intense. In the main street, at the corner of the court, some labourers
were repairing the gas-pipes, and had lighted a great fire in a brazier,
round which a party of ragged men and boys were gathered: warming
their hands and winking their eyes before the blaze in rapture. The
water-plug being left in solitude, its overflowings sullenly congealed,
and turned to misanthropic ice. The brightness of the shops where
holly sprigs and berries crackled in the lamp heat of the windows,
made pale faces ruddy as they passed. Poulterers' and grocers' trades
became a splendid joke: a glorious pageant, with which it was next
to impossible to believe that such dull principles as bargain and sale
had anything to do. The Lord Mayor, in the stronghold of the mighty
Mansion House, gave orders to his fifty cooks and butlers to keep
Christmas as a Lord Mayor's household should; and even the little
tailor, whom he had fined five shillings on the previous Monday for
being drunk and bloodthirsty in the streets, stirred up to-morrow's
pudding in his garret, while his lean wife and the baby sallied out
to buy the beef.

Foggier yet, and colder. Piercing, searching, biting cold. If the good
Saint Dunstan had but nipped the Evil Spirit's nose with a touch
of such weather as that, instead of using his familiar weapons, then
indeed he would have roared to lusty purpose. The owner of one
scant young nose, gnawed and mumbled by the hungry cold as bones

are gnawed by dogs, stooped down at Scrooge's keyhole to regale
him with a Christmas carol: but at the first sound of
                    "God bless you, merry gentleman!
                    May nothing you dismay!"
Scrooge seized the ruler with such energy of action, that the singer
fled in terror, leaving the keyhole to the fog and even more congenial
frost.

At length the hour of shutting up the counting-house arrived. With
an ill-will Scrooge dismounted from his stool, and tacitly admitted
the fact to the expectant clerk in the Tank, who instantly snuffed
his candle out, and put on his hat.

"You'll want all day to-morrow, I suppose?" said Scrooge.

"If quite convenient, sir."

"It's not convenient," said Scrooge, "and it's not fair. If I was to
stop half-a-crown for it, you'd think yourself ill-used, I'll be bound."

The clerk smiled faintly.

"And yet," said Scrooge, "you don't think *me* ill-used, when I
pay a day's wages for no work."

The clerk observed that it was only once a year.

"A poor excuse for picking a man's pocket every twenty-fifth of
December!" said Scrooge, buttoning his great-coat to the chin. "But I
suppose you must have the whole day. Be here all the earlier next
morning."

The clerk promised that he would; and Scrooge walked out with a
growl. The office was closed in a twinkling, and the clerk, with the
long ends of his white comforter dangling below his waist (for he
boasted no great-coat), went down a slide on Cornhill, at the end
of a lane of boys, twenty times, in honour of its being Christmas Eve,
and then ran home to Camden Town as hard as he could pelt, to
play at blindman's buff.

Scrooge took his melancholy dinner in his usual melancholy tavern;
and having read all the newspapers, and beguiled the rest of the
evening with his banker's-book, went home to bed. He lived in chambers which had once belonged to his deceased partner. They were a
gloomy suite of rooms, in a lowering pile of building up a yard, where
it had so little business to be, that one could scarcely help fancying it
must have run there when it was a young house, playing at hide-and-
seek with other houses, and forgotten the way out again. It was old
enough now, and dreary enough, for nobody lived in it but Scrooge,
the other rooms being all let out as offices. The yard was so dark that
even Scrooge, who knew its every stone, was fain to grope with his
hands. The fog and frost so hung about the black old gateway of
the house, that it seemed as if the Genius of the Weather sat in
mournful meditation on the threshold.

Now, it is a fact, that there was nothing at all particular about the knocker on the door, except that it was very large. It is also a fact, that Scrooge had seen it, night and morning, during his whole residence in that place; also that Scrooge had as little of what is called fancy about him as any man in the city of London, even including—which is a bold word—the corporation, aldermen, and livery. Let it also be borne in mind that Scrooge had not bestowed one thought on Marley, since his last mention of his seven-years' dead partner that afternoon. And then let any man explain to me, if he can, how it happened that Scrooge, having his key in the lock of the door, saw in the knocker, without its undergoing any intermediate process of change—not a knocker, but Marley's face.

Marley's face. It was not in impenetrable shadow as the other objects in the yard were, but had a dismal light about it, like a bad lobster in a dark cellar. It was not angry or ferocious, but looked at Scrooge as Marley used to look: with ghostly spectacles turned up on its ghostly forehead. The hair was curiously stirred, as if by breath or hot air; and, though the eyes were wide open, they were perfectly motionless. That, and its livid colour, made it horrible; but its horror seemed to be in spite of the face and beyond its control, rather than a part of its own expression.

As Scrooge looked fixedly at this phenomenon, it was a knocker again.

To say that he was not startled, or that his blood was not conscious of a terrible sensation to which it had been a stranger from infancy, would be untrue. But he put his hand upon the key he had relinquished, turned it sturdily, walked in, and lighted his candle.

He *did* pause, with a moment's irresolution, before he shut the door; and he *did* look cautiously behind it first, as if he half expected to be terrified with the sight of Marley's pigtail sticking out into the hall. But there was nothing on the back of the door, except the screws and nuts that held the knocker on, so he said "Pooh, pooh!" and closed it with a bang.

The sound resounded through the house like thunder. Every room above, and every cask in the wine-merchant's cellars below, appeared to have a separate peal of echoes of its own. Scrooge was not a man to be frightened by echoes. He fastened the door, and walked across the hall, and up the stairs; slowly too: trimming his candle as he went.

You may talk vaguely about driving a coach-and-six up a good old flight of stairs, or through a bad young Act of Parliament; but I mean to say you might have got a hearse up that staircase, and taken it broadwise, with the splinter-bar towards the wall and the door towards the balustrades: and done it easy. There was plenty of width for that, and room to spare; which is perhaps the reason why Scrooge thought he saw a locomotive hearse going on before him in the gloom. Half-a-dozen gas-lamps out of the street wouldn't have lighted the entry too well, so you may suppose that it was pretty dark with Scrooge's dip.

Up Scrooge went, not caring a button for that. Darkness is cheap, and Scrooge liked it. But before he shut his heavy door, he walked through his rooms to see that all was right. He had just enough recollection of the face to desire to do that.

Sitting-room, bed-room, lumber-room. All as they should be. Nobody under the table, nobody under the sofa; a small fire in the grate; spoon and basin ready; and the little saucepan of gruel (Scrooge had a cold in his head) upon the hob. Nobody under the bed; nobody in the closet; nobody in his dressing-gown, which was hanging up in a suspicious attitude against the wall. Lumber-room as usual. Old fire-guard, old shoes, two fish-baskets, washing-stand on three legs, and a poker.

Quite satisfied, he closed his door, and locked himself in; double-locked himself in, which was not his custom. Thus secured against surprise, he took off his cravat; put on his dressing-gown and slippers, and his nightcap; and sat down before the fire to take his gruel.

It was a very low fire indeed; nothing on such a bitter night. He was obliged to sit close to it, and brood over it, before he could extract the least sensation of warmth from such a handful of fuel. The fireplace was an old one, built by some Dutch merchant long ago, and paved all round with quaint Dutch tiles, designed to illustrate the Scriptures. There were Cains and Abels, Pharaoh's daughters, Queens of Sheba, Angelic messengers descending through the air on clouds like feather-beds, Abrahams, Belshazzars, Apostles putting off to sea in butter-boats, hundreds of figures to attract his thoughts; and yet that face of Marley, seven years dead, came like the ancient Prophet's rod, and swallowed up the whole. If each smooth tile had been a blank at first, with power to shape some picture on its surface from the disjointed fragments of his thoughts, there would have been a copy of old Marley's head on every one.

"Humbug!" said Scrooge; and walked across the room.

After several turns, he sat down again. As he threw his head back in the chair, his glance happened to rest upon a bell, a disused bell, that hung in the room, and communicated for some purpose now forgotten with a chamber in the highest story of the building. It was with great astonishment, and with a strange, inexplicable dread, that as he looked, he saw this bell begin to swing. It swung so softly in the outset that it scarcely made a sound; but soon it rang out loudly, and so did every bell in the house.

This might have lasted half a minute, or a minute, but it seemed an hour. The bells ceased as they had begun, together. They were succeeded by a clanking noise, deep down below; as if some person were dragging a heavy chain over the casks in the wine-merchant's cellar. Scrooge then remembered to have heard that ghosts in haunted houses were described as dragging chains.

The cellar-door flew open with a booming sound, and then he heard the noise much louder, on the floors below; then coming up the stairs; then coming straight towards his door.

"It's humbug still!" said Scrooge. "I won't believe it."

His colour changed though, when, without a pause, it came on through the heavy door, and passed into the room before his eyes. Upon its coming in, the dying flame leaped up, as though it cried, "I know him; Marley's Ghost!" and fell again.

The same face: the very same. Marley in his pigtail, usual waistcoat, tights and boots; the tassels on the latter bristling, like his pigtail, and his coat-skirts, and the hair upon his head. The chain he drew was clasped about his middle. It was long, and wound about him like a tail; and it was made (for Scrooge observed it closely) of cash-boxes, keys, padlocks, ledgers, deeds, and heavy purses wrought in steel. His body was transparent; so that Scrooge, observing him, and looking through his waistcoat, could see the two buttons on his coat behind.

Scrooge had often heard it said that Marley had no bowels, but he had never believed it until now.

No, nor did he believe it even now. Though he looked the phantom through and through, and saw it standing before him; though he felt the chilling influence of its death-cold eyes; and marked the very texture of the folded kerchief bound about its head and chin, which wrapper he had not observed before; he was still incredulous, and fought against his senses.

"How now!" said Scrooge, caustic and cold as ever. "What do you want with me?"

"Much!"—Marley's voice, no doubt about it.

"Who are you?"

"Ask me who I *was*."

"Who *were* you then?" said Scrooge, raising his voice. "You're particular, for a shade." He was going to say "*to* a shade," but substituted this, as more appropriate.

"In life I was your partner, Jacob Marley."

"Can you—can you sit down?" asked Scrooge, looking doubtfully at him.

"I can."

"Do it, then."

Scrooge asked the question, because he didn't know whether a ghost so transparent might find himself in a condition to take a chair; and felt that in the event of its being impossible, it might involve the necessity of an embarrassing explanation. But the ghost sat down on the opposite side of the fireplace, as if he were quite used to it.

"You don't believe in me," observed the Ghost.

"I don't," said Scrooge.

"What evidence would you have of my reality beyond that of your senses?"

"I don't know," said Scrooge.

"Why do you doubt your senses?"

"Because," said Scrooge, "a little thing affects them. A slight disorder of the stomach makes them cheats. You may be an undigested bit of beef, a blot of mustard, a crumb of cheese, a fragment of an underdone potato. There's more of gravy than of grave about you, whatever you are!"

Scrooge was not much in the habit of cracking jokes, nor did he feel, in his heart, by any means waggish then. The truth is, that he tried to be smart, as a means of distracting his own attention, and keeping down his terror; for the spectre's voice disturbed the very marrow in his bones.

To sit, staring at those fixed glazed eyes, in silence for a moment, would play, Scrooge felt, the very deuce with him. There was something very awful, too, in the spectre's being provided with an infernal atmosphere of its own. Scrooge could not feel it himself, but this was clearly the case; for though the Ghost sat perfectly motionless, its hair, and skirts, and tassels, were still agitated as by the hot vapour from an oven.

"You see this toothpick?" said Scrooge, returning quickly to the charge, for the reason just assigned; and wishing, though it were only for a second, to divert the vision's stony gaze from himself.

"I do," replied the Ghost.

"You are not looking at it," said Scrooge.

"But I see it," said the Ghost, "notwithstanding."

"Well!" returned Scrooge, "I have but to swallow this, and be for the rest of my days persecuted by a legion of goblins, all of my own creation. Humbug, I tell you! humbug!"

At this the spirit raised a frightful cry, and shook its chain with such a dismal and appalling noise, that Scrooge held on tight to his chair, to save himself from falling in a swoon. But how much greater was his horror, when the phantom taking off the bandage round its head, as if it were too warm to wear indoors, its lower jaw dropped down upon its breast!

Scrooge fell upon his knees, and clasped his hands before his face.

"Mercy!" he said. "Dreadful apparition, why do you trouble me?"

"Man of the worldly mind!" replied the Ghost, "do you believe in me or not?"

"I do," said Scrooge. "I must. But why do spirits walk the earth, and why do they come to me?"

"It is required of every man," the Ghost returned, "that the spirit within him should walk abroad among his fellow-men, and travel far and wide; and if that spirit goes not forth in life, it is condemned to do so after death. It is doomed to wander through the world—oh, woe is me!—and witness what it cannot share, but might have shared on earth, and turned to happiness!"

Again the spectre raised a cry, and shook its chain and wrung its shadowy hands.

"You are fettered," said Scrooge, trembling. "Tell me why."

"I wear the chain I forged in life," replied the Ghost. "I made it link by link, and yard by yard; I girded it on of my own free will, and of my own free will I wore it. Is its pattern strange to *you*?"

Scrooge trembled more and more.

"Or would you know," pursued the Ghost, "the weight and length of the strong coil you bear yourself? It was full as heavy and as long as this, seven Christmas Eves ago. You have laboured on it since. It is a ponderous chain!"

Scrooge glanced about him on the floor, in the expectation of finding himself surrounded by some fifty or sixty fathoms of iron cable: but he could see nothing.

"Jacob," he said, imploringly. "Old Jacob Marley, tell me more. Speak comfort to me, Jacob!"

"I have none to give," the Ghost replied. "It comes from other regions, Ebenezer Scrooge, and is conveyed by other ministers, to other kinds of men. Nor can I tell you what I would. A very little more is all permitted to me. I cannot rest, I cannot stay, I cannot linger anywhere. My spirit never walked beyond our counting-house —mark me!—in life my spirit never roved beyond the narrow limits of our money-changing hole; and weary journeys lie before me!"

It was a habit with Scrooge, whenever he became thoughtful, to put his hands in his breeches pockets. Pondering on what the Ghost had said, he did so now, but without lifting up his eyes, or getting off his knees.

"You must have been very slow about it, Jacob," Scrooge observed, in a business-like manner, though with humility and deference.

"Slow!" the Ghost repeated.

"Seven years dead," mused Scrooge. "And travelling all the time!"

"The whole time," said the Ghost. "No rest, no peace. Incessant torture of remorse."

"You travel fast?" said Scrooge.

"On the wings of the wind," replied the Ghost.

"You might have got over a great quantity of ground in seven years," said Scrooge.

The Ghost, on hearing this, set up another cry, and clanked its chain so hideously in the dead silence of the night, that the Ward would have been justified in indicting it for a nuisance.

"Oh! captive, bound, and double-ironed," cried the phantom, "not to know that ages of incessant labour by immortal creatures for this earth must pass into eternity before the good of which it is susceptible is all developed. Not to know that any Christian spirit working kindly in its little sphere, whatever it may be, will find its mortal life too short for its vast means of usefulness. Not to know that no space of regret can make amends for one life's opportunity misused! Yet such was I! Oh! such was I!"

"But you were always a good man of business, Jacob," faltered Scrooge, who now began to apply this to himself.

"Business!" cried the Ghost, wringing its hands again. "Mankind was my business. The common welfare was my business; charity, mercy, forbearance, and benevolence, were all my business. The dealings of my trade were but a drop of water in the comprehensive ocean of my business!"

It held up its chain at arm's length, as if that were the cause of all its unavailing grief, and flung it heavily upon the ground again.

"At this time of the rolling year," the spectre said, "I suffer most. Why did I walk through crowds of fellow-beings with my eyes turned down, and never raise them to that blessed Star which led the Wise Men to a poor abode! Were there no poor homes to which its light would have conducted *me!*"

Scrooge was very much dismayed to hear the spectre going on at this rate, and began to quake exceedingly.

"Hear me!" cried the Ghost. "My time is nearly gone."

"I will," said Scrooge. "But don't be hard upon me! Don't be flowery, Jacob! Pray!"

"How it is that I appear before you in a shape that you can see, I may not tell. I have sat invisible beside you many and many a day."

It was not an agreeable idea. Scrooge shivered, and wiped the perspiration from his brow.

"That is no light part of my penance," pursued the Ghost. "I am here to-night to warn you, that you have yet a chance and hope of escaping my fate. A chance and hope of my procuring, Ebenezer."

"You were always a good friend to me," said Scrooge. "Thank'ee!"

"You will be haunted," resumed the Ghost, "by Three Spirits."

Scrooge's countenance fell almost as low as the Ghost's had done.

"Is that the chance and hope you mentioned, Jacob?" he demanded, in a faltering voice.

"It is."

"I—I think I'd rather not," said Scrooge.

"Without their visits," said the Ghost, "you cannot hope to shun the path I tread. Expect the first to-morrow, when the bell tolls One."

"Couldn't I take 'em all at once, and have it over, Jacob?" hinted Scrooge.

"Expect the second on the next night at the same hour. The third upon the next night when the last stroke of Twelve has ceased to vibrate. Look to see me no more; and look that, for your own sake, you remember what has passed between us!"

When it had said these words, the spectre took its wrapper from the table, and bound it round its head, as before. Scrooge knew this, by the smart sound its teeth made, when the jaws were brought together by the bandage. He ventured to raise his eyes again, and found his supernatural visitor confronting him in an erect attitude, with its chain wound over and about its arm.

The apparition walked backward from him; and at every step it took the window raised itself a little, so that when the spectre reached it, it was wide open.

It beckoned Scrooge to approach, which he did. When they were within two paces of each other, Marley's Ghost held up its hand, warning him to come no nearer. Scrooge stopped.

Not so much in obedience, as in surprise and fear: for on the raising of the hand, he became sensible of confused voices in the air; incoherent sounds of lamentation and regret; wailings inexpressibly sorrowful and self-accusatory. The spectre, after listening for a moment, joined in the mournful dirge; and floated out upon the bleak, dark night.

Scrooge followed to the window: desperate in his curiosity. He looked out.

The air was filled with phantoms, wandering hither and thither in restless haste, and moaning as they went. Every one of them wore chains like Marley's Ghost; some few (they might be guilty governments) were linked together; none were free. Many had been personally known to Scrooge in their lives. He had been quite familiar with one old ghost, in a white waistcoat, with a monstrous iron safe attached to its ankle, who cried piteously at being unable to assist a wretched woman with an infant, whom it saw below, upon a doorstep. The misery with them all was, clearly, that they sought to interfere, for good, in human matters, and had lost the power for ever.

Whether these creatures faded into mist, or mist enshrouded them, he could not tell. But they and their spirit voices faded together; and the night became as it had been when he walked home.

Scrooge closed the window, and examined the door by which the Ghost had entered. It was double-locked, as he had locked it with his own hands, and the bolts were undisturbed. He tried to say "Humbug!" but stopped at the first syllable. And being, from the emotion he had undergone, or the fatigues of the day, or his glimpse of the Invisible World, or the dull conversation of the Ghost, or the lateness of the hour, much in need of repose; went straight to bed, without undressing, and fell asleep upon the instant.

STAVE II   *THE FIRST OF THE THREE SPIRITS*

When Scrooge awoke, it was so dark that, looking out of bed, he could scarcely distinguish the transparent window from the opaque walls of his chamber. He was endeavouring to pierce the darkness with his ferret eyes, when the chimes of a neighbouring church struck the four quarters. So he listened for the hour.

To his great astonishment the heavy bell went on from six to seven, and from seven to eight, and regularly up to twelve; then stopped. Twelve! It was past two when he went to bed. The clock was wrong. An icicle must have got into the works. Twelve!

He touched the spring of his repeater, to correct this most preposterous clock. Its rapid little pulse beat twelve: and stopped.

"Why, it isn't possible," said Scrooge, "that I can have slept through a whole day and far into another night. It isn't possible that anything has happened to the sun, and this is twelve at noon!"

The idea being an alarming one, he scrambled out of bed, and groped his way to the window. He was obliged to rub the frost off with the sleeve of his dressing-gown before he could see anything; and could see very little then. All he could make out was, that it was still very foggy and extremely cold, and that there was no noise of people running to and fro, and making a great stir, as there unquestionably would have been if night had beaten off bright day, and taken possession of the world. This was a great relief, because "three days after sight of this First of Exchange pay to Mr. Ebenezer Scrooge or his order," and so forth, would have become a mere United States' security if there were no days to count by.

Scrooge went to bed again, and thought, and thought, and thought it over and over and over, and could make nothing of it. The more he thought, the more perplexed he was; and the more he endeavoured not to think, the more he thought.

Marley's Ghost bothered him exceedingly. Every time he resolved within himself, after mature inquiry, that it was all a dream, his mind flew back again, like a strong spring released, to its first position, and presented the same problem to be worked all through, "Was it a dream or not?"

Scrooge lay in this state until the chime had gone three quarters more, when he remembered, on a sudden, that the Ghost had warned him of a visitation when the bell tolled one. He resolved to lie awake until the hour was passed; and, considering that he could no more go to sleep than go to Heaven, this was perhaps the wisest resolution in his power.

The quarter was so long, that he was more than once convinced he must have sunk into a doze unconsciously, and missed the clock. At length it broke upon his listening ear.

"Ding, dong!"

"A quarter past," said Scrooge, counting.

"Ding, dong!"

"Half-past!" said Scrooge.

"Ding, dong!"

"A quarter to it," said Scrooge.

"Ding, dong!"

"The hour itself," said Scrooge, triumphantly, "and nothing else!"

He spoke before the hour bell sounded, which it now did with a deep, dull, hollow, melancholy ONE. Light flashed up in the room upon the instant, and the curtains of his bed were drawn.

The curtains of his bed were drawn aside, I tell you, by a hand. Not the curtains at his feet, nor the curtains at his back, but those to which his face was addressed. The curtains of his bed were drawn aside; and Scrooge, starting up into a half-recumbent attitude, found himself face to face with the unearthly visitor who drew them: as close to it as I am now to you, and I am standing in the spirit at your elbow.

It was a strange figure—like a child: yet not so like a child as like an old man, viewed through some supernatural medium, which gave him the appearance of having receded from the view, and being diminished to a child's proportions. Its hair, which hung about its neck and down its back, was white as if with age; and yet the face had not a wrinkle in it, and the tenderest bloom was on the skin. The arms were very long and muscular; the hands the same, as if its hold were of uncommon strength. Its legs and feet, most delicately formed, were, like those upper members, bare. It wore a tunic of the purest white; and round its waist was bound a lustrous belt, the sheen of which was beautiful. It held a branch of fresh green holly in its hand; and, in singular contradiction of that wintry emblem, had its dress trimmed with summer flowers. But the strangest thing about it was, that from the crown of its head there sprung a bright clear jet of light, by which all this was visible; and which was doubtless the occasion of its using, in its duller moments, a great extinguisher for a cap, which it now held under its arm.

Even this, though, when Scrooge looked at it with increasing steadiness, was *not* its strangest quality. For as its belt sparkled and glittered now in one part and now in another, and what was light one instant, at another time was dark, so the figure itself fluctuated in its distinctness: being now a thing with one arm, now with one leg, now with twenty legs, now a pair of legs without a head, now a head without a body: of which dissolving parts, no outline would be visible in the dense gloom wherein they melted away. And in the very wonder of this, it would be itself again, distinct and clear as ever.

"Are you the Spirit, sir, whose coming was foretold to me?" asked Scrooge.

"I am!"

The voice was soft and gentle. Singularly low, as if instead of being so close beside him, it were at a distance.

"Who, and what are you?" Scrooge demanded.

"I am the Ghost of Christmas Past."

"Long past?" inquired Scrooge: observant of its dwarfish stature.

"No. Your past."

Perhaps Scrooge could not have told anybody why, if anybody could have asked him; but he had a special desire to see the Spirit in his cap, and begged him to be covered.

"What!" exclaimed the Ghost, "would you so soon put out, with worldly hands, the light I give? Is it not enough that you are one of those whose passions made this cap, and force me through whole trains of years to wear it low upon my brow!"

Scrooge reverently disclaimed all intention to offend or any knowledge of having wilfully "bonneted" the Spirit at any period of his life. He then made bold to inquire what business brought him there.

"Your welfare!" said the Ghost.

Scrooge expressed himself much obliged, but could not help thinking that a night of unbroken rest would have been more conducive to that end. The Spirit must have heard him thinking, for it said immediately:

"Your reclamation, then. Take heed!"

It put out its strong hand as it spoke, and clasped him gently by the arm.

"Rise! and walk with me!"

It would have been in vain for Scrooge to plead that the weather and the hour were not adapted to pedestrian purposes; that bed was warm, and the thermometer a long way below freezing; that he was clad but lightly in his slippers, dressing-gown, and nightcap; and that he had a cold upon him at that time. The grasp, though gentle as a woman's hand, was not to be resisted. He rose: but finding that the Spirit made towards the window, clasped his robe in supplication.

"I am a mortal," Scrooge remonstrated, "and liable to fall."

"Bear but a touch of my hand *there*," said the Spirit, laying it upon his heart, "and you shall be upheld in more than this!"

As the words were spoken, they passed through the wall, and stood

upon an open country road, with fields on either hand. The city had
entirely vanished. Not a vestige of it was to be seen. The darkness and
the mist had vanished with it, for it was a clear, cold, wintry day, with
snow upon the ground.

"Good Heaven!" said Scrooge, clasping his hands together, as he
looked about him. "I was bred in this place. I was a boy here!"

The Spirit gazed upon him mildly. Its gentle touch, though it had
been light and instantaneous, appeared still present to the old man's
sense of feeling. He was conscious of a thousand odours floating
in the air, each one connected with a thousand thoughts, and hopes,
and joys, and cares long, long, forgotten!

"Your lip is trembling," said the Ghost. "And what is that upon
your cheek?"

Scrooge muttered, with an unusual catching in his voice, that it
was a pimple; and begged the Ghost to lead him where he would.

"You recollect the way?" inquired the Spirit.

"Remember it!" cried Scrooge with fervour; "I could walk it blind-
fold."

"Strange to have forgotten it for so many years!" observed the
Ghost. "Let us go on."

They walked along the road, Scrooge recognising every gate, and
post, and tree; until a little market-town appeared in the distance,
with its bridge, its church, and winding river. Some shaggy ponies
now were seen trotting towards them with boys upon their backs,
who called to other boys in country gigs and carts, driven by farmers.
All these boys were in great spirits, and shouted to each other, until
the broad fields were so full of merry music, that the crisp air laughed
to hear it!

"These are but shadows of the things that have been," said the
Ghost. "They have no consciousness of us."

The jocund travellers came on; and as they came, Scrooge knew
and named them every one. Why was he rejoiced beyond all bounds
to see them! Why did his cold eye glisten, and his heart leap up as
they went past! Why was he filled with gladness when he heard them
give each other Merry Christmas, as they parted at cross-roads and
bye-ways, for their several homes! What was merry Christmas to
Scrooge? Out upon merry Christmas! What good had it ever done
to him?

"The school is not quite deserted," said the Ghost. "A solitary child,
neglected by his friends, is left there still."

Scrooge said he knew it. And he sobbed.

They left the high-road, by a well-remembered lane, and soon approached a mansion of dull red brick, with a little weathercock-
surmounted cupola on the roof, and a bell hanging in it. It was a
large house, but one of broken fortunes; for the spacious offices were

little used, their walls were damp and mossy, their windows broken, and their gates decayed. Fowls clucked and strutted in the stables; and the coach-houses and sheds were over-run with grass. Nor was it more retentive of its ancient state, within; for entering the dreary hall, and glancing through the open doors of many rooms, they found them poorly furnished, cold, and vast. There was an earthy savour in the air, a chilly bareness in the place, which associated itself somehow with too much getting up by candle-light, and not too much to eat.

They went, the Ghost and Scrooge, across the hall, to a door at the back of the house. It opened before them, and disclosed a long, bare, melancholy room, made barer still by lines of plain deal forms and desks. At one of these a lonely boy was reading near a feeble fire; and Scrooge sat down upon a form, and wept to see his poor forgotten self as he used to be.

Not a latent echo in the house, not a squeak and scuffle from the mice behind the panelling, not a drip from the half-thawed water-spout in the dull yard behind, not a sigh among the leafless boughs of one despondent poplar, not the idle swinging of an empty store-house door, no, not a clicking in the fire, but fell upon the heart of Scrooge with a softening influence, and gave a freer passage to his tears.

The Spirit touched him on the arm, and pointed to his younger self, intent upon his reading. Suddenly a man, in foreign garments: wonderfully real and distinct to look at: stood outside the window, with an axe stuck in his belt, and leading by the bridle an ass laden with wood.

"Why, it's Ali Baba!" Scrooge exclaimed in ecstasy. "It's dear old honest Ali Baba! Yes, yes, I know! One Christmas time, when yonder solitary child was left here all alone, he *did* come, for the first time, just like that. Poor boy! And Valentine," said Scrooge, "and his wild brother, Orson; there they go! And what's his name, who was put down in his drawers, asleep, at the Gate of Damascus; don't you see him! And the Sultan's Groom turned upside down by the Genii; there he is upon his head! Serve him right. I'm glad of it. What business had *he* to be married to the Princess!"

To hear Scrooge expending all the earnestness of his nature on such subjects, in a most extraordinary voice between laughing and crying; and to see his heightened and excited face; would have been a surprise to his business friends in the city, indeed.

"There's the Parrot!" cried Scrooge. "Green body and yellow tail, with a thing like a lettuce growing out of the top of his head; there he is! Poor Robin Crusoe, he called him, when he came home again after sailing round the island. 'Poor Robin Crusoe, where have you been, Robin Crusoe?' The man thought he was dreaming, but he wasn't. It was the Parrot, you know. There goes Friday, running for his life to the little creek! Halloa! Hoop! Halloo!"

Then, with a rapidity of transition very foreign to his usual character, he said, in pity for his former self, "Poor boy!" and cried again.

"I wish," Scrooge muttered, putting his hand in his pocket, and looking about him, after drying his eyes with his cuff: "but it's too late now."

"What is the matter?" asked the Spirit.

"Nothing," said Scrooge. "Nothing. There was a boy singing a Christmas Carol at my door last night. I should like to have given him something: that's all."

The Ghost smiled thoughtfully, and waved its hand: saying as it did so, "Let us see another Christmas!"

Scrooge's former self grew larger at the words, and the room became a little darker and more dirty. The panels shrunk, the windows cracked; fragments of plaster fell out of the ceiling, and the naked laths were shown instead; but how all this was brought about, Scrooge knew no more than you do. He only knew that it was quite correct; that everything had happened so; that there he was, alone again, when all the other boys had gone home for the jolly holidays.

He was not reading now, but walking up and down despairingly. Scrooge looked at the Ghost, and with a mournful shaking of his head, glanced anxiously towards the door.

It opened; and a little girl, much younger than the boy, came darting in, and putting her arms about his neck, and often kissing him, addressed him as her "Dear, dear brother."

"I have come to bring you home, dear brother!" said the child, clapping her tiny hands, and bending down to laugh. "To bring you home, home, home!"

"Home, little Fan?" returned the boy.

"Yes!" said the child, brimful of glee. "Home, for good and all. Home, for ever and ever. Father is so much kinder than he used to be, that home's like Heaven! He spoke so gently to me one dear night when I was going to bed, that I was not afraid to ask him once more if you might come home; and he said Yes, you should; and sent me in a coach to bring you. And you're to be a man!" said the child, opening her eyes, "and are never to come back here; but first, we're to be together all the Christmas long, and have the merriest time in all the world."

"You are quite a woman, little Fan!" exclaimed the boy.

She clapped her hands and laughed, and tried to touch his head; but being too little, laughed again, and stood on tiptoe to embrace him. Then she began to drag him, in her childish eagerness, towards the door; and he, nothing loth to go, accompanied her.

A terrible voice in the hall cried, "Bring down Master Scrooge's box, there!" and in the hall appeared the school-master himself, who glared on Master Scrooge with a ferocious condescension, and threw him into a dreadful state of mind by shaking hands with him. He then conveyed him and his sister into the veriest old well of a shivering best-parlour that ever was seen, where the maps upon the wall, and the celestial and terrestrial globes in the windows, were waxy with cold. Here he produced a decanter of curiously light wine, and a block of curiously heavy cake, and administered instalments of those dainties to the young people: at the same time, sending out a meagre servant to offer a glass of "something" to the postboy, who answered that he thanked the gentleman, but if it was the same tap as he had tasted before, he had rather not. Master Scrooge's trunk being by this time tied on to the top of the chaise, the children bade the school-master good-bye right willingly; and getting into it, drove gaily down the garden-sweep: the quick wheels dashing the hoar-frost and snow from off the dark leaves of the evergreens like spray.

"Always a delicate creature, whom a breath might have withered," said the Ghost. "But she had a large heart!"

"So she had," cried Scrooge. "You're right. I will not gainsay it, Spirit. God forbid!"

"She died a woman," said the Ghost, "and had, as I think, children."

"One child," Scrooge returned.

"True," said the Ghost. "Your nephew!"

Scrooge seemed uneasy in his mind; and answered briefly, "Yes."

Although they had but that moment left the school behind them, they were now in the busy thoroughfares of a city, where shadowy passengers passed and repassed; where shadowy carts and coaches battled for the way, and all the strife and tumult of a real city were. It was made plain enough, by the dressing of the shops, that here too it was Christmas again; but it was evening, and the streets were lighted up.

The Ghost stopped at a certain warehouse door, and asked Scrooge if he knew it.

"Know it!" said Scrooge. "Was I not apprenticed here!"

They went in. At sight of an old gentleman in a Welsh wig, sitting behind such a high desk, that if he had been two inches taller he must have knocked his head against the ceiling, Scrooge cried in great excitement:

"Why, it's old Fezziwig! Bless his heart; it's Fezziwig alive again!"

Old Fezziwig laid down his pen, and looked up at the clock, which pointed to the hour of seven. He rubbed his hands; adjusted his capacious waistcoat; laughed all over himself, from his shoes to his organ of benevolence; and called out in a comfortable, oily, rich, fat, jovial voice:

"Yo ho, there! Ebenezer! Dick!"

Scrooge's former self, now grown a young man, came briskly in, accompanied by his fellow-'prentice.

"Dick Wilkins, to be sure!" said Scrooge to the Ghost. "Bless me, yes. There he is. He was very much attached to me, was Dick. Poor Dick! Dear, dear!"

"Yo ho, my boys!" said Fezziwig. "No more work to-night. Christmas Eve, Dick. Christmas, Ebenezer! Let's have the shutters up," cried old Fezziwig, with a sharp clap of his hands, "before a man can say Jack Robinson!"

You wouldn't believe how those two fellows went at it! They charged into the street with the shutters—one, two, three—had 'em up in their places—four, five, six—barred 'em and pinned 'em—seven, eight, nine—and came back before you could have got to twelve, panting like race-horses.

"Hilli-ho!" cried old Fezziwig, skipping down from the high desk, with wonderful agility. "Clear away, my lads, and let's have lots of room here! Hilli-ho Dick! Chirrup, Ebenezer!"

Clear away! There was nothing they wouldn't have cleared away, or couldn't have cleared away, with old Fezziwig looking on. It was done in a minute. Every movable was packed off, as if it were dismissed from public life for evermore; the floor was swept and watered, the lamps were trimmed, fuel was heaped upon the fire; and the warehouse was as snug, and warm, and dry, and bright a ball-room, as you would desire to see upon a winter's night.

In came a fiddler with a music-book, and went up to the lofty desk, and made an orchestra of it, and tuned like fifty stomachaches. In came Mrs. Fezziwig, one vast substantial smile. In came the three Miss Fezziwigs, beaming and lovable. In came the six young followers whose hearts they broke. In came all the young men and women employed in the business. In came the housemaid, with her cousin, the baker. In came the cook, with her brother's particular friend, the milkman. In came the boy from over the way, who was suspected of not having board enough from his master; trying to hide himself behind the girl from next door but one, who was proved to have had her ears pulled by her mistress. In they all came, one after another; some shyly, some boldly, some gracefully, some awkwardly, some pushing, some pulling; in they all came, anyhow and everyhow. Away they all went, twenty couple at once; hands half round and back again the other way; down the middle and up again; round and round in various stages of affectionate grouping; old top couple always turning up in the wrong place; new top couple starting off again, as soon as they got there; all top couples at last, and not a bottom one to help them! When this result was brought about, old Fezziwig, clapping his hands to stop the dance, cried out, "Well done!" and the fiddler plunged his hot face into a pot of porter, especially provided for that purpose. But scorning rest, upon his reappearance, he instantly began again, though there were no dancers yet, as if the other fiddler had been carried home, exhausted, on a shutter, and he were a bran-new man resolved to beat him out of sight, or perish.

There were more dances, and there were forfeits, and more dances, and there was cake, and there was negus, and there was a great piece of Cold Roast, and there was a great piece of Cold Boiled, and there were mince-pies, and plenty of beer. But the great effect of the evening came after the Roast and Boiled, when the fiddler (an artful dog, mind! The sort of man who knew his business better than you or I could have told it him!) struck up "Sir Roger de Coverley." Then old Fezziwig stood out to dance with Mrs. Fezziwig. Top couple, too; with a good stiff piece of work cut out for them; three or four and twenty pair of partners; people who were not to be trifled with; people who *would* dance, and had no notion of walking.

But if they had been twice as many—ah, four times—old Fezziwig would have been a match for them, and so would Mrs. Fezziwig. As to *her*, she was worthy to be his partner in every sense of the term. If that's not high praise, tell me higher, and I'll use it. A positive light appeared to issue from Fezziwig's calves. They shone in every part of the dance like moons. You couldn't have predicted, at any given time, what would have become of them next. And when old Fezziwig and Mrs. Fezziwig had gone all through the dance; advance and retire, both hands to your partner, bow and curtsey, corkscrew, thread-the-needle, and back again to your place; Fezziwig "cut"—cut so deftly, that he appeared to wink with his legs, and came upon his feet again without a stagger.

When the clock struck eleven, this domestic ball broke up. Mr. and Mrs. Fezziwig took their stations, one on either side of the door, and shaking hands with every person individually as he or she went out, wished him or her a Merry Christmas. When everybody had retired but the two 'prentices, they did the same to them; and thus the cheerful voices died away, and the lads were left to their beds; which were under a counter in the backshop.

During the whole of this time, Scrooge had acted like a man out of his wits. His heart and soul were in the scene, and with his former self. He corroborated everything, remembered everything, enjoyed everything, and underwent the strangest agitation. It was not until now, when the bright faces of his former self and Dick were turned from them, that he remembered the Ghost, and became conscious that it was looking full upon him, while the light upon its head burnt very clear.

"A small matter," said the Ghost, "to make these silly folks so full of gratitude."

"Small!" echoed Scrooge.

The Spirit signed to him to listen to the two apprentices, who were pouring out their hearts in praise of Fezziwig: and when he had done so, said,

"Why! Is it not? He has spent but a few pounds of your mortal money: three or four perhaps. Is that so much that he deserves this praise?"

"It isn't that," said Scrooge, heated by the remark, and speaking unconsciously like his former, not his latter, self. "It isn't that, Spirit. He has the power to render us happy or unhappy; to make our service light or burdensome; a pleasure or a toil. Say that his power lies in words and looks; in things so slight and insignificant that it is impossible to add and count 'em up: what then? The happiness he gives, is quite as great as if it cost a fortune."

He felt the Spirit's glance, and stopped.

"What is the matter?" asked the Ghost.

"Nothing particular," said Scrooge.

"Something, I think?" the Ghost insisted.

"No," said Scrooge. "No. I should like to be able to say a word or two to my clerk just now. That's all."

His former self turned down the lamps as he gave utterance to the wish; and Scrooge and the Ghost again stood side by side in the open air.

"My time grows short," observed the Spirit. "Quick!"

This was not addressed to Scrooge, or to any one whom he could see, but it produced an immediate effect. For again Scrooge saw himself. He was older now; a man in the prime of life. His face had not the harsh and rigid lines of later years; but it had begun to wear the signs of care and avarice. There was an eager, greedy, restless motion in the eye, which showed the passion that had taken root, and where the shadow of the growing tree would fall.

He was not alone, but sat by the side of a fair young girl in a mourning-dress: in whose eyes there were tears, which sparkled in the light that shone out of the Ghost of Christmas Past.

"It matters little," she said, softly. "To you, very little. Another idol has displaced me; and if it can cheer and comfort you in time to come, as I would have tried to do, I have no just cause to grieve."

"What idol has displaced you?" he rejoined.

"A golden one."

"This is the even-handed dealing of the world!" he said. "There is nothing on which it is so hard as poverty; and there is nothing it professes to condemn with such severity as the pursuit of wealth!"

"You fear the world too much," she answered, gently. "All your other hopes have merged into the hope of being beyond the chance of its sordid reproach. I have seen your nobler aspirations fall off one by one, until the master-passion, Gain, engrosses you. Have I not?"

"What then?" he retorted. "Even if I have grown so much wiser, what then? I am not changed towards you."

She shook her head.

"Am I?"

"Our contract is an old one. It was made when we were both poor and content to be so, until, in good season, we could improve our worldly fortune by our patient industry. You *are* changed. When it was made, you were another man."

"I was a boy," he said impatiently.

"Your own feeling tells you that you were not what you are," she returned. "I am. That which promised happiness when we were one in heart, is fraught with misery now that we are two. How often and how keenly I have thought of this, I will not say. It is enough that I *have* thought of it, and can release you."

"Have I ever sought release?"

"In words. No. Never."

"In what, then?"

"In a changed nature; in an altered spirit; in another atmosphere of life; another Hope as its great end. In everything that made my love of any worth or value in your sight. If this had never been between us," said the girl, looking mildly, but with steadiness, upon him; "tell me, would you seek me out and try to win me now? Ah, no!"

He seemed to yield to the justice of this supposition, in spite of himself. But he said with a struggle, "You think not."

"I would gladly think otherwise if I could," she answered, "Heaven knows! When I have learned a Truth like this, I know how strong and irresistible it must be. But if you were free to-day, to-morrow, yesterday, can even I believe that you would choose a dowerless girl—you who, in your very confidence with her, weigh everything by Gain: or, choosing her, if for a moment you were false enough to your one guiding principle to do so, do I not know that your repentance and regret would surely follow? I do; and I release you. With a full heart, for the love of him you once were."

He was about to speak; but with her head turned from him, she resumed.

"You may—the memory of what is past half makes me hope you will—have pain in this. A very, very brief time, and you will dismiss the recollection of it, gladly, as an unprofitable dream, from which it happened well that you awoke. May you be happy in the life you have chosen!"

She left him, and they parted.

"Spirit!" said Scrooge, "show me no more! Conduct me home. Why do you delight to torture me?"

"One shadow more!" exclaimed the Ghost.

"No more!" cried Scrooge. "No more. I don't wish to see it. Show me no more!"

But the relentless Ghost pinioned him in both his arms, and forced him to observe what happened next.

They were in another scene and place; a room, not very large or handsome, but full of comfort. Near to the winter fire sat a beautiful young girl, so like that last that Scrooge believed it was the same until he saw *her*, now a comely matron, sitting opposite her daughter. The noise in this room was perfectly tumultuous, for there were more children there, than Scrooge in his agitated state of mind could count; and, unlike the celebrated herd in the poem, they were not forty children conducting themselves like one, but every child was conducting itself like forty. The consequences were uproarious beyond belief; but no one seemed to care; on the contrary, the mother and daughter laughed heartily, and enjoyed it very much; and the latter, soon beginning to mingle in the sports, got pillaged by the young brigands most ruthlessly. What would I not have given to be one of them! Though I never could have been so rude, no, no! I wouldn't for the wealth of all the world have crushed that braided hair, and torn it down; and for the precious little shoe, I wouldn't have plucked it off, God bless my soul! to save my life. As to measuring her waist in sport, as they did, bold young brood, I couldn't have done it; I should have expected my arm to have grown round it for a punishment, and never come straight again. And yet I should have dearly liked, I own, to have touched her lips; to have questioned her, that she might have opened them; to have looked upon the lashes of her downcast eyes, and never raised a blush; to have let loose waves of hair, an inch of which would be a keepsake beyond price: in short, I should have liked, I do confess, to have had the lightest licence of a child, and yet to have been man enough to know its value.

But now a knocking at the door was heard, and such a rush immediately ensued that she with laughing face and plundered dress was borne towards it the centre of a flushed and boisterous group, just in time to greet the father, who came home attended by a man laden with Christmas toys and presents. Then the shouting and the struggling, and the onslaught that was made on the defenceless porter! The scaling him with chairs for ladders to dive into his pockets, despoil him of brown-paper parcels, hold on tight by his cravat, hug him round his neck, pommel his back, and kick his legs in irrepressible affection! The shouts of wonder and delight with which the development of every package was received! The terrible announcement that the baby had been taken in the act of putting a doll's frying-pan into his mouth, and was more than suspected of having swallowed a fictitious turkey, glued on a wooden platter! The immense relief of finding this a false alarm! The joy, and gratitude, and ecstasy! They are all indescribable alike. It is enough that by degrees the children and their emotions got out of the parlour, and by one stair at a time, up to the top of the house; where they went to bed, and so subsided.

And now Scrooge looked on more attentively than ever, when the master of the house, having his daughter leaning fondly on him, sat down with her and her mother at his own fireside; and when he thought that such another creature, quite as graceful and as full of promise, might have called him father, and been a spring-time in the haggard winter of his life, his sight grew very dim indeed.

"Belle," said the husband, turning to his wife with a smile, "I saw an old friend of yours this afternoon."

"Who was it?"

"Guess!"

"How can I? Tut, don't I know?" she added in the same breath, laughing as he laughed. "Mr. Scrooge."

"Mr. Scrooge it was. I passed his office window; and as it was not shut up, and he had a candle inside, I could scarcely help seeing him. His partner lies upon the point of death, I hear; and there he sat alone. Quite alone in the world, I do believe."

"Spirit!" said Scrooge in a broken voice, "remove me from this place."

"I told you these were shadows of the things that have been," said the Ghost. "That they are what they are, do not blame me!"

"Remove me!" Scrooge exclaimed, "I cannot bear it!"

He turned upon the Ghost, and seeing that it looked upon him with a face, in which in some strange way there were fragments of all the faces it had shown him, wrestled with it.

"Leave me! Take me back. Haunt me no longer!"

In the struggle, if that can be called a struggle in which the Ghost with no visible resistance on its own part was undisturbed by any effort of its adversary, Scrooge observed that its light was burning high and bright; and dimly connecting that with its influence over him, he seized the extinguisher-cap, and by a sudden action pressed it down upon its head.

The Spirit dropped beneath it, so that the extinguisher covered its whole form; but though Scrooge pressed it down with all his force, he could not hide the light, which streamed from under it, in an unbroken flood upon the ground.

He was conscious of being exhausted, and overcome by an irresistible drowsiness; and, further, of being in his own bedroom. He gave the cap a parting squeeze, in which his hand relaxed; and had barely time to reel to bed, before he sank into a heavy sleep.

STAVE III *THE SECOND OF THE THREE SPIRITS*

Awaking in the middle of a prodigiously tough snore, and sitting up in bed to get his thoughts together, Scrooge had no occasion to be told that the bell was again upon the stroke of One. He felt that he was restored to consciousness in the right nick of time, for the especial purpose of holding a conference with the second messenger despatched to him through Jacob Marley's intervention. But, finding that he turned uncomfortably cold when he began to wonder which of his curtains this new spectre would draw back, he put them every one aside with his own hands, and lying down again, established a sharp look-out all round the bed. For he wished to challenge the Spirit on the moment of its appearance, and did not wish to be taken by surprise, and made nervous.

Gentlemen of the free-and-easy sort, who plume themselves on being acquainted with a move or two, and being usually equal to the time-of-day, express the wide range of their capacity for adventure by observing that they are good for anything from pitch-and-toss to man-slaughter; between which opposite extremes, no doubt, there lies a tolerably wide and comprehensive range of subjects. Without venturing for Scrooge quite as hardily as this, I don't mind calling on you to believe that he was ready for a good broad field of strange appearances, and that nothing between a baby and rhinoceros would have astonished him very much.

Now, being prepared for almost anything, he was not by any means prepared for nothing; and, consequently, when the Bell struck One, and no shape appeared, he was taken with a violent fit of trembling. Five minutes, ten minutes, a quarter of an hour went by, yet nothing came. All this time, he lay upon his bed, the very core and centre of a blaze of ruddy light, which streamed upon it when the clock proclaimed the hour; and which, being only light, was more alarming than a dozen ghosts, as he was powerless to make out what it meant, or would be at; and was sometimes apprehensive that he might be at that very moment an interesting case of spontaneous combustion, without having the consolation of knowing it. At last, however, he began to think—as you or I would have thought at first; for it is always the person not in the predicament who knows what ought to have been done in it, and would unquestionably have done it too—at last, I say, he began to think that the source and secret of this ghostly light might be in the adjoining room, from whence, on further tracing it, it seemed to shine. This idea taking full possession of his mind, he got up softly and shuffled in his slippers to the door.

The moment Scrooge's hand was on the lock, a strange voice called him by his name, and bade him enter. He obeyed.

It was his own room. There was no doubt about that. But it had undergone a surprising transformation. The walls and ceiling were so hung with living green, that it looked a perfect grove; from every part of which, bright gleaming berries glistened. The crisp leaves of holly, mistletoe, and ivy reflected back the light, as if so many little mirrors had been scattered there; and such a mighty blaze went roaring up the chimney, as that dull petrification of a hearth had never known in Scrooge's time, or Marley's, or for many and many a winter season gone. Heaped up on the floor, to form a kind of throne, were turkeys, geese, game, poultry, brawn, great joints of meat, sucking-pigs, long wreaths of sausages, mince-pies, plum-puddings, barrels of oysters, red-hot chestnuts, cherry-cheeked apples, juicy oranges, luscious pears, immense twelfth-cakes, and seething bowls of punch, that made the chamber dim with their delicious steam. In easy state upon this couch, there sat a jolly Giant, glorious to see; who bore a glowing torch, in shape not unlike Plenty's horn, and held it up, high up, to shed its light on Scrooge, as he came peeping round the door.

"Come in!" exclaimed the Ghost. "Come in! and know me better, man!"

Scrooge entered timidly, and hung his head before this Spirit. He was not the dogged Scrooge he had been; and though the Spirit's eyes were clear and kind, he did not like to meet them.

"I am the Ghost of Christmas Present," said the Spirit. "Look upon me!"

Scrooge reverently did so. It was clothed in one simple green robe, or mantle, bordered with white fur. This garment hung so loosely on the figure, that its capacious breast was bare, as if disdaining to be warded or concealed by any artifice. Its feet, observable beneath the ample folds of the garment, were also bare; and on its head it wore no other covering than a holly wreath, set here and there with shining icicles. Its dark brown curls were long and free; free as its genial face, its sparkling eye, its open hand, its cheery voice, its unconstrained demeanour, and its joyful air. Girded round its middle was an antique scabbard; but no sword was in it, and the ancient sheath was eaten up with rust.

"You have never seen the like of me before!" exclaimed the Spirit.

"Never," Scrooge made answer to it.

"Have you never walked forth with the younger members of my family; meaning (for I am very young) my elder brothers born in these later years?" pursued the Phantom.

"I don't think I have," said Scrooge. "I am afraid I have not. Have you had many brothers, Spirit?"

"More than eighteen hundred," said the Ghost.

"A tremendous family to provide for!" muttered Scrooge.

The Ghost of Christmas Present rose.

"Spirit," said Scrooge submissively, "conduct me where you will. I went forth last night on compulsion, and I learnt a lesson which is working now. To-night, if you have aught to teach me, let me profit by it."

"Touch my robe!"

Scrooge did as he was told, and held it fast.

Holly, mistletoe, red berries, ivy, turkeys, geese, game, poultry, brawn, meat, pigs, sausages, oysters, pies, puddings, fruit, and punch, all vanished instantly. So did the room, the fire, the ruddy glow, the hour of night, and they stood in the city streets on Christmas morning, where (for the weather was severe) the people made a rough, but brisk and not unpleasant kind of music, in scraping the snow from the pavement in front of their dwellings, and from the tops of their houses, whence it was mad delight to the boys to see it come plumping down into the road below, and splitting into artificial little snow-storms.

The house fronts looked black enough, and the windows blacker, contrasting with the smooth white sheet of snow upon the roofs, and with the dirtier snow upon the ground; which last deposit had been ploughed up in deep furrows by the heavy wheels of carts and waggons; furrows that crossed and re-crossed each other hundreds of times where the great streets branched off; and made intricate channels, hard to trace in the thick yellow mud and icy water. The sky was gloomy, and the shortest streets were choked up with a dingy mist, half thawed, half frozen, whose heavier particles descended in a shower of sooty atoms, as if all the chimneys in Great Britain had, by one consent, caught fire, and were blazing away to their dear hearts' content. There was nothing very cheerful in the climate or the town, and yet was there an air of cheerfulness abroad that the clearest summer air and brightest summer sun might have endeavoured to diffuse in vain.

For the people who were shovelling away on the house-tops were jovial and full of glee; calling out to one another from the parapets, and now and then exchanging a facetious snowball—better-natured missile far than many a wordy jest—laughing heartily if it went right and not less heartily if it went wrong. The poulterers' shops were still half open, and the fruiterers' were radiant in their glory. There were great, round, pot-bellied baskets of chestnuts, shaped like the waistcoats of jolly old gentlemen, lolling at the doors, and tumbling out into the street in their apoplectic opulence. There were ruddy, brown-faced, broad-girthed Spanish Onions, shining in the fatness of their growth like Spanish Friars, and winking from their shelves in wanton slyness at the girls as they went by, and glanced demurely at the hung-up mistletoe. There were pears and apples, clustered high in blooming pyramids; there were bunches of grapes, made in the shopkeepers' benevolence to dangle from conspicuous hooks, that people's mouths might water gratis as they passed; there were piles of filberts, mossy and brown, recalling, in their fragrance, ancient walks among the woods, and pleasant shufflings ankle deep through withered leaves; there were Norfolk Biffins, squab and swarthy, setting off the yellow of the oranges and lemons, and, in the great compactness of their juicy persons, urgently entreating and beseeching to be carried home in paper bags and eaten after dinner. The very gold and silver fish, set forth among these choice fruits in a bowl, though members of a dull and stagnant-blooded race, appeared to know that there was something going on; and, to a fish, went gasping round and round their little world in slow and passionless excitement.

The Grocers'! oh the Grocers'! nearly closed, with perhaps two shutters down, or one; but through those gaps such glimpses! It was not alone that the scales descending on the counter made a merry sound, or that the twine and roller parted company so briskly, or that the canisters were rattled up and down like juggling tricks, or even that the blended scents of tea and coffee were so grateful to the nose, or even that the raisins were so plentiful and rare, the almonds so extremely white, the sticks of cinnamon so long and straight, the other spices so delicious, the candied fruits so caked and spotted with molten sugar as to make the coldest lookers-on feel faint and subsequently bilious. Nor was it that the figs were moist and pulpy, or that the French plums blushed in modest tartness from their highly-decorated boxes, or that everything was good to eat and in its Christmas dress; but the customers were all so hurried and so eager in the hopeful promise of the day, that they tumbled up against each other at the door, crashing their wicker baskets wildly, and left their purchases upon the counter, and came running back to fetch them, and committed hundreds of the like mistakes, in the best humour possible; while the Grocer and his people were so frank and fresh that the polished hearts with which they fastened their aprons behind might have been their own, worn outside for general inspection, and for Christmas daws to peck at if they chose.

But soon the steeples called good people all, to church and chapel, and away they came, flocking through the streets in their best clothes, and with their gayest faces. And at the same time there emerged from scores of bye-streets, lanes, and nameless turnings, innumerable people, carrying their dinners to the bakers' shops. The sight of these poor revellers appeared to interest the Spirit very much, for he stood with Scrooge beside him in a baker's doorway, and taking off the covers as their bearers passed, sprinkled incense on their dinners from his torch. And it was a very uncommon kind of torch, for once or twice when there were angry words between some dinner-carriers who had jostled each other, he shed a few drops of water on them from it, and their good humour was restored directly. For they said it was a shame to quarrel upon Christmas Day. And so it was! God love it, so it was!

In time the bells ceased, and the bakers were shut up; and yet there was a genial shadowing forth of all these dinners and the progress of their cooking, in the thawed blotch of wet above each baker's oven; where the pavement smoked as if its stones were cooking too.

"Is there a peculiar flavour in what you sprinkle from your torch?" asked Scrooge.

"There is. My own."

"Would it apply to any kind of dinner on this day?" asked Scrooge.

"To any kindly given. To a poor one most."

"Why to a poor one most?" asked Scrooge.

"Because it needs it most."

"Spirit," said Scrooge, after a moment's thought, "I wonder you, of all the beings in the many worlds about us, should desire to cramp these people's opportunities of innocent enjoyment."

"I!" cried the Spirit.

"You would deprive them of their means of dining every seventh day, often the only day on which they can be said to dine at all," said Scrooge. "Wouldn't you?"

"I!" cried the Spirit.

"You seek to close these places on the Seventh Day?" said Scrooge. "And it comes to the same thing."

"I seek!" exclaimed the Spirit.

"Forgive me if I am wrong. It has been done in your name, or at least in that of your family," said Scrooge.

"There are some upon this earth of yours," returned the Spirit, "who lay claim to know us, and who do their deeds of passion, pride, ill-will, hatred, envy, bigotry, and selfishness in our name, who are as strange to us and all our kith and kin, as if they had never lived. Remember that, and charge their doings on themselves, not us."

Scrooge promised that he would; and they went on, invisible, as they had been before, into the suburbs of the town. It was a remarkable quality of the Ghost (which Scrooge had observed at the baker's), that notwithstanding his gigantic size, he could accommodate himself to any place with ease; and that he stood beneath a low roof quite as gracefully and like a supernatural creature, as it was possible he could have done in any lofty hall.

And perhaps it was the pleasure the good Spirit had in showing off this power of his, or else it was his own kind, generous, hearty nature, and his sympathy with all poor men, that led him straight to Scrooge's clerk's; for there he went, and took Scrooge with him, holding to his robe; and on the threshold of the door the Spirit smiled, and stopped to bless Bob Cratchit's dwelling with the sprinkling of his torch. Think of that! Bob had but fifteen "Bob" a-week himself; he pocketed on

Saturdays but fifteen copies of his Christian name; and yet the Ghost of Christmas Present blessed his four-roomed house!

Then up rose Mrs. Cratchit, Cratchit's wife, dressed out but poorly in a twice-turned gown, but brave in ribbons, which are cheap and make a goodly show for sixpence; and she laid the cloth, assisted by Belinda Cratchit, second of her daughters, also brave in ribbons; while Master Peter Cratchit plunged a fork into the saucepan of potatoes, and getting the corners of his monstrous shirt collar (Bob's private property, conferred upon his son and heir in honour of the day) into his mouth, rejoiced to find himself so gallantly attired, and yearned to show his linen in the fashionable Parks. And now two smaller Cratchits, boy and girl, came tearing in, screaming that outside the baker's they had smelt the goose, and known it for their own; and basking in luxurious thoughts of sage and onion, these young Cratchits danced about the table, and exalted Master Peter Cratchit to the skies, while he (not proud, although his collars nearly choked him) blew the fire, until the slow potatoes bubbling up, knocked loudly at the saucepan-lid to be let out and peeled.

"Whatever has got your precious father then?" said Mrs. Cratchit. "And your brother, Tiny Tim! And Martha warn't as late last Christmas Day by half-an-hour."

"Here's Martha, mother!" said a girl, appearing as she spoke.

"Here's Martha, mother!" cried the two young Cratchits. "Hurrah! There's *such* a goose, Martha!"

"Why, bless your heart alive, my dear, how late you are!" said Mrs. Cratchit, kissing her a dozen times, and taking off her shawl and bonnet for her with officious zeal.

"We'd a deal of work to finish up last night," replied the girl, "and had to clear away this morning, mother!"

"Well! Never mind so long as you are come," said Mrs. Cratchit. "Sit ye down before the fire, my dear, and have a warm, Lord bless ye!"

"No, no! There's father coming," cried the two young Cratchits, who were everywhere at once. "Hide, Martha, hide!"

So Martha hid herself, and in came little Bob, the father, with at least three feet of comforter exclusive of the fringe, hanging down before him; and his threadbare clothes darned up and brushed, to look seasonable; and Tiny Tim upon his shoulder. Alas for Tiny Tim, he bore a little crutch, and had his limbs supported by an iron frame!

"Why, where's our Martha?" cried Bob Cratchit, looking round.

"Not coming," said Mrs. Cratchit.

"Not coming!" said Bob, with a sudden declension in his high spirits; for he had been Tim's blood horse all the way from church, and had come home rampant. "Not coming upon Christmas Day!"

Martha didn't like to see him disappointed, if it were only in joke;

so she came out prematurely from behind the closet door, and ran into his arms, while the two young Cratchits hustled Tiny Tim, and bore him off into the wash-house, that he might hear the pudding singing in the copper.

"And how did little Tim behave?" asked Mrs. Cratchit, when she had rallied Bob on his credulity, and Bob had hugged his daughter to his heart's content.

"As good as gold," said Bob, "and better. Somehow he gets thoughtful, sitting by himself so much, and thinks the strangest things you ever heard. He told me, coming home, that he hoped the people saw him in the church, because he was a cripple, and it might be pleasant to them to remember upon Christmas Day, who made lame beggars walk, and blind men see."

Bob's voice was tremulous when he told them this, and trembled more when he said that Tiny Tim was growing strong and hearty.

His active little crutch was heard upon the floor, and back came Tiny Tim before another word was spoken, escorted by his brother and sister to his stool before the fire; and while Bob, turning up his cuffs—as if, poor fellow, they were capable of being made more shabby—compounded some hot mixture in a jug with gin and lemons, and stirred it round and round and put it on the hob to simmer; Master Peter, and the two ubiquitous young Cratchits went to fetch the goose, with which they soon returned in high procession.

Such a bustle ensued that you might have thought a goose the rarest of all birds; a feathered phenomenon, to which a black swan was a matter of course—and in truth it was something very like it in that house. Mrs. Cratchit made the gravy (ready beforehand in a little saucepan) hissing hot; Master Peter mashed the potatoes with incredible vigour; Miss Belinda sweetened up the apple-sauce; Martha dusted the hot plates; Bob took Tiny Tim beside him in a tiny corner at the table; the two young Cratchits set chairs for everybody, not forgetting themselves, and mounting guard upon their posts, crammed spoons into their mouths, lest they should shriek for goose before their turn came to be helped. At last the dishes were set on, and grace was said. It was succeeded by a breathless pause, as Mrs. Cratchit, looking slowly all along the carving-knife, prepared to plunge it in the breast; but when she did, and when the long expected gush of stuffing issued forth, one murmur of delight arose all round the board, and even Tiny Tim, excited by the two young Cratchits, beat on the table with the handle of his knife, and feebly cried Hurrah!

There never was such a goose. Bob said he didn't believe there ever was such a goose cooked. Its tenderness and flavour, size and cheapness, were the themes of universal admiration. Eked out by apple-sauce and mashed potatoes, it was a sufficient dinner for the whole family; indeed, as Mrs. Cratchit said with great delight (surveying one small atom of a bone upon the dish), they hadn't ate it all at last! Yet every one had had enough, and the youngest Cratchits in particular, were steeped in sage and onion to the eyebrows! But now, the plates being changed by Miss Belinda, Mrs. Cratchit left the room alone—too nervous to bear witnesses—to take the pudding up and bring it in.

Suppose it should not be done enough! Suppose it should break in turning out! Suppose somebody should have got over the wall of the back-yard, and stolen it, while they were merry with the goose—a supposition at which the two young Cratchits became livid! All sorts of horrors were supposed.

Hallo! A great deal of steam! The pudding was out of the copper. A smell like a washing-day! That was the cloth. A smell like an eating-house and a pastrycook's next door to each other, with a laundress's next door to that! That was the pudding! In half a minute Mrs. Cratchit entered—flushed, but smiling proudly—with the pudding, like a speckled cannon-ball, so hard and firm, blazing in half of half-a-quartern of ignited brandy, and bedight with Christmas holly stuck into the top.

Oh, a wonderful pudding! Bob Cratchit said, and calmly too, that he regarded it as the greatest success achieved by Mrs. Cratchit since their marriage. Mrs. Cratchit said that now the weight was off her mind, she would confess she had had her doubts about the quantity of flour. Everybody had something to say about it, but nobody said or thought it was at all a small pudding for a large family. It would have been flat heresy to do so. Any Cratchit would have blushed to hint at such a thing.

At last the dinner was all done, the cloth was cleared, the hearth swept, and the fire made up. The compound in the jug being tasted, and considered perfect, apples and oranges were put upon the table, and a shovel-full of chestnuts on the fire. Then all the Cratchit family drew round the hearth, in what Bob Cratchit called a circle, meaning half a one; and at Bob Cratchit's elbow stood the family display of glass. Two tumblers, and a custard-cup without a handle.

These held the hot stuff from the jug, however, as well as golden goblets would have done; and Bob served it out with beaming looks, while the chestnuts on the fire sputtered and cracked noisily. Then Bob proposed:

"A Merry Christmas to us all, my dears. God bless us!"

Which all the family re-echoed.

"God bless us every one!" said Tiny Tim, the last of all.

He sat very close to his father's side upon his little stool. Bob held his withered little hand in his, as if he loved the child, and wished to keep him by his side, and dreaded that he might be taken from him.

"Spirit," said Scrooge, with an interest he had never felt before, "tell me if Tiny Tim will live."

"I see a vacant seat," replied the Ghost, "in the poor chimney corner, and a crutch without an owner, carefully preserved. If these shadows remain unaltered by the Future, the child will die."

"No, no," said Scrooge. "Oh, no, kind Spirit! say he will be spared."

"If these shadows remain unaltered by the Future, none other of my race," returned the Ghost, "will find him here. What then? If he be like to die, he had better do it, and decrease the surplus population."

Scrooge hung his head to hear his own words quoted by the Spirit, and was overcome with penitence and grief.

"Man," said the Ghost, "if man you be in heart, not adamant, forbear that wicked cant until you have discovered What the surplus is, and Where it is. Will you decide what men shall live, what men shall die? It may be, that in the sight of Heaven, you are more worthless and less fit to live than millions like this poor man's child. Oh God! to hear the Insect on the leaf pronouncing on the too much life among his hungry brothers in the dust!"

Scrooge bent before the Ghost's rebuke, and trembling cast his eyes upon the ground. But he raised them speedily, on hearing his own name.

"Mr. Scrooge!" said Bob; "I'll give you Mr. Scrooge, the Founder of the Feast!"

"The Founder of the Feast indeed!" cried Mrs. Cratchit, reddening. "I wish I had him here. I'd give him a piece of my mind to feast upon, and I hope he'd have a good appetite for it."

"My dear," said Bob, "the children! Christmas Day."

"It should be Christmas Day, I am sure," said she, "on which one drinks the health of such an odious, stingy, hard, unfeeling man as Mr. Scrooge. You know he is, Robert! Nobody knows it better than you do, poor fellow!"

"My dear," was Bob's mild answer, "Christmas Day."

"I'll drink his health for your sake and the Day's," said Mrs. Cratchit, "not for his. Long life to him! A merry Christmas and a happy new year! He'll be very merry and very happy, I have no doubt!"

The children drank the toast after her. It was the first of their proceedings which had no heartiness. Tiny Tim drank it last of all, but he didn't care twopence for it. Scrooge was the Ogre of the family. The mention of his name cast a dark shadow on the party, which was not dispelled for full five minutes.

After it had passed away, they were ten times merrier than before, from the mere relief of Scrooge the Baleful being done with. Bob Cratchit told them how he had a situation in his eye for Master Peter, which would bring in, if obtained, full five-and-sixpence weekly. The two young Cratchits laughed tremendously at the idea of Peter's being a man of business; and Peter himself looked thoughtfully at the fire from between his collars, as if he were deliberating what particular investments he should favour when he came into the receipt of that bewildering income. Martha, who was a poor apprentice at a milliner's, then told them what kind of work she had to do, and how many hours she worked at a stretch, and how she meant to lie abed to-morrow morning for a good long rest; to-morrow being a holiday she passed at home. Also how she had seen a countess and a lord some days before, and how the lord "was much about as tall as Peter;" at which Peter pulled up his collars so high that you couldn't have seen his head if you had been there. All this time the chestnuts and the jug went round and round; and by-and-bye they had a song, about a lost child travelling in the snow, from Tiny Tim, who had a plaintive little voice, and sang it very well indeed.

There was nothing of high mark in this. They were not a handsome family; they were not well dressed; their shoes were far from being water-proof; their clothes were scanty; and Peter might have known, and very likely did, the inside of a pawnbroker's. But they were happy, grateful, pleased with one another, and contented with the time; and when they faded, and looked happier yet in the bright sprinklings of the Spirit's torch at parting, Scrooge had his eye upon them, and especially on Tiny Tim, until the last.

By this time it was getting dark, and snowing pretty heavily; and as Scrooge and the Spirit went along the streets, the brightness of the roaring fires in kitchens, parlours, and all sorts of rooms, was wonderful. Here, the flickering of the blaze showed preparations for a cosy dinner, with hot plates baking through and through before the fire, and deep red curtains, ready to be drawn to shut out cold and darkness. There all the children of the house were running out into the snow to meet their married sisters, brothers, cousins, uncles, aunts, and be the first to greet them. Here, again, were shadows on the window-blind of guests assembling; and there a group of handsome girls, all hooded and fur-booted, and all chattering at once, tripped lightly off to some near neighbour's house; where, woe upon the single man who saw them enter—artful witches, well they knew it—in a glow!

But, if you had judged from the numbers of people on their way to friendly gatherings, you might have thought that no one was at home to give them welcome when they got there, instead of every house expecting company, and piling up its fires half-chimney high. Blessings on it, how the Ghost exulted! How it bared its breadth of breast, and opened its capacious palm, and floated on, outpouring, with a generous hand, its bright and harmless mirth on everything within its reach! The very lamplighter, who ran on before, dotting the dusky street with specks of light, and who was dressed to spend the evening somewhere, laughed out loudly as the Spirit passed, though little kenned the lamp-lighter that he had any company but Christmas!

And now, without a word of warning from the Ghost, they stood upon a bleak and desert moor, where monstrous masses of rude stone were cast about, as though it were the burial-place of giants; and water spread itself wheresoever it listed, or would have done so, but for the frost that held it prisoner; and nothing grew but moss and furze, and coarse rank grass. Down in the west the setting sun had left a streak of fiery red, which glared upon the desolation for an instant, like a sullen eye, and frowning lower, lower, lower yet, was lost in the thick gloom of darkest night.

"What place is this?" asked Scrooge.

"A place where Miners live, who labour in the bowels of the earth," returned the Spirit. "But they know me. See!"

A light shone from the window of a hut, and swiftly they advanced towards it. Passing through the wall of mud and stone, they found a cheerful company assembled round a glowing fire. An old, old man and woman, with their children and their children's children, and another generation beyond that, all decked out gaily in their holiday attire. The old man, in a voice that seldom rose above the howling of the wind upon the barren waste, was singing them a Christmas song—it had been a very old song when he was a boy—and from time to time they all joined in the chorus. So surely as they raised their voices, the old man got quite blithe and loud; and so surely as they stopped, his vigour sank again.

The Spirit did not tarry here, but bade Scrooge hold his robe, and passing on above the moor, sped—whither? Not to sea? To sea. To Scrooge's horror, looking back, he saw the last of the land, a frightful range of rocks, behind them; and his ears were deafened by the thundering of water, as it rolled and roared, and raged among the dreadful caverns it had worn, and fiercely tried to undermine the earth.

Built upon a dismal reef of sunken rocks, some league or so from shore, on which the waters chafed and dashed, the wild year through, there stood a solitary lighthouse. Great heaps of sea-weed clung to its base, and storm-birds—born of the wind one might suppose, as sea-weed of the water—rose and fell about it, like the waves they skimmed.

But even here, two men who watched the light had made a fire, that through the loophole in the thick stone wall shed out a ray of brightness on the awful sea. Joining their horny hands over the rough table at which they sat, they wished each other Merry Christmas in their can of grog; and one of them: the elder, too, with his face all damaged and scarred with hard weather, as the figure-head of an old ship might be: struck up a sturdy song that was like a Gale in itself.

Again the Ghost sped on, above the black and heaving sea—on, on—until, being far away, as he told Scrooge, from any shore, they lighted on a ship. They stood beside the helmsman at the wheel, the look-out in the bow, the officers who had the watch; dark, ghostly figures in their several stations; but every man among them hummed a Christmas tune, or had a Christmas thought, or spoke below his breath to his companion of some bygone Christmas Day, with homeward hopes belonging to it. And every man on board, waking or sleeping, good or bad, had had a kinder word for another on that day than on any day in the year; and had shared to some extent in its festivities; and had remembered those he cared for at a distance, and had known that they delighted to remember him.

It was a great surprise to Scrooge, while listening to the moaning of the wind, and thinking what a solemn thing it was to move on through the lonely darkness over an unknown abyss, whose depths were secrets as profound as Death: it was a great surprise to Scrooge, while thus engaged, to hear a hearty laugh. It was a much greater surprise to Scrooge to recognise it as his own nephew's, and to find himself in a bright, dry, gleaming room, with the Spirit standing smiling by his side, and looking at that same nephew with approving affability!

"Ha, ha!" laughed Scrooge's nephew. "Ha, ha, ha!"

If you should happen, by any unlikely chance, to know a man more blest in a laugh than Scrooge's nephew, all I can say is, I should like to know him too. Introduce him to me, and I'll cultivate his acquaintance.

It is a fair, even-handed, noble adjustment of things, that while there is infection in disease and sorrow, there is nothing in the world so irresistibly contagious as laughter and good-humour. When Scrooge's nephew laughed in this way: holding his sides, rolling his head, and twisting his face into the most extravagant contortions: Scrooge's niece, by marriage, laughed as heartily as he. And their assembled friends being not a bit behindhand, roared out lustily.

"Ha, ha! Ha, ha, ha, ha!"

"He said that Christmas was a humbug, as I live!" cried Scrooge's nephew. "He believed it too!"

"More shame for him, Fred!" said Scrooge's niece, indignantly. Bless those women; they never do anything by halves. They are always in earnest.

She was very pretty: exceedingly pretty. With a dimpled, surprised-looking, capital face; a ripe little mouth, that seemed made to be kissed—as no doubt it was; all kinds of good little dots about her chin, that melted into one another when she laughed; and the sunniest pair of eyes you ever saw in any little creature's head. Altogether

she was what you would have called provoking, you know; but satisfactory, too. Oh, perfectly satisfactory.

"He's a comical old fellow," said Scrooge's nephew, "that's the
truth: and not so pleasant as he might be. However, his offences
carry their own punishment, and I have nothing to say against him."

"I'm sure he is very rich, Fred," hinted Scrooge's niece. "At least
you always tell *me* so."

"What of that, my dear!" said Scrooge's nephew. "His wealth is
of no use to him. He don't do any good with it. He don't make
himself comfortable with it. He hasn't the satisfaction of thinking—
ha, ha, ha!—that he is ever going to benefit US with it."

"I have no patience with him," observed Scrooge's niece. Scrooge's
niece's sisters, and all the other ladies, expressed the same opinion.

"Oh, I have!" said Scrooge's nephew. "I am sorry for him; I couldn't
be angry with him if I tried. Who suffers by his ill whims! Himself,
always. Here, he takes it into his head to dislike us, and he won't
come and dine with us. What's the consequence? He don't lose much
of a dinner."

"Indeed, I think he loses a very good dinner," interrupted Scrooge's
niece. Everybody else said the same, and they must be allowed to
have been competent judges, because they had just had dinner; and,
with the dessert upon the table, were clustered round the fire, by
lamplight.

"Well! I'm very glad to hear it," said Scrooge's nephew, "because I
haven't great faith in these young housekeepers. What do *you* say,
Topper?"

Topper had clearly got his eye upon one of Scrooge's niece's sisters,
for he answered that a bachelor was a wretched outcast, who had
no right to express an opinion on the subject. Whereat Scrooge's
niece's sister—the plump one with the lace tucker: not the one with
the roses—blushed.

"Do go on, Fred," said Scrooge's niece, clapping her hands. "He
never finishes what he begins to say! He is such a ridiculous fellow!"

Scrooge's nephew revelled in another laugh, and as it was impossible to keep the infection off; though the plump sister tried hard
to do it with aromatic vinegar; his example was unanimously followed.

"I was only going to say," said Scrooge's nephew, "that the consequences of his taking a dislike to us, and not making merry with
us, is, as I think, that he loses some pleasant moments, which could
do him no harm. I am sure he loses pleasanter companions than he
can find in his own thoughts, either in his mouldy old office, or his
dusty chambers. I mean to give him the same chance every year,
whether he likes it or not, for I pity him. He may rail at Christmas
till he dies, but he can't help thinking better of it—I defy him—

if he finds me going there, in good temper, year after year, and saying,
Uncle Scrooge, how are you? If it only puts him in the vein to leave
his poor clerk fifty pounds, *that's* something; and I think I shook
him yesterday."

It was their turn to laugh now at the notion of his shaking Scrooge.
But being thoroughly good-natured, and not much caring what they
laughed at, so that they laughed at any rate, he encouraged them in
their merriment, and passed the bottle joyously.

After tea, they had some music. For they were a musical family, and
knew what they were about, when they sung a Glee or Catch, I can
assure you: especially Topper, who could growl away in the bass like
a good one, and never swell the large veins in his forehead, or get red
in the face over it. Scrooge's niece played well upon the harp; and
played among other tunes a simple little air (a mere nothing: you
might learn to whistle it in two minutes), which had been familiar to
the child who fetched Scrooge from the boarding-school, as he had
been reminded by the Ghost of Christmas Past. When this strain of
music sounded, all the things that Ghost had shown him, came upon
his mind; he softened more and more; and thought that if he could
have listened to it often, years ago, he might have cultivated the kind-
nesses of life for his own happiness with his own hands, without resorting to the sexton's spade that buried Jacob Marley.

But they didn't devote the whole evening to music. After a while
they played at forfeits; for it is good to be children sometimes, and
never better than at Christmas, when its mighty Founder was a child
himself. Stop! There was first a game at blindman's buff. Of course
there was. And I no more believe Topper was really blind than I
believe he had eyes in his boots. My opinion is, that it was a done
thing between him and Scrooge's nephew; and that the Ghost of
Christmas Present knew it. The way he went after that plump sister in
the lace tucker, was an outrage on the credulity of human nature.
Knocking down the fire-irons, tumbling over the chairs, bumping
against the piano, smothering himself among the curtains, wherever
she went, there went he! He always knew where the plump sister was.
He wouldn't catch anybody else. If you had fallen up against him (as
some of them did), on purpose, he would have made a feint of endeavouring to seize you, which would have been an affront to your
understanding, and would instantly have sidled off in the direction of
the plump sister. She often cried out that it wasn't fair; and it really
was not. But when at last, he caught her; when, in spite of all her
silken rustlings, and her rapid flutterings past him, he got her into a
corner whence there was no escape; then his conduct was the most
execrable. For his pretending not to know her; his pretending that it
was necessary to touch her head-dress, and further to assure himself of
her identity by pressing a certain ring upon her finger, and a certain

chain about her neck; was vile, monstrous! No doubt she told him her opinion of it, when, another blind-man being in office, they were so very confidential together, behind the curtains.

Scrooge's niece was not one of the blindman's buff party, but was made comfortable with a large chair and a footstool, in a snug corner, where the Ghost and Scrooge were close behind her. But she joined in the forfeits, and loved her love to admiration with all the letters of the alphabet. Likewise at the game of How, When, and Where, she was very great, and to the secret joy of Scrooge's nephew, beat her sisters hollow: though they were sharp girls too, as Topper could have told you. There might have been twenty people there, young and old, but they all played, and so did Scrooge; for wholly forgetting in the interest he had in what was going on, that his voice made no sound in their ears, he sometimes came out with his guess quite loud, and very often guessed quite right, too; for the sharpest needle, best White-chapel, warranted not to cut in the eye, was not sharper than Scrooge; blunt as he took it in his head to be.

The Ghost was greatly pleased to find him in this mood, and looked upon him with such favour, that he begged like a boy to be allowed to stay until the guests departed. But this the Spirit said could not be done.

"Here is a new game," said Scrooge. "One half hour, Spirit, only one!"

It was a game called Yes and No, where Scrooge's nephew had to think of something, and the rest must find out what; he only answering to their questions yes or no, as the case was. The brisk fire of questioning to which he was exposed, elicited from him that he was thinking of an animal, a live animal, rather a disagreeable animal, a savage animal, an animal that growled and grunted sometimes, and talked sometimes, and lived in London, and walked about the streets, and wasn't made a show of, and wasn't led by anybody, and didn't live in a menagerie, and was never killed in a market, and was not a horse, or an ass, or a cow, or a bull, or a tiger, or a dog, or a pig, or a cat, or a bear. At every fresh question that was put to him, this nephew burst into a fresh roar of laughter; and was so inexpressibly tickled, that he was obliged to get up off the sofa and stamp. At last the plump sister, falling into a similar state, cried out:

"I have found it out! I know what it is, Fred! I know what it is!"

"What is it?" cried Fred.

"It's your Uncle Scro-o-o-o-oge!"

Which it certainly was. Admiration was the universal sentiment, though some objected that the reply to "Is it a bear?" ought to have been "Yes;" inasmuch as an answer in the negative was sufficient to have diverted their thoughts from Mr. Scrooge, supposing they had ever had any tendency that way.

"He has given us plenty of merriment, I am sure," said Fred, "and it would be ungrateful not to drink his health. Here is a glass of mulled wine ready to our hand at the moment; and I say, 'Uncle Scrooge!'"

"Well! Uncle Scrooge!" they cried.

"A Merry Christmas and a Happy New Year to the old man, whatever he is!" said Scrooge's nephew. "He wouldn't take it from me, but may he have it, nevertheless. Uncle Scrooge!"

Uncle Scrooge had imperceptibly become so gay and light of heart, that he would have pledged the unconscious company in return, and thanked them in an inaudible speech, if the Ghost had given him time. But the whole scene passed off in the breath of the last word spoken by his nephew; and he and the Spirit were again upon their travels.

Much they saw, and far they went, and many homes they visited, but always with a happy end. The Spirit stood beside sick beds, and they were cheerful; on foreign lands, and they were close at home; by struggling men, and they were patient in their greater hope; by poverty, and it was rich. In almshouse, hospital, and jail, in misery's every refuge, where vain man in his little brief authority had not made fast the door, and barred the Spirit out, he left his blessing, and taught Scrooge his precepts.

It was a long night, if it were only a night; but Scrooge had his doubts of this, because the Christmas Holidays appeared to be condensed into the space of time they passed together. It was strange, too, that while Scrooge remained unaltered in his outward form, the Ghost grew older, clearly older. Scrooge had observed this change, but never spoke of it, until they left a children's Twelfth Night party, when, looking at the Spirit as they stood together in an open place, he noticed that its hair was grey.

"Are spirits' lives so short?" asked Scrooge.

"My life upon this globe, is very brief," replied the Ghost. "It ends to-night."

"To-night!" cried Scrooge.

"To-night at midnight. Hark! The time is drawing near."

The chimes were ringing the three quarters past eleven at that moment.

"Forgive me if I am not justified in what I ask," said Scrooge, looking intently at the Spirit's robe, "but I see something strange, and not belonging to yourself, protruding from your skirts. Is it a foot or a claw?"

"It might be a claw, for the flesh there is upon it," was the Spirit's sorrowful reply. "Look here."

From the foldings of its robe, it brought two children; wretched, abject, frightful, hideous, miserable. They knelt down at its feet, and clung upon the outside of its garment.

"Oh, Man! look here. Look, look, down here!" exclaimed the Ghost.

They were a boy and girl. Yellow, meagre, ragged, scowling, wolfish; but prostrate, too, in their humility. Where graceful youth should have filled their features out, and touched them with its freshest tints, a stale and shrivelled hand, like that of age, had pinched, and twisted them, and pulled them into shreds. Where angels might have sat enthroned, devils lurked, and glared out menacing. No change, no degradation, no perversion of humanity, in any grade, through all the mysteries of wonderful creation, has monsters half so horrible and dread.

Scrooge started back, appalled. Having them shown to him in this way, he tried to say they were fine children, but the words choked themselves, rather than be parties to a lie of such enormous magnitude.

"Spirit! are they yours?" Scrooge could say no more.

"They are Man's," said the Spirit, looking down upon them. "And they cling to me, appealing from their fathers. This boy is Ignorance. This girl is Want. Beware them both, and all of their degree, but most of all beware this boy, for on his brow I see that written which is Doom, unless the writing be erased. Deny it!" cried the Spirit, stretching out its hand towards the city. "Slander those who tell it ye! Admit it for your factious purposes, and make it worse. And bide the end!"

"Have they no refuge or resource?" cried Scrooge.

"Are there no prisons?" said the Spirit, turning on him for the last time with his own words. "Are there no workhouses?"

The bell struck twelve.

Scrooge looked about him for the Ghost, and saw it not. As the last stroke ceased to vibrate, he remembered the prediction of old Jacob Marley, and lifting up his eyes, beheld a solemn Phantom, draped and hooded, coming, like a mist along the ground, towards him.

STAVE IV   *THE LAST OF THE SPIRITS*

The Phantom slowly, gravely, silently approached. When it came near him, Scrooge bent down upon his knee; for in the very air through which this Spirit moved it seemed to scatter gloom and mystery.

It was shrouded in a deep black garment, which concealed its head, its face, its form, and left nothing of it visible save one outstretched hand. But for this it would have been difficult to detach its figure from the night, and separate it from the darkness by which it was surrounded.

He felt that it was tall and stately when it came beside him, and that its mysterious presence filled him with a solemn dread. He knew no more, for the Spirit neither spoke nor moved.

"I am in the presence of the Ghost of Christmas Yet To Come?" said Scrooge.

The Spirit answered not, but pointed onward with its hand.

"You are about to show me shadows of the things that have not happened, but will happen in the time before us," Scrooge pursued. "Is that so, Spirit?"

The upper portion of the garment was contracted for an instant in its folds, as if the Spirit had inclined its head. That was the only answer he received.

Although well used to ghostly company by this time, Scrooge feared the silent shape so much that his legs trembled beneath him, and he found that he could hardly stand when he prepared to follow it. The Spirit paused a moment, as observing his condition, and giving him time to recover.

But Scrooge was all the worse for this. It thrilled him with a vague uncertain horror, to know that behind the dusky shroud, there were ghostly eyes intently fixed upon him, whilst he, though he stretched his own to the utmost, could see nothing but a spectral hand and one great heap of black.

"Ghost of the Future!" he exclaimed, "I fear you more than any spectre I have seen. But as I know your purpose is to do me good, and as I hope to live to be another man from what I was, I am prepared to bear you company, and do it with a thankful heart. Will you not speak to me?"

It gave him no reply. The hand was pointed straight before them.

"Lead on!" said Scrooge. "Lead on! The night is waning fast, and it is precious time to me, I know. Lead on, Spirit!"

The Phantom moved away as it had come towards him. Scrooge followed in the shadow of its dress, which bore him up, he thought, and carried him along.

They scarcely seemed to enter the city; for the city rather seemed to spring up about them, and encompass them of its own act. But there they were, in the heart of it; on 'Change, amongst the merchants; who hurried up and down, and chinked the money in their pockets, and conversed in groups, and looked at their watches, and trifled thoughtfully with their great gold seals; and so forth, as Scrooge had seen them often.

The Spirit stopped beside one little knot of business men. Observing that the hand was pointed to them, Scrooge advanced to listen to their talk.

"No," said a great fat man with a monstrous chin, "I don't know much about it, either way. I only know he's dead."

"When did he die?" inquired another.

"Last night, I believe."

"Why, what was the matter with him?" asked a third, taking a vast quantity of snuff out of a very large snuff-box. "I thought he'd never die."

"God knows," said the first, with a yawn.

"What has he done with his money?" asked a red-faced gentleman with a pendulous excrescence on the end of his nose, that shook like the gills of a turkey-cock.

"I haven't heard," said the man with the large chin, yawning again. "Left it to his company, perhaps. He hasn't left it to *me*. That's all I know."

This pleasantry was received with a general laugh.

"It's likely to be a very cheap funeral," said the same speaker; "for upon my life I don't know of anybody to go to it. Suppose we make up a party and volunteer?"

"I don't mind going if a lunch is provided," observed the gentleman with the excrescence on his nose. "But I must be fed, if I make one."

Another laugh.

"Well, I am the most disinterested among you, after all," said the first speaker, "for I never wear black gloves, and I never eat lunch. But I'll offer to go, if anybody else will. When I come to think of it, I'm not at all sure that I wasn't his most particular friend; for we used to stop and speak whenever we met. Bye, bye!"

Speakers and listeners strolled away, and mixed with other groups. Scrooge knew the men, and looked towards the Spirit for an explanation.

The Phantom glided on into a street. Its finger pointed to two persons meeting. Scrooge listened again, thinking that the explanation might lie here.

He knew these men, also, perfectly. They were men of business: very wealthy, and of great importance. He had made a point always of standing well in their esteem: in a business point of view, that is; strictly in a business point of view.

"How are you?" said one.

"How are you?" returned the other.

"Well!" said the first. "Old Scratch has got his own at last, hey?"

"So I am told," returned the second. "Cold, isn't it?"

"Seasonable for Christmas time. You're not a skater, I suppose?"

"No. No. Something else to think of. Good morning!"

Not another word. That was their meeting, their conversation, and their parting.

Scrooge was at first inclined to be surprised that the Spirit should attach importance to conversations apparently so trivial; but feeling assured that they must have some hidden purpose, he set himself to

consider what it was likely to be. They could scarcely be supposed to
have any bearing on the death of Jacob, his old partner, for that was
Past, and this Ghost's province was the Future. Nor could he think of
any one immediately connected with himself, to whom he could apply
them. But nothing doubting that to whomsoever they applied they
had some latent moral for his own improvement, he resolved to treasure up every word he heard, and everything he saw; and especially to
observe the shadow of himself when it appeared. For he had an expectation that the conduct of his future self would give him the clue
he missed, and would render the solution of these riddles easy.

He looked about in that very place for his own image; but another
man stood in his accustomed corner, and though the clock pointed to
his usual time of day for being there, he saw no likeness of himself
among the multitudes that poured in through the Porch. It gave him
little surprise, however; for he had been revolving in his mind a change
of life, and thought and hoped he saw his new-born resolutions carried
out in this.

Quiet and dark, beside him stood the Phantom, with its outstretched hand. When he roused himself from his thoughtful quest,
he fancied from the turn of the hand, and its situation in reference to
himself, that the Unseen Eyes were looking at him keenly. It made
him shudder, and feel very cold.

They left the busy scene, and went into an obscure part of the town,
where Scrooge had never penetrated before, although he recognised
its situation, and its bad repute. The ways were foul and narrow; the
shops and houses wretched; the people half-naked, drunken, slipshod,
ugly. Alleys and archways, like so many cesspools, disgorged their
offences of smell, and dirt, and life, upon the straggling streets; and
the whole quarter reeked with crime, with filth, and misery.

Far in this den of infamous resort, there was a low-browed, beetling
shop, below a pent-house roof, where iron, old rags, bottles, bones,
and greasy offal, were bought. Upon the floor within, were piled up
heaps of rusty keys, nails, chains, hinges, files, scales, weights, and refuse iron of all kinds. Secrets that few would like to scrutinise were
bred and hidden in mountains of unseemly rags, masses of corrupted
fat, and sepulchres of bones. Sitting in among the wares he dealt in,
by a charcoal stove, made of old bricks, was a grey-haired rascal, nearly
seventy years of age; who had screened himself from the cold air without, by a frousy curtaining of miscellaneous tatters, hung upon a line;
and smoked his pipe in all the luxury of calm retirement.

Scrooge and the Phantom came into the presence of this man, just
as a woman with a heavy bundle slunk into the shop. But she had
scarcely entered, when another woman, similarly laden, came in too;
and she was closely followed by a man in faded black, who was no less
startled by the sight of them, than they had been upon the recognition

of each other. After a short period of blank astonishment, in which the old man with the pipe had joined them, they all three burst into a laugh.

"Let the charwoman alone to be the first!" cried she who had entered first. "Let the laundress alone to be the second; and let the undertaker's man alone to be the third. Look here, old Joe, here's a chance! If we haven't all three met here without meaning it!"

"You couldn't have met in a better place," said old Joe, removing his pipe from his mouth. "Come into the parlour. You were made free of it long ago, you know; and the other two an't strangers. Stop till I shut the door of the shop. Ah! How it skreeks! There an't such a rusty bit of metal in the place as its own hinges, I believe; and I'm sure there's no such old bones here, as mine. Ha, ha! We're all suitable to our calling, we're well matched. Come into the parlour. Come into the parlour."

The parlour was the space behind the screen of rags. The old man raked the fire together with an old stair-rod, and having trimmed his smoky lamp (for it was night), with the stem of his pipe, put it in his mouth again.

While he did this, the woman who had already spoken threw her bundle on the floor, and sat down in a flaunting manner on a stool; crossing her elbows on her knees, and looking with a bold defiance at the other two.

"What odds then! What odds, Mrs. Dilber?" said the woman. "Every person has a right to take care of themselves. *He* always did."

"That's true, indeed!" said the laundress. "No man more so."

"Why then, don't stand staring as if you was afraid, woman; who's the wiser? We're not going to pick holes in each other's coats, I suppose?"

"No, indeed!" said Mrs. Dilber and the man together. "We should hope not."

"Very well, then!" cried the woman. "That's enough. Who's the worse for the loss of a few things like these? Not a dead man, I suppose?"

"No, indeed," said Mrs. Dilber, laughing.

"If he wanted to keep 'em after he was dead, a wicked old screw," pursued the woman, "why wasn't he natural in his lifetime? If he had been, he'd have had somebody to look after him when he was struck with death, instead of lying gasping out his last there, alone by himself."

"It's the truest word that ever was spoke," said Mrs. Dilber. "It's a judgment on him."

"I wish it was a little heavier judgment," replied the woman; "and it should have been, you may depend upon it, if I could have laid my hands on anything else. Open that bundle, old Joe, and let me know the value of it. Speak out plain. I'm not afraid to be the first, nor afraid for them to see it. We knew pretty well that we were helping ourselves, before we met here, I believe. It's no sin. Open the bundle, Joe."

But the gallantry of her friends would not allow of this; and the man in faded black, mounting the breach first, produced *his* plunder. It was not extensive. A seal or two, a pencil-case, a pair of sleeve-buttons, and a brooch of no great value, were all. They were severally examined and appraised by old Joe, who chalked the sums he was disposed to give for each, upon the wall, and added them up into a total when he found there was nothing more to come.

"That's your account," said Joe, "and I wouldn't give another six-pence, if I was to be boiled for not doing it. Who's next?"

Mrs. Dilber was next. Sheets and towels, a little wearing apparel, two old-fashioned silver teaspoons, a pair of sugar-tongs, and a few boots. Her account was stated on the wall in the same manner.

"I always give too much to ladies. It's a weakness of mine, and that's the way I ruin myself," said old Joe. "That's your account. If you asked me for another penny, and made it an open question, I'd repent of being so liberal and knock off half-a-crown."

"And now undo *my* bundle, Joe," said the first woman.

Joe went down on his knees for the greater convenience of opening it, and having unfastened a great many knots, dragged out a large and heavy roll of some dark stuff.

"What do you call this?" said Joe. "Bed-curtains!"

"Ah!" returned the woman, laughing and leaning forward on her crossed arms. "Bed-curtains!"

"You don't mean to say you took 'em down, rings and all, with him lying there?" said Joe.

"Yes, I do," replied the woman. "Why not?"

"You were born to make your fortune," said Joe, "and you'll cer-tainly do it."

"I certainly shan't hold my hand, when I can get anything in it by reaching it out, for the sake of such a man as *he* was, I promise you, Joe," returned the woman coolly. "Don't drop that oil upon the blankets, now."

"His blankets?" asked Joe.

"Whose else's do you think?" replied the woman. "He isn't likely to take cold without 'em, I dare say."

"I hope he didn't die of anything catching? Eh?" said old Joe, stop-ping in his work, and looking up.

"Don't you be afraid of that," returned the woman. "I an't so fond of his company that I'd loiter about him for such things, if he did. Ah! you may look through that shirt till your eyes ache; but you won't find a hole in it, nor a threadbare place. It's the best he had, and a fine one too. They'd have wasted it, if it hadn't been for me."

"What do you call wasting of it?" asked old Joe.

"Putting it on him to be buried in, to be sure," replied the woman with a laugh. "Somebody was fool enough to do it, but I took it off again. If calico an't good enough for such a purpose, it isn't good enough for anything. It's quite as becoming to the body. He can't look uglier than he did in that one."

Scrooge listened to this dialogue in horror. As they sat grouped about their spoil, in the scanty light afforded by the old man's lamp, he viewed them with a detestation and disgust, which could hardly have been greater, though they had been obscene demons, marketing the corpse itself.

"Ha, ha!" laughed the same woman, when old Joe, producing a flannel bag with money in it, told out their several gains upon the ground. "This is the end of it, you see! He frightened every one away from him when he was alive, to profit us when he was dead! Ha, ha, ha!"

"Spirit!" said Scrooge, shuddering from head to foot. "I see, I see. The case of this unhappy man might be my own. My life tends that way, now. Merciful Heaven, what is this!"

He recoiled in terror, for the scene had changed, and now he almost touched a bed: a bare, uncurtained bed: on which, beneath a ragged sheet, there lay a something covered up, which, though it was dumb, announced itself in awful language.

The room was very dark, too dark to be observed with any accuracy, though Scrooge glanced round it in obedience to a secret impulse, anxious to know what kind of room it was. A pale light, rising in the outer air, fell straight upon the bed; and on it, plundered and bereft, unwatched, unwept, uncared for, was the body of this man.

Scrooge glanced towards the Phantom. Its steady hand was pointed to the head. The cover was so carelessly adjusted that the slightest raising of it, the motion of a finger upon Scrooge's part, would have disclosed the face. He thought of it, felt how easy it would be to do, and longed to do it; but had no more power to withdraw the veil than to dismiss the spectre at his side.

Oh cold, cold, rigid, dreadful Death, set up thine altar here, and dress it with such terrors as thou hast at thy command: for this is thy dominion! But of the loved, revered, and honoured head, thou canst not turn one hair to thy dread purposes, or make one feature odious. It is not that the hand is heavy and will fall down when released; it is not that the heart and pulse are still; but that the hand was open, generous, and true; the heart brave, warm, and tender; and the pulse a man's. Strike, Shadow, strike! And see his good deeds springing from the wound, to sow the world with life immortal!

No voice pronounced these words in Scrooge's ears, and yet he heard them when he looked upon the bed. He thought, if this man could be raised up now, what would be his foremost thoughts? Avarice, hard-dealing, griping cares? They have brought him to a rich end, truly!

He lay, in the dark empty house, with not a man, a woman, or a child, to say that he was kind to me in this or that, and for the memory of one kind word I will be kind to him. A cat was tearing at the door, and there was a sound of gnawing rats beneath the hearth-stone. What *they* wanted in the room of death, and why they were so restless and disturbed, Scrooge did not dare to think.

"Spirit!" he said, "this is a fearful place. In leaving it, I shall not leave its lesson, trust me. Let us go!"

Still the Ghost pointed with an unmoved finger to the head.

"I understand you," Scrooge returned, "and I would do it, if I could. But I have not the power, Spirit. I have not the power."

Again it seemed to look upon him.

"If there is any person in the town, who feels emotion caused by this man's death," said Scrooge quite agonised, "show that person to me, Spirit, I beseech you!"

The Phantom spread its dark robe before him for a moment, like a wing; and withdrawing it, revealed a room by daylight, where a mother and her children were.

She was expecting some one, and with anxious eagerness; for she walked up and down the room; started at every sound; looked out from the window; glanced at the clock; tried, but in vain, to work with her needle; and could hardly bear the voices of the children in their play.

At length the long-expected knock was heard. She hurried to the door, and met her husband; a man whose face was careworn and depressed, though he was young. There was a remarkable expression in it now; a kind of serious delight of which he felt ashamed, and which he struggled to repress.

He sat down to the dinner that had been hoarding for him by the fire; and when she asked him faintly what news (which was not until after a long silence), he appeared embarrassed how to answer.

"Is it good?" she said, "or bad?"—to help him.

"Bad," he answered.

"We are quite ruined?"

"No. There is hope yet, Caroline."

"If *he* relents," she said, amazed, "there is! Nothing is past hope, if such a miracle has happened."

"He is past relenting," said her husband. "He is dead."

She was a mild and patient creature if her face spoke truth; but she was thankful in her soul to hear it, and she said so, with clasped hands. She prayed forgiveness the next moment, and was sorry; but the first was the emotion of her heart.

"What the half-drunken woman whom I told you of last night, said to me, when I tried to see him and obtain a week's delay; and what I thought was a mere excuse to avoid me; turns out to have been quite true. He was not only very ill, but dying, then."

"To whom will our debt be transferred?"

"I don't know. But before that time we shall be ready with the money; and even though we were not, it would be a bad fortune indeed to find so merciless a creditor in his successor. We may sleep to-night with light hearts, Caroline!"

Yes. Soften it as they would, their hearts were lighter. The children's faces, hushed and clustered round to hear what they so little understood, were brighter; and it was a happier house for this man's death! The only emotion that the Ghost could show him, caused by the event, was one of pleasure.

"Let me see some tenderness connected with a death," said Scrooge; "or that dark chamber, Spirit, which we left just now, will be for ever present to me."

The Ghost conducted him through several streets familiar to his feet; and as they went along, Scrooge looked here and there to find himself, but nowhere was he to be seen. They entered Poor Bob Cratchit's house; the dwelling he had visited before; and found the mother and the children seated round the fire.

Quiet. Very quiet. The noisy little Cratchits were as still as statues in one corner, and sat looking up at Peter, who had a book before him. The mother and her daughters were engaged in sewing. But surely they were very quiet!

"'And He took a child, and set him in the midst of them.'"

Where had Scrooge heard those words? He had not dreamed them. The boy must have read them out, as he and the Spirit crossed the threshold. Why did he not go on?

The mother laid her work upon the table, and put her hand up to her face.

"The colour hurts my eyes," she said.

The colour? Ah, poor Tiny Tim!

"They're better now again," said Cratchit's wife. "It makes them weak by candle-light; and I wouldn't show weak eyes to your father when he comes home, for the world. It must be near his time."

"Past it rather," Peter answered, shutting up his book. "But I think he has walked a little slower than he used, these few last evenings, mother."

They were very quiet again. At last she said, and in a steady, cheerful voice, that only faltered once:

"I have known him walk with—I have known him walk with Tiny Tim upon his shoulder, very fast indeed."

"And so have I," cried Peter. "Often."

"And so have I," exclaimed another. So had all.

"But he was very light to carry," she resumed, intent upon her work, "and his father loved him so, that it was no trouble: no trouble. And there is your father at the door!"

She hurried out to meet him; and little Bob in his comforter—he had need of it, poor fellow—came in. His tea was ready for him on the hob, and they all tried who should help him to it most. Then the two young Cratchits got upon his knees and laid, each child a little cheek, against his face, as if they said, "Don't mind it, father. Don't be grieved!"

Bob was very cheerful with them, and spoke pleasantly to all the family. He looked at the work upon the table, and praised the industry and speed of Mrs. Cratchit and the girls. They would be done long before Sunday, he said.

"Sunday! You went to-day, then, Robert?" said his wife.

"Yes, my dear," returned Bob. "I wish you could have gone. It would have done you good to see how green a place it is. But you'll see it often. I promised him that I would walk there on a Sunday. My little, little child!" cried Bob. "My little child!"

He broke down all at once. He couldn't help it. If he could have helped it, he and his child would have been farther apart perhaps than they were.

He left the room, and went up-stairs into the room above, which was lighted cheerfully, and hung with Christmas. There was a chair set close beside the child, and there were signs of some one having been there, lately. Poor Bob sat down in it, and when he had thought a little and composed himself, he kissed the little face. He was reconciled to what had happened, and went down again quite happy.

They drew about the fire, and talked; the girls and mother working still. Bob told them of the extraordinary kindness of Mr. Scrooge's nephew, whom he had scarcely seen but once, and who, meeting him in the street that day, and seeing that he looked a little—"just a little down you know," said Bob, inquired what had happened to distress him. "On which," said Bob, "for he is the pleasantest-spoken gentleman you ever heard, I told him. 'I am heartily sorry for it Mr. Cratchit,' he said, 'and heartily sorry for your good wife.' By the bye, how he ever knew *that*, I don't know."

"Knew what, my dear?"

"Why, that you were a good wife," replied Bob.

"Everybody knows that!" said Peter.

"Very well observed, my boy!" cried Bob. "I hope they do. 'Heartily sorry,' he said, 'for your good wife. If I can be of service to you in any way,' he said, giving me his card, 'that's where I live. Pray come to me.' Now, it wasn't," cried Bob, "for the sake of anything he might be able to do for us, so much as for his kind way, that this was quite delightful. It really seemed as if he had known our Tiny Tim, and felt with us."

"I'm sure he's a good soul!" said Mrs. Cratchit.

"You would be surer of it, my dear," returned Bob, "if you saw and spoke to him. I shouldn't be at all surprised—mark what I say!—if he got Peter a better situation."

"Only hear that, Peter," said Mrs. Cratchit.

"And then," cried one of the girls, "Peter will be keeping company with some one, and setting up for himself."

"Get along with you!" retorted Peter, grinning.

"It's just as likely as not," said Bob, "one of these days; though there's plenty of time for that, my dear. But however and whenever we part from one another, I am sure we shall none of us forget poor Tiny Tim—shall we—or this first parting that there was among us?"

"Never, father!" cried they all.

"And I know," said Bob, "I know, my dears, that when we recollect how patient and how mild he was; although he was a little, little child; we shall not quarrel easily among ourselves, and forget poor Tiny Tim in doing it."

"No, never father!" they all cried again.

"I am very happy," said little Bob, "I am very happy!"

Mrs. Cratchit kissed him, his daughters kissed him, the two young Cratchits kissed him, and Peter and himself shook hands. Spirit of Tiny Tim, thy childish essence was from God!

"Spectre," said Scrooge, "something informs me that our parting moment is at hand. I know it, but I know not how. Tell me what man that was whom we saw lying dead?"

The Ghost of Christmas Yet To Come conveyed him, as before—though at a different time, he thought: indeed, there seemed no order in these latter visions, save that they were in the Future—into the resorts of business men, but showed him not himself. Indeed, the Spirit did not stay for anything, but went straight on, as to the end just now desired, until besought by Scrooge to tarry for a moment.

"This court," said Scrooge, "through which we hurry now, is where my place of occupation is, and has been for a length of time. I see the house. Let me behold what I shall be, in days to come!"

The Spirit stopped; the hand was pointed elsewhere.

"The house is yonder," Scrooge exclaimed. "Why do you point away?"

The inexorable finger underwent no change.

Scrooge hastened to the window of his office, and looked in. It was an office still, but not his. The furniture was not the same, and the figure in the chair was not himself. The Phantom pointed as before.

He joined it once again, and wondering why and whither he had gone, accompanied it until they reached an iron gate. He paused to look round before entering.

A churchyard. Here, then, the wretched man whose name he had now to learn, lay underneath the ground. It was a worthy place. Walled in by houses; overrun by grass and weeds, the growth of vegetation's death, not life; choked up with too much burying; fat with repleted appetite. A worthy place!

The Spirit stood among the graves, and pointed down to One. He advanced towards it trembling. The Phantom was exactly as it had been, but he dreaded that he saw new meaning in its solemn shape.

"Before I draw nearer to that stone to which you point," said Scrooge, "answer me one question. Are these the shadows of the things that Will be, or are they shadows of things that May be, only?"

Still the Ghost pointed downward to the grave by which it stood.

"Men's courses will foreshadow certain ends, to which, if persevered in, they must lead," said Scrooge. "But if the courses be departed from, the ends will change. Say it is thus with what you show me!"

The Spirit was immovable as ever.

Scrooge crept towards it, trembling as he went; and following the finger, read upon the stone of the neglected grave his own name, EBENEZER SCROOGE.

"Am I that man who lay upon the bed?" he cried, upon his knees.

The finger pointed from the grave to him, and back again.

"No, Spirit! Oh, no, no!"

The finger still was there.

"Spirit!" he cried, tight clutching at its robe, "hear me! I am not the man I was. I will not be the man I must have been but for this intercourse. Why show me this, if I am past all hope?"

For the first time the hand appeared to shake.

"Good Spirit," he pursued, as down upon the ground he fell before it: "Your nature intercedes for me, and pities me. Assure me that I yet may change these shadows you have shown me, by an altered life!"

The kind hand trembled.

"I will honour Christmas in my heart, and try to keep it all the year. I will live in the Past, the Present, and the Future. The Spirits of all Three shall strive within me. I will not shut out the lessons that they teach. Oh, tell me I may sponge away the writing on this stone!"

In his agony, he caught the spectral hand. It sought to free itself, but he was strong in his entreaty, and detained it. The Spirit, stronger yet, repulsed him.

Holding up his hands in a last prayer to have his fate reversed, he saw an alteration in the Phantom's hood and dress. It shrunk, collapsed, and dwindled down into a bedpost.

STAVE V   *THE END OF IT*

Yes! and the bedpost was his own. The bed was his own, the room was his own. Best and happiest of all, the Time before him was his own, to make amends in!

"I will live in the Past, the Present, and the Future!" Scrooge repeated, as he scrambled out of bed. "The Spirits of all Three shall strive within me. Oh Jacob Marley! Heaven, and the Christmas Time be praised for this! I say it on my knees, old Jacob, on my knees!"

He was so fluttered and so glowing with his good intentions, that his broken voice would scarcely answer to his call. He had been sobbing violently in his conflict with the Spirit, and his face was wet with tears.

"They are not torn down," cried Scrooge, folding one of his bed-curtains in his arms, "they are not torn down, rings and all. They are here—I am here—the shadows of the things that would have been, may be dispelled. They will be. I know they will!"

His hands were busy with his garments all this time; turning them inside out, putting them on upside down, tearing them, mislaying them, making them parties to every kind of extravagance.

"I don't know what to do!" cried Scrooge, laughing and crying in the same breath; and making a perfect Laocoön of himself with his stockings. "I am as light as a feather, I am as happy as an angel, I am as merry as a schoolboy. I am as giddy as a drunken man. A merry Christmas to everybody! A happy New Year to all the world! Hallo here! Whoop! Hallo!"

He had frisked into the sitting-room, and was now standing there: perfectly winded.

"There's the saucepan that the gruel was in!" cried Scrooge, starting off again, and going round the fireplace. "There's the door, by which the Ghost of Jacob Marley entered! There's the corner where the Ghost of Christmas Present, sat! There's the window where I saw the wandering Spirits! It's all right, it's all true, it all happened. Ha ha ha!"

Really, for a man who had been out of practice for so many years, it was a splendid laugh, a most illustrious laugh. The father of a long, long line of brilliant laughs!

"I don't know what day of the month it is!" said Scrooge. "I don't know how long I've been among the Spirits. I don't know anything. I'm quite a baby. Never mind. I don't care. I'd rather be a baby. Hallo! Whoop! Hallo here!"

He was checked in his transports by the churches ringing out the lustiest peals he had ever heard. Clash, clang, hammer; ding, dong, bell. Bell, dong, ding; hammer, clang, clash! Oh, glorious, glorious!

Running to the window, he opened it, and put out his head. No fog, no mist; clear, bright, jovial, stirring, cold; cold, piping for the blood to dance to; Golden sunlight; Heavenly sky; sweet fresh air; merry bells. Oh, glorious! Glorious!

"What's to-day?" cried Scrooge, calling downward to a boy in Sunday clothes, who perhaps had loitered in to look about him.

"Eh?" returned the boy, with all his might of wonder.

"What's to-day, my fine fellow?" said Scrooge.

"To-day!" replied the boy. "Why, Christmas Day."

"It's Christmas Day!" said Scrooge to himself. "I haven't missed it. The Spirits have done it all in one night. They can do anything they like. Of course they can. Of course they can. Hallo, my fine fellow!"

"Hallo!" returned the boy.

"Do you know the Poulterer's, in the next street but one at the corner?" Scrooge inquired.

"I should hope I did," replied the lad.

"An intelligent boy!" said Scrooge. "A remarkable boy! Do you know whether they've sold the prize Turkey that was hanging up there?—Not the little prize Turkey: the big one?"

"What, the one as big as me?" returned the boy.

"What a delightful boy!" said Scrooge. "It's a pleasure to talk to him. Yes, my buck!"

"It's hanging there now," replied the boy.

"Is it?" said Scrooge. "Go and buy it."

"Walk-er!" exclaimed the boy.

"No, no," said Scrooge, "I am in earnest. Go and buy it, and tell 'em to bring it here, that I may give them the direction where to take it. Come back with the man, and I'll give you a shilling. Come back with him in less than five minutes and I'll give you half-a-crown!"

The boy was off like a shot. He must have had a steady hand at a trigger who could have got a shot off half so fast.

"I'll send it to Bob Cratchit's!" whispered Scrooge, rubbing his hands, and splitting with a laugh. "He sha'n't know who sends it. It's twice the size of Tiny Tim. Joe Miller never made such a joke as sending it to Bob's will be!"

The hand in which he wrote the address was not a steady one, but write it he did, somehow, and went down-stairs to open the street door, ready for the coming of the poulterer's man. As he stood there, waiting his arrival, the knocker caught his eye.

"I shall love it, as long as I live!" cried Scrooge, patting it with his hand. "I scarcely ever looked at it before. What an honest expression it has in its face! It's a wonderful knocker!—Here's the Turkey. Hallo! Whoop! How are you! Merry Christmas!"

It *was* a Turkey! He never could have stood upon his legs, that bird. He would have snapped 'em short off in a minute, like sticks of sealing-wax.

"Why, it's impossible to carry that to Camden Town," said Scrooge. "You must have a cab."

The chuckle with which he said this, and the chuckle with which he paid for the Turkey, and the chuckle with which he paid for the cab, and the chuckle with which he recompensed the boy, were only to be exceeded by the chuckle with which he sat down breathless in his chair again, and chuckled till he cried.

Shaving was not an easy task, for his hand continued to shake very much; and shaving requires attention, even when you don't dance while you are at it. But if he had cut the end of his nose off, he would have put a piece of sticking-plaister over it, and been quite satisfied.

He dressed himself "all in his best," and at last got out into the streets. The people were by this time pouring forth, as he had seen them with the Ghost of Christmas Present; and walking with his hands behind him, Scrooge regarded every one with a delighted smile. He looked so irresistibly pleasant, in a word, that three or four good-humoured fellows said, "Good morning, sir! A merry Christmas to you!" And Scrooge said often afterwards, that of all the blithe sounds he had ever heard, those were the blithest in his ears.

He had not gone far, when coming on towards him he beheld the portly gentleman, who had walked into his counting-house the day before, and said, "Scrooge and Marley's, I believe?" It sent a pang across his heart to think how this old gentleman would look upon him when they met; but he knew what path lay straight before him, and he took it.

"My dear sir," said Scrooge, quickening his pace, and taking the old gentleman by both his hands. "How do you do? I hope you succeeded yesterday. It was very kind of you. A merry Christmas to you, sir!"

"Mr. Scrooge?"

"Yes," said Scrooge. "That is my name, and I fear it may not be pleasant to you. Allow me to ask your pardon. And will you have the goodness"—here Scrooge whispered in his ear.

"Lord bless me!" cried the gentleman, as if his breath were taken away. "My dear Mr. Scrooge, are you serious?"

"If you please," said Scrooge. "Not a farthing less. A great many back-payments are included in it, I assure you. Will you do me that favour?"

"My dear sir," said the other, shaking hands with him. "I don't know what to say to such munifi—"

"Don't say anything, please," retorted Scrooge. "Come and see me. Will you come and see me?"

"I will!" cried the old gentleman. And it was clear he meant to do it.

"Thank'ee," said Scrooge. "I am much obliged to you. I thank you fifty times. Bless you!"

He went to church, and walked about the streets, and watched the people hurrying to and fro, and patted children on the head, and questioned beggars, and looked down into the kitchens of houses, and up to the windows, and found that everything could yield him pleasure. He had never dreamed that any walk—that anything—could give him so much happiness. In the afternoon he turned his steps towards his nephew's house.

He passed the door a dozen times, before he had the courage to go up and knock. But he made a dash, and did it:

"Is your master at home, my dear?" said Scrooge to the girl. Nice girl! Very.

"Yes, sir."

"Where is he, my love?" said Scrooge.

"He's in the dining-room, sir, along with mistress. I'll show you upstairs, if you please."

"Thank'ee. He knows me," said Scrooge, with his hand already on the dining-room lock. "I'll go in here, my dear."

He turned it gently, and sidled his face in, round the door. They were looking at the table (which was spread out in great array); for these young housekeepers are always nervous on such points, and like to see that everything is right.

"Fred!" said Scrooge.

Dear heart alive, how his niece by marriage started! Scrooge had forgotten, for the moment, about her sitting in the corner with the footstool, or he wouldn't have done it, on any account.

"Why bless my soul!" cried Fred, "who's that?"

"It's I. Your uncle Scrooge. I have come to dinner. Will you let me in, Fred?"

Let him in! It is a mercy he didn't shake his arm off. He was at home in five minutes. Nothing could be heartier. His niece looked just the same. So did Topper when *he* came. So did the plump sister when *she* came. So did every one when *they* came. Wonderful party, wonderful games, wonderful unanimity, wonderful happiness!

But he was early at the office next morning. Oh, he was early there. If he could only be there first, and catch Bob Cratchit coming late! That was the thing he had set his heart upon.

And he did it; yes, he did! The clock struck nine. No Bob. A quarter past. No Bob. He was full eighteen minutes and a half behind his time. Scrooge sat with his door wide open, that he might see him come into the Tank.

His hat was off, before he opened the door; his comforter too. He was on his stool in a jiffy; driving away with his pen, as if he were trying to overtake nine o'clock.

"Hallo!" growled Scrooge, in his accustomed voice, as near as he could feign it. "What do you mean by coming here at this time of day?"

"I am very sorry, sir," said Bob. "I *am* behind my time."

"You are?" repeated Scrooge. "Yes. I think you are. Step this way, sir, if you please."

"It's only once a year, sir," pleaded Bob, appearing from the Tank. "It shall not be repeated. I was making rather merry yesterday, sir."

"Now, I'll tell you what, my friend," said Scrooge, "I am not going to stand this sort of thing any longer. And therefore," he continued, leaping from his stool, and giving Bob such a dig in the waistcoat that he staggered back into the Tank again; "and therefore I am about to raise your salary!"

Bob trembled, and got a little nearer to the ruler. He had a momentary idea of knocking Scrooge down with it, holding him, and calling to the people in the court for help and a strait-waistcoat.

"A merry Christmas, Bob!" said Scrooge, with an earnestness that could not be mistaken, as he clapped him on the back. "A merrier Christmas, Bob, my good fellow, then I have given you, for many a year! I'll raise your salary, and endeavour to assist your struggling family, and we will discuss your affairs this very afternoon, over a Christmas bowl of smoking bishop, Bob! Make up the fires, and buy another coal-scuttle before you dot another i, Bob Cratchit!"

Scrooge was better than his word. He did it all, and infinitely more; and to Tiny Tim, who did NOT die, he was a second father. He became as good a friend, as good a master, and as good a man, as the good old city knew, or any other good old city, town, or borough, in the good old world. Some people laughed to see the alteration in him, but he let them laugh, and little heeded them; for he was wise enough to know that nothing ever happened on this globe, for good, at which some people did not have their fill of laughter in the outset; and knowing that such as these would be blind anyway, he thought it quite as well that they should wrinkle up their eyes in grins, as have the malady in less attractive forms. His own heart laughed; and that was quite enough for him.

He had no further intercourse with Spirits, but lived upon the Total Abstinence Principle, ever afterwards; and it was always said of him, that he knew how to keep Christmas well, if any man alive possessed the knowledge. May that be truly said of us, and all of us! And so, as Tiny Tim observed, God bless Us, Every One!

—1843

The Chimes A GOBLIN STORY

OF SOME BELLS THAT RANG AN OLD YEAR OUT AND A NEW YEAR IN

~~~~~~

FIRST QUARTER

There are not many people—and as it is desirable that a story-teller and a story-reader should establish a mutual understanding as soon as possible, I beg it to be noticed that I confine this observation neither to young people nor to little people, but extend it to all conditions of people: little and big, young and old: yet growing up, or already growing down again—there are not, I say, many people who would care to sleep in a church. I don't mean at sermon-time in warm weather (when the thing has actually been done, once or twice), but in the night, and alone. A great multitude of persons will be violently astonished, I know, by this position, in the broad bold Day. But it applies to Night. It must be argued by night, and I will undertake to maintain it successfully on any gusty winter's night appointed for the purpose, with any one opponent chosen from the rest, who will meet me singly in an old churchyard, before an old church-door; and will previously empower me to lock him in, if needful to his satisfaction, until morning.

For the night-wind has a dismal trick of wandering round and round a building of that sort, and moaning as it goes; and of trying, with its unseen hand, the windows and the doors; and seeking out some crevices by which to enter. And when it has got in; as one not finding what it seeks, whatever that may be, it wails and howls to issue forth again: and not content with stalking through the aisles, and gliding round and round the pillars, and tempting the deep organ, soars up to the roof, and strives to rend the rafters: then flings itself despairingly upon the stones below, and passes, muttering, into the vaults. Anon, it comes up stealthily, and creeps along the walls, seeming to read, in whispers, the Inscriptions sacred to the Dead. At some of these, it breaks out shrilly, as with laughter; and at others, moans and cries as if it were lamenting. It has a ghostly sound too, lingering within the altar; where it seems to chaunt, in its wild way, of Wrong and Murder done, and false Gods worshipped, in defiance of the Tables of the Law, which look so fair and smooth, but are so flawed and broken.

Ugh! Heaven preserve us, sitting snugly round the fire! It has an awful voice, that wind at Midnight, singing in a church!

But, high up in the steeple! There the foul blast roars and whistles! High up in the steeple, where it is free to come and go through many an airy arch and loophole, and to twist and twine itself about the giddy stair, and twirl the groaning weathercock, and make the very tower shake and shiver! High up in the steeple, where the belfry is, and iron rails are ragged with rust, and sheets of lead and copper, shrivelled by the changing weather, crackle and heave beneath the unaccustomed tread; and birds stuff shabby nests into corners of old oaken joists and beams; and dust grows old and grey; and speckled spiders, indolent and fat with long security, swing idly to and fro in the vibration of the bells, and never loose their hold upon their thread-spun castles in the air, or climb up sailor-like in quick alarm, or drop upon the ground and ply a score of nimble legs to save one life! High up in the steeple of an old church, far above the light and murmur of the town and far below the flying clouds that shadow it, is the wild and dreary place at night: and high up in the steeple of an old church, dwelt the Chimes I tell of.

They were old Chimes, trust me. Centuries ago, these bells had been baptized by bishops: so many centuries ago, that the register of their baptism was lost long, long before the memory of man, and no one knew their names. They had had their Godfathers and God-mothers, these Bells (for my own part, by the way, I would rather incur the responsibility of being Godfather to a Bell than a Boy), and had their silver mugs no doubt, besides. But Time had mowed down their sponsors, and Henry the Eighth had melted down their mugs; and they now hung, nameless and mugless, in the church-tower.

Not speechless, though. Far from it. They had clear, loud, lusty, sounding voices, had these Bells; and far and wide they might be heard upon the wind. Much too sturdy Chimes were they, to be dependent on the pleasure of the wind, moreover; for, fighting gallantly against it when it took an adverse whim, they would pour their cheerful notes into a listening ear right royally; and bent on being heard on stormy nights, by some poor mother watching a sick child, or some lone wife whose husband was at sea, they had been sometimes known to beat a blustering Nor' Wester; aye, "all to fits," as Toby Veck said;—for though they chose to call him Trotty Veck, his name was Toby, and nobody could make it anything else either (except Tobias) without a special act of parliament; he having been as lawfully christened in his day as the Bells had been in theirs, though with not quite so much of solemnity or public rejoicing.

For my part, I confess myself of Toby Veck's belief, for I am sure he had opportunities enough of forming a correct one. And whatever

Toby Veck said, I say. And I take my stand by Toby Veck, although he *did* stand all day long (and weary work it was) just outside the church-door. In fact he was a ticket-porter, Toby Veck, and waited there for jobs.

And a breezy, goose-skinned, blue-nosed, red-eyed, stony-toed, tooth-chattering place it was, to wait in, in the winter-time, as Toby Veck well knew. The wind came tearing round the corner—especially the east wind—as if it had sallied forth, express, from the confines of the earth, to have a blow at Toby. And oftentimes it seemed to come upon him sooner than it had expected, for bouncing round the corner, and passing Toby, it would suddenly wheel round again, as if it cried "Why, here he is!" Incontinently his little white apron would be caught up over his head like a naughty boy's garments, and his feeble little cane would be seen to wrestle and struggle unavailingly in his hand, and his legs would undergo tremendous agitation, and Toby himself all aslant, and facing now in this direction, now in that, would be so banged and buffeted, and touzled, and worried, and hustled, and lifted off his feet, as to render it a state of things but one degree removed from a positive miracle, that he wasn't carried up bodily into the air as a colony of frogs or snails or other very portable creatures sometimes are, and rained down again, to the great astonishment of the natives, on some strange corner of the world where ticket-porters are unknown.

But, windy weather, in spite of its using him so roughly, was, after all, a sort of holiday for Toby. That's the fact. He didn't seem to wait so long for a sixpence in the wind, as at other times; the having to fight with that boisterous element took off his attention, and quite freshened him up, when he was getting hungry and low-spirited. A hard frost too, or a fall of snow, was an Event; and it seemed to do him good, somehow or other—it would have been hard to say in what respect though, Toby! So wind and frost and snow, and perhaps a good stiff storm of hail, were Toby Veck's red-letter days.

Wet weather was the worst; the cold, damp, clammy wet, that wrapped him up like a moist great-coat—the only kind of great-coat Toby owned, or could have added to his comfort by dispensing with. Wet days, when the rain came slowly, thickly, obstinately down; when the street's throat, like his own, was choked with mist; when smoking umbrellas passed and repassed, spinning round and round like so many teetotums, as they knocked against each other on the crowded footway, throwing off a little whirlpool of uncomfortable sprinklings; when gutters brawled and waterspouts were full and noisy; when the wet from the projecting stones and ledges of the church fell drip, drip, drip, on Toby, making the wisp of straw on which he stood mere mud in no time; those were the days that tried him. Then, indeed, you might see Toby looking anxiously out from his shelter in an angle of the church wall—such a meagre shelter that in summer-time it never cast a shadow thicker than a good-sized walking stick upon the sunny pavement—with a disconsolate and lengthened face. But coming out, a minute afterwards, to warm himself by exercise, and trotting up and down some dozen times, he would brighten even then, and go back more brightly to his niche.

They called him Trotty from his pace, which meant speed if it didn't make it. He could have walked faster perhaps; most likely; but rob him of his trot, and Toby would have taken to his bed and died. It bespattered him with mud in dirty weather; it cost him a world of trouble; he could have walked with infinitely greater ease; but that was one reason for his clinging to it so tenaciously. A weak, small, spare old man, he was a very Hercules, this Toby, in his good intentions. He loved to earn his money. He delighted to believe— Toby was very poor, and couldn't well afford to part with a delight —that he was worth his salt. With a shilling or an eighteenpenny message or small parcel in hand, his courage always high, rose higher. As he trotted on, he would call out to fast Postmen ahead of him, to get out of the way; devoutly believing that in the natural course of things he must inevitably overtake and run them down; and he had perfect faith—not often tested—in his being able to carry anything that man could lift.

Thus, even when he came out of his nook to warm himself on a wet day, Toby trotted. Making, with his leaky shoes, a crooked line of slushy footprints in the mire; and blowing on his chilly hands and rubbing them against each other, poorly defended from the searching cold by threadbare mufflers of grey worsted, with a private apartment only for the thumb, and a common room or tap for the rest of the fingers; Toby, with his knees bent and his cane beneath his arm, still trotted. Falling out into the road to look up at the belfry when the Chimes resounded, Toby trotted still.

He made this last excursion several times a day, for they were company to him; and when he heard their voices, he had an interest in glancing at their lodging-place, and thinking how they were moved, and what hammers beat upon them. Perhaps he was the more curious about these Bells, because there were points of resemblance between themselves and him. They hung there, in all weathers, with the wind and rain driving in upon them; facing only the outsides of all those houses; never getting any nearer to the blazing fires that gleamed and shone upon the windows, or came puffing out of the chimney tops; and incapable of participation in any of the good things that were constantly being handed, through the street doors and the area railings, to prodigious cooks. Faces came and went at many windows: sometimes pretty faces, youthful faces, pleasant faces: sometimes the reverse: but Toby knew no more (though he often speculated on these trifles, standing idle in the streets) whence they came, or where they went, or whether, when the lips moved, one kind word was said of him in all the year, than did the Chimes themselves.

Toby was not a casuist—that he knew of, at least—and I don't mean to say that when he began to take to the Bells, and to knit up his first rough acquaintance with them into something of a closer and more delicate woof, he passed through these considerations one by one, or held any formal review or great field-day in his thoughts. But what I mean to say, and do say is, that as the functions of Toby's body, his digestive organs for example, did of their own cunning, and by a great many operations of which he was altogether ignorant, and the knowledge of which would have astonished him very much, arrive at a certain end; so his mental faculties, without his privity or concurrence, set all these wheels and springs in motion, with a thousand others, when they worked to bring about his liking for the Bells.

And though I had said his love, I would not have recalled the word, though it would scarcely have expressed his complicated feeling. For, being but a simple man, he invested them with a strange and solemn character. They were so mysterious, often heard and never seen; so high up, so far off, so full of such a deep strong melody, that he regarded them with a species of awe; and sometimes when he looked up at the dark arched windows in the tower, he half expected to be beckoned to by something which was not a Bell, and yet was what he had heard so often sounding in the Chimes. For all this, Toby scouted with indignation a certain flying rumour that the Chimes were haunted, as implying the possibility of their being connected with any Evil thing. In short, they were very often in his ears, and he very often got such a crick in his neck by staring with his mouth wide open, at the steeple where they hung, that he was fain to take an extra trot or two, afterwards, to cure it.

The very thing he was in the act of doing one cold day, when the last drowsy sound of Twelve o'clock, just struck, was humming like a melodious monster of a Bee, and not by any means a busy bee, all through the steeple!

"Dinner-time, eh!" said Toby, trotting up and down before the church. "Ah!"

Toby's nose was very red, and his eyelids were very red, and he winked very much, and his shoulders were very near his ears, and his legs were very stiff, and altogether he was evidently a long way upon the frosty side of cool.

"Dinner-time, eh!" repeated Toby, using his right-hand muffler like an infantine boxing-glove, and punishing his chest for being cold. "Ah-h-h-h!"

He took a silent trot, after that, for a minute or two.

"There's nothing," said Toby, breaking forth afresh—but here he stopped short in his trot, and with a face of great interest and some alarm, felt his nose carefully all the way up. It was but a little way (not being much of a nose) and he had soon finished.

"I thought it was gone," said Toby, trotting off again. "It's all right, however. I am sure I couldn't blame it if it was to go. It has a precious hard service of it in the bitter weather, and precious little to look forward to; for I don't take snuff myself. It's a good deal tried, poor creetur, at the best of times; for when it *does* get hold of a pleasant whiff or so (which an't too often), it's generally from somebody else's dinner, a-coming home from the baker's."

The reflection reminded him of that other reflection, which he had left unfinished.

"There's nothing," said Toby, "more regular in its coming round than dinner-time, and nothing less regular in its coming round than dinner. That's the great difference between 'em. It's took me a long time to find it out. I wonder whether it would be worth any gentleman's while, now, to buy that obserwation for the Papers; or the Parliament!"

Toby was only joking, for he gravely shook his head in self-depreciation.

"Why! Lord!" said Toby. "The Papers is full of obserwations as it is; and so's the Parliament. Here's last week's paper, now;" taking a very dirty one from his pocket, and holding it from him at arm's length; "full of obserwations! Full of obserwations! I like to know the news as well as any man," said Toby, slowly; folding it a little smaller, and putting it in his pocket again: "but it almost goes against the grain with me to read a paper now. It frightens me almost. I don't know what we poor people are coming to. Lord send we may be coming to something better in the New Year nigh upon us!"

"Why, father, father!" said a pleasant voice, hard by.

But Toby, not hearing it, continued to trot backwards and forwards: musing as he went, and talking to himself.

"It seems as if we can't go right, or do right, or be righted," said Toby. "I hadn't much schooling, myself, when I was young; and I can't make out whether we have any business on the face of the earth, or not. Sometimes I think we must have—a little; and sometimes I think we must be intruding. I get so puzzled sometimes that I am not even able to make up my mind whether there is any good at all in us, or whether we are born bad. We seem to be dreadful things; we seem to give a deal of trouble; we are always being complained of and guarded against. One way or other, we fill the papers. Talk of a New Year!" said Toby, mournfully. "I can bear up as well as another man at most times; better than a good many, for I am as strong as a lion, and all men an't; but supposing it should really be that we have no right to a New Year—supposing we really *are* intruding——"

"Why, father, father!" said the pleasant voice again.

Toby heard it this time; started; stopped; and shortening his sight, which had been directed a long way off as seeking the enlightenment in the very heart of the approaching year, found himself face to face with his own child, and looking close into her eyes.

Bright eyes they were. Eyes that would bear a world of looking in, before their depth was fathomed. Dark eyes, that reflected back the eyes which searched them; not flashingly, or at the owner's will, but with a clear, calm, honest, patient radiance, claiming kindred with that light which Heaven called into being. Eyes that were beautiful and true, and beaming with Hope. With Hope so young and fresh; with Hope so buoyant, vigorous, and bright, despite the twenty years of work and poverty on which they had looked; that they became a voice to Trotty Veck, and said: "I think we have some business here—a little!"

Trotty kissed the lips belonging to the eyes, and squeezed the blooming face between his hands.

"Why, Pet," said Trotty. "What's to do? I didn't expect you to-day, Meg."

"Neither did I expect to come, father," cried the girl, nodding her head and smiling as she spoke. "But here I am! And not alone; not alone!"

"Why you don't mean to say," observed Trotty, looking curiously at a covered basket which she carried in her hand, "that you——"

"Smell it, father dear," said Meg. "Only smell it!"

Trotty was going to lift up the cover at once, in a great hurry, when she gaily interposed her hand.

"No, no, no," said Meg, with the glee of a child. "Lengthen it out a little. Let me just lift up the corner; just the lit-tle ti-ny cor-ner, you know," said Meg, suiting the action to the word with the utmost gentleness, and speaking very softly, as if she were afraid of being overheard by something inside the basket; "there. Now. What's that?"

Toby took the shortest possible sniff at the edge of the basket, and cried out in a rapture:

"Why, it's hot!"

"It's burning hot!" cried Meg. "Ha, ha, ha! It's scalding hot!"

"Ha, ha, ha!" roared Toby, with a sort of kick. "It's scalding hot!"

"But what is it, father?" said Meg. "Come. You haven't guessed what it is. And you must guess what it is. I can't think of taking it out, till you guess what it is. Don't be in such a hurry! Wait a minute! A little bit more of the cover. Now guess!"

Meg was in a perfect fright lest he should guess right too soon; shrinking away, as she held the basket towards him; curling up her pretty shoulders; stopping her ear with her hand, as if by so doing she could keep the right word out of Toby's lips; and laughing softly the whole time.

Meanwhile Toby, putting a hand on each knee, bent down his nose to the basket, and took a long inspiration at the lid; the grin upon his withered face expanding in the process, as if he were inhaling laughing gas.

"Ah! It's very nice," said Toby. "It an't—I suppose it an't polonies?"

"No, no, no!" cried Meg, delighted. "Nothing like polonies!"

"No," said Toby, after another sniff. "It's—it's mellower than polonies. It's very nice. It improves every moment. It's too decided for trotters. An't it?"

Meg was in an ecstasy. He could not have gone wider of the mark than trotters—except polonies.

"Liver?" said Toby, communing with himself. "No. There's a mildness about it that don't answer to liver. Pettitoes? No. It an't faint enough for pettitoes. It wants the stringiness of cocks' heads. And I know it an't sausages. I'll tell you what it is. It's chitterlings!"

"No, it an't!" cried Meg, in a burst of delight. "No, it an't!"

"Why, what am I a-thinking of!" said Toby, suddenly recovering a position as near the perpendicular as it was possible for him to assume. "I shall forget my own name next. It's tripe!"

Tripe it was; and Meg, in high joy, protested he should say, in half a minute more, it was the best tripe ever stewed.

"And so," said Meg, busying herself exultingly with the basket, "I'll lay the cloth at once, father; for I have brought the tripe in a basin, and tied the basin up in a pocket-handkerchief; and if I like to be proud for once, and spread that for a cloth, and call it a cloth, there's no law to prevent me; is there, father?"

"Not that I know of, my dear," said Toby. "But they're always a-bringing up some new law or other."

"And according to what I was reading you in the paper the other day, father; what the Judge said, you know; we poor people are supposed to know them all. Ha ha! What a mistake! My goodness me, how clever they think us!"

"Yes, my dear," said Trotty; "and they'd be very fond of any one of us that *did* know 'em all. He'd grow fat upon the work he'd get, that man, and be popular with the gentlefolks in his neighbourhood. Very much so!"

"He'd eat his dinner with an appetite, whoever he was, if it smelt like this," said Meg, cheerfully. "Make haste, for there's a hot potato besides, and half a pint of fresh-drawn beer in a bottle. Where will you dine, father? On the Post, or on the Steps? Dear, dear, how grand we are. Two places to choose from!"

"The steps to-day, my Pet," said Trotty. "Steps in dry weather.

Post in wet. There's a greater conveniency in the steps at all times, because of the sitting down; but they're rheumatic in the damp."

"Then here," said Meg, clapping her hands, after a moment's bustle; "here it is, all ready! And beautiful it looks! Come, father. Come!"

Since his discovery of the contents of the basket, Trotty had been standing looking at her—and had been speaking too—in an abstracted manner, which showed that though she was the object of his thoughts and eyes, to the exclusion even of tripe, he neither saw nor thought about her as she was at that moment, but had before him some imaginary rough sketch or drama of her future life. Roused, now, by her cheerful summons, he shook off a melancholy shake of the head which was just coming upon him, and trotted to her side. As he was stooping to sit down, the Chimes rang.

"Amen!" said Trotty, pulling off his hat and looking up towards them.

"Amen to the Bells, father?" cried Meg.

"They broke in like a grace, my dear," said Trotty, taking his seat. "They'd say a good one, I am sure, if they could. Many's the kind thing they say to me."

"The Bells do, father?" laughed Meg, as she set the basin, and a knife and fork, before him. "Well!"

"Seem to, my Pet," said Trotty, falling to with great vigour. "And where's the difference? If I hear 'em, what does it matter whether they speak it or not? Why bless you, my dear," said Toby, pointing at the tower with his fork, and becoming more animated under the influence of dinner, "how often have I heard them Bells say, 'Toby Veck, Toby Veck, keep a good heart, Toby! Toby Veck, Toby Veck, keep a good heart, Toby!' A million times? More!"

"Well, I never!" cried Meg.

She had, though—over and over again. For it was Toby's constant topic.

"When things is very bad," said Trotty; "very bad indeed, I mean; almost at the worst; then it's 'Toby Veck, Toby Veck, job coming soon, Toby! Toby Veck, Toby Veck, job coming soon, Toby!' That way."

"And it comes—at last, father," said Meg, with a touch of sadness in her pleasant voice.

"Always," answered the unconscious Toby. "Never fails."

While this discourse was holding, Trotty made no pause in his attack upon the savoury meat before him, but cut and ate, and cut and drank, and cut and chewed, and dodged about, from tripe to hot potato, and from hot potato back again to tripe, with an unctuous and unflagging relish. But happening now to look all round the street—in case anybody should be beckoning from any door or window for a porter—his eyes, in coming back again, encountered Meg: sitting opposite to him, with her arms folded: and only busy in watching his progress with a smile of happiness.

"Why, Lord forgive me!" said Trotty, dropping his knife and fork. "My dove! Meg! why didn't you tell me what a beast I was?"

"Father?"

"Sitting here," said Trotty, in penitent explanation, "cramming, and stuffing, and gorging myself; and you before me there, never so much as breaking your precious fast, nor wanting to, when——"

"But I have broken it, father," interposed his daughter, laughing, "all to bits. I have had my dinner."

"Nonsense," said Trotty. "Two dinners in one day! It an't possible! You might as well tell me that two New Year's Days will come together, or that I have had a gold head all my life, and never changed it."

"I have had my dinner, father, for all that," said Meg, coming nearer to him. "And if you'll go on with yours, I'll tell you how and where; and how your dinner came to be brought; and—and something else besides."

Toby still appeared incredulous; but she looked into his face with her clear eyes, and laying her hand upon his shoulder, motioned him to go on while the meat was hot. So Trotty took up his knife and fork again, and went to work. But much more slowly than before, and shaking his head, as if he were not at all pleased with himself.

"I had my dinner, father," said Meg, after a little hesitation, "with —with Richard. His dinner-time was early; and as he brought his dinner with him when he came to see me, we—we had it together, father."

Trotty took a little beer, and smacked his lips. Then he said, "Oh!" —because she waited.

"And Richard says, father—" Meg resumed. Then stopped.

"What does Richard say, Meg?" asked Toby.

"Richard says, father—" Another stoppage.

"Richard's a long time saying it," said Toby.

"He says then, father," Meg continued, lifting up her eyes at last, and speaking in a tremble, but quite plainly; "another year is nearly gone, and where is the use of waiting on from year to year, when it is so unlikely we shall ever be better off than we are now? He says we are poor now, father, and we shall be poor then, but we are young now, and years will make us old before we know it. He says that if we wait: people in our condition: until we see our way quite clearly, the way will be a narrow one indeed—the common way—the Grave, father."

A bolder man than Trotty Veck must needs have drawn upon his boldness largely, to deny it. Trotty held his peace.

"And how hard, father, to grow old, and die, and think we might have cheered and helped each other! How hard in all our lives to love each other; and to grieve, apart, to see each other working, changing, growing old and grey. Even if I got the better of it, and forgot him (which I never could), oh father dear, how hard to have a heart so full as mine is now, and live to have it slowly drained out every drop, without the recollection of one happy moment of a woman's life, to stay behind and comfort me, and make me better!"

Trotty sat quite still. Meg dried her eyes, and said more gaily: that is to say, with here a laugh, and there a sob, and here a laugh and sob together:

"So Richard says, father; as his work was yesterday made certain for some time to come, and as I love him, and have loved him full three years—ah! longer than that, if he knew it!—will I marry him on New Year's Day; the best and happiest day, he says, in the whole year, and one that is almost sure to bring good fortune with it. It's a short notice, father—isn't it?—but I haven't my fortune to be settled, or my wedding dresses to be made, like the great ladies, father, have I? And he said so much, and said it in his way; so strong and earnest, and all the time so kind and gentle; that I said I'd come and talk to you, father. And as they paid the money for that work of mine this morning (unexpectedly, I am sure!) and as you have fared very poorly for a whole week, and as I couldn't help wishing there should be something to make this day a sort of holiday to you as well as a dear and happy day to me, father, I made a little treat and brought it to surprise you."

"And see how he leaves it cooling on the step," said another voice.

It was the voice of this same Richard, who had come upon them unobserved, and stood before the father and daughter; looking down upon them with a face as glowing as the iron on which his stout sledge-hammer daily rung. A handsome, well-made, powerful youngster he was; with eyes that sparkled like the red-hot droppings from a furnace fire; black hair that curled about his swarthy temples rarely; and a smile—a smile that bore out Meg's eulogium on his style of conversation.

"See how he leaves it cooling on the step!" said Richard. "Meg don't know what he likes. Not she!"

Trotty, all action and enthusiasm, immediately reached up his hand to Richard, and was going to address him in a great hurry, when the house-door opened without any warning, and a footman very nearly put his foot into the tripe.

"Out of the vays here, will you! You must always go and be a-settin on our steps, must you! You can't go and give a turn to none of the neighbours never, can't you! Will you clear the road, or won't you?"

Strictly speaking, the last question was irrelevant, as they had already done it.

"What's the matter, what's the matter!" said the gentleman for whom the door was opened; coming out of the house at that kind of light-heavy pace—that peculiar compromise between a walk and a jog-trot—with which a gentleman upon the smooth down-hill of life, wearing creaking boots, a watch-chain, and clean linen, *may* come out of his house: not only without any abatement of his dignity, but with an expression of having important and wealthy engagements elsewhere. "What's the matter! What's the matter!"

"You're always a-being begged, and prayed, upon your bended knees you are," said the footman with great emphasis to Trotty Veck, "to let our door-steps be. Why don't you let 'em be? CAN'T you let 'em be?"

"There! That'll do, that'll do!" said the gentleman. "Halloa there! Porter!" beckoning with his head to Trotty Veck. "Come here. What's that? Your dinner?"

"Yes, sir," said Trotty, leaving it behind him in a corner.

"Don't leave it there," exclaimed the gentleman. "Bring it here, bring it here. So! This is your dinner, is it?"

"Yes, sir," repeated Trotty, looking with a fixed eye and a watery mouth, at the piece of tripe he had reserved for a last delicious tit-bit; which the gentleman was now turning over and over on the end of the fork.

Two other gentlemen had come out with him. One was a low-spirited gentleman of middle age, of a meagre habit, and a disconsolate face; who kept his hands continually in the pockets of his scanty pepper-and-salt trousers, very large and dog's-eared from that custom; and was not particularly well brushed or washed. The other, a full-sized, sleek, well-conditioned gentleman, in a blue coat with bright buttons, and a white cravat. This gentleman had a very red face, as if an undue proportion of the blood in his body were squeezed up into his head; which perhaps accounted for his having also the appearance of being rather cold about the heart.

He who had Toby's meat upon the fork, called to the first one by the name of Filer; and they both drew near together. Mr. Filer being exceedingly short-sighted, was obliged to go so close to the remnant of Toby's dinner before he could make out what it was, that Toby's heart leaped up into his mouth. But Mr. Filer didn't eat it.

"This is a description of animal food, Alderman," said Filer, making little punches in it with a pencil-case, "commonly known to the labouring population of this country, by the name of tripe."

The Alderman laughed, and winked; for he was a merry fellow, Alderman Cute. Oh, and a sly fellow too! A knowing fellow. Up

to everything. Not to be imposed upon. Deep in the people's hearts!
He knew them, Cute did. I believe you!

"But who eats tripe?" said Mr. Filer, looking round. "Tripe is without an exception the least economical, and the most wasteful article
of consumption that the markets of this country can by possibility
produce. The loss upon a pound of tripe has been found to be, in
the boiling, seven-eights of a fifth more than the loss upon a pound
of any other animal substance whatever. Tripe is more expensive,
properly understood, then the hot-house pine-apple. Taking into account the number of animals slaughtered yearly within the bills of
mortality alone; and forming a low estimate of the quantity of tripe
which the carcases of those animals, reasonably well butchered, would
yield; I find that the waste on that amount of tripe, if boiled, would
victual a garrison of five hundred men for five months of thirty-one
days each, and a February over. The Waste, the Waste!"

Trotty stood aghast, and his legs shook under him. He seemed
to have starved a garrison of five hundred men with his own hand.

"Who eats tripe?" said Mr. Filer, warmly. "Who eats tripe?"

Trotty made a miserable bow.

"You do, do you?" said Mr. Filer. "Then I'll tell you something.
You snatch your tripe, my friend, out of the mouths of widows and
orphans."

"I hope not, sir," said Trotty, faintly. "I'd sooner die of want!"

"Divide the amount of tripe before-mentioned, Alderman," said
Mr. Filer, "by the estimated number of existing widows and orphans,
and the result will be one pennyweight of tripe to each. Not a grain
is left for that man. Consequently, he's a robber."

Trotty was so shocked, that it gave him no concern to see the
red-faced gentleman in the blue coat. "You have heard friend Filer.
What do *you* say?"

"What's it possible to say?" returned the gentleman. "What *is* to
be said? Who can take any interest in a fellow like this," meaning
Trotty; "in such degenerate times as these? Look at him. What an
object! The good old times, the grand old times, the great old times!
Those were the times for a bold peasantry, and all that sort of thing.
Those were the times for every sort of thing, in fact. There's nothing
now-a-days. Ah!" sighed the red-faced gentleman. "The good old
times, the good old times!"

The gentleman didn't specify what particular times he alluded to;
nor did he say whether he objected to the present times, from a disinterested consciousness that they had done nothing very remarkable
in producing himself.

"The good old times, the good old times," repeated the gentleman.
"What times they were! They were the only times. It's of no use
talking about any other times, or discussing what the people are in

these times. You don't call these, times, do you? I don't. Look into Strutt's Costumes, and see what a Porter used to be, in any of the good old English reigns."

"He hadn't, in his very best circumstances, a shirt to his back, or a stocking to his foot; and there was scarcely a vegetable in all England for him to put into his mouth," said Mr. Filer. "I can prove it, by tables."

But still the red-faced gentleman extolled the good old times, the grand old times, the great old times. No matter what anybody else said, he still went turning round and round in one set form of words concerning them; as a poor squirrel turns and turns in its revolving cage; touching the mechanism, and trick of which, it has probably quite as distinct perceptions, as ever this red-faced gentleman had of his deceased Millennium.

It is possible that poor Trotty's faith in these very vague Old Times was not entirely destroyed, for he felt vague enough, at that moment. One thing, however, was plain to him, in the midst of his distress; to wit, that however these gentlemen might differ in details, his misgivings of that morning, and of many other mornings, were well founded. "No, no. We can't go right or do right," thought Trotty in despair. "There is no good in us. We are born bad!"

But Trotty had a father's heart within him; which had somehow got into his breast in spite of this decree; and he could not bear that Meg, in the blush of her brief joy, should have her fortune read by these wise gentlemen. "God help her," thought poor Trotty. "She will know it soon enough."

He anxiously signed, therefore, to the young smith, to take her away. But he was so busy, talking to her softly at a little distance, that he only became conscious of this desire, simultaneously with Alderman Cute. Now, the Alderman had not yet had his say, but *he* was a philosopher, too—practical, though! Oh, very practical—and, as he had no idea of losing any portion of his audience, he cried, "Stop!"

"Now, you know," said the Alderman, addressing his two friends, with a self-complacent smile upon his face which was habitual to him, "I am a plain man, and a practical man; and I go to work in a plain practical way. That's my way. There is not the least mystery or difficulty in dealing with this sort of people if you only understand 'em, and can talk to 'em in their own manner. Now, you Porter! Don't you ever tell me, or anybody else, my friend, that you haven't always enough to eat, and of the best; because I know better. I have tasted your tripe, you know, and you can't 'chaff' me. You understand what 'chaff' means, eh? That's the right word, isn't it? Ha, ha, ha! Lord bless you," said the Alderman, turning to his friends again, "it's the easiest thing on earth to deal with this sort of people, if you understand 'em."

Famous man for the common people, Alderman Cute! Never out
of temper with them! Easy, affable, joking, knowing gentleman!

"You see, my friend," pursued the Alderman, "there's a great deal
of nonsense talked about Want—'hard up,' you know; that's the
phrase, isn't it? Ha! ha! ha!—and I intend to Put it Down. There's a
certain amount of cant in vogue about Starvation, and I mean to
Put it Down. That's all! Lord bless you," said the Alderman, turning
to his friends again, "you may Put Down anything among this sort of
people, if you only know the way to set about it."

Trotty took Meg's hand and drew it through his arm. He didn't
seem to know what he was doing though.

"Your daughter, eh?" said the Alderman, chucking her familiarly
under the chin.

Always affable with the working classes, Alderman Cute! Knew
what pleased them! Not a bit of pride!

"Where's her mother?" asked that worthy gentleman.

"Dead," said Toby. "Her mother got up linen; and was called to
Heaven when she was born."

"Not to get up linen *there*, I suppose," remarked the Alderman
pleasantly.

Toby might or might not have been able to separate his wife in
Heaven from her old pursuits. But query: If Mrs. Alderman Cute had
gone to Heaven, would Mr. Alderman Cute have pictured her as
holding any state or station there?

"And you're making love to her, are you?" said Cute to the young
smith.

"Yes," returned Richard quickly, for he was nettled by the question.
"And we are going to be married on New Year's Day."

"What do you mean!" cried Filer sharply. "Married!"

"Why, yes, we're thinking of it, Master," said Richard. "We're
rather in a hurry, you see, in case it should be Put Down first."

"Ah!" cried Filer, with a groan. "Put *that* down, indeed, Alderman,
and you'll do something. Married! Married!! The ignorance of the
first principles of political economy on the part of these people; their
improvidence; their wickedness; is, by Heavens! enough to— Now look
at that couple, will you!"

Well? They were worth looking at. And marriage seemed as reasonable and fair a deed as they need have in contemplation.

"A man may live to be as old as Methuselah," said Mr. Filer, "and
may labour all his life for the benefit of such people as those; and
may heap up facts on figures, facts on figures, facts on figures, mountains high and dry; and he can no more hope to persuade 'em that
they have no right or business to be married, than he can hope to
persuade 'em that they have no earthly right or business to be born.

And *that* we know they haven't. We reduced it to a mathematical certainty long ago!"

Alderman Cute was mightily diverted, and laid his right fore-finger on the side of his nose, as much as to say to both his friends, "Observe me, will you! Keep your eye on the practical man!"—and called Meg to him.

"Come here, my girl!" said Alderman Cute.

The young blood of her lover had been mounting, wrathfully, within the last few minutes; and he was indisposed to let her come. But, setting a constraint upon himself, he came forward with a stride as Meg approached, and stood beside her. Trotty kept her hand within his arm still, but looked from face to face as wildly as a sleeper in a dream.

"Now, I'm going to give you a word or two of good advice, my girl," said the Alderman, in his nice easy way. "It's my place to give advice, you know, because I'm a Justice. You know I'm a Justice, don't you?"

Meg timidly said, "Yes." But everybody knew Alderman Cute was a Justice! O dear, so active a Justice always! Who such a mote of brightness in the public eye, as Cute!

"You are going to be married, you say," pursued the Alderman. "Very unbecoming and indelicate in one of your sex! But never mind that. After you are married, you'll quarrel with your husband and come to be a distressed wife. You may think not; but you will, because I tell you so. Now, I give you fair warning, that I have made up my mind to Put distressed wives Down. So, don't be brought before me. You'll have children—boys. Those boys will grow up bad, of course, and run wild in the streets, without shoes and stockings. Mind, my young friend! I'll convict 'em summarily, every one, for I am determined to Put boys without shoes and stockings Down. Perhaps your husband will die young (most likely) and leave you with a baby. Then you'll be turned out of doors, and wander up and down the streets. Now, don't wander near me, my dear, for I am resolved to Put all wandering mothers Down. All young mothers, of all sorts and kinds, it's my determination to Put Down. Don't think to plead illness as an excuse with me; or babies as an excuse with me; for all sick persons and young children (I hope you know the church-service, but I'm afraid not) I am determined to Put Down. And if you attempt, desperately, and ungratefully, and impiously, and fraudulently attempt, to drown yourself, or hang yourself, I'll have no pity for you, for I have made up my mind to Put all suicide Down! If there is one thing," said the Alderman, with his self-satisfied smile, "on which I can be said to have made up my mind more than on another, it is to Put suicide Down. So don't try it on. That's the phrase, isn't it? Ha, ha! now we understand each other."

Toby knew not whether to be agonised or glad, to see that Meg had turned a deadly white, and dropped her lover's hand.

"And as for you, you dull dog," said the Alderman, turning with even increased cheerfulness and urbanity to the young smith, "what are you thinking of being married for? What do you want to be married for, you silly fellow? If I was a fine, young, strapping chap like you, I should be ashamed of being milksop enough to pin myself to a woman's apron-strings! Why, she'll be an old woman before you're a middle-aged man! And a pretty figure you'll cut then, with a draggle-tailed wife and a crowd of squalling children crying after you wherever you go!"

O, he knew how to banter the common people, Alderman Cute!

"There! Go along with you," said the Alderman, "and repent. Don't make such a fool of yourself as to get married on New Year's Day. You'll think very differently of it, long before next New Year's Day: a trim young fellow like you, with all the girls looking after you. There! Go along with you!"

They went along. Not arm in arm, or hand in hand, or interchanging bright glances; but, she in tears; he, gloomy and down-looking. Were these the hearts that had so lately made old Toby's leap up from its faintness? No, no. The Alderman (a blessing on his head!) had Put *them* Down.

"As you happen to be here," said the Alderman to Toby, "you shall carry a letter for me. Can you be quick? You're an old man."

Toby, who had been looking after Meg, quite stupidly, made shift to murmur out that he was very quick, and very strong.

"How old are you?" inquired the Alderman.

"I'm over sixty, sir," said Toby.

"O! This man's a great deal past the average age, you know, cried Mr. Filer, breaking in as if his patience would bear some trying, but this really was carrying matters a little too far.

"I feel I'm intruding, sir," said Toby. "I—I misdoubted it this morning. Oh dear me!"

The Alderman cut him short by giving him the letter from his pocket. Toby would have got a shilling too; but Mr. Filer clearly showing that in that case he would rob a certain given number of persons of ninepence-halfpenny a-piece, he only got sixpence; and thought himself very well off to get that.

Then the Alderman gave an arm to each of his friends, and walked off in high feather; but, he immediately came hurrying back alone, as if he had forgotten something.

"Porter!" said the Alderman.

"Sir!" said Toby.

"Take care of that daughter of yours. She's much too handsome."

"Even her good looks are stolen from somebody or other, I suppose," thought Toby, looking at the sixpence in his hand, and thinking of the tripe. "She's been and robbed five hundred ladies of a bloom a-piece, I shouldn't wonder. It's very dreadful!"

"She's much too handsome, my man," repeated the Alderman. "The chances are, that she'll come to no good, I clearly see. Observe what I say. Take care of her!" With which he hurried off again.

"Wrong every way. Wrong every way!" said Trotty, clasping his hands. "Born bad. No business here!"

The Chimes came clashing in upon him as he said the words. Full, loud, and sounding—but with no encouragement. No, not a drop.

"The tune's changed," cried the old man, as he listened. "There's not a word of all that fancy in it. Why should there be? I have no business with the New Year nor with the Old one neither. Let me die!"

Still the Bells, pealing forth their changes, made the very air spin. Put 'em down, Put 'em down! Good old Times, Good old Times! Facts and Figures, Facts and Figures! Put 'em down, Put 'em down! If they said anything they said this, until the brain of Toby reeled.

He pressed his bewildered head between his hands, as if to keep it from splitting asunder. A well-timed action, as it happened; for finding the letter in one of them, and being by that means reminded of his charge, he fell, mechanically, into his usual trot, and trotted off.

THE SECOND QUARTER

The letter Toby had received from Alderman Cute, was addressed to a great man in the great district of the town. The greatest district of the town. It must have been the greatest district of the town, because it was commonly called "the world" by its inhabitants.

The letter positively seemed heavier in Toby's hand than another letter. Not because the Alderman had sealed it with a very large coat of arms and no end of wax, but because of the weighty name on the superscription, and the ponderous amount of gold and silver with which it was associated.

"How different from us!" thought Toby, in all simplicity and earnestness, as he looked at the direction. "Divide the lively turtles in the bills of mortality, by the number of gentlefolks able to buy 'em; and whose share does he take but his own! As to snatching tripe from anybody's mouth—he'd scorn it!"

With the involuntary homage due to such an exalted character, Toby interposed a corner of his apron between the letter and his fingers.

"His children," said Trotty, and a mist rose before his eyes; "his daughters— Gentlemen may win their hearts and marry them; they may be happy wives and mothers; they may be handsome like my darling M—e—"

He couldn't finish the name. The final letter swelled in his throat, to the size of the whole alphabet.

"Never mind," thought Trotty. "I know what I mean. That's more than enough for me." And with this consolatory rumination, trotted on.

It was a hard frost, that day. The air was bracing, crisp, and clear. The wintry sun, though powerless for warmth, looked brightly down upon the ice it was too weak to melt, and set a radiant glory there. At other times, Trotty might have learned a poor man's lesson from the wintry sun; but he was past that, now.

The Year was Old, that day. The patient Year had lived through the reproaches and misuses of its slanderers, and faithfully performed its work. Spring, summer, autumn, winter. It had laboured through the destined round, and now laid down its weary head to die. Shut out from hope, high impulse, active happiness, itself, but active messenger of many joys to others, it made appeal in its decline to have its toiling days and patient hours remembered, and to die in peace. Trotty might have read a poor man's allegory in the fading year; but he was past that, now.

And only he? Or has the like appeal been ever made, by seventy years at once upon an English labourer's head, and made in vain!

The streets were full of motion, and the shops were decked out gaily. The New Year, like an Infant Heir to the whole world, was waited for, with welcomes, presents, and rejoicings. There were books and toys for the New Year, glittering trinkets for the New Year, dresses for the New Year, schemes of fortune for the New Year; new inventions to beguile it. Its life was parcelled out in almanacks and pocket-books; the coming of its moons, and stars, and tides, was known beforehand to the moment; all the workings of its seasons in their days and nights, were calculated with as much precision as Mr. Filer could work sums in men and women.

The New Year, the New Year. Everywhere the New Year! The Old Year was already looked upon as dead; and its effects were selling cheap, like some drowned mariner's aboardship. Its patterns were Last Year's, and going at a sacrifice, before its breath was gone. Its treasures were mere dirt, beside the riches of its unborn successor!

Trotty had no portion, to his thinking, in the New Year or the Old.

"Put 'em down, Put 'em down! Facts and Figures, Facts and Figures! Good old Times, Good old Times! Put 'em down, Put 'em down!"—his trot went to that measure, and would fit itself to nothing else.

But, even that one, melancholy as it was, brought him, in due time, to the end of his journey. To the mansion of Sir Joseph Bowley, Member of Parliament.

The door was opened by a Porter. Such a Porter! Not of Toby's order. Quite another thing. His place was the ticket though; not Toby's.

This Porter underwent some hard panting before he could speak; having breathed himself by coming incautiously out of his chair, without first taking time to think about it and compose his mind. When he had found his voice—which it took him a long time to do, for it was a long way off, and hidden under a load of meat—he said in a fat whisper:

"Who's it from?"

Toby told him.

"You're to take it in, yourself," said the Porter, pointing to a room at the end of a long passage, opening from the hall. "Everything goes straight in, on this day of the year. You're not a bit too soon; for the carriage is at the door now, and they have only come to town for a couple of hours, a' purpose."

Toby wiped his feet (which were quite dry already) with great care, and took the way pointed out to him; observing as he went that it was an awfully grand house, but hushed and covered up, as if the family were in the country. Knocking at the room-door, he was told to enter from within; and doing so found himself in a spacious library, where, at a table strewn with files and papers, were a stately lady in a bonnet; and a not very stately gentleman in black who wrote from her dictation; while another, and an older, and a much statelier gentleman, whose hat and cane were on the table, walked up and down, with one hand in his breast, and looked complacently from time to time at his own picture—a full length; a very full length—hanging over the fireplace.

"What is this?" said the last-named gentleman. "Mr. Fish, will you have the goodness to attend?"

Mr. Fish begged pardon, and taking the letter from Toby, handed it, with great respect.

"From Alderman Cute, Sir Joseph."

"Is this all? Have you nothing else, Porter?" inquired Sir Joseph. Toby replied in the negative.

"You have no bill or demand upon me—my name is Bowley, Sir Joseph Bowley—of any kind from anybody, have you?" said Sir Joseph. "If you have, present it. There is a cheque-book by the side of Mr. Fish. I allow nothing to be carried into the New Year. Every description of account is settled in this house at the close of the old one. So that if death was to—to—"

"To cut," suggested Mr. Fish.

"To sever, sir," returned Sir Joseph, with great asperity, "the cord
of existence—my affairs would be found, I hope, in a state of preparation."

"My dear Sir Joseph!" said the lady, who was greatly younger than
the gentleman. "How shocking!"

"My lady Bowley," returned Sir Joseph, floundering now and then,
as in the great depth of his observations, "at this season of the year
we should think of—of—ourselves. We should look into our—our accounts. We should feel that every return of so eventful a period in
human transactions, involves a matter of deep moment between a
man and his—and his banker."

Sir Joseph delivered these words as if he felt the full morality of
what he was saying; and desired that even Trotty should have an
opportunity of being improved by such discourse. Possibly he had
this end before him in still forbearing to break the seal of the letter,
and in telling Trotty to wait where he was, a minute.

"You were desiring Mr. Fish to say, my lady—" observed Sir Joseph.

"Mr. Fish has said that, I believe," returned his lady, glancing
at the letter. "But, upon my word, Sir Joseph, I don't think I can
let it go after all. It is so very dear."

"What is dear?" inquired Sir Joseph.

"That Charity, my love. They only allow two votes for a subscription of five pounds. Really monstrous!"

"My lady Bowley," returned Sir Joseph, "you surprise me. Is the
luxury of feeling in proportion to the number of votes; or is it, to a
rightly constituted mind, in proportion to the number of applicants,
and the wholesome state of mind to which their canvassing reduces
them? Is there no excitement of the purest kind in having two votes
to dispose of among fifty people?"

"Not to me, I acknowledge," replied the lady. "It bores one. Besides, one can't oblige one's acquaintance. But you are the Poor
Man's Friend, you know, Sir Joseph. You think otherwise."

"I *am* the Poor Man's Friend," observed Sir Joseph, glancing at
the poor man present. "As such I may be taunted. As such I have
been taunted. But I ask no other title."

"Bless him for a noble gentleman!" thought Trotty.

"I don't agree with Cute here, for instance," said Sir Joseph, holding out the letter. "I don't agree with the Filer party. I don't agree
with any party. My friend the Poor Man has no business with anything of that sort, and nothing of that sort has any business with
him. My friend the Poor Man, in my district, is my business. No
man or body of men has any right to interfere between my friend
and me. That is the ground I take. I assume a—a paternal character
towards my friend. I say, 'My good fellow, I will treat you paternally.'"

Toby listened with great gravity, and began to feel more comfortable.

"Your only business, my good fellow," pursued Sir Joseph, looking abstractedly at Toby; "your only business in life is with me. You needn't trouble yourself to think about anything. I will think for you; I know what is good for you; I am your perpetual parent. Such is the dispensation of an all-wise Providence! Now, the design of your creation is—not that you should swill, and guzzle, and associate your enjoyments, brutally, with food;" Toby thought remorsefully of the tripe; "but that you should feel the Dignity of Labour. Go forth erect into the cheerful morning air, and—and stop there. Live hard and temperately, be respectful, exercise your self-denial, bring up your family on next to nothing, pay your rent as regularly as the clock strikes, be punctual in your dealings (I set you a good example; you will find Mr. Fish, my confidential secretary, with a cash-box before him at all times); and you may trust to me to be your Friend and Father."

"Nice children, indeed, Sir Joseph!" said the lady, with a shudder. "Rheumatisms, and fevers, and crooked legs, and asthmas, and all kinds of horrors!"

"My lady," returned Sir Joseph, with solemnity, "not the less am I the Poor Man's Friend and Father. Not the less shall he receive encouragement at my hands. Every quarter-day he will be put in communication with Mr. Fish. Every New Year's Day, myself and friends will drink his health. Once every year, myself and friends will address him with the deepest feeling. Once in his life, he may even perhaps receive—in public, in the presence of the gentry—a Trifle from a Friend. And when, upheld no more by these stimulants, and the Dignity of Labour, he sinks into his comfortable grave, then, my lady"—here Sir Joseph blew his nose—"I will be a Friend and a Father—on the same terms—to his children."

Toby was greatly moved.

"O! You have a thankful family, Sir Joseph!" cried his wife.

"My lady," said Sir Joseph, quite majestically, "ingratitude is known to be the sin of that class. I expect no other return."

"Ah! Born bad!" thought Toby. "Nothing melts us."

"What man can do, I do," pursued Sir Joseph. "I do my duty as the Poor Man's Friend and Father; and I endeavour to educate his mind, by inculcating on all occasions the one great moral lesson which that class requires. That is, entire Dependence on myself. They have no business whatever with—with themselves. If wicked and designing persons tell them otherwise, and they become impatient and discontented, and are guilty of insubordinate conduct and black-hearted ingratitude—which is undoubtedly the case—I am their Friend and Father still. It is so Ordained. It is in the nature of things."

With that great sentiment, he opened the Alderman's letter, and read it.

"Very polite and attentive, I am sure!" exclaimed Sir Joseph. "My lady, the Alderman is so obliging as to remind me that he has had 'the distinguished honour'—he is very good—of meeting me at the house of our mutual friend Deedles, the banker; and he does me the favour to inquire whether it will be agreeable to me to have Will Fern put down."

"*Most* agreeable!" replied my Lady Bowley. "The worst man among them! He has been committing a robbery, I hope?"

"Why, no," said Sir Joseph, referring to the letter. "Not quite. Very near. Not quite. He came up to London, it seems, to look for employment (trying to better himself—that's his story), and being found at night asleep in a shed, was taken into custody, and carried next morning before the Alderman. The Alderman observes (very properly) that he is determined to put this sort of thing down; and that if it will be agreeable to me to have Will Fern put down, he will be happy to begin with him."

"Let him be made an example of, by all means," returned the lady. "Last winter, when I introduced pinking and eyelet-holing among the men and boys in the village, as a nice evening employment, and had the lines,

> O let us love our occupations,
> Bless the squire and his relations
> Live upon our daily rations,
> And always know our proper stations,

set to music on the new system, for them to sing the while; this very Fern—I see him now—touched that hat of his, and said, 'I humbly ask your pardon, my lady, but *an't* I something different from a great girl?' I expected it, of course; who can expect anything but insolence and ingratitude from that class of people! That is not to the purpose, however. Sir Joseph! Make an example of him!"

"Hem!" coughed Sir Joseph. "Mr. Fish, if you'll have the goodness to attend—"

Mr. Fish immediately seized his pen, and wrote from Sir Joseph's dictation.

"Private. My dear Sir. I am very much indebted to you for your courtesy in the matter of the man William Fern, of whom, I regret to add, I can say nothing favourable. I have uniformly considered myself in the light of his Friend and Father, but have been repaid (a common case, I grieve to say) with ingratitude, and constant opposition to my plans. He is a turbulent and rebellious spirit. His character will not bear investigation. Nothing will persuade him to be happy when he might. Under these circumstances, it appears to me, I own, that when he comes before you again (as you informed me he promised to do to-morrow, pending your inquiries, and I think he may be so far relied upon), his committal for some short term as a Vagabond, would be a service to society, and would be a salutary example in a country where—for the sake of those who are, through good and evil report, the Friends and Fathers of the Poor, as well as with a view to that, generally speaking, misguided class themselves—examples are greatly needed. And I am," and so forth.

"It appears," remarked Sir Joseph when he had signed this letter, and Mr. Fish was sealing it, "as if this were Ordained: really. At the close of the year, I wind up my account and strike my balance, even with William Fern!"

Trotty, who had long ago relapsed, and was very low-spirited, stepped forward with a rueful face to take the letter.

"With my compliments and thanks," said Sir Joseph. "Stop!"

"Stop!" echoed Mr. Fish.

"You have heard, perhaps," said Sir Joseph, oracularly, "certain remarks into which I have been led respecting the solemn period of time at which we have arrived, and the duty imposed upon us of settling our affairs, and being prepared. You have observed that I don't shelter myself behind my superior standing in society, but that Mr. Fish—that gentleman—has a cheque-book at his elbow, and is in fact here, to enable me to turn over a perfectly new leaf, and enter on the epoch before us with a clean account. Now, my friend, can you lay your hand upon your heart, and say, that you also have made preparations for a New Year?"

"I am afraid, sir," stammered Trotty, looking meekly at him, "that I am a—a—little behind-hand with the world."

"Behind-hand with the world!" repeated Sir Joseph Bowley, in a tone of terrible distinctness.

"I am afraid, sir," faltered Trotty, "that there's a matter of ten or twelve shillings owing to Mrs. Chickenstalker."

"To Mrs. Chickenstalker!" repeated Sir Joseph, in the same tone as before.

"A shop, sir," exclaimed Toby, "in the general line. Also a—a little money on account of rent. A very little, sir. It oughtn't to be owing, I know, but we have been hard put to it, indeed!"

Sir Joseph looked at his lady, and at Mr. Fish, and at Trotty, one after another, twice all round. He then made a despondent gesture with both hands at once, as if he gave the thing up altogether.

"How a man, even among this improvident and impracticable race; an old man; a man grown grey; can look a New Year in the face, with his affairs in this condition; how he can lie down on his bed at night, and get up again in the morning, and— There!" he said, turning his back on Trotty. "Take the letter. Take the letter!"

"I heartily wish it was otherwise, sir," said Trotty, anxious to excuse himself. "We have been tried very hard."

Sir Joseph still repeating "Take the letter, take the letter!" and Mr. Fish not only saying the same thing, but giving additional force to the request by motioning the bearer to the door, he had nothing for it but to make his bow and leave the house. And in the street, poor Trotty pulled his worn old hat down on his head, to hide the grief he felt at getting no hold on the New Year, anywhere.

He didn't even lift his hat to look up at the Bell tower when he came to the old church on his return. He halted there a moment, from habit: and knew that it was growing dark, and that the steeple rose above him, indistinct and faint, in the murky air. He knew, too, that the Chimes would ring immediately; and that they sounded to his fancy, at such a time, like voices in the clouds. But he only made the more haste to deliver the Alderman's letter, and get out of the way before they began; for he dreaded to hear them tagging "Friends and Fathers, Friends and Fathers," to the burden they had rung out last.

Toby discharged himself of his commission, therefore, with all possible speed, and set off trotting homeward. But what with his pace, which was at best an awkward one in the street; and what with his hat, which didn't improve it; he trotted against somebody in less than no time, and was sent staggering out into the road.

"I beg your pardon, I'm sure!" said Trotty, pulling up his hat in great confusion, and between the hat and the torn lining, fixing his head into a kind of bee-hive. "I hope I haven't hurt you."

As to hurting anybody, Toby was not such an absolute Samson, but that he was much more likely to be hurt himself: and indeed, he had flown out into the road, like a shuttlecock. He had such an opinion of his own strength, however, that he was in real concern for the other party: and said again,

"I hope I haven't hurt you?"

The man against whom he had run; a sun-browned, sinewy, country-looking man, with grizzled hair, and a rough chin; stared at him for a moment, as if he suspected him to be in jest. But, satisfied of his good faith, he answered:

"No, friend. You have not hurt me."

"Nor the child, I hope?" said Trotty.

"Nor the child," returned the man. "I thank you kindly."

As he said so, he glanced at a little girl he carried in his arms, asleep: and shading her face with the long end of the poor handkerchief he wore about his throat, went slowly on.

The tone in which he said "I thank you kindly," penetrated Trotty's heart. He was so jaded and foot-sore, and so soiled with travel, and looked about him so forlorn and strange, that it was a comfort to him to be able to thank any one: no matter for how little. Toby stood gazing after him as he plodded wearily away, with the child's arm clinging round his neck.

Before he merged into the darkness the traveller stopped; and looking round, and seeing Trotty standing there yet, seemed undecided whether to return or go on. After doing first the one and then the other, he came back, and Trotty went half-way to meet him.

"You can tell me, perhaps," said the man with a faint smile, "and if you can I am sure you will, and I'd rather ask you than another—where Alderman Cute lives."

"Close at hand," replied Toby. "I'll show you his house with pleasure."

"I was to have gone to him elsewhere to-morrow," said the man, accompanying Toby, "but I'm uneasy under suspicion, and want to clear myself, and to be free to go and seek my bread—I don't know where. So, maybe he'll forgive my going to his house to-night."

"It's impossible," cried Toby with a start, "that your name's Fern!"

"Eh!" cried the other, turning on him in astonishment.

"Fern! Will Fern!" said Trotty.

"That's my name," replied the other.

"Why then," cried Trotty, seizing him by the arm, and looking cautiously round, "for Heaven's sake don't go to him! Don't go to him! He'll put you down as sure as ever you were born. Here, come up this alley, and I'll tell you what I mean. Don't go to *him*."

His new acquaintance looked as if he thought him mad; but he bore him company nevertheless. When they were shrouded from observation, Trotty told him what he knew, and what character he had received, and all about it.

The subject of his history listened to it with a calmness that surprised him. He did not contradict or interrupt it, once. He nodded his head now and then—more in corroboration of an old and worn-out story, it appeared, than in refutation of it; and once or twice threw back his hat, and passed his freckled hand over a brow, where every furrow he had ploughed seemed to have set its image in little. But he did no more.

"It's true enough in the main," he said, "master, I could sift grain from husk here and there, but let it be as 'tis. What odds? I have gone against his plans; to my misfortun'. I can't help it; I should do the like to-morrow. As to character, them gentlefolks will search and search, and pry and pry, and have it as free from spot or speck in us, afore they'll help us to a dry good word!— Well! I hope they don't lose good opinion as easy as we do, or their lives is strict indeed, and hardly worth the keeping. For myself, master, I never took with that hand"—holding it before him—"what wasn't my own; and never held it back from work, however hard, or poorly paid. Whoever can deny it, let him chop it off! But when work won't maintain me like a human creetur; when my living is so bad, that I am hungry, out of doors and in; when I see a whole working life begin that way, go on that way, and end that way, without a chance or change; then I say to the gentle-folks 'Keep away from me! Let my cottage be. My doors is dark enough without your darkening of 'em more. Don't look for me to come up into the park to help the show when there's a birthday, or a fine speechmaking, or what not. Act your plays and games without me, and be welcome to 'em, and enjoy 'em. We've nowt to do with one another. I'm best let alone!'"

Seeing that the child in his arms had opened her eyes, and was looking about her in wonder, he checked himself to say a word or two of foolish prattle in her ear, and stand her on the ground beside him. Then slowly winding one of her long tresses round and round his rough forefinger like a ring, while she hung about his dusty leg, he said to Trotty:

"I'm not a cross-grained man by natur', I believe; and easy satisfied, I'm sure. I bear no ill-will against none of 'em. I only want to live like one of the Almighty's creeturs. I can't—I don't—and so there's a pit dug between me, and them that can and do. There's others like me. You might tell 'em off by hundreds and by thousands, sooner than by ones."

Trotty knew he spoke the Truth in this, and shook his head to signify as much.

"I've got a bad name this way," said Fern; "and I'm not likely, I'm afeared, to get a better. 'Tan't lawful to be out of sorts, and I AM out of sorts, though God knows I'd sooner bear a cheerful spirit if I could. Well! I don't know as this Alderman could hurt *me* much by sending me to jail; but without a friend to speak a word for me, he might do it; and you see—!" pointing downward with his finger, at the child.

"She has a beautiful face," said Trotty.

"Why, yes!" replied the other in a low voice, as he gently turned it up with both his hands towards his own, and looked upon it stead-fastly. "I've thought so, many times. I've thought so, when my hearth was very cold, and cupboard very bare. I thought so t'other night, when we were taken like two thieves. But they—they shouldn't try the little face too often, should they, Lilian? That's hardly fair upon a man!"

He sunk his voice so low, and gazed upon her with an air so stern and strange, that Toby, to divert the current of his thoughts, inquired if his wife were living.

"I never had one," he returned, shaking his head. "She's my brother's child: a orphan. Nine year old, though you'd hardly think it; but she's tired and worn out now. They'd have taken care on her, the Union—eight-and-twenty miles away from where we live—between four walls (as they took care of my old father when he couldn't work no more, though he didn't trouble 'em long); but I took her instead, and she's lived with me ever since. Her mother had a friend once, in London here. We are trying to find her, and to find work too; but it's a large place. Never mind. More room for us to walk about in, Lilly!"

Meeting the child's eyes with a smile which melted Toby more than tears, he shook him by the hand.

"I don't so much as know your name," he said, "but I've opened my heart free to you, for I'm thankful to you; with good reason. I'll take your advice, and keep clear of this—"

"Justice," suggested Toby.

"Ah!" he said. "If that's the name they give him. This Justice. And to-morrow will try whether there's better fortun' to be met with, somewheres near London. Good night. A Happy New Year!"

"Stay!" cried Trotty, catching at his hand, as he relaxed his grip. "Stay! The New Year never can be happy to me, if we part like this. The New Year never can be happy to me, if I see the child and you go wandering away, you don't know where, without a shelter for your heads. Come home with me! I'm a poor man, living in a poor place; but I can give you lodging for one night and never miss it. Come home with me! Here! I'll take her!" cried Trotty, lifting up the child. "A pretty one! I'd carry twenty times her weight, and never know I'd got it. Tell me if I go too quick for you. I'm very fast. I always was!" Trotty said this, taking about six of his trotting paces to one stride of his fatigued companion; and with his thin legs quivering again, beneath the load he bore.

"Why, she's as light," said Trotty, trotting in his speech as well as in his gait; for he couldn't bear to be thanked, and dreaded a moment's pause; "as light as a feather. Lighter than a Peacock's feather—a great deal lighter. Here we are and here we go! Round this first turning to the right, Uncle Will, and past the pump, and sharp off up the passage to the left, right opposite the public-house. Here we are and here we go! Cross over, Uncle Will, and mind the kidney pieman at the corner! Here we are and here we go! Down the Mews here, Uncle Will, and stop at the black door, with 'T. Veck, Ticket Porter,' wrote upon a board; and here we are and here we go, and here we are indeed, my precious Meg, surprising you!"

With which words Trotty, in a breathless state, set the child down before his daughter in the middle of the floor. The little visitor looked once at Meg; and doubting nothing in that face, but trusting everything she saw there; ran into her arms.

"Here we are and here we go!" cried Trotty, running round the room, and choking audibly. "Here, Uncle Will, here's a fire you know! Why don't you come to the fire? Oh here we are and here we go! Meg, my precious darling, where's the kettle? Here it is and here it goes, and it'll bile in no time!"

Trotty really had picked up the kettle somewhere or other in the course of his wild career, and now put it on the fire: while Meg, seating the child in a warm corner, knelt down on the ground before her, and pulled off her shoes, and dried her wet feet on a cloth. Ay, and she laughed at Trotty too—so pleasantly, so cheerfully, that Trotty could have blessed her where she kneeled; for he had seen that, when they entered, she was sitting by the fire in tears.

"Why, father!" said Meg. "You're crazy to-night, I think. I don't know what the Bells would say to that. Poor little feet. How cold they are!"

"Oh, they're warmer now!" exclaimed the child. "They're quite warm now!"

"No, no, no," said Meg. "We haven't rubbed 'em half enough. We're so busy. So busy! And when they're done, we'll brush out the damp hair; and when that's done, we'll bring some colour to the poor face with fresh water; and when that's done, we'll be so gay, and brisk, and happy—!"

The child, in a burst of sobbing, clasped her round the neck; caressed her fair cheek with its hand; and said, "Oh Meg! oh dear Meg!"

Toby's blessing could have done no more. Who could do more!

"Why, father!" cried Meg, after a pause.

"Here I am and here I go, my dear!" said Trotty.

"Good gracious me!" cried Meg. "He's crazy! He's put the dear child's bonnet on the kettle, and hung the lid behind the door!"

"I didn't for to do it, my love," said Trotty, hastily repairing this mistake. "Meg, my dear?"

Meg looked towards him and saw that he had elaborately stationed himself behind the chair of their male visitor, where with many mysterious gestures he was holding up the sixpence he had earned.

"I see, my dear," said Trotty, "as I was coming in, half an ounce of tea lying somewhere on the stairs; and I'm pretty sure there was a bit of bacon too. As I don't remember where it was exactly, I'll go myself and try to find 'em."

With this inscrutable artifice, Toby withdrew to purchase the viands he had spoken of, for ready money, at Mrs. Chickenstalker's; and presently came back, pretending he had not been able to find them, at first, in the dark.

"But here they are at last," said Trotty, setting out the tea-things, "all correct! I was pretty sure it was tea, and a rasher. So it is. Meg, my pet, if you'll just make the tea, while your unworthy father toasts the bacon, we shall be ready, immediate. It's a curious circumstance," said Trotty, proceeding in his cookery, with the assistance of the toasting-fork, "curious, but well known to my friends, that I never care, myself, for rashers, nor for tea. I like to see other people enjoy 'em," said Trotty, speaking very loud, to impress the fact upon his guest, "but to me, as food, they're disagreeable."

No. Trotty's occupation was, to see Will Fern and Lilian eat and drink; and so was Meg's. And never did spectators at a city dinner or court banquet find such high delight in seeing others feast: although it were a monarch or a pope: as those two did, in looking on that night. Meg smiled at Trotty, Trotty laughed at Meg. Meg shook her head, and made belief to clap her hands, applauding Trotty; Trotty conveyed, in dumb-show, unintelligible narratives of how and when and where he had found their visitors, to Meg; and they were happy. Very happy.

"Although," thought Trotty, sorrowfully, as he watched Meg's face; "that match is broken off, I see!"

"Now, I'll tell you what," said Trotty after tea. "The little one, she sleeps with Meg, I know."

"With good Meg!" cried the child, caressing her. "With Meg."

"That's right," said Trotty. "And I shouldn't wonder if she kiss Meg's father, won't she? I'm Meg's father."

Mightily delighted Trotty was, when the child went timidly towards him, and having kissed him, fell back upon Meg again.

"She's as sensible as Solomon," said Trotty. "Here we come and here we—no, we don't—I don't mean that—I—what was I saying, Meg, my precious?"

Meg looked towards their guest, who leaned upon her chair, and with his face turned from her, fondled the child's head, half hidden in her lap.

"To be sure," said Toby. "To be sure! I don't know what I'm rambling on about, to-night. My wits are wool-gathering, I think. Will Fern, you come along with me. You're tired to death, and broken down for want of rest. You come along with me."

The man still played with the child's curls, still leaned upon Meg's chair, still turned away his face. He didn't speak, but in his rough coarse fingers, clenching and expanding in the fair hair of the child, there was an eloquence that said enough.

"Yes, yes," said Trotty, answering unconsciously what he saw expressed in his daughter's face. "Take her with you, Meg. Get her to bed. There! Now, Will, I'll show you where you lie. It's not much of a place: only a loft; but having a loft, I always say, is one of the great conveniences of living in a mews; and till this coach-house and stable gets a better let, we live here cheap. There's plenty of sweet hay up there, belonging to a neighbour; and it's as clean as hands, and Meg, can make it. Cheer up! Don't give way. A new heart for a New Year, always!"

The hand released from the child's hair, had fallen, trembling, into

Trotty's hand. So Trotty, talking without intermission, led him out as tenderly and easily as if he had been a child himself.

Returning before Meg, he listened for an instant at the door of her little chamber; an adjoining room. The child was murmuring a simple Prayer before lying down to sleep, and when she had remembered Meg's name, "Dearly, Dearly"—so her words ran—Trotty heard her stop and ask for his.

It was some short time before the foolish little old fellow could compose himself to mend the fire, and draw his chair to the warm hearth. But when he had done so, and had trimmed the light, he took his newspaper from his pocket, and began to read. Carelessly at first, and skimming up and down the columns; but with an earnest and a sad attention, very soon.

For this same dreaded paper re-directed Trotty's thoughts into the channel they had taken all that day, and which the day's events had so marked out and shaped. His interest in the two wanderers had set him on another course of thinking, and a happier one, for the time; but being alone again, and reading of the crimes and violences of the people, he relapsed into his former train.

In this mood, he came to an account (and it was not the first he had ever read) of a woman who had laid her desperate hands not only on her own life but on that of her young child. A crime so terrible, and so revolting to his soul, dilated with the love of Meg, that he let the journal drop, and fell back in his chair, appalled!

"Unnatural and cruel!" Toby cried. "Unnatural and cruel! None but people who were bad at heart, born bad, who had no business on the earth, could do such deeds. It's too true, all I've heard to-day; too just, too full of proof. We're Bad!"

The Chimes took up the words so suddenly—burst out so loud, and clear, and sonorous—that the Bells seemed to strike him in his chair.

And what was that, they said?

"Toby Veck, Toby Veck, waiting for you Toby! Toby Veck, Toby Veck, waiting for you Toby! Come and see us, come and see us, Drag him to us, drag him to us, Haunt and hunt him, haunt and hunt him, Break his slumbers, break his slumbers! Toby Veck, Toby Veck, door open wide Toby, Toby Veck, Toby Veck, door open wide Toby—" then fiercely back to their impetuous strain again, and ringing in the very bricks and plaster on the walls.

Toby listened. Fancy, fancy! His remorse for having run away from them that afternoon! No, no. Nothing of the kind. Again, again, and yet a dozen times again. "Haunt and hunt him, haunt and hunt him, Drag him to us, drag him to us!" Deafening the whole town!

"Meg," said Trotty softly: tapping at her door. "Do you hear anything?"

"I hear the Bells, father. Surely they're very loud to-night."

"Is she asleep?" said Toby, making an excuse for peeping in.

"So peacefully and happily! I can't leave her yet though, father. Look how she holds my hand!"

"Meg," whispered Trotty. "Listen to the Bells!"

She listened, with her face towards him all the time. But it underwent no change. She didn't understand them.

Trotty withdrew, resumed his seat by the fire, and once more listened by himself. He remained there a little time.

It was impossible to bear it; their energy was dreadful.

"If the tower-door is really open," said Toby, hastily laying aside his apron, but never thinking of his hat, "what's to hinder me from going up into the steeple and satisfying myself? If it's shut, I don't want any other satisfaction. That's enough."

He was pretty certain as he slipped out quietly into the street that he should find it shut and locked, for he knew the door well, and had so rarely seen it open, that he couldn't reckon above three times in all. It was a low arched portal, outside the church, in a dark nook behind a column; and had such great iron hinges, and such a monstrous lock, that there was more hinge and lock than door.

But what was his astonishment when, coming bare-headed to the church; and putting his hand into this dark nook, with a certain misgiving that it might be unexpectedly seized, and a shivering propensity to draw it back again; he found that the door, which opened outwards, actually stood ajar!

He thought, on the first surprise, of going back; or of getting a light, or a companion, but his courage aided him immediately, and he determined to ascend alone.

"What have I to fear?" said Trotty. "It's a church! Besides, the ringers may be there, and have forgotten to shut the door."

So he went in; feeling his way as he went, like a blind man; for it was very dark. And very quiet, for the Chimes were silent.

The dust from the street had blown into the recess; and lying there, heaped up, made it so soft and velvet-like to the foot, that there was something startling, even in that. The narrow stair was so close to the door, too, that he stumbled at the very first; and shutting the door upon himself, by striking it with his foot, and causing it to rebound back heavily, he couldn't open it again.

This was another reason, however, for going on. Trotty groped his way, and went on. Up, up, up, and round, and round; and up, up, up; higher, higher, higher up!

It was a disagreeable staircase for that groping work; so low and narrow, that his groping hand was always touching something; and it often felt so like a man or ghostly figure standing up erect and making room for him to pass without discovery, that he would rub the smooth wall upward searching for its face, and downward searching for its feet, while a chill tingling crept all over him. Twice or thrice, a door or niche broke the monotonous surface; and then it seemed a gap as wide as the whole church; and he felt on the brink of an abyss, and going to tumble headlong down, until he found the wall again.

Still up, up, up; and round and round; and up, up, up; higher, higher, higher up!

At length, the dull and stifling atmosphere began to freshen: presently to feel quite windy: presently it blew so strong, that he could hardly keep his legs. But he got to an arched window in the tower, breast high, and holding tight, looked down upon the house-tops, on the smoking chimneys, on the blurr and blotch of lights (towards the place where Meg was wondering where he was and calling to him perhaps), all kneaded up together in a leaven of mist and darkness.

This was the belfry, where the ringers came. He had caught hold of one of the frayed ropes which hung down through apertures in the oaken roof. At first he started, thinking it was hair then trembled at the very thought of waking the deep Bell. The Bells themselves were higher. Higher, Trotty, in his fascination, or in working out the spell upon him, groped his way. By ladders now, and toilsomely, for it was steep, and not too certain holding for the feet.

Up, up, up; and climb and clamber; up, up, up; higher, higher, higher up!

Until, ascending through the floor, and pausing with his head just raised above its beams, he came among the Bells. It was barely possible to make out their great shapes in the gloom; but there they were. Shadowy, and dark, and dumb.

A heavy sense of dread and loneliness fell instantly upon him, as he climbed into this airy nest of stone and metal. His head went round and round. He listened, and then raised a wild "Halloa!"

Halloa! was mournfully protracted by the echoes.

Giddy, confused, and out of breath, and frightened, Toby looked about him vacantly, and sunk down in a swoon.

THIRD QUARTER

Black are the brooding clouds and troubled the deep waters, when the Sea of Thought, first heaving from a calm, gives up its Dead. Monsters uncouth and wild, arise in premature, imperfect resurrection; the several parts and shapes of different things are joined and mixed by chance; and when, and how, and by what wonderful degrees, each separates from each, and every sense and object of the mind resumes its usual form and lives again, no man—though every man is every day the casket of this type of the Great Mystery—can tell.

So, when and how the darkness of the night-black steeple changed to shining light; when and how the solitary tower was peopled with a myriad figures; when and how the whispered "Haunt and hunt him," breathing monotonously through his sleep or swoon, became a voice exclaiming in the waking ears of Trotty, "Break his slumbers;" when and how he ceased to have a sluggish and confused idea that such things were, companioning a host of others that were not; there are no dates or means to tell. But, awake and standing on his feet upon the boards where he had lately lain, he saw this Goblin Sight.

He saw the tower, whither his charmed footsteps had brought him, swarming with dwarf phantoms, spirits, elfin creatures of the Bells. He saw them leaping, flying, dropping, pouring from the Bells without a pause. He saw them, round him on the ground; above him, in the air; clambering from him, by the ropes below; looking down upon him, from the massive iron-girded beams; peeping in upon him, through the chinks and loopholes in the walls; spreading away and away from him in enlarging circles, as the water ripples give way to a huge stone that suddenly comes plashing in among them. He saw them, of all aspects and all shapes. He saw them ugly, handsome, crippled, exquisitely formed. He saw them young, he saw them old, he saw them kind, he saw them cruel, he saw them merry, he saw them grim; he saw them dance, and heard them sing; he saw them tear their hair, and heard them howl. He saw the air thick with them. He saw them come and go, incessantly. He saw them riding downward, soaring upward, sailing off afar, perching near at hand, all restless and all violently active. Stone, and brick, and slate, and tile, became transparent to him as to them. He saw them *in* the houses, busy at the sleepers' beds. He saw them soothing people in their dreams; he saw them beating them with knotted whips; he saw them yelling in their ears; he saw them playing softest music on their pillows; he saw them cheering some with the songs of birds and the perfume of flowers; he saw them flashing awful faces on the troubled rest of others, from enchanted mirrors which they carried in their hands.

He saw these creatures, not only among sleeping men but waking also, active in pursuits irreconcilable with one another, and possessing or assuming natures the most opposite. He saw one buckling on innumerable wings to increase his speed; another loading himself with chains and weights, to retard his. He saw some putting the hands of clocks forward, some putting the hands of clocks backward, some endeavouring to stop the clock entirely. He saw them representing, here a marriage ceremony, there a funeral; in this chamber an election, in that a ball; he saw, everywhere, restless and untiring motion.

Bewildered by the host of shifting and extraordinary figures, as well as by the uproar of the Bells, which all this while were ringing, Trotty clung to a wooden pillar for support, and turned his white face here and there, in mute and stunned astonishment.

As he gazed, the Chimes stopped. Instantaneous change! The whole swarm fainted! their forms collapsed, their speed deserted them; they sought to fly, but in the act of falling died and melted into air. No fresh supply succeeded them. One straggler leaped down pretty briskly from the surface of the Great Bell, and alighted on his feet, but he was dead and gone before he could turn round. Some few of the late company who had gambolled in the tower, remained there, spinning over and over a little longer; but these became at every turn more faint, and few, and feeble, and soon went the way of the rest. The last of all was one small hunchback, who had got into an echoing corner, where he twirled and twirled, and floated by himself a long time; showing such perseverance, that at last he dwindled to a leg and even to a foot, before he finally retired; but he vanished in the end, and then the tower was silent.

Then and not before, did Trotty see in every Bell a bearded figure of the bulk and stature of the Bell—incomprehensibly, a figure and the Bell itself. Gigantic, grave, and darkly watchful of him, as he stood rooted to the ground.

Mysterious and awful figures! Resting on nothing; poised in the night air of the tower, with their draped and hooded heads merged in the dim roof; motionless and shadowy. Shadowy and dark, although he saw them by some light belonging to themselves—none else was there —each with its muffled hand upon its goblin mouth.

He could not plunge down wildly through the opening in the floor; for all power of motion had deserted him. Otherwise he would have done so—aye, would have thrown himself, head foremost, from the steeple-top, rather than have seen them watching him with eyes that would have waked and watched although the pupils had been taken out.

Again, again, the dread and terror of the lonely place, and of the wild and fearful night that reigned there, touched him like a spectral hand. His distance from all help; the long, dark, winding, ghost-be-leaguered way that lay between him and the earth on which men lived; his being high, high, high, up there, where it had made him dizzy to see the birds fly in the day; cut off from all good people, who at such an hour were safe at home and sleeping in their beds; all this struck coldly through him, not as a reflection but a bodily sensation. Meantime his eyes and thoughts and fears, were fixed upon the watchful figures; which rendered unlike any figures of this world by the deep gloom and shade enwrapping and enfolding them, as well as by their looks and forms and supernatural hovering above the floor, were nevertheless as plainly to be seen as were the stalwart oaken frames, cross-pieces, bars and beams, set up there to support the Bells.

These hemmed them, in a very forest of hewn timber; from the entanglements, intricacies, and depths of which, as from among the boughs of a dead wood blighted for their phantom use, they kept their darksome and unwinking watch.

A blast of air—how cold and shrill!—came moaning through the tower. As it died away, the great Bell, or the Goblin of the Great Bell, spoke.

"What visitor is this!" it said. The voice was low and deep, and Trotty fancied that it sounded in the other figures as well.

"I thought my name was called by the Chimes!" said Trotty, raising his hands in an attitude of supplication. "I hardly know why I am here, or how I came. I have listened to the Chimes these many years. They have cheered me often."

"And you have thanked them?" said the Bell.

"A thousand times!" said Trotty.

"How?"

"I am a poor man," faltered Trotty, "and could only thank them in words."

"And always so?" inquired the Goblin of the Bell. "Have you never done us wrong in words?"

"No!" cried Trotty eagerly.

"Never done us foul, and false, and wicked wrong, in words?" pursued the Goblin of the Bell.

Trotty was about to answer, "Never!" But he stopped, and was confused.

"The voice of Time," said the Phantom, "cries to man, Advance! Time is for his advancement and improvement; for his greater worth, his greater happiness, his better life; his progress onward to that goal within its knowledge and its view, and set there, in the period when Time and He began. Ages of darkness, wickedness, and violence, have come and gone—millions uncountable, have suffered, lived, and died —to point the way before him. Who seeks to turn him back, or stay him on his course, arrests a mighty engine which will strike the meddler dead; and be the fiercer and the wilder, ever, for its momentary check!"

"I never did so to my knowledge, sir," said Trotty. "It was quite by accident if I did. I wouldn't go to do it, I'm sure."

"Who puts into the mouth of Time, or of its servants," said the Goblin of the Bell, "a cry of lamentation for days which have had their trial and their failure, and have left deep traces of it which the blind may see—a cry that only serves the present time, by showing men how much it needs their help when any ears can listen to regrets for such a past—who does this, does a wrong. And you have done that wrong, to us, the Chimes."

Trotty's first excess of fear was gone. But he had felt tenderly and gratefully towards the Bells, as you have seen; and when he heard himself arraigned as one who had offended them so weightily, his heart was touched with penitence and grief.

"If you knew," said Trotty, clasping his hands earnestly—"or perhaps you do know—if you know how often you have kept me company; how often you have cheered me up when I've been low; how you were quite the plaything of my little daughter Meg (almost the only one she ever had) when first her mother died, and she and me were left alone; you won't bear malice for a hasty word!"

"Who hears in us, the Chimes, one note bespeaking disregard, or stern regard, of any hope, or joy, or pain, or sorrow, of the many-sorrowed throng; who hears us make response to any creed that gauges human passions and affections, as it gauges the amount of miserable food on which humanity may pine and wither; does us wrong. That wrong you have done us!" said the Bell.

"I have!" said Trotty. "Oh forgive me!"

"Who hears us echo the dull vermin of the earth: the Putters Down of crushed and broken natures, formed to be raised up higher than such maggots of the time can crawl or can conceive," pursued the Goblin of the Bell; "who does so, does us wrong. And you have done us wrong!"

"Not meaning it," said Trotty. "In my ignorance. Not meaning it!"

"Lastly, and most of all," pursued the Bell. "Who turns his back upon the fallen and disfigured of his kind; abandons them as vile; and does not trace and track with pitying eyes the unfenced precipice by which they fell from good—grasping in their fall some tufts and shreds of that lost soil, and clinging to them still when bruised and dying in the gulf below; does wrong to Heaven and man, to time and to eternity. And you have done that wrong!"

"Spare me," cried Trotty, falling on his knees; "for Mercy's sake!"

"Listen!" said the Shadow.

"Listen!" cried the other Shadows.

"Listen!" said a clear and childlike voice, which Trotty thought he recognised as having heard before.

The organ sounded faintly in the church below. Swelling by degrees, the melody ascended to the roof, and filled the choir and nave. Expanding more and more, it rose up, up; up, up; higher, higher, higher up; awakening agitated hearts within the burly piles of oak, the hollow bells, the iron-bound doors, the stairs of solid stone; until the tower walls were insufficient to contain it, and it soared into the sky.

No wonder that an old man's breast could not contain a sound so vast and mighty. It broke from that weak prison in a rush of tears; and Trotty put his hands before his face.

"Listen!" said the Shadow.

"Listen!" said the other Shadows.

"Listen!" said the child's voice.

A solemn strain of blended voices rose into the tower.

It was a very low and mournful strain—a Dirge—and as he listened, Trotty heard his child among the singers.

"She is dead!" exclaimed the old man. "Meg is dead! Her Spirit calls to me. I hear it!"

"The Spirit of your child bewails the dead, and mingles with the dead—dead hopes, dead fancies, dead imaginings of youth," returned the Bell, "but she is living. Learn from her life, a living truth. Learn from the creature dearest to your heart, how bad the bad are born. See every bud and leaf plucked one by one from off the fairest stem, and know how bare and wretched it may be. Follow her! To desperation!"

Each of the shadowy figures stretched its right arm forth, and pointed downward.

"The Spirit of the Chimes is your companion," said the figure. "Go! It stands behind you!"

Trotty turned, and saw—the child! The child Will Fern had carried in the street; the child whom Meg had watched, but now, asleep!

"I carried her myself, to-night," said Trotty. "In these arms!"

"Show him what he calls himself," said the dark figures, one and all.

The tower opened at his feet. He looked down, and beheld his own form, lying at the bottom, on the outside: crushed and motionless.

"No more a living man!" cried Trotty. "Dead!"

"Dead!" said the figures all together.

"Gracious Heaven! And the New Year—"

"Past," said the figures.

"What!" he cried, shuddering. "I missed my way, and coming on the outside of this tower in the dark, fell down—a year ago?"

"Nine years ago!" replied the figures.

As they gave the answer, they recalled their outstretched hands; and where their figures had been, there the Bells were.

And they rung; their time being come again. And once again, vast multitudes of phantoms sprung into existence; once again were incoherently engaged, as they had been before; once again, faded on the stopping of the Chimes; and dwindled into nothing.

"What are these?" he asked his guide. "If I am not mad, what are these?"

"Spirits of the Bells. Their sound upon the air," returned the child. "They take such shapes and occupations as the hopes and thoughts of mortals, and the recollections they have stored up, give them."

"And you," said Trotty wildly. "What are you?"

"Hush, hush!" returned the child. "Look here!"

In a poor, mean room; working at the same kind of embroidery which he had often, often seen before her; Meg, his own dear daughter,

was presented to his view. He made no effort to imprint his kisses on
her face; he did not strive to clasp her to his loving heart; he knew that
such endearments were, for him, no more. But he held his trembling
breath, and brushed away the blinding tears, that he might look upon
her; that he might only see her.

Ah! Changed. Changed. The light of the clear eye, how dimmed.
The bloom, how faded from the cheek. Beautiful she was, as she had
ever been, but Hope, Hope, Hope, oh where was the fresh Hope that
had spoken to him like a voice!

She looked up from her work, at a companion. Following her eyes,
the old man started back.

In the woman grown, he recognised her at a glance. In the long
silken hair, he saw the self-same curls; around the lips, the child's expression lingering still. See! In the eyes, now turned inquiringly on
Meg, there shone the very look that scanned those features when he
brought her home!

Then what was this, beside him!

Looking with awe into its face, he saw a something reigning there:
a lofty something, undefined and indistinct, which made it hardly
more than a remembrance of that child—as yonder figure might be—
yet it was the same: the same: and wore the dress.

Hark! They were speaking!

"Meg," said Lilian, hesitating. "How often you raise your head from
your work to look at me!"

"Are my looks so altered, that they frighten you?" asked Meg.

"Nay, dear! But you smile at that, yourself! Why not smile, when
you look at me, Meg?"

"I do so. Do I not?" she answered: smiling on her.

"Now you do," said Lilian, "but not usually. When you think I'm
busy, and don't see you, you look so anxious and so doubtful, that I
hardly like to raise my eyes. There is little cause for smiling in this hard
and toilsome life, but you were once so cheeful."

"Am I not now?" cried Meg, speaking in a tone of strange alarm,
and rising to embrace her. "Do I make our weary life more weary to
you, Lilian?"

"You have been the only thing that made it life," said Lilian, fervently kissing her; "sometimes the only thing that made me care to
live so, Meg. Such work, such work! So many hours, so many days, so
many long, long nights of hopeless, cheerless, never-ending work—not
to heap up riches, not to live grandly or gaily, not to live upon enough,
however coarse; but to earn bare bread; to scrape together just enough
to toil upon, and want upon, and keep alive in us the consciousness of
our hard fate! Oh Meg, Meg!" she raised her voice and twined her
arms about her as she spoke, like one in pain. "How can the cruel
world go round, and bear to look upon such lives?"

"Lilly!" said Meg, soothing her, and putting back her hair from her wet face. "Why, Lilly! You! So pretty and so young!"

"Oh Meg!" she interrupted, holding her at arm's-length, and looking in her face imploringly. "The worst of all, the worst of all! Strike me old, Meg! Wither me, and shrivel me, and free me from the dreadful thoughts that tempt me in my youth!"

Trotty turned to look upon his guide. But the Spirit of the child had taken flight. Was gone.

Neither did he himself remain in the same place; for Sir Joseph Bowley, Friend and Father of the Poor, held a great festivity at Bowley Hall, in honour of the natal day of Lady Bowley. And as Lady Bowley had been born on New Year's Day (which the local newspapers considered an especial pointing of the finger of Providence to number One, as Lady Bowley's destined figure in Creation), it was on a New Year's Day that this festivity took place.

Bowley Hall was full of visitors. The red-faced gentleman was there, Mr. Filer was there, the great Alderman Cute was there—Alderman Cute had a sympathetic feeling with great people, and had considerably improved his acquaintance with Sir Joseph Bowley on the strength of his attentive letter: indeed had become quite a friend of the family since then—and many guests were there. Trotty's ghost was there, wandering about, poor phantom, drearily; and looking for its guide.

There was to be a great dinner in the Great Hall. At which Sir Joseph Bowley, in his celebrated character of Friend and Father of the Poor, was to make his great speech. Certain plum-puddings were to be eaten by his Friends and Children in another Hall first; and, at a given signal, Friends and Children flocking in among their Friends and Fathers, were to form a family assemblage, with not one manly eye therein unmoistened by emotion.

But there was more than this to happen. Even more than this. Sir Joseph Bowley, Baronet and Member of Parliament, was to play a match at skittles—real skittles—with his tenants!

"Which quite reminds me," said Alderman Cute, "of the days of old King Hal, stout King Hal, bluff King Hal. Ah. Fine character!"

"Very," said Mr. Filer, dryly. "For marrying women and murdering 'em. Considerably more than the average number of wives, by the bye."

"You'll marry the beautiful ladies, and not murder 'em, eh?" said Alderman Cute to the heir of Bowley, aged twelve. "Sweet boy! We shall have this little gentleman in Parliament now," said the Alderman, holding him by the shoulders, and looking as reflective as he could, "before we know where we are. We shall hear of his successes at the poll; his speeches in the House; his overtures from Governments; his brilliant achievements of all kinds; ah! we shall make our little orations about him in the Common Council, I'll be bound; before we have time to look about us!"

"Oh, the difference of shoes and stockings!" Trotty thought. But his heart yearned towards the child, for the love of those same shoeless and stockingless boys, predestined (by the Alderman) to turn out bad, who might have been the children of poor Meg.

"Richard," moaned Trotty, roaming among the company, to and fro; "where is he? I can't find Richard! Where is Richard?"

Not likely to be there, if still alive! But Trotty's grief and solitude confused him; and he still went wandering among the gallant company, looking for his guide, and saying, "Where is Richard? Show me Richard!"

He was wandering thus, when he encountered Mr. Fish, the confidential Secretary: in great agitation.

"Bless my heart and soul!" cried Mr. Fish. "Where's Alderman Cute? Has anybody seen the Alderman?"

Seen the Alderman? Oh dear! Who could ever help seeing the Alderman? He was so considerate, so affable, he bore so much in mind the natural desires of folks to see him, that if he had a fault, it was the being constantly On View. And wherever the great people were, there, to be sure, attracted by the kindred sympathy between great souls, was Cute.

Several voices cried that he was in the circle round Sir Joseph. Mr. Fish made way there; found him; and took him secretly into a window near at hand. Trotty joined them. Not of his own accord. He felt that his steps were led in that direction.

"My dear Alderman Cute," said Mr. Fish. "A little more this way. The most dreadful circumstance has occurred. I have this moment received the intelligence. I think it will be best not to acquaint Sir Joseph with it till the day is over. You understand Sir Joseph, and will give me your opinion. The most frightful and deplorable event!"

"Fish!" returned the Alderman. "Fish! My good fellow, what is the matter? Nothing revolutionary, I hope! No—no attempted interference with the magistrates?"

"Deedles, the banker," gasped the Secretary. "Deedles Brothers—who was to have been here to-day—high in office in the Goldsmiths' Company—"

"Not stopped!" exclaimed the Alderman. "It can't be!"

"Shot himself."

"Good God!"

"Put a double-barrelled pistol to his mouth, in his own counting-house," said Mr. Fish, "and blew his brains out. No motive. Princely circumstances!"

"Circumstances!" exclaimed the Alderman. "A man of noble fortune. One of the most respectable of men. Suicide, Mr. Fish! By his own hand!"

"This very morning," returned Mr. Fish.

"Oh the brain, the brain!" exclaimed the pious Alderman, lifting up his hands. "Oh the nerves, the nerves; the mysteries of this machine called Man! Oh the little that unhinges it: poor creatures that we are! Perhaps a dinner, Mr. Fish. Perhaps the conduct of his son, who, I have heard, ran very wild, and was in the habit of drawing bills upon him without the least authority! A most respectable man. One of the most respectable men I ever knew! A lamentable instance, Mr. Fish. A public calamity! I shall make a point of wearing the deepest mourning. A most respectable man! But there is One above. We must submit, Mr. Fish. We must submit!"

What, Alderman! No word of Putting Down? Remember, Justice, your high moral boast and pride. Come, Alderman! Balance those scales. Throw me into this, the empty one, no dinner, and Nature's founts in some poor woman, dried by starving misery and rendered obdurate to claims for which her offspring *has* authority in holy mother Eve. Weigh me the two, you Daniel, going to judgment, when your day shall come! Weigh them, in the eyes of suffering thousands, audience (not unmindful) of the grim farce you play. Or supposing that you strayed from your five wits—it's not so far to go, but that it might be—and laid hands upon that throat of yours, warning your fellows (if you have a fellow) how they croak their comfortable wickedness to raving heads and stricken hearts. What then?

The words rose up in Trotty's breast, as if they had been spoken by some other voice within him. Alderman Cute pledged himself to Mr. Fish that he would assist him in breaking the melancholy catastrophe to Sir Joseph when the day was over. Then, before they parted, wringing Mr. Fish's hand in bitterness of soul he said, "The most respectable of men!" And added that he hardly knew (not even he), why such afflictions were allowed on earth.

"It's almost enough to make one think, if one didn't know better," said Alderman Cute, "that at times some motion of a capsizing nature was going on in things, which affected the general economy of the social fabric. Deedles Brothers!"

The skittle-playing came off with immense success. Sir Joseph knocked the pins about quite skilfully; Master Bowley took an innings at a shorter distance also; and everybody said that now, when a Baronet and the Son of a Baronet played at skittles, the country was coming round again, as fast as it could come.

At its proper time, the Banquet was served up. Trotty involuntarily repaired to the Hall with the rest, for he felt himself conducted thither by some stronger impulse than his own free will. The sight was gay in the extreme; the ladies were very handsome; the visitors delighted, cheerful, and good-tempered. When the lower doors were opened, and the people flocked in, in their rustic dresses, the beauty of the spectacle was at its height; but Trotty only murmured more and more, "Where is Richard? He should help and comfort her! I can't see Richard!"

There had been some speeches made; and Lady Bowley's health had been proposed; and Sir Joseph Bowley had returned thanks, and had made his great speech, showing by various pieces of evidence that he was born Friend and Father, and so forth; and had given as a Toast, his Friends and Children, and the Dignity of Labour; when a slight disturbance at the bottom of the Hall attracted Toby's notice. After some confusion, noise, and opposition, one man broke through the rest, and stood forward by himself.

Not Richard. No. But one whom he had thought of, and had looked for, many times. In a scantier supply of light, he might have doubted the identity of that worn man, so old, and grey, and bent; but with a blaze of lamps upon his gnarled and knotted head, he knew Will Fern as soon as he stepped forth.

"What is this!" exclaimed Sir Joseph, rising. "Who gave this man admittance? This is a criminal from prison! Mr. Fish, sir, *will* you have the goodness—"

"A minute!" said Will Fern. "A minute! My Lady, you was born on this day along with a New Year. Get me a minute's leave to speak."

She made some intercession for him. Sir Joseph took his seat again, with native dignity.

The ragged visitor—for he was miserably dressed—looked round upon the company, and made his homage to them with a humble bow.

"Gentlefolks!" he said. "You've drunk the Labourer. Look at me!"

"Just come from jail," said Mr. Fish.

"Just come from jail," said Will. "And neither for the first time, nor the second, nor the third, nor yet the fourth."

Mr. Filer was heard to remark testily, that four times was over the average; and he ought to be ashamed of himself.

"Gentlefolks!" repeated Will Fern. "Look at me! You see I'm at the worst. Beyond all hurt or harm; beyond your help; for the time when your kind words or kind actions could have done ME good,"—he struck his hand upon his breast, and shook his head, "is gone, with the scent of last year's beans or clover on the air. Let me say a word for these," pointing to the labouring people in the Hall; "and when you're met together, hear the real Truth spoke out for once."

"There's not a man here," said the host, "who would have him for a spokesman."

"Like enough, Sir Joseph. I believe it. Not the less true, perhaps, is what I say. Perhaps that's a proof on it. Gentlefolks, I've lived many a year in this place. You may see the cottage from the sunk fence over yonder. I've seen the ladies draw it in their books, a hundred times.

It looks well in a picter, I've heerd say; but there ain't weather in picters, and maybe 'tis fitter for that, than for a place to live in. Well! I lived there. How hard—how bitter hard, I lived there, I won't say. Any day in the year, and every day, you can judge for your own selves."

He spoke as he had spoken on the night when Trotty found him in the street. His voice was deeper and more husky, and had a trembling in it now and then; but he never raised it, passionately, and seldom lifted it above the firm stern level of the homely facts he stated.

" 'Tis harder than you think for, gentlefolks, to grow up decent: commonly decent: in such a place. That I growed up a man and not a brute, says something for me—as I was then. As I am now, there's nothing can be said for me or done for me. I'm past it."

"I am glad this man has entered," observed Sir Joseph, looking round serenely. "Don't disturb him. It appears to be Ordained. He is an example: a living example. I hope and trust, and confidently expect, that it will not be lost upon my Friends here."

"I dragged on," said Fern, after a moment's silence, "somehow. Neither me nor any other man knows how; but so heavy, that I couldn't put a cheerful face upon it, or make believe that I was anything but what I was. Now, gentlemen—you gentlemen that sits at Sessions—when you see a man with discontent writ on his face, you says to one another, 'He's suspicious. I has my doubts,' says you, 'about Will Fern. Watch that fellow!' I don't say, gentlemen, it ain't quite nat'ral, but I say 'tis so; and from that hour, whatever Will Fern does, or lets alone—all one—it goes against him."

Alderman Cute stuck his thumbs in his waistcoat-pockets, and leaning back in his chair, and smiling, winked at a neighbouring chandelier. As much as to say, "Of course! I told you so. The common cry! Lord bless you, we are up to all this sort of thing—myself and human nature."

"Now, gentlemen," said Will Fern, holding out his hands, and flushing for an instant in his haggard face, "see how your laws are made to trap and hunt us when we're brought to this. I tries to live elsewhere. And I'm a vagabond. To jail with him! I comes back here. I goes a-nutting in your woods, and breaks—who don't?—a limber branch or two. To jail with him! One of your keepers sees me in the broad day, near my own patch of garden, with a gun. To jail with him! I has a nat'ral angry word with that man, when I'm free again. To jail with him! I cuts a stick. To jail with him! I eats a rotten apple or a turnip. To jail with him. It's twenty mile away; and coming back I begs a trifle on the road. To jail with him! At last, the constable, the keeper—anybody—finds me anywhere, a-doing anything. To jail with him, for he's a vagrant, and a jail-bird known; and jail's the only home he's got."

The Alderman nodded sagaciously, as who should say, "A very good home too!"

"Do I say this to serve MY cause?" cried Fern. "Who can give me back my liberty, who can give me back my good name, who can give me back my innocent niece? Not all the Lords and Ladies in wide England. But, gentlemen, gentlemen, dealing with other men like me, begin at the right end. Give us, in mercy, better homes when we're a-lying in our cradles; give us better food when we're a-working for our lives; give us kinder laws to bring us back when we're a-going wrong; and don't set Jail, Jail, Jail, afore us, everywhere we turn. There an't a condescension you can show the Labourer then, that he won't take, as ready and as grateful as a man can be; for he has a patient, peaceful, willing heart. But you must put his rightful spirit in him first; for whether he's a wreck and ruin such as me, or is like one of them that stand here now, his spirit is divided from you at this time. Bring it back, gentlefolks, bring it back! Bring it back, afore the day comes when even his Bible changes in his altered mind, and the words seem to him to read, as they have sometimes read in my own eyes—in Jail: 'Whither thou goest, I can Not go; where thou lodgest, I do Not lodge; thy people are Not my people; Nor thy God my God!' "

A sudden stir and agitation took place in the Hall. Trotty thought at first that several had risen to eject the man; and hence this change in its appearance. But another moment showed him that the room and all the company had vanished from his sight, and that his daughter was again before him, seated at her work. But in a poorer, meaner garret than before; and with no Lilian by her side.

The frame at which she had worked, was put away upon a shelf and covered up. The chair in which she had sat, was turned against the wall. A history was written in these little things, and in Meg's grief-worn face. Oh! who could fail to read it!

Meg strained her eyes upon her work until it was too dark to see the threads; and when the night closed in, she lighted her feeble candle and worked on. Still her old father was invisible about her; looking down upon her; loving her—how dearly loving her!—and talking to her in a tender voice about the old times, and the Bells. Though he knew, poor Trotty, though he knew she could not hear him. A great part of the evening had worn away, when a knock came at her door. She opened it. A man was on the threshold. A slouching, moody, drunken sloven, wasted by intemperance and vice, and with his matted hair and unshorn beard in wild disorder; but with some traces on him, too, of having been a man of good proportion and good features in his youth.

He stopped until he had her leave to enter; and she, retiring a pace or two from the open door, silently and sorrowfully looked upon him. Trotty had his wish. He saw Richard.

"May I come in, Margaret?"

"Yes! Come in. Come in!"

It was well that Trotty knew him before he spoke; for with any doubt remaining on his mind, the harsh discordant voice would have persuaded him that it was not Richard but some other man.

There were but two chairs in the room. She gave him hers, and stood at some short distance from him, waiting to hear what he had to say.

He sat, however, staring vacantly at the floor; with a lustreless and stupid smile. A spectacle of such deep degradation, of such abject hopelessness, of such a miserable downfall, that she put her hands before her face and turned away, lest he should see how much it moved her.

Roused by the rustling of her dress, or some such trifling sound, he lifted his head, and began to speak as if there had been no pause since he entered.

"Still at work, Margaret? You work late."

"I generally do."

"And early?"

"And early."

"So she said. She said you never tired; or never owned that you tired. Not all the time you lived together. Not even when you fainted, between work and fasting. But I told you that, the last time I came."

"You did," she answered. "And I implored you to tell me nothing more; and you made me a solemn promise, Richard, that you never would."

"A solemn promise," he repeated, with a drivelling laugh and vacant stare. "A solemn promise. To be sure. A solemn promise!" Awakening, as it were, after a time; in the same manner as before; he said with sudden animation:

"How can I help it, Margaret? What am I to do? She has been to me again!"

"Again!" cried Meg, clasping her hands. "O, does she think of me so often? Has she been again?"

"Twenty times again," said Richard. "Margaret, she haunts me. She comes behind me in the street, and thrusts it in my hand. I hear her foot upon the ashes when I'm at my work (ha, ha! that an't often), and before I can turn my head, her voice is in my ear, saying, 'Richard, don't look round. For Heaven's love, give her this!' She brings it where I live; she sends it in letters; she taps at the window and lays it on the sill. What *can* I do? Look at it!"

He held out in his hand a little purse, and chinked the money it enclosed.

"Hide it," said Meg. "Hide it! When she comes again, tell her,

Richard, that I love her in my soul. That I never lie down to sleep, but I bless her, and pray for her. That, in my solitary work, I never cease to have her in my thoughts. That she is with me, night and day. That if I died to-morrow, I would remember her with my last breath. But, that I cannot look upon it!"

He slowly recalled his hand, and crushing the purse together, said with a kind of drowsy thoughtfulness:

"I told her so. I told her so, as plain as words could speak. I've taken this gift back and left it at her door, a dozen times since then. But when she came at last, and stood before me, face to face, what could I do?"

"You saw her!" exclaimed Meg. "You saw her! O, Lilian, my sweet girl! O, Lilian, Lilian!"

"I saw her," he went on to say, not answering, but engaged in the same slow pursuit of his own thoughts. "There she stood: trembling! 'How does she look, Richard? Does she ever speak of me? Is she thinner? My old place at the table: what's in my old place? And the frame she taught me our old work on—has she burnt it, Richard?' There she was. I heard her say it."

Meg checked her sobs, and with the tears streaming from her eyes, bent over him to listen. Not to lose a breath.

With his arms resting on his knees; and stooping forward in his chair, as if what he said were written on the ground in some half legible character, which it was his occupation to decipher and connect; he went on.

"'Richard, I have fallen very low; and you may guess how much I have suffered in having this sent back, when I can bear to bring it in my hand to you. But you loved her once, even in my memory, dearly. Others stepped in between you; fears, and jealousies, and doubts, and vanities, estranged you from her; but you did love her, even in my memory!' I suppose I did," he said, interrupting himself for a moment. "I did! That's neither here nor there. 'O Richard, if you ever did; if you have any memory for what is gone and lost, take it to her once more. Once more! Tell her how I laid my head upon your shoulder, where her own head might have lain, and was so humble to you, Richard. Tell her that you looked into my face, and saw the beauty which she used to praise, all gone: all gone: and in its place, a poor, wan, hollow cheek, that she would weep to see. Tell her everything, and take it back, and she will not refuse again. She will not have the heart!'"

So he sat musing, and repeating the last words, until he woke again, and rose.

"You won't take it, Margaret?"

She shook her head, and motioned an entreaty to him to leave her.

"Good night, Margaret."

"Good night!"

He turned to look upon her; struck by her sorrow, and perhaps by the pity for himself which trembled in her voice. It was a quick and rapid action; and for the moment some flash of his old bearing kindled in his form. In the next he went as he had come. Nor did this glimmer of a quenched fire seem to light him to a quicker sense of his debasement.

In any mood, in any grief, in any torture of the mind or body, Meg's work must be done. She sat down to her task, and plied it. Night, midnight. Still she worked.

She had a meagre fire, the night being very cold; and rose at intervals to mend it. The Chimes rang half-past twelve while she was thus engaged; and when they ceased she heard a gentle knocking at the door. Before she could so much as wonder who was there, at that unusual hour, it opened.

O Youth and Beauty, happy as ye should be, look at this. O Youth and Beauty, blest and blessing all within your reach, and working out the ends of your Beneficent Creator, look at this!

She saw the entering figure; screamed its name; cried "Lilian!"

It was swift, and fell upon its knees before her: clinging to her dress.

"Up, dear! Up! Lilian! My own dearest!"

"Never more, Meg; never more! Here! Here! Close to you, holding to you, feeling your dear breath upon my face!"

"Sweet Lilian! Darling Lilian! Child of my heart—no mother's love can be more tender—lay your head upon my breast!"

"Never more, Meg. Never more! When I first looked into your face, you knelt before me. On my knees before you, let me die. Let it be here!"

"You have come back. My Treasure! We will live together, work together, hope together, die together!"

"Ah! Kiss my lips, Meg; fold your arms about me; press me to your bosom; look kindly on me; but don't raise me. Let it be here. Let me see the last of your dear face upon my knees!"

O Youth and Beauty, happy as ye should be, look at this! O Youth and Beauty, working out the ends of your Beneficent Creator, look at this!

"Forgive me, Meg! So dear, so dear! Forgive me! I know you do, I see you do, but say so, Meg!"

She said so, with her lips on Lilian's cheek. And with her arms twined round—she knew it now—a broken heart.

"His blessing on you, dearest love. Kiss me once more! He suffered her to sit beside His feet, and dry them with her hair. O Meg, what Mercy and Compassion!"

As she died, the Spirit of the child returning, innocent and radiant, touched the old man with its hand, and beckoned him away.

Some new remembrance of the ghostly figures in the Bells; some faint impression of the ringing of the Chimes; some giddy consciousness of having seen the swarm of phantoms reproduced and reproduced until the recollection of them lost itself in the confusion of their numbers; some hurried knowledge, how conveyed to him he knew not, that more years had passed; and Trotty, with the Spirit of the child attending him, stood looking on at mortal company.

Fat company, rosy-cheeked company, comfortable company. They were but two, but they were red enough for ten. They sat before a bright fire, with a small low table between them; and unless the fragrance of hot tea and muffins lingered longer in that room than in most others, the table had seen service very lately. But all the cups and saucers being clean, and in their proper places in the corner-cupboard; and the brass toasting-fork hanging in its usual nook and spreading its four idle fingers out as if it wanted to be measured for a glove; there remained no other visible tokens of the meal just finished, than such as purred and washed their whiskers in the person of the basking cat, and glistened in the gracious, not to say the greasy, faces of her patrons.

This cosy couple (married, evidently) had made a fair division of the fire between them, and sat looking at the glowing sparks that dropped into the grate; now nodding off into a doze; now waking up again when some hot fragment, larger than the rest, came rattling down, as if the fire were coming with it.

It was in no danger of sudden extinction, however; for it gleamed not only in the little room, and on the panes of window-glass in the door, and on the curtain half drawn across them, but in the little shop beyond. A little shop, quite crammed and choked with the abundance of its stock; a perfectly voracious little shop, with a maw as accommodating and full as any shark's. Cheese, butter, firewood, soap, pickles, matches, bacon, table-beer, peg-tops, sweetmeats, boys' kites, bird-seed, cold ham, birch brooms, hearth-stones, salt, vinegar, blacking, red-herrings, stationery, lard, mushroom-ketchup, staylaces, loaves of bread, shuttle-cocks, eggs, and slate pencil; everything was fish that came to the net of this greedy little shop, and all articles were in its net. How many other kinds of petty merchandise were there, it would be difficult to say; but balls of packthread, ropes of onions, pounds of candles, cabbage-nets, and brushes, hung in bunches from the ceiling, like extraordinary fruit; while various odd canisters emitting aromatic smells, established the veracity of the inscription over the outer door, which informed the public that the keeper of this little shop was a licensed dealer in tea, coffee, tobacco, pepper, and snuff.

Glancing at such of these articles as were visible in the shining of the blaze, and the less cheerful radiance of two smoky lamps which burnt but dimly in the shop itself, as though its plethora sat heavy on their lungs; and glancing, then, at one of the two faces by the parlour-fire; Trotty had small difficulty in recognising in the stout old lady, Mrs. Chickenstalker: always inclined to corpulency, even in the days when he had known her as established in the general line, and having a small balance against him in her books.

The features of her companion were less easy to him. The great broad chin, with creases in it large enough to hide a finger in; the astonished eyes, that seemed to expostulate with themselves for sinking deeper and deeper into the yielding fat of the soft face; the nose afflicted with that disordered action of its functions which is generally termed The Snuffles; the short thick throat and labouring chest, with other beauties of the like description; though calculated to impress the memory, Trotty could at first allot to nobody he had ever known: and yet he had some recollection of them too. At length, in Mrs. Chickenstalker's partner in the general line, and in the crooked and eccentric line of life, he recognised the former porter of Sir Joseph Bowley; an apoplectic innocent, who had connected himself in Trotty's mind with Mrs. Chickenstalker years ago, by giving him admission to the mansion where he had confessed his obligations to that lady, and drawn on his unlucky head such grave reproach.

Trotty had little interest in a change like this, after the changes he had seen; but association is very strong sometimes; and he looked involuntarily behind the parlour-door, where the accounts of credit customers were usually kept in chalk. There was no record of his name. Some names were there, but they were strange to him, and infinitely fewer than of old; from which he argued that the porter was an advocate of ready-money transactions, and on coming into the business had looked pretty sharp after the Chickenstalker defaulters.

So desolate was Trotty, and so mournful for the youth and promise of his blighted child, that it was a sorrow to him, even to have no place in Mrs. Chickenstalker's ledger.

"What sort of a night is it, Anne?" inquired the former porter of Sir Joseph Bowley, stretching out his legs before the fire, and rubbing as much of them as his short arms could reach; with an air that added, "Here I am if it's bad, and I don't want to go out if it's good."

"Blowing and sleeting hard," returned his wife; "and threatening snow. Dark. And very cold."

"I'm glad to think we had muffins," said the former porter, in the tone of one who had set his conscience at rest. "It's a sort of night that's meant for muffins. Likewise crumpets. Also Sally Lunns."

The former porter mentioned each successive kind of eatable, as if he were musingly summing up his good actions. After which he rubbed his fat legs as before, and jerking them at the knees to get the fire upon the yet unroasted parts, laughed as if somebody had tickled him.

"You're in spirits, Tugby, my dear," observed his wife.

The firm was Tugby, late Chickenstalker.

"No," said Tugby. "No. Not particular. I'm a little elewated. The muffins came so pat!"

With that he chuckled until he was black in the face; and had so much ado to become any other colour, that his fat legs took the strangest excursions into the air. Nor were they reduced to anything like decorum until Mrs. Tugby had thumped him violently on the back, and shaken him as if he were a great bottle.

"Good gracious, goodness, lord-a-mercy bless and save the man!" cried Mrs. Tugby, in great terror. "What's he doing?"

Mr. Tugby wiped his eyes, and faintly repeated that he found himself a little elewated.

"Then don't be so again, that's a dear good soul," said Mrs. Tugby, "if you don't want to frighten me to death, with your struggling and fighting!"

Mr. Tugby said he wouldn't; but his whole existence was a fight, in which, if any judgment might be founded on the constantly-increasing shortness of his breath, and the deepening purple of his face, he was always getting the worst of it.

"So it's blowing, and sleeting, and threatening snow; and it's dark, and very cold, is it, my dear?" said Mr. Tugby, looking at the fire, and reverting to the cream and marrow of his temporary elevation.

"Hard weather indeed," returned his wife, shaking her head.

"Aye, aye! Years," said Mr. Tugby, "are like Christians in that respect. Some of 'em die hard; some of 'em die easy. This one hasn't many days to run, and is making a fight for it. I like him all the better. There's a customer, my love!"

Attentive to the rattling door, Mrs. Tugby had already risen.

"Now then!" said the lady, passing out into the little shop. "What's wanted? Oh! I beg your pardon, sir, I'm sure. I didn't think it was you."

She made this apology to a gentleman in black, who, with his wristbands tucked up, and his hat cocked loungingly on one side, and his hands in his pockets, sat down astride on the table-beer barrel, and nodded in return.

"This is a bad business up-stairs, Mrs. Tugby," said the gentleman. "The man can't live."

"Not the back-attic can't!" cried Tugby, coming out into the shop to join the conference.

"The back-attic, Mr. Tugby," said the gentleman, "is coming down-stairs fast, and will be below the basement very soon."

Looking by turns at Tugby and his wife, he sounded the barrel with his knuckles for the depth of beer, and having found it, played a tune upon the empty part.

"The back-attic, Mr. Tugby," said the gentleman: Tugby having stood in silent consternation for some time: "is Going."

"Then," said Tugby, turning to his wife, "he must Go, you know, before he's Gone."

"I don't think you can move him," said the gentleman, shaking his head. "I wouldn't take the responsibility of saying it could be done, myself. You had better leave him where he is. He can't live long."

"It's the only subject," said Tugby, bringing the butter-scale down upon the counter with a crash, by weighing his fist on it, "that we've ever had a word upon; she and me; and look what it comes to! He's going to die here, after all. Going to die upon the premises. Going to die in our house!"

"And where should he have died, Tugby?" cried his wife.

"In the workhouse," he returned. "What are workhouses made for?"

"Not for that," said Mrs. Tugby, with great energy. "Not for that! Neither did I marry you for that. Don't think it, Tugby. I won't have it. I won't allow it. I'd be separated first, and never see your face again. When my widow's name stood over that door, as it did for many years: this house being known as Mrs. Chickenstalker's far and wide, and never known but to its honest credit and its good report: when my widow's name stood over that door, Tugby, I knew him as a hand-some, steady, manly, independent youth; I knew her as the sweetest-looking, sweetest-tempered girl, eyes ever saw; I knew her father (poor old creetur, he fell down from the steeple walking in his sleep, and killed himself), for the simplest, hardest-working, childest-hearted man, that ever drew the breath of life; and when I turn them out of house and home, may angels turn me out of Heaven. As they would! And serve me right!"

Her old face, which had been a plump and dimpled one before the changes which had come to pass, seemed to shine out of her as she said these words; and when she dried her eyes, and shook her head and her handkerchief at Tugby, with an expression of firmness which it was quite clear was not to be easily resisted, Trotty said, "Bless her! Bless her!"

Then he listened, with a panting heart, for what should follow. Knowing nothing yet, but that they spoke of Meg.

If Tugby had been a little elevated in the parlour, he more than balanced that account by being not a little depressed in the shop, where he now stood staring at his wife, without attempting a reply; secretly conveying, however—either in a fit of abstraction or as a precautionary measure—all the money from the till into his own pockets, as he looked at her.

The gentleman upon the table-beer cask, who appeared to be some authorised medical attendant upon the poor, was far too well accustomed, evidently, to little differences of opinion between man and wife, to interpose any remark in this instance. He sat softly whistling, and turning little drops of beer out of the tap upon the ground, until there was a perfect calm: when he raised his head, and said to Mrs. Tugby, late Chickenstalker:

"There's something interesting about the woman, even now. How did she come to marry him?"

"Why that," said Mrs. Tugby, taking a seat near him, "is not the least cruel part of her story, sir. You see they kept company, she and Richard, many years ago. When they were a young and beautiful couple, everything was settled, and they were to have been married on a New Year's Day. But, somehow, Richard got it into his head, through what the gentlemen told him, that he might do better, and that he'd soon repent it, and that she wasn't good enough for him, and that a young man of spirit had no business to be married. And the gentlemen frightened her, and made her melancholy, and timid of his deserting her, and of her children coming to the gallows, and of its being wicked to be man and wife, and a good deal more of it. And in short, they lingered and lingered, and their trust in one another was broken, and so at last was the match. But the fault was his. She would have married him, sir, joyfully. I've seen her heart swell many times afterwards, when he passed her in a proud and careless way; and never did a woman grieve more truly for a man, than she for Richard when he first went wrong."

"Oh! he went wrong, did he?" said the gentleman, pulling out the vent-peg of the table-beer, and trying to peep down into the barrel through the hole.

"Well, sir, I don't know that he rightly understood himself, you see. I think his mind was troubled by their having broke with one another; and that but for being ashamed before the gentlemen, and perhaps for being uncertain too, how she might take it, he'd have gone through any suffering or trial to have had Meg's promise and Meg's hand again. That's my belief. He never said so; more's the pity! He took to drinking, idling, bad companions: all the fine resources that were to be so much better for him than the Home he might have had. He lost his looks, his character, his health, his strength, his friends, his work: everything!"

"He didn't lose everything, Mrs. Tugby," returned the gentleman, "because he gained a wife; and I want to know how he gained her."

"I'm coming to it, sir, in a moment. This went on for years and years; he sinking lower and lower; she enduring, poor thing, miseries enough to wear her life away. At last, he was so cast down, and cast out, that no one would employ or notice him; and doors were shut upon him, go where he would. Applying from place to place, and door to door; and coming for the hundredth time to one gentleman who had often and often tried him (he was a good workman to the very end); that gentleman, who knew his history, said 'I believe you are incorrigible; there is only one person in the world who has a chance of reclaiming you; ask me to trust you no more, until she tries to do it.' Something like that, in his anger and vexation."

"Ah!" said the gentleman. "Well?"

"Well, sir, he went to her, and kneeled to her; said it was so; said it ever had been so; and made a prayer to her to save him."

"And she?— Don't distress yourself, Mrs. Tugby."

"She came to me that night to ask me about living here. 'What he was once to me,' she said, 'is buried in a grave, side by side with what I was to him. But I have thought of this; and I will make the trial. In the hope of saving him; for the love of the light-hearted girl (you remember her) who was to have been married on a New Year's Day; and for the love of her Richard.' And she said he had come to her from Lilian, and Lilian had trusted to him, and she never could forget that. So they were married; and when they came home here, and I saw them, I hoped that such prophecies as parted them when they were young, may not often fulfil themselves as they did in this case, or I wouldn't be the makers of them for a Mine of Gold."

The gentleman got off the cask, and stretched himself, observing:

"I suppose he used her ill, as soon as they were married?"

"I don't think he ever did that," said Mrs. Tugby, shaking her head, and wiping her eyes. "He went on better for a short time; but his habits were too old and strong to be got rid of; he soon fell back a little; and was falling fast back, when his illness came so strong upon him. I think he has always felt for her. I am sure he has. I have seen him, in his crying fits and tremblings, try to kiss her hand; and I have heard him call her 'Meg,' and say it was her nineteenth birthday. There he has been lying, now, these weeks and months. Between him and her baby, she has not been able to do her old work; and by not being able to be regular, she has lost it, even if she could have done it. How they have lived, I hardly know!"

"*I* know," muttered Mr. Tugby; looking at the till, and round the shop, and at his wife; and rolling his head with immense intelligence. "Like Fighting Cocks!"

He was interrupted by a cry—a sound of lamentation—from the upper story of the house. The gentleman moved hurriedly to the door.

"My friend," he said, looking back, "you needn't discuss whether he shall be removed or not. He has spared you that trouble, I believe."

Saying so, he ran up-stairs, followed by Mrs. Tugby; while Mr.

Tugby panted and grumbled after them at leisure: being rendered
more than commonly short-winded by the weight of the till, in which
there had been an inconvenient quantity of copper. Trotty, with the
child beside him, floated up the staircase like mere air.

"Follow her! Follow her! Follow her!" He heard the ghostly voices
in the Bells repeat their words as he ascended. "Learn it from the
creature dearest to your heart!"

It was over. It was over. And this was she, her father's pride and joy!
This haggard, wretched woman, weeping by the bed, if it deserved
that name, and pressing to her breast, and hanging down her head
upon, an infant. Who can tell how spare, how sickly, and how poor an
infant! Who can tell how dear!

"Thank God!" cried Trotty, holding up his folded hands. "O God
be thanked! She loves her child!"

The gentleman, not otherwise hard-hearted or indifferent to such
scenes, than that he saw them every day, and knew that they were
figures of no moment in the Filer sums—mere scratches in the working
of these calculations—laid his hand upon the heart that beat no more,
and listened for the breath, and said, "His pain is over. It's better as
it is!" Mrs. Tugby tried to comfort her with kindness. Mr. Tugby tried
philosophy.

"Come, come!" he said, with his hands in his pockets, "you mustn't
give way, you know. That won't do. You must fight up. What would
have become of me if I had given way when I was porter, and we had
as many as six runaway carriage-doubles at our door in one night! But I
fell back upon my strength of mind, and didn't open it!"

Again Trotty heard the voices saying, "Follow her!" He turned towards his guide, and saw it rising from him, passing through the air.
"Follow her!" it said. And vanished.

He hovered round her; sat down at her feet; looked up into her face
for one trace of her old self; listened for one note of her old pleasant
voice. He flitted round the child: so wan, so prematurely old, so dreadful in its gravity, so plaintive in its feeble, mournful, miserable wail.
He almost worshipped it. He clung to it as her only safeguard; as the
last unbroken link that bound her to endurance. He set his father's
hope and trust on the frail baby; watched her every look upon it as she
held it in her arms; and cried a thousand times, "She loves it! God be
thanked, she loves it!"

He saw the woman tend her in the night; return to her when her
grudging husband was asleep, and all was still; encourage her, shed
tears with her, set nourishment before her. He saw the day come, and
the night again; the day, the night; the time go by; the house of death
relieved of death; the room left to herself and to the child; he heard
it moan and cry; he saw it harass her, and tire her out, and when she
slumbered in exhaustion, drag her back to consciousness, and hold her

with its little hands upon the rack; but she was constant to it, gentle with it, patient with it. Patient! Was its loving mother in her inmost heart and soul, and had its Being knitted up with hers as when she carried it unborn.

All this time, she was in want: languishing away, in dire and pining want. With the baby in her arms, she wandered here and there, in quest of occupation; and with its thin face lying in her lap, and looking up in hers, did any work for any wretched sum; a day and night of labour for as many farthings as there were figures on the dial. If she had quarrelled with it; if she had neglected it; if she had looked upon it with a moment's hate; if, in the frenzy of an instant, she had struck it! No. His comfort was, She loved it always.

She told no one of her extremity, and wandered abroad in the day lest she should be questioned by her only friend: for any help she received from her hands, occasioned fresh disputes between the good woman and her husband; and it was new bitterness to be the daily cause of strife and discord, where she owed so much.

She loved it still. She loved it more and more. But a change fell on the aspect of her love. One night.

She was singing faintly to it in its sleep, and walking to and fro to hush it, when her door was softly opened, and a man looked in.

"For the last time," he said.

"William Fern!"

"For the last time."

He listened like a man pursued: and spoke in whispers.

"Margaret, my race is nearly run. I couldn't finish it, without a parting word with you. Without one grateful word."

"What have you done?" she asked: regarding him with terror.

He looked at her, but gave no answer.

After a short silence, he made a gesture with his hand, as if he set her question by; as if he brushed it aside; and said:

"It's long ago, Margaret, now: but that night is as fresh in my memory as ever 'twas. We little thought, then," he added, looking round, "that we should ever meet like this. Your child, Margaret? Let me have it in my arms. Let me hold your child."

He put his hat upon the floor, and took it. And he trembled as he took it, from head to foot.

"Is it a girl?"

"Yes."

He put his hand before its little face.

"See how weak I'm grown, Margaret, when I want the courage to look at it! Let her be, a moment. I won't hurt her. It's long ago, but— What's her name?"

"Margaret," she answered, quickly.

"I'm glad of that," he said. "I'm glad of that!"

He seemed to breathe more freely; and after pausing for an instant, took away his hand, and looked upon the infant's face. But covered it again, immediately.

"Margaret!" he said; and gave her back the child. "It's Lilian's."

"Lilian's!"

"I held the same face in my arms when Lilian's mother died and left her."

"When Lilian's mother died and left her!" she repeated, wildly.

"How shrill you speak! Why do you fix your eyes upon me so? Margaret!"

She sunk down in a chair, and pressed the infant to her breast, and wept over it. Sometimes, she released it from her embrace, to look anxiously in its face: then strained it to her bosom again. At those times, when she gazed upon it, then it was that something fierce and terrible began to mingle with her love. Then it was that her old father quailed.

"Follow her!" was sounded through the house. "Learn it from the creature dearest to your heart!"

"Margaret," said Fern, bending over her, and kissing her upon the brow: "I thank you for the last time. Good night. Good bye! Put your hand in mine, and tell me you'll forget me from this hour, and try to think the end of me was here."

"What have you done?" she asked again.

"There'll be a Fire to-night," he said, removing from her. "There'll be Fires this winter-time, to light the dark nights, East, West, North, and South. When you see the distant sky red, they'll be blazing. When you see the distant sky red, think of me no more; or, if you do, remember what a Hell was lighted up inside of me, and think you see its flames reflected in the clouds. Good night. Good bye!"

She called to him; but he was gone. She sat down stupefied, until her infant roused her to a sense of hunger, cold, and darkness. She paced the room with it the live-long night, hushing it and soothing it. She said at intervals, "Like Lilian, when her mother died and left her!" Why was her step so quick, her eye so wild, her love so fierce and terrible, whenever she repeated those words?

"But it is Love," said Trotty. "It is Love. She'll never cease to love it. My poor Meg!"

She dressed the child next morning with unusual care—ah, vain expenditure of care upon such squalid robes!—and once more tried to find some means of life. It was the last day of the Old Year. She tried till night, and never broke her fast. She tried in vain.

She mingled with an abject crowd, who tarried in the snow, until it pleased some officer appointed to dispense the public charity (the lawful charity; not that once preached upon a Mount), to call them in, and question them, and say to this one, "Go to such a place;" to that one, "Come next week;" to make a football of another wretch, and pass him here and there, from hand to hand, from house to house, until he wearied and lay down to die; or started up and robbed, and so became a higher sort of criminal, whose claims allowed of no delay. Here, too, she failed.

She loved her child, and wished to have it lying on her breast. And that was quite enough.

It was night: a bleak, dark, cutting night: when, pressing the child close to her for warmth, she arrived outside the house she called her home. She was so faint and giddy, that she saw no one standing in the doorway until she was close upon it, and about to enter. Then she recognised the master of the house, who had so disposed himself—with his person it was not difficult—as to fill up the whole entry.

"O!" he said softly. "You have come back?"

She looked at the child, and shook her head.

"Don't you think you have lived here long enough without paying any rent? Don't you think that, without any money, you've been a pretty constant customer at this shop, now?" said Mr. Tugby.

She repeated the same mute appeal.

"Suppose you try and deal somewhere else," he said. "And suppose you provide yourself with another lodging. Come! Don't you think you could manage it?"

She said in a low voice, that it was very late. To-morrow.

"Now I see what you want," said Tugby; "and what you mean. You know there are two parties in this house about you, and you delight in setting 'em by the ears. I don't want any quarrels; I'm speaking soft to avoid a quarrel; but if you don't go away, I'll speak out loud, and you shall cause words high enough to please you. But you shan't come in. That I am determined."

She put her hair back with her hand, and looked in a sudden manner at the sky, and the dark lowering distance.

"This is the last night of an Old Year, and I won't carry ill-blood and quarrellings and disturbances into a New One, to please you nor anybody else," said Tugby, who was quite a retail Friend and Father. "I wonder you an't ashamed of yourself, to carry such practices into a New Year. If you haven't any business in the world, but to be always giving way, and always making disturbances between man and wife, you'd be better out of it. Go along with you."

"Follow her! To desperation!"

Again the old man heard the voices. Looking up, he saw the figures hovering in the air, and pointing where she went, down the dark street.

"She loves it!" he exclaimed, in agonised entreaty for her. "Chimes! she loves it still!"

"Follow her!" The shadow swept upon the track she had taken, like a cloud.

He joined in the pursuit; he kept close to her; he looked into her face. He saw the same fierce and terrible expression mingling with her love, and kindling in her eyes. He heard her say, "Like Lilian! To be changed like Lilian!" and her speed redoubled.

O, for something to awaken her! For any sight, or sound, or scent, to call up tender recollections in a brain on fire! For any gentle image of the Past to rise before her!

"I was her father! I was her father!" cried the old man, stretching out his hands to the dark shadows flying on above. "Have mercy on her, and on me! Where does she go? Turn her back! I was her father!"

But they only pointed to her, as she hurried on; and said, "To desperation! Learn it from the creature dearest to your heart!"

A hundred voices echoed it. The air was made of breath expended in those words. He seemed to take them in at every gasp he drew. They were everywhere, and not to be escaped. And still she hurried on; the same light in her eyes, the same words in her mouth, "Like Lilian! To be changed like Lilian!"

All at once she stopped.

"Now, turn her back!" exclaimed the old man, tearing his white hair. "My child! Meg! Turn her back! Great Father, turn her back!"

In her own scanty shawl, she wrapped the baby warm. With her fevered hands she smoothed its limbs, composed its face, arranged its mean attire. In her wasted arms she folded it, as though she never would resign it more. And with her dry lips, kissed it in a final pang, and last long agony of Love.

Putting its tiny hand up to her neck, and holding it there, within her dress, next to her distracted heart, she set its sleeping face against her: closely, steadily, against her: and sped onward to the River.

To the rolling River, swift and dim, where Winter Night sat brooding like the last dark thoughts of many who had sought a refuge there before her. Where scattered lights upon the banks gleamed sullen, red, and dull, as torches that were burning there, to show the way to Death. Where no abode of living people cast its shadow on the deep, impenetrable, melancholy shade.

To the River! To that portal of Eternity, her desperate footsteps tended with the swiftness of its rapid waters running to the sea. He tried to touch her as she passed him, going down to its dark level: but the wild distempered form, the fierce and terrible love, the desperation that had left all human check or hold behind, swept by him like the wind.

He followed her. She paused a moment on the brink, before the dreadful plunge. He fell down on his knees, and in a shriek addressed the figures in the Bells now hovering above them.

"I have learnt it!" cried the old man. "From the creature dearest to my heart! O, save her, save her!"

He could wind his fingers in her dress; could hold it! As the words escaped his lips, he felt his sense of touch return, and knew that he detained her.

The figures looked down steadfastly upon him.

"I have learnt it!" cried the old man. "O, have mercy on me in this hour, if, in my love for her, so young and good, I slandered Nature in the breasts of mothers rendered desperate! Pity my presumption, wickedness, and ignorance, and save her."

He felt his hold relaxing. They were silent still.

"Have mercy on her!" he exclaimed, "as one in whom this dreadful crime has sprung from Love perverted; from the strongest, deepest Love we fallen creatures know! Think what her misery must have been, when such seed bears such fruit! Heaven meant her to be good. There is no loving mother on the earth who might not come to this, if such a life had gone before. O, have mercy on my child, who, even at this pass, means mercy to her own, and dies herself, and perils her immortal soul, to save it!"

She was in his arms. He held her now. His strength was like a giant's.

"I see the Spirit of the Chimes among you!" cried the old man, singling out the child, and speaking in some inspiration, which their looks conveyed to him. "I know that our inheritance is held in store for us by Time. I know there is a sea of Time to rise one day, before which all who wrong us or oppress us will be swept away like leaves. I see it, on the flow! I know that we must trust and hope, and neither doubt ourselves, nor doubt the good in one another. I have learnt it from the creature dearest to my heart. I clasp her in my arms again. O Spirits, merciful and good, I take your lesson to my breast along with her! O Spirits, Merciful and good, I am grateful!"

He might have said more; but the Bells, the old familiar Bells, his own dear, constant, steady friends, the Chimes, began to ring the joy-peals for a New Year: so lustily, so merrily, so happily, so gaily, that he leapt upon his feet, and broke the spell that bound him.

"And whatever you do, father," said Meg, "don't eat tripe again, without asking some doctor whether it's likely to agree with you; for how you *have* been going on, Good gracious!"

She was working with her needle, at the little table by the fire; dressing her simple gown with ribbons for her wedding. So quietly happy, so blooming and youthful, so full of beautiful promise, that he uttered a great cry as if it were an Angel in his house; then flew to clasp her in his arms.

But he caught his feet in the newspaper, which had fallen on the hearth; and somebody came rushing in between them.

"No!" cried the voice of this same somebody; a generous and jolly voice it was! "Not even you. Not even you. The first kiss of Meg in the New Year is mine. Mine! I have been waiting outside the house, this hour, to hear the Bells and claim it. Meg, my precious prize, a happy year! A life of happy years, my darling wife!"

And Richard smothered her with kisses.

You never in all your life saw anything like Trotty after this. I don't care where you have lived or what you have seen; you never in all your life saw anything at all approaching him! He sat down in his chair and beat his knees and cried; he sat down in his chair and beat his knees and laughed; he sat down in his chair and beat his knees and laughed and cried together; he got out of his chair and hugged Meg; he got out of his chair and hugged Richard; he got out of his chair and hugged them both at once; he kept running up to Meg, and squeezing her fresh face between his hands and kissing it, going from her backwards not to lose sight of it, and running up again like a figure in a magic lantern; and whatever he did, he was constantly sitting himself down in his chair, and never stopping in it for one single moment; being— that's the truth—beside himself with joy.

"And to-morrow's your wedding-day, my pet!" cried Trotty. "Your real, happy wedding-day!"

"To-day!" cried Richard, shaking hands with him. "To-day. The Chimes are ringing in the New Year. Hear them!"

They WERE ringing! Bless their sturdy hearts, they WERE ringing! Great Bells as they were; melodious, deep-mouthed, noble Bells; cast in no common metal; made by no common founder; when had they ever chimed like that, before!

"But to-day, my pet!" said Trotty. "You and Richard had some words to-day."

"Because he's such a bad fellow, father," said Meg. "An't you Richard? Such a headstrong, violent man! He'd have made no more of speaking his mind to that great Alderman, and putting *him* down I don't know where, than he would of—"

"—Kissing Meg," suggested Richard. Doing it too!

"No. Not a bit more," said Meg. "But I wouldn't let him, father. Where would have been the use!"

"Richard, my boy!" cried Trotty. "You was turned up Trumps originally; and Trumps you must be, till you die! But you were crying by the fire to-night, my pet, when I came home! Why did you cry by the fire?"

"I was thinking of the years we've passed together, father. Only that. And thinking that you might miss me, and be lonely."

Trotty was backing off to that extraordinary chair again, when the

child, who had been awakened by the noise, came running in half-
dressed.

"Why, here she is!" cried Trotty, catching her up. "Here's little
Lilian! Ha ha ha! Here we are and here we go! O here we are and here
we go again! And here we are and here we go! and Uncle Will too!"
Stopping in his trot to greet him heartily. "O, Uncle Will, the vision
that I've had to-night, through lodging you! O, Uncle Will, the obligations that you've laid me under, by your coming, my good friend!"

Before Will Fern could make the least reply, a band of music burst
into the room, attended by a lot of neighbours, screaming "A Happy
New Year, Meg!" "A Happy Wedding!" "Many of 'em!" and other
fragmentary good wishes of that sort. The Drum (who was a private
friend of Trotty's) then stepped forward, and said:

"Trotty Veck, my boy! It's got about, that your daughter is going to
be married to-morrow. There an't a soul that knows you that don't
wish you well, or that knows her and don't wish her well. Or that
knows you both, and don't wish you both all the happiness the New
Year can bring. And here we are, to play it in and dance it in, accordingly."

Which was received with a general shout. The Drum was rather
drunk, by-the-bye; but never mind.

"What a happiness it is, I'm sure," said Trotty, "to be so esteemed!
How kind and neighbourly you are! It's all along of my dear daughter.
She deserves it!"

They were ready for a dance in half a second (Meg and Richard at
the top); and the Drum was on the very brink of leathering away with
all his power; when a combination of prodigious sounds was heard
outside, and a good-humoured comely woman of some fifty years of
age, or thereabouts, came running in, attended by a man bearing a
stone pitcher of terrific size, and closely followed by the marrow-bones
and cleavers, and the bells; not *the* Bells, but a portable collection on
a frame.

Trotty said, "It's Mrs. Chickenstalker!" And sat down and beat his
knees again.

"Married, and not tell me, Meg!" cried the good woman. "Never! I
couldn't rest on the last night of the Old Year without coming to wish
you joy. I couldn't have done it, Meg. Not if I had been bed-ridden.
So here I am; and as it's New Year's Eve, and the Eve of your wedding
too, my dear, I had a little flip made, and brought it with me."

Mrs. Chickenstalker's notion of a little flip did honour to her
character. The pitcher steamed and smoked and reeked like a volcano;
and the man who had carried it was faint.

"Mrs. Tugby!" said Trotty, who had been going round and round
her, in an ecstasy.—"I *should* say, Chickenstalker— Bless your heart
and soul! A happy New Year, and many of 'em! Mrs. Tugby," said

Trotty when he had saluted her;— "I *should* say, Chickenstalker— This is William Fern and Lilian."

The worthy dame, to his surprise, turned very pale and very red.

"Not Lilian Fern whose mother died in Dorsetshire!" said she.

Her uncle answered "Yes," and meeting hastily, they exchanged some hurried words together; of which the upshot was, that Mrs. Chickenstalker shook him by both hands; saluted Trotty on his cheek again of her own free will; and took the child to her capacious breast.

"Will Fern!" said Trotty, pulling on his right-hand muffler. "Not the friend you was hoping to find?"

"Ay!" returned Will, putting a hand on each of Trotty's shoulders. "And like to prove a'most as good a friend, if that can be, as one I found."

"Oh!" said Trotty. "Please to play up there. Will you have the goodness?"

To the music of the band, the bells, the marrow-bones and cleavers, all at once; and while the Chimes were yet in lusty operation out of doors; Trotty, making Meg and Richard second couple, led off Mrs. Chickenstalker down the dance, and danced it in a step unknown before or since; founded on his own peculiar trot.

Had Trotty dreamed? Or are his joys and sorrows, and the actors in them, but a dream; himself a dream; the teller of this tale a dreamer, waking but now? If it be so, O listener, dear to him in all his visions, try to bear in mind the stern realities from which these shadows come; and in your sphere—none is too wide, and none too limited for such an end—endeavour to correct, improve, and soften them. So may the New Year be a happy one to you, happy to many more whose happiness depends on you! So may each year be happier than the last, and not the meanest of our brethren or sisterhood debarred their rightful share, in what our Great Creator formed them to enjoy.

—1844

The Cricket on the Hearth

A FAIRY TALE OF HOME

TO LORD JEFFREY THIS LITTLE STORY IS INSCRIBED WITH THE
AFFECTION AND ATTACHMENT OF HIS FRIEND THE AUTHOR

December 1845

CHIRP THE FIRST

The kettle began it! Don't tell me what Mrs. Peerybingle said. I
know better. Mrs. Peerybingle may leave it on record to the end of
time that she couldn't say which of them began it; but I say the kettle
did. I ought to know, I hope! The kettle began it, full five minutes by
the little waxy-faced Dutch clock in the corner, before the Cricket
uttered a chirp.

As if the clock hadn't finished striking, and the convulsive little
Haymaker at the top of it, jerking away right and left with a scythe in
front of a Moorish Palace, hadn't mowed down half an acre of
imaginary grass before the Cricket joined in at all!

Why, I am not naturally positive. Every one knows that. I wouldn't
set my own opinion against the opinion of Mrs. Peerybingle, unless
I were quite sure, on any account whatever. Nothing should induce
me. But, this is a question of fact. And the fact is, that the kettle
began it, at least five minutes before the Cricket gave any sign of being
in existence. Contradict me, and I'll say ten.

Let me narrate exactly how it happened. I should have proceeded
to do so in my very first word, but for this plain consideration—if I am
to tell a story I must begin at the beginning; and how is it possible to
begin at the beginning, without beginning at the kettle?

It appeared as if there were a sort of match, or trial of skill, you
must understand, between the kettle and the Cricket. And this is what
led to it, and how it came about.

Mrs. Peerybingle, going out into the raw twilight, and clicking over
the wet stones in a pair of pattens that worked innumerable rough
impressions of the first proposition in Euclid all about the yard—Mrs.
Peerybingle filled the kettle at the water-butt. Presently returning, less
the pattens (and a good deal less, for they were tall and Mrs. Perry-

bingle was but short), she set the kettle on the fire. In doing which she lost her temper, or mislaid it for an instant; for, the water being uncomfortably cold, and in that slippy, slushy, sleety sort of state wherein it seems to penetrate through every kind of substance, patten rings included—had laid hold of Mrs. Peerybingle's toes, and even splashed her legs. And when we rather plume ourselves (with reason too) upon our legs, and keep ourselves particularly neat in point of stockings, we find this, for the moment, hard to bear.

Besides, the kettle was aggravating and obstinate. It wouldn't allow itself to be adjusted on the top bar; it wouldn't hear of accommodating itself kindly to the knobs of coal; it *would* lean forward with a drunken air, and dribble, a very Idiot of a kettle, on the hearth. It was quarrelsome, and hissed and spluttered morosely at the fire. To sum up all, the lid, resisting Mrs. Peerybingle's fingers, first of all turned topsyturvy, and then, with an ingenious pertinacity deserving of a better cause, dived sideways in—down to the very bottom of the kettle. And the hull of the *Royal George* has never made half the monstrous resistance to coming out of the water, which the lid of that kettle employed against Mrs. Peerybingle, before she got it up again.

It looked sullen and pig-headed enough, even then; carrying its handle with an air of defiance, and cocking its spout pertly and mockingly at Mrs. Peerybingle, as if it said, "I won't boil. Nothing shall induce me!"

But Mrs. Peerybingle, with restored good humour, dusted her chubby little hands against each other, and sat down before the kettle, laughing. Meantime, the jolly blaze uprose and fell, flashing and gleaming on the little Haymaker at the top of the Dutch clock, until one might have thought he stood stock still before the Moorish Palace, and nothing was in motion but the flame.

He was on the move, however; and had his spasms, two to the second, all right and regular. But his sufferings, when the clock was going to strike, were frightful to behold; and when a Cuckoo looked out of a trap-door in the Palace, and gave note six times, it shook him, each time, like a spectral voice—or like a something wiry, plucking at his legs.

It was not until a violent commotion and a whirring noise among the weights and ropes below him had quite subsided, that this terrified Haymaker became himself again. Nor was he startled without reason; for these rattling, bony skeletons of clocks are very disconcerting in their operation, and I wonder very much how any set of men, but most of all how Dutchmen, can have had a liking to invent them. There is a popular belief that Dutchmen love broad cases and much clothing for their own lower selves; and they might know better than to leave their clocks so very lank and unprotected, surely.

Now it was, you observe, that the kettle began to spend the evening.

Now it was that the kettle, growing mellow and musical, began to have irrepressible gurglings in its throat, and to indulge in short vocal snorts, which it checked in the bud, as if it hadn't quite made up its mind yet to be good company. Now it was that after two or three such vain attempts to stifle its convivial sentiments, it threw off all moroseness, all reserve, and burst into a stream of song so cosy and hilarious, as never maudlin nightingale yet formed the least idea of.

So plain too! Bless you, you might have understood it like a book—better than some books you and I could name, perhaps. With its warm breath gushing forth in a light cloud which merrily and gracefully ascended a few feet, then hung about the chimney-corner as its own domestic Heaven, it trolled its song with that strong energy of cheerfulness, that its iron body hummed and stirred upon the fire; and the lid itself, the recently rebellious lid—such is the influence of a bright example—performed a sort of jig, and clattered like a deaf and dumb young cymbal that had never known the use of its twin brother.

That this song of the kettle's was a song of invitation and welcome to somebody out of doors: to somebody at that moment coming on, towards the snug small home and the crisp fire: there is no doubt whatever. Mrs. Peerybingle knew it, perfectly, as she sat musing before the hearth. It's a dark night, sang the kettle, and the rotten leaves are lying by the way; and, above, all is mist and darkness, and, below, all is mire and clay; and there's only one relief in all the sad and murky air; and I don't know that it is one, for it's nothing but a glare; of deep and angry crimson, where the sun and wind together; set a brand upon the clouds for being guilty of such weather; and the widest open country is a long dull streak of black; and there's hoar-frost on the finger-post, and thaw upon the track; and the ice it isn't water, and the water isn't free; and you couldn't say that anything is what it ought to be; but he's coming, coming, coming!——

And here, if you like, the Cricket DID chime in! with a Chirrup, Chirrup, Chirrup of such magnitude, by way of chorus; with a voice so astoundingly disproportionate to its size, as compared with the kettle; (size! you couldn't see it!) that if it had then and there burst itself like an overcharged gun, if it had fallen a victim on the spot, and chirruped its little body into fifty pieces, it would have seemed a natural and inevitable consequence, for which it had expressly laboured.

The kettle had had the last of its solo performance. It persevered with undiminished ardour; but the Cricket took first fiddle and kept it. Good Heaven, how it chirped! Its shrill, sharp, piercing voice resounded through the house, and seemed to twinkle in the outer darkness like a star. There was an indescribable little trill and tremble in it, at its loudest, which suggested its being carried off its legs, and made to leap again, by its own intense enthusiasm. Yet they went very well together. The Cricket and the kettle. The burden of the song was still the same; and louder, louder, louder still, they sang it in their emulation.

The fair little listener—for fair she was, and young, though something of what is called the dumpling shape; but I don't myself object to that—lighted a candle, glanced at the Haymaker on the top of the clock, who was getting in a pretty average crop of minutes; and looked out of the window, where she saw nothing, owing to the darkness, but her own face imaged in the glass. And my opinion is (and so would yours have been) that she might have looked a long way, and seen nothing half so agreeable. When she came back, and sat down in her former seat, the Cricket and the kettle were still keeping it up, with a perfect fury of competition. The kettle's weak side clearly being, that he didn't know when he was beat.

There was all the excitement of a race about it. Chirp, chirp, chirp! Cricket a mile ahead. Hum, hum, hum—m—m! Kettle making play in the distance, like a great top. Chirp, chirp, chirp! Cricket round the corner. Hum, hum, hum—m—m! Kettle sticking to him in his own way; no idea of giving in. Chirp, chirp, chirp! Cricket fresher than ever. Hum, hum, hum—m—m! Kettle slow and steady. Chirp, chirp, chirp! Cricket going in to finish him. Hum, hum, hum—m—m! Kettle not to be finished. Until at last they got so jumbled together, in the hurry-skurry, helter-skelter of the match, that whether the kettle chirped and the Cricket hummed, or the Cricket chirped and the kettle hummed, or they both chirped and both hummed, it would have taken a clearer head than yours or mine to have decided with anything like certainty. But of this there is no doubt: that the kettle and the Cricket, at one and the same moment, and by some power of amalgamation best known to themselves, sent, each, his fireside song of comfort streaming into a ray of the candle that shone out through the window, and a long way down the lane. And this light, bursting on a certain person who, on the instant, approached towards it through the gloom, expressed the whole thing to him, literally in a twinkling, and cried, "Welcome home, old fellow! Welcome home, my boy!"

This end attained, the kettle, being dead beat, boiled over, and was taken off the fire. Mrs. Peerybingle then went running to the door, where, what with the wheels of a cart, the tramp of a horse, the voice of a man, the tearing in and out of an excited dog, and the surprising and mysterious appearance of a baby, there was soon the very What's-his-name to pay.

Where the baby came from, or how Mrs. Peerybingle got hold of it in that flash of time, I don't know. But a live baby there was in Mrs. Peerybingle's arms; and a pretty tolerable amount of pride she seemed to have in it, when she was drawn gently to the fire, by a sturdy figure of a man, much taller and much older than herself, who had to stoop a long way down to kiss her. But she was worth the trouble. Six foot six, with the lumbago, might have done it.

"Oh goodness, John!" said Mrs. P. "What a state you are in with the weather!"

He was something the worse for it, undeniably. The thick mist hung in clots upon his eyelashes like candied thaw; and between the fog and fire together, there were rainbows in his very whiskers.

"Why, you see, Dot," John made answer, slowly, as he unrolled a shawl from about his throat; and warmed his hands; "it—it ain't exactly summer weather. So, no wonder."

"I wish you wouldn't call me Dot, John. I don't like it," said Mrs. Peerybingle: pouting in a way that clearly showed she *did* like it, very much.

"Why what else are you?" returned John, looking down upon her with a smile, and giving her waist as light a squeeze as his huge hand and arm could give. "A dot and"—here he glanced at the baby—"a dot and carry—I won't say it, for fear I should spoil it; but I was very near a joke. I don't know as ever I was nearer."

He was often near to something or other very clever, by his own account: this lumbering, slow, honest John; this John so heavy, but so light of spirit; so rough upon the surface, but so gentle at the core; so dull without, so quick within; so stolid, but so good! Oh Mother Nature, give thy children the true poetry of heart that hid itself in this poor Carrier's breast—he was but a Carrier by the way—and we can bear to have them talking prose, and leading lives of prose; and bear to bless thee for their company!

It was pleasant to see Dot, with her little figure, and her baby in her arms: a very doll of a baby: glancing with a coquettish thoughtfulness at the fire, and inclining her delicate little head just enough on one side to let it rest in an odd, half-natural, half-affected, wholly nestling and agreeable manner, on the great rugged figure of the Carrier. It was pleasant to see him, with his tender awkwardness, endeavouring to adapt his rude support to her slight need, and make his burly middle-age a leaning-staff not inappropriate to her blooming youth. It was pleasant to observe how Tilly Slowboy, waiting in the background for the baby, took special cognizance (though in her earliest teens) of this grouping; and stood with her mouth and eyes wide open, and her head thrust forward, taking it in as if it were air. Nor was it less agreeable to obseve how John the Carrier, reference being made by Dot to the aforesaid baby, checked his hand when on the point of touching the infant, as if he thought he might crack it; and bending down, surveyed it from a safe distance, with a kind of puzzled pride, such as an amiable mastiff might be supposed to show, if he found himself, one day, the father of a young canary.

"An't he beautiful, John? Don't he look precious in his sleep?"

"Very precious," said John. "Very much so. He generally *is* asleep, an't he?"

"Lor, John! Good gracious no!"

"Oh," said John, pondering, "I thought his eyes was generally shut. Halloa!"

"Goodness, John, how you startle one!"

"It an't right for him to turn 'em up in that way!" said the astonished Carrier, "is it? See how he's winking with both of 'em at once! And look at his mouth! Why he's gasping like a gold and silver fish!"

"You don't deserve to be a father, you don't," said Dot, with all the dignity of an experienced matron. "But how should you know what little complaints children are troubled with, John! You wouldn't so much as know their names, you stupid fellow." And when she had turned the baby over on her left arm, and had slapped its back as a restorative, she pinched her husband's ear, laughing.

"No," said John, pulling off his outer coat. "It's very true, Dot. I don't know much about it. I only know that I've been fighting pretty stiffly with the wind to-night. It's been blowing north-east, straight into the cart, the whole way home."

"Poor old man, so it has!" cried Mrs. Peerybingle, instantly becoming very active. "Here! Take the precious darling, Tilly, while I make myself of some use. Bless it, I could smother it with kissing it, I could! Hie then, good dog! Hie, Boxer, boy! Only let me make the tea first, John; and then I'll help you with the parcels, like a busy bee. 'How doth the little'—and all the rest of it, you know, John. Did you ever learn 'how doth the little,' when you went to school, John?"

"Not to quite know it," John returned. "I was very near it once. But I should only have spoilt it, I dare say."

"Ha, ha," laughed Dot. She had the blithest little laugh you ever heard. "What a dear old darling of a dunce you are, John, to be sure!"

Not at all disputing this position, John went out to see that the boy with the lantern, which had been dancing to and fro before the door and window, like a Will of the Wisp, took due care of the horse; who was fatter than you would quite believe if I gave you his measure, and so old that his birthday was lost in the mists of antiquity. Boxer, feeling that his attentions were due to the family in general, and must be impartially distributed, dashed in and out with bewildering inconstancy; now, describing a circle of short barks round the horse, where he was being rubbed down at the stable-door; now, feigning to make savage rushes at his mistress, and facetiously bringing himself to sudden stops; now eliciting a shriek from Tilly Slowboy, in the low nursing-chair near the fire, by the unexpected application of his moist nose to her countenance; now, exhibiting an obtrusive interest in the baby; now, going round and round upon the hearth, and lying down as if he had established himself for the night; now, getting up again, and taking that nothing of a fag-end of a tail of his, out into the weather, as if he had just remembered an appointment, and was off, at a round trot, to keep it.

"There! There's the teapot, ready on the hob!" said Dot; as briskly busy as a child at play at keeping house. "And there's the old knuckle of ham; and there's the butter; and there's the crusty loaf, and all! Here's the clothes-basket for the small parcels, John, if you've got any there—where are you, John? Don't let the dear child fall under the grate, Tilly, whatever you do!"

It may be noted of Miss Slowboy, in spite of her rejecting the caution with some vivacity, that she had a rare and surprising talent for getting this baby into difficulties: and had several times imperilled its short life, in a quiet way peculiarly her own. She was of a spare and straight shape, this young lady, insomuch that her garments appeared to be in constant danger of sliding off those sharp pegs, her shoulders, on which they were loosely hung. Her costume was remarkable for the partial development, on all possible occasions, of some flannel vestment of a singular structure; also for affording glimpses, in the region of the back, of a corset, or pair of stays, in colour a dead-green. Being always in a state of gaping admiration at everything, and absorbed, besides, in the perpetual contemplation of her mistress's perfections and the baby's, Miss Slowboy, in her little errors of judgment, may be said to have done equal honour to her head and to her heart; and though these did less honour to the baby's head, which they were the occasional means of bringing into contact with deal doors, dressers, stair-rails, bed-posts, and other foreign substances, still they were the honest results of Tilly Slowboy's constant astonishment at finding herself so kindly treated, and installed in such a comfortable home. For the maternal and paternal Slowboy were alike unknown to Fame, and Tilly had been bred by public charity, a foundling; which word, though only differing from fondling by one vowel's length, is very different in meaning, and expresses quite another thing.

To have seen little Mrs. Peerybingle come back with her husband, tugging at the clothes-basket, and making the most strenuous exertions to do nothing at all (for he carried it), would have amused you almost as much as it amused him. It may have entertained the Cricket too, for anything I know; but, certainly, it now began to chirp again, vehemently.

"Heyday!" said John, in his slow way. "It's merrier than ever, tonight, I think."

"And it's sure to bring us good fortune, John! It always has done so. To have a Cricket on the Hearth, is the luckiest thing in all the world!"

John looked at her as if he had very nearly got the thought into his head, that she was his Cricket in chief, and he quite agreed with her. But, it was probably one of his narrow escapes, for he said nothing.

"The first time I heard its cheerful little note, John, was on that night when you brought me home—when you brought me to my new home here; its little mistress. Nearly a year ago. You recollect, John?"

O yes. John remembered. I should think so!

"Its chirp was such a welcome to me! It seemed so full of promise and encouragement. It seemed to say, you would be kind and gentle with me, and would not expect (I had a fear of that, John, then) to find an old head on the shoulders of your foolish little wife."

John thoughtfully patted one of the shoulders, and then the head, as though he would have said No, no; he had had no such expectation; he had been quite content to take them as they were. And really he had reason. They were very comely.

"It spoke the truth, John, when it seemed to say so; for you have ever been, I am sure, the best, the most considerate, the most affectionate of husbands to me. This has been a happy home, John; and I love the Cricket for its sake!"

"Why, so do I then," said the Carrier. "So do I, Dot."

"I love it for the many times I have heard it, and the many thoughts its harmless music has given me. Sometimes, in the twilight, when I have felt a little solitary and downhearted, John—before baby was here to keep me company and make the house gay—when I have thought how lonely you would be if I should die; how lonely I should be if I could know that you had lost me, dear; its Chirp, Chirp, Chirp upon the hearth, has seemed to tell me of another little voice, so sweet, so very dear to me, before whose coming sound my trouble vanished like a dream. And when I used to fear—I did fear once, John, I was very young you know—that ours might prove to be an ill-assorted marriage, I being such a child, and you more like my guardian than my husband; and that you might not, however hard you tried, be able to learn to love me, as you hoped and prayed you might; its Chirp, Chirp, Chirp has cheered me up again, and filled me with new trust and confidence. I was thinking of these things to-night, dear, when I sat expecting you; and I love the Cricket for their sake!"

"And so do I," repeated John. "But, Dot? I hope and pray that I might learn to love you? How you talk! I had learnt that, long before I brought you here, to be the Cricket's little mistress, Dot!"

She laid her hand, an instant, on his arm, and looked up at him with an agitated face, as if she would have told him something. Next moment she was down upon her knees before the basket, speaking in a sprightly voice, and busy with the parcels.

"There are not many of them to-night, John, but I saw some goods behind the cart, just now; and though they give more trouble, perhaps, still they pay as well; so we have no reason to grumble, have we? Besides, you have been delivering, I dare say, as you came along?"

"Oh yes," John said. "A good many."

"Why what's this round box? Heart alive, John, it's a wedding-cake!"

"Leave a woman alone to find out that," said John, admiringly. "Now a man would never have thought of it. Whereas, it's my belief that if you was to pack a wedding-cake up in a tea-chest, or a turn-up bedstead, or a pickled salmon keg, or any unlikely thing, a woman would be sure to find it out directly. Yes; I called for it at the pastry-cook's."

"And it weighs I don't know what—whole hundredweights!" cried Dot, making a great demonstration of trying to lift it. "Whose is it, John? Where is it going?"

"Read the writing on the other side," said John.

"Why, John! My Goodness, John!

"Ah! who'd have thought it!" John returned.

"You never mean to say," pursued Dot, sitting on the floor and shaking her head at him, "that it's Gruff and Tackleton the toy-maker!"

John nodded.

Mrs. Peerybingle nodded also, fifty times at least. Not in assent—in dumb and pitying amazement; screwing up her lips the while with all their little force (they were never made for screwing up; I am clear of that), and looking the good Carrier through and through, in her abstraction. Miss Slowboy, in the mean time, who had a mechanical power of reproducing scraps of current conversation for the delectation of the baby, with all the sense struck out of them, and all the nouns changed into the plural number, inquired aloud of that young creature, Was it Gruffs and Tackletons the toymakers then, and Would it call at Pastry-cooks for wedding-cakes, and Did its mothers know the boxes when its fathers brought them homes; and so on.

"And that is really to come about!" said Dot. "Why, she and I were girls at school together, John."

He might have been thinking of her, or nearly thinking of her, perhaps, as she was in that same school time. He looked upon her with a thoughtful pleasure, but he made no answer.

"And he's as old! As unlike her!— Why, how many years older than you, is Gruff and Tackleton, John?"

"How many more cups of tea shall I drink to-night at one sitting, than Gruff and Tackleton ever took in four, I wonder!" replied John, good-humouredly, as he drew a chair to the round table, and began at the cold ham. "As to eating, I eat but little; but that little I enjoy, Dot."

Even this, his usual sentiment at meal times, one of his innocent

delusions (for his appetite was always obstinate, and flatly contradicted him), awoke no smile in the face of his little wife, who stood
among the parcels, pushing the cake-box slowly from her with her
foot, and never once looked, though her eyes were cast down too,
upon the dainty shoe she generally was so mindful of. Absorbed in
thought, she stood there, heedless alike of the tea and John (although
he called to her, and rapped the table with his knife to startle her),
until he rose and touched her on the arm; when she looked at him
for a moment, and hurried to her place behind the teaboard, laughing
at her negligence. But not as she had laughed before. The manner
and the music were quite changed.

The Cricket, too, had stopped. Somehow the room was not so cheerful as it had been. Nothing like it.

"So these are all the parcels, are they, John?" she said, breaking a
long silence, which the honest Carrier had devoted to the practical
illustration of one part of his favourite sentiment—certainly enjoying
what he ate, if it couldn't be admitted that he ate but little. "So these
are all the parcels; are they John?"

"That's all," said John. "Why—no—I—" laying down his knife and
fork, and taking a long breath. "I declare—I've clean forgotten the
old gentleman!"

"The old gentleman?"

"In the cart," said John. "He was asleep, among the straw, the last
time I saw him. I've very nearly remembered him, twice, since I came
in; but he went out of my head again. Halloa! Yahip there! Rouse
up! That's my hearty!"

John said these latter words outside the door, whither he had hurried
with the candle in his hand.

Miss Slowboy, conscious of some mysterious reference to The Old
Gentleman, and connecting in her mystified imagination certain
associations of a religious nature with the phrase, was so disturbed,
that hastily rising from the low chair by the fire to seek protection
near the skirts of her mistress, and coming into contact as she crossed
the doorway with an ancient Stranger, she instinctively made a charge
or butt at him with the only offensive instrument within her reach.
This instrument happening to be the baby, great commotion and
alarm ensued, which the sagacity of Boxer rather tended to increase;
for that good dog, more thoughtful than its master, had, it seemed,
been watching the old gentleman in his sleep, lest he should walk
off with a few young poplar trees that were tied up behind the cart;
and he still attended on him very closely, worrying his gaiters in fact,
and making dead sets at the buttons.

"You're such an undeniable good sleeper, sir," said John, when
tranquillity was restored; in the mean time the old gentleman had
stood, bareheaded and motionless, in the centre of the room; "that

I have half a mind to ask you where the other six are—only that would be a joke, and I know I should spoil it. Very near though," murmured the Carrier, with a chuckle; "very near!"

The Stranger, who had long white hair, good features, singularly bold and well defined for an old man, and dark, bright, penetrating eyes, looked round with a smile, and saluted the Carrier's wife by gravely inclining his head.

His garb was very quaint and odd—a long, long way behind the time. Its hue was brown, all over. In his hand he held a great brown club or walking-stick; and striking this upon the floor, it fell asunder, and became a chair. On which he sat down, quite composedly.

"There!" said the Carrier, turning to his wife. "That's the way I found him, sitting by the roadside! Upright as a milestone. And almost as deaf."

"Sitting in the open air, John!"

"In the open air," replied the Carrier, "just at dusk. 'Carriage Paid,' he said; and gave me eighteenpence. Then he got in. And there he is."

"He's going, John, I think!"

Not at all. He was only going to speak.

"If you please, I was to be left till called for," said the Stranger mildly. "Don't mind me."

With that, he took a pair of spectacles from one of his large pockets, and a book from another, and leisurely began to read. Making no more of Boxer than if he had been a house lamb!

The Carrier and his wife exchanged a look of perplexity. The Stranger raised his head; and glancing from the latter to the former, said,

"Your daughter, my good friend?"

"Wife," returned John.

"Niece?" said the Stranger.

"Wife," roared John.

"Indeed?" observed the Stranger. "Surely? Very young!"

He quietly turned over, and resumed his reading. But, before he could have read two lines, he again interrupted himself to say:

"Baby, yours?"

John gave him a gigantic nod; equivalent to an answer in the affirmative, delivered through a speaking trumpet.

"Girl?"

"Bo-o-oy!" roared John.

"Also very young, eh?"

Mrs. Peerybingle instantly struck in. "Two months, and three da-ays! Vaccinated just six weeks ago-o! Took very fine-ly! Considered, by the doctor, a remarkable beautiful chi-ild! Equal to the general run of children at five months o-old! Takes notice, in a way quite won-der-ful! May seem impossible to you, but feels his legs al-ready!"

Here the breathless little mother, who had been shrieking these short sentences into the old man's ear, until her pretty face was crimsoned, held up the Baby before him as a stubborn and triumphant fact; while Tilly Slowboy, with a melodious cry of 'Ketcher, Ketcher'—which sounded like some unknown words, adapted to a popular Sneeze—performed some cow-like gambols round that all-unconscious Innocent.

"Hark! He's called for, sure enough," said John. "There's somebody at the door. Open it, Tilly."

Before she could reach it, however, it was opened from without; being a primitive sort of door, with a latch, that any one could lift if he chose—and a good many people did choose, for all kinds of neighbours liked to have a cheerful word or two with the Carrier, though he was no great talker himself. Being opened, it gave admission to a little, meagre, thoughtful, dingy-faced man, who seemed to have made himself a great-coat from the sack-cloth covering of some old box; for when he turned to shut the door, and keep the weather out, he disclosed upon the back of that garment, the inscription G & T in large black capitals. Also the word GLASS in bold characters.

"Good evening, John!" said the little man. "Good evening, Mum. Good evening, Tilly. Good evening, Unbeknown! How's Baby, Mum? Boxer's pretty well, I hope?"

"All thriving, Caleb," replied Dot. "I am sure you need only look at the dear child, for one, to know that."

"And I'm sure I need only look at you for another," said Caleb.

He didn't look at her though; he had a wandering and thoughtful eye which seemed to be always projecting itself into some other time and place, no matter what he said; a description which will equally apply to his voice.

"Or at John for another," said Caleb. "Or at Tilly, as far as that goes. Or certainly at Boxer."

"Busy just now, Caleb?" asked the Carrier.

"Why, pretty well, John," he returned, with the distraught air of a man who was casting about for the Philosopher's stone, at least. "Pretty much so. There's rather a run on Noah's Arks at present. I could have wished to improve upon the Family, but I don't see how it's to be done at the price. It would be a satisfaction to one's mind, to make it clearer which was Shems and Hams, and which was Wives. Flies an't on that scale neither, as compared with elephants you know! Ah! well! Have you got anything in the parcel line for me, John?"

The Carrier put his hand into a pocket of the coat he had taken off; and brought out, carefully preserved in moss and paper, a tiny flower-pot.

"There it is!" he said, adjusting it with great care. "Not so much as a leaf damaged. Full of buds!"

Caleb's dull eye brightened, as he took it, and thanked him.

"Dear, Caleb," said the Carrier. "Very dear at this season."

"Never mind that. It would be cheap to me, whatever it cost," returned the little man. "Anything else, John?"

"A small box," replied the Carrier. "Here you are!"

"'For Caleb Plummer,'" said the little man, spelling out the direction. "'With Cash.' With Cash, John? I don't think it's for me."

"With Care," returned the Carrier, looking over his shoulder. "Where do you make out cash?"

"Oh! To be sure!" said Caleb. "It's all right. With care! Yes, yes; that's mine. It might have been with cash, indeed, if my dear Boy in the Golden South Americas had lived, John. You loved him like a son; didn't you? You needn't say you did. I know, of course. 'Caleb Plummer. With care.' Yes, yes, it's all right. It's a box of doll's eyes for my daughter's work. I wish it was her own sight in a box, John."

"I wish it was, or could be!" cried the Carrier.

"Thank'ee," said the little man. "You speak very hearty. To think that she should never see the Dolls—and them a-staring at her, so bold, all day long! That's where it cuts. What's the damage, John?"

"I'll damage you," said John, "if you inquire. Dot! Very near?"

"Well! it's like you to say so," observed the little man. "It's your kind way. Let me see. I think that's all."

"I think not," said the Carrier. "Try again."

"Something for our Governor, eh?" said Caleb, after pondering a little while. "To be sure. That's what I came for; but my head's so running on them Arks and things! He hasn't been here, has he?"

"Not he," returned the Carrier. "He's too busy, courting."

"He's coming round though," said Caleb; "for he told me to keep on the near side of the road going home, and it was ten to one he'd take me up. I had better go, by the bye.—You couldn't have the goodness to let me pinch Boxer's tail, Mum, for half a moment, could you?"

"Why, Caleb! what a question!"

"Oh never mind, Mum," said the little man. "He mightn't like it perhaps. There's a small order just come in, for barking dogs; and I should wish to go as close to Natur' as I could, for sixpence. That's all. Never mind, Mum."

It happened opportunely, that Boxer, without receiving the proposed stimulus, began to bark with great zeal. But, as this implied the approach of some new visitor, Caleb, postponing his study from the life to a more convenient season, shouldered the round box, and took a hurried leave. He might have spared himself the trouble, for he met the visitor upon the threshold.

"Oh! You are here, are you? Wait a bit. I'll take you home. John

Peerybingle, my service to you. More of my service to your pretty wife. Handsomer every day! Better too, if possible! And younger," mused the speaker, in a low voice; "that's the Devil of it!"

"I should be astonished at your paying compliments, Mr. Tackleton," said Dot, not with the best grace in the world; "but for your condition."

"You know all about it, then?"

"I have got myself to believe it, somehow," said Dot.

"After a hard struggle, I suppose?"

"Very."

Tackleton the Toy-merchant, pretty generally known as Gruff and Tackleton—for that was the firm, though Gruff had been bought out long ago; only leaving his name, and as some said his nature, according to its Dictionary meaning, in the business—Tackleton the Toy-merchant was a man whose vocation had been quite misunderstood by his Parents and Guardians. If they had made him a Money Lender, or a sharp Attorney, or a Sheriff's Officer, or a Broker, he might have sown his discontented oats in his youth, and, after having had the full run of himself in ill-natured transactions, might have turned out amiable, at last, for the sake of a little freshness and novelty. But, cramped and chafing in the peaceable pursuit of toy-making, he was a domestic Ogre, who had been living on children all his life, and was their implacable enemy. He despised all toys; wouldn't have bought one for the world; delighted, in his malice, to insinuate grim expressions into the faces of brown-paper farmers who drove pigs to market, bellmen who advertised lost lawyers' consciences, movable old ladies who darned stockings or carved pies; and other like samples of his stock in trade. In appalling masks; hideous, hairy, red-eyed Jacks in Boxes; Vampire Kites; demoniacal Tumblers who wouldn't lie down, and were perpetually flying forward, to stare infants out of countenance; his soul perfectly revelled. They were his only relief and safety-valve. He was great in such inventions. Anything suggestive of a Pony-nightmare was delicious to him. He had even lost money (and he took to that toy very kindly) by getting up Goblin slides for magic-lanterns, whereon the Powers of Darkness were depicted as a sort of supernatural shell-fish, with human faces. In intensifying the portraiture of Giants, he had sunk quite a little capital; and, though no painter himself, he could indicate, for the instruction of his artists, with a piece of chalk, a certain furtive leer for the countenances of those monsters, which was safe to destroy the peace of mind of any young gentleman between the ages of six and eleven, for the whole Christmas or Midsummer Vacation.

What he was in toys, he was (as most men are) in other things. You may easily suppose, therefore, that within the great green cape, which reached down to the calves of his legs, there was buttoned up to the chin an uncommonly pleasant fellow; and that he was about as choice a spirit, and as agreeable a companion, as ever stood in a pair of bull-headed-looking boots with mahogany-coloured tops.

Still, Tackleton the Toy-merchant was going to be married. In spite of all this, he was going to be married. And to a young wife too, a beautiful young wife.

He didn't look much like a bridegroom, as he stood in the Carrier's kitchen, with a twist in his dry face, and a screw in his body, and his hat jerked over the bridge of his nose, and his hands tucked down into the bottoms of his pockets, and his whole sarcastic ill-conditioned self peering out of one little corner of one little eye, like the concentrated essence of any number of ravens. But, a Bridegroom he designed to be.

"In three days' time. Next Thursday. The last day of the first month in the year. That's my wedding-day," said Tackleton.

Did I mention that he had always one eye wide open, and one eye nearly shut; and that the one eye nearly shut, was always the expressive eye? I don't think I did.

"That's my wedding-day!" said Tackleton, rattling his money.

"Why, it's our wedding-day too," exclaimed the Carrier.

"Ha, ha!" laughed Tackleton. "Odd! You're just such another couple. Just!"

The indignation of Dot at this presumptuous assertion is not to be described. What next? His imagination would compass the possibility of just such another Baby, perhaps. The man was mad.

"I say! A word with you," murmured Tackleton, nudging the Carrier with his elbow, and taking him a little apart. "You'll come to the wedding? We're in the same boat, you know."

"How in the same boat?" inquired the Carrier.

"A little disparity, you know," said Tackleton, with another nudge. "Come and spend an evening with us, beforehand."

"Why?" demanded John, astonished at this pressing hospitality.

"Why?" returned the other. "That's a new way of receiving an invitation. Why, for pleasure—sociability, you know, and all that!"

"I thought you were never sociable," said John, in his plain way.

"Tchah! It's of no use to be anything but free with you, I see," said Tackleton. "Why, then, the truth is you have a—what tea-drinking people call a sort of a comfortable appearance together, you and your wife. We know better, you know, but—"

"No, we don't know better," interposed John. "What are you talking about?"

"Well! We don't know better, then," said Tackleton. "We'll agree that we don't. As you like; what does it matter? I was going to say, as you have that sort of appearance, your company will produce a favourable effect on Mrs. Tackleton that will be. And, though I don't think your good lady's very friendly to me, in this matter, still she can't help herself from falling into my views, for there's a compactness and cosiness of appearance about her that always tells, even in an indifferent case. You'll say you'll come?"

"We have arranged to keep our Wedding-Day (as far as that goes) at home," said John. "We have made the promise to ourselves these six months. We think, you see, that home—"

"Bah! what's home?" cried Tackleton. "Four walls and a ceiling! (why don't you kill that Cricket? I would! I always do. I hate their noise.) There are four walls and a ceiling at my house. Come to me!"

"You kill your Crickets, eh?" said John.

"Scrunch 'em, sir," returned the other, setting his heel heavily on the floor. "You'll say you'll come? It's as much your interest as mine, you know, that the women should persuade each other that they're quiet and contented, and couldn't be better off. I know their way. Whatever one woman says, another woman is determined to clinch, always. There's that spirit of emulation among 'em, sir, that if your wife says to my wife, 'I'm the happiest woman in the world, and mine's the best husband in the world, and I dote on him,' my wife will say the same to yours, or more, and half believe it."

"Do you mean to say she don't, then?" asked the Carrier.

"Don't!" cried Tackleton, with a short, sharp laugh. "Don't what?"

The Carrier had some faint idea of adding, "dote upon you." But, happening to meet the half-closed eye, as it twinkled upon him over the turned-up collar of the cape, which was within an ace of poking it out, he felt it such an unlikely part and parcel of anything to be doted on, that he substituted, "that she don't believe it?"

"Ah, you dog! You're joking," said Tackleton.

But the Carrier, though slow to understand the full drift of his meaning, eyed him in such a serious manner, that he was obliged to be a little more explanatory.

"I have the humour," said Tackleton: holding up the fingers of his left hand, and tapping the forefinger, to imply "there I am, Tackleton to wit:" "I have the humour, sir, to marry a young wife, and a pretty wife:" here he rapped his little finger, to express the Bride; not sparingly, but sharply; with a sense of power. "I'm able to gratify that humour and I do. It's my whim. But—now look there!"

He pointed to where Dot was sitting, thoughtfully, before the fire; leaning her dimpled chin upon her hand, and watching the bright blaze. The Carrier looked at her, and then at him, and then at her, and then at him again.

"She honours and obeys, no doubt, you know," said Tackleton; "and that, as I am not a man of sentiment, is quite enough for *me*. But do you think there's anything more in it?"

"I think," observed the Carrier, "that I should chuck any man out of the window, who said there wasn't."

"Exactly so," returned the other with an unusual alacrity of assent. "To be sure! Doubtless you would. Of course. I'm certain of it. Good night. Pleasant dreams!"

The Carrier was puzzled, and made uncomfortable and uncertain, in spite of himself. He couldn't help showing it, in his manner.

"Good night, my dear friend!" said Tackleton, compassionately. "I'm off. We're exactly alike, in reality, I see. You won't give us to-morrow evening? Well! Next day you go out visiting, I know. I'll meet you there, and bring my wife that is to be. It'll do her good. You're agreeable? Thank'ee. What's that?"

It was a loud cry from the Carrier's wife: a loud, sharp, sudden cry, that made the room ring, like a glass vessel. She had risen from her seat, and stood like one transfixed by terror and surprise. The Stranger had advanced towards the fire to warm himself, and stood within a short stride of her chair. But quite still.

"Dot!" cried the Carrier "Mary! Darling! What's the matter?"

They were all about her in a moment. Caleb, who had been dozing on the cake-box, in the first imperfect recovery of his suspended presence of mind, seized Miss Slowboy by the hair of her head, but immediately apologised.

"Mary!" exclaimed the Carrier, supporting her in his arms. "Are you ill! What is it? Tell me, dear!"

She only answered by beating her hands together, and falling into a wild fit of laughter. Then, sinking from his grasp upon the ground, she covered her face with her apron, and wept bitterly. And then she laughed again, and then she cried again, and then she said how cold it was, and suffered him to lead her to the fire, where she sat down as before. The old man standing, as before, quite still.

"I'm better, John," she said. "I'm quite well now—I—"

"John!" But John was on the other side of her. Why turn her face towards the strange old gentleman, as if addressing him! Was her brain wandering?

"Only a fancy, John dear—a kind of shock—a something coming suddenly before my eyes—I don't know what it was. It's quite gone, quite gone."

"I'm glad it's gone," muttered Tackleton, turning the expressive eye all round the room. "I wonder where it's gone, and what it was. Humph! Caleb, come here! Who's that with the grey hair?"

"I don't know, sir," returned Caleb in a whisper. "Never see him before, in all my life. A beautiful figure for a nutcracker; quite a new model. With a screw-jaw opening down into his waistcoat, he'd be lovely."

"Not ugly enough," said Tackleton.

"Or for a firebox, either," observed Caleb, in deep contemplation, "what a model! Unscrew his head to put the matches in; turn him heels up'ards for the light; and what a firebox for a gentleman's mantel-shelf, just as he stands!"

"Not half ugly enough," said Tackleton. "Nothing in him at all! Come! Bring that box! All right now, I hope?"

"Oh quite gone! Quite gone!" said the little woman, waving him hurriedly away. "Good night!"

"Good night," said Tackleton. "Good night, John Peerybingle! Take care how you carry that box, Caleb. Let it fall, and I'll murder you! Dark as pitch, and weather worse than ever, eh? Good night!"

So, with another sharp look round the room, he went out at the door; followed by Caleb with the wedding-cake on his head.

The Carrier had been so much astounded by his little wife, and so busily engaged in soothing and tending her, that he had scarcely been conscious of the Stranger's presence, until now, when he again stood there, their only guest.

"He don't belong to them, you see," said John. "I must give him a hint to go."

"I beg your pardon, friend," said the old gentleman, advancing to him; "the more so, as I fear your wife has not been well; but the Attendant whom my infirmity," he touched his ears and shook his head, "renders almost indispensable, not having arrived, I fear there must be some mistake. The bad night which made the shelter of your comfortable cart (may I never have a worse!) so acceptable, is still as bad as ever. Would you, in your kindness, suffer me to rent a bed here?"

"Yes, yes," cried Dot. "Yes! Certainly!"

"Oh!" said the Carrier, surprised by the rapidity of this consent. "Well! I don't object; but, still I'm not quite sure that—"

"Hush!" she interrupted. "Dear John!"

"Why, he's stone deaf," urged John.

"I know he is, but— Yes, sir, certainly. Yes! certainly! I'll make him up a bed, directly, John."

As she hurried off to do it, the flutter of her spirits, and the agitation of her manner, were so strange that the Carrier stood looking after her, quite confounded.

"Did its mothers make it up a Beds then!" cried Miss Slowboy to the Baby; "and did its hair grow brown and curly, when its caps was lifted off, and frighten it, a precious Pets, a-sitting by the fires!"

With that unaccountable attraction of the mind to trifles, which is often incidental to a state of doubt and confusion, the Carrier, as he walked slowly to and fro, found himself mentally repeating even these absurd words, many times. So many times that he got them by heart, and was still conning them over and over, like a lesson, when Tilly, after administering as much friction to the little bald head with her hand as she thought wholesome (according to the practice of nurses), had once more tied the Baby's cap on.

"And frighten it, a precious Pets, a-sitting by the fires. What frightened Dot, I wonder!" mused the Carrier, pacing to and fro.

He scouted, from his heart, the insinuations of the Toy-merchant, and yet they filled him with a vague, indefinite uneasiness. For, Tackleton was quick and sly; and he had that painful sense, himself, of being a man of slow perception, that a broken hint was always worrying to him. He certainly had no intention in his mind of linking anything that Tackleton had said, with the unusual conduct of his wife, but the two subjects of reflection came into his mind together, and he could not keep them asunder.

The bed was soon made ready; and the visitor, declining all refreshment but a cup of tea, retired. Then, Dot—quite well again, she said, quite well again—arranged the great chair in the chimney-corner for her husband; filled his pipe and gave it him; and took her usual little stool beside him on the hearth.

She always *would* sit on that little stool. I think she must have had a kind of notion that it was a coaxing, wheedling, little stool.

She was, out and out, the very best filler of a pipe, I should say, in the four quarters of the globe. To see her put that chubby little finger in the bowl, and then blow down the pipe to clear the tube, and, when she had done so, affect to think that there was really something in the tube, and blow a dozen times, and hold it to her eye like a telescope, with a most provoking twist in her capital little face, as she looked down it, was quite a brilliant thing. As to the tobacco, she was perfect mistress of the subject; and her lighting of the pipe, with a wisp of paper, when the Carrier had it in his mouth—going so very near his nose, and yet not scorching it—was Art, high Art.

And the Cricket and the kettle, turning up again, acknowledged it! The bright fire, blazing up again, acknowledged it! The little Mower on the clock, in his unheeded work, acknowledged it! The Carrier, in his smoothing forehead and expanding face, acknowledged it, the readiest of all.

And as he soberly and thoughtfully puffed at his old pipe; and as the Dutch clock ticked; and as the red fire gleamed; and as the Cricket chirped; the Genius of his Hearth and Home (for such the Cricket was) came out, in fairy shape, into the room, and summoned many forms of Home about him. Dots of all ages, and all sizes, filled the chamber. Dots who were merry children, running on before him gathering flowers in the fields; coy Dots, half shrinking from, half yielding to, the pleading of his own rough image; newly-married Dots, alighting at the door, and taking wondering possession of the household keys; motherly little Dots, attended by fictitious Slowboys, bearing babies to be christened; matronly Dots, still young and blooming, watching Dots of daughters, as they danced at rustic balls; fat Dots, encircled and beset by troops of rosy grandchildren; withered Dots, who leaned on sticks, and tottered as they crept along. Old Carriers, too, appeared, with blind old Boxers lying at their feet; and newer carts with younger drivers ("Peerybingle Brothers" on the tilt); and sick old Carriers, tended by the gentlest hands; and graves of dead and gone old Carriers, green in the churchyard. And as the Cricket showed him all these things—he saw them plainly, though his eyes were fixed upon the fire—the Carrier's heart grew light and happy, and he thanked his Household Gods with all his might, and cared no more for Gruff and Tackleton than you do.

But what was that young figure of a man, which the same Fairy Cricket set so near Her stool, and which remained there, singly and alone? Why did it linger still, so near her, with its arm upon the chimney-piece, ever repeating "Married! and not to me!"

O Dot! O failing Dot! There is no place for it in all your husband's visions; why has its shadow fallen on his hearth?

CHIRP THE SECOND

Caleb Plummer and his Blind Daughter lived all alone by themselves, as the Story-books say—and my blessing, with yours to back it, I hope, on the Story-books, for saying anything in this workaday world!— Caleb Plummer and his Blind Daughter lived all alone by themselves, in a little cracked nutshell of a wooden house, which was, in truth, no better than a pimple on the prominent red-brick nose of Gruff and Tackleton. The premises of Gruff and Tackleton were the great feature of the street; but you might have knocked down Caleb Plummer's dwelling with a hammer or two, and carried off the pieces in a cart.

If any one had done the dwelling-house of Caleb Plummer the honour to miss it after such an inroad, it would have been, no doubt, to commend its demolition as a vast improvement. It stuck to the premises of Gruff and Tackleton, like a barnacle to a ship's keel, or a snail to a door, or a little bunch of toadstools to the stem of a tree. But it was the germ from which the full-grown trunk of Gruff and Tackleton had sprung; and, under its crazy roof, the Gruff before last, had, in a small way, made toys for a generation of old boys and girls, who had played with them, and found them out, and broken them, and gone to sleep.

I have said that Caleb and his poor Blind Daughter lived here. I should have said that Caleb lived here, and his poor Blind Daughter somewhere else—in an enchanted home of Caleb's furnishing, where scarcity and shabbiness were not, and trouble never entered. Caleb was no sorcerer, but in the only magic art that still remains to us, the magic of devoted, deathless love, Nature had been the mistress of his study; and from her teaching all the wonder came.

The Blind Girl never knew that ceilings were discoloured, walls blotched and bare of plaster here and there, high crevices unstopped and widening every day, beams mouldering and tending downward. The Blind Girl never knew that iron was rusting, wood rotting, paper peeling off; the size, and shape, and true proportion of the dwelling, withering away. The Blind Girl never knew that ugly shapes of delf and earthenware were on the board; that sorrow and faintheartedness were in the house; that Caleb's scanty hairs were turning greyer and more grey, before her sightless face. The Blind Girl never knew they had a master, cold, exacting, and uninterested—never knew that Tackleton was Tackleton in short; but lived in the belief of an eccentric humourist who loved to have his jest with them, and who, while he was the Guardian Angel of their lives, disdained to hear one word of thankfulness.

And all was Caleb's doing; all the doing of her simple father! But he too had a Cricket on his Hearth; and listening sadly to its music when the motherless Blind Child was very young, that Spirit had inspired him with the thought that even her great deprivation might be almost changed into a blessing, and the girl made happy by these little means. For all the Cricket tribe are potent Spirits, even though the people who hold converse with them do not know it (which is frequently the case); and there are not, in the unseen world, voices more gentle and more true, that may be so implicitly relied on, or that are so certain to give none but tenderest counsel, as the Voices in which the Spirits of the Fireside and the Hearth address themselves to human kind.

Caleb and his daughter were at work together in their usual working-room, which served them for their ordinary living-room as well; and a strange place it was. There were houses in it, finished and unfinished, for Dolls of all stations in life. Suburban tenements for Dolls of moderate means; kitchens and single apartments for Dolls of the lower classes; capital town residences for Dolls of high estate. Some of these establishments were already furnished according to estimate, with a view to the convenience of Dolls of limited income; others could be fitted on the most expensive scale, at a moment's notice, from whole shelves of chairs and tables, sofas, bedsteads, and upholstery. The nobility and gentry, and public in general, for whose accommodation these tenements were designed, lay, here and there, in baskets, staring straight up at the ceiling; but in denoting their degrees in society, and confining them to their respective stations (which experience shows to be lamentably difficult in real life), the makers of these Dolls had far improved on Nature, who is often froward and perverse; for they, not resting on such arbitrary marks as satin, cotton-print, and bits of rag, had superadded striking personal differences which allowed of no mistake. Thus, the Doll-lady of distinction had wax limbs of perfect symmetry; but only she and her compeers. The next grade in the social scale being made of leather, and the next of coarse linen stuff. As to the common-people, they had just so many matches out of tinder-boxes, for their arms and legs, and there they were—established in their sphere at once, beyond the possibility of getting out of it.

There were various other samples of his handicraft, besides Dolls, in Caleb Plummer's room. There were Noah's Arks, in which the Birds and Beasts were an uncommonly tight fit, I assure you; though they could be crammed in, anyhow, at the roof, and rattled and shaken into the smallest compass. By a bold poetical licence, most of these Noah's Arks had knockers on the doors; inconsistent appendages, perhaps, as suggestive of morning callers and a Postman, yet a pleasant finish to the outside of the building. There were scores of melancholy little carts which, when the wheels went round, performed most doleful music. Many small fiddles, drums, and other instruments of torture; no end of cannon, shields, swords, spears, and guns. There were little tumblers in red breeches, incessantly swarming up high obstacles of red-tape, and coming down, head first, on the other side; and there were innumerable old gentlemen of respectable, not to say venerable, appearance, insanely flying over horizontal pegs, inserted, for the purpose, in their own street doors. There were beasts of all sorts; horses, in particular, of every breed, from the spotted barrel on four pegs, with a small tippet for a mane, to the thoroughbred rocker on his highest mettle. As it would have been hard to count the dozens upon dozens of grotesque figures that were ever ready to commit all sorts of absurdities on the turning of a handle, so it would have been no easy task to mention any human folly, vice, or weakness, that had not its type, immediate or remote, in Caleb Plummer's room. And not in an exaggerated form, for very little handles will move men and women to as strange performances as any Toy was ever made to undertake.

In the midst of all these objects, Caleb and his daughter sat at work. The Blind Girl busy as a Doll's dressmaker; Caleb painting and glazing the four-pair front of a desirable family mansion.

The care imprinted in the lines of Caleb's face, and his absorbed and dreamy manner, which would have sat well on some alchemist or abstruse student, were at first sight an odd contrast to his occupation, and the trivialities about him. But trivial things, invented and pursued for bread, become very serious matters of fact; and, apart from this consideration, I am not at all prepared to say, myself, that if Caleb had been a Lord Chamberlain, or a Member of Parliament, or a law-yer, or even a great speculator, he would have dealt in toys one whit less whimsical, while I have a very great doubt whether they would have been as harmless.

"So you were out in the rain last night, father, in your beautiful new great-coat," said Caleb's daughter.

"In my beautiful new great-coat," answered Caleb, glancing to-wards a clothes-line in the room, on which the sack-cloth garment previously described was carefully hung up to dry.

"How glad I am you bought it, father!"

"And of such a tailor, too," said Caleb. "Quite a fashionable tailor. It's too good for me."

The Blind Girl rested from her work, and laughed with delight. "Too good, father! What can be too good for you?"

"I'm half-ashamed to wear it though," said Caleb, watching the effect of what he said, upon her brightening face; "upon my word! When I hear the boys and people say behind me, "Halloa! Here's a swell!" I don't know which way to look. And when the beggar wouldn't go away last night; and when I said I was a very common man, said, 'No, your Honour! Bless your Honour, don't say that!' I was quite ashamed. I really felt as if I hadn't a right to wear it."

Happy Blind Girl! How merry she was, in her exultation!

"I see you, father," she said, clasping her hands, "as plainly as if I had the eyes I never want when you are with me. A blue coat—"

"Bright blue," said Caleb.

"Yes, yes! Bright blue!" exclaimed the girl, turning up her radiant face; "the colour I can just remember in the blessed sky! You told me it was blue before! A bright blue coat—"

"Made loose to the figure," suggested Caleb.

"Made loose to the figure!" cried the Blind Girl, laughing heartily; "and in it, you, dear father, with your merry eyes, your smiling face, your free step, and your dark hair—looking so young and handsome!"

"Halloa! Halloa!" said Caleb. "I shall be vain, presently!"

"I think you are, already," cried the Blind Girl, pointing at him, in her glee. "I know you, father! Ha, ha, ha! I've found you out, you see!"

How different the picture in her mind, from Caleb, as he sat observ-ing her! She had spoken of his free step. She was right in that. For years and years he had never once crossed that threshold at his own slow pace, but with a footfall counterfeited for her ear; and never had he, when his heart was heaviest, forgotten the light tread that was to render hers so cheerful and courageous!

Heaven knows! But I think Caleb's vague bewilderment of manner may have half originated in his having confused himself about him-self, and everything around, for the love of his Blind Daughter. How could the little man be otherwise than bewildered, after labouring for so many years to destroy his own identity, and that of all the objects that had any bearing on it!

"There we are," said Caleb, falling back a pace or two to form the better judgment of his work; "as near the real thing as sixpenn'orth of halfpence is to sixpence. What a pity that the whole front of the house opens at once! If there was only a staircase in it, now, and regular doors to the rooms to go in at! But that's the worst of my calling, I'm always deluding myself, and swindling myself."

"You are speaking quite softly. You are not tired, father?"

"Tired!" echoed Caleb, with a great burst of animation, "what should tire me, Bertha? I was never tired. What does it mean?"

To give the greater force to his words, he checked himself in an involuntary imitation of two half-length stretching and yawning figures on the mantel-shelf, who were represented as in one eternal state of weariness from the waist upwards; and hummed a fragment of a song. It was a Bacchanalian song, something about a Sparkling Bowl. He sang it with an assumption of a devil-may-care voice, that made his face a thousand times more meagre and more thoughtful than ever.

"What! You're singing, are you?" said Tackleton, putting his head in at the door. "Go it! I can't sing."

Nobody would have suspected him of it. He hadn't what is generally termed a singing face, by any means.

"I can't afford to sing," said Tackleton. "I'm glad you can. I hope you can afford to work too. Hardly time for both, I should think?"

"If you could only see him, Bertha, how he's winking at me!" whispered Caleb. "Such a man to joke! you'd think, if you didn't know him, he was in earnest—wouldn't you now?"

The Blind Girl smiled and nodded.

"The bird that can sing and won't sing must be made to sing, they say," grumbled Tackleton. "What about the owl that can't sing, and oughtn't to sing, and will sing; is there anything that he should be made to do?"

"The extent to which he's winking at this moment!" whispered Caleb to his daughter. "O, my gracious!"

"Always merry and light-hearted with us!" cried the smiling Bertha.

"O, you're there, are you?" answered Tackleton. "Poor Idiot!"

He really did believe she was an Idiot; and he founded the belief, I can't say whether consciously or not, upon her being fond of him.

"Well! and being there,—how are you?" said Tackleton, in his grudging way.

"Oh! well; quite well. And as happy as even you can wish me to be. As happy as you would make the whole world, if you could!"

"Poor Idiot!" muttered Tackleton. "No gleam of reason. Not a gleam!"

The Blind Girl took his hand and kissed it; held it for a moment in her own two hands; and laid her cheek against it tenderly, before releasing it. There was such unspeakable affection and such fervent gratitude in the act, that Tackleton himself was moved to say, in a milder growl than usual:

"What's the matter now?"

"I stood it close beside my pillow when I went to sleep last night, and remembered it in my dreams. And when the day broke, and the glorious red sun—the *red* sun, father?"

"Red in the mornings and the evenings, Bertha," said poor Caleb, with a woeful glance at his employer.

"When it rose, and the bright light I almost fear to strike myself against in walking, came into the room, I turned the little tree towards it, and blessed Heaven for making things so precious, and blessed you for sending them to cheer me!"

"Bedlam broke loose!" said Tackleton under his breath. "We shall arrive at the strait-waistcoat and mufflers soon. We're getting on!"

Caleb, with his hands hooked loosely in each other, stared vacantly before him while his daughter spoke, as if he really were uncertain (I believe he was) whether Tackleton had done anything to deserve her thanks, or not. If he could have been a perfectly free agent, at that moment, required, on pain of death, to kick the Toy-merchant, or fall at his feet, according to his merits, I believe it would have been an even chance which course he would have taken. Yet Caleb knew that with his own hands he had brought the little rose-tree home for her so carefully, and that with his own lips he had forged the innocent deception which should help to keep her from suspecting how much, how very much, he every day denied himself, that she might be the happier.

"Bertha!" said Tackleton, assuming, for the nonce, a little cordiality. "Come here."

"Oh! I can come straight to you! You needn't guide me!" she rejoined.

"Shall I tell you a secret, Bertha?"

"If you will!" she answered, eagerly.

How bright the darkened face! How adorned with light, the listening head!

"This is the day on which little what's-her-name, the spoilt child, Peerybingle's wife, pays her regular visit to you—makes her fantastic Pic-Nic here; an't it?" said Tackleton, with a strong expression of distaste for the whole concern.

"Yes," replied Bertha. "This is the day."

"I thought so," said Tackleton. "I should like to join the party."

"Do you hear that, father?" cried the Blind Girl in an ecstasy.

"Yes, yes, I hear it," murmured Caleb, with the fixed look of a sleep-walker; "but I don't believe it. It's one of my lies, I've no doubt."

"You see I—I want to bring the Peerybingles a little more into company with May Fielding," said Tackleton. "I am going to be married to May."

"Married!" cried the Blind Girl, starting from him.

"She's such a con-founded Idiot," muttered Tackleton, "that I was afraid she'd never comprehend me. Ah, Bertha! Married! Church, parson, clerk, beadle, glass-coach, bells, breakfast, bride-cake, favours, marrow-bones, cleavers, and all the rest of the tom-foolery. A wedding, you know; a wedding. Don't you know what a wedding is?"

"I know," replied the Blind Girl, in a gentle tone. "I understand!"

"Do you?" muttered Tackleton. "It's more than I expected. Well! On that account I want to join the party, and to bring May and her mother. I'll send in a little something or other, before the afternoon. A cold leg of mutton, or some comfortable trifle of that sort. You'll expect me?"

"Yes," she answered.

She had drooped her head, and turned away; and so stood, with her hands crossed, musing.

"I don't think you will," muttered Tackleton, looking at her; "for you seem to have forgotten all about it, already. Caleb!"

"I may venture to say I'm here, I suppose," thought Caleb. "Sir!"

"Take care she don't forget what I've been saying to her."

"*She* never forgets," returned Caleb. "It's one of the few things she an't clever in."

"Every man thinks his own geese swans," observed the Toy-merchant, with a shrug. "Poor devil!"

Having delivered himself of which remark, with infinite contempt, old Gruff and Tackleton withdrew.

Bertha remained where he had left her, lost in meditation. The gaiety had vanished from her downcast face, and it was very sad. Three or four times, she shook her head, as if bewailing some remembrance or some loss; but her sorrowful reflections found no vent in words.

It was not until Caleb had been occupied, some time, in yoking a team of horses to a waggon by the summary process of nailing the harness to the vital parts of their bodies, that she drew near to his working-stool, and sitting down beside him, said:

"Father, I am lonely in the dark. I want my eyes, my patient, willing eyes."

"Here they are," said Caleb. "Always ready. They are more yours than mine, Bertha, any hour in the four-and-twenty. What shall your eyes do for you, dear?"

"Look round the room, father."

"All right," said Caleb. "No sooner said than done, Bertha."

"Tell me about it."

"It's much the same as usual," said Caleb. "Homely, but very snug. The gay colours on the walls; the bright flowers on the plates and dishes; the shining wood, where there are beams or panels; the general cheerfulness and neatness of the building; make it very pretty."

Cheerful and neat it was wherever Bertha's hands could busy themselves. But nowhere else were cheerfulness and neatness possible, in the old crazy shed which Caleb's fancy so transformed.

"You have your working dress on, and are not so gallant as when you wear the handsome coat?" said Bertha, touching him.

"Not quite so gallant," answered Caleb. "Pretty brisk though."

"Father," said the Blind Girl, drawing close to his side, and stealing one arm round his neck, "tell me something about May. She is very fair?"

"She is indeed," said Caleb. And she was indeed. It was quite a rare thing to Caleb, not to have to draw on his invention.

"Her hair is dark," said Bertha, pensively, "darker than mine. Her voice is sweet and musical, I know. I have often loved to hear it. Her shape—"

"There's not a Doll's in all the room to equal it," said Caleb. "And her eyes!—"

He stopped; for Bertha had drawn closer round his neck, and from the arm that clung about him, came a warning pressure which he understood too well.

He coughed a moment, hammered for a moment, and then fell back upon the song about the sparkling bowl; his infallible resource in all such difficulties.

"Our friend, father, our benefactor. I am never tired, you know, of hearing about him.— Now, was I ever?" she said hastily.

"Of course not," answered Caleb, "and with reason."

"Ah! With how much reason!" cried the Blind Girl. With such fervency, that Caleb, though his motives were so pure, could not endure to meet her face; but dropped his eyes, as if she could have read in them his innocent deceit.

"Then, tell me again about him, dear father," said Bertha. "Many times again! His face is benevolent, kind, and tender. Honest and true, I am sure it is. The manly heart that tries to cloak all favours with a show of roughness and unwillingness, beats in its every look and glance."

"And makes it noble!" added Caleb, in his quiet desperation.

"And makes it noble!" cried the Blind Girl. "He is older than May, father."

"Ye-es," said Caleb, reluctantly. "He's a little older than May. But that don't signify."

"Oh father, yes! To be his patient companion in infirmity and age;

to be his gentle nurse in sickness, and his constant friend in suffering and sorrow; to know no weariness in working for his sake; to watch him, tend him, sit beside his bed and talk to him awake, and pray for him asleep; what privileges these would be! What opportunities for proving all her truth and devotion to him! Would she do all this, dear father?"

"No doubt of it," said Caleb.

"I love her, father; I can love her from my soul!" exclaimed the Blind Girl. And saying so, she laid her poor blind face on Caleb's shoulder, and so wept and wept, that he was almost sorry to have brought that tearful happiness upon her.

In the mean time, there had been a pretty sharp commotion at John Peerybingle's, for little Mrs. Peerybingle naturally couldn't think of going anywhere without the Baby; and to get the Baby under weigh took time. Not that there was much of the Baby, speaking of it as a thing of weight and measure, but there was a vast deal to do about and about it, and it all had to be done by easy stages. For instance, when the Baby was got, by hook and by crook, to a certain point of dressing, and you might have rationally supposed that another touch or two would finish him off, and turn him out a tip-top Baby challenging the world, he was unexpectedly extinguished in a flannel cap, and hustled off to bed; where he simmered (so to speak) between two blankets for the best part of an hour. From this state of inaction he was then recalled, shining very much and roaring violently, to partake of—well? I would rather say, if you'll permit me to speak generally—of a slight repast. After which, he went to sleep again. Mrs. Peerybingle took advantage of this interval, to make herself as smart in a small way as ever you saw anybody in all your life; and, during the same short truce, Miss Slowboy insinuated herself into a spencer of a fashion so surprising and ingenious, that it had no connection with herself, or anything else in the universe, but was a shrunken, dog's-eared, independent fact, pursuing its lonely course without the least regard to anybody. By this time, the Baby, being all alive again, was invested, by the united efforts of Mrs. Peerybingle and Miss Slowboy, with a cream-coloured mantle for its body and a sort of nankeen raised-pie for its head; and so in course of time they all three got down to the door, where the old horse had already taken more than the full value of his day's toll out of the Turnpike Trust, by tearing up the road with his impatient autographs; and whence Boxer might be dimly seen in the remote perspective, standing looking back, and tempting him to come on without orders.

As to a chair, or anything of that kind for helping Mrs. Peerybingle into the cart, you know very little of John, if you think *that* was necessary. Before you could have seen him lift her from the ground, there she was in her place, fresh and rosy, saying, "John! How *can* you! Think of Tilly!"

If I might be allowed to mention a young lady's legs, on any terms, I would observe of Miss Slowboy's that there was a fatality about them which rendered them singularly liable to be grazed; and that she never effected the smallest ascent or descent, without recording the circumstance upon them with a notch, as Robinson Crusoe marked the days upon his wooden calendar. But as this might be considered ungenteel, I'll think of it.

"John! You've got the Basket with the Veal and Ham Pie and things, and the bottles of Beer?" said Dot. "If you haven't, you must turn round again, this very minute."

"You're a nice little article," returned the Carrier, "to be talking about turning round, after keeping me a full quarter of an hour behind my time."

"I am sorry for it, John," said Dot in a great bustle, "but I really could not think of going to Bertha's—I would not do it, John, on any account—without the Veal and Ham Pie and things, and the bottles of Beer. Way!"

This monosyllable was addressed to the horse, who didn't mind it at all.

"Oh *do* way, John!" said Mrs. Peerybingle. "Please!"

"It'll be time enough to do that," returned John, "when I begin to leave things behind me. The basket's here, safe enough."

"What a hard-hearted monster you must be, John, not to have said so, at once, and save me such a turn! I declared I wouldn't go to Bertha's without the Veal and Ham Pie and things, and the bottles of Beer, for any money. Regularly once a fortnight ever since we have been married, John, have we made our little Pic-Nic there. If anything was to go wrong with it, I should almost think we were never to be lucky again."

"It was a kind thought in the first instance," said the Carrier: "and I honour you for it, little woman."

"My dear John," replied Dot, turning very red, "don't talk about honouring *me*. Good Gracious!"

"By the bye—" observed the Carrier. "That old gentleman—"

Again so visibly, and instantly embarrassed!

"He's an odd fish," said the Carrier, looking straight along the road before them. "I can't make him out. I don't believe there's any harm in him."

"None at all. I'm—I'm sure there's none at all."

"Yes," said the Carrier, with his eyes attracted to her face by the great earnestness of her manner. "I am glad you feel so certain of it, because it's a confirmation to me. It's curious that he should have taken it into his head to ask leave to go on lodging with us; an't it? Things come about so strangely."

"So very strangely," she rejoined in a low voice, scarcely audible.

"However, he's a good-natured old gentleman," said John, "and pays as a gentleman, and I think his word is to be relied upon, like a gentleman's. I had quite a long talk with him this morning: he can hear me better already, he says, as he gets more used to my voice. He told me a great deal about himself, and I told him a great deal about myself, and a rare lot of questions he asked me. I gave him information about my having two beats, you know, in my business; one day to the right from our house and back again; another day to the left from our house and back again (for he's a stranger and don't know the names of places about here); and he seemed quite pleased. 'Why, then I shall be returning home to-night your way,' he says, 'when I thought you'd be coming in an exactly opposite direction. That's capital! I may trouble you for another lift perhaps, but I'll engage not to fall so sound asleep again.' He *was* sound asleep, sure-ly!— Dot! what are you thinking of?"

"Thinking of, John? I—I was listening to you."

"O! That's all right!" said the honest Carrier. "I was afraid, from the look of your face, that I had gone rambling on so long, as to set you thinking about something else. I was very near it, I'll be bound."

Dot making no reply, they jogged on, for some little time, in silence. But it was not easy to remain silent very long in John Peerybingle's cart, for everybody on the road had something to say. Though it might only be "How are you?" and indeed it was very often nothing else, still, to give that back again in the right spirit of cordiality, required, not merely a nod and a smile, but as wholesome an action of the lungs withal, as a long-winded Parliamentary speech. Sometimes, passengers on foot, or horseback, plodded on a little way beside the cart, for the express purpose of having a chat; and then there was a great deal to be said, on both sides.

Then, Boxer gave occasion to more good-natured recognitions of, and by, the Carrier, than half-a-dozen Christians could have done! Everybody knew him, all along the road—especially the fowls and pigs, who when they saw him approaching, with his body all on one side, and his ears pricked up inquisitively, and that knob of a tail making the most of itself in the air, immediately withdrew into remote back settlements, without waiting for the honour of a nearer acquaintance. He had business everywhere; going down all the turnings, looking into all the wells, bolting in and out of all the cottages, dashing into the midst of all the Dame-Schools, fluttering all the pigeons, magnifying the tails of all the cats, and trotting into the public houses like a regular customer. Wherever he went, somebody or other might have been heard to cry, "Halloa! Here's Boxer!" and out came that somebody forthwith, accompanied by at least two or three other somebodies, to give John Peerybingle and his pretty wife, Good Day.

The packages and parcels for the errand cart were numerous; and there were many stoppages to take them in and give them out, which were not by any means the worst parts of the journey. Some people were so full of expectation about their parcels, and other people were so full of wonder about their parcels, and other people were so full of inexhaustible directions about their parcels, and John had such a lively interest in all the parcels, that it was as good as a play. Likewise, there were articles to carry, which required to be considered and discussed, and in reference to the adjustment and disposition of which, councils had to be holden by the Carrier and the senders: at which Boxer usually assisted, in short fits of the closest attention, and long fits of tearing round and round the assembled sages and barking himself hoarse. Of all these little incidents, Dot was the amused and open-eyed spectatress from her chair in the cart; and as she sat there, looking on—a charming little portrait framed to admiration by the tilt—there was no lack of nudgings and glancings and whisperings and envyings among the younger men. And this delighted John the Carrier, beyond measure; for he was proud to have his little wife admired, knowing that she didn't mind it—that, if anything, she rather liked it perhaps.

The trip was a little foggy, to be sure, in the January weather; and was raw and cold. But who cared for such trifles? Not Dot, decidedly. Not Tilly Slowboy, for she deemed sitting in a cart, on any terms, to be the highest point of human joys; the crowning circumstance of earthly hopes. Not the Baby, I'll be sworn; for it's not in Baby nature to be warmer or more sound asleep, though its capacity is great in both respects, than the blessed young Peerybingle was, all the way.

You couldn't see very far in the fog, of course; but you could see a deal! It's astonishing how much you may see, in a thicker fog than that, if you will only take the trouble to look for it. Why, even to sit watching for the Fairy-rings in the fields, and for the patches of hoarfrost still lingering in the shade, near hedges and by trees, was a pleasant occupation; to make no mention of the unexpected shapes in which the trees themselves came starting out of the mist, and glided into it again. The hedges were tangled and bare, and waved a multitude of blighted garlands in the wind; but there was no discouragement in this. It was agreeable to contemplate; for it made the fireside warmer in possession, and the summer greener in expectancy. The river looked chilly; but it was in motion, and moving a good pace—which was a great point. The canal was rather slow and torpid; that must be admitted. Never mind. It would freeze the sooner when the frost set fairly in, and then there would be skating, and sliding; and the heavy old barges, frozen up somewhere near a wharf, would smoke their rusty iron chimney pipes all day, and have a lazy time of it.

In one place, there was a great mound of weeds or stubble burning; and they watched the fire, so white in the daytime, flaring through the fog, with only here and there a dash of red in it, until, in consequence, as she observed, of the smoke "getting up her nose," Miss Slowboy choked—she could do anything of that sort, on the smallest provocation—and woke the Baby, who wouldn't go to sleep again. But Boxer, who was in advance some quarter of a mile or so, had already passed the outposts of the town, and gained the corner of the street where Caleb and his daughter lived; and long before they had reached the door, he and the Blind Girl were on the pavement waiting to receive them.

Boxer, by the way, made certain delicate distinctions of his own, in his communication with Bertha, which persuade me fully that he knew her to be blind. He never sought to attract her attention by looking at her, as he often did with other people, but touched her invariably. What experience he could ever have had of blind people or blind dogs, I don't know. He had never lived with a blind master; nor had Mr. Boxer the elder, nor Mrs. Boxer, nor any of his respectable family on either side, ever been visited with blindness, that I am aware of. He may have found it out for himself, perhaps, but he had got hold of it somehow; and therefore he had hold of Bertha too, by the skirt, and kept hold, until Mrs. Peerybingle and the Baby, and Miss Slowboy, and the basket, were all got safely within doors.

May Fielding was already come; and so was her mother—a little querulous chip of an old lady with a peevish face, who, in right of having preserved a waist like a bed-post, was supposed to be a most transcendent figure; and who, in consequence of having once been better off, or of labouring under an impression that she might have been, if something had happened which never did happen, and seemed to have never been particularly likely to come to pass—but it's all the same—was very genteel and patronising indeed. Gruff and Tackleton was also there, doing the agreeable, with the evident sensation of being as perfectly at home, and as unquestionably in his own element, as a fresh young salmon on the top of the Great Pyramid.

"May! My dear old friend!" cried Dot, running up to meet her. "What a happiness to see you."

Her old friend was, to the full, as hearty and as glad as she; and it really was, if you'll believe me, quite a pleasant sight to see them embrace. Tackleton was a man of taste beyond all question. May was very pretty.

You know sometimes, when you are used to a pretty face, how, when it comes into contact and comparison with another pretty face, it seems for the moment to be homely and faded, and hardly to deserve the high opinion you have had of it. Now, this was not at all the case, either with Dot or May; for May's face set off Dot's, and

Dot's face set off May's, so naturally and agreeably, that, as John Peerybingle was very near saying when he came into the room, they ought to have been born sisters—which was the only improvement you could have suggested.

Tackleton had brought his leg of mutton, and, wonderful to relate, a tart besides—but we don't mind a little dissipation when our brides are in the case; we don't get married every day—and in addition to these dainties, there were the Veal and Ham Pie, and "things," as Mrs. Peerybingle called them; which were chiefly nuts and oranges, and cakes, and such small deer. When the repast was set forth on the board, flanked by Caleb's contribution, which was a great wooden bowl of smoking potatoes (he was prohibited, by solemn compact, from producing any other viands), Tackleton led his intended mother-in-law to the post of honour. For the better gracing of this place at the high festival, the majestic old soul had adorned herself with a cap, calculated to inspire the thoughtless with sentiments of awe. She also wore her gloves. But let us be genteel, or die!

Caleb sat next his daughter; Dot and her old schoolfellow were side by side; the good Carrier took care of the bottom of the table. Miss Slowboy was isolated, for the time being, from every article of furniture but the chair she sat on, that she might have nothing else to knock the Baby's head against.

As Tilly stared about her at the dolls and toys, they stared at her and at the company. The venerable old gentlemen at the street doors (who were all in full action) showed especial interest in the party: pausing occasionally before leaping, as if they were listening to the conversation, and then plunging wildly over and over, a great many times, without halting for breath—as in a frantic state of delight with the whole proceedings.

Certainly, if these old gentlemen were inclined to have a fiendish joy in the contemplation of Tackleton's discomfiture, they had good reason to be satisfied. Tackleton couldn't get on at all; and the more cheerful his intended bride became in Dot's society, the less he liked it, though he had brought them together for that purpose. For he was a regular dog in the manger, was Tackleton; and when they laughed and he couldn't, he took it into his head, immediately, that they must be laughing at him.

"Ah, May!" said Dot. "Dear, dear, what changes! To talk of those merry school-days makes one young again."

"Why, you an't particularly old, at any time; are you?" said Tackleton.

"Look at my sober plodding husband there," returned Dot. "He adds twenty years to my age at least. Don't you, John?"

"Forty," John replied.

"How many *you'll* add to May's, I am sure I don't know," said

Dot, laughing. "But she can't be much less than a hundred years of age on her next birthday."

"Ha ha!" laughed Tackleton. Hollow as a drum that laugh though. And he looked as if he could have twisted Dot's neck, comfortably.

"Dear, dear!" said Dot. "Only to remember how we used to talk, at school, about the husbands we would choose. I don't know how young, and how handsome, and how gay, and how lively, mine was not to be! And as to May's!— Ah dear! I don't know whether to laugh or cry, when I think what silly girls we were."

May seemed to know which to do; for the colour flushed into her face, and tears stood in her eyes.

"Even the very persons themselves—real live young men—were fixed on sometimes," said Dot. "We little thought how things would come about. I never fixed on John, I'm sure; I never so much as thought of him. And if I had told you, you were ever to be married to Mr. Tackleton, why you'd have slapped me. Wouldn't you, May?"

Though May didn't say yes, she certainly didn't say no, or express no, by any means.

Tackleton laughed—quite shouted, he laughed so loud. John Peerybingle laughed too, in his ordinary good-natured and contented manner; but his was a mere whisper of a laugh, to Tackleton's.

"You couldn't help yourselves, for all that. You couldn't resist us, you see," said Tackleton. "Here we are! Here we are! Where are your gay young bridegrooms now?"

"Some of them are dead," said Dot; "and some of them forgotten. Some of them, if they could stand among us at this moment, would not believe we were the same creatures; would not believe that what they saw and heard was real, and we *could* forget them so. No! they would not believe one word of it!"

"Why, Dot!" exclaimed the Carrier. "Little woman!"

She had spoken with such earnestness and fire, that she stood in need of some recalling to herself, without doubt. Her husband's check was very gentle, for he merely interfered, as he supposed, to shield old Tackleton; but it proved effectual, for she stopped, and said no more. There was an uncommon agitation, even in her silence, which the wary Tackleton, who had brought his half-shut eye to bear upon her, noted closely, and remembered to some purpose too.

May uttered no word, good or bad, but sat quite still, with her eyes cast down, and made no sign of interest in what had passed. The good lady her mother now interposed, observing, in the first instance, that girls were girls, and byegones byegones, and that so long as young people were young and thoughtless, they would probably conduct themselves like young and thoughtless persons: with two or three other positions of a no less sound and incontrovertible character. She then remarked, in a devout spirit, that she thanked Heaven she had always found in her daughter May, a dutiful and obedient child; for which she took no credit to herself, though she had every reason to believe it was entirely owing to herself. With regard to Mr. Tackleton she said, That he was in a moral point of view an undeniable individual, and That he was in an eligible point of view a son-in-law to be desired, no one in their senses could doubt. (She was very emphatic here.) With regard to the family into which he was so soon about, after some solicitation, to be admitted, she believed Mr. Tackleton knew that, although reduced in purse, it had some pretensions to gentility; and if certain circumstances, not wholly unconnected, she would go so far as to say, with the Indigo Trade, but to which she would not more particularly refer, had happened differently, it might perhaps have been in possession of wealth. She then remarked that she would not allude to the past, and would not mention that her daughter had for some time rejected the suit of Mr. Tackleton; and that she would not say a great many other things which she did say, at great length. Finally, she delivered it as the general result of her observation and experience, that those marriages in which there was least of what was romantically and sillily called love, were always the happiest; and that she anticipated the greatest possible amount of bliss—not rapturous bliss; but the solid, steady-going article—from the approaching nuptials. She concluded by informing the company that to-morrow was the day she had lived for, expressly; and that when it was over, she would desire nothing better than to be packed up and disposed of, in any genteel place of burial.

As these remarks were quite unanswerable—which is the happy property of all remarks that are sufficiently wide of the purpose—they changed the current of the conversation, and diverted the general attention to the Veal and Ham Pie, the cold mutton, the potatoes, and the tart. In order that the bottled beer might not be slighted, John Peerybingle proposed To-morrow: the Wedding-Day; and called upon them to drink a bumper to it, before he proceeded on his journey.

For you ought to know that he only rested there, and gave the old horse a bait. He had to go some four or five miles farther on; and when he returned in the evening, he called for Dot, and took another rest on his way home. This was the order of the day on all the Pic-Nic occasions, had been, ever since their institution.

There were two persons present, besides the bride and bridegroom elect, who did but indifferent honour to the toast. One of these was Dot, too flushed and discomposed to adapt herself to any small occurrence of the moment; the other, Bertha, who rose up hurriedly, before the rest, and left the table.

"Good bye!" said stout John Peerybingle, pulling on his dreadnought coat. "I shall be back at the old time. Good bye all!"

"Good bye, John," returned Caleb.

He seemed to say it by rote, and to wave his hand in the same unconscious manner; for he stood observing Bertha with an anxious wondering face, that never altered its expression.

"Good bye, young shaver!" said the jolly Carrier, bending down to kiss the child; which Tilly Slowboy, now intent upon her knife and fork, had deposited asleep (and strange to say, without damage) in a little cot of Bertha's furnishing; "good bye! Time will come, I suppose, when *you'll* turn out into the cold, my little friend, and leave your old father to enjoy his pipe and his rheumatics in the chimney-corner; eh? Where's Dot?"

"I'm here, John!" she said, starting.

"Come come!" returned the Carrier, clapping his sounding hands. "Where's the pipe?"

"I quite forgot the pipe, John."

Forgot the pipe! Was such a wonder ever heard of! She! Forgot the pipe!

"I'll—I'll fill it directly. It's soon done."

But it was not so soon done, either. It lay in the usual place—the Carrier's dreadnought pocket—with the little pouch, her own work, from which she was used to fill it; but her hand shook so, that she entangled it (and yet her hand was small enough to have come out easily, I am sure), and bungled terribly. The filling of the pipe and lighting it, those little offices in which I have commended her discretion, were vilely done, from first to last. During the whole process, Tackleton stood looking on maliciously with the half-closed eye; which, whenever it met hers—or caught it, for it can hardly be said to have ever met another eye: rather being a kind of trap to snatch it up—augmented her confusion in a most remarkable degree.

"Why, what a clumsy Dot you are, this afternoon!" said John. "I could have done it better myself, I verily believe!"

With these good-natured words, he strode away, and presently was heard, in company with Boxer, and the old horse, and the cart, making lively music down the road. What time the dreamy Caleb still stood, watching his blind daughter, with the same expression on his face.

"Bertha!" said Caleb, softly. "What has happened? How changed you are, my darling, in a few hours—since this morning. *You* silent and dull all day! What is it? Tell me!"

"Oh father, father!" cried the Blind Girl, bursting into tears. "Oh my hard, hard fate!"

Caleb drew his hand across his eyes before he answered her.

"But think how cheerful and how happy you have been, Bertha! How good, and how much loved, by many people."

"That strikes me to the heart, dear father! Always so mindful of me! Always so kind to me!"

Caleb was very much perplexed to understand her.

"To be—to be blind, Bertha, my poor dear," he faltered, "is a great affliction; but——"

"I have never felt it!" cried the Blind Girl. "I have never felt it, in its fulness. Never! I have sometimes wished that I could see you, or could see him—only once, dear father, only for one little minute—that I might know what it is I treasure up," she laid her hands upon her breast, "and hold here! That I might be sure and have it right! And sometimes (but then I was a child) I have wept in my prayers at night, to think that when your images ascended from my heart to Heaven, they might not be the true resemblance of yourselves. But I have never had these feelings long. They have passed away and left me tranquil and contented."

"And they will again," said Caleb.

"But, father! Oh my good, gentle father, bear with me, if I am wicked!" said the Blind Girl. "This is not the sorrow that so weighs me down!"

Her father could not choose but let his moist eyes overflow; she was so earnest and pathetic, but he did not understand her, yet.

"Bring her to me," said Bertha. "I cannot hold it closed and shut within myself. Bring her to me, father!"

She knew he hesitated, and said, "May. Bring May!"

May heard the mention of her name, and coming quietly towards her, touched her on the arm. The Blind Girl turned immediately, and held her by both hands.

"Look into my face, Dear heart, Sweet heart!" said Bertha. "Read it with your beautiful eyes, and tell me if the truth is written on it."

"Dear Bertha, Yes!"

The Blind Girl, still upturning the blank sightless face, down which the tears were coursing fast, addressed her in these words:

"There is not, in my soul, a wish or thought that is not for your good, bright May! There is not, in my soul, a grateful recollection stronger than the deep remembrance which is stored there, of the many many times when, in the full pride of sight and beauty, you have had consideration for Blind Bertha, even when we two were children, or when Bertha was as much a child as ever blindness can be! Every blessing on your head! Light upon your happy course! Not the less, my dear May;" and she drew towards her, in a closer grasp; "not the less, my bird, because, to-day, the knowledge that you are to be His wife has wrung my heart almost to breaking! Father, May, Mary! oh forgive me that it is so, for the sake of all he has done to relieve the weariness of my dark life: and for the sake of the belief you have in me, when I call Heaven to witness that I could not wish him married to a wife more worthy of his goodness!"

While speaking, she had released May Fielding's hands, and clasped her garments in an attitude of mingled supplication and love. Sinking lower and lower down, as she proceeded in her strange confession, she dropped at last at the feet of her friend, and hid her blind face in the folds of her dress.

"Great Power!" exclaimed her father, smitten at one blow with the truth, "have I deceived her from her cradle, but to break her heart at last?"

It was well for all of them that Dot, that beaming, useful, busy little Dot—for such she was, whatever faults she had, and however you may learn to hate her, in good time—it was well for all of them, I say, that she was there: or where this would have ended, it were hard to tell. But Dot, recovering her self-possession, interposed, before May could reply, or Caleb say another word.

"Come, come, dear Bertha! come away with me! Give her your arm, May. So! How composed she is, you see, already; and how good it is of her to mind us," said the cheery little woman, kissing her upon the forehead. "Come away, dear Bertha. Come! and here's her good father will come with her; won't you, Caleb? To—be—sure!"

Well, well! she was a noble little Dot in such things, and it must have been an obdurate nature that could have withstood her influence. When she had got poor Caleb and his Bertha away, that they might comfort and console each other, as she knew they only could, she presently came bouncing back,—the saying is, as fresh as any daisy; I say fresher—to mount guard over that bridling little piece of consequence in the cap and gloves, and prevent the dear old creature from making discoveries.

"So bring me the precious Baby, Tilly," said she, drawing a chair to the fire; "and while I have it in my lap, here's Mrs. Fielding, Tilly, will tell me all about the management of Babies, and put me right in twenty points where I'm as wrong as can be. Won't you, Mrs. Fielding?"

Not even the Welsh Giant, who, according to the popular expression, was so "slow" as to perform a fatal surgical operation upon himself, in emulation of a juggling-trick achieved by his arch-enemy at breakfast-time; not even he fell half so readily into the snare prepared for him, as the old lady did into this artful pitfall. The fact of Tackleton having walked out; and furthermore, of two or three people having been talking together at a distance, for two minutes, leaving her to her own resources; was quite enough to have put her on her dignity, and the bewailment of that mysterious convulsion in the Indigo Trade, for four-and-twenty hours. But this becoming deference to her experience, on the part of the young mother, was so irresistible, that after a short affectation of humility, she began to enlighten her with the best grace in the world; and sitting bolt upright before the wicked Dot, she did, in half an hour, deliver more infallible domestic recipes and precepts, than would (if acted on) have utterly destroyed and done up that Young Peerybingle, though he had been an Infant Samson.

To change the theme, Dot did a little needlework—she carried the contents of a whole workbox in her pocket; however she contrived it, I don't know—then did a little nursing; then a little more needlework; then had a little whispering chat with May, while the old lady dozed; and so in little bits of bustle, which was quite her manner always, found it a very short afternoon. Then, as it grew dark, and as it was a solemn part of this Institution of the Pic-Nic that she should perform all Bertha's household tasks, she trimmed the fire, and swept the hearth, and set the teaboard out, and drew the curtain, and lighted a candle. Then she played an air or two on a rude kind of harp, which Caleb had contrived for Bertha, and played them very well; for Nature had made her delicate little ear as choice a one for music as it would have been for jewels, if she had had any to wear. By this time it was the established hour for having tea; and Tackleton came back again, to share the meal, and spend the evening.

Caleb and Bertha had returned some time before, and Caleb had sat down to his afternoon's work. But he couldn't settle to it, poor fellow, being anxious and remorseful for his daughter. It was touching to see him sitting idle on his working-stool, regarding her so wistfully, and always saying in his face, "Have I deceived her from her cradle, but to break her heart!"

When it was night, and tea was done, and Dot had nothing more to do in washing up the cups and saucers; in a word—for I must come to it, and there is no use in putting it off—when the time drew nigh for expecting the Carrier's return in every sound of distant wheels, her manner changed again, her colour came and went, and she was very restless. Not as good wives are, when listening for their husbands. No, no, no. It was another sort of restlessness from that.

Wheels heard. A horse's feet. The barking of a dog. The gradual approach of all the sounds. The scratching paw of Boxer at the door!

"Whose step is that?" cried Bertha, starting up.

"Whose step?" returned the Carrier, standing in the portal, with his brown face ruddy as a winter berry from the keen night air. "Why, mine."

"The other step," said Bertha. "The man's tread behind you!"

"She is not to be deceived," observed the Carrier, laughing. "Come along, sir. You'll be welcome, never fear!"

He spoke in a loud tone; and as he spoke, the deaf old gentleman entered.

"He's not so much a stranger, that you haven't seen him once, Caleb," said the Carrier. "You'll give him house-room till we go?"

"Oh surely, John, and take it as an honour."

"He's the best company on earth, to talk secrets in," said John. "I have reasonable good lungs, but he tries 'em, I can tell you. Sit down, sir. All friends here, and glad to see you!"

When he had imparted this assurance, in a voice that amply corroborated what he had said about his lungs, he added in his natural tone, "A chair in the chimney-corner, and leave to sit quite silent and look pleasantly about him, is all he cares for. He's easily pleased."

Bertha had been listening intently. She called Caleb to her side, when he had set the chair, and asked him, in a low voice, to describe their visitor. When he had done so (truly now; with scrupulous fidelity), she moved, for the first time since he had come in, and sighed, and seemed to have no further interest concerning him.

The Carrier was in high spirits, good fellow that he was, and fonder of his little wife than ever.

"A clumsy Dot she was, this afternoon!" he said, encircling her with his rough arm, as she stood, removed from the rest; "and yet I like her somehow. See yonder, Dot!"

He pointed to the old man. She looked down. I think she trembled.

"He's—ha, ha ha!—he's full of admiration for you!" said the Carrier. "Talked of nothing else, the whole way here. Why, he's a brave old boy. I like him for it!"

"I wish he had had a better subject, John," she said, with an uneasy glance about the room. At Tackleton especially.

"A better subject!" cried the jovial John. "There's no such thing. Come, off with the great-coat, off with the thick shawl, off with the heavy wrappers! and a cosy half-hour by the fire! My humble service, Mistress. A game at cribbage, you and I? That's hearty. The cards and board, Dot. And a glass of beer here, if there's any left, small wife!"

His challenge was addressed to the old lady, who accepting it with gracious readiness, they were soon engaged upon the game. At first, the Carrier looked about him sometimes, with a smile, or now and then called Dot to peep over his shoulder at his hand, and advise him on some knotty point. But his adversary being a rigid disciplinarian, and subject to an occasional weakness in respect of pegging more than she was entitled to, required such vigilance on his part, as left him neither eyes nor ears to spare. Thus his whole attention gradually became absorbed upon the cards; and he thought of nothing else, until a hand upon his shoulder restored him to a consciousness of Tackleton.

"I am sorry to disturb you—but a word, directly."

"I'm going to deal," returned the Carrier. "It's a crisis."

"It is," said Tackleton. "Come here, man!"

There was that in his pale face which made the other rise immediately, and ask him, in a hurry, what the matter was.

"Hush! John Peerybingle," said Tackleton. "I am sorry for this. I am indeed. I have been afraid of it. I have suspected it from the first."

"What is it?" asked the Carrier, with a frightened aspect.

"Hush! I'll show you, if you'll come with me."

The Carrier accompanied him, without another word. They went across a yard, where the stars were shining, and by a little side-door, into Tackleton's own counting-house, where there was a glass window, commanding the ware-room, which was closed for the night. There was no light in the counting-house itself, but there were lamps in the long narrow ware-room; and consequently the window was bright.

"A moment!" said Tackleton. "Can you bear to look through that window, do you think?"

"Why not?" returned the Carrier.

"A moment more," said Tackleton. "Don't commit any violence. It's of no use. It's dangerous too. You're a strong-made man; and you might do murder before you know it."

The Carrier looked him in the face, and recoiled a step as if he had been struck. In one stride he was at the window, and he saw—

Oh Shadow on the Hearth! Oh truthful Cricket! Oh perfidious Wife!

He saw her, with the old man—old no longer, but erect and gallant—bearing in his hand the false white hair that had won his way into their desolate and miserable home. He saw her listening to him, as he bent his head to whisper in her ear; and suffering him to clasp her round the waist, as they moved slowly down the dim wooden gallery towards the door by which they had entered it. He saw them stop, and saw her turn—to have the face, the face he loved so, so presented to his view!—and saw her, with her own hands, adjust the lie upon his head, laughing, as she did it, at his unsuspicious nature!

He clenched his strong right hand at first, as if it would have beaten down a lion. But opening it immediately again, he spread it out before the eyes of Tackleton (for he was tender of her, even then), and so, as they passed out, fell down upon a desk, and was as weak as any infant.

He was wrapped up to the chin, and busy with his horse and parcels, when she came into the room, prepared for going home.

"Now, John, dear! Good night, May! Good night, Bertha!"

Could she kiss them? Could she be blithe and cheerful in her parting? Could she venture to reveal her face to them without a blush? Yes. Tackleton observed her closely, and she did all this.

Tilly was hushing the Baby, and she crossed and recrossed Tackleton, a dozen times, repeating drowsily:

"Did the knowledge that it was to be its wifes, then, wring its hearts almost to breaking; and did its fathers deceive it from its cradles but to break its hearts at last!"

"Now, Tilly, give me the Baby! Good night, Mr. Tackleton. Where's John, for goodness' sake?"

"He's going to walk beside the horse's head," said Tackleton, who helped her to her seat.

"My dear John. Walk? To-night?"

The muffled figure of her husband made a hasty sign in the affirmative; and the false stranger and the little nurse being in their places, the old horse moved off. Boxer, the unconscious Boxer, running on before, running back, running round and round the cart, and barking as triumphantly and merrily as ever.

When Tackleton had gone off likewise, escorting May and her mother home, poor Caleb sat down by the fire beside his daughter; anxious and remorseful at the core; and still saying in his wistful contemplation of her, "Have I deceived her from her cradle, but to break her heart at last!"

The toys that had been set in motion for the Baby, had all stopped, and run down, long ago. In the faint light and silence, the imperturbably calm dolls, the agitated rocking-horses with distended eyes and nostrils, the old gentlemen at the street-doors, standing half doubled up upon their failing knees and ankles, the wry-faced nut-crackers, the very Beasts upon their way into the Ark, in twos, like a Boarding School out walking, might have been imagined to be stricken motionless with fantastic wonder, at Dot being false, or Tackleton beloved, under any combination of circumstances.

CHIRP THE THIRD

The Dutch clock in the corner struck Ten, when the Carrier sat down by his fireside. So troubled and grief-worn, that he seemed to scare the Cuckoo, who having cut his ten melodious announcements as short as possible, plunged back into the Moorish Palace again, and clapped his little door behind him, as if the unwonted spectacle were too much for his feelings.

If the little Haymaker had been armed with the sharpest of scythes, and had cut at every stroke into the Carrier's heart, he never could have gashed and wounded it, as Dot had done.

It was a heart so full of love for her; so bound up and held together by innumerable threads of winning remembrance, spun from the daily working of her many qualities of endearment; it was a heart in which she had enshrined herself so gently and so closely; a heart so single and so earnest in its Truth, so strong in right, so weak in wrong; that it could cherish neither passion nor revenge at first, and had only room to hold the broken image of its Idol.

But, slowly, slowly, as the Carrier sat brooding on his hearth, now cold and dark, other and fiercer thoughts began to rise within him, as an angry wind comes rising in the night. The Stranger was neath his outraged roof. Three steps would take him to his chamber-door. One blow would beat it in. "You might do murder before you know it," Tackleton had said. How could it be murder, if he gave the villain time to grapple with him hand to hand! He was the younger man.

It was an ill-timed thought, bad for the dark mood of his mind. It was an angry thought, goading him to some avenging act, that should change the cheerful house into a haunted place which lonely travellers would dread to pass by night; and where the timid would see shadows struggling in the ruined windows when the moon was dim, and hear wild noises in the stormy weather.

He was the younger man! Yes, yes; some lover who had won the heart that *he* had never touched. Some lover of her early choice, of whom she had thought and dreamed, for whom she had pined and pined, when he had fancied her so happy by his side. O agony to think of it!

She had been above-stairs with the Baby, getting it to bed. As he sat brooding on the hearth, she came close beside him, without his knowledge—in the turning of the rack of his great misery, he lost all other sounds—and put her little stool at his feet. He only knew it, when he felt her hand upon his own, and saw her looking up into his face.

With wonder? No. It was his first impression, and he was fain to look at her again, to set it right. No, not with wonder. With an eager and inquiring look; but not with wonder. At first it was alarmed and serious; then, it changed into a strange, wild, dreadful smile of recognition of his thoughts; then, there was nothing but her clasped hands on her brow, and her bent head, and falling hair.

Though the power of Omnipotence had been his to wield at that moment, he had too much of its diviner property of Mercy in his breast, to have turned one feather's weight of it against her. But he could not bear to see her crouching down upon the little seat where he had often looked on her, with love and pride, so innocent and gay; and, when she rose and left him, sobbing as she went, he felt it a relief to have the vacant place beside him rather than her so long-cherished presence. This in itself was anguish keener than all, reminding him how desolate he was become, and how the great bond of his life was rent asunder.

The more he felt this, and the more he knew he could have better borne to see her lying prematurely dead before him with their little child upon her breast, the higher and the stronger rose his wrath against his enemy. He looked about him for a weapon.

There was a gun, hanging on the wall. He took it down, and moved a pace or two towards the door of the perfidious Stranger's room. He knew the gun was loaded. Some shadowy idea that it was just to shoot this man like a wild beast, seized him, and dilated in his mind until it grew into a monstrous demon in complete possession of him, casting out all milder thoughts and setting up its undivided empire.

That phrase is wrong. Not casting out his milder thoughts, but artfully transforming them. Changing them into scourges to drive him on. Turning water into blood, love into hate, gentleness into blind ferocity. Her image, sorrowing, humbled, but still pleading to his tenderness and mercy with resistless power, never left his mind; but, staying there, it urged him to the door; raised the weapon to his shoulder; fitted and nerved his finger to the trigger; and cried "Kill him! In his bed!"

He reversed the gun to beat the stock upon the door; he already held it lifted in the air; some indistinct design was in his thoughts of calling out to him to fly, for God's sake, by the window—

When, suddenly, the struggling fire illumined the whole chimney with a glow of light; and the Cricket on the Hearth began to Chirp!

No sound he could have heard, no human voice, not even hers, could so have moved and softened him. The artless words in which she had told him of her love for this same Cricket, were once more freshly spoken; her trembling, earnest manner at the moment, was again before him; her pleasant voice— O what a voice it was, for making household music at the fireside of an honest man!—thrilled through and through his better nature, and awoke it into life and action.

He recoiled from the door, like a man walking in his sleep, awakened from a frightful dream; and put the gun aside. Clasping his hands before his face, he then sat down again beside the fire, and found relief in tears.

The Cricket on the Hearth came out into the room, and stood in Fairy shape before him.

"'I love it,'" said the Fairy Voice, repeating what he well remembered, "'for the many times I have heard it, and the many thoughts its harmless music has given me.'"

"She said so!" cried the Carrier. "True!"

"'This has been a happy home, John; and I love the Cricket for its sake!'"

"It has been, Heaven knows," returned the Carrier. "She made it happy, always,—until now."

"So gracefully sweet-tempered; so domestic, joyful, busy, and light-hearted!" said the Voice.

"Otherwise I never could have loved her as I did," returned the Carrier.

The Voice, correcting him, said "do."

The Carrier repeated "as I did." But not firmly. His faltering tongue resisted his control, and would speak in its own way, for itself and him.

The Figure, in an attitude of invocation, raised its hand and said: "Upon your own hearth—"

"The hearth she has blighted," interposed the Carrier.

"The hearth she has—how often!—blessed and brightened," said the Cricket; "the hearth which, but for her, were only a few stones and bricks and rusty bars, but which has been, through her, the Altar of your Home; on which you have nightly sacrificed some petty passion, selfishness, or care, and offered up the homage of a tranquil mind, a trusting nature, and an overflowing heart; so that the smoke from this poor chimney has gone upward with a better fragrance than the richest incense that is burnt before the richest shrines in all the gaudy temples of this world!— Upon your own hearth; in its quiet sanctuary; surrounded by its gentle influences and associations; hear her! Hear me! Hear everything that speaks the language of your hearth and home!"

"And pleads for her?" inquired the Carrier.

"All things that speak the language of your hearth and home, *must* plead for her!" returned the Cricket. "For they speak the truth."

And while the Carrier, with his head upon his hands, continued to sit meditating in his chair, the Presence stood beside him, suggesting his reflections by its power, and presenting them before him, as in a glass or picture. It was not a solitary Presence. From the hearthstone, from the chimney, from the clock, the pipe, the kettle, and the cradle; from the floor, the walls, the ceiling, and the stairs; from the cart without and the cupboard within, and the household implements; from every thing and every place with which she had ever been familiar, and with which she had ever entwined one recollection of herself in her unhappy husband's mind; Fairies came trooping forth. Not to stand beside him as the Cricket did, but to busy and bestir themselves. To do all honour to her image. To pull him by the skirts, and point to it when it appeared. To cluster round it, and embrace it, and strew flowers for it to tread on. To try to crown its fair head with their tiny hands. To show that they were fond of it and loved it; and that there was not one ugly, wicked, or accusatory creature to claim knowledge of it—none but their playful and approving selves.

His thoughts were constant to her image. It was always there.

She sat plying her needle, before the fire, and singing to herself. Such a blithe, thriving, steady little Dot! The fairy figures turned upon him all at once, by one consent, with one prodigious concentrated stare, and seemed to say, "Is this the light wife you are mourning for?"

There were sounds of gaiety outside, musical instruments, and noisy tongues, and laughter. A crowd of young merrymakers came pouring in, among whom were May Fielding and a score of pretty girls. Dot was the fairest of them all; as young as any of them too. They came to summon her to join their party. It was a dance. If ever little foot were made for dancing, hers was, surely. But she laughed, and shook her head, and pointed to her cookery on the fire, and her table ready spread: with an exulting defiance that rendered her more charming than she was before. And so she merrily dismissed them, nodding to her would-be partners, one by one, as they passed, but with a comical indifference, enough to make them go and drown themselves immediately if they were her admirers—and they must have been so, more or less; they couldn't help it. And yet indifference was not her character. O no! For presently, there came a certain Carrier to the door; and bless her, what a welcome she bestowed upon him!

Again the staring figures turned upon him all at once, and seemed to say, "Is this the wife who has forsaken you?"

A shadow fell upon the mirror or the picture: call it what you will. A great shadow of the Stranger, as he first stood underneath their roof; covering its surface, and blotting out all other objects. But the nimble Fairies worked like bees to clear it off again. And Dot again was there. Still bright and beautiful.

Rocking her little Baby in its cradle, singing to it softly, and resting her head upon a shoulder which had its counterpart in the musing figure by which the Fairy Cricket stood.

The night—I mean the real night: not going by Fairy clocks— was wearing now; and in this stage of the Carrier's thoughts, the moon burst out, and shone brightly in the sky. Perhaps some calm and quiet light had risen also, in his mind; and he could think more soberly of what had happened.

Although the shadow of the Stranger fell at intervals upon the glass—always distinct, and big, and thoroughly defined—it never fell so darkly as at first. Whenever it appeared, the Fairies uttered a general cry of consternation, and plied their little arms and legs, with inconceivable activity, to rub it out. And whenever they got at Dot again, and showed her to him once more, bright and beautiful, they cheered in the most inspiring manner.

They never showed her, otherwise than beautiful and bright, for they were Household Spirits to whom falsehood is annihilation; and being so, what Dot was there for them, but the one active, beaming, pleasant little creature who had been the light and sun of the Carrier's Home!

The Fairies were prodigiously excited when they showed her, with the Baby, gossiping among a knot of sage old matrons, and affecting to be wondrous old and matronly herself, and leaning in a staid, demure old way upon her husband's arm, attempting—she! such a bud of a little woman—to convey the idea of having abjured the vanities of the world in general, and of being the sort of person to whom it was no novelty at all to be a mother; yet in the same breath, they showed her, laughing at the Carrier for being awkward, and pulling up his shirt-collar to make him smart, and mincing merrily about that very room to teach him how to dance!

They turned, and stared immensely at him when they showed her with the Blind Girl; for though she carried cheerfulness and animation with her wheresoever she went, she bore those influences into Caleb Plummer's home, heaped up and running over. The Blind Girl's love for her, and trust in her, and gratitude to her; her own good busy way of setting Bertha's thanks aside; her dexterous little arts for filling up each moment of the visit in doing something useful to the house, and really working hard while feigning to make holiday; her bountiful provision of those standing delicacies, the Veal and Ham Pie and the bottles of Beer; her radiant little face arriving at the door, and taking leave; the wonderful expression in her whole self, from her neat foot to the crown of her head, of being a part of the establishment—a something necessary to it, which it couldn't be without; all this the Fairies revelled in, and loved her for. And once again they looked upon him all at once, appealingly, and seemed to say, while some among them nestled in her dress and fondled her, "Is this the wife who has betrayed your confidence?"

More than once, or twice, or thrice, in the long thoughtful night, they showed her to him sitting on her favourite seat, with her bent head, her hands clasped on her brow, her falling hair. As he had seen her last. And when they found her thus, they neither turned nor looked upon him, but gathered close round her, and comforted and kissed her, and pressed on one another to show sympathy and kindness to her, and forgot him altogether.

Thus the night passed. The moon went down; the stars grew pale; the cold day broke; the sun rose. The Carrier still sat, musing in the chimney-corner. He had sat there, with his head upon his hands, all night. All night the faithful Cricket had been Chirp, Chirp, Chirping on the Hearth. All night he had listened to its voice. All night the household Fairies had been busy with him. All night she had been amiable and blameless in the glass, except when that one shadow fell upon it.

He rose up when it was broad day, and washed and dressed himself. He couldn't go about his customary cheerful avocations—he wanted spirit for them—but it mattered the less, that it was Tackleton's wedding-day, and he had arranged to make his rounds by proxy. He thought to have gone merrily to church with Dot. But such plans were at an end. It was their own wedding-day too. Ah! how little he had looked for such a close to such a year!

The Carrier had expected that Tackleton would pay him an early visit; and he was right. He had not walked to and fro before his own door, many minutes, when he saw the Toy-merchant coming in his chaise along the road. As the chaise drew nearer, he perceived that Tackleton was dressed out sprucely for his marriage, and that he had decorated his horse's head with flowers and favours.

The horse looked much more like a bridegroom than Tackleton, whose half-closed eye was more disagreeably expressive than ever. But the Carrier took little heed of this. His thoughts had other occupation.

"John Peerybingle!" said Tackleton, with an air of condolence. "My good fellow, how do you find yourself this morning?"

"I have had but a poor night, Master Tackleton," returned the Carrier, shaking his head: "for I have been a good deal disturbed in my mind. But it's over now! Can you spare me half an hour or so, for some private talk?"

"I came on purpose," returned Tackleton, alighting. "Never mind the horse. He'll stand quiet enough, with the reins over this post, if you'll give him a mouthful of hay."

The Carrier having brought it from his stable, and set it before him, they turned into the house.

"You are not married before noon," he said, "I think?"

"No," answered Tackleton. "Plenty of time. Plenty of time."

When they entered the kitchen, Tilly Slowboy was rapping at the Stranger's door; which was only removed from it by a few steps. One of her very red eyes (for Tilly had been crying all night long, because her mistress cried) was at the keyhole; and she was knocking very loud; and seemed frightened.

"If you please I can't make nobody hear," said Tilly, looking round. "I hope nobody an't gone and been and died if you please!"

This philanthropic wish, Miss Slowboy emphasised with various new raps and kicks at the door; which led to no result whatever.

"Shall I go?" said Tackleton. "It's curious."

The Carrier, who had turned his face from the door, signed to him to go if he would.

So Tackleton went to Tilly Slowboy's relief; and he too kicked and knocked; and he too failed to get the least reply. But he thought of trying the handle of the door; and as it opened easily, he peeped in, looked in, went in, and soon came running out again.

"John Peerybingle," said Tackleton, in his ear. "I hope there has been nothing—nothing rash in the night?"

The Carrier turned upon him quickly.

"Because he's gone!" said Tackleton; "and the window's open. I don't see any marks—to be sure it's almost on a level with the garden: but I was afraid there might have been some—some scuffle. Eh?"

He nearly shut up the expressive eye altogether; he looked at him so hard. And he gave his eye, and his face, and his whole person, a sharp twist. As if he would have screwed the truth out of him.

"Make yourself easy," said the Carrier. "He went into that room last night, without harm in word or deed from me, and no one has entered it since. He is away of his own free will. I'd go out gladly at that door, and beg my bread from house to house, for life, if I could so change the past that he had never come. But he has come and gone. And I have done with him!"

"Oh!— Well, I think he has got off pretty easy," said Tackleton, taking a chair.

The sneer was lost upon the Carrier, who sat down too, and shaded his face with his hand, for some little time, before proceeding.

"You showed me last night," he said at length, "my wife; my wife that I love; secretly—"

"And tenderly," insinuated Tackleton.

"Conniving at that man's disguise, and giving him opportunities of meeting her alone. I think there's no sight I wouldn't have rather seen than that. I think there's no man in the world I wouldn't have rather had to show it me."

"I confess to having had my suspicions always," said Tackleton. "And that has made me objectionable here, I know."

"But as you did show it me," pursued the Carrier, not minding him; "and as you saw her, my wife, my wife that I love"—his voice, and eye, and hand, grew steadier and firmer as he repeated these words: evidently in pursuance of a steadfast purpose—"as you saw her at this disadvantage, it is right and just that you should also see with my eyes, and look into my breast, and know what my mind is upon the subject. For it's settled," said the Carrier, regarding him attentively. "And nothing can shake it now."

Tackleton muttered a few general words of assent, about its being necessary to vindicate something or other; but he was overawed by the manner of his companion. Plain and unpolished as it was, it had a something dignified and noble in it, which nothing but the soul of generous honour dwelling in the man could have imparted.

"I am a plain, rough man," pursued the Carrier, "with very little to recommend me. I am not a clever man, as you very well know. I am not a young man. I loved my little Dot, because I had seen her grow up, from a child, in her father's house; because I knew how precious she was; because she had been my life, for years and years. There's many men I can't compare with, who never could have loved my little Dot like me, I think!"

He paused, and softly beat the ground a short time with his foot, before resuming.

"I often thought that though I wasn't good enough for her, I should make her a kind husband, and perhaps know her value better than another; and in this way I reconciled it to myself, and came to think it might be possible that we should be married. And in the end it came about, and we *were* married."

"Hah!" said Tackleton, with a significant shake of the head.

"I had studied myself; I had had experience of myself; I knew how much I loved her, and how happy I should be," pursued the Carrier. "But I had not—I feel it now—sufficiently considered her."

"To be sure," said Tackleton. "Giddiness, frivolity, fickleness, love of admiration! Not considered! All left out of sight! Hah!"

"You had best not interrupt me," said the Carrier, with some sternness, "till you understand me; and you're wide of doing so. If, yesterday, I'd have struck that man down at a blow, who dared to breathe a word against her, to-day I'd set foot upon his face, if he was my brother!"

The Toy-merchant gazed at him in astonishment. He went on in a softer tone:

"Did I consider," said the Carrier, "that I took her—at her age, and with her beauty—from her young companions, and the many scenes of which she was the ornament; in which she was the brightest little star that ever shone, to shut her up from day to day in my dull house, and keep my tedious company? Did I consider how little suited I was to her sprightly humour, and how wearisome a plodding man like me must be, to one of her quick spirit? Did I consider that it was no merit in me, or claim in me, that I loved her, when everybody must, who knew her? Never. I took advantage of her hopeful nature and her cheerful disposition; and I married her. I wish I never had! For her sake; not for mine!"

The Toy-merchant gazed at him, without winking. Even the half-shut eye was open now.

"Heaven bless her!" said the Carrier, "for the cheerful constancy with which she tried to keep the knowledge of this from me! And Heaven help me, that, in my slow mind, I have not found it out before! Poor child! Poor Dot! *I* not to find it out, who have seen her eyes fill with tears, when such a marriage as our own was spoken of! I, who have seen the secret trembling on her lips a hundred times, and never suspected it till last night! Poor girl! That I could ever hope she would be fond of me! That I could ever believe she was!"

"She made a show of it," said Tackleton. "She made such a show of it, that to tell you the truth it was the origin of my misgivings."

And here he asserted the superiority of May Fielding, who certainly made no sort of show of being fond of *him*.

"She has tried," said the poor Carrier, with greater emotion than he had exhibited yet; "I only now begin to know how hard she has tried, to be my dutiful and zealous wife. How good she has been; how much she has done; how brave and strong a heart she has; let the happiness I have known under this roof bear witness! It will be some help and comfort to me, when I am here alone."

"Here alone?" said Tackleton. "Oh! Then you do mean to take some notice of this?"

"I mean," returned the Carrier, "to do her the greatest kindness, and make her the best reparation, in my power. I can release her from the daily pain of an unequal marriage, and the struggle to conceal it. She shall be as free as I can render her."

"Make *her* reparation!" exclaimed Tackleton, twisting and turning his great ears with his hands. "There must be something wrong here. You didn't say that, of course."

The Carrier set his grip upon the collar of the Toy-merchant, and shook him like a reed.

"Listen to me!" he said. "And take care that you hear me right. Listen to me. Do I speak plainly?"

"Very plainly indeed," answered Tackleton.

"As if I meant it?"

"Very much as if you meant it."

"I sat upon that hearth, last night, all night," exclaimed the Carrier. "On the spot where she has often sat beside me, with her sweet face looking into mine. I called up her whole life, day by day. I had her dear self, in its every passage, in review before me. And upon my soul she is innocent, if there is One to judge the innocent and guilty!"

Staunch Cricket on the Hearth! Loyal household Fairies!

"Passion and distrust have left me!" said the Carrier; "and nothing but my grief remains. In an unhappy moment some old lover, better suited to her tastes and years than I; forsaken, perhaps, for me, against her will; returned. In an unhappy moment, taken by surprise, and wanting time to think of what she did, she made herself a party to his treachery, by concealing it. Last night she saw him, in the interview we witnessed. It was wrong. But otherwise than this she is innocent if there is truth on earth!"

"If that is your opinion"—Tackleton began.

"So, let her go!" pursued the Carrier. "Go, with my blessing for the many happy hours she has given me, and my forgiveness for any pang she has caused me. Let her go, and have the peace of mind I wish her! She'll never hate me. She'll learn to like me better, when I'm not a drag upon her, and she wears the chain I have riveted, more lightly. This is the day on which I took her, with so little thought for her enjoyment, from her home. Today she shall return to it, and I will trouble her no more. Her father and mother will be here to-day—we had made a little plan for keeping it together—and they shall take her home. I can trust her, there, or anywhere. She leaves me without blame, and she will live so I am sure. If I should die—I may perhaps while she is still young; I have lost some courage in a few hours—

she'll find that I remembered her, and loved her to the last! This is the end of what you showed me. Now, it's over!"

"O no, John, not over. Do not say it's over yet! Not quite yet. I have heard your noble words. I could not steal away, pretending to be ignorant of what has affected me with such deep gratitude. Do not say it's over, 'till the clock has struck again!"

She had entered shortly after Tackleton, and had remained there. She never looked at Tackleton, but fixed her eyes upon her husband. But she kept away from him, setting as wide a space as possible between them; and though she spoke with most impassioned earnestness, she went no nearer to him even then. How different in this from her old self!

"No hand can make the clock which will strike again for me the hours that are gone," replied the Carrier, with a faint smile. "But let it be so, if you will, my dear. It will strike soon. It's of little matter what we say. I'd try to please you in a harder case than that."

"Well!" muttered Tackleton. "I must be off, for when the clock strikes again, it'll be necessary for me to be upon my way to church. Good morning, John Peerybingle. I'm sorry to be deprived of the pleasure of your company. Sorry for the loss, and the occasion of it too!"

"I have spoken plainly?" said the Carrier, accompanying him to the door.

"Oh, quite!"

"And you'll remember what I have said?"

"Why, if you compel me to make the observation," said Tackleton, previously taking the precaution of getting into his chaise; "I must say that it was so very unexpected, that I'm far from being likely to forget it."

"The better for us both," returned the Carrier. "Good bye. I give you joy!"

"I wish I could give it to *you*," said Tackleton. "As I can't; thank'ee. Between ourselves (as I told you before, eh?), I don't much think I shall have the less joy in my married life, because May hasn't been too officious about me, and too demonstrative. Good bye! Take care of yourself."

The Carrier stood looking after him until he was smaller in the distance than his horse's flowers and favours near at hand; and then, with a deep sigh, went strolling like a restless, broken man, among some neighbouring elms; unwilling to return until the clock was on the eve of striking.

His little wife, being left alone, sobbed piteously; but often dried her eyes and checked herself, to say how good he was, how excellent he was! and once or twice she laughed; so heartily, triumphantly, and incoherently (still crying all the time), that Tilly was quite horrified.

"Ow if you please don't!" said Tilly. "It's enough to dead and bury the Baby, so it is if you please."

"Will you bring him sometimes, to see his father, Tilly," inquired her mistress, drying her eyes; "when I can't live here, and have gone to my old home?"

"Ow if you please don't!" cried Tilly, throwing back her head, and bursting out into a howl—she looked at the moment uncommonly like Boxer. "Ow if you please don't! Ow, what has everybody gone and been and done with everybody, making everybody else so wretched! Ow-w-w-w!"

The soft-hearted Slowboy trailed off at this juncture, into such a deplorable howl, the more tremendous from its long suppression, that she must infallibly have awakened the Baby, and frightened him into something serious (probably convulsions), if her eyes had not encountered Caleb Plummer, leading in his daughter. This spectacle restoring her to a sense of the proprieties, she stood for some few moments silent, with her mouth wide open; and then, posting off to the bed on which the Baby lay asleep, danced in a weird, Saint Vitus manner on the floor, and at the same time rummaged with her face and head among the bed-clothes, apparently deriving much relief from those extraordinary operations.

"Mary!" said Bertha. "Not at the marriage!"

"I told her you would not be there, mum," whispered Caleb. "I heard as much last night. But bless you," said the little man, taking her tenderly by both hands, "I don't care for what they say. I don't believe them. There an't much of me, but that little should be torn to pieces sooner than I'd trust a word against you!"

He put his arms about her and hugged her, as a child might have hugged one of his own dolls.

"Bertha couldn't stay at home this morning," said Caleb. "She was afraid, I know, to hear the bells ring, and couldn't trust herself to be so near them on their wedding-day. So we started in good time, and came here. I have been thinking of what I have done," said Caleb, after a moment's pause; "I have been blaming myself till I hardly knew what to do or where to turn, for the distress of mind I have caused her; and I've come to the conclusion that I'd better, if you'll stay with me, mum, the while, tell her the truth. You'll stay with me the while?" he inquired, trembling from head to foot. "I don't know what effect it may have upon her; I don't know what she'll think of me; I don't know that she'll ever care for her poor father afterwards. But it's best for her that she should be undeceived, and I must bear the consequences as I deserve!"

"Mary," said Bertha, "where is your hand! Ah! Here it is; here it is!" pressing it to her lips, with a smile, and drawing it through her arm. "I heard them speaking softly among themselves, last night, of some blame against you. They were wrong."

The Carrier's wife was silent. Caleb answered for her.

"They were wrong," he said.

"I knew it!" cried Bertha, proudly. "I told them so. I scorned to hear a word! Blame *her* with justice!" she pressed the hand between her own, and the soft cheek against her face. "No! I am not so blind as that."

Her father went on one side of her, while Dot remained upon the other: holding her hand.

"I know you all," said Bertha, "better than you think. But none so well as her. Not even you, father. There is nothing half so real and so true about me, as she is. If I could be restored to sight this instant, and not a word were spoken, I could choose her from a crowd! My sister!"

"Bertha, my dear!" said Caleb, "I have something on my mind I want to tell you, while we three are alone. Hear me kindly! I have a confession to make to you, my darling."

"A confession, father?"

"I have wandered from the truth and lost myself, my child," said Caleb, with a pitiable expression in his bewildered face. "I have wandered from the truth, intending to be kind to you; and have been cruel."

She turned her wonder-stricken face towards him, and repeated "Cruel!"

"He accuses himself too strongly, Bertha," said Dot. "You'll say so, presently. You'll be the first to tell him so."

"He cruel to me!" cried Bertha, with a smile of incredulity.

"Not meaning it, my child," said Caleb. "But I have been; though I never suspected it, till yesterday. My dear blind daughter, hear me and forgive me! The world you live in, heart of mine, doesn't exist as I have represented it. The eyes you have trusted in, have been false to you."

She turned her wonder-stricken face towards him still; but drew back, and clung closer to her friend.

"Your road in life was rough, my poor one," said Caleb, "and I meant to smooth it for you. I have altered objects, changed the characters of people, invented many things that never have been, to make you happier. I have had concealments from you, put deceptions on you, God forgive me! and surrounded you with fancies."

"But living people are not fancies!" she said hurriedly, and turning very pale, and still retiring from him. "You can't change them."

"I have done so, Bertha," pleaded Caleb. "There is one person that you know, my dove—"

"Oh father! why do you say, I know?" she answered, in a term of keen reproach. "What and whom do I know! I who have no leader! I so miserably blind."

In the anguish of her heart, she stretched out her hands, as if she were groping her way; then spread them, in a manner most forlorn and sad, upon her face.

"The marriage that takes place to-day," said Caleb, "is with a stern, sordid, grinding man. A hard master to you and me, my dear, for many years. Ugly in his looks, and in his nature. Cold and callous always. Unlike what I have painted him to you in everything, my child. In everything."

"Oh why," cried the Blind Girl, tortured, as it seemed, almost beyond endurance, "why did you ever do this? Why did you ever fill my heart so full, and then come in like Death, and tear away the objects of my love? O Heaven, how blind I am! How helpless and alone!"

Her afflicted father hung his head, and offered no reply but in his penitence and sorrow.

She had been but a short time in this passion of regret, when the Cricket on the Hearth, unheard by all but her, began to chirp. Not merrily, but in a low, faint, sorrowing way. It was so mournful that her tears began to flow; and when the Presence which had been beside the Carrier all night, appeared behind her, pointing to her father, they fell down like rain.

She heard the Cricket-voice more plainly soon, and was conscious, through her blindness, of the Presence hovering about her father.

"Mary," said the Blind Girl, "tell me what my home is. What it truly is."

"It is a poor place, Bertha; very poor and bare indeed. The house will scarcely keep out wind and rain another winter. It is roughly shielded from the weather, Bertha," Dot continued in a low, clear voice, "as your poor father in his sack-cloth coat."

The Blind Girl, greatly agitated, rose, and led the Carrier's little wife aside.

"Those presents that I took such care of; that came almost at my wish, and were so dearly welcome to me," she said, trembling; "where did they come from? Did you send them?"

"No."

"Who then?"

Dot saw she knew, already, and was silent. The Blind Girl spread her hands before her face again. But in quite another manner now.

"Dear Mary, a moment. One moment? More this way. Speak softly to me. You are true, I know. You'd not deceive me now; would you?"

"No, Bertha, indeed!"

"No, I am sure you would not. You have too much pity for me.

Mary, look across the room to where we were just now—to where my father is—my father, so compassionate and loving to me—and tell me what you see."

"I see," said Dot, who understood her well, "an old man sitting in a chair, and leaning sorrowfully on the back, with his face resting on his hand. As if his child should comfort him, Bertha."

"Yes, yes. She will. Go on."

"He is an old man, worn with care and work. He is a spare, dejected, thoughtful, grey-haired man. I see him now, despondent and bowed down, and striving against nothing. But, Bertha, I have seen him many times before, and striving hard in many ways for one great sacred object. And I honour his grey head, and bless him!"

The Blind Girl broke away from her; and throwing herself upon her knees before him, took the grey head to her breast.

"It is my sight restored. It is my sight!" she cried. "I have been blind, and now my eyes are open. I never knew him! To think I might have died, and never truly seen the father who has been so loving to me!"

There were no words for Caleb's emotion.

"There is not a gallant figure on this earth," exclaimed the Blind Girl, holding him in her embrace, "that I would love so dearly, and would cherish so devotedly, as this! The greyer, and more worn, the dearer, father! Never let them say I am blind again. There's not a furrow in his face, there's not a hair upon his head, that shall be forgotten in my prayers and thanks to Heaven!"

Caleb managed to articulate "My Bertha!"

"And in my blindness, I believed him," said the girl, caressing him with tears of exquisite affection, "to be so different! And having him beside me, day by day, so mindful of me always, never dreamed of this!"

"The fresh smart father in the blue coat, Bertha," said poor Caleb. "He's gone!"

"Nothing is gone," she answered. "Dearest father, no! Everything is here—in you. The father that I loved so well; the father that I never loved enough, and never knew; the benefactor whom I first began to reverence and love, because he had such sympathy for me; all are here in you. Nothing is dead to me. The soul of all that was most dear to me is here—here, with the worn face, and the grey head. And I am NOT blind, father, any longer!"

Dot's whole attention had been concentrated, during this discourse, upon the father and daughter; but looking, now, towards the little Haymaker in the Moorish meadow, she saw that the clock was within a few minutes of striking, and fell, immediately, into a nervous and excited state.

"Father," said Bertha, hesitating. "Mary."

"Yes, my dear," returned Caleb. "Here she is."

There is no change in *her*. You never told me anything of *her* that was not true?"

"I should have done it, my dear, I am afraid," returned Caleb, "if I could have made her better than she was. But I must have changed her for the worse, if I had changed her at all. Nothing could improve her, Bertha."

Confident as the Blind Girl had been when she asked the question, her delight and pride in the reply and her renewed embrace of Dot, were charming to behold.

"More changes than you think for, may happen though, my dear," said Dot. "Changes for the better, I mean; changes for great joy to some of us. You mustn't let them startle you too much, if any such should ever happen, and affect you. Are those wheels upon the road? You've a quick ear, Bertha. Are they wheels?"

"Yes. Coming very fast."

"I—I—I know you have a quick ear," said Dot, placing her hand upon her heart, and evidently talking on, as fast as she could to hide its palpitating state, "because I have noticed it often, and because you were so quick to find out that strange step last night. Though why you should have said, as I very well recollect you did say, Bertha, "Whose step is that!" and why you should have taken any greater observation of it than of any other step, I don't know. Though as I said just now, there are great changes in the world: great changes: and we can't do better than prepare ourselves to be surprised at hardly anything."

Caleb wondered what this meant; perceiving that she spoke to him, no less than to his daughter. He saw her, with astonishment, so fluttered and distressed that she could scarcely breathe; and holding to a chair, to save herself from falling.

"They are wheels indeed!" she panted. "Coming nearer! Nearer! Very close! And now you hear them stopping at the garden-gate! And now you hear a step outside the door—the same step, Bertha, is it not!—and now!"—

She uttered a wild cry of uncontrollable delight; and running up to Caleb put her hands upon his eyes, as a young man rushed into the room, and flinging away his hat into the air, came sweeping down upon them.

"Is it over?" cried Dot.

"Yes!"

"Happily over?"

"Yes!"

"Do you recollect the voice, dear Caleb? Did you ever hear the like of it before?" cried Dot.

"If my boy in the Golden South Americas was alive"—said Caleb, trembling.

"He is alive!" shrieked Dot, removing her hands from his eyes, and clapping them in ecstasy; "look at him! See where he stands before you, healthy and strong! Your own dear son! Your own dear living, loving brother, Bertha!"

All honour to the little creature for her transports! All honour to her tears and laughter, when the three were locked in one another's arms! All honour to the heartiness with which she met the sunburnt sailor-fellow, with his dark streaming hair, half-way, and never turned her rosy little mouth aside, but suffered him to kiss it, freely, and to press her to his bounding heart!

And honour to the Cuckoo too—why not!—for bursting out of the trap-door in the Moorish Palace like a house-breaker, and hiccoughing twelve times on the assembled company, as if he had got drunk for joy!

The Carrier, entering, started back. And well he might, to find himself in such good company.

"Look, John!" said Caleb, exultingly, "look here! My own boy from the Golden South Americas! My own son! Him that you fitted out, and sent away yourself! Him that you were always such a friend to!"

The Carrier advanced to seize him by the hand; but, recoiling, as some feature in his face awakened a remembrance of the Deaf Man in the Cart, said:

"Edward! Was it you?"

"Now tell him all!" cried Dot. "Tell him all, Edward; and don't spare me, for nothing shall make me spare myself in his eyes, ever again."

"I was the man," said Edward.

"And could you steal, disguised, into the house of your old friend?" rejoined the Carrier. "There was a frank boy once—how many years is it, Caleb, since we heard that he was dead, and had it proved, we thought?—who never would have done that."

"There was a generous friend of mine, once; more a father to me than a friend;" said Edward, "who never would have judged me, or any other man, unheard. You were he. So I am certain you will hear me now."

The Carrier, with a troubled glance at Dot, who still kept far away from him, replied, "Well! that's but fair. I will."

"You must know that when I left here, a boy," said Edward, "I was in love, and my love was returned. She was a very young girl, who perhaps (you may tell me) didn't know her own mind. But I knew mine, and I had a passion for her."

"You had!" exclaimed the Carrier. "You!"

"Indeed I had," returned the other. "And she returned it. I have ever since believed she did, and now I am sure she did."

"Heaven help me!" said the Carrier. "This is worse than all."

"Constant to her," said Edward, "and returning, full of hope, after many hardships and perils, to redeem my part of our old contract, I heard, twenty miles away, that she was false to me; that she had forgotten me; and had bestowed herself upon another and a richer man. I had no mind to reproach her; but I wished to see her, and to prove beyond dispute that this was true. I hoped she might have been forced into it, against her own desire and recollection. It would be small comfort, but it would be some, I thought, and on I came. That I might have the truth, the real truth; observing freely for myself, and judging for myself, without obstruction on the one hand, or presenting my own influence (if I had any) before her, on the other; I dressed myself unlike myself—you know how; and waited on the road—you know where. You had no suspicion of me; neither had—had she," pointing to Dot, "until I whispered in her ear at that fireside, and she so nearly betrayed me."

"But when she knew that Edward was alive, and had come back," sobbed Dot, now speaking for herself, as she had burned to do, all through this narrative; "and when she knew his purpose, she advised him by all means to keep his secret close; for his old friend John Peerybingle was much too open in his nature, and too clumsy in all artifice—being a clumsy man in general," said Dot, half laughing and half crying—"to keep it for him. And when she—that's me, John," sobbed the little woman—"told him all, and how his sweetheart had believed him to be dead; and how she had at last been over-persuaded by her mother into a marriage which the silly, dear old thing called advantageous; and when she—that's me again, John—told him they were not yet married (though close upon it), and that it would be nothing but a sacrifice if it went on, for there was no love on her side; and when he went nearly mad with joy to hear it; then she—that's me again—said she would go between them, as she had often done before in old times, John, and would sound his sweetheart and be sure that what she—me again, John—said and thought was right. And it was right, John! And they were brought together, John! And they were married, John, an hour ago! And here's the Bride! And Gruff and Tackleton may die a bachelor! And I'm a happy little woman, May, God bless you!"

She was an irresistible little woman, if that be anything to the purpose; and never so completely irresistible as in her present transports. There never were congratulations so endearing and delicious, as those she lavished on herself and on the Bride.

Amid the tumult of emotions in his breast, the honest Carrier had stood confounded. Flying, now, towards her, Dot stretched out her hand to stop him, and retreated as before.

"No, John, no! Hear all! Don't love me any more, John, till you've heard every word I have to say. It was wrong to have a secret from you,

John. I'm very sorry. I didn't think it any harm, till I came and sat down by you on the little stool last night. But when I knew by what was written in your face, that you had seen me walking in the gallery with Edward, and when I knew what you thought, I felt how giddy and how wrong it was. But oh, dear John, how could you, could you, think so!"

Little woman, how she sobbed again! John Peerybingle would have caught her in his arms. But no; she wouldn't let him.

"Don't love me yet, please John! Not for a long time yet! When I was sad about this intended marriage, dear, it was because I remembered May and Edward such young lovers; and knew that her heart was far away from Tackleton. You believe that, now. Don't you, John?"

John was going to make another rush at this appeal; but she stopped him again.

"No; keep there, please, John! When I laugh at you, as I sometimes do, John, and call you clumsy and a dear old goose, and names of that sort, it's because I love you, John, so well, and take such pleasure in your ways, and wouldn't see you altered in the least respect to have you made a King to-morrow."

"Hooroar!" said Caleb with unusual vigour. "My opinion!"

"And when I speak of people being middle-aged, and steady, John, and pretend that we are a humdrum couple, going on in a jog-trot sort of way, it's only because I'm such a silly little thing, John, that I like, sometimes, to act a kind of Play with Baby, and all that: and make believe."

She saw that he was coming; and stopped him again. But she was very nearly too late.

"No, don't love me for another minute or two, if you please, John! What I want most to tell you, I have kept to the last. My dear, good, generous John, when we were talking the other night about the Cricket, I had it on my lips to say, that at first I did not love you quite so dearly as I do now; that when I first came home here, I was half afraid I mightn't learn to love you every bit as well as I hoped and prayed I might—being so very young, John! But, dear John, every day and hour I loved you more and more. And if I could have loved you better than I do, the noble words I heard you say this morning, would have made me. But I can't. All the affection that I had (it was a great deal, John) I gave you, as you well deserve, long, long ago, and I have no more left to give. Now, my dear husband, take me to your heart again! That's my home, John; and never, never think of sending me to any other!"

You never will derive so much delight from seeing a glorious little woman in the arms of a third party, as you would have felt if you had seen Dot run into the Carrier's embrace. It was the most complete, unmitigated, soul-fraught little piece of earnestness that ever you beheld in all your days.

You may be sure the Carrier was in a state of perfect rapture; and you may be sure Dot was likewise; and you may be sure they all were, inclusive of Miss Slowboy, who wept copiously for joy, and wishing to include her young charge in the general interchange of congratulations, handed round the Baby to everybody in succession, as if it were something to drink.

But, now, the sound of wheels was heard again outside the door; and somebody exclaimed that Gruff and Tackleton was coming back. Speedily that worthy gentleman appeared, looking warm and flustered.

"Why, what the Devil's this, John Peerybingle!" said Tackleton. "There's some mistake. I appointed Mrs. Tackleton to meet me at the church, and I'll swear I passed her on the road, on her way here. Oh! here she is! I beg your pardon, sir; I haven't the pleasure of knowing you; but if you can do me the favour to spare this young lady, she has rather a particular engagement this morning."

"But I can't spare her," returned Edward. "I couldn't think of it."

"What do you mean, you vagabond?" said Tackleton.

"I mean, that as I can make allowance for your being vexed," returned the other, with a smile, "I am as deaf to harsh discourse this morning, as I was to all discourse last night."

The look that Tackleton bestowed upon him, and the start he gave!

"I am sorry, sir," said Edward, holding out May's left hand, and especially the third finger; "that the young lady can't accompany you to church; but as she has been there once this morning, perhaps you'll excuse her."

Tackleton looked hard at the third finger, and took a little piece of silver-paper, apparently containing a ring, from his waistcoat-pocket.

"Miss Slowboy," said Tackleton. "Will you have the kindness to throw that in the fire? Thank'ee."

"It was a previous engagement, quite an old engagement, that prevented my wife from keeping her appointment with you, I assure you," said Edward.

"Mr. Tackleton will do me the justice to acknowledge that I revealed it to him faithfully; and that I told him, many times, I never could forget it," said May, blushing.

"Oh certainly!" said Tackleton. "Oh to be sure. Oh it's all right. It's quite correct. Mrs. Edward Plummer, I infer?"

"That's the name," returned the bridegroom.

"Ah, I shouldn't have known you, sir," said Tackleton, scrutinising his face narrowly, and making a low bow. "I give you joy, sir!"

"Thank'ee."

"Mrs. Peerybingle," said Tackleton, turning suddenly to where she stood with her husband; "I am sorry. You haven't done me a very great kindness, but, upon my life I am sorry. You are better than I thought you. John Peerybingle, I am sorry. You understand me; that's enough. It's quite correct, ladies and gentlemen all, and perfectly satisfactory. Good morning!"

With these words he carried it off, and carried himself off too: merely stopping at the door, to take the flowers and favours from his horse's head, and to kick that animal once, in the ribs, as a means of informing him that there was a screw loose in his arrangements.

Of course it became a serious duty now, to make such a day of it, as should mark these events for a high Feast and Festival in the Peerybingle Calendar for evermore. Accordingly, Dot went to work to produce such an entertainment, as should reflect undying honour on the house and on every one concerned; and in a very short space of time, she was up to her dimpled elbows in flour, and whitening the Carrier's coat, every time he came near her, by stopping him to give him a kiss. That good fellow washed the greens, and peeled the turnips, and broke the plates, and upset iron pots full of cold water on the fire, and made himself useful in all sorts of ways: while a couple of professional assistants, hastily called in from somewhere in the neighbourhood, as on a point of life or death, ran against each other in all the doorways and round all the corners, and everybody tumbled over Tilly Slowboy and the Baby, everywhere. Tilly never came out in such force before. Her ubiquity was the theme of general admiration. She was a stumbling-block in the passage at five-and-twenty minutes past two; a man-trap in the kitchen at half-past two precisely; and a pitfull in the garret at five-and-twenty minutes to three. The Baby's head was, as it were, a test and touchstone for every description of matter,—animal, vegetable, and mineral. Nothing was in use that day that didn't come, at some time or other, into close acquaintance with it.

Then, there was a great Expedition set on foot to go and find out Mrs. Fielding; and to be dismally penitent to that excellent gentlewoman; and to bring her back, by force, if needful, to be happy and forgiving. And when the Expedition first discovered her, she would listen to no terms at all, but said, an unspeakable number of times, that ever she should have lived to see the day! and couldn't be got to say anything else, except, "Now carry me to the grave:" which seemed absurd, on account of her not being dead, or anything at all like it. After a time, she lapsed into a state of dreadful calmness, and observed, that when that unfortunate train of circumstances had occurred in the Indigo Trade, she had foreseen that she would be exposed, during her whole life, to every piece of insult and contumely; and that she was glad to find it was the case; and begged they wouldn't trouble themselves about her,—for what was she? oh, dear! a nobody! —but would forget that such a being lived, and would take their course

in life without her. From this bitterly sarcastic mood, she passed into
an angry one, in which she gave vent to the remarkable expression that
the worm would turn if trodden on; and, after that, she yielded to a
soft regret, and said, if they had only given her their confidence, what
might she not have had it in her power to suggest! Taking advantage of
this crisis in her feelings, the Expedition embraced her; and she very
soon had her gloves on, and was on her way to John Peerybingle's in
a state of unimpeachable gentility; with a paper parcel at her side containing a cap of state, almost as tall, and quite as stiff, as a mitre.

Then, there were Dot's father and mother to come, in another little
chaise; and they were behind their time; and fears were entertained;
and there was much looking out for them down the road; and Mrs.
Fielding always would look in the wrong and morally impossible direction; and being apprised thereof hoped she might take the liberty of
looking where she pleased. At last they came: a chubby little couple,
jogging along in a snug and comfortable little way that quite belonged
to the Dot family; and Dot and her mother, side by side, were wonderful to see. They were so like each other.

Then, Dot's mother had to renew her acquaintance with May's
mother; and May's mother always stood on her gentility; and Dot's
mother never stood on anything but her active little feet. And old Dot
—so to call Dot's father, I forgot it wasn't his right name, but never
mind—took liberties, and shook hands at first sight, and seemed to
think a cap but so much starch and muslin, and didn't defer himself
at all to the Indigo Trade, but said there was no help for it now; and,
in Mrs. Fielding's summing up, was a good-natured kind of man—but
coarse, my dear.

I wouldn't have missed Dot, doing the honours in her wedding-
gown, my benison on her bright face! for any money. No! nor the
good Carrier, so jovial and so ruddy, at the bottom of the table. Nor
the brown, fresh sailor-fellow, and his handsome wife. Nor any one
among them. To have missed the dinner would have been to miss as
jolly and as stout a meal as man need eat; and to have missed the overflowing cups in which they drank The Wedding-Day, would have been
the greatest miss of all.

After dinner, Caleb sang the song about the Sparkling Bowl. As I'm
a living man, hoping to keep so, for a year or two, he sang it through.

And, by the by, a most unlooked-for incident occurred, just as he
finished the last verse.

There was a tap at the door; and a man came staggering in, without
saying with your leave, or by your leave, with something heavy on his
head. Setting this down in the middle of the table, symmetrically in
the centre of the nuts and apples, he said:

"Mr. Tackleton's compliments, and as he hasn't got no use for the
cake himself, p'raps you'll eat it."

And with those words he walked off.

There was some surprise among the company, as you may imagine. Mrs. Fielding, being a lady of infinite discernment, suggested that the cake was poisoned, and related a narrative of a cake, which, within her knowledge, had turned a seminary for young ladies, blue. But she was overruled by acclamation; and the cake was cut by May, with much ceremony and rejoicing.

I don't think any one had tasted it, when there came another tap at the door, and the same man appeared again, having under his arm a vast brown-paper parcel.

"Mr. Tackleton's compliments, and he's sent a few toys for the Babby. They ain't ugly."

After the delivery of which expressions, he retired again.

The whole party would have experienced great difficulty in finding words for their astonishment, even if they had had ample time to seek them. But they had none at all; for the messenger had scarcely shut the door behind him, when there came another tap, and Tackleton himself walked in.

"Mrs. Peerybingle!" said the Toy-merchant, hat in hand. "I'm sorry. I'm more sorry than I was this morning. I have had time to think of it. John Peerybingle! I'm sour by disposition; but I can't help being sweetened, more or less, by coming face to face with such a man as you. Caleb! This unconscious little nurse gave me a broken hint last night, of which I have found the thread. I blush to think how easily I might have bound you and your daughter to me, and what a miserable idiot I was, when I took her for one! Friends, one and all, my house is very lonely to-night. I have not so much as a Cricket on my Hearth. I have scared them all away. Be gracious to me; let me join this happy party!"

He was at home in five minutes. You never saw such a fellow. What *had* he been doing with himself all his life, never to have known, before, his great capacity of being jovial! Or what had the Fairies been doing with him, to have effected such a change!

"John! you won't send me home this evening; will you?" whispered Dot.

He had been very near it though!

There wanted but one living creature to make the party complete; and, in the twinkling of an eye, there he was, very thirsty with hard running, and engaged in hopeless endeavours to squeeze his head into a narrow pitcher. He had gone with the cart to its journey's end, very much disgusted with the absence of his master, and stupendously rebellious to the Deputy. After lingering about the stable for some little time, vainly attempting to incite the old horse to the mutinous act of returning on his own account, he had walked into the tap-room and laid himself down before the fire. But suddenly yielding to the conviction that the Deputy was a humbug, and must be abandoned, he had got up again, turned tail, and come home.

There was a dance in the evening. With which general mention of that recreation, I should have left it alone, if I had not some reason to suppose that it was quite an original dance, and one of a most uncommon figure. It was formed in an odd way; in this way. Edward, that sailor-fellow—a good free dashing sort of a fellow he was—had been telling them various marvels concerning parrots, and mines, and Mexicans, and gold dust, when all at once he took it in his head to jump up from his seat and propose a dance; for Bertha's harp was there, and she had such a hand upon it as you seldom hear. Dot (sly little piece of affectation when she chose) said her dancing days were over; I think because the Carrier was smoking his pipe, and she liked sitting by him, best. Mrs. Fielding had no choice, of course, but to say her dancing days were over, after that; and everybody said the same, except May; May was ready.

So, May and Edward get up, amid great applause, to dance alone; and Bertha plays her liveliest tune.

Well! if you'll believe me, they have not been dancing five minutes, when suddenly the Carrier flings his pipe away, takes Dot round the waist, dashes out into the room, and starts off with her, toe and heel, quite wonderfully. Tackleton no sooner sees this, than he skims across to Mrs. Fielding, takes her round the waist, and follows suit. Old Dot no sooner sees this, than up he is, all alive, whisks off Mrs. Dot in the middle of the dance, and is the foremost there. Caleb no sooner sees this, than he clutches Tilly Slowboy by both hands and goes off at score; Miss Slowboy, firm in the belief that diving hotly in among the other couples, and effecting any number of concussions with them, is your only principle of footing it.

Hark! how the Cricket joins the music with its Chirp, Chirp, Chirp; and how the kettle hums!

But what is this! even as I listen to them, blithely, and turn towards Dot, for one last glimpse of a little figure very pleasant to me, she and the rest have vanished into air, and I am left alone. A Cricket sings upon the Hearth; a broken child's-toy lies upon the ground; and nothing else remains.

—1845

The Battle of Life A LOVE STORY

THIS CHRISTMAS BOOK IS CORDIALLY INSCRIBED TO MY ENGLISH FRIENDS IN SWITZERLAND

~~~~~~

PART THE FIRST

Once upon a time, it matters little when, and in stalwart England, it matters little where, a fierce battle was fought. It was fought upon a long summer day when the waving grass was green. Many a wild flower formed by the Almighty Hand to be a perfumed goblet for the dew, felt its enamelled cup filled high with blood that day, and shrinking dropped. Many an insect deriving its delicate colour from harmless leaves and herbs, was stained anew that day by dying men, and marked its frightened way with an unnatural track. The painted butterfly took blood into the air upon the edges of its wings. The stream ran red. The trodden ground became a quagmire, whence, from sullen pools collected in the prints of human feet and horses' hoofs, the one prevailing hue still lowered and glimmered at the sun.

Heaven keep us from a knowledge of the sights the moon beheld upon that field, when, coming up above the black line of distant rising-ground, softened and blurred at the edge by trees, she rose into the sky and looked upon the plain, strewn with upturned faces that had once at mothers' breasts sought mothers' eyes, or slumbered happily. Heaven keep us from a knowledge of the secrets whispered afterwards upon the tainted wind that blew across the scene of that day's work and that night's death and suffering! Many a lonely moon was bright upon the battle-ground, and many a star kept mournful watch upon it, and many a wind from every quarter of the earth blew over it, before the traces of the fight were worn away.

They lurked and lingered for a long time, but survived in little things; for Nature, far above the evil passions of men, soon recovered Her serenity, and smiled upon the guilty battle-ground as she had done before, when it was innocent. The larks sang high above it; the swallows skimmed and dipped and flitted to and fro; the shadows of the flying clouds pursued each other swiftly, over grass and corn and turnip-field and wood, and over roof and church-spire in the nestling town among the trees, away into the bright distance on the borders of the sky and earth, where the red sunsets faded. Crops were sown, and grew up, and were gathered in; the stream that had been crimsoned, turned a water-mill; men whistled at the plough; gleaners and hay-makers were seen in quiet groups at work; sheep and oxen pastured; boys whooped and called, in fields, to scare away the birds; smoke rose from cottage chimneys; sabbath bells rang peacefully; old people lived and died; the timid creatures of the field, and simple flowers of the bush and garden, grew and withered in their destined terms: and all upon the fierce and bloody battle-ground, where thousands upon thousands had been killed in the great fight.

But there were deep green patches in the growing corn at first, that people looked at awfully. Year after year they reappeared; and it was known that underneath those fertile spots, heaps of men and horses lay buried, indiscriminately, enriching the ground. The husbandmen who ploughed those places, shrunk from the great worms abounding there; and the sheaves they yielded were, for many a long year, called the Battle Sheaves, and set apart; and no one ever knew a Battle Sheaf to be among the last load at a Harvest Home. For a long time, every furrow that was turned, revealed some fragments of the fight. For a long time, there were wounded trees upon the battle-ground; and scraps of hacked and broken fence and wall, where deadly struggles had been made; and trampled parts where not a leaf or blade would grow. For a long time, no village girl would dress her hair or bosom with the sweetest flower from the field of death: and after many a year had come and gone, the berries growing there, were still believed to leave too deep a stain upon the hand that plucked them.

The Seasons in their course, however, though they passed as lightly as the summer clouds themselves, obliterated, in the lapse of time, even these remains of the old conflict; and wore away such legend-ary traces of it as the neighbouring people carried in their minds, until they dwindled into old wives' tales, dimly remembered round the win-ter fire, and waning every year. Where the wild flowers and berries had so long remained upon the stem untouched, gardens arose, and houses were built, and children played at battles on the turf. The wounded trees had long ago made Christmas logs, and blazed and roared away. The deep green patches were no greener now than the memory of those who lay in dust below. The ploughshare still turned up from time to time some rusty bits of metal, but it was hard to say what use they had ever served, and those who found them wondered and dis-puted. An old dinted corselet, and a helmet, had been hanging in the church so long, that the same weak half-blind old man who tried in vain to make them out above the whitewashed arch, had marvelled at them as a baby. If the host slain upon the field, could have been for a moment reanimated in the forms in which they fell, each upon the spot that was the bed of his untimely death, gashed and ghastly soldiers would have stared in, hundreds deep, at household door and window; and would have risen on the hearths of quiet homes; and would have been the garnered store of barns and granaries; and would have started up between the cradled infant and its nurse; and would have floated with the stream, and whirled round on the mill, and crowded the orchard, and burdened the meadow, and piled the rickyard high with dying men. So altered was the battle-ground, where thousands upon thousands had been killed in the great fight.

Nowhere more altered, perhaps, about a hundred years ago, than in one little orchard attached to an old stone house with a honeysuckle porch; where, on a bright autumn morning, there were sounds of music and laughter, and where two girls danced merrily together on the grass, while some half-dozen peasant women standing on ladders, gathering the apples from the trees, stopped in their work to look down, and share their enjoyment. It was a pleasant, lively, natural scene; a beautiful day, a retired spot; and the two girls, quite unconstrained and careless, danced in the freedom and gaiety of their hearts.

If there were no such thing as display in the world, my private opinion is, and I hope you agree with me, that we might get on a great deal better than we do, and might be infinitely more agreeable company than we are. It was charming to see how these girls danced. They had no spectators but the apple-pickers on the ladders. They were very glad to please them, but they danced to please themselves (or at least you would have supposed so) and you could no more help admiring, than they could help dancing. How they did dance!

Not like opera-dancers. Not at all. And not like Madame Anybody's finished pupils. Not the least. It was not quadrille dancing, nor minuet dancing, nor even country-dance dancing. It was neither in the old style, nor the new style, nor the French style, nor the English style: though it may have been, by accident, a trifle in the Spanish style, which is a free and joyous one, I am told, deriving a delightful air of off-hand inspiration, from the chirping little castanets. As they danced among the orchard trees, and down the groves of stems and back again, and twirled each other lightly round and round, the influence of their airy motion seemed to spread and spread, in the sunlighted scene, like an expanding circle in the water. Their streaming hair and fluttering skirts, the elastic grass beneath their feet, the boughs that rustled in the morning air—the flashing leaves, the speckled shadows on the soft green ground—the balmy wind that swept along the landscape, glad to turn the distant windmill, cheerily—everything between the two girls, and the man and team at plough upon the ridge of land, where they showed against the sky as if they were the last things in the world—seemed dancing too.

At last, the younger of the dancing sisters, out of breath, and laughing gaily, threw herself upon a bench to rest. The other leaned against a tree hard by. The music, a wandering harp and fiddle, left off with a flourish, as if it boasted of its freshness; though the truth is, it had gone at such a pace, and worked itself to such a pitch of competition with the dancing, that it never could have held on, half a minute longer. The apple-pickers on the ladders raised a hum and murmur of applause, and then, in keeping with the sound, bestirred themselves to work again like bees.

The more actively, perhaps, because an elderly gentleman, who was no other than Doctor Jeddler himself—it was Doctor Jeddler's house and orchard, you should know, and these were Doctor Jeddler's daughters—came bustling out to see what was the matter, and who the deuce played music on his property, before breakfast. For he was a great philosopher, Doctor Jeddler, and not very musical.

"Music and dancing to-day!" said the Doctor, stopping short and speaking to himself. "I thought they dreaded to-day. But it's a world of contradictions. Why, Grace, why, Marion!" he added, aloud, "is the world more mad than usual this morning?"

"Make some allowance for it, father, if it be," replied his younger daughter, Marion, going close to him, and looking into his face, "for it's somebody's birth-day."

"Somebody's birth-day, Puss!" replied the Doctor. "Don't you know it's always somebody's birth-day? Did you never hear how many new performers enter on this—ha! ha! ha!—it's impossible to speak gravely on it—on this preposterous and ridiculous business called Life, every minute?"

"No, father!"

"No, not you, of course; you're a woman—almost," said the Doctor. "By-the-by," and he looked into the pretty face, still close to his, "I suppose it's your birth-day."

"No! Do you really, father?" cried his pet daughter, pursing up her red lips to be kissed.

"There! Take my love with it," said the Doctor, imprinting his upon them; "and many happy returns of the—the idea!—of the day. The notion of wishing happy returns in such a farce as this," said the Doctor to himself, "is good! Ha! ha! ha!"

Doctor Jeddler was, as I have said, a great philosopher, and the heart and mystery of his philosophy was, to look upon the world as a gigantic practical joke; as something too absurd to be considered seriously, by any rational man. His system of belief had been, in the beginning, part and parcel of the battle-ground on which he lived, as you shall presently understand.

"Well! But how did you get the music?" asked the Doctor. "Poultry-stealers, of course! Where did the minstrels come from?"

"Alfred sent the music," said his daughter Grace, adjusting a few simple flowers in her sister's hair, with which, in her admiration of that

youthful beauty, she had herself adorned it half-an-hour before, and
which the dancing had disarranged.

"Oh! Alfred sent the music, did he?" returned the Doctor.

"Yes. He met it coming out of the town as he was entering early.
The men are travelling on foot, and rested there last night; and as it
was Marion's birth-day, and he thought it would please her, he sent
them on, with a pencilled note to me, saying that if I thought so too,
they had come to serenade her."

"Ay, ay," said the Doctor, carelessly, "he always takes your opinion."

"And my opinion being favourable," said Grace, good-humouredly;
and pausing for a moment to admire the pretty head she decorated,
with her own thrown back; "and Marion being in high spirits, and
beginning to dance, I joined her. And so we danced to Alfred's music
till we were out of breath. And we thought the music all the gayer for
being sent by Alfred. Didn't we, dear Marion?"

"Oh, I don't know, Grace. How you tease me about Alfred."

"Tease you by mentioning your lover?" said her sister.

"I am sure I don't much care to have him mentioned," said the
wilful beauty, stripping the petals from some flowers she held, and
scattering them on the ground. "I am almost tired of hearing of him;
and as to his being my lover——"

"Hush! Don't speak lightly of a true heart, which is all your own,
Marion," cried her sister, "even in jest. There is not a truer heart than
Alfred's in the world!"

"No—no," said Marion, raising her eyebrows with a pleasant air of
careless consideration, "perhaps not. But I don't know that there's any
great merit in that. I—I don't want him to be so very true. I never
asked him. If he expects that I—— But, dear Grace, why need we talk
of him at all, just now?"

It was agreeable to see the graceful figures of the blooming sisters,
twined together, lingering among the trees, conversing thus, with earnestness opposed to lightness, yet, with love responding tenderly to
love. And it was very curious indeed to see the younger sister's eyes
suffused with tears, and something fervently and deeply felt, breaking
through the wilfulness of what she said, and striving with it painfully.

The difference between them, in respect of age, could not exceed
four years at most; but Grace, as often happens in such cases, when no
mother watches over both (the Doctor's wife was dead), seemed, in
her gentle care of her young sister, and in the steadiness of her devotion to her, older than she was; and more removed, in course of nature,
from all competition with her, or participation, otherwise than through
her sympathy and true affection, in her wayward fancies, than their
ages seemed to warrant. Great character of mother, that, even in this
shadow and faint reflection of it, purifies the heart, and raises the
exalted nature nearer to the angels!

The Doctor's reflections, as he looked after them, and heard the purport of their discourse, were limited at first to certain merry meditations on the folly of all loves and likings, and the idle imposition practised on themselves by young people, who believed for a moment, that there could be anything serious in such bubbles, and were always undeceived—always!

But the home-adorning, self-denying qualities of Grace, and her sweet temper, so gentle and retiring, yet including so much constancy and bravery of spirit, seemed all expressed to him in the contrast between her quiet household figure and that of his younger and more beautiful child; and he was sorry for her sake—sorry for them both—that life should be such a very ridiculous business as it was.

The Doctor never dreamed of inquiring whether his children, or either of them, helped in any way to make the scheme a serious one. But then he was a Philosopher.

A kind and generous man by nature, he had stumbled, by chance, over that common Philosopher's stone (much more easily discovered than the object of the alchemist's researches), which sometimes trips up kind and generous men, and has the fatal property of turning gold to dross and every precious thing to poor account.

"Britain!" cried the Doctor. "Britain! Holloa!"

A small man, with an uncommonly sour and discontented face, emerged from the house, and returned to this call the unceremonious acknowledgment of "Now then!"

"Where's the breakfast table?" said the Doctor.

"In the house," returned Britain.

"Are you going to spread it out here, as you were told last night?" said the Doctor. "Don't you know that there are gentlemen coming? That there's business to be done this morning, before the coach comes by? That this is a very particular occasion?"

"I couldn't do anything, Dr. Jeddler, till the women had done getting in the apples, could I?" said Britain, his voice rising with his reasoning, so that it was very loud at last.

"Well, have they done now?" replied the Doctor, looking at his watch, and clapping his hands. "Come! make haste! where's Clemency?"

"Here am I, Mister," said a voice from one of the ladders, which a pair of clumsy feet descended briskly. "It's all done now. Clear away, gals. Everything shall be ready for you in half a minute, Mister."

With that she began to bustle about most vigorously; presenting, as she did so, an appearance sufficiently peculiar to justify a word of introduction.

She was about thirty years old, and had a sufficiently plump and cheerful face, though it was twisted up into an odd expression of tightness that made it comical. But the extraordinary homeliness of her

gait and manner would have superseded any face in the world. To say
that she had two left legs, and somebody else's arms, and that all four
limbs seemed to be out of joint, and to start from perfectly wrong
places when they were set in motion, is to offer the mildest outline of
the reality. To say that she was perfectly content and satisfied with
these arrangements, and regarded them as being no business of hers,
and that she took her arms and legs as they came, and allowed them to
dispose of themselves just as it happened, is to render faint justice to
her equanimity. Her dress was a prodigious pair of self-willed shoes,
that never wanted to go where her feet went; blue stockings; a printed
gown of many colours, and the most hideous pattern procurable for
money; and a white apron. She always wore short sleeves, and always
had, by some accident, grazed elbows, in which she took so lively an
interest, that she was continually trying to turn them round and get
impossible views of them. In general, a little cap placed somewhere on
her head; though it was rarely to be met with in the place usually
occupied in other subjects, by that article of dress; but from head to
foot she was scrupulously clean, and maintained a kind of dislocated
tidiness. Indeed, her laudable anxiety to be tidy and compact in her
own conscience as well as in the public eye, gave rise to one of her
most startling evolutions, which was to grasp herself sometimes by a
sort of wooden handle (part of her clothing, and familiarly called a
busk), and wrestle as it were with her garments, until they fell into a
symmetrical arrangement.

Such, in outward form and garb, was Clemency Newcome; who was
supposed to have unconsciously originated a corruption of her own
Christian name, from Clementina (but nobody knew, for the deaf old
mother, a very phenomenon of age, whom she had supported almost
from a child, was dead, and she had no other relation); who now
busied herself in preparing the table, and who stood, at intervals, with
her bare red arms crossed, rubbing her grazed elbows with opposite
hands, and staring at it very composedly, until she suddenly remembered something else she wanted, and jogged off to fetch it.

"Here are them two lawyers a-coming, Mister!" said Clemency, in
a tone of no very great good-will.

"Ah!" cried the Doctor, advancing to the gate to meet them. "Good
morning, good morning! Grace, my dear! Marion! Here are Messrs.
Snitchey and Craggs. Where's Alfred?"

"He'll be back directly, father, no doubt," said Grace. "He had so
much to do this morning in his preparations for departure, that he was
up and out by daybreak. Good morning, gentlemen."

"Ladies!" said Mr. Snitchey, "for Self and Craggs," who bowed,
"good morning! Miss," to Marion, "I kiss your hand." Which he did.
"And I wish you"—which he might or might not, for he didn't look,
at first sight, like a gentleman troubled with many warm outpourings

of soul, in behalf of other people, "a hundred happy returns of this auspicious day."

"Ha, ha, ha!" laughed the Doctor thoughtfully, with his hands in his pockets. "The great farce in a hundred acts!"

"You wouldn't, I am sure," said Mr. Snitchey, standing a small professional blue bag against one leg of the table, "cut the great farce short for this actress, at all events, Doctor Jeddler."

"No," returned the Doctor. "God forbid! May she live to laugh at it, as long as she *can* laugh, and then say, with the French wit, 'The farce is ended; draw the curtain.'"

"The French wit," said Mr. Snitchey, peeping sharply into his blue bag, "was wrong, Doctor Jeddler, and your philosophy is altogether wrong, depend upon it, as I have often told you. Nothing serious in life! What do you call law?"

"A joke," replied the Doctor.

"Did you ever go to law?" asked Mr. Snitchey, looking out of the blue bag.

"Never," returned the Doctor.

"If you ever do," said Mr. Snitchey, "perhaps you'll alter that opinion."

Craggs, who seemed to be represented by Snitchey, and to be conscious of little or no separate existence or personal individuality, offered a remark of his own in this place. It involved the only idea of which he did not stand seized and possessed in equal moieties with Snitchey; but he had some partners in it among the wise men of the world.

"It's made a great deal too easy," said Mr. Craggs.

"Law is?" asked the Doctor.

"Yes," said Mr. Craggs, "everything is. Everything appears to me to be made too easy, now-a-days. It's the vice of these times. If the world is a joke (I am not prepared to say it isn't), it ought to be made a very difficult joke to crack. It ought to be as hard a struggle, sir, as possible. That's the intention. But it's being made far too easy. We are oiling the gates of life. They ought to be rusty. We shall have them beginning to turn, soon, with a smooth sound. Whereas they ought to grate upon their hinges, sir."

Mr. Craggs seemed positively to grate upon his own hinges, as he delivered this opinion; to which he communicated immense effect—being a cold, hard, dry man, dressed in grey and white, like a flint; with small twinkles in his eyes, as if something struck sparks out of them. The three natural kingdoms, indeed, had each a fanciful representative among this brotherhood of disputants; for Snitchey was like a magpie or raven (only not so sleek), and the Doctor had a streaked face like a winter-pippin, with here and there a dimple to express the peckings of the birds, and a very little bit of pigtail behind that stood for the stalk.

As the active figure of a handsome young man, dressed for a journey, and followed by a porter bearing several packages and baskets, entered the orchard at a brisk pace, and with an air of gaiety and hope that accorded well with the morning, these three drew together, like the brothers of the sister Fates, or like the Graces most effectually disguised, or like the three weird prophets on the heath, and greeted him.

"Happy returns, Alf!" said the Doctor, lightly.

"A hundred happy returns of this auspicious day, Mr. Heathfield!" said Snitchey, bowing low.

"Returns!" Craggs murmured in a deep voice, all alone.

"Why, what a battery!" exclaimed Alfred, stopping short, "and one —two—three—all foreboders of no good, in the great sea before me. I am glad you are not the first I have met this morning: I should have taken it for a bad omen. But Grace was the first—sweet, pleasant Grace—so I defy you all!"

"If you please, Mister, I was the first, you know," said Clemency Newcome. "She was walking out here, before sunrise, you remember. I was in the house."

"That's true! Clemency was the first," said Alfred. "So I defy you with Clemency."

"Ha, ha, ha,—for Self and Craggs," said Snitchey. "What a defiance!"

"Not so bad a one as it appears, may be," said Alfred, shaking hands heartily with the Doctor, and also with Snitchey and Craggs, and then looking round. "Where are the— Good Heavens!"

With a start, productive for the moment of a closer partnership between Jonathan Snitchey and Thomas Craggs than the subsisting articles of agreement in that wise contemplated, he hastily betook himself to where the sisters stood together, and—however, I needn't more particularly explain his manner of saluting Marion first, and Grace afterwards, than by hinting that Mr. Craggs may possibly have considered it "too easy."

Perhaps to change the subject, Dr. Jeddler made a hasty move towards the breakfast, and they all sat down at table. Grace presided; but so discreetly stationed herself, as to cut off her sister and Alfred from the rest of the company. Snitchey and Craggs sat at opposite corners, with the blue bag between them for safety; the Doctor took his usual position, opposite to Grace. Clemency hovered galvanically about the table, as waitress; and the melancholy Britain, at another and a smaller board, acted as Grand Carver of a round of beef and a ham.

"Meat?" said Britain, approaching Mr. Snitchey, with the carving knife and fork in his hands, and throwing the question at him like a missile.

"Certainly," returned the lawyer.

"Do *you* want any?" to Craggs.

"Lean and well done," replied that gentleman.

Having executed these orders, and moderately supplied the Doctor (he seemed to know that nobody else wanted anything to eat), he lingered as near the Firm as he decently could, watching with an austere eye their disposition of the viands, and but once relaxing the severe expression of his face. This was on the occasion of Mr. Craggs, whose teeth were not the best, partially choking, when he cried out with great animation, "I thought he was gone!"

"Now, Alfred," said the Doctor, "for a word or two of business, while we are yet at breakfast."

"While we are yet at breakfast," said Snitchey and Craggs, who seemed to have no present idea of leaving off.

Although Alfred had not been breakfasting, and seemed to have quite enough business on his hands as it was, he respectfully answered:

"If you please, sir."

"If anything could be serious," the Doctor began, "in such a—"

"Farce as this, sir," hinted Alfred.

"In such a farce as this," observed the Doctor, "it might be this recurrence, on the eve of separation, of a double birth-day, which is connected with many associations pleasant to us four, and with the recollection of a long and amicable intercourse. That's not to the purpose."

"Ah! yes, yes, Dr. Jeddler," said the young man. "It is to the purpose. Much to the purpose, as my heart bears witness this morning; and as yours does too, I know, if you would let it speak. I leave your house to-day; I cease to be your ward to-day; we part with tender relations stretching far behind us, that never can be exactly renewed, and with others dawning yet before us," he looked down at Marion beside him, "fraught with such considerations as I must not trust myself to speak of now. Come, come!" he added, rallying his spirits and the Doctor at once, "there's a serious grain in this large foolish dust-heap, Doctor. Let us allow to-day, that there is One."

"To-day!" cried the Doctor. "Hear him! Ha, ha, ha! Of all days in the foolish year. Why, on this day, the great battle was fought on this ground. On this ground where we now sit, where I saw my two girls dance this morning, where the fruit has just been gathered for our eating from these trees, the roots of which are struck in Men, not earth,— so many lives were lost, that within my recollection, generations afterwards, a churchyard full of bones, and dust of bones, and chips of cloven skulls, has been dug up from underneath our feet here. Yet not a hundred people in that battle knew for what they fought, or why;

not a hundred of the inconsiderate rejoicers in the victory, why they rejoiced. Not half a hundred people were the better for the gain or loss. Not half-a-dozen men agree to this hour on the cause or merits; and nobody, in short, ever knew anything distinct about it, but the mourners of the slain. Serious, too!" said the Doctor, laughing. "Such a system!"

"But all this seems to me," said Alfred, "to be very serious."

"Serious!" cried the Doctor. "If you allowed such things to be serious, you must go mad, or die, or climb up to the top of a mountain, and turn hermit."

"Besides—so long ago," said Alfred.

"Long ago!" returned the Doctor. "Do you know what the world has been doing, ever since? Do you know what else it has been doing? I don't!"

"It has gone to law a little," observed Mr. Snitchey, stirring his tea.

"Although the way out has been always made too easy," said his partner.

"And you'll excuse my saying, Doctor," pursued Mr. Snitchey, "having been already put a thousand times in possession of my opinion, in the course of our discussions, that, in its having gone to law, and in its legal system altogether, I do observe a serious side—now, really, a something tangible, and with a purpose and intention in it—"

Clemency Newcome made an angular tumble against the table, occasioning a sounding clatter among the cups and saucers.

"Heyday! what's the matter there?" exclaimed the Doctor.

"It's this evil-inclined blue bag," said Clemency, "always tripping up somebody!"

"With a purpose and intention in it, I was saying," resumed Snitchey, "that commands respect. Life a farce, Dr. Jeddler? With law in it?"

The Doctor laughed, and looked at Alfred.

"Granted, if you please, that war is foolish," said Snitchey. "There we agree. For example. Here's a smiling country," pointing it out with his fork, "once overrun by soldiers—trespassers every man of 'em—and laid waste by fire and sword. He, he, he! The idea of any man exposing himself, voluntarily, to fire and sword! Stupid, wasteful, positively ridiculous; you laugh at your fellow-creatures, you know, when you think of it! But take this smiling country as it stands. Think of the laws appertaining to real property; to the bequest and devise of real property; to the mortgage and redemption of real property; to lease-hold, freehold, and copyhold estate; think," said Mr. Snitchey, with such great emotion that he actually smacked his lips, "of the complicated laws relating to title and proof of title, with all the contradictory precedents and numerous acts of parliament connected with them; think of the infinite number of ingenious and interminable chancery suits, to which this pleasant prospect may give rise; and acknowledge, Dr. Jeddler, that there is a green spot in the scheme about us! I believe," said Mr. Snitchey, looking at his partner, "that I speak for Self and Craggs?"

Mr. Craggs having signified assent, Mr. Snitchey, somewhat freshened by his recent eloquence, observed that he would take a little more beef and another cup of tea.

"I don't stand up for life in general," he added, rubbing his hands and chuckling, "it's full of folly; full of something worse. Professions of trust, and confidence, and unselfishness, and all that! Bah, bah, bah! We see what they're worth. But you mustn't laugh at life; you've got a game to play; a very serious game indeed! Everybody's playing against you, you know, and you're playing against them. Oh! it's a very interesting thing. There are deep moves upon the board. You must only laugh, Dr. Jeddler, when you win—and then not much. He, he, he! And then not much," repeated Snitchey, rolling his head and winking his eye, as if he would have added, "you may do this instead!"

"Well, Alfred!" cried the Doctor, "what do you say now?"

"I say, sir," replied Alfred, "that the greatest favour you could do me, and yourself too, I am inclined to think, would be to try sometimes to forget this battle-field and others like it in that broader battle-field of Life, on which the sun looks every day."

"Really, I'm afraid that wouldn't soften his opinions, Mr. Alfred," said Snitchey. "The combatants are very eager and very bitter in that same battle of Life. There's a great deal of cutting and slashing, and firing into people's heads from behind. There is terrible treading down, and trampling on. It is rather a bad business."

"I believe, Mr. Snitchey," said Alfred, "there are quiet victories and struggles, great sacrifices of self, and noble acts of heroism, in it—even in many of its apparent lightnesses and contradictions—not the less difficult to achieve, because they have no earthly chronicle or audience—done every day in nooks and corners, and in the little households, and in men's and women's hearts—any one of which might reconcile the sternest man to such a world, and fill him with belief and hope in it, though two-fourths of its people were at war, and another fourth at law; and that's a bold word."

Both the sisters listened keenly.

"Well, well!" said the Doctor, "I am too old to be converted, even by my friend Snitchey here, or my good spinster sister, Martha Jeddler; who had what she calls her domestic trials ages ago, and has led a sympathising life with all sorts of people ever since; and who is so much of your opinion (only she's less reasonable and more obstinate, being a woman), that we can't agree, and seldom meet. I was born upon this battle-field. I began, as a boy, to have my thoughts directed to the real history of a battle-field. Sixty years have gone over my head, and I have never seen the Christian world, including Heaven knows how many loving mothers and good enough girls like mine here, anything but mad for a battle-field. The same contradictions prevail in everything. One must either laugh or cry at such stupendous inconsistencies; and I prefer to laugh."

Britain, who had been paying the profoundest and most melancholy attention to each speaker in his turn, seemed suddenly to decide in favour of the same preference, if a deep sepulchral sound that escaped him might be construed into a demonstration of risibility. His face, however, was so perfectly unaffected by it, both before and afterwards, that although one or two of the breakfast party looked round as being startled by a mysterious noise, nobody connected the offender with it.

Except his partner in attendance, Clemency Newcome; who rousing him with one of those favourite joints, her elbows, inquired, in a reproachful whisper, what he laughed at.

"Not you!" said Britain.

"Who then?"

"Humanity," said Britain. "That's the joke!"

"What between master and them lawyers, he's getting more and more addle-headed every day!" cried Clemency, giving him a lunge with the other elbow, as a mental stimulant. "Do you know where you are? Do you want to get warning?"

"I don't know anything," said Britain, with a leaden eye and an immovable visage. "I don't care for anything. I don't make out anything. I don't believe anything. And I don't want anything."

Although this forlorn summary of his general condition may have been overcharged in an access of despondency, Benjamin Britain—sometimes called Little Britain, to distinguish him from Great; as we might say Young England, to express Old England with a decided difference—had defined his real state more accurately than might be supposed. For, serving as a sort of man Miles to the Doctor's Friar Bacon, and listening day after day to innumerable orations addressed by the Doctor to various people, all tending to show that his very existence was at best a mistake and an absurdity, this unfortunate servitor had fallen, by degrees, into such an abyss of confused and contradictory suggestions from within and without, that Truth at the bottom of her well, was on the level surface as compared with Britain in the depths of his mystification. The only point he clearly comprehended, was, that the new element usually brought into these discussions by Snitchey and Craggs, never served to make them clearer, and always seemed to give the Doctor a species of advantage and confirmation. Therefore, he looked upon the Firm as one of the proximate causes of his state of mind, and held them in abhorrence accordingly.

"But this is not our business, Alfred," said the Doctor. "Ceasing to be my ward (as you have said) today; and leaving us full to the brim of such learning as the Grammar School down here was able to give you, and your studies in London could add to that, and such practical knowledge as a dull old country Doctor like myself could graft upon both; you are away, now, into the world. The first term of probation appointed by your poor father, being over, away you go now, your own master, to fulfil his second desire. And long before your three years' tour among the foreign schools of medicine is finished, you'll have forgotten us. Lord, you'll forget us easily in six months!"

"If I do—but you know better; why should I speak to you!" said Alfred, laughing.

"I don't know anything of the sort," returned the Doctor. "What do you say, Marion?"

Marion, trifling with her teacup, seemed to say—but she didn't say it—that he was welcome to forget, if he could. Grace pressed the blooming face against her cheek, and smiled.

"I haven't been, I hope, a very unjust steward in the execution of my trust," pursued the Doctor; "but I am to be, at any rate, formally discharged, and released, and what not, this morning; and here are our good friends Snitchey and Craggs, with a bagful of papers, and accounts, and documents, for the transfer of the balance of the trust fund to you (I wish it was a more difficult one to dispose of, Alfred, but you must get to be a great man and make it so), and other drolleries of that sort, which are to be signed, sealed, and delivered."

"And duly witnessed as by law required," said Snitchey, pushing away his plate, and taking out the papers, which his partner proceeded to spread upon the table; "and Self and Craggs having been co-trustees with you, Doctor, in so far as the fund was concerned, we shall want your two servants to attest the signatures—can you read, Mrs. Newcome?"

"I an't married, Mister," said Clemency.

"Oh! I beg your pardon. I should think not," chuckled Snitchey, casting his eyes over her extraordinary figure. "You *can* read?"

"A little," answered Clemency.

"The marriage service, night and morning, eh?" observed the lawyer, jocosely.

"No," said Clemency. "Too hard. I only reads a thimble."

"Read a thimble!" echoed Snitchey. "What are you talking about, young woman?"

Clemency nodded. "And a nutmeg-grater."

"Why, this is a lunatic! a subject for the Lord High Chancellor!" said Snitchey, staring at her.

—"If possessed of any property," stipulated Craggs.

Grace, however, interposing, explained that each of the articles in question bore an engraved motto, and so formed the pocket library of Clemency Newcome, who was not much given to the study of books.

"Oh, that's it, is it, Miss Grace!" said Snitchey.

"Yes, yes. Ha, ha, ha! I thought our friend was an idiot. She looks uncommonly like it," he muttered, with a supercilious glance. "And what does the thimble say, Mrs. Newcome?"

"I an't married, Mister," observed Clemency.

"Well, Newcome. Will that do?" said the lawyer. "What does the thimble say, Newcome?"

How Clemency, before replying to this question, held one pocket open, and looked down into its yawning depths for the thimble which wasn't there,—and how she then held an opposite pocket open, and seeming to descry it, like a pearl of great price, at the bottom, cleared away such intervening obstacles as a handkerchief, an end of wax candle, a flushed apple, an orange, a lucky penny, a cramp bone, a padlock, a pair of scissors in a sheath more expressively describable as promising young shears, a handful or so of loose beads, several balls of cotton, a needle-case, a cabinet collection of curl-papers, and a biscuit, all of which articles she entrusted individually and separately to Britain to hold,—is of no consequence.

Nor how, in her determination to grasp this pocket by the throat and keep it prisoner (for it had a tendency to swing, and twist itself round the nearest corner), she assumed and calmly maintained, an attitude apparently inconsistent with the human anatomy and the laws of gravity. It is enough that at last she triumphantly produced the thimble on her finger, and rattled the nutmeg-grater: the literature of both those trinkets being obviously in course of wearing out and wasting away, through excessive friction.

"That's the thimble, is it, young woman?" said Mr. Snitchey, diverting himself at her expense. "And what does the thimble say?"

"It says," replied Clemency, reading slowly round as if it were a tower, "For-get and For-give."

Snitchey and Craggs laughed heartily. "So new!" said Snitchey. "So easy!" said Craggs. "Such a knowledge of human nature in it!" said Snitchey. "So applicable to the affairs of life!" said Craggs.

"And the nutmeg-grater?" inquired the head of the Firm.

"The grater says," returned Clemency, "Do as you—wold—be —done by."

"Do, or you'll be done brown, you mean," said Mr. Snitchey.

"I don't understand," retorted Clemency, shaking her head vaguely. "I an't no lawyer."

"I am afraid that if she was, Doctor," said Mr. Snitchey, turning to him suddenly, as if to anticipate any effect that might otherwise be consequent on this retort, "she'd find it to be the golden rule of half her clients. They are serious enough in that—whimsical as your world is—and lay the blame on us afterwards. We, in our profession, are little else than mirrors after all, Mr. Alfred; but we are generally consulted by angry and quarrelsome people who are not in their best looks, and it's rather hard to quarrel with us if we reflect unpleasant aspects. I think," said Mr. Snitchey, "that I speak for Self and Craggs?"

"Decidedly," said Craggs.

"And so, if Mr. Britain will oblige us with a mouthful of ink," said Mr. Snitchey, returning to the papers, "we'll sign, seal, and deliver as soon as possible, or the coach will be coming past before we know where we are."

If one might judge from his appearance, there was every probability of the coach coming past before Mr. Britain knew where *he* was; for he stood in a state of abstraction, mentally balancing the Doctor against the lawyers, and the lawyers against the Doctor, and their clients against both, and engaged in feeble attempts to make the thimble and nutmeg-grater (a new idea to him) square with anybody's system of philosophy; and, in short, bewildering himself as much as ever his great namesake has done with theories and schools. But Clemency, who was his good Genius—though he had the meanest possible opinion of her understanding, by reason of her seldom troubling herself with abstract speculations, and being always at hand to do the right thing at the right time—having produced the ink in a twinkling, tendered him the further service of recalling him to himself by the application of her elbows; with which gentle flappers she so jogged his memory, in a more literal construction of that phrase than usual, that he soon became quite fresh and brisk.

How he laboured under an apprehension not uncommon to persons in his degree, to whom the use of pen and ink is an event, that he couldn't append his name to a document, not of his own writing, without committing himself in some shadowy manner, or somehow signing away vague and enormous sums of money; and how he approached the deeds under protest, and by dint of the Doctor's coercion, and insisted on pausing to look at them before writing (the cramped hand, to say nothing of the phraseology, being so much Chinese to him), and also on turning them round to see whether there was anything fraudulent underneath; and how, having signed his name, he became desolate as one who had parted with his property and rights; I want the time to tell. Also, how the blue bag containing his signature, afterwards had a mysterious interest for him, and he couldn't leave it; also how Clemency Newcome, in an ectasy of laughter at the idea of her own importance and dignity, brooded over the whole table with her two elbows, like a spread eagle, and reposed her head upon her left arm as a preliminary to the formation of certain cabalistic characters, which required a deal of ink, and imaginary counterparts whereof she executed at the same time with her tongue.

Also, how, having once tasted ink, she became thirsty in that regard, as tame tigers are said to be after tasting another sort of fluid, and wanted to sign everything, and put her name in all kinds of places. In brief, the Doctor was discharged of his trust and all its responsibilities; and Alfred, taking it on himself, was fairly started on the journey of life.

"Britain!" said the Doctor. "Run to the gate, and watch for the coach. Time flies, Alfred."

"Yes, sir, yes," returned the young man, hurriedly. "Dear Grace! a moment! Marion—so young and beautiful, so winning and so much admired, dear to my heart as nothing else in life is—remember! I leave Marion to you!"

"She has always been a sacred charge to me, Alfred. She is doubly so, now. I will be faithful to my trust, believe me."

"I do believe it, Grace. I know it well. Who could look upon your face, and hear your voice, and not know it! Ah, Grace! If I had your well-governed heart, and tranquil mind, how bravely I would leave this place to-day!"

"Would you?" she answered with a quiet smile.

"And yet, Grace— Sister, seems the natural word."

"Use it!" she said quickly. "I am glad to hear it. Call me nothing else."

"And yet, sister, then," said Alfred, "Marion and I had better have your true and steadfast qualities serving us here, and making us both happier and better. I wouldn't carry them away, to sustain myself, if I could!"

"Coach upon the hill-top!" exclaimed Britain.

"Time flies, Alfred," said the Doctor.

Marion had stood apart, with her eyes fixed upon the ground; but, this warning being given, her young lover brought her tenderly to where her sister stood, and gave her into her embrace.

"I have been telling Grace, dear Marion," he said, "that you are her charge; my precious trust at parting. And when I come back and reclaim you, dearest, and the bright prospect of our married life lies stretched before us, it shall be one of our chief pleasures to consult how we can make Grace happy; how we can anticipate her wishes; how we can show our gratitude and love to her; how we can return her something of the debt she will have heaped upon us."

The younger sister had one hand in his; the other rested on her sister's neck. She looked into that sister's eyes, so calm, serene, and cheerful, with a gaze in which affection, admiration, sorrow, wonder, almost veneration, were blended. She looked into that sister's face, as if it were the face of some bright angel. Calm, serene, and cheerful, the face looked back on her and on her lover.

"And when the time comes, as it must one day," said Alfred,—"I wonder it has never come yet, but Grace knows best, for Grace is always right—when *she* will want a friend to open her whole heart to, and to be to her something of what she has been to us—then, Marion, how faithful we will prove, and what delight to us to know that she, our dear good sister, loves and is loved again, as we would have her!"

Still the younger sister looked into her eyes, and turned not—even towards him. And still those honest eyes looked back, so calm, serene, and cheerful, on herself and on her lover.

"And when all that is past, and we are old, and living (as we must!) together—close together—talking often of old times," said Alfred—"these shall be our favourite times among them—this day most of all; and, telling each other what we thought and felt, and hoped and feared at parting; and how we couldn't bear to say good bye——"

"Coach coming through the wood!" cried Britain.

"Yes! I am ready—and how we met again, so happily in spite of all; we'll make this day the happiest in all the year, and keep it as a treble birth-day. Shall we, dear?"

"Yes!" interposed the elder sister, eagerly, and with a radiant smile. "Yes! Alfred, don't linger. There's no time. Say good bye to Marion. And Heaven be with you!"

He pressed the younger sister to his heart. Released from his embrace, she again clung to her sister; and her eyes, with the same blended look, again sought those so calm, serene, and cheerful.

"Farewell, my boy!" said the Doctor. "To talk about any serious correspondence or serious affections, and engagements and so forth, in such a—ha, ha, ha!—you know what I mean—why that, of course, would be sheer nonsense. All I can say is, that if you and Marion should continue in the same foolish minds, I shall not object to have you for a son-in-law one of these days."

"Over the bridge!" cried Britain.

"Let it come!" said Alfred, wringing the Doctor's hand stoutly. "Think of me sometimes, my old friend and guardian, as seriously as you can! Adieu, Mr. Snitchey! Farewell, Mr. Craggs!"

"Coming down the road!" cried Britain.

"A kiss of Clemency Newcome for long acquaintance' sake! Shake hands, Britain! Marion, dearest heart, good bye! Sister Grace! remember!"

The quiet household figure, and the face so beautiful in its serenity, were turned towards him in reply; but Marion's look and attitude remained unchanged.

The coach was at the gate. There was a bustle with the luggage. The coach drove away. Marion never moved.

"He waves his hat to you, my love," said Grace. "Your chosen husband, darling. Look!"

The younger sister raised her head, and, for a moment, turned it.

Then, turning back again, and fully meeting, for the first time, those calm eyes, fell sobbing on her neck.

"Oh, Grace. God bless you! But I cannot bear to see it, Grace! It breaks my heart."

PART THE SECOND

Snitchey and Craggs had a snug little office on the old Battle Ground, where they drove a snug little business, and fought a great many small pitched battles for a great many contending parties. Though it could hardly be said of these conflicts that they were running fights—for in truth they generally proceeded at a snail's pace—the part the Firm had in them came so far within the general denomination, that now they took a shot at this Plaintiff, and now aimed a chop at that Defendant, now made a heavy charge at an estate in Chancery, and now had some light skirmishing among an irregular body of small debtors, just as the occasion served, and the enemy happened to present himself. The Gazette was an important and profitable feature in some of their fields, as in fields of greater renown; and in most of the Actions wherein they showed their generalship, it was afterwards observed by the combatants that they had had great difficulty in making each other out, or in knowing with any degree of distinctness what they were about, in consequence of the vast amount of smoke by which they were surrounded.

The offices of Messrs. Snitchey and Craggs stood convenient, with an open door down two smooth steps, in the market-place; so that any angry farmer inclining towards hot water, might tumble into it at once. Their special council-chamber and hall of conference was an old back-room up-stairs, with a low dark ceiling, which seemed to be knitting its brows gloomily in the consideration of tangled points of law. It was furnished with some high-backed leathern chairs, garnished with great goggle-eyed brass nails, of which, every here and there, two or three had fallen out—or had been picked out, perhaps, by the wandering thumbs and forefingers of bewildered clients. There was a framed print of a great judge in it, every curl in whose dreadful wig had made a man's hair stand on end. Bales of papers filled the dusty closets, shelves, and tables; and round the wainscot there were tiers of boxes, padlocked and fire-proof, with people's names painted outside, which anxious visitors felt themselves, by a cruel enchantment, obliged to spell backwards and forwards, and to make anagrams of, while they sat, seeming to listen to Snitchey and Craggs, without comprehending one word of what they said.

Snitchey and Craggs had each, in private life as in professional existence, a partner of his own. Snitchey and Craggs were the best friends in the world, and had a real confidence in one another; but Mrs. Snitchey, by a dispensation not uncommon in the affairs of life, was on principle suspicious of Mr. Craggs; and Mrs. Craggs was on principle suspicious of Mr. Snitchey. "Your Snitcheys indeed," the latter lady would observe, sometimes, to Mr. Craggs; using that imaginative plural as if in disparagement of an objectionable pair of pantaloons, or other articles not possessed of a singular number; "I don't see what you want with your Snitcheys, for my part. You trust a great deal too much to your Snitcheys, I think, and I hope you may never find my words come true." While Mrs. Snitchey would observe to Mr. Snitchey, of Craggs, "that if ever he was led away by man he was led away by that man, and that if ever she read a double purpose in a mortal eye, she read that purpose in Craggs's eye." Notwithstanding this, however, they were all very good friends in general: and Mrs. Snitchey and Mrs. Craggs maintained a close bond of alliance against "the office," which they both considered the Blue chamber, and common enemy, full of dangerous (because unknown) machinations.

In this office, nevertheless, Snitchey and Craggs made honey for their several hives. Here, sometimes, they would linger, of a fine evening, at the window of their council-chamber overlooking the old battle-ground, and wonder (but that was generally at assize time, when much business had made them sentimental) at the folly of mankind, who couldn't always be at peace with one another and go to law comfortably. Here, days, and weeks, and months, and years, passed over them: their calendar, the gradually diminishing number of brass nails in the leathern chairs, and the increasing bulk of papers on the tables. Here, nearly three years' flight had thinned the one and swelled the other, since the breakfast in the orchard; when they sat together in consultation at night.

Not alone; but with a man of thirty, or about that time of life, negligently dressed, and somewhat haggard in the face, but wellmade, well-attired, and well-looking, who sat in the arm-chair of state, with one hand in his breast, and the other in his dishevelled hair, pondering moodily. Messrs. Snitchey and Craggs sat opposite each other at a neighbouring desk. One of the fire-proof boxes, unpadlocked and opened, was upon it; a part of its contents lay strewn upon the table, and the rest was then in course of passing through the hands of Mr. Snitchey, who brought it to the candle, document by document, looked at every paper singly, as he produced it, shook his head, and handed it to Mr. Craggs; who looked it over also, shook his head, and laid it down. Sometimes they would stop, and shaking their heads in concert, look towards the abstracted client. And the name on the box being Michael Warden, Esquire, we may conclude from these premises that the name and the box were both his, and that the affairs of Michael Warden, Esquire, were in a bad way.

"That's all," said Mr. Snitchey, turning up the last paper. "Really there's no other resource. No other resource."

"All lost, spent, wasted, pawned, borrowed, and sold, eh?" said' the client, looking up.

"All," returned Mr. Snitchey.

"Nothing else to be done, you say?"

"Nothing at all."

The client bit his nails, and pondered again.

"And I am not even personally safe in England? You hold to that, do you?"

"In no part of the United Kingdom of Great Britain and Ireland'," replied Mr. Snitchey.

"A mere prodigal son with no father to go back to, no swine to keep, and no husks to share with them? Eh?" pursued the client, rocking one leg over the other, and searching the ground with his eyes.

Mr. Snitchey coughed, as if to deprecate the being supposed to participate in any figurative illustration of a legal position. Mr. Craggs, as if to express that it was a partnership view of the subject, also coughed.

"Ruined at thirty!" said the client. "Humph!"

"Not ruined, Mr. Warden," returned Snitchey. "Not so bad as that. You have done a good deal towards it, I must say, but you are not ruined. A little nursing—"

"A little Devil," said the client.

"Mr. Craggs," said Snitchey, "will you oblige me with a pinch of snuff? Thank you, sir."

As the imperturbable lawyer applied it to his nose with great apparent relish and a perfect absorption of his attention in the proceeding, the client gradually broke into a smile, and, looking up, said:

"You talk of nursing. How long nursing?"

"How long nursing?" repeated Snitchey, dusting the snuff from his fingers, and' making a slow calculation in his mind. "For your involved estate, sir? In good hands? S. and C.'s, say? Six or seven years."

"To starve for six or seven years!" said the client with a fretful laugh, and an impatient change of his position.

"To starve for six or seven years, Mr. Warden," said Snitchey, "would be very uncommon indeed. You might get another estate by showing yourself, the while. But we don't think you could do it—speaking for Self and Craggs—and consequently don't advise it."

"What *do* you advise?"

"Nursing, I say," repeated Snitchey. "Some few years of nursing be Self and Craggs would bring it round. But to enable us to make terms, and hold terms, and you to keep terms, you must go away; you must live abroad. As to starvation, we could ensure you some hundreds a-year to starve upon, even in the beginning—I dare say, Mr. Warden."

"Hundreds," said the client. "And I have spent thousands!"

"That," retorted Mr. Snitchey, putting the papers slowly back into the cast-iron box, "there is no doubt about. No doubt a—bout," he repeated to himself, as he thoughtfully pursued his occupation.

The lawyer very likely knew *his* man; at any rate his dry, shrewd, whimsical manner, had a favourable influence on the client's moody state, and disposed him to be more free and unreserved. Or perhaps the client knew *his* man, and had elicited such encouragement as he had received, to render some purpose he was about to disclose the more defensible in appearance. Gradually raising his head, he sat looking at his immovable adviser with a smile, which presently broke into a laugh.

"After all," he said, "my iron-headed friend—"

Mr. Snitchey pointed out his partner. "Self and—excuse me—Craggs."

"I beg Mr. Craggs's pardon," said the client. "After all, my iron-headed friends," he leaned forward in his chair, and dropped his voice a little, "you don't know half my ruin yet."

Mr. Snitchey stopped and stared at him. Mr. Craggs also stared.

"I am not only deep in debt," said the client, "but I am deep in—"

"Not in love!" cried Snitchey.

"Yes!" said the client, falling back in his chair, and surveying the Firm with his hands in his pockets. "Deep in love."

"And not with an heiress, sir?" said Snitchey.

"Not with an heiress."

"Nor a rich lady?"

"Nor a rich lady that I know of—except in beauty and merit."

"A single lady, I trust?" said Mr. Snitchey, with great expression.

"Certainly."

"It's not one of Dr. Jeddler's daughters?" said Snitchey, suddenly squaring his elbows on his knees, and advancing his face at least a yard.

"Yes!" returned the client.

"Not his younger daughter?" said Snitchey.

"Yes!" returned the client.

"Mr. Craggs," said Snitchey, much relieved, "will you oblige me with another pinch of snuff? Thank you! I am happy to say it don't signify, Mr. Warden; she's engaged, sir, she's bespoke. My partner can corroborate me. We know the fact."

"We know the fact," repeated Craggs.

"Why, so do I perhaps," returned the client quietly. "What of that! Are you men of the world, and did you never hear of a woman changing her mind?"

"There certainly have been actions for breach," said Mr. Snitchey, "brought against both spinsters and widows, but, in the majority of cases—"

"Cases!" interposed the client, impatiently. "Don't talk to me of cases. The general precedent is in a much larger volume than any of your law books. Besides, do you think I have lived six weeks in the Doctor's house for nothing?"

"I think, sir," observed Mr. Snitchey, gravely addressing himself to his partner, "that of all the scrapes Mr. Warden's horses have brought him into at one time and another—and they have been pretty numerous, and pretty expensive, as none know better than himself, and you, and I—the worst scrape may turn out to be, if he talks in this way, this having ever been left by one of them at the Doctor's garden wall, with three broken ribs, a snapped collar-bone, and the Lord knows how many bruises. We didn't think so much of it, at the time when we knew he was going on well under the Doctor's hands and roof; but it looks bad now, sir. Bad? It looks very bad. Doctor Jeddler too—our client, Mr. Craggs."

"Mr. Alfred Heathfield too—a sort of client, Mr. Snitchey," said Craggs.

"Mr. Michael Warden too, a kind of client," said the careless visitor, "and no bad one either: having played the fool for ten or twelve years. However, Mr. Michael Warden has sown his wild oats now—there's their crop, in that box; and he means to repent and be wise. And in proof of it, Mr. Michael Warden means, if he can, to marry Marion, the Doctor's lovely daughter, and to carry her away with him."

"Really, Mr. Craggs," Snitchey began.

"Really, Mr. Snitchey, and Mr. Craggs, partners both," said the client, interrupting him; "you know your duty to your clients, and you know well enough, I am sure, that it is no part of it to interfere in a mere love affair, which I am obliged to confide to you. I am not going to carry the young lady off, without her own consent. There's nothing illegal in it. I never was Mr. Heathfield's bosom friend. I violate no confidence of his. I love where he loves, and I mean to win where he would win, if I can."

"He can't, Mr. Craggs," said Snitchey, evidently anxious and discomfited. "He can't do it, sir. She dotes on Mr. Alfred."

"Does she?" returned the client.

"Mr. Craggs, she dotes on him, sir," persisted Snitchey.

"I didn't live six weeks, some few months ago, in the Doctor's house for nothing; and I doubted that soon," observed the client.

"She would have doted on him, if her sister could have brought it about; but I watched them. Marion avoided his name, avoided the subject: shrunk from the least allusion to it, with evident distress."

"Why should she, Mr. Craggs, you know? Why should she, sir?" inquired Snitchey.

"I don't know why she should, though there are many likely reasons," said the client, smiling at the attention and perplexity expressed in Mr. Snitchey's shining eye, and at his cautious way of carrying on the conversation, and making himself informed upon the subject; "but I know she does. She was very young when she made the engagement —if it may be called one, I am not even sure of that—and has repented of it, perhaps. Perhaps—it seems a foppish thing to say, but upon my soul I don't mean it in that light—she may have fallen in love with me, as I have fallen in love with her."

"He, he! Mr. Alfred, her old playfellow too, you remember, Mr. Craggs," said Snitchey, with a disconcerted laugh; "knew her almost from a baby!"

"Which makes it the more probable that she may be tired of his idea," calmly pursued the client, "and not indisposed to exchange it for the newer one of another lover, who presents himself (or is presented by his horse) under romantic circumstances; has the not unfavourable reputation—with a country girl—of having lived thoughtlessly and gaily, without doing much harm to anybody; and who, for his youth and figure, and so forth—this may seem foppish again, but upon my soul I don't mean it in that light—might perhaps pass muster in a crowd with Mr. Alfred himself."

There was no gainsaying that last clause, certainly; and Mr. Snitchey, glancing at him, thought so. There was something naturally graceful and pleasant in the very carelessness of his air. It seemed to suggest, of his comely face and well-knit figure, that they might be greatly better if he chose: and that, once roused and made earnest (but he never had been earnest yet), he could be full of fire and purpose. "A dangerous sort of libertine," thought the shrewd lawyer, "to seem to catch the spark he wants, from a young lady's eyes."

"Now, observe, Snitchey," he continued, rising and taking him by the button, "and Craggs," taking him by the button also, and placing one partner on either side of him, so that neither might evade him. "I don't ask you for any advice. You are right to keep quite aloof from all parties in such a matter, which is not one in which grave men like you could interfere, on any side. I am briefly going to review in half-a-dozen words, my position and intention, and then I shall leave it to you to do the best for me, in money matters, that you can: seeing that, if I run away with the Doctor's beautiful daughter (as I hope to do, and to become another man under her bright influence), it will be, for the moment, more chargeable than running away alone. But I shall soon make all that up in an altered life."

"I think it will be better not to hear this, Mr. Craggs?" said Snitchey, looking at him across the client.

"I think not," said Craggs.— Both listened attentively.

"Well! You needn't hear it," replied their client. "I'll mention it, however. I don't mean to ask the Doctor's consent, because he wouldn't give it me. But I mean to do the Doctor no wrong or harm, because (besides there being nothing serious in such trifles, as he says) I hope to rescue his child, my Marion, from what I see—I *know*—she dreads, and contemplates with misery: that is, the return of this old lover. If anything in the world is true, it is true that she dreads his return. Nobody is injured so far. I am so harried and worried here just now, that I lead the life of a flying-fish. I skulk about in the dark, I am shut out of my own house, and warned off my own grounds; but that house, and those grounds, and many an acre besides, will come back to me one day, as you know and say; and Marion will probably be richer—on your showing, who are never sanguine—ten years hence as my wife, than as the wife of Alfred Heathfield, whose return she dreads (remember that), and in whom or in any man, my passion is not surpassed. Who is injured yet? It is a fair case throughout. My right is as good as his, if she decide in my favour; and I will try my right by her alone. You will like to know no more after this, and I will tell you no more. Now you know my purpose, and wants. When must I leave here?"

"In a week," said Snitchey. "Mr. Craggs?"

"In something less, I should say," responded Craggs.

"In a month," said the client, after attentively watching the two faces. "This day month. To-day is Thursday. Succeed or fail, on this day month I go."

"It's too long a delay," said Snitchey; "much too long. But let it be so. I thought he'd have stipulated for three," he murmured to himself. "Are you going? Good night, sir!"

"Good night!" returned the client, shaking hands with the Firm. "You'll live to see me making a good use of riches yet. Henceforth the star of my destiny is Marion!"

"Take care of the stairs, sir," replied Snitchey; "for she don't shine there. Good night!"

"Good night!"

So they both stood at the stair-head with a pair of office-candles, watching him down. When he had gone away, they stood looking at each other.

"What do you think of all this, Mr. Craggs?" said Snitchey.

Mr. Craggs shook his head.

"It was our opinion, on the day when that release was executed, that there was something curious in the parting of that pair, I recollect," said Snitchey.

"It was," said Mr. Craggs.

"Perhaps he deceives himself altogether," pursued Mr. Snitchey, locking up the fire-proof box, and putting it away; "or, if he don't, a little bit of fickleness and perfidy is not a miracle, Mr. Craggs. And yet I thought that pretty face was very true. I thought," said Mr. Snitchey, putting on his great-coat (for the weather was very cold), drawing on his gloves, and snuffing out one candle, "that I had even seen her character becoming stronger and more resolved of late. More like her sister's."

"Mrs. Craggs was of the same opinion," returned Craggs.

"I'd really give a trifle to-night," observed Mr. Snitchey, who was a good-natured man, "if I could believe that Mr. Warden was reckoning without his host; but light-headed, capricious, and unballasted as he is, he knows something of the world and its people (he ought to, for he has bought what he does know, dear enough); and I can't quite think that. We had better not interfere: we can do nothing, Mr. Craggs, but keep quiet."

"Nothing," returned Craggs.

"Our friend the Doctor makes light of such things," said Mr. Snitchey, shaking his head. "I hope he mayn't stand in need of his philosophy. Our friend Alfred talks of the battle of life," he shook his head again, "I hope he mayn't be cut down early in the day. Have you got your hat, Mr. Craggs? I am going to put the other candle out."

Mr. Craggs replying in the affirmative, Mr. Snitchey suited the action to the word, and they groped their way out of the council-chamber, now dark as the subject, or the law in general.

My story passes to a quiet little study, where, on that same night, the sisters and the hale old Doctor sat by a cheerful fireside. Grace was working at her needle. Marion read aloud from a book before her. The Doctor, in his dressing-gown and slippers, with his feet spread out upon the warm rug, leaned back in his easy-chair, and listened to the book, and looked upon his daughters.

They were very beautiful to look upon. Two better faces for a fireside, never made a fireside bright and sacred. Something of the difference between them had been softened down in three years' time; and enthroned upon the clear brow of the younger sister, looking through her eyes, and thrilling in her voice, was the same earnest nature that her own motherless youth had ripened in the elder sister long ago. But she still appeared at once the lovelier and weaker of the two; still seemed to rest her head upon her sister's breast, and put her trust in her, and look into her eyes for counsel and reliance. Those loving eyes, so calm, serene, and cheerful, as of old.

" 'And being in her own home,' " read Marion, from the book; " 'her home made exquisitely dear by these remembrances, she now began to know that the great trial of her heart must soon come on, and could not be delayed. O Home, our comforter and friend when others fall away, to part with whom, at any step between the cradle and the grave' "—

"Marion, my love!" said Grace.

"Why, Puss!" exclaimed her father, "what's the matter?"

She put her hand upon the hand her sister stretched towards her, and read on; her voice still faltering and trembling, though she made an effort to command it when thus interrupted.

" 'To part with whom, at any step between the cradle and the grave, is always sorrowful. O Home, so true to us, so often slighted in return, be lenient to them that turn away from thee, and do not haunt their erring footsteps too reproachfully! Let no kind looks, no well-remembered smiles, be seen upon thy phantom face. Let no ray of affection, welcome, gentleness, forbearance, cordiality, shine from thy white head. Let no old loving word, or tone, rise up in judgment against thy deserter; but if thou canst look harshly and severely, do, in mercy to the Penitent!' "

"Dear Marion, read no more to-night," said Grace—for she was weeping.

"I cannot," she replied, and closed the book. "The words seem all on fire!"

The Doctor was amused at this; and laughed as he patted her on the head.

"What! overcome by a story-book!" said Doctor Jeddler. "Print and paper! Well, well, it's all one. It's as rational to make a serious matter of print and paper as of anything else. But dry your eyes, love, dry your eyes. I dare say the heroine has got home again long ago, and made it up all round—and if she hasn't, a real home is only four walls; and a fictitious one, mere rags and ink. What's the matter now?"

"It's only me, Mister," said Clemency, putting in her head at the door.

"And what's the matter with *you?*" said the Doctor.

"Oh, bless you, nothing an't the matter with me," returned Clemency—and truly too, to judge from her well-soaped face, in which there gleamed as usual the very soul of good-humour, which, ungainly as she was, made her quite engaging. Abrasions on the elbows are not generally understood, it is true, to range within that class of personal charms called beauty-spots. But it is better, going through the world, to have the arms chafed in that narrow passage, than the temper: and Clemency's was sound and whole as any beauty's in the land.

"Nothing an't the matter with me," said Clemency, entering, "but —come a little closer, Mister."

The Doctor, in some astonishment, complied with this invitation.

"You said I wasn't to give you one before them, you know," said Clemency.

A novice in the family might have supposed, from her extraordinary ogling as she said it, as well as from a singular rapture or ecstasy which pervaded her elbows, as if she were embracing herself, that "one," in its most favourable interpretation, meant a chaste salute. Indeed the Doctor himself seemed alarmed, for the moment; but quickly regained his composure, as Clemency, having had recourse to both her pockets—beginning with the right one, going away to the wrong one, and afterwards coming back to the right one again— produced a letter from the Post-office.

"Britain was riding by on a errand," she chuckled, handing it to the Doctor, "and see the mail come in, and waited for it. There's A. H. in the corner. Mr. Alfred's on his journey home, I bet. We shall have a wedding in the house—there was two spoons in my saucer this morning. Oh Luck, how slow he opens it!"

All this she delivered, by way of soliloquy, gradually rising higher and higher on tiptoe, in her impatience to hear the news, and making a corkscrew of her apron, and a bottle of her mouth. At last, arriving at a climax of suspense, and seeing the Doctor still engaged in the perusal of the letter, she came down flat upon the soles of her feet again, and cast her apron, as a veil, over her head, in a mute despair, and inability to bear it any longer.

"Here! Girls!" cried the Doctor. "I can't help it: I never could keep a secret in my life. There are not many secrets, indeed, worth being kept in such a—well! never mind that. Alfred's coming home, my dears, directly."

"Directly!" exclaimed Marion.

"What! The story-book is soon forgotten!" said the Doctor, pinching her cheek. "I thought the news would dry those tears. Yes. 'Let it be a surprise,' he says, here. But I can't let it be a surprise. He must have a welcome."

"Directly!" repeated Marion.

"Why, perhaps not what your impatience calls 'directly,'" returned the Doctor; "but pretty soon too. Let us see. Let us see. To-day is Thursday, is it not? Then he promises to be here, this day month."

"This day month!" repeated Marion, softly.

"A gay day and a holiday for us," said the cheerful voice of her sister Grace, kissing her in congratulation. "Long looked forward to, dearest, and come at last."

She answered with a smile; a mournful smile, but full of sisterly affection. As she looked in her sister's face, and listened to the quiet music of her voice, picturing the happiness of this return, her own face glowed with hope and joy.

And with a something else; a something shining more and more through all the rest of its expression; for which I have no name. It was not exultation, triumph, proud enthusiasm. They are not so calmly shown. It was not love and gratitude alone, though love and gratitude were part of it. It emanated from no sordid thought, for sordid thoughts do not light up the brow, and hover on the lips, and move the spirit like a fluttered light, until the sympathetic figure trembles.

Dr. Jeddler, in spite of his system of philosophy—which he was continually contradicting and denying in practice, but more famous philosophers have done that—could not help having as much interest in the return of his old ward and pupil as if it had been a serious event. So he sat himself down in his easy-chair again, stretched out his slippered feet once more upon the rug, read the letter over and over a great many times, and talked it over more times still.

"Ah! The day was," said the Doctor, looking at the fire, "when you and he, Grace, used to trot about arm-in-arm, in his holiday time, like a couple of walking dolls. You remember?"

"I remember," she answered, with her pleasant laugh, and plying her needle busily.

"This day month, indeed!" mused the Doctor. "That hardly seems a twelvemonth ago. And where was my little Marion then!"

"Never far from her sister," said Marion, cheerily, "however little. Grace was everything to me, even when she was a young child herself."

"True, Puss, true," returned the Doctor. "She was a staid little woman, was Grace, and a wise housekeeper, and a busy, quiet, pleasant body; bearing with our humours and anticipating our wishes, and always ready to forget her own, even in those times. I never knew you positive or obstinate, Grace, my darling, even then, on any subject but one."

"I am afraid I have changed sadly for the worse, since," laughed Grace, still busy at her work. "What was that one, father?"

"Alfred, of course," said the Doctor. "Nothing would serve you but you must be called Alfred's wife; so we called you Alfred's wife; and you liked it better, I believe (odd as it seems now), than being called a Duchess, if we could have made you one."

"Indeed?" said Grace, placidly.

"Why, don't you remember?" inquired the Doctor.

"I think I remember something of it," she returned, "but not much. It's so long ago." And as she sat at work, she hummed the burden of an old song, which the Doctor liked.

"Alfred will find a real wife soon," she said, breaking off; "and that will be a happy time indeed for all of us. My three years' trust is nearly at an end, Marion. It has been a very easy one. I shall tell Alfred, when I give you back to him, that you have loved him dearly all the time, and that he has never once needed my good services. May I tell him so, love?"

"Tell him, dear Grace," replied Marion, "that there never was a trust so generously, nobly, steadfastly, discharged; and that I have loved *you*, all the time, dearer and dearer every day; and O! how dearly now!"

"Nay," said her cheerful sister, returning her embrace, "I can scarcely tell him that; we will leave my deserts to Alfred's imagination. It will be liberal enough, dear Marion; like your own."

With that, she resumed the work she had for a moment laid down, when her sister spoke so fervently: and with it the old song the Doctor liked to hear. And the Doctor, still reposing in his easy-chair, with his slippered feet stretched out before him on the rug, listened to the tune, and beat time on his knee with Alfred's letter, and looked at his two daughters, and thought that among the many trifles of the trifling world, these trifles were agreeable enough.

Clemency Newcome, in the meantime, having accomplished her mission and lingered in the room until she had made herself a party to the news, descended to the kitchen, where her coadjutor, Mr. Britain, was regaling after supper, surrounded by such a plentiful collection of bright pot-lids, well-scoured saucepans, burnished dinner-covers, gleaming kettles, and other tokens of her industrious habits, arranged upon the walls and shelves, that he sat as in the centre of a hall of mirrors. The majority did not give forth very flattering portraits of him, certainly; nor were they by any means unanimous in their reflections; as some made him very long-faced, others very broad-faced, some tolerably well-looking, others vastly ill-looking, according to their several manners of reflecting: which were as various, in respect of one fact, as those of so many kinds of men. But they all agreed that in the midst of them sat, quite at his ease, an individual with a pipe in his mouth, and a jug of beer at his elbow, who nodded condescendingly to Clemency, when she stationed herself at the same table.

"Well, Clemmy," said Britain, "how are you by this time, and what's the news?"

Clemency told him the news, which he received very graciously. A gracious change had come over Benjamin from head to foot. He was much broader, much redder, much more cheerful, and much jollier in all respects. It seemed as if his face had been tied up in a knot before, and was now untwisted and smoothed out.

"There'll be another job for Snitchey and Craggs, I suppose," he observed, puffing slowly at his pipe. "More witnessing for you and me, perhaps, Clemmy!"

"Lor!" replied his fair companion, with her favourite twist of her favourite joints. "I wish it was me, Britain!"

"Wish what was you?"

"A-going to be married," said Clemency.

Benjamin took his pipe out of his mouth and laughed heartily. "Yes! you're a likely subject for that!" he said. "Poor Clem!" Clemency for her part laughed as heartily as he, and seemed as much amused by the idea. "Yes," she assented, "I'm a likely subject for that; an't I?"

"*You'll* never be married, you know," said Mr. Britain, resuming his pipe.

"Don't you think I ever shall though?" said Clemency, in perfect good faith.

Mr. Britain shook his head. "Not a chance of it!"

"Only think!" said Clemency. "Well!—I suppose you mean to, Britain, one of these days; don't you?"

A question so abrupt, upon a subject so momentous, required consideration. After blowing out a great cloud of smoke, and looking at it with his head now on this side and now on that, as if it were actually the question, and he were surveying it in various aspects, Mr. Britain replied that he wasn't altogether clear about it, but—ye-es— he thought he might come to that at last.

"I wish her joy, whoever she may be!" cried Clemency.

"Oh she'll have that," said Benjamin, "safe enough."

"But she wouldn't have led quite such a joyful life as she will lead, and wouldn't have had quite such a sociable sort of husband as she will have," said Clemency, spreading herself half over the table, and staring retrospectively at the candle, "if it hadn't been for—not that I went to do it, for it was accidental, I am sure—if it hadn't been for me; now would she, Britain?"

"Certainly not," returned Mr. Britain, by this time in that high state of appreciation of his pipe, when a man can open his mouth but a very little way for speaking purposes; and sitting luxuriously immovable in his chair, can afford to turn only his eyes towards a companion, and that very passively and gravely. "Oh! I'm greatly beholden to you, you know, Clem."

"Lor, how nice that is to think of!" said Clemency.

At the same time, bringing her thoughts as well as her sight to bear upon the candle-grease, and becoming abruptly reminiscent of its healing qualities as a balsam, she anointed her left elbow with a plentiful application of that remedy.

"You see I've made a good many investigations of one sort and another in my time," pursued Mr. Britain, with the profundity of a sage, "having been always of an inquiring turn of mind; and I've read a good many books about the general Rights of things and Wrongs of things, for I went into the literary line myself, when I began life."

"Did you though!" cried the admiring Clemency.

"Yes," said Mr. Britain: "I was hid for the best part of two years behind a bookstall, ready to fly out if anybody pocketed a volume; and after that, I was light porter to a stay and mantua maker, in which capacity I was employed to carry about, in oilskin baskets, nothing but deceptions—which soured my spirits and disturbed my confidence in human nature; and after that, I heard a world of discussions in this house, which soured my spirits fresh; and my opinion after all is, that, as a safe and comfortable sweetener of the same, and as a pleasant guide through life, there's nothing like a nutmeg-grater."

Clemency was about to offer a suggestion, but he stopped her by anticipating it.

"Com-bined," he added gravely, "with a thimble."

"Do as you wold, you know, and cetrer, eh!" observed Clemency, folding her arms comfortably in her delight at this avowal, and patting her elbows. "Such a short cut, an't it?"

"I'm not sure," said Mr. Britain, "that it's what would be considered good philosophy. I've my doubts about that; but it wears well, and saves a quantity of snarling, which the genuine article don't always."

"See how you used to go on once, yourself, you know!" said Clemency.

"Ah!" said Mr. Britain. "But the most extraordinary thing, Clemmy, is that I should live to be brought round, through you. That's the strange part of it. Through you! Why, I suppose you haven't so much as half an idea in your head."

Clemency, without taking the least offence, shook it, and laughed, and hugged herself, and said, "No, she didn't suppose she had."

"I'm pretty sure of it," said Mr. Britain.

"Oh! I dare say you're right," said Clemency. "I don't pretend to none. I don't want any."

Benjamin took his pipe from his lips, and laughed till the tears ran down his face. "What a natural you are, Clemmy!" he said, shaking his head, with an infinite relish of the joke, and wiping his eyes. Clemency, without the smallest inclination to dispute it, did the like, and laughed as heartily as he.

"I can't help liking you," said Mr. Britain; "you're a regular good creature in your way, so shake hands, Clem. Whatever happens, I'll always take notice of you, and be a friend to you."

"Will you?" returned Clemency. "Well! that's very good of you."

"Yes, yes," said Mr. Britain, giving her his pipe to knock the ashes out of it; "I'll stand by you. Hark! That's a curious noise!"

"Noise!" repeated Clemency.

"A footstep outside. Somebody dropping from the wall, it sounded like," said Britain. "Are they all a-bed up-stairs?"

"Yes, all a-bed by this time," she replied.

"Didn't you hear anything?"

"No."

They both listened, but heard nothing.

"I tell you what," said Benjamin, taking down a lantern. "I'll have a look round, before I go to bed myself, for satisfaction's sake. Undo the door while I light this, Clemmy."

Clemency complied briskly; but observed as she did so, that he would only have his walk for his pains, that it was all his fancy, and so forth. Mr. Britain said "Very likely;" but sallied out, nevertheless, armed with the poker, and casting the light of the lantern far and near in all directions.

"It's as quiet as a churchyard," said Clemency, looking after him; "and almost as ghostly too!"

Glancing back into the kitchen, she cried fearfully, as a light figure stole into her view, "What's that!"

"Hush!" said Marion in an agitated whisper. "You have always loved me, have you not?"

"Loved you, child! You may be sure I have."

"I am sure. And I may trust you, may I not? There is no one else just now, in whom I *can* trust."

"Yes," said Clemency, with all her heart.

"There is some one out there," pointing to the door, "whom I must see, and speak with, to-night. Michael Warden, for God's sake, retire! Not now!"

Clemency started with surprise and trouble as, following the direction of the speaker's eyes, she saw a dark figure standing in the doorway.

"In another moment you may be discovered," said Marion. "Not now! Wait, if you can, in some concealment. I will come presently."

He waved his hand to her, and was gone.

"Don't go to bed. Wait here for me!" said Marion, hurriedly. "I have been seeking to speak to you for an hour past. Oh, be true to me!"

Eagerly seizing her bewildered hand, and pressing it with both her own to her breast—an action more expressive, in its passion of entreaty, than the most eloquent appeal in words,—Marion withdrew; as the light of the returning lantern flashed into the room.

"All still and peaceable. Nobody there. Fancy, I suppose," said Mr.

Britain, as he locked and barred the door. "One of the effects of having a lively imagination. Halloa! Why, what's the matter?"

Clemency, who could not conceal the effects of her surprise and concern, was sitting in a chair: pale, and trembling from head to foot.

"Matter!" she repeated, chafing her hands and elbows nervously, and looking anywhere but at him. "That's good in you, Britain, that is! After going and frightening one out of one's life with noises and lanterns, and I don't know what all. Matter! Oh, yes!"

"If you're frightened out of your life by a lantern, Clemmy," said Mr. Britain, composedly blowing it out and hanging it up again, "that apparition's very soon got rid of. But you're as bold as brass in general," he said, stopping to observe her; "and were, after the noise and the lantern too. What have you taken into your head? Not an idea, eh?"

But as Clemency bade him good night very much after her usual fashion, and began to bustle about with a show of going to bed herself immediately, Little Britain, after giving utterance to the original remark that it was impossible to account for a woman's whims, bade her good night in return, and taking up his candle strolled drowsily away to bed.

When all was quiet, Marion returned.

"Open the door," she said; "and stand there close beside me, while I speak to him, outside."

Timid as her manner was, it still evinced a resolute and settled purpose, such as Clemency could not resist. She softly unbarred the door: but before turning the key, looked round on the young creature waiting to issue forth when she should open it.

The face was not averted or cast down, but looking full upon her, in its pride of youth and beauty. Some simple sense of the slightness of the barrier that interposed itself between the happy home and honoured love of the fair girl, and what might be the desolation of that home and shipwreck of its dearest treasure, smote so keenly on the tender heart of Clemency, and so filled it to overflowing with sorrow and compassion, that, bursting into tears, she threw her arms round Marion's neck.

"It's little that I know, my dear," cried Clemency, "very little; but I know that this should not be. Think of what you do!"

"I have thought of it many times," said Marion, gently.

"Once more," urged Clemency. "Till to-morrow." Marion shook her head.

"For Mr. Alfred's sake," said Clemency, with homely earnestness. "Him that you used to love so dearly, once!"

She hid her face upon the instant in her hands, repeating "Once!" as if it rent her heart.

"Let me go out," said Clemency, soothing her. "I'll tell him what you like. Don't cross the door-step to-night. I'm sure no good will come of it. Oh, it was an unhappy day when Mr. Warden was ever brought here! Think of your good father, darling—of your sister."

"I have," said Marion, hastily raising her head. "You don't know what I do. I *must* speak to him. You are the best and truest friend in all the world for what you have said to me, but I must take this step. Will you go with me, Clemency," she kissed her on her friendly face, "or shall I go alone?"

Sorrowing and wondering, Clemency turned the key, and opened the door. Into the dark and doubtful night that lay beyond the threshold, Marion passed quickly, holding by her hand.

In the dark night he joined her, and they spoke together earnestly and long; and the hand that held so fast by Clemency's, now trembled, now turned deadly cold, now clasped and close on hers, in the strong feeling of the speech it emphasised unconsciously. When they returned, he followed to the door, and pausing there a moment, seized the other hand, and pressed it to his lips. Then, stealthily withdrew.

The door was barred and locked again, and once again she stood beneath her father's roof. Not bowed down by the secret that she brought there, though so young; but with that same expression on her face for which I had no name before, and shining through her tears.

Again she thanked and thanked her humble friend, and trusted to her, as she said, with confidence, implicitly. Her chamber safely reached, she fell upon her knees; and with her secret weighing on her heart, could pray!

Could rise up from her prayers, so tranquil and serene, and bending over her fond sister in her slumber, look upon her face and smile —though sadly: murmuring as she kissed her forehead, how that Grace had been a mother to her, ever, and she loved her as a child!

Could draw the passive arm about her neck when lying down to rest—it seemed to cling there, of its own will, protectingly and tenderly even in sleep—and breathe upon the parted lips, God bless her!

Could sink into a peaceful sleep herself; but for one dream, in which she cried out, in her innocent and touching voice, that she was quite alone, and they had all forgotten her.

A month soon passes, even at its tardiest pace. The month appointed to elapse between that night and the return, was quick of foot, and went by like a vapour.

The day arrived. A raging winter day, that shook the old house, sometimes, as if it shivered in the blast. A day to make home doubly home. To give the chimney-corner new delights. To shed a ruddier glow upon the faces gathered round the hearth, and draw each fireside group into a closer and more social league, against the roaring

elements without. Such a wild winter day as best prepares the way
for shut-out night; for curtained rooms, and cheerful look; for music,
laughter, dancing, light, and jovial entertainment!

All these the Doctor had in store to welcome Alfred back. They
knew that he could not arrive till night; and they would make the
night air ring, he said, as he approached. All his old friends should
congregate about him. He should not miss a face that he had known
and liked. No! They should every one be there!

So guests were bidden, and musicians were engaged, and tables
spread, and floors prepared for active feet, and bountiful provision
made, of every hospitable kind. Because it was the Christmas season,
and his eyes were all unused to English holly and its sturdy green, the
dancing-room was garlanded and hung with it; and the red berries
gleamed an English welcome to him, peeping from among the leaves.

It was a busy day for all of them: a busier day for none of them
than Grace, who noiselessly presided everywhere, and was the cheerful
mind of all the preparations. Many a time that day (as well as many
a time within the fleeting month preceding it), did Clemency glance
anxiously, and almost fearfully, at Marion. She saw her paler, perhaps, than usual; but there was a sweet composure on her face that
made it lovelier than ever.

At night when she was dressed, and wore upon her head a wreath
that Grace had proudly twined about it—its mimic flowers were Alfred's favourites, as Grace remembered when she chose them—that
old expression, pensive, almost sorrowful, and yet so spiritual, high,
and stirring, sat again upon her brow, enhanced a hundred-fold.

"The next wreath I adjust on this fair head, will be a marriage
wreath," said Grace; "or I am no true prophet, dear."

Her sister smiled, and held her in her arms.

"A moment, Grace. Don't leave me yet. Are you sure that I want
nothing more?"

Her care was not for that. It was her sister's face she thought of,
and her eyes were fixed upon it, tenderly.

"My art," said Grace, "can go no farther, dear girl; nor your beauty.
I never saw you look so beautiful as now."

"I never was so happy," she returned.

"Ay, but there is a greater happiness in store. In such another home,
as cheerful and as bright as this looks now," said Grace, "Alfred and
his young wife will soon be living."

She smiled again. "It is a happy home, Grace, in your fancy. I can
see it in your eyes. I know it *will* be happy, dear. How glad I am to
know it."

"Well," cried the Doctor, bustling in. "Here we are, all ready for
Alfred, eh? He can't be here until pretty late—an hour or so before
midnight—so there'll be plenty of time for making merry before he

comes. He'll not find us with the ice unbroken. Pile up the fire here, Britain! Let it shine upon the holly till it winks again. It's a world of nonsense, Puss; true lovers and all the rest of it—all nonsense; but we'll be nonsensical with the rest of 'em, and give our true lover a mad welcome. Upon my word!" said the old Doctor, looking at his daughters proudly, "I'm not clear to-night, among other absurdities, but that I'm the father of two handsome girls."

"All that one of them has ever done, or may do—may do, dearest father—to cause you pain or grief, forgive her," said Marion, "forgive her now, when her heart is full. Say that you forgive her. That you will forgive her. That she shall always share your love, and—," and the rest was not said, for her face was hidden on the old man's shoulder.

"Tut, tut, tut," said the Doctor gently. "Forgive! What have I to forgive? Heyday, if our true lovers come back to flurry us like this, we must hold 'em at a distance; we must send expresses out to stop 'em short upon the road, and bring 'em on a mile or two a day, until we're properly prepared to meet 'em. Kiss me, Puss. Forgive! Why, what a silly child you are! If you had vexed and crossed me fifty times a day, instead of not at all, I'd forgive you everything, but such a supplication. Kiss me again, Puss. There! Prospective and retrospective—a clear score between us. Pile up the fire here! Would you freeze the people on this bleak December night! Let us be light, and warm, and merry, or I'll not forgive some of you!"

So gaily the old Doctor carried it! And the fire was piled up, and the lights were bright, and company arrived, and murmuring of lively tongues began, and already there was a pleasant air of cheerful excitement stirring through all the house.

More and more company came flocking in. Bright eyes sparkled upon Marion; smiling lips gave her joy of his return; sage mothers fanned themselves, and hoped she mightn't be too youthful and inconstant for the quiet round of home; impetuous fathers fell into disgrace for too much exaltation of her beauty; daughters envied her; sons envied him; innumerable pairs of lovers profited by the occasion; all were interested, animated, and expectant.

Mr. and Mrs. Craggs came arm in arm, but Mrs. Snitchey came alone. "Why, what's become of *him?*" inquired the Doctor.

The feather of a Bird of Paradise in Mrs. Snitchey's turban, trembled as if the Bird of Paradise were alive again, when she said that doubtless Mr. Craggs knew. *She* was never told.

"That nasty office," said Mrs. Craggs.

"I wish it was burnt down," said Mrs. Snitchey.

"He's—he's—there's a little matter of business that keeps my partner rather late," said Mr. Craggs, looking uneasily about him.

"Oh—h! Business. Don't tell me!" said Mrs. Snitchey.

"*We* know what business means," said Mrs. Craggs.

But their not knowing what it meant, was perhaps the reason why Mrs. Snitchey's Bird of Paradise feather quivered so portentously, and why all the pendant bits on Mrs. Craggs's earrings shook like little bells.

"I wonder *you* could come away, Mr. Craggs," said his wife.

"Mr. Craggs is fortunate, I'm sure!" said Mrs. Snitchey.

"That office so engrosses 'em," said Mrs. Craggs.

"A person with an office has no business to be married at all," said Mrs. Snitchey.

Then, Mrs. Snitchey said, within herself, that that look of hers had pierced to Craggs's soul, and he knew it; and Mrs. Craggs observed to Craggs, that "his Snitcheys" were deceiving him behind his back, and he would find it out when it was too late.

Still, Mr. Craggs, without much heeding these remarks, looked uneasily about until his eye rested on Grace, to whom he immediately presented himself.

"Good evening, ma'am," said Craggs. "You look charmingly. Your—Miss—your sister, Miss Marion, is she——"

"Oh, she's quite well, Mr. Craggs."

"Yes—I—is she here?" asked Craggs.

"Here! Don't you see her yonder? Going to dance?" said Grace.

Mr. Craggs put on his spectacles to see the better; looked at her through them, for some time; coughed; and put them, with an air of satisfaction, in their sheath again, and in his pocket.

Now the music struck up, and the dance commenced. The bright fire crackled and sparkled, rose and fell, as though it joined the dance itself, in right good fellowship. Sometimes, it roared as if it would make music too. Sometimes, it flashed and beamed as if it were the eye of the old room: it winked too, sometimes, like a knowing patriarch, upon the youthful whisperers in corners. Sometimes, it sported with the holly-boughs; and, shining on the leaves by fits and starts, made them look as if they were in the cold winter night again, and fluttering in the wind. Sometimes its genial humour grew obstreperous, and passed all bounds; and then it cast into the room, among the twinkling feet, with a loud burst, a shower of harmless little sparks, and in its exultation leaped and bounded, like a mad thing, up the broad old chimney.

Another dance was near its close, when Mr. Snitchey touched his partner, who was looking on, upon the arm.

Mr. Craggs started, as if his familiar had been a spectre.

"Is he gone?" he asked.

"Hush! He has been with me," said Snitchey, "for three hours and more. He went over everything. He looked into all our arrangements for him, and was very particular indeed. He— Humph!"

The dance was finished. Marion passed close before him, as he spoke. She did not observe him, or his partner; but looked over her shoulder towards her sister in the distance, as she slowly made her way into the crowd, and passed out of their view.

"You see! All safe and well," said Mr. Craggs. "He didn't recur to that subject, I suppose?"

"Not a word."

"And is he really gone? Is he safe away?"

"He keeps to his word. He drops down the river with the tide in that shell of a boat of his, and so goes out to sea on this dark night!— a dare-devil he is—before the wind. There's no such lonely road anywhere else. That's one thing. The tide flows, he says, an hour before midnight—about this time. I'm glad it's over." Mr. Snitchey wiped his forehead, which looked hot and anxious.

"What do you think," said Mr. Craggs, "about—"

"Hush!" replied his cautious partner, looking straight before him. "I understand you. Don't mention names, and don't let us seem to be talking secrets. I don't know what to think; and to tell you the truth, I don't care now. It's a great relief. His self-love deceived him, I suppose. Perhaps the young lady coquetted a little. The evidence would seem to point that way. Alfred not arrived?"

"Not yet," said Mr. Craggs. "Expected every minute."

"Good." Mr. Snitchey wiped his forehead again. "It's a great relief. I haven't been so nervous since we've been in partnership. I intend to spend the evening now, Mr. Craggs."

Mrs. Craggs and Mrs. Snitchey joined them as he announced this intention. The Bird of Paradise was in a state of extreme vibration, and the little bells were ringing quite audibly.

"It has been the theme of general comment, Mr. Snitchey," said Mrs. Snitchey. "I hope the office is satisfied."

"Satisfied with what, my dear?" asked Mr. Snitchey.

"With the exposure of a defenceless woman to ridicule and remark," returned his wife. "That is quite in the way of the office, *that* is."

"I really, myself," said Mrs. Craggs, "have been so long accustomed to connect the office with everything opposed to domesticity, that I am glad to know it as the avowed enemy of my peace. There is something honest in that, at all events."

"My dear," urged Mr. Craggs, "your good opinion is invaluable, but I never avowed that the office was the enemy of your peace."

"No," said Mrs. Craggs, ringing a perfect peal upon the little bells. "Not you, indeed. You wouldn't be worthy of the office, if you had the candour to."

"As to my having been away to-night, my dear," said Mr. Snitchey, giving her his arm, "the deprivation has been mine, I'm sure; but, as Mr. Craggs knows—"

Mrs. Snitchey cut this reference very short by hitching her husband to a distance, and asking him to look at that man. To do her the favour to look at him!

"At which man, my dear?" said Mr. Snitchey.

"Your chosen companion; I'm no companion to you, Mr. Snitchey."

"Yes, yes, you are, my dear," he interposed.

"No, no, I'm not," said Mrs. Snitchey with a majestic smile. "I know my station. Will you look at your chosen companion, Mr. Snitchey; at your referee, at the keeper of your secrets, at the man you trust; at your other self, in short?"

The habitual association of Self with Craggs, occasioned Mr. Snitchey to look in that direction.

"If you can look that man in the eye this night," said Mrs. Snitchey, "and not know that you are deluded, practised upon, made the victim of his arts, and bent down prostrate to his will by some unaccountable fascination which it is impossible to explain and against which no warning of mine is of the least avail, all I can say is—I pity you!"

At the very same moment Mrs. Craggs was oracular on the cross subject. Was it possible, she said, that Craggs could so blind himself to his Snitcheys, as not to feel his true position? Did he mean to say that he had seen his Snitcheys come into that room and didn't plainly see that there was reservation, cunning, treachery, in the man? Would he tell her that his very action, when he wiped his forehead and looked so stealthily about him, didn't show that there was something weighing on the conscience of his precious Snitcheys (if he had a conscience), that wouldn't bear the light? Did anybody but his Snitcheys come to festive entertainments like a burglar?—which, by the way, was hardly a clear illustration of the case, as he had walked in very mildly at the door. And would he still assert to her at noonday (it being nearly midnight), that his Snitcheys were to be justified through thick and thin, against all facts, and reason, and experience?

Neither Snitchey nor Craggs openly attempted to stem the current which had thus set in, but both were content to be carried gently along it, until its force abated. This happened at about the same time as a general movement for a country dance; when Mr. Snitchey proposed himself as a partner to Mrs. Craggs, and Mr. Craggs gallantly offered himself to Mrs. Snitchey; and after some such slight evasions as "why don't you ask somebody else?" and "you'll be glad, I know, if I decline," and "I wonder you can dance out of the office" (but this jocosely now), each lady graciously accepted, and took her place.

It was an old custom among them, indeed, to do so, and to pair off, in like manner, at dinners and suppers; for they were excellent friends, and on a footing of easy familiarity. Perhaps the false Craggs and the wicked Snitchey were a recognised fiction with the two wives, as Doe and Roe, incessantly running up and down bailiwicks, were with the two husbands: or, perhaps the ladies had instituted, and taken upon themselves, these two shares in the business, rather than be left out of it altogether. But certain it is, that each wife went as gravely and steadily to work in her vocation as her husband did in his, and would have considered it almost impossible for the Firm to maintain a successful and respectable existence, without her laudable exertions.

But now the Bird of Paradise was seen to flutter down the middle; and the little bells began to bounce and jingle in poussette; and the Doctor's rosy face spun round and round, like an expressive pegtop highly varnished; and breathless Mr. Craggs began to doubt already, whether country dancing had been made "too easy," like the rest of life; and Mr. Snitchey, with his nimble cuts and capers, footed it for Self and Craggs, and half-a-dozen more.

Now, too, the fire took fresh courage, favoured by the lively wind the dance awakened, and burnt clear and high. It was the Genius of the room, and present everywhere. It shone in people's eyes, it sparkled in the jewels on the snowy necks of girls, it twinkled at their ears as if it whispered to them slyly, it flashed about their waists, it flickered on the ground and made it rosy for their feet, it bloomed upon the ceiling that its glow might set off their bright faces, and it kindled up a general illumination in Mrs. Craggs's little belfry.

Now, too, the lively air that fanned it, grew less gentle as the music quickened and the dance proceeded with new spirit; and a breeze arose that made the leaves and berries dance upon the wall, as they had often done upon the trees; and the breeze rustled in the room as if an invisible company of fairies, treading in the footsteps of the good substantial revellers, were whirling after them. Now, too, no feature of the Doctor's face could be distinguished as he spun and spun; and now there seemed a dozen Birds of Paradise in fitful flight; and now there were a thousand little bells at work; and now a fleet of flying skirts was ruffled by a little tempest, when the music gave in, and the dance was over.

Hot and breathless as the Doctor was, it only made him the more impatient for Alfred's coming.

"Anything been seen, Britain? Anything been heard?"

"Too dark to see far, sir. Too much noise inside the house to hear."

"That's right! The gayer welcome for him. How goes the time?"

"Just twelve, sir. He can't be long, sir."

"Stir up the fire, and throw another log upon it," said the Doctor. "Let him see his welcome blazing out upon the night—good boy!— as he comes along!"

He saw it—Yes! From the chaise he caught the light, as he turned the corner by the old church. He knew the room from which it shone. He saw the wintry branches of the old trees between the light and him. He knew that one of those trees rustled musically in the summer time at the window of Marion's chamber.

The tears were in his eyes. His heart throbbed so violently that he could hardly bear his happiness. How often he had thought of this time—pictured it under all circumstances—feared that it might never come—yearned, and wearied for it—far away!

Again the light! Distinct and ruddy; kindled, he knew, to give him welcome, and to speed him home. He beckoned with his hand, and waved his hat, and cheered out, loud, as if the light were they, and they could see and hear him, as he dashed towards them through the mud and mire, triumphantly.

Stop! He knew the Doctor, and understood what he had done. He would not let it be a surprise to them. But he could make it one, yet, by going forward on foot. If the orchard-gate were open, he could enter there; if not, the wall was easily climbed, as he knew of old; and he would be among them in an instant.

He dismounted from the chaise, and telling the driver—even that was not easy in his agitation—to remain behind for a few minutes, and then to follow slowly, ran on with exceeding swiftness, tried the gate, scaled the wall, jumped down on the other side, and stood panting in the old orchard.

There was a frosty rime upon the trees, which, in the faint light of the clouded moon, hung upon the smaller branches like dead garlands. Withered leaves crackled and snapped beneath his feet, as he crept softly on towards the house. The desolation of a winter night sat brooding on the earth, and in the sky. But, the red light came cheerily towards him from the windows; figures passed and repassed there; and the hum and murmur of voices greeted his ear sweetly.

Listening for hers: attempting, as he crept on, to detach it from the rest, and half believing that he heard it: he had nearly reached the door, when it was abruptly opened, and a figure coming out encountered his. It instantly recoiled with a half-suppressed cry.

"Clemency," he said, "don't you know me?"

"Don't come in!" she answered, pushing him back. "Go away. Don't ask me why. Don't come in."

"What is the matter?" he exclaimed.

"I don't know. I—I am afraid to think. Go back. Hark!"

There was a sudden tumult in the house. She put her hands upon her ears. A wild scream, such as no hands could shut out, was heard; and Grace—distraction in her looks and manner—rushed out at the door.

"Grace!" He caught her in his arms. "What is it! Is she dead!"

She disengaged herself, as if to recognise his face, and fell down at his feet.

A crowd of figures came about them from the house. Among them was her father, with a paper in his hand.

"What is it!" cried Alfred, grasping his hair with his hands, and looking in an agony from face to face, as he bent upon his knee beside the insensible girl. "Will no one look at me? Will no one speak to me? Does no one know me? Is there no voice among you all, to tell me what it is?"

There was a murmur among them. "She is gone."

"Gone!" he echoed.

"Fled, my dear Alfred!" said the Doctor, in a broken voice, and with his hands before his face. "Gone from her home and us. To-night! She writes that she has made her innocent and blameless choice —entreats that we will forgive her—prays that we will not forget her— and is gone."

"With whom? Where?"

He started up, as if to follow in pursuit; but, when they gave way to let him pass, looked wildly round upon them, staggered back, and sunk down in his former attitude, clasping one of Grace's cold hands in his own.

There was a hurried running to and fro, confusion, noise, disorder, and no purpose. Some proceeded to disperse themselves about the roads, and some took horse, and some got lights, and some conversed together, urging that there was no trace or track to follow. Some approached him kindly, with the view of offering consolation; some admonished him that Grace must be removed into the house, and that he prevented it. He never heard them, and he never moved.

The snow fell fast and thick. He looked up for a moment in the air, and thought that those white ashes strewn upon his hopes and misery, were suited to them well. He looked round on the whitening ground, and thought how Marion's footprints would be hushed and covered up, as soon as made, and even that remembrance of her blotted out. But he never felt the weather and he never stirred.

PART THE THIRD

The world had grown six years older since that night of the return. It was a warm autumn afternoon, and there had been heavy rain. The sun burst suddenly from among the clouds; and the old battle-ground, sparkling brilliantly and cheerfully at sight of it in one green place, flashed a responsive welcome there, which spread along the country side as if a joyful beacon had been lighted up, and answered from a thousand stations.

How beautiful the landscape kindling in the light, and that luxuriant influence passing on like a celestial presence, brightening everything! The wood, a sombre mass before, revealed its varied tints of yellow, green, brown, red: its different forms of trees, with raindrops glittering on their leaves and twinkling as they fell. The verdant meadowland, bright and glowing, seemed as if it had been blind, a minute since, and now had found a sense of sight wherewith to look up at the shining sky. Corn-fields, hedgerows, fences, homesteads, and clustered roofs, and steeple of the church, the stream, the water-mill, all sprang out of the gloomy darkness smiling. Birds sang sweetly, flowers raised their drooping heads, fresh scents arose from the invigorated ground; the blue expanse above extended and diffused itself; already the sun's slanting rays pierced mortally the sullen bank of cloud that lingered in its flight; and a rainbow, spirit of all the colours that adorned the earth and sky, spanned the whole arch with its triumphant glory.

At such a time, one little roadside inn, snugly sheltered behind a great elm-tree with a rare seat for idlers encircling its capacious bole, addressed a cheerful front towards the traveller, as a house of entertainment ought, and tempted him with many mute but significant assurances of a comfortable welcome. The ruddy sign-board perched up in the tree, with its golden letters winking in the sun, ogled the passerby, from among the green leaves, like a jolly face, and promised good cheer. The horse-trough, full of clear fresh water, and the ground below it sprinkled with droppings of fragrant hay, made every horse that passed, prick up his ears. The crimson curtains in the lower rooms, and the pure white hangings in the little bed-chambers above, beckoned, Come in! with every breath of air. Upon the bright green shutters, there were golden legends about beer and ale, and neat wines, and good beds; and an affecting picture of a brown jug frothing over at the top. Upon the window-sills were flowering plants in bright red pots, which made a lively show against the white front of the house; and in the darkness of the doorway there were streaks of light, which glanced off from the surfaces of bottles and tankards.

On the door-step appeared a proper figure of a landlord, too; for, though he was a short man, he was round and broad, and stood with his hands in his pockets, and his legs just wide enough apart to express a mind at rest upon the subject of the cellar, and an easy confidence—too calm and virtuous to become a swagger—in the general resources of the Inn. The super-abundant moisture, trickling from everything after the late rain, set him off well. Nothing near him was thirsty. Certain top-heavy dahlias, looking over the palings of his neat well-ordered garden, had swilled as much as they could carry—perhaps a

trifle more—and may have been the worse for liquor; but the sweet-
briar, roses, wall-flowers, the plants at the windows, and the leaves on
the old tree, were in the beaming state of moderate company that had
taken no more than was wholesome for them, and had served to de-
velop their best qualities. Sprinkling dewy drops about them on the
ground, they seemed profuse of innocent and sparkling mirth, that
did good where it lighted, softening neglected corners which the
steady rain could seldom reach, and hurting nothing.

This village Inn had assumed, on being established, an uncommon
sign. It was called The Nutmeg-Grater. And underneath that household word was inscribed, up in the tree, on the same flaming board,
and in the like golden characters, By Benjamin Britain.

At a second glance, and on a more minute examination of his face,
you might have known that it was no other than Benjamin Britain
himself who stood in the doorway—reasonably changed by time, but
for the better; a very comfortable host indeed.

"Mrs. B.," said Mr. Britain, looking down the road, "is rather late.
It's tea-time."

As there was no Mrs. Britain coming, he strolled leisurely out into
the road and looked up at the house, very much to his satisfaction.
"It's just the sort of house," said Benjamin, "I should wish to stop at,
if I didn't keep it."

Then, he strolled towards the garden-paling, and took a look at the
dahlias. They looked over at him, with a helpless drowsy hanging of
their heads: which bobbed again, as the heavy drops of wet dripped
off them.

"You must be looked after," said Benjamin. "Memorandum, not to
forget to tell her so. She's a long time coming!"

Mr. Britain's better half seemed to be by so very much his better
half, that his own moiety of himself was utterly cast away and helpless
without her.

"She hadn't much to do, I think," said Ben. "There were a few
little matters of business after market, but not many. Oh! here we are
at last!"

A chaise-cart, driven by a boy, came clattering along the road: and
seated in it, in a chair, with a large well-saturated umbrella spread out
to dry behind her, was the plump figure of a matronly woman, with
her bare arms folded across a basket which she carried on her knee,
several other baskets and parcels lying crowded around her, and a
certain bright good nature in her face and contented awkwardness in her manner, as she jogged to and fro with the motion of her
carriage, which smacked of old times, even in the distance. Upon her
nearer approach, this relish of by-gone days was not diminished; and
when the cart stopped at the Nutmeg-Grater door, a pair of shoes,
alighting from it, slipped nimbly through Mr. Britain's open arms,

and came down with a substantial weight upon the pathway, which shoes could hardly have belonged to any one but Clemency Newcome.

In fact they did belong to her, and she stood in them, and a rosy comfortable-looking soul she was: with as much soap on her glossy face as in times of yore, but with whole elbows now, that had grown quite dimpled in her improved condition.

"You're late, Clemmy!" said Mr. Britain.

"Why, you see, Ben, I've had a deal to do!" she replied, looking busily after the safe removal into the house of all the packages and baskets: "eight, nine, ten,—where's eleven? Oh! my basket's eleven! It's all right. Put the horse up, Harry, and if he coughs again give him a warm mash to-night. Eight, nine, ten. Why, where's eleven? Oh I forgot, it's all right. How's the children, Ben?"

"Hearty, Clemmy, hearty."

"Bless their precious faces!" said Mrs. Britain, unbonneting her own round countenance (for she and her husband were by this time in the bar), and smoothing her hair with her open hands. "Give us a kiss, old man!"

Mr. Britain promptly complied.

"I think," said Mrs. Britain, applying herself to her pockets and drawing forth an immense bulk of thin books and crumpled papers: a very kennel of dogs'-ears: "I've done everything. Bills all settled—turnips sold—brewer's account looked into and paid—'bacco pipes ordered—seventeen pound four, paid into the Bank—Doctor Heathfield's charge for little Clem—you'll guess what that is—Doctor Heathfield won't take nothing again, Ben."

"I thought he wouldn't," returned Ben.

"No. He says whatever family you was to have, Ben, he'd never put you to the cost of a halfpenny. Not if you was to have twenty."

Mr. Britain's face assumed a serious expression, and he looked hard at the wall.

"An't it kind of him?" said Clemency.

"Very," returned Mr. Britain. "It's the sort of kindness that I wouldn't presume upon, on any account."

"No," retorted Clemency. "Of course not. Then there's the pony—he fetched eight pound two; and that an't bad, is it?"

"It's very good," said Ben.

"I'm glad you're pleased!" exclaimed his wife. "I thought you would be; and I think thats all, and so no more at present from yours and cetrer, C. Britain. Ha, ha, ha! There! Take all the papers, and lock 'em up. Oh! Wait a minute. Here's a printed bill to stick on the wall. Wet from the printer's. How nice it smells!"

"What's this?" said Ben, looking over the document.

"I don't know," replied his wife. "I haven't read a word of it."

"'To be sold by Auction,'" read the host of the Nutmeg-Grater, "'unless previously disposed of by private contract.'"

"They always put that," said Clemency.

"Yes, but they don't always put this," he returned. "Look here, 'Mansion,' &c.—'offices,' &c., 'shrubberies,' &c., 'ring fence,' &c. 'Messrs. Snitchey and Craggs,' &c., 'ornamental portion of the unencumbered freehold property of Michael Warden, Esquire, intending to continue to reside abroad'!"

"Intending to continue to reside abroad!" repeated Clemency.

"Here it is," said Britain. "Look!"

"And it was only this very day that I heard it whispered at the old house, that better and plainer news had been half promised of her, soon!" said Clemency, shaking her head sorrowfully, and patting her elbows as if the recollection of old times unconsciously awakened her old habits. "Dear, dear, dear! There'll be heavy hearts, Ben, yonder."

Mr. Britain heaved a sigh, and shook his head, and said he couldn't make it out: he had left off trying long ago. With that remark, he applied himself to putting up the bill just inside the bar window. Clemency, after meditating in silence for a few moments, roused herself, cleared her thoughtful brow, and bustled off to look after the children.

Though the host of the Nutmeg-Grater had a lively regard for his good-wife, it was of the old patronising kind, and she amused him mightily. Nothing would have astonished him so much, as to have known for certain from any third party, that it was she who managed the whole house, and made him, by her plain straightforward thrift, good-humour, honesty, and industry, a thriving man. So easy it is, in any degree of life (as the world very often finds it), to take those cheerful natures that never assert their merit, at their own modest valuation; and to conceive a flippant liking of people for their outward oddities and eccentricities, whose innate worth, if we would look so far, might make us blush in the comparison!

It was comfortable to Mr. Britain, to think of his own condescension in having married Clemency. She was a perpetual testimony to him of the goodness of his heart, and the kindness of his disposition; and he felt that her being an excellent wife was an illustration of the old precept that virtue is its own reward.

He had finished wafering up the bill, and had locked the vouchers for her day's proceedings in the cupboard—chuckling all the time, over her capacity for business—when, returning with the news that the two Master Britains were playing in the coach-house under the superintendence of one Betsey, and that little Clem was sleeping "like a picture," she sat down to tea, which had awaited her arrival, on a little table. It was a very neat little bar, with the usual display of bottles and glasses; a sedate clock, right to the minute (it was half-past five); everything in its place, and everything furbished and polished up to the very utmost.

"It's the first time I've sat down quietly to-day, I declare," said Mrs. Britain, taking a long breath, as if she had sat down for the night; but getting up again immediately to hand her husband his tea, and cut him his bread-and-butter; "how that bill does set me thinking of old times!"

"Ah!" said Mr. Britain, handling his saucer like an oyster, and disposing of its contents on the same principle.

"That same Mr. Michael Warden," said Clemency, shaking her head at the notice of sale, "lost me my old place."

"And got you your husband," said Mr. Britain.

"Well! So he did," retorted Clemency, "and many thanks to him."

"Man's the creature of habit," said Mr. Britain, surveying her over his saucer. "I had somehow got used to you, Clem; and I found I shouldn't be able to get on without you. So we went and got made man and wife. Ha! ha! We! Who'd have thought it!"

"Who indeed!" cried Clemency. "It was very good of you, Ben."

"No, no, no," replied Mr. Britain, with an air of self-denial. "Nothing worth mentioning."

"Oh yes it was, Ben," said his wife, with great simplicity; "I'm sure I think so, and am very much obliged to you. Ah!" looking again at the bill; "when she was known to be gone, and out of reach, dear girl, I couldn't help telling—for her sake quite as much as theirs—what I knew, could I?"

"You told it, anyhow," observed her husband.

"And Dr. Jeddler," pursued Clemency, putting down her teacup, and looking thoughtfully at the bill, "in his grief and passion turned me out of house and home! I never have been so glad of anything in all my life, as that I didn't say an angry word to him, and hadn't any angry feeling towards him, even then; for he repented that truly, afterwards. How often he has sat in this room, and told me over and over again he was sorry for it!—the last time, only yesterday, when you were out. How often he has sat in this room, and talked to me, hour after hour, about one thing and another, in which he made believe to be interested!—but only for the sake of the days that are gone by, and because he knows she used to like me, Ben!"

"Why, how did you ever come to catch a glimpse of that, Clem?" asked her husband: astonished that she should have a distinct perception of a truth which had only dimly suggested itself to his inquiring mind.

"I don't know, I'm sure," said Clemency, blowing her tea, to cool it. "Bless you, I couldn't tell you, if you was to offer me a reward of a hundred pound."

He might have pursued this metaphysical subject but for her catching a glimpse of a substantial fact behind him, in the shape of a gentleman attired in mourning, and cloaked and booted like a rider on horseback, who stood at the bar-door. He seemed attentive to their conversation, and not at all impatient to interrupt it.

Clemency hastily rose at this sight. Mr. Britain also rose and saluted the guest. "Will you please to walk up-stairs, sir? There's a very nice room up-stairs, sir."

"Thank you," said the stranger, looking earnestly at Mr. Britain's wife. "May I come in here?"

"Oh surely, if you like sir," returned Clemency, admitting him. "What would you please to want, sir?"

The bill had caught his eye, and he was reading it.

"Excellent property that, sir," observed Mr. Britain.

He made no answer; but, turning round, when he had finished reading, looked at Clemency with the same observant curiosity as before. "You were asking me,"—he said, still looking at her,—

"What you would please to take, sir," answered Clemency, stealing a glance at him in return.

"If you will let me have a draught of ale," he said, moving to a table by the window, "and will let me have it here, without being any interruption to your meal, I shall be much obliged to you."

He sat down as he spoke, without any further parley, and looked out at the prospect. He was an easy, well-knit figure of a man in the prime of life. His face, much browned by the sun, was shaded by a quantity of dark hair; and he wore a moustache. His beer being set before him, he filled out a glass, and drank, good-humouredly, to the house; adding, as he put the tumbler down again:

"It's a new house, is it not?"

"Not particularly new, sir," replied Mr. Britain.

"Between five and six years old," said Clemency; speaking very distinctly.

"I think I heard you mention Dr. Jeddler's name, as I came in," inquired the stranger. "That bill reminds me of him; for I happen to know something of that story, by hearsay, and through certain connexions of mine.— Is the old man living?"

"Yes, he's living, sir," said Clemency.

"Much changed?"

"Since when, sir?" returned Clemency, with remarkable emphasis and expression.

"Since his daughter—went away."

"Yes! he's greatly changed since then," said Clemency. "He's grey and old, and hasn't the same way with him at all; but I think he's happy now. He has taken on with his sister since then, and goes to see her very often. That did him good, directly. At first, he was sadly broken down; and it was enough to make one's heart bleed, to see him wandering about, railing at the world; but a great change for the better came over him after a year or two, and then he began to like to talk about his lost daughter, and to praise her, ay and the world too! and was never tired of saying, with the tears in his poor eyes, how beautiful and good she was. He had forgiven her then. That was about the same time as Miss Grace's marriage. Britain, you remember?"

Mr. Britain remembered very well.

"The sister *is* married then," returned the stranger. He paused for some time before he asked, "To whom?"

Clemency narrowly escaped oversetting the tea-board, in her emotion at this question.

"Did *you* never hear?" she said.

"I should like to hear," he replied, as he filled his glass again, and raised it to his lips.

"Ah! It would be a long story, if it was properly told," said Clemency, resting her chin on the palm of her left hand, and supporting that elbow on her right hand, as she shook her head, and looked back through the intervening years, as if she were looking at a fire. "It would be a long story, I am sure."

"But told as a short one," suggested the stranger.

"Told as a short one," repeated Clemency in the same thoughtful tone, and without any apparent reference to him, or consciousness of having auditors, "what would there be to tell? That they grieved together, and remembered her together, like a person dead; that they were so tender of her, never would reproach her, called her back to one another as she used to be, and found excuses for her! Every one knows that. I'm sure I do. No one better," added Clemency, wiping her eyes with her hand.

"And so," suggested the stranger.

"And so," said Clemency, taking him up mechanically, and without any change in her attitude or manner, "they at last were married. They were married on her birth-day—it comes round again to-morrow—very quiet, very humble like, but very happy. Mr. Alfred said, one night when they were walking in the orchard, 'Grace, shall our wedding-day be Marion's birth-day?' And it was."

"And they have lived happily together?" said the stranger.

"Ay," said Clemency. "No two people ever more so. They have had no sorrow but this."

She raised her head as with a sudden attention to the circumstances under which she was recalling these events, and looked quickly at the stranger. Seeing that his face was turned toward the window, and that he seemed intent upon the prospect, she made some eager signs to her husband, and pointed to the bill, and moved her mouth as if she were repeating with great energy, one word or phrase to him over and over again. As she uttered no sound, and as her dumb motions like most of her gestures were of a very extraordinary kind, this unintelligible conduct reduced Mr. Britain to the confines of despair. He stared at the table, at the stranger, at the spoons, at his wife—followed her panto-mime with looks of deep amazement and perplexity—asked in the same language, was it property in danger, was it he in danger, was it she—answered her signals with other signals expressive of the deepest distress and confusion—followed the motions of her lips—guessed half aloud "milk and water," "monthly warning," "mice and walnuts"—and couldn't approach her meaning.

Clemency gave it up at last, as a hopeless attempt; and moving her chair by very slow degrees a little nearer to the stranger, sat with her eyes apparently cast down but glancing sharply at him now and then, waiting until he should ask some other question. She had not to wait long; for he said, presently:

"And what is the after history of the young lady who went away? They know it, I suppose?"

Clemency shook her head. "I've heard," she said, "that Doctor Jeddler is thought to know more of it than he tells. Miss Grace has had letters from her sister, saying that she was well and happy, and made much happier by her being married to Mr. Alfred: and has written letters back. But there's a mystery about her life and fortunes, altogether, which nothing has cleared up to this hour, and which—"

She faltered here, and stopped.

"And which"—repeated the stranger.

"Which only one other person, I believe, could explain," said Clemency, drawing her breath quickly.

"Who may that be?" asked the stranger.

"Mr. Michael Warden!" answered Clemency, almost in a shriek: at once conveying to her husband what she would have had him under-stand before, and letting Michael Warden know that he was recog-nised.

"You remember me, sir?" said Clemency, trembling with emotion; "I saw just now you did! You remember me, that night in the garden. I was with her!"

"Yes. You were," he said.

"Yes, sir," returned Clemency. "Yes, to be sure. This is my husband, if you please. Ben, my dear Ben, run to Miss Grace—run to Mr. Alfred —run somewhere, Ben! Bring somebody here, directly!"

"Stay!" said Michael Warden, quietly interposing himself between the door and Britain. "What would you do?"

"Let them know that you are here, sir," answered Clemency, clap-ping her hands in sheer agitation. "Let them know that they may hear of her, from your own lips; let them know that she is not quite lost to them, but that she will come home again yet, to bless her father and her loving sister—even her old servant, even me," she struck herself upon the breast with both hands, "with a sight of her sweet face. Run,

Ben, run!" And still she pressed him on towards the door, and still Mr.
Warden stood before it, with his hand stretched out, not angrily, but
sorrowfully.

"Or perhaps," said Clemency, running past her husband, and catching in her emotion at Mr. Warden's cloak, "perhaps she's here now;
perhaps she's close by. I think from your manner she is. Let me see
her, sir, if you please. I waited on her when she was a little child. I
saw her grow to be the pride of all this place. I knew her when she
was Mr. Alfred's promised wife. I tried to warn her when you tempted
her away. I know what her old home was when she was like the soul
of it, and how it changed when she was gone and lost. Let me speak
to her, if you please!"

He gazed at her with compassion, not unmixed with wonder: but
he made no gesture of assent.

"I don't think she *can* know," pursued Clemency, "how truly they
forgive her; how they love her; what joy it would be to them, to see
her once more. She may be timorous of going home. Perhaps if she
sees me, it may give her new heart. Only tell me truly, Mr. Warden,
is she with you?"

"She is not," he answered, shaking his head.

This answer, and his manner, and his black dress, and his coming
back so quietly, and his announced intention of continuing to live
abroad, explained it all. Marion was dead.

He didn't contradict her; yes, she was dead! Clemency sat down, hid
her face upon the table, and cried.

At that moment, a grey-headed old gentleman came running in:
quite out of breath, and panting so much that his voice was scarcely to
be recognised as the voice of Mr. Snitchey.

"Good Heaven, Mr. Warden!" said the lawyer, taking him aside,
"what wind has blown——" He was so blown himself, that he couldn't
get on any further until after a pause, when he added, feebly, "you
here?"

"An ill wind, I am afraid," he answered. "If you could have heard
what has just passed—how I have been besought and entreated to
perform impossibilities—what confusion and affliction I carry with
me!"

"I can guess it all. But why did you ever come here, my good sir?"
retorted Snitchey.

"Come! How should I know who kept the house? When I sent my
servant on to you, I strolled in here because the place was new to me;
and I had a natural curiosity in everything new and old, in these old
scenes; and it was outside the town. I wanted to communicate with
you, first, before appearing there. I wanted to know what people would
say to me. I see by your manner that you can tell me. If it were not for

your confounded caution, I should have been possessed of everything long ago."

"Our caution!" returned the lawyer, "speaking for Self and Craggs —deceased," here Mr. Snitchey, glancing at his hat-band, shook his head, "how can you reasonably blame us, Mr. Warden? It was understood between us that the subject was never to be renewed, and that it wasn't a subject on which grave and sober men like us (I made a note of your observations at the time) could interfere. Our caution too! When Mr. Craggs, sir, went down to his respected grave in the full belief——"

"I had given a solemn promise of silence until I should return, whenever that might be," interrupted Mr. Warden; "and I have kept it."

"Well, sir, and I repeat it," returned Mr. Snitchey, "we were bound to silence too. We were bound to silence in our duty towards ourselves, and in our duty towards a variety of clients, you among them, who were as close as wax. It was not our place to make inquiries of you on such a delicate subject. I had my suspicions, sir; but it is not six months since I have known the truth, and been assured that you lost her."

"And you know it?" said his client.

"By Doctor Jeddler himself, sir, who at last reposed that confidence in me voluntarily. He, and only he, has known the whole truth, years and years."

"And you know it?" said his client.

"I do, sir!" replied Snitchey; "and I have also reason to know that it will be broken to her sister to-morrow evening. They have given her that promise. In the meantime, perhaps you'll give me the honour of your company at my house; being unexpected at your own. But, not to run the chance of any more such difficulties as you have had here, in case you should be recognised—though you're a good deal changed; I think I might have passed you myself, Mr. Warden—we had better dine here, and walk on in the evening. It's a very good place to dine at, Mr. Warden: your own property, by-the-bye. Self and Craggs (deceased) took a chop here sometimes, and had it very comfortably served. Mr. Craggs, sir," said Snitchey, shutting his eyes tight for an instant, and opening them again, "was struck off the roll of life too soon."

"Heaven forgive me for not condoling with you," returned Michael Warden, passing his hand across his forehead, "but I'm like a man in a dream at present. I seem to want my wits. Mr. Craggs—yes—I am very sorry we have lost Mr. Craggs." But he looked at Clemency as he said it, and seemed to sympathise with Ben, consoling her.

"Mr. Craggs, sir," observed Snitchey, "didn't find life, I regret to say, as easy to have and to hold as his theory made it out, or he would have been among us now. It's a great loss to me. He was my right arm, my right leg, my right ear, my right eye, was Mr. Craggs. I am paralytic without him. He bequeathed his share of the business to Mrs. Craggs, her executors, administrators, and assigns. His name remains in the Firm to this hour. I try, in a childish sort of a way, to make believe, sometimes, he's alive. You may observe that I speak for Self and Craggs —deceased, sir—deceased," said the tender-hearted attorney, waving his pocket-handkerchief.

Michael Warden, who had still been observant of Clemency, turned to Mr. Snitchey when he ceased to speak, and whispered in his ear.

"Ah, poor thing!" said Snitchey, shaking his head. "Yes. She was always very faithful to Marion. She was always very fond of her. Pretty Marion. Poor Marion! Cheer up, Mistress—you *are* married now, you know, Clemency."

Clemency only sighed, and shook her head.

"Well, well! Wait till to-morrow," said the lawyer, kindly.

"To-morrow can't bring back the dead to life, Mister," said Clemency, sobbing.

"No. It can't do that, or it would bring back Mr. Craggs, deceased," returned the lawyer. "But it may bring some soothing circumstances; it may bring some comfort. Wait till to-morrow!"

So Clemency, shaking his proffered hand, said she would; and Britain, who had been terribly cast down at sight of his despondent wife (which was like the business hanging its head), said that was right; and Mr. Snitchey and Michael Warden went upstairs; and there they were soon engaged in a conversation so cautiously conducted, that no murmur of it was audible above the clatter of plates and dishes, the hissing of the frying-pan, the bubbling of saucepans, the low monotonous waltzing of the jack—with a dreadful click every now and then as if it had met with some mortal accident to its head, in a fit of giddiness— and all the other preparations in the kitchen for their dinner.

To-morrow was a bright and peaceful day; and nowhere were the autumn tints more beautifully seen, than from the quiet orchard of the Doctor's house. The snows of many winter nights had melted from that ground, the withered leaves of many summer times had rustled there, since she had fled. The porch was green again, the trees cast bountiful and changing shadows on the grass, the landscape was as tranquil and serene as it had ever been; but where was she!

Not there. Not there. She would have been a stranger sight in her old home now, even than that home had been at first, without her. But a lady sat in the familiar place, from whose heart she had never passed away; in whose true memory she lived, unchanging, youthful, radiant with all promise and all hope; in whose affection—and it was a mother's now, there was a cherished little daughter playing by her side—she had no rival, no successor; upon whose gentle lips her name was trembling then.

The spirit of the lost girl looked out of those eyes. Those eyes of Grace, her sister, sitting with her husband in the orchard, on their wedding-day, and his and Marion's birth-day.

He had not become a great man; he had not grown rich; he had not forgotten the scenes and friends of his youth; he had not fulfilled any one of the Doctor's old predictions. But in his useful, patient, unknown visiting of poor men's homes; and in his watching of sick beds; and in his daily knowledge of the gentleness and goodness flowering the by-paths of this world, not to be trodden down beneath the heavy foot of poverty, but springing up, elastic, in its track, and making its way beautiful; he had better learned and proved, in each succeeding year, the truth of his old faith. The manner of his life, though quiet and remote, had shown him how often men still entertained angels, unawares, as in the olden time; and how the most unlikely forms— even some that were mean and ugly to the view, and poorly clad— became irradiated by the couch of sorrow, want, and pain, and changed to ministering spirits with a glory round their heads.

He lived to better purpose on the altered battle-ground, perhaps, than if he had contended restlessly in more ambitious lists; and he was happy with his wife, dear Grace.

And Marion. Had *he* forgotten her?

"The time has flown, dear Grace," he said, "since then;" they had been talking of that night; "and yet it seems a long long while ago. We count by changes and events within us. Not by years."

"Yet we have years to count by, too, since Marion was with us," returned Grace. "Six times, dear husband, counting to-night as one, we have sat here on her birth-day, and spoken together of that happy return, so eagerly expected and so long deferred. Ah, when will it be? When will it be?"

Her husband attentively observed her, as the tears collected in her eyes; and drawing nearer, said:

"But Marion told you, in that farewell letter which she left for you upon your table, love, and which you read so often, that years must pass away before it *could* be. Did she not?"

She took a letter from her breast, and kissed it, and said "Yes."

"That through these intervening years, however happy she might be, she would look forward to the time when you would meet again, and all would be made clear; and that she prayed you, trustfully and hopefully to do the same. The letter runs so, does it not, my dear?"

"Yes, Alfred."

"And every other letter she has written since?"

"Except the last—some months ago—in which she spoke of you, and what you then knew, and what I was to learn to-night."

He looked towards the sun, then fast declining, and said that the appointed time was sunset.

"Alfred!" said Grace, laying her hand upon his shoulder earnestly, "there is something in this letter—this old letter, which you say I read so often—that I have never told you. But to-night, dear husband, with that sunset drawing near, and all our life seeming to soften and become hushed with the departing day, I cannot keep it secret."

"What is it, love?"

"When Marion went away, she wrote me, here, that you had once left her a sacred trust to me, and that now she left you, Alfred, such a trust in my hands: praying and beseeching me, as I loved her, and as I loved you, not to reject the affection she believed (she knew, she said) you would transfer to me when the new wound was healed, but to encourage and return it."

"—And make me a proud, and happy man again, Grace. Did she say so?"

"She meant, to make myself so blest and honoured in your love," was his wife's answer, as he held her in his arms.

"Hear me, my dear!" he said.—"No. Hear me so!"—and as he spoke, he gently laid the head she had raised, again upon his shoulder. "I know why I have never heard this passage in the letter until now. I know why no trace of it ever showed itself in any word or look of yours at that time. I know why Grace, although so true a friend to me, was hard to win to be my wife. And knowing it, my own! I know the priceless value of the heart I gird within my arms, and thank GOD for the rich possession!"

She wept, but not for sorrow, as he pressed her to his heart. After a brief space, he looked down at the child, who was sitting at their feet playing with a little basket of flowers, and bade her look how golden and how red the sun was.

"Alfred," said Grace, raising her head quickly at these words. "The sun is going down. You have not forgotten what I am to know before it sets."

"You are to know the truth of Marion's history, my love," he answered.

"All the truth," she said, imploringly. "Nothing veiled from me, any more. That was the promise. Was it not?"

"It was," he answered.

"Before the sun went down on Marion's birth-day. And you see it, Alfred? It is sinking fast."

He put his arm about her waist, and, looking steadily into her eyes, rejoined:

"That truth is not reserved so long for me to tell, dear Grace. It is to come from other lips."

"From other lips!" she faintly echoed.

"Yes. I know your constant heart, I know how brave you are, I know that to you a word of preparation is enough. You have said, truly, that the time is come. It is. Tell me that you have present fortitude to bear a trial—a surprise—a shock: and the messenger is waiting at the gate."

"What messenger?" she said. "And what intelligence does he bring?"

"I am pledged," he answered her, preserving his steady look, "to say no more. Do you think you understand me?"

"I am afraid to think," she said.

There was that emotion in his face, despite its steady gaze, which frightened her. Again she hid her own face on his shoulder, trembling, and entreated him to pause—a moment.

"Courage, my wife! When you have firmness to receive the messenger, the messenger is waiting at the gate. The sun is setting on Marion's birth-day. Courage, courage, Grace!"

She raised her head, and, looking at him, told him she was ready. As she stood, and looked upon him going away, her face was so like Marion's as it had been in her later days at home, that it was wonderful to see. He took the child with him. She called her back—she bore the lost girl's name—and pressed her to her bosom. The little creature, being released again, sped after him, and Grace was left alone.

She knew not what she dreaded, or what hoped; but remained there, motionless, looking at the porch by which they had disappeared.

Ah! what was that, emerging from its shadow; standing on its threshold! That figure, with its white garments rustling in the evening air; its head laid down upon her father's breast, and pressed against it to his loving heart! O God! was it a vision that came bursting from the old man's arms, and with a cry, and with a waving of its hands, and with a wild precipitation of itself upon her in its boundless love, sank down in her embrace!

"Oh, Marion, Marion! Oh, my sister! Oh, my heart's dear love! Oh, joy and happiness unutterable, so to meet again!"

It was no dream, no phantom conjured up by hope and fear, but Marion, sweet Marion! So beautiful, so happy, so unalloyed by care and trial, so elevated and exalted in her loveliness, that as the setting sun shone brightly on her upturned face, she might have been a spirit visiting the earth upon some healing mission.

Clinging to her sister, who had dropped upon a seat and bent down over her—and smiling through her tears—and kneeling, close before her, with both arms twining round her, and never turning for an instant from her face—and with the glory of the setting sun upon her brow, and with the soft tranquillity of evening gathering around them —Marion at length broke silence; her voice, so calm, low, clear, and pleasant, well-tuned to the time.

"When this was my dear home, Grace, as it will be now again—"

"Stay, my sweet love! A moment! O Marion, to hear you speak again!"

She could not bear the voice she loved so well, at first.

"When this was my dear home, Grace, as it will be now again, I loved him from my soul. I loved him most devotedly. I would have died for him, though I was so young. I never slighted his affection in my secret breast for one brief instant. It was far beyond all price to me. Although it is so long ago, and past, and gone, and everything is wholly changed, I could not bear to think that you, who love so well, should think I did not truly love him once. I never loved him better, Grace, than when he left this very scene upon this very day. I never loved him better, dear one, than I did that night when *I* left here."

Her sister, bending over her, could look into her face, and hold her fast.

"But he had gained, unconsciously," said Marion, with a gentle smile, "another heart, before I knew that I had one to give him. That heart—yours, my sister!—was so yielded up, in all its other tenderness, to me; was so devoted, and so noble; that it plucked its love away, and kept its secret from all eyes but mine— Ah! what other eyes were quickened by such tenderness and gratitude!—and was content to sacrifice itself to me. But I knew something of its depths. I knew the struggle it had made. I knew its high, inestimable worth to him, and his appreciation of it, let him love me as he would. I knew the debt I owed it. I had its great example every day before me. What you had done for me, I knew that I could do, Grace, if I would, for you. I never laid my head down on my pillow, but I prayed with tears to do it. I never laid my head down on my pillow, but I thought of Alfred's own words on the day of his departure, and how truly he had said (for I knew that, knowing you) that there were victories gained every day, in struggling hearts, to which these fields of battle were nothing. Thinking more and more upon the great endurance cheerfully sustained, and never known or cared for, that there must be, every day and hour, in that great strife of which he spoke, my trial seemed to grow light and easy. And He who knows our hearts, my dearest, at this moment, and who knows there is no drop of bitterness or grief—of anything but unmixed happiness—in mine, enabled me to make the resolution that I never would be Alfred's wife. That he should be my brother, and your husband, if the course I took could bring that happy end to pass; but that I never would (Grace, I then loved him dearly, dearly!) be his wife!"

"O Marion! O Marion!"

"I had tried to seem indifferent to him;" and she pressed her sister's face against her own; "but that was hard, and you were always his true advocate. I had tried to tell you of my resolution, but you would never hear me; you would never understand me. The time was drawing near for his return. I felt that I must act, before the daily intercourse between us was renewed. I knew that one great pang, undergone at that time, would save a lengthened agony to all of us. I knew that if I went away then, that end must follow which *has* followed, and which has made us both so happy, Grace! I wrote to good Aunt Martha, for a refuge in her house: I did not then tell her all, but something of my story, and she freely promised it. While I was contesting that step with myself, and with my love of you, and home, Mr. Warden, brought here by an accident, became, for some time, our companion."

"I have sometimes feared of late years, that this might have been," exclaimed her sister; and her countenance was ashy-pale. "You never loved him—and you married him in your self-sacrifice to me!"

"He was then," said Marion, drawing her sister closer to her, "on the eve of going secretly away for a long time. He wrote to me, after leaving here; told me what his condition and prospects really were; and offered me his hand. He told me he had seen I was not happy in the prospect of Alfred's return. I believe he thought my heart had had no part in that contract; perhaps thought I might have loved him once, and did not then; perhaps thought that when I tried to seem indifferent, I tried to hide indifference—I cannot tell. But I wished that you should feel me wholly lost to Alfred—hopeless to him —dead. Do you understand me, love?"

Her sister looked into her face, attentively. She seemed in doubt.

"I saw Mr. Warden, and confided in his honour; charged him with my secret, on the eve of his and my departure. He kept it. Do you understand me, dear?"

Grace looked confusedly upon her. She scarcely seemed to hear.

"My love, my sister!" said Marion, "recall your thoughts a moment; listen to me. Do not look so strangely on me. There are countries, dearest, where those who would abjure a misplaced passion, or would strive against some cherished feeling of their hearts and conquer it, retire into a hopeless solitude, and close the world against themselves and worldly loves and hopes for ever. When women do so, they assume that name which is so dear to you and me, and call each other Sisters. But there may be sisters, Grace, who, in the broad world out of doors, and underneath its free sky, and in its crowded places, and among its busy life, and trying to assist and cheer it and to do some good,—learn the same lesson; and who, with hearts still fresh and young, and open to all happiness and means of happiness, can say the battle is long past, the victory long won. And such a one am I! You understand me now?"

Still she looked fixedly upon her, and made no reply.

"Oh Grace, dear Grace," said Marion, clinging yet more tenderly and fondly to that breast from which she had been so long exiled, "if you were not a happy wife and mother—if I had no little namesake here—if Alfred, my kind brother, were not your own fond husband—

from whence could I derive the ecstasy I feel to-night! But as I left here, so I have returned. My heart has known no other love, my hand has never been bestowed apart from it. I am still your maiden sister, unmarried, unbetrothed: your own loving old Marion, in whose affection you exist alone and have no partner, Grace!"

She understood her now. Her face relaxed: sobs came to her relief; and falling on her neck, she wept and wept, and fondled her as if she were a child again.

When they were more composed, they found that the Doctor, and his sister good Aunt Martha, were standing near at hand, with Alfred.

"This is a weary day for me," said good Aunt Martha, smiling through her tears, as she embraced her nieces; "for I lose my dear companion in making you all happy; and what can you give me, in return for my Marion?"

"A converted brother," said the Doctor.

"That's something, to be sure," retorted Aunt Martha, "in such a farce as—"

"No, pray don't," said the Doctor penitently.

"Well, I won't," replied Aunt Martha. "But I consider myself ill used. I don't know what's to become of me without my Marion, after we have lived together half-a-dozen years."

"You must come and live here, I suppose," replied the Doctor. "We shan't quarrel now, Martha."

"Or you must get married, Aunt," said Alfred.

"Indeed," returned the old lady, "I think it might be a good speculation if I were to set my cap at Michael Warden, who, I hear, is come home much the better for his absence in all respects. But as I knew him when he was a boy, and I was not a very young woman then, perhaps he mightn't respond. So I'll make up my mind to go and live with Marion, when she marries, and until then (it will not be very long, I dare say) to live alone. What do *you* say, Brother?"

"I've a great mind to say it's a ridiculous world altogether, and there's nothing serious in it," observed the poor old Doctor.

"You might take twenty affidavits of it if you chose, Anthony," said his sister; "but nobody would believe you with such eyes as those."

"It's a world full of hearts," said the Doctor, hugging his younger daughter, and bending across her to hug Grace—for he couldn't separate the sisters; "and a serious world, with all its folly—even with mine, which was enough to have swamped the whole globe; and it is a world on which the sun never rises, but it looks upon a thousand bloodless battles that are some set-off against the miseries and wickedness of Battle-Fields; and it is a world we need be careful how we libel, Heaven forgive us, for it is a world of sacred mysteries, and its Creator only knows what lies beneath the surface of His lightest image!"

You would not be the better pleased with my rude pen, if it dissected and laid open to your view the transports of this family, long severed and now reunited. Therefore, I will not follow the poor Doctor through his humbled recollection of the sorrow he had had when Marion was lost to him; nor will I tell how serious he had found that world to be, in which some love, deep-anchored, is the portion of all human creatures; nor how such a trifle as the absence of one little unit in the great absurd account, had stricken him to the ground. Nor how, in compassion for his distress, his sister had, long ago, revealed the truth to him by slow degrees, and brought him to the knowledge of the heart of his self-banished daughter, and to that daughter's side.

Nor how Alfred Heathfield had been told the truth, too, in the course of that then current year; and Marion had seen him, and had promised him, as her brother, that on her birth-day, in the evening, Grace should know it from her lips at last.

"I beg your pardon, Doctor," said Mr. Snitchey, looking into the orchard, "but have I liberty to come in?"

Without waiting for permission, he came straight to Marion, and kissed her hand, quite joyfully.

"If Mr. Craggs had been alive, my dear Miss Marion," said Mr. Snitchey, "he would have had great interest in this occasion. It might have suggested to him, Mr. Alfred, that our life is not too easy perhaps: that, taken altogether, it will bear any little smoothing we can give it; but Mr. Craggs was a man who could endure to be convinced, sir. He was always open to conviction. If he were open to conviction, now, I —this is weakness. Mrs. Snitchey, my dear,"—at his summons that lady appeared from behind the door, "you are among old friends."

Mrs. Snitchey having delivered her congratulations, took her husband aside.

"One moment, Mr. Snitchey," said that lady. "It is not in my nature to rake up the ashes of the departed."

"No, my dear," returned her husband.

"Mr. Craggs is—"

"Yes, my dear, he is deceased," said Snitchey.

"But I ask you if you recollect," pursued his wife, "that evening of the ball? I only ask you that. If you do; and if your memory has not entirely failed you, Mr. Snitchey; and if you are not absolutely in your dotage; I ask you to connect this time with that—to remember how I begged and prayed you, on my knees—"

"Upon your knees, my dear?" said Mr. Snitchey.

"Yes," said Mrs. Snitchey, confidently, "and you know it—to beware of that man—to observe his eye—and now to tell me whether I was right, and whether at that moment he knew secrets which he didn't choose to tell."

"Mrs. Snitchey," returned her husband, in her ear, "Madam. Did you ever observe anything in *my* eye?"

"No," said Mrs. Snitchey, sharply. "Don't flatter yourself."

"Because, Madam, that night," he continued, twitching her by the sleeve, "it happens that we both knew secrets which we didn't choose to tell, and both knew just the same professionally. And so the less you say about such things the better, Mrs. Snitchey; and take this as a warning to have wiser and more charitable eyes another time. Miss Marion, I brought a friend of yours along with me. Here! Mistress!"

Poor Clemency, with her apron to her eyes, came slowly in, escorted by her husband; the latter doleful with the presentiment that if she abandoned herself to grief the Nutmeg-Grater was done for.

"Now, Mistress," said the lawyer, checking Marion as she ran towards her, and interposing himself between them, "what's the matter with *you?*"

"The matter!" cried poor Clemency.— When, looking up in wonder, and in indignant remonstrance, and in the added emotion of a great roar from Mr. Britain, and seeing that sweet face so well remembered close before her, she stared, sobbed, laughed, cried, screamed, embraced her, held her fast, released her, fell on Mr. Snitchey and embraced him (much to Mrs. Snitchey's indignation), fell on the Doctor and embraced him, fell on Mr. Britain and embraced him, and concluded by embracing herself, throwing her apron over her head, and going into hysterics behind it.

A stranger had come into the orchard after Mr. Snitchey, and had remained apart, near the gate, without being observed by any of the group; for they had little spare attention to bestow, and that had been monopolised by the ecstasies of Clemency. He did not appear to wish to be observed, but stood alone, with downcast eyes; and there was an air of dejection about him (though he was a gentleman of a gallant appearance) which the general happiness rendered more remarkable.

None but the quick eyes of Aunt Martha, however, remarked him at all; but almost as soon as she espied him, she was in conversation with him. Presently, going to where Marion stood with Grace and her little namesake, she whispered something in Marion's ear at which she started, and appeared surprised; but soon recovering from her confusion, she timidly approached the stranger, in Aunt Martha's company, and engaged in conversation with him too.

"Mr. Britain," said the lawyer, putting his hand in his pocket, and bringing out a legal-looking document, while this was going on, "I congratulate you. You are now the whole and sole proprietor of that freehold tenement, at present occupied and held by yourself as a licensed tavern, or house of public entertainment, and commonly called or known by the sign of the Numeg-Grater. Your wife lost one house, through my client Mr. Michael Warden; and now gains another. I shall have the pleasure of canvassing you for the county, one of these fine mornings."

"Would it make any difference in the vote if the sign was altered, sir?" asked Britain.

"Not in the least," replied the lawyer.

"Then," said Mr. Britain, handing him back the conveyance, "just clap in the words, 'and Thimble,' will you be so good; and I'll have the two mottoes painted up in the parlour instead of my wife's portrait."

"And let me," said a voice behind them; it was the stranger's— Michael Warden's; "let me claim the benefit of those inscriptions. Mr. Heathfield and Dr. Jeddler, I might have deeply wronged you both. That I did not, is no virtue of my own. I will not say that I am six years wiser than I was, or better. But I have known, at any rate, that term of self-reproach. I can urge no reason why you should deal gently with me. I abused the hospitality of this house; and learnt by my own demerits, with a shame I never have forgotten, yet with some profit too, I would fain hope, from one," he glanced at Marion, "to whom I made my humble supplication for forgiveness, when I knew her merit and my deep unworthiness. In a few days I shall quit this place for ever. I entreat your pardon. Do as you would be done by! Forget and forgive!"

TIME—from whom I had the latter portion of this story, and with whom I have the pleasure of a personal acquaintance of some five-and-thirty years' duration—informed me, leaning easily upon his scythe, that Michael Warden never went away again, and never sold his house, but opened it afresh, maintained a golden means of hospitality, and had a wife, the pride and honour of that country-side, whose name was Marion. But, as I have observed that Time confuses facts occasionally, I hardly know what weight to give to his authority.
—1846

The Haunted Man and The Ghost's Bargain

A FANCY FOR CHRISTMAS TIME

~~~~~~

CHAPTER I *The Gift Bestowed*

Everybody said so.

Far be it from me to assert that what everybody says must be true. Everybody is, often, as likely to be wrong as right. In the general experience, everybody has been wrong so often, and it has taken in most instances such a weary while to find out how wrong, that the authority is proved to be fallible. Everybody may sometimes be right; "but *that's* no rule," as the ghost of Giles Scroggins says in the ballad.

The dread word, GHOST, recalls me.

Everybody said he looked like a haunted man. The extent of my present claim for everybody is, that they were so far right. He did.

Who could have seen his hollow cheek, his sunken brilliant eye; his black attired figure, indefinably grim, although well-knit and well-proportioned; his grizzled hair hanging, like tangled sea-weed about his face,—as if he had been, through his whole life, a lonely mark for the chafing and beating of the great deep of humanity,—but might have said he looked like a haunted man?

Who could have observed his manner, taciturn, thoughtful, gloomy, shadowed by habitual reserve, retiring always and jocund never, with a distraught air of reverting to a bygone place and time, or of listening to some old echoes in his mind, but might have said it was the manner of a haunted man?

Who could have heard his voice, slow-speaking, deep, and grave, with a natural fulness and melody in it which he seemed to set himself against and stop, but might have said it was the voice of a haunted man?

Who that had seen him in his inner chamber, part library and part laboratory,—for he was, as the world knew, far and wide, a learned man in chemistry, and a teacher on whose lips and hands a crowd of aspiring ears and eyes hung daily,—who that had seen him there, upon a winter night, alone, surrounded by his drugs and instruments and books; the shadow of his shaded lamp a monstrous beetle on the wall, motionless among a crowd of spectral shapes raised there by the flickering of the fire upon the quaint objects around him; some of these phantoms (the reflection of glass vessels that held liquids), trembling at heart like things that knew his power to uncombine them, and to give back their component parts to fire and vapour;—who that had seen him then, his work done, and he pondering in his chair before the rusted grate and red flame, moving his thin mouth as if in speech, but silent as the dead, would not have said that the man seemed haunted and the chamber too?

Who might not, by a very easy flight of fancy, have believed that everything about him took this haunted tone, and that he lived on haunted ground?

His dwelling was so solitary and vault-like,—an old, retired part of an ancient endowment for students, once a brave edifice planted in an open place, but now the obsolete whim of forgotten architects; smoke-age-and-weather-darkened, squeezed on every side by the over-growing of the great city, and choked, like an old well, with stones and bricks; its small quadrangles, lying down in very pits formed by the streets and buildings, which, in course of time, had been con-structed above its heavy chimney stacks; its old trees, insulted by the neighbouring smoke, which deigned to droop so low when it was very feeble and the weather very moody; its grass-plots, struggling with the mildewed earth to be grass, or to win any show of compromise; its silent pavements, unaccustomed to the tread of feet, and even to the observation of eyes, except when a stray face looked down from the upper world, wondering what nook it was; its sun-dial in a little bricked-up corner, where no sun had straggled for a hundred years, but where, in compensation for the sun's neglect, the snow would lie for weeks when it lay nowhere else, and the black east wind would spin like a huge humming-top, when in all other places it was silent and still.

His dwelling, at its heart and core—within doors—at his fireside—was so lowering and old, so crazy, yet so strong, with its worm-eaten beams of wood in the ceiling, and its sturdy floor shelving downward to the great oak chimney-piece; so environed and hemmed in by the pressure of the town, yet so remote in fashion, age and custom; so quiet, yet so thundering with echoes when a distant voice was raised or a door was shut,—echoes, not confined to the many low passages and empty rooms, but rumbling and grumbling till they were stifled in the heavy air of the forgotten Crypt where the Norman arches were half-buried in the earth.

You should have seen him in his dwelling about twilight, in the dead winter time.

When the wind was blowing, shrill and shrewd, with the going down of the blurred sun. When it was just so dark, as that the forms of things were indistinct and big—but not wholly lost. When sitters by the fire began to see wild faces and figures, mountains and abysses, ambuscades and armies, in the coals. When people in the streets bent down their heads and ran before the weather. When those who were obliged to meet it, were stopped at angry corners, stung by wandering snow-flakes alighting on the lashes of their eyes,—which fell too sparingly, and were blown away too quickly, to leave a trace upon the frozen ground. When windows of private houses closed up tight and warm. When lighted gas began to burst forth in the busy and the quiet streets fast blackening otherwise. When stray pedestrians, shivering along the latter, looked down at the glowing fires in kitchens, and sharpened their sharp appetites by sniffing up the fragrance of whole miles of dinner.

When travellers by land were bitter cold, and looked wearily on gloomy landscapes, rustling and shuddering in the blast. When mariners at sea, outlying upon icy yards, were tossed and swung above the howling ocean dreadfully. When lighthouses, on rocks and headlands, showed solitary and watchful; and benighted sea-birds breasted on against their ponderous lanterns, and fell dead. When little readers of story-books, by the firelight, trembled to think of Cassim Baba cut into quarters, hanging in the Robbers' Cave, or had some small misgivings that the fierce little old woman with the crutch, who used to start out of the box in the merchant Abudah's bedroom, might, one of these nights, be found upon the stairs, in the long, cold, dusky journey up to bed.

When, in rustic places, the last glimmering of daylight died away from the ends of avenues; and the trees, arching overhead, were sullen and black. When, in parks and woods, the high wet fern and sodden moss and beds of fallen leaves, and trunks of trees, were lost to view, in masses of impenetrable shade. When mists arose from dyke, and fen, and river. When lights in old halls and in cottage windows, were a cheerful sight. When the mill stopped, the wheelwright and the blacksmith shut their workshops, the turnpike-gate closed, the plough and harrow were left lonely in the fields, the labourer and team went home, and the striking of the church clock had a deeper sound than at noon, and the churchyard wicket would be swung no more that night.

When twilight everywhere released the shadows, prisoned up all day, that now closed in and gathered like mustering swarms of ghosts. When they stood lowering, in corners of rooms, and frowned out from behind half-opened doors. When they had full possession of unoccupied apartments. When they danced upon the floors, and walls, and ceilings of inhabited chambers, while the fire was low, and withdrew like ebbing waters when it sprung into a blaze. When they fantastically mocked the shapes of household objects, making the nurse an ogress, the rocking-horse a monster, the wondering child half-scared and half-amused, a stranger to itself,—the very tongs upon the hearth, a straddling giant with his arms a-kimbo, evidently smelling the blood of Englishmen, and wanting to grind people's bones to make his bread.

When these shadows brought into the minds of older people, other thoughts, and showed them different images. When they stole from their retreats, in the likenesses of forms and faces from the past, from the grave, from the deep, deep gulf, where the things that might have been, and never were, are always wandering.

When he sat, as already mentioned, gazing at the fire. When, as it rose and fell, the shadows went and came. When he took no heed of them with his bodily eyes; but let them come or let them go, looked fixedly at the fire. You should have seen him then.

When the sounds that had arisen with the shadows, and come out of their lurking places at the twilight summons, seemed to make a deeper stillness all about him. When the wind was rumbling in the chimney, and sometimes crooning, sometimes howling, in the house. When the old trees outside were so shaken and beaten, that one querulous old rook, unable to sleep, protested now and then, in a feeble, dozy, high-up "Caw!" When, at intervals, the window trembled, the rusty vane upon the turret-top complained, the clock beneath it recorded that another quarter of an hour was gone, or the fire collapsed and fell in with a rattle.

—When a knock came at his door, in short, as he was sitting so, and roused him.

"Who's that?" said he. "Come in!"

Surely there had been no figure leaning on the back of his chair, no face looking over it. It is certain that no gliding footstep touched the floor, as he lifted up his head with a start, and spoke. And yet there was no mirror in the room on whose surface his own form could have cast its shadow for a moment; and Something had passed darkly and gone!

"I'm humbly fearful, sir," said a fresh-coloured busy man, holding the door open with his foot for the admission of himself and a wooden tray he carried, and letting it go again by very gentle and careful degrees, when he and the tray had got in, lest it should close noisily, "that it's a good bit past the time to-night. But Mrs. William has been taken off her legs so often——"

"By the wind? Ay! I have heard it rising."

"—By the wind, sir—that it's a mercy she got home at all. Oh dear, yes. Yes. It was by the wind, Mr. Redlaw. By the wind."

He had, by this time, put down the tray for dinner, and was employed in lighting the lamp, and spreading a cloth on the table. From this employment he desisted in a hurry, to stir and feed the fire, and then resumed it; the lamp he had lighted, and the blaze that rose under his hand, so quickly changing the appearance of the room, that it seemed as if the mere coming in of his fresh red face and active manner had made the pleasant alteration.

"Mrs. William is of course subject at any time, sir, to be taken off her balance by the elements. She is not formed superior to *that*."

"No," returned Mr. Redlaw good-naturedly, though abruptly.

"No, sir. Mrs. William may be taken off her balance by Earth; as, for example, last Sunday week, when sloppy and greasy, and she going out to tea with her newest sister-in-law, and having a pride in herself, and wishing to appear perfectly spotless though pedestrian. Mrs. William may be taken off her balance by Air; as being once over-persuaded by a friend to try a swing at Peckham Fair, which acted on her constitution instantly like a steamboat. Mrs. William may be taken off her balance by Fire; as on a false alarm of engines at her mother's, when she went two miles in her nightcap. Mrs. William may be taken off her balance by Water; as at Battersea, when rowed into the piers by her young nephew, Charley Swidger junior, aged twelve, which had no idea of boats whatever. But these are elements. Mrs. William must be taken out of elements for the strength of *her* character to come into play."

As he stopped for a reply, the reply was "Yes," in the same tone as before.

"Yes, sir. Oh dear, yes!" said Mr. Swidger, still proceeding with his preparations, and checking them off as he made them. "That's where it is, sir. That's what I always say myself, sir. Such a many of us Swidgers!—Pepper. Why there's my father, sir, superannuated keeper and custodian of this Institution, eighty-seven year old. He's a Swidger!—Spoon."

"True, William," was the patient and abstracted answer, when he stopped again.

"Yes, sir," said Mr. Swidger. "That's what I always say, sir. You may call him the trunk of the tree!—Bread. Then you come to his successor, my unworthy self—Salt—and Mrs. William, Swidgers both. —Knife and fork. Then you come to all my brothers and their families, Swidgers, man and woman, boy and girl. Why, what with cousins, uncles, aunts, and relationships of this, that, and t'other degree, and what-not degree, and marriages, and lyings-in, the Swidgers—Tumblers—might take hold of hands, and make a ring round England!"

Receiving no reply at all here, from the thoughtful man whom he addressed, Mr. William approached him nearer, and made a feint of accidentally knocking the table with a decanter, to rouse him. The moment he succeeded, he went on, as if in great alacrity of acquiescence.

"Yes, sir! That's just what I say myself, sir. Mrs. William and me have often said so. 'There's Swidgers enough,' we say, 'without *our* voluntary contributions,'—Butter. In fact, sir, my father is a family in

himself—Castors—to take care of; and it happens all for the best that
we have no child of our own, though it's made Mrs. William rather
quiet-like too. Quite ready for the fowl and mashed potatoes, sir? Mrs.
William said she'd dish in ten minutes when I left the Lodge."

"I am quite ready," said the other, waking as from a dream, and
walking slowly to and fro.

"Mrs. William has been at it again, sir!" said the keeper, as he
stood warming a plate at the fire, and pleasantly shading his face
with it. Mr. Redlaw stopped in his walking, and an expression of
interest appeared in him.

"What I always say myself, sir. She *will* do it! There's a motherly
feeling in Mrs. William's breast that must and will have went."

"What has she done?"

"Why, sir, not satisfied with being a sort of mother to all the young
gentlemen that come up from a wariety of parts, to attend your course
of lectures at this ancient foundation—it's surprising how stone-
chaney catches the heat this frosty weather, to be sure!" Here he
turned the plate, and cooled his fingers.

"Well?" said Mr. Redlaw.

"That's just what I say myself, sir," returned Mr. William, speaking
over his shoulder, as if in ready and delighted assent. "That is exactly
where it is, sir! There ain't one of our students but appears to regard
Mrs. William in that light. Every day, right through the course, they
puts their heads into the Lodge, one after another, and have all got
something to tell her, or something to ask her. 'Swidge' is the ap-
pellation by which they speak of Mrs. William in general, among
themselves, I'm told; but that's what I say, sir. Better be called ever
so far out of your name, if it's done in real liking, than have it made
ever so much of, and not cared about! What's a name for? To know a
person by. If Mrs. William is known by something better than her
name—I allude to Mrs. William's qualities and disposition—never
mind her name, though it *is* Swidger, by rights. Let 'em call her
Swidge, Widge, Bridge—Lord! London Bridge, Blackfriars, Chelsea,
Putney, Waterloo, or Hammersmith Suspension—if they like!"

The close of this triumphant oration brought him and the plate
to the table, upon which he half laid and half dropped it, with a
lively sense of its being thoroughly heated, just as the subject of his
praises entered the room, bearing another tray and a lantern, and
followed by a venerable old man with long grey hair.

Mrs. William, like Mr. William, was a simple, innocent-looking person, in whose smooth cheeks the cheerful red of her husband's official
waistcoat was very pleasantly repeated. But whereas Mr. William's
light hair stood on end all over his head, and seemed to draw his
eyes up with it in an excess of bustling readiness for anything, the
dark brown hair of Mrs. William was carefully smoothed down, and

waved away under a trim tidy cap, in the most exact and quiet manner imaginable. Whereas Mr. William's very trousers hitched themselves up at the ankles, as if it were not in their iron-grey nature to
rest without looking about them, Mrs. William's neatly-flowered skirts
—red and white, like her own pretty face—were as composed and
orderly, as if the very wind that blew so hard out of doors could not
disturb one of their folds. Whereas his coat had something of a fly-
away and half-off appearance about the collar and breast, her little
bodice was so placid and neat, that there should have been protection
for her in it, had she needed any, with the roughest people. Who
could have had the heart to make so calm a bosom swell with grief,
or throb with fear, or flutter with a thought of shame! To whom
would its repose and peace have not appealed against disturbance,
like the innocent slumber of a child!

"Punctual of course, Milly," said her husband, relieving her of the
tray, "or it wouldn't be you. Here's Mrs. William, sir!—He looks
lonelier than ever to-night," whispering to his wife, as he was taking
the tray, "and ghostlier altogether."

Without any show of hurry or noise, or any show of herself even,
she was so calm and quiet, Milly set the dishes she had brought upon
the table,—Mr. William, after much clattering and running about,
having only gained possession of a butter-boat of gravy, which he stood
ready to serve.

"What is that the old man has in his arms?" asked Mr. Redlaw,
as he sat down to his solitary meal.

"Holly, sir," replied the quiet voice of Milly.

"That's what I say myself, sir," interposed Mr. William, striking in
with the butter-boat. "Berries is so seasonable to the time of year!—
Brown gravy!"

"Another Christmas come, another year gone!" murmured the
Chemist, with a gloomy sigh. "More figures in the lengthening sum
of recollection that we work and work at to our torment, till Death
idly jumbles all together, and rubs all out. So, Philip!" breaking off,
and raising his voice, as he addressed the old man standing apart,
with his glistening burden in his arms, from which the quiet Mrs.
William took small branches, which she noiselessly trimmed with
her scissors, and decorated the room with, while her aged father-in-
law looked on much interested in the ceremony.

"My duty to you, sir," returned the old man. "Should have spoke
before, sir, but know your ways, Mr. Redlaw—proud to say—and
wait till spoke to! Merry Christmas, sir, and happy New Year, and
many of 'em. Have had a pretty many of 'em myself—ha, ha!—and
may take the liberty of wishing 'em. I'm eighty-seven!"

"Have you had so many that were merry and happy?" asked the
other.

"Ay, sir, ever so many," returned the old man.

"Is his memory impaired with age? It is to be expected now," said Mr. Redlaw, turning to the son, and speaking lower.

"Not a morsel of it, sir," replied Mr. William. "That's exactly what I say myself, sir. There never was such a memory as my father's. He's the most wonderful man in the world. He don't know what forgetting means. It's the very observation I'm always making to Mrs. William, sir, if you'll believe me!"

Mr. Swidger, in his polite desire to seem to acquiesce at all events, delivered this as if there were no iota of contradiction in it, and it were all said in unbounded and unqualified assent.

The Chemist pushed his plate away, and, rising from the table, walked across the room to where the old man stood looking at a little sprig of holly in his hand.

"It recalls the time when many of those years were old and new, then?" he said, observing him attentively, and touching him on the shoulder. "Does it?"

"Oh many, many!" said Philip, half awaking from his reverie. "I'm eighty-seven!"

"Merry and happy, was it?" asked the Chemist, in a low voice. "Merry and happy, old man?"

"May-be as high as that, no higher," said the old man, holding out his hand a little way above the level of his knee, and looking retrospectively at his questioner, "when I first remember 'em! Cold, sunshiny day it was, out a-walking, when some one—it was my mother as sure as you stand there, though I don't know what her blessed face was like, for she took ill and died that Christmas-time—told me they were food for birds. The pretty little fellow thought—that's me, you understand—that birds' eyes were so bright, perhaps, because the berries that they lived on in the winter were so bright. I recollect that. And I'm eighty-seven!"

"Merry and happy!" mused the other, bending his dark eyes upon the stooping figure, with a smile of compassion. "Merry and happy—and remember well!"

"Ay, ay, ay!" resumed the old man, catching the last words. "I remember 'em well in my school time, year after year, and all the merry-making that used to come along with them. I was a strong chap then, Mr. Redlaw; and, if you'll believe me, hadn't my match at foot-ball within ten mile. Where's my son, William? Hadn't my match at foot-ball, William, within ten mile!"

"That's what I always say, father!" returned the son promptly, and with great respect. "You ARE a Swidger, if ever there was one of the family!"

"Dear!" said the old man, shaking his head as he again looked at the holly. "His mother—my son William's my youngest son—and I,

have sat among 'em all, boys and girls, like children and babies, many
a year, when the berries like these were not shining half so bright all
round us, as their bright faces. Many of 'em are gone; she's gone; and
my son George (our eldest, who was her pride more than all the rest!)
is fallen very low: but I can see them, when I look here, alive and
healthy, as they used to be in those days; and I can see him, thank
God, in his innocence. It's a blessed thing to me, at eighty-seven."

The keen look that had been fixed upon him with so much earnestness, had gradually sought the ground.

"When my circumstances got to be not so good as formerly,
through not being honestly dealt by, and I first come here to be
custodian," said the old man, "—which was upwards of fifty years
ago—where's my son William? More than half a century ago, William!"

"That's what I say, father," replied the son, as promptly and duti-
fully as before, "that's exactly where it is. Two times ought's an ought,
and twice five ten, and there's a hundred of 'em."

"It was quite a pleasure to know that one of our founders—or
more correctly speaking," said the old man, with a great glory in
his subject and his knowledge of it, "one of the learned gentlemen
that helped endow us in Queen Elizabeth's time, for we were founded
afore her day—left in his will, among the other bequests he made us,
so much to buy holly, for garnishing the walls and windows, come
Christmas. There was something homely and friendly in it. Being but
strange here, then, and coming at Christmas-time, we took a liking for
his very picter that hangs in what used to be, anciently, afore our
ten poor gentlemen commuted for an annual stipend in money, our
great Dinner Hall.—A sedate gentleman in a peaked beard, with a
ruff round his neck, and a scroll below him, in old English letters,
"Lord! keep my memory green!" You know all about him, Mr. Redlaw?"

"I know the portrait hangs there, Philip."

"Yes, sure, it's the second on the right, above the panelling. I
was going to say—he has helped to keep *my* memory green, I thank
him; for, going round the building every year, as I'm a-doing now,
and freshening up the bare rooms with these branches and berries,
freshens up my bare old brain. One year brings back another, and
that year another, and those others numbers! At last, it seems to me
as if the birth-time of our Lord was the birth-time of all I have ever
had affection for, or mourned for, or delighted in,—and they're a
pretty many, for I'm eighty-seven!"

"Merry and happy," murmured Redlaw to himself.

The room began to darken strangely.

"So you see, sir" pursued old Philip, whose hale wintry cheek had
warmed into a ruddier glow, and whose blue eyes had brightened

while he spoke, "I have plenty to keep, when I keep this present season. Now, where's my quiet Mouse? Chattering's the sin of my time of life, and there's half the building to do yet, if the cold don't freeze us first, or the wind don't blow us away, or the darkness don't swallow us up."

The quiet Mouse had brought her calm face to his side, and silently taken his arm, before he finished speaking.

"Come away, my dear," said the old man. "Mr. Redlaw won't settle to his dinner, otherwise, till it's cold as the winter. I hope you'll excuse me rambling on, sir, and I wish you good night, and, once again, a merry—"

"Stay!" said Mr. Redlaw, resuming his place at the table, more, it would have seemed from his manner, to reassure the old keeper, than in any remembrance of his own appetite. "Spare me another moment, Philip. William, you were going to tell me something to your excellent wife's honour. It will not be disagreeable to her to hear you praise her. What was it?"

"Why, that's where it is, you see, sir," returned Mr. William Swidger, looking towards his wife in considerable embarrassment. "Mrs. William's got her eye upon me."

"But you're not afraid of Mrs. William's eye?"

"Why, no, sir," returned Mr. Swidger, "that's what I say myself. It wasn't made to be afraid of. It wouldn't have been made so mild, if that was the intention. But I wouldn't like to—Milly!—him, you know. Down in the Buildings."

Mr. William, standing behind the table, and rummaging disconcertedly among the objects upon it, directed persuasive glances at Mrs. William, and secret jerks of his head and thumb at Mr. Redlaw, as alluring her towards him.

"Him, you know, my love," said Mr. William. "Down in the Buildings. Tell, my dear. You're the works of Shakspeare in comparison with myself. Down in the Buildings, you know, my love.—Student."

"Student?" repeated Mr. Redlaw, raising his head.

"That's what I say, sir!" cried Mr. William, in the utmost animation of assent. "If it wasn't the poor student down in the Buildings, why should you wish to hear it from Mrs. William's lips? Mrs. William, my dear—Buildings."

"I didn't know," said Milly, with a quiet frankness, free from any haste or confusion, "that William had said anything about it, or I wouldn't have come. I asked him not to. It's a sick young gentleman, sir—and very poor, I am afraid—who is too ill to go home this holiday-time, and lives, unknown to any one, in but a common kind of lodging for a gentleman, down in Jerusalem Buildings. That's all, sir."

"Why have I never heard of him?" said the Chemist, rising hurriedly.

"Why has he not made his situation known to me? Sick!—give me my hat and cloak. Poor!—what house?—what number?"

"Oh, you mustn't go there, sir," said Milly, leaving her father-in-law, and calmly confronting him with her collected little face and folded hands.

"Not go there?"

"Oh dear, no!" said Milly, shaking her head as at a most manifest and self-evident impossibility. "It couldn't be thought of!"

"What do you mean? Why not?"

"Why, you see, sir," said Mr. William Swidger, persuasively and confidentially, "that's what I say. Depend upon it, the young gentleman would never have made his situation known to one of his own sex. Mrs. William has got into his confidence, but that's quite different. They all confide in Mrs. William; they all trust *her*. A man, sir, couldn't have got a whisper out of him; but woman, sir, and Mrs. William combined—!"

"There is good sense and delicacy in what you say, William," returned Mr. Redlaw, observant of the gentle and composed face at his shoulder. And laying his finger on his lip, he secretly put his purse into her hand.

"Oh dear no, sir!" cried Milly, giving it back again. "Worse and worse! Couldn't be dreamed of!"

Such a staid matter-of-fact housewife she was, and so unruffled by the momentary haste of this rejection, that, an instant afterwards, she was tidily picking up a few leaves which had strayed from between her scissors and her apron, when she had arranged the holly.

Finding, when she rose from her stooping posture, that Mr. Redlaw was still regarding her with doubt and astonishment, she quietly repeated—looking about the while for any other fragments that might have escaped her observation:

"Oh dear no, sir! He said that of all the world he would not be known to you, or receive help from you—though he is a student in your class. I have made no terms of secrecy with you, but I trust to your honour completely."

"Why did he say so?"

"Indeed I can't tell, sir," said Milly, after thinking a little, "because I am not at all clever, you know; and I wanted to be useful to him in making things neat and comfortable about him, and employed myself that way. But I know he is poor, and lonely, and I think he is somehow neglected too.—How dark it is!"

The room had darkened more and more. There was a very heavy gloom and shadow gathering behind the Chemist's chair.

"What more about him?" he asked.

"He is engaged to be married when he can afford it," said Milly, "and is studying, I think, to qualify himself to earn a living. I have

seen, a long time, that he has studied hard and denied himself much.
—How very dark it is!"

"It's turned colder, too," said the old man, rubbing his hands.
"There's a chill and dismal feeling in the room. Where's my son
William? William, my boy, turn the lamp, and rouse the fire."

Milly's voice resumed, like quiet music very softly played:

"He muttered in his broken sleep yesterday afternoon, after talking
to me" (this was to herself) "about some one dead, and some great
wrong done that could never be forgotten; but whether to him or to
another person, I don't know. Not *by* him, I am sure."

"And, in short, Mrs. William, you see—which she wouldn't say
herself, Mr. Redlaw, if she was to stop here till the new year after
this next one—" said Mr. William, coming up to him to speak in his
ear, "has done him worlds of good! Bless you, worlds of good! All at
home just the same as ever—my father made as snug and comfortable
—not a crumb of litter to be found in the house, if you were to offer
fifty pound ready money for it—Mrs. William apparently never out of
the way—yet Mrs. William backwards and forwards, backwards and
forwards, up and down, up and down, a mother to him!"

The room turned darker and colder, and the gloom and shadow
gathering behind the chair was heavier.

"Not content with this, sir, Mrs. William goes and finds, this very
night, when she was coming home (why it's not above a couple of
hours ago), a creature more like a young wild beast than a young
child, shivering upon a door-step. What does Mrs. William do, but
brings it home to dry it, and feed it, and keep it till our old Bounty
of food and flannel is given away, on Christmas morning! If it ever
felt a fire before, it's as much as ever it did; for it's sitting in the
old Lodge chimney, staring at ours as if its ravenous eyes would never
shut again. It's sitting there, at least," said Mr. William, correcting
himself, on reflection, "unless it's bolted!"

"Heaven keep her happy!" said the Chemist aloud, "and you too,
Philip! and you, William! I must consider what to do in this. I may
desire to see this student, I'll not detain you longer now. Good night!"

"I thank'ee, sir, I thank'ee!" said the old man, "for Mouse, and for
my son William, and for myself. Where's my son William? William,
you take the lantern and go on first, through them long dark passages,
as you did last year and the year afore. Ha, ha! I remember—though
I'm eighty-seven! 'Lord, keep my memory green!' It's a very good
prayer, Mr. Redlaw, that of the learned gentleman in the peaked
beard, with a ruff round his neck—hangs up, second on the right
above the panelling, in what used to be, afore our ten poor gentlemen commuted, our great Dinner Hall. 'Lord, keep my memory green!'
It's very good and pious, sir. Amen! Amen!"

As they passed out and shut the heavy door, which, however carefully withheld, fired a long train of thundering reverberations when it shut at last, the room turned darker.

As he fell a-musing in his chair alone, the healthy holly withered on the wall, and dropped—dead branches.

As the gloom and shadow thickened behind him, in that place where it had been gathering so darkly, it took, by slow degrees,—or out of it there came, by some unreal, unsubstantial process—not to be traced by any human sense,—an awful likeness of himself.

Ghastly and cold, colourless in its leaden face and hands, but with his features, and his bright eyes, and his grizzled hair, and dressed in the gloomy shadow of his dress, it came into his terrible appearance of existence, motionless, without a sound. As *he* leaned his arm upon the elbow of his chair, ruminating before the fire, *it* leaned upon the chair-back, close above him, with its appalling copy of his face looking where his face looked, and bearing the expression his face bore.

This, then, was the Something that had passed and gone already. This was the dread companion of the haunted man!

It took, for some moments, no more apparent heed of him, than he of it. The Christmas Waits were playing somewhere in the distance, and, through his thoughtfulness, he seemed to listen to the music. It seemed to listen too.

At length he spoke; without moving or lifting up his face.

"Here again!" he said.

"Here again!" replied the Phantom.

"I see you in the fire," said the haunted man; "I hear you in music, in the wind, in the dead stillness of the night."

The Phantom moved its head, assenting.

"Why do you come, to haunt me thus?"

"I come as I am called," replied the Ghost.

"No. Unbidden," exclaimed the Chemist.

"Unbidden be it," said the Spectre. "It is enough. I am here."

Hitherto the light of the fire had shone on the two faces—if the dread lineaments behind the chair might be called a face—both addressed towards it, as at first, and neither looking at the other. But, now, the haunted man turned, suddenly, and stared upon the Ghost. The Ghost, as sudden in its motion, passed to before the chair, and stared on him.

The living man, and the animated image of himself dead, might so have looked, the one upon the other. An awful survey, in a lonely and remote part of an empty old pile of building, on a winter night, with the loud wind going by upon its journey of mystery—whence, or whither, no man knowing since the world began—and the stars, in unimaginable millions, glittering through it, from eternal space, where the world's bulk is as a grain, and its hoary age is infancy.

"Look upon me!" said the Spectre. "I am he, neglected in my youth, and miserably poor, who strove and suffered, and still strove and suffered, until I hewed out knowledge from the mine where it was buried, and made rugged steps thereof, for my worn feet to rest and rise on."

"I *am* that man," returned the Chemist.

"No mother's self-denying love," pursued the Phantom, "no father's counsel, aided *me*. A stranger came into my father's place when I was but a child, and I was easily an alien from my mother's heart. My parents, at the best, were of that sort whose care soon ends, and whose duty is soon done; who cast their off-spring loose, early, as birds do theirs; and, if they do well, claim the merit; and, if ill, the pity."

It paused, and seemed to tempt and goad him with its look, and with the manner of its speech, and with its smile.

"I am he," pursued the Phantom, "who, in this struggle upward, found a friend. I made him—won him—bound him to me! We worked together, side by side. All the love and confidence that in my earlier youth had had no outlet, and found no expression, I bestowed on him."

"Not all," said Redlaw, hoarsely.

"No, not all," returned the Phantom. "I had a sister."

The haunted man, with his head resting on his hands, replied "I had!" The Phantom, with an evil smile, drew closer to the chair, and resting its chin upon its folded hands, its folded hands upon the back, and looking down into his face with searching eyes, that seemed instinct with fire, went on:

"Such glimpses of the light of home as I had ever known, had streamed from her. How young she was, how fair, how loving! I took her to the first poor roof that I was master of, and made it rich. She came into the darkness of my life, and made it bright.—She is before me!"

"I saw her, in the fire, but now. I hear her in music, in the wind, in the dead stillness of the night," returned the haunted man.

"*Did* he love her?" said the Phantom, echoing his contemplative tone. "I think he did once. I am sure he did. Better had she loved him less—less secretly, less dearly, from the shallower depths of a more divided heart!"

"Let me forget it," said the Chemist, with an angry motion of his hand. "Let me blot it from my memory!"

The Spectre, without stirring, and with its unwinking, cruel eyes still fixed upon his face, went on:

"A dream, like hers, stole upon my life."

"It did," said Redlaw.

"A love, as like hers," pursued the Phantom, "as my inferior nature might cherish, arose in my own heart. I was too poor to bind its object to my fortune then, by any thread of promise or entreaty. I loved her far too well, to seek to do it. But, more than ever I had striven in my life, I strove to climb! Only an inch gained, brought me something nearer to the height. I toiled up! In the late pauses of my labour at that time—my sister (sweet companion!) still sharing with me the expiring embers and the cooling hearth,—when day was breaking, what pictures of the future did I see!"

"I saw them, in the fire, but now," he murmured. "They come back to me in music, in the wind, in the dead stillness of the night, in the revolving years."

"—Pictures of my own domestic life, in after-time, with her who was the inspiration of my toil. Pictures of my sister, made the wife of my dear friend, on equal terms—for he had some inheritance, we none—pictures of our sobered age and mellowed happiness, and of the golden links, extending back so far, that should blind us, and our children, in a radiant garland," said the Phantom.

"Pictures," said the haunted man, "that were delusions. Why is it my doom to remember them too well!"

"Delusions," echoed the Phantom in its changeless voice, and glaring on him with its changeless eyes. "For my friend (in whose breast my confidence was locked as in my own), passing between me and the centre of the system of my hopes and struggles, won her to himself, and shattered my frail universe. My sister, doubly dear, doubly devoted, doubly cheerful in my home, lived on to see me famous, and my old ambition so rewarded when its spring was broken, and then—"

"Then died," he interposed. "Died, gentle as ever, happy, and with no concern but for her brother. Peace!"

The Phantom watched him silently.

"Remembered!" said the haunted man, after a pause. "Yes. So well remembered, that even now, when years have passed, and nothing is more idle or more visionary to me than the boyish love so long outlived, I think of it with sympathy, as if it were a younger brother's or a son's. Sometimes I even wonder when her heart first inclined to him, and how it had been affected towards me.—Not lightly, once, I think.—But that is nothing. Early unhappiness, a wound from a hand I loved and trusted, and a loss that nothing can replace, outlive such fancies."

"Thus," said the Phantom, "I bear within me a Sorrow and a Wrong. Thus I prey upon myself. Thus, memory is my curse; and, if I could forget my sorrow and my wrong, I would!"

"Mocker!" said the Chemist, leaping up, and making, with a wrathful hand, at the throat of his other self. "Why have I always that taunt in my ears?"

"Forbear!" exclaimed the Spectre in an awful voice. "Lay a hand on me, and die!"

He stopped midway, as if its words had paralysed him, and stood looking on it. It had glided from him; it had its arm raised high in warning; and a smile passed over its unearthly features as it reared its dark figure in triumph.

"If I could forget my sorrow and wrong, I would," the Ghost repeated. "If I could forget my sorrow and wrong, I would!"

"Evil spirit of myself," returned the haunted man, in a low, trembling tone, "my life is darkened by that incessant whisper."

"It is an echo," said the Phantom.

"If it be an echo of my thoughts—as now, indeed, I know it is," rejoined the haunted man, "why should I, therefore, be tormented? It is not a selfish thought. I suffer it to range beyond myself. All men and women have their sorrows,—most of them their wrongs; ingratitude, and sordid jealousy, and interest, besetting all degrees of life. Who would not forget their sorrows and their wrongs?"

"Who would not, truly, and be the happier and better for it?" said the Phantom.

"These revolutions of years, which we commemorate," proceeded Redlaw, "what do *they* recall! Are there any minds in which they do not re-awaken some sorrow, or some trouble? What is the remembrance of the old man who was here to-night? A tissue of sorrow and trouble."

"But common natures," said the Phantom, with its evil smile upon its glassy face, "unenlightened minds and ordinary spirits, do not feel or reason on these things like men of higher cultivation and profounder thought."

"Tempter," answered Redlaw, "whose hollow look and voice I dread more than words can express, and from whom some dim foreshadowing of greater fear is stealing over me while I speak, I hear again an echo of my own mind."

"Receive it as a proof that I am powerful," returned the Ghost. "Hear what I offer! Forget the sorrow, wrong, and trouble you have known!"

"Forget them!" he repeated.

"I have the power to cancel their remembrance—to leave but very faint, confused traces of them, that will die out soon," returned the Spectre. "Say! It is done?"

"Stay!" cried the haunted man, arresting by a terrified gesture the uplifted hand. "I tremble with distrust and doubt of you; and the dim fear you cast upon me deepens into a nameless horror I can hardly bear.—I would not deprive myself of any kindly recollection, or any sympathy that is good for me, or others. What shall I lose, if I assent to this? What else will pass from my remembrance?"

"No knowledge; no result of study; nothing but the intertwisted chain of feelings and associations, each in its turn dependent on, and nourished by, the banished recollections. Those will go."

"Are they so many?" said the haunted man, reflecting in alarm.

"They have been wont to show themselves in the fire, in music, in the wind, in the dead stillness of the night, in the revolving years," returned the Phantom scornfully.

"In nothing else?"

The Phantom held its peace.

But, having stood before him, silent, for a little while, it moved towards the fire; then stopped.

"Decide!" it said, "before the opportunity is lost!"

"A moment! I call Heaven to witness," said the agitated man, "that I have never been a hater of my kind,—never morose, indifferent, or hard, to anything around me. If, living here alone, I have made too much of all that was and might have been, and too little of what is, the evil, I believe, has fallen on me, and not on others. But, if there were poison in my body, should I not, possessed of antidotes and knowledge how to use them, use them? If there be poison in my mind, and through this fearful shadow I can cast it out, shall I not cast it out?"

"Say," said the Spectre, "is it done?"

"A moment longer!" he answered hurriedly. "*I would forget it if I could!* Have I thought that, alone, or has it been the thought of thousands upon thousands, generation after generation? All human memory is fraught with sorrow and trouble. My memory is as the memory of other men, but other men have not this choice. Yes, I close the bargain. Yes! I WILL forget my sorrow, wrong, and trouble!"

"Say," said the Spectre, "is it done?"

"It is!"

"IT IS. And take this with you, man whom I here renounce! The gift that I have given, you shall give again, go where you will. Without recovering yourself the power that you have yielded up, you shall henceforth destroy its like in all whom you approach. Your wisdom has discovered that the memory of sorrow, wrong, and trouble is the lot of all mankind, and that mankind would be the happier, in its other memories, without it. Go! Be its benefactor! Freed from such remembrance, from this hour, carry involuntarily the blessing of such freedom with you. Its diffusion is inseparable and inalienable from you. Go! Be happy in the good you have won, and in the good you do!"

The Phantom, which had held its bloodless hand above him while it spoke, as if in some unholy invocation, or some ban; and which had gradually advanced its eyes so close to his, that he could see how they did not participate in the terrible smile upon its face, but were a fixed, unalterable, steady horror; melted before him and was gone.

As he stood rooted to the spot, possessed by fear and wonder, and imagining he heard repeated in melancholy echoes, dying away fainter and fainter, the words, "Destroy its like in all whom you approach!" a shrill cry reached his ears. It came, not from the passage beyond the door, but from another part of the old building, and sounded like the cry of some one in the dark who had lost the way.

He looked confusedly upon his hands and limbs, as if to be assured of his identity, and then shouted in reply, loudly and wildly; for there was a strangeness and terror upon him, as if he too were lost.

The cry responding, and being nearer, he caught up the lamp, and raised a heavy curtain in the wall, by which he was accustomed to pass into and out of the theatre where he lectured,—which adjoined his room. Associated with youth and animation, and a high amphi-theatre of faces which his entrance charmed to interest in a moment, it was a ghostly place when all this life was faded out of it, and stared upon him like an emblem of Death.

"Halloa!" he cried. "Halloa! This way! Come to the light!" When, as he held the curtain with one hand, and with the other raised the lamp and tried to pierce the gloom that filled the place, something rushed past him into the room like a wild-cat, and crouched down in a corner.

"What is it?" he said, hastily.

He might have asked "What is it?" even had he seen it well, as presently he did when he stood looking at it gathered up in its corner.

A bundle of tatters, held together by a hand, in size and form al-most an infant's, but, in its greedy, desperate little clutch, a bad old man's. A face rounded and smoothed by some half-dozen years, but pinched and twisted by the experiences of a life. Bright eyes, but not youthful. Naked feet, beautiful in their childish delicacy,—ugly in the blood and dirt that cracked upon them. A baby savage, a young monster, a child who had never been a child, a creature who might live to take the outward form of man, but who, within, would live and perish a mere beast.

Used, already, to be worried and hunted like a beast, the boy crouched down as he was looked at, and looked back again, and inter-posed his arm to ward off the expected blow.

"I'll bite," he said, "if you hit me!"

The time had been, and not many minutes since, when such a sight as this would have wrung the Chemist's heart. He looked upon it now, coldly; but, with a heavy effort to remember something—he did not know what—he asked the boy what he did there, and whence he came.

"Where's the woman?" he replied. "I want to find the woman."

"Who?"

"The woman. Her that brought me here, and set me by the large fire. She was so long gone, that I went to look for her, and lost myself. I don't want you. I want the woman."

He made a spring, so suddenly, to get away, that the dull sound of his naked feet upon the floor was near the curtain, when Redlaw caught him by his rags.

"Come! you let me go!" muttered the boy, struggling, and clenching his teeth. "I've done nothing to you. Let me go, will you, to the woman!"

"That is not the way. There is a nearer one," said Redlaw, detaining him, in the same blank effort to remember some association that ought, of right, to bear upon this monstrous object. "What is your name?"

"Got none."

"Where do you live?"

"Live! What's that?"

The boy shook his hair from his eyes to look at him for a moment, and then, twisting round his legs and wrestling with him, broke again into his repetition of "You let me go, will you? I want to find the woman."

The Chemist led him to the door. "This way," he said, looking at him still confusedly, but with repugnance and avoidance, growing out of his coldness. "I'll take you to her."

The sharp eyes in the child's head, wandering round the room, lighted on the table where the remnants of the dinner were.

"Give me some of that!" he said, covetously.

"Has she not fed you?"

"I shall be hungry again to-morrow, sha'n't I? Ain't I hungry every day?"

Finding himself released, he bounded at the table like some small animal of prey, and hugging to his breast bread and meat, and his own rags, all together, said:

"There! Now take me to the woman!"

As the Chemist, with a new-born dislike to touch him, sternly motioned him to follow, and was going out of the door, he trembled and stopped.

"The gift that I have given, you shall give again, go where you will!"

The Phantom's words were blowing in the wind, and the wind blew chill upon him.

"I'll not go there, to-night," he murmured faintly.

"I'll go nowhere to-night. Boy! straight down this long-arched passage, and past the great dark door into the yard,—you see the fire shining on the window there."

"The woman's fire?" inquired the boy.

He nodded, and the naked feet had sprung away. He came back with his lamp, locked his door hastily, and sat down in his chair, covering his face like one who was frightened at himself.

For now he was, indeed, alone. Alone, alone.

CHAPTER II *The Gift Diffused*

A small man sat in a small parlour, partitioned off from a small shop by a small screen, pasted all over with small scraps of newspapers. In company with the small man, was almost any amount of small children you may please to name—at least, it seemed so; they made, in that very limited sphere of action, such an imposing effect, in point of numbers.

Of these small fry, two had, by some strong machinery, been got into bed in a corner, where they might have reposed snugly enough in the sleep of innocence, but for a constitutional propensity to keep awake, and also to scuffle in and out of bed. The immediate occasion of these predatory dashes at the waking world, was the construction of an oyster-shell wall in a corner, by two other youths of tender age; on which fortification the two in bed made harassing descents (like those accursed Picts and Scots who beleaguer the early historical studies of most young Britons), and then withdrew to their own territory.

In addition to the stir attendant on these inroads, and the retorts of the invaded, who pursued hotly, and made lunges at the bed-clothes, under which the marauders took refuge, another little boy, in another little bed, contributed his mite of confusion to the family stock, by casting his boots upon the waters; in other words, by launching these and several small objects inoffensive in themselves, though of a hard substance considered as missiles, at the disturbers of his repose,—who were not slow to return these compliments.

Besides which, another little boy—the biggest there, but still little —was tottering to and fro, bent on one side, and considerably affected in his knees by the weight of a large baby, which he was supposed, by a fiction that obtains sometimes in sanguine families, to be hushing to sleep. But oh! the inexhaustible regions of contemplation and watchfulness into which this baby's eyes were then only beginning to compose themselves to stare, over his unconscious shoulder!

It was a very Moloch of a baby, on whose insatiate altar the whole existence of this particular young brother was offered up a daily sacrifice. Its personality may be said to have consisted in its never being quiet, in any one place, for five consecutive minutes, and never going to sleep when required. "Tetterby's baby" was as well known in the neighbourhood as the postman or the pot-boy. It roved from door-step to door-step, in the arms of little Johnny Tetterby, and lagged heavily at the rear of troops of juveniles who followed the Tumblers or the Monkey, and came up, all on one side, a little too late for everything that was attractive, from Monday morning until Saturday night. Wherever childhood congregated to play, there was little Moloch making Johnny fag and toil. Wherever Johnny desired to stay, little Moloch became fractious, and would not remain. Whenever Johnny wanted to go out, Moloch was asleep, and must be watched. Whenever Johnny wanted to stay at home, Moloch was awake, and must be taken out. Yet Johnny was verily persuaded that it was a faultless baby, without its peer in the realm of England; and was quite content to catch meek glimpses of things in general from behind its skirts, or over its limp flapping bonnet, and to go staggering about with it like a very little porter with a very large parcel, which was not directed to anybody, and could never be delivered anywhere.

The small man who sat in the small parlour, making fruitless attempts to read his newspaper peaceably in the midst of this disturbance, was the father of the family, and the chief of the firm described in the inscription over the little shop front, by the name and title of A. TETTERBY AND CO., NEWSMEN. Indeed, strictly speaking, he was the only personage answering to that designation; as Co. was a mere poetical abstraction, altogether baseless and impersonal.

Tetterby's was the corner shop in Jerusalem Buildings. There was a good show of literature in the window, chiefly consisting of picture-newspapers out of date, and serial pirates, and foot-pads. Walking-sticks, likewise, and marbles, were included in the stock in trade. It had once extended into the light confectionery line; but it would seem that those elegancies of life were not in demand about Jerusalem Buildings, for nothing connected with that branch of commerce remained in the window, except a sort of small glass lantern containing a languishing mass of bull's-eyes, which had melted in the summer and congealed in the winter until all hope of ever getting them out, or of eating them without eating the lantern too, was gone for ever. Tetterby's had tried its hand at several things. It had once made a feeble little dart at the toy business; for, in another lantern, there was a heap of minute wax dolls, all sticking together upside down, in the direst confusion, with their feet on one another's heads, and a precipitate of broken arms and legs at the bottom. It had made a move in the millinery direction, which a few dry, wiry bonnet-shapes remained in a corner of the window to attest. It had fancied that a living might lie hidden in the tobacco trade, and had stuck up a representation of a native of each of the three integral portions of the

British empire, in the act of consuming that fragrant weed; with a poetic legend attached, importing that in one cause they sat and joked, one chewed tobacco, one took snuff, one smoked; but nothing seemed to have come of it,—except flies. Time had been when it had put a forlorn trust in imitative jewellery, for in one pane of glass there was a card of cheap seals, and another of pencil-cases, and a mysterious black amulet of inscrutable intention, labelled ninepence. But, to that hour, Jerusalem Buildings had bought none of them. In short, Tetterby's had tried so hard to get a livelihood out of Jerusalem Buildings in one way or other, and appeared to have done so indifferently in all, that the best position in the firm was too evidently Co.'s; Co., as a bodiless creation, being untroubled with the vulgar inconveniences of hunger and thirst, being chargeable neither to the poor's-rates nor the assessed taxes, and having no young family to provide for.

Tetterby himself, however, in his little parlour, as already mentioned, having the presence of a young family impressed upon his mind in a manner too clamorous to be disregarded, or to comport with the quiet perusal of a newspaper, laid down his paper, wheeled, in his distraction, a few times round the parlour, like an undecided carrier-pigeon, made an ineffectual rush at one or two flying little figures in bed-gowns that skimmed past him, and then, bearing suddenly down upon the only unoffending member of the family, boxed the ears of little Moloch's nurse.

"You bad boy!" said Mr. Tetterby, "haven't you any feeling for your poor father after the fatigues and anxieties of a hard winter's day, since five o'clock in the morning, but must you wither his rest, and corrode his latest intelligence, with *your* wicious tricks? Isn't it enough, sir, that your brother 'Dolphus is toiling and moiling in the fog and cold, and you rolling in the lap of luxury with a—with a baby, and everything you can wish for," said Mr. Tetterby, heaping this up as a great climax of blessings, "but must you make a wilderness of home, and maniacs of your parents? Must you, Johnny? Hey?" At each interrogation, Mr. Tetterby made a feint of boxing his ears again, but thought better of it, and held his hand.

"Oh, father!" whimpered Johnny, "when I wasn't doing anything, I'm sure, but taking such care of Sally, and getting her to sleep. Oh, father!"

"I wish my little woman would come home!" said Mr. Tetterby, relenting and repenting, "I only wish my little woman would come home! I ain't fit to deal with 'em. They make my head go round, and get the better of me. Oh, Johnny! Isn't it enough that your dear mother has provided you with that sweet sister?" indicating Moloch; "isn't it enough that you were seven boys before, without a ray of gal, and that your dear mother went through what she *did* go through, on purpose that you might all of you have a little sister, but must you so behave yourself as to make my head swim?"

Softening more and more, as his own tender feelings and those of his injured son were worked on, Mr. Tetterby concluded by embracing him, and immediately breaking away to catch one of the real delinquents. A reasonably good start occurring, he succeeded, after a short but smart run, and some rather severe cross-country work under and over the bedsteads, and in and out among the intricacies of the chairs, in capturing his infant, whom he condignly punished, and bore to bed. This example had a powerful, and apparently, mesmeric influence on him of the boots, who instantly fell into a deep sleep, though he had been, but a moment before, broad awake, and in the highest possible feather. Nor was it lost upon the two young architects, who retired to bed, in an adjoining closet, with great privacy and speed. The comrade of the Intercepted One also shrinking into his nest with similar discretion, Mr. Tetterby, when he paused for breath, found himself unexpectedly in a scene of peace.

"My little woman herself," said Mr. Tetterby, wiping his flushed face, "could hardly have done it better! I only wish my little woman had had it to do, I do indeed!"

Mr. Tetterby sought upon his screen for a passage appropriate to be impressed upon his children's minds on the occasion, and read the following.

"'It is an undoubted fact that all remarkable men have had remarkable mothers, and have respected them in after life as their best friends.' Think of your own remarkable mother, my boys," said Mr. Tetterby, "and know her value while she is still among you!"

He sat down in his chair by the fire, and composed himself, cross-legged, over his newspaper.

"Let anybody, I don't care who it is, get out of bed again," said Tetterby, as a general proclamation, delivered in a very softhearted manner, "and astonishment will be the portion of that respected contemporary!"—which expression Mr. Tetterby selected from his screen. "Johnny, my child, take care of your only sister, Sally; for she's the brightest gem that ever sparkled on your early brow."

Johnny sat down on a little stool, and devotedly crushed himself beneath the weight of Moloch.

"Ah, what a gift that baby is to you, Johnny!" said his father, "and how thankful you ought to be! 'It is not generally known,' Johnny," he was now referring to the screen again, "'but it is a fact ascertained, by accurate calculations, that the following immense per-centage of babies never attain to two years old; that is to say—'"

"Oh, don't, father, please!" cried Johnny. "I can't bear it, when I think of Sally."

Mr. Tetterby desisting, Johnny, with a profounder sense of his trust, wiped his eyes, and hushed his sister.

"Your brother 'Dolphus," said his father, poking the fire, "is late to-night, Johnny, and will come home like a lump of ice. What's got your precious mother?"

"Here's mother, and 'Dolphus too, father!" exclaimed Johnny, "I think."

"You're right!" returned his father, listening. "Yes, that's the footstep of my little woman."

The process of induction, by which Mr. Tetterby had come to the conclusion that his wife was a little woman, was his own secret. She would have made two editions of himself, very easily. Considered as an individual, she was rather remarkable for being robust and portly; but considered with reference to her husband, her dimensions became magnificent. Nor did they assume a less imposing proportion, when studied with reference to the size of her seven sons, who were but diminutive. In the case of Sally, however, Mrs. Tetterby had asserted herself, at last; as nobody knew better than the victim Johnny, who weighed and measured that exacting idol every hour in the day.

Mrs. Tetterby, who had been marketing, and carried a basket, threw back her bonnet and shawl, and sitting down, fatigued, commanded Johnny to bring his sweet charge to her straightway, for a kiss. Johnny having complied, and gone back to his stool, and again crushed himself, Master Adolphus Tetterby, who had by this time unwound his Torso out of a prismatic comforter, apparently interminable, requested the same favour. Johnny having again complied, and again gone back to his stool, and again crushed himself, Mr. Tetterby, struck by a sudden thought, preferred the same claim on his own parental part. The satisfaction of this third desire completely exhausted the sacrifice, who had hardly breath enough left to get back to his stool, crush himself again, and pant at his relations.

"Whatever you do, Johnny," said Mrs. Tetterby, shaking her head, "take care of her, or never look your mother in the face again."

"Nor your brother," said Adolphus.

"Nor your father, Johnny," added Mr. Tetterby.

Johnny, much affected by this conditional renunciation of him, looked down at Moloch's eyes to see that they were all right, so far, and skilfully patted her back (which was uppermost), and rocked her with his foot.

"Are you wet, 'Dolphus, my boy?" said his father. "Come and take my chair, and dry yourself."

"No, father, thank'ee," said Adolphus, smoothing himself down with his hands. "I an't very wet, I don't think. Does my face shine much, father?"

"Well, it *does* look waxy, my boy," returned Mr. Tetterby.

"It's the weather, father," said Adolphus, polishing his cheeks on the worn sleeve of his jacket. "What with rain, and sleet, and wind, and snow, and fog, my face gets quite brought out into a rash sometimes. And shines, it does—oh, don't it, though!"

Master Adolphus was also in the newspaper line of life, being employed by a more thriving firm than his father and Co., to vend newspapers at a railway station, where his chubby little person, like a shabbily disguised Cupid, and his shrill little voice (he was not much more than ten years old), were as well known as the hoarse panting of the locomotives, running in and out. His juvenility might have been at some loss for a harmless outlet, in his early application to traffic, but for a fortunate discovery he made of a means of entertaining himself, and of dividing the long day into stages of interest, without neglecting business. This ingenious invention, remarkable, like many great discoveries, for its simplicity, consisted in varying the first vowel in the word "paper," and substituting, in its stead, at different periods of the day, all the other vowels in grammatical succession. Thus, before daylight in the winter time, he went to and fro, in his little oilskin cap and cape, and his big comforter, piercing the heavy air with his cry of "Morn-ing Pa-per!" which, about an hour before noon, changed to "Morn-ing Pep-per!" which, at about two, changed to "Morn-ing Pip-per!" which, in a couple of hours, changed to "Morn-ing Pop-per!" and so declined with the sun into "Eve-ning Pup-per!" to the great relief and comfort of this young gentleman's spirits.

Mrs. Tetterby, his lady-mother, who had been sitting with her bonnet and shawl thrown back, as aforesaid, thoughtfully turning her wedding-ring round and round upon her finger, now rose, and divesting herself of her out-of-door attire, began to lay the cloth for supper.

"Ah, dear me, dear me, dear me!" said Mrs. Tetterby. "That's the way the world goes!"

"Which is the way the world goes, my dear?" asked Mr. Tetterby, looking round.

"Oh, nothing!" said Mrs. Tetterby.

Mr. Tetterby elevated his eyebrows, folded his newspaper afresh, and carried his eyes up it, and down it, and across it, but was wandering in his attention, and not reading it.

Mrs. Tetterby, at the same time, laid the cloth, but rather as if she were punishing the table than preparing the family supper; hitting it unnecessarily hard with the knives and forks, slapping it with the plates, dinting it with the salt-cellar, and coming heavily down upon it with the loaf.

"Ah, dear me, dear me, dear me!" said Mrs. Tetterby. "That's the way the world goes!"

"My duck," returned her husband, looking round again, "you said that before. Which is the way the world goes?"

"Oh, nothing!" said Mrs. Tetterby.

"Sophia!" remonstrated her husband, "you said *that* before, too."

"Well, I'll say it again if you like," returned Mrs. Tetterby. "Oh nothing—there! And again if you like, oh nothing—there! And again if you like, oh nothing—now then!"

Mr. Tetterby brought his eye to bear upon the partner of his bosom, and said, in mild astonishment:

"My little woman, what has put you out?"

"I'm sure *I* don't know," she retorted. "Don't ask me. Who said I was put out at all? *I* never did."

Mr. Tetterby gave up the perusal of his newspaper as a bad job, and, taking a slow walk across the room, with his hands behind him, and his shoulders raised—his gait according perfectly with the resignation of his manner—addressed himself to his two eldest offspring.

"Your supper will be ready in a minute, 'Dolphus," said Mr. Tetterby. "Your mother has been out in the wet, to the cook's shop, to buy it. It was very good of your mother so to do. *You* shall get some supper too, very soon, Johnny. Your mother's pleased with you, my man, for being so attentive to your precious sister."

Mrs. Tetterby, without any remark, but with a decided subsidence of her animosity towards the table, finished her preparations, and took, from her ample basket, a substantial slab of hot pease pudding wrapped in paper, and a basin covered with a saucer, which, on being uncovered, sent forth an odour so agreeable, that the three pair of eyes in the two beds opened wide and fixed themselves upon the banquet. Mr. Tetterby, without regarding this tacit invitation to be seated, stood repeating slowly, "Yes, yes, your supper will be ready in a minute, 'Dolphus—your mother went out in the wet, to the cook's shop, to buy it. It was very good of your mother so to do'—until Mrs. Tetterby, who had been exhibiting sundry tokens of contrition behind him, caught him round the neck, and wept.

"Oh, 'Dolphus!" said Mrs. Tetterby, "how could I go and behave so?"

This reconciliation affected Adolphus the younger and Johnny to that degree, that they both, as with one accord, raised a dismal cry, which had the effect of immediately shutting up the round eyes in the beds, and utterly routing the two remaining little Tetterbys, just then stealing in from the adjoining closet to see what was going on in the eating way.

"I am sure, 'Dolphus," sobbed Mrs. Tetterby, "coming home, I had no more idea than a child unborn——"

Mr. Tetterby seemed to dislike this figure of speech, and observed, "Say than the baby, my dear."

"—Had no more idea than the baby," said Mrs. Tetterby.—"Johnny, don't look at me, but look at her, or she'll fall out of your lap and be killed, and then you'll die in agonies of a broken heart, and serve you right.—No more idea I hadn't than that darling, of being cross when I came home; but somehow, 'Dolphus——" Mrs. Tetterby paused, and again turned her wedding-ring round and round upon her finger.

"I see!" said Mr. Tetterby. "I understand! My little woman was put out. Hard times, and hard weather, and hard work, make it trying now and then. I see, bless your soul! No wonder! 'Dolf, my man," continued Mr. Tetterby, exploring the basin with a fork, "here's your mother been and bought, at the cook's shop, besides pease pudding, a whole knuckle of a lovely roast leg of pork, with lots of crackling left upon it, and with seasoning gravy and mustard quite unlimited. Hand in your plate, my boy, and begin while it's simmering."

Master Adolphus, needing no second summons, received his portion with eyes rendered moist by appetite, and withdrawing to his particular stool, fell upon his supper tooth and nail. Johnny was not forgotten, but received his rations on bread, lest he should, in a flush of gravy, trickle any on the baby. He was required, for similar reasons, to keep his pudding, when not on active service, in his pocket.

There might have been more pork on the knucklebone,—which knucklebone the carver at the cook's shop had assuredly not forgotten in carving for previous customers—but there was no stint of seasoning, and that is an accessory dreamily suggesting pork, and pleasantly cheating the sense of taste. The pease pudding, too, the gravy and mustard, like the Eastern rose in respect of the nightingale, if they were not absolutely pork, had lived near it; so, upon the whole, there was the flavour of a middle-sized pig. It was irresistible to the Tetterbys in bed, who, though professing to slumber peacefully, crawled out when unseen by their parents, and silently appealed to their brothers for any gastronomic token of fraternal affection. They, not hard of heart, presenting scraps in return, it resulted that a party of light skirmishers in night-gowns were careering about the parlour all through supper, which harassed Mr. Tetterby exceedingly, and once or twice imposed upon him the necessity of a charge, before which these guerilla troops retired in all directions and in great confusion.

Mrs. Tetterby did not enjoy her supper. There seemed to be something on Mrs. Tetterby's mind. At one time she laughed without reason, and at another time she cried without reason, and at last she laughed and cried together in a manner so very unreasonable that her husband was confounded.

"My little woman," said Mr. Tetterby, "if the world goes that way, it appears to go the wrong way, and to choke you."

"Give me a drop of water," said Mrs. Tetterby, struggling with herself, "and don't speak to me for the present, or take any notice of me. Don't do it!"

Mr. Tetterby having administered the water, turned suddenly on the unlucky Johnny (who was full of sympathy), and demanded why he was wallowing there, in gluttony and idleness, instead of coming forward with the baby, that the sight of her might revive his mother. Johnny immediately approached, borne down by its weight; but Mrs. Tetterby holding out her hand to signify that she was not in a condition to bear that trying appeal to her feelings, he was interdicted from advancing another inch, on pain of perpetual hatred from all his dearest connections; and accordingly retired to his stool again, and crushed himself as before.

After a pause, Mrs. Tetterby said she was better now, and began to laugh.

"My little woman," said her husband, dubiously, "are you quite sure you're better? Or are you, Sophia, about to break out in a fresh direction?"

"No, 'Dolphus, no," replied his wife. "I'm quite myself." With that, settling her hair, and pressing the palms of her hands upon his eyes, she laughed again.

"What a wicked fool I was, to think so for a moment!" said Mrs. Tetterby. "Come nearer, 'Dolphus, and let me ease my mind, and tell you what I mean. Let me tell you all about it."

Mr. Tetterby bringing his chair closer, Mrs. Tetterby laughed again, gave him a hug, and wiped her eyes.

"You know, 'Dolphus, my dear," said Mrs. Tetterby, "that when I was single, I might have given myself away in several directions. At one time, four after me at once; two of them were sons of Mars."

"We're all sons of Ma's, my dear," said Mr. Tetterby, "jointly with Pa's."

"I don't mean that," replied his wife, "I mean soldiers—serjeants."

"Oh!" said Mr. Tetterby.

"Well, 'Dolphus, I'm sure I never think of such things now, to regret them; and I'm sure I've got as good a husband, and would do as much to prove that I was fond of him, as——"

"As any little woman in the world," said Mr. Tetterby. "Very good. Very good."

If Mr. Tetterby had been ten feet high, he could not have expressed a gentler consideration for Mrs. Tetterby's fairy-like stature; and if Mrs. Tetterby had been two feet high, she could not have felt it more appropriately her due.

"But you see, 'Dolphus," said Mrs. Tetterby, "this being Christmas-time, when all people who can, make holiday, and when all people who have got money, like to spend some, I did, somehow, get a little out of sorts when I was in the streets just now. There were so many things to be sold—such delicious things to eat, such fine things to look at, such delightful things to have—and there was so much calculating

and calculating necessary, before I durst lay out a sixpence for the
commonest thing; and the basket was so large, and wanted so much
in it; and my stock of money was so small, and would go such a little
way;—you hate me, don't you, 'Dolphus?"

"Not quite," said Mr. Tetterby, "as yet."

"Well! I'll tell you the whole truth," pursued his wife, penitently,
"and then perhaps you will. I felt all this, so much, when I was trudging about in the cold, and when I saw a lot of other calculating faces
and large baskets trudging about, too, that I began to think whether I
mightn't have done better, and been happier, if—I hadn't—" the wedding-ring went round again, and Mrs. Tetterby shook her downcast
head as she turned it.

"I see," said her husband quietly; "if you hadn't married at all, or
if you had married somebody else?"

"Yes," sobbed Mrs. Tetterby. "That's really what I thought. Do you
hate me now, 'Dolphus?"

"Why no," said Mr. Tetterby, "I don't find that I do, as yet."

Mrs. Tetterby gave him a thankful kiss, and went on.

"I begin to hope you won't, now, 'Dolphus, though I am afraid I
haven't told you the worst. I can't think what came over me. I don't
know whether I was ill, or mad, or what I was, but I couldn't call up
anything that seemed to bind us to each other, or to reconcile me to
my fortune. All the pleasures and enjoyments we had ever had—*they*
seemed so poor and insignificant, I hated them. I could have trodden
on them. And I could think of nothing else, except our being poor,
and the number of mouths there were at home."

"Well, well, my dear," said Mr. Tetterby, shaking her hand encouragingly, "that's truth after all. We *are* poor, and there *are* a number of
mouths at home here."

"Ah! but, Dolf, Dolf!" cried his wife, laying her hands upon his
neck, "my good, kind, patient fellow, when I had been at home a very
little while—how different! Oh, Dolf, dear, how different it was! I felt
as if there was a rush of recollection on me, all at once, that softened
my hard heart, and filled it up till it was bursting. All our struggles for
a livelihood, all our cares and wants since we have been married, all
the times of sickness, all the hours of watching, we have ever had, by
one another, or by the children, seemed to speak to me, and say that
they had made us one, and that I never might have been, or could
have been, or would have been, any other than the wife and mother
I am. Then, the cheap enjoyments that I could have trodden on so
cruelly, got to be so precious to me—oh, so priceless, and dear!—that I
couldn't bear to think how much I had wronged them; and I said, and
say again a hundred times, how could I ever behave so, 'Dolphus, how
could I ever have the heart to do it!"

The good woman, quite carried away by her honest tenderness and remorse, was weeping with all her heart, when she started up with a scream, and ran behind her husband. Her cry was so terrified, that the children started from their sleep and from their beds, and clung about her. Nor did her gaze belie her voice, as she pointed to a pale man in a black cloak who had come into the room.

"Look at that man! Look there! What does he want?"

"My dear," returned her husband, "I'll ask him if you'll let me go. What's the matter? How you shake!"

"I saw him in the street, when I was out just now. He looked at me, and stood near me. I am afraid of him."

"Afraid of him! Why?"

"I don't know why—I—stop! husband!" for he was going towards the stranger.

She had one hand pressed upon her forehead, and one upon her breast; and there was a peculiar fluttering all over her, and a hurried unsteady motion of her eyes, as if she had lost something.

"Are you ill, my dear?"

"What is it that is going from me again?" she muttered, in a low voice. "What *is* this that is going away?"

Then she abruptly answered: "Ill? No, I am quite well," and stood looking vacantly at the floor.

Her husband, who had not been altogether free from the infection of her fear at first, and whom the present strangeness of her manner did not tend to reassure, addressed himself to the pale visitor in the black cloak, who stood still, and whose eyes were bent upon the ground.

"What may be your pleasure, sir," he asked, "with us?"

"I fear that my coming in unperceived," returned the visitor, "has alarmed you; but you were talking and did not hear me."

"My little woman says—perhaps you heard her say it," returned Mr. Tetterby, "that it's not the first time you have alarmed her to-night."

"I am sorry for it. I remember to have observed her, for a few moments only, in the street. I had no intention of frightening her."

As he raised his eyes in speaking, she raised hers. It was extraordinary to see what dread she had of him, and with what dread he observed it—and yet how narrowly and closely.

"My name," he said, "is Redlaw. I come from the old college hard by. A young gentleman who is a student there, lodges in your house, does he not?"

"Mr. Denham?" said Tetterby.

"Yes."

It was a natural action, and so slight as to be hardly noticeable; but the little man, before speaking again, passed his hand across his forehead, and looked quickly round the room, as though he were sensible of some change in its atmosphere. The Chemist, instantly transferring to him the look of dread he had directed towards the wife, stepped back, and his face turned paler.

"The gentleman's room," said Tetterby, "is up-stairs, sir. There's a more convenient private entrance; but as you have come in here, it will save your going out into the cold, if you'll take this little staircase," showing one communicating directly with the parlour, "and go up to him that way, if you wish to see him."

"Yes, I wish to see him," said the Chemist. "Can you spare a light?"

The watchfulness of his haggard look, and the inexplicable distrust that darkened it, seemed to trouble Mr. Tetterby. He paused; and looking fixedly at him in return, stood for a minute or so, like a man stupefied, or fascinated.

At length he said, "I'll light you, sir, if you'll follow me."

"No," replied the Chemist, "I don't wish to be attended, or announced to him. He does not expect me. I would rather go alone. Please to give me the light, if you can spare it, and I'll find the way."

In the quickness of his expression of this desire, and in taking the candle from the newsman, he touched him on the breast. Withdrawing his hand hastily, almost as though he had wounded him by accident (for he did not know in what part of himself his new power resided, or how it was communicated, or how the manner of its reception varied in different persons), he turned and ascended the stair.

But when he reached the top, he stopped and looked down. The wife was standing in the same place, twisting her ring round and round upon her finger. The husband, with his head bent forward on his breast, was musing heavily and sullenly. The children, still clustering about the mother, gazed timidly after the visitor, and nestled together when they saw him looking down.

"Come!" said the father, roughly. "There's enough of this. Get to bed here!"

"The place is inconvenient and small enough," the mother added, "without you. Get to bed!"

The whole brood, scared and sad, crept away; little Johnny and the baby lagging last. The mother, glancing contemptuously round the sordid room, and tossing from her the fragments of their meal, stopped on the threshold of her task of clearing the table, and sat down, pondering idly and dejectedly. The father betook himself to the chimney-corner, and impatiently raking the small fire together, bent over it as if he would monopolise it all. They did not interchange a word.

The Chemist, paler than before, stole upward like a thief; looking back upon the change below, and dreading equally to go on or return.

"What have I done!" he said, confusedly. "What am I going to do!"

"To be the benefactor of mankind," he thought he heard a voice reply.

He looked round, but there was nothing there; and a passage now shutting out the little parlour from his view, he went on, directing his eyes before him at the way he went.

"It is only since last night," he muttered gloomily, "that I have remained shut up, and yet all things are strange to me. I am strange to myself. I am here, as in a dream. What interest have I in this place, or in any place that I can bring to my remembrance? My mind is going blind!"

There was a door before him, and he knocked at it. Being invited, by a voice within, to enter, he complied.

"Is that my kind nurse?" said the voice. "But I need not ask her. There is no one else to come here."

It spoke cheerfully, though in a languid tone, and attracted his attention to a young man lying on a couch, drawn before the chimney-piece, with the back towards the door. A meagre scanty stove, pinched and hollowed like a sick man's cheeks, and bricked into the centre of a hearth that it could scarcely warm, contained the fire, to which his face was turned. Being so near the windy house-top, it wasted quickly, and with a busy sound, and the burning ashes dropped down fast.

"They chink when they shoot out here," said the student, smiling, "so, according to the gossips, they are not coffins, but purses. I shall be well and rich yet, some day, if it please God, and shall live perhaps to love a daughter Milly, in remembrance of the kindest nature and the gentlest heart in the world."

He put up his hand as if expecting her to take it, but, being weakened, he lay still, with his face resting on his other hand, and did not turn round.

The Chemist glanced about the room;—at the student's books and papers, piled upon a table in a corner, where they, and his extinguished reading-lamp, now prohibited and put away, told of the attentive hours that had gone before this illness, and perhaps caused it;—at such signs of his old health and freedom, as the out-of-door attire that hung idle on the wall;—at those remembrances of other and less solitary scenes, the little miniatures upon the chimney-piece, and the drawing of home;—at that token of his emulation, perhaps, in some sort, of his personal attachment too, the framed engraving of himself, the looker-on. The time had been, only yesterday, when not one of these objects, in its remotest association of interest with the living figure before him, would have been lost on Redlaw. Now, they were but objects; or, if any gleam of such connexion shot upon him, it perplexed, and not enlightened him, as he stood looking round with a dull wonder.

The student, recalling the thin hand which had remained so long untouched, raised himself on the couch, and turned his head.

"Mr. Redlaw!" he exclaimed, and started up.

Redlaw put out his arm.

"Don't come nearer to me. I will sit here. Remain you, where you are!"

He sat down on a chair near the door, and having glanced at the young man standing leaning with his hand upon the couch, spoke with his eyes averted towards the ground.

"I heard, by an accident, by what accident is no matter, that one of my class was ill and solitary. I received no other description of him, than that he lived in this street. Beginning my inquiries at the first house in it, I have found him."

"I have been ill, sir," returned the student, not merely with a modest hesitation, but with a kind of awe of him, "but am greatly better. An attack of fever—of the brain, I believe—has weakened me, but I am much better. I cannot say I have been solitary, in my illness, or I should forget the ministering hand that has been near me."

"You are speaking of the keeper's wife," said Redlaw.

"Yes." The student bent his head, as if he rendered her some silent homage.

The Chemist, in whom there was a cold, monotonous apathy, which rendered him more like a marble image on the tomb of the man who had started from his dinner yesterday at the first mention of this student's case, than the breathing man himself, glanced again at the student leaning with his hand upon the couch, and looked upon the ground, and in the air, as if for light for his blinded mind.

"I remembered your name," he said, "when it was mentioned to me down-stairs, just now; and I recollect your face. We have held but very little personal communication together?"

"Very little."

"You have retired and withdrawn from me, more than any of the rest, I think?"

The student signified assent.

"And why?" said the Chemist; not with the least expression of interest, but with a moody, wayward kind of curiosity. "Why? How comes it that you have sought to keep especially from me, the knowledge of your remaining here, at this season, when all the rest have dispersed, and of your being ill? I want to know why this is?"

The young man, who had heard him with increasing agitation, raised his downcast eyes to his face, and clasping his hands together, cried with sudden earnestness and with trembling lips:

"Mr. Redlaw! You have discovered me. You know my secret!"

"Secret?" said the Chemist, harshly. "I know?"

"Yes! Your manner, so different from the interest and sympathy which endear you to so many hearts, your altered voice, the constraint there is in everything you say, and in your looks," replied the student, "warn me that you know me. That you would conceal it, even now, is but a proof to me (God knows I need none!) of your natural kindness, and of the bar there is between us."

A vacant and contemptuous laugh was all his answer.

"But Mr. Redlaw," said the student, "as a just man, and a good man, think how innocent I am, except in name and descent, of participation in any wrong inflicted on you, or in any sorrow you have borne."

"Sorrow!" said Redlaw, laughing. "Wrong! What are those to me?"

"For Heaven's sake," entreated the shrinking student, "do not let the mere interchange of a few words with me change you like this, sir! Let me pass again from your knowledge and notice. Let me occupy my old reserved and distant place among those whom you instruct. Know me only by the name I have assumed, and not by that of Longford—"

"Longford!" exclaimed the other.

He clasped his head with both his hands, and for a moment turned upon the young man his own intelligent and thoughtful face. But the light passed from it, like the sunbeam of an instant, and it clouded as before.

"The name my mother bears, sir," faltered the young man, "the name she took, when she might, perhaps, have taken one more honoured. Mr. Redlaw," hesitating, "I believe I know that history. Where my information halts, my guesses at what is wanting may supply something not remote from the truth. I am the child of a marriage that has not proved itself a well-assorted or a happy one. From infancy, I have heard you spoken of with honour and respect—with something that was almost reverence. I have heard of such devotion, of such fortitude and tenderness, of such rising up against the obstacles which press men down, that my fancy, since I learnt my little lesson from my mother, has shed a lustre on your name. At last, a poor student myself, from whom could I learn but you?"

Redlaw, unmoved, unchanged, and looking at him with a staring frown, answered by no word or sign.

"I cannot say," pursued the other, "I should try in vain to say, how much it has impressed me, and affected me, to find the gracious traces of the past, in that certain power of winning gratitude and confidence which is associated among us students (among the humblest of us, most) with Mr. Redlaw's generous name. Our ages and positions are so different, sir, and I am so accustomed to regard you from a distance, that I wonder at my own presumption when I touch, however lightly, on that theme. But to one who—I may say, who felt no common interest in my mother once—it may be something to hear, now that is all past, with what indescribable feelings of affection I have, in my obscurity, regarded him; with what pain and reluctance I have kept aloof from his encouragement, when a word of it would have made me rich; yet how I have felt it fit that I should hold my course, content to know him, and to be unknown. Mr. Redlaw," said the student, faintly, "what I would have said, I have said ill, for my strength is strange to me as yet; but for anything unworthy in this fraud of mine, forgive me, and for all the rest forget me!"

The staring frown remained on Redlaw's face, and yielded to no other expression until the student, with these words, advanced towards him, as if to touch his hand, when he drew back and cried to him:

"Don't come nearer to me!"

The young man stopped, shocked by the eagerness of his recoil, and by the sternness of his repulsion; and he passed his hand, thoughtfully, across his forehead.

"The past is past," said the Chemist. "It dies like the brutes. Who talks to me of its traces in my life? He raves or lies! What have I to do with your distempered dreams? If you want money, here it is. I came to offer it; and that is all I came for. There can be nothing else that brings me here," he muttered, holding his head again, with both his hands. "There *can* be nothing else, and yet——"

He had tossed his purse upon the table. As he fell into this dim cogitation with himself, the student took it up, and held it out to him.

"Take it back, sir," he said proudly, though not angrily. "I wish you could take from me, with it, the remembrance of your words and offer."

"You do?" he retorted, with a wild light in his eyes. "You do?"

"I do!"

The Chemist went close to him, for the first time, and took the purse, and turned him by the arm, and looked him in the face.

"There is sorrow and trouble in sickness, is there not?" he demanded, with a laugh.

The wondering student answered, "Yes."

"In its unrest, in its anxiety, in its suspense, in all its train of physical and mental miseries?" said the Chemist, with a wild unearthly exultation. "All best forgotten, are they not?"

The student did not answer, but again passed his hand, confusedly, across his forehead. Redlaw still held him by the sleeve, when Milly's voice was heard outside.

"I can see very well now," she said, "thank you, Dolf. Don't cry, dear. Father and mother will be comfortable again, to-morrow, and home will be comfortable too. A gentleman with him, is there!"

Redlaw released his hold, as he listened.

"I have feared, from the first moment," he murmured to himself, "to meet her. There is a steady quality of goodness in her, that I dread to influence. I may be the murderer of what is tenderest and best within her bosom."

She was knocking at the door.

"Shall I dismiss it as an idle foreboding, or still avoid her?" he muttered, looking uneasily around.

She was knocking at the door again.

"Of all the visitors who could come here," he said, in a hoarse alarmed voice, turning to his companion, "this is the one I should desire most to avoid. Hide me!"

The student opened a frail door in the wall, communicating where the garret-roof began to slope towards the floor, with a small inner room. Redlaw passed in hastily, and shut it after him.

The student then resumed his place upon the couch, and called to her to enter.

"Dear Mr. Edmund," said Milly, looking round, "they told me there was a gentleman here."

"There is no one here but I."

"There has been some one?"

"Yes, yes, there has been some one."

She put her little basket on the table, and went up to the back of the couch, as if to take the extended hand—but it was not there. A little surprised, in her quiet way, she leaned over to look at his face, and gently touched him on the brow.

"Are you quite as well to-night? Your head is not so cool as in the afternoon."

"Tut!" said the student, petulantly, "very little ails me."

A little more surprise, but no reproach, was expressed in her face, as she withdrew to the other side of the table, and took a small packet of needlework from her basket. But she laid it down again, on second thoughts, and going noiselessly about the room, set every thing exactly in its place, and in the neatest order; even to the cushions on the couch, which she touched with so light a hand, that he hardly seemed to know it, as he lay looking at the fire. When all this was done, and she had swept the hearth, she sat down, in her modest little bonnet, to her work, and was quietly busy on it directly.

"It's the new muslin curtain for the window, Mr. Edmund," said Milly, stitching away as she talked. "It will look very clean and nice, though it costs very little, and will save your eyes, too, from the light. My William says the room should not be too light just now, when you are recovering so well, or the glare might make you giddy."

He said nothing; but there was something so fretful and impatient in his change of position, that her quick fingers stopped, and she looked at him anxiously.

"The pillows are not comfortable," she said, laying down her work and rising. "I will soon put them right."

"They are very well," he answered. "Leave them alone, pray. You make so much of everything."

He raised his head to say this, and looked at her so thanklessly, that, after he had thrown himself down again, she stood timidly pausing. However, she resumed her seat, and her needle, without having directed even a murmuring look towards him, and was soon as busy as before.

"I have been thinking, Mr. Edmund, that you have been often thinking of late, when I have been sitting by, how true the saying is, that adversity is a good teacher. Health will be more precious to you, after this illness, than it has ever been. And years hence, when this time of year comes round, and you remember the days when you lay here sick, alone, that the knowledge of your illness might not afflict those who are dearest to you, your home will be doubly dear and doubly blest. Now, isn't that a good, true thing?"

She was too intent upon her work, and too earnest in what she said, and too composed and quiet altogether, to be on the watch for any look he might direct towards her in reply; so the shaft of his ungrateful glance fell harmless, and did not wound her.

"Ah!" said Milly, with her pretty head inclining thoughtfully on one side, as she looked down, following her busy fingers with her eyes. "Even on me—and I am very different from you, Mr. Edmund, for I have no learning, and don't know how to think properly—this view of such things has made a great impression, since you have been lying ill. When I have seen you so touched by the kindness and attention of the people down-stairs, I have felt that you thought even that experience some repayment for the loss of health, and I have read in your face, as plain as if it was a book, that but for some trouble and sorrow we should never know half the good there is about us."

His getting up from the couch, interrupted her, or she was going on to say more.

"We needn't magnify the merit, Mrs. William," he rejoined slightingly. "The people down-stairs will be paid in good time, I dare say, for any little extra service they may have rendered me; and perhaps they anticipate no less. I am much obliged to you, too."

Her fingers stopped, and she looked at him.

"I can't be made to feel the more obliged by your exaggerating the case," he said. "I am sensible that you have been interested in me, and I say I am much obliged to you. What more would you have?"

Her work fell on her lap, as she still looked at him walking to and fro with an intolerant air, and stopping now and then.

"I say again, I am much obliged to you. Why weaken my sense of what is your due in obligation, by preferring enormous claims upon me? Trouble, sorrow, afflictions, adversity! One might suppose I had been dying a score of deaths here!"

"Do you believe, Mr. Edmund," she asked, rising and going nearer to him, "that I spoke of the poor people of the house, with any reference to myself? To me?" laying her hand upon her bosom with a simple and innocent smile of astonishment.

"Oh! I think nothing about it, my good creature," he returned. "I have had an indisposition, which your solicitude—observe! I say solicitude—makes a great deal more of, than it merits; and it's over, and we can't perpetuate it."

He coldly took a book, and sat down at the table.

She watched him for a little while, until her smile was quite gone, and then returning to where her basket was, said gently:

"Mr. Edmund, would you rather be alone?"

"There is no reason why I should detain you here," he replied.

"Except—" said Milly, hesitating, and showing her work.

"Oh! the curtain," he answered, with a supercilious laugh. "That's not worth staying for."

She made up the little packet again, and put it in her basket. Then, standing before him with such an air of patient entreaty that he could not choose but look at her, she said:

"If you should want me, I will come back willingly. When you did want me, I was quite happy to come; there was no merit in it. I think you must be afraid, that, now you are getting well, I may be troublesome to you; but I should not have been, indeed. I should have come no longer than your weakness and confinement lasted. You owe me nothing; but it is right that you should deal as justly by me as if I was a lady—even the very lady that you love; and if you suspect me of meanly making much of the little I have tried to do to comfort your sick room, you do yourself more wrong than ever you can do me. That is why I am sorry. That is why I am very sorry."

If she had been as passionate as she was quiet, as indignant as she was calm, as angry in her look as she was gentle, as loud of tone as she was low and clear, she might have left no sense of her departure in the room, compared with that which fell upon the lonely student when she went away.

He was gazing drearily upon the place where she had been, when Redlaw came out of his concealment, and came to the door.

"When sickness lays its hand on you again," he said, looking fiercely back at him, "—may it be soon!—Die here! Rot here!"

"What have you done?" returned the other, catching at his cloak. "What change have you wrought in me? What curse have you brought upon me? Give me back myself!"

"Give me back *myself*!" exclaimed Redlaw like a madman. "I am infected! I am infectious! I am charged with poison for my own mind, and the minds of all mankind. Where I felt interest, compassion, sympathy, I am turning into stone. Selfishness and ingratitude spring up in my blighted footsteps. I am only so much less base than the wretches whom I make so, that in the moment of their transformation I can hate them."

As he spoke—the young man still holding to his cloak—he cast him off, and struck him: then, wildly hurried out into the night air where the wind was blowing, the snow falling, the cloud-drift sweeping on, the moon dimly shining, and where, blowing in the wind, falling with the snow, drifting with the clouds, shining in the moonlight, and heavily looming in the darkness, were the Phantom's words, "The gift that I have given, you shall give again, go where you will!"

Wither he went, he neither knew nor cared, so that he avoided company. The change he felt within him made the busy streets a desert, and himself a desert, and the multitude around him, in their manifold endurances and ways of life, a mighty waste of sand, which the winds tossed into unintelligible heaps and made a ruinous confusion of. Those traces in his breast which the Phantom had told him would "die out soon," were not, as yet, so far upon their way to death, but that he understood enough of what he was, and what he made of others, to desire to be alone.

This put it in his mind—he suddenly bethought himself, as he was going along, of the boy who had rushed into his room. And then he recollected, that of those with whom he had communicated since the Phantom's disappearance, that boy alone had shown no sign of being changed.

Monstrous and odious as the wild thing was to him, he determined to seek it out, and prove if this were really so; and also to seek it with another intention, which came into his thoughts at the same time.

So, resolving with some difficulty where he was, he directed his steps back to the old college, and to that part of it where the general porch was, and where, alone, the pavement was worn by the tread of the students' feet.

The keeper's house stood just within the iron gates, forming a part of the chief quadrangle. There was a little cloister outside, and from that sheltered place he knew he could look in at the window of their ordinary room, and see who was within. The iron gates were shut, but his hand was familiar with the fastening, and drawing it back by thrusting in his wrist between the bars, he passed through softly, shut it again, and crept up to the window, crumbling the thin crust of snow with his feet.

The fire, to which he had directed the boy last night, shining brightly through the glass, made an illuminated place upon the ground. Instinctively avoiding this, and going round it, he looked in at the window. At first, he thought that there was no one there, and that the blaze was reddening only the old beams in the ceiling and the dark walls; but peering in more narrowly, he saw the object of his search coiled asleep before it on the floor. He passed quickly to the door, opened it, and went in.

The creature lay in such a fiery heat, that, as the Chemist stooped to rouse him, it scorched his head. So soon as he was touched, the boy, not half awake, clutched his rags together with the instinct of flight upon him, half rolled and half ran into a distant corner of the room, where, heaped upon the ground, he struck his foot out to defend himself.

"Get up!" said the Chemist. "You have not forgotten me?"

"You let me alone!" returned the boy. "This is the woman's house—not yours."

The Chemist's steady eye controlled him somewhat, or inspired him with enough submission to be raised upon his feet, and looked at.

"Who washed them, and put those bandages where they were bruised and cracked?" asked the Chemist, pointing to their altered state.

"The woman did."

"And is it she who has made you cleaner in the face, too?"

"Yes, the woman."

Redlaw asked these questions to attract his eyes towards himself, and with the same intent now held him by the chin, and threw his wild hair back, though he loathed to touch him. The boy watched his eyes keenly, as if he thought it needful to his own defence, not knowing what he might do next; and Redlaw could see well that no change came over him.

"Where are they?" he inquired.

"The woman's out."

"I know she is. Where is the old man with the white hair, and his son?"

"The woman's husband, d'ye mean?" inquired the boy.

"Aye. Where are those two?"

"Out. Something's the matter, somewhere. They were fetched out in a hurry, and told me to stop here."

"Come with me," said the Chemist, "and I'll give you money."

"Come where? and how much will you give?"

"I'll give you more shillings than you ever saw, and bring you back soon. Do you know your way to where you came from?"

"You let me go," returned the boy, suddenly twisting out of his grasp. "I'm not a-going to take you there. Let me be, or I'll heave some fire at you!"

He was down before it, and ready, with his savage little hand, to pluck the burning coals out.

What the Chemist had felt, in observing the effect of his charmed influence stealing over those with whom he came in contact, was not nearly equal to the cold vague terror with which he saw this baby-monster put it at defiance. It chilled his blood to look on the immovable impenetrable thing, in the likeness of a child, with its sharp malignant face turned up to his, and its almost infant hand, ready at the bars.

"Listen, boy!" he said. "You shall take me where you please, so that you take me where the people are very miserable or very wicked. I want to do them good, and not to harm them. You shall have money, as I have told you, and I will bring you back. Get up! Come quickly!" He made a hasty step towards the door, afraid of her returning.

"Will you let me walk by myself, and never hold me, nor yet touch me?" said the boy, slowly withdrawing the hand with which he threatened, and beginning to get up.

"I will!"

"And let me go before, behind, or anyways I like?"

"I will!"

"Give me some money first then, and I'll go."

The Chemist laid a few shillings, one by one, in his extended hand. To count them was beyond the boy's knowledge, but he said "one," every time, and avariciously looked at each as it was given, and at the donor. He had nowhere to put them, out of his hand, but in his mouth; and he put them there.

Redlaw then wrote with his pencil on a leaf of his pocketbook, that the boy was with him; and laying it on the table, signed to him to follow. Keeping his rags together, as usual, the boy complied, and went out with his bare head and his naked feet into the winter night.

Preferring not to depart by the iron gate by which he had entered, where they were in danger of meeting her whom he so anxiously avoided, the Chemist led the way, through some of those passages among which the boy had lost himself, and by that portion of the building where he lived, to a small door of which he had the key. When they got into the street, he stopped to ask his guide—who instantly retreated from him—if he knew where they were.

The savage thing looked here and there, and at length, nodding his head, pointed in the direction he designed to take. Redlaw going on at once, he followed, somewhat less suspiciously; shifting his money from his mouth into his hand, and back again into his mouth, and stealthily rubbing it bright upon his shreds of clothes, as he went along.

Three times, in their progress, they were side by side. Three times they stopped, being side by side. Three times the Chemist glanced down at his face, and shuddered as it forced upon him one reflection.

The first occasion was when they were crossing an old churchyard, and Redlaw stopped among the graves, utterly at a loss how to connect them with any tender, softening, or consolatory thought.

The second was, when the breaking forth of the moon induced him to look up at the Heavens, where he saw her in her glory, surrounded by a host of stars he still knew by the names and histories which human science has appended to them; but where he saw nothing else he had been wont to see, felt nothing he had been wont to feel, in looking up there, on a bright night.

The third was when he stopped to listen to a plaintive strain of music, but could only hear a tune, made manifest to him by the dry mechanism of the instruments and his own ears, with no address to any mystery within him, without a whisper in it of the past, or of the future, powerless upon him as the sound of last year's running water, or the rushing of last year's wind.

At each of these three times, he saw with horror that, in spite of the vast intellectual distance between them, and their being unlike each other in all physical respects, the expression on the boy's face was the expression on his own.

They journeyed on for some time—now through such crowded places, that he often looked over his shoulder thinking he had lost his guide, but generally finding him within his shadow on his other side; now by ways so quiet, that he could have counted his short, quick, naked footsteps coming on behind—until they arrived at a ruinous collection of houses, and the boy touched him and stopped.

"In there!" he said, pointing out one house where there were scattered lights in the windows, and a dim lantern in the doorway, with "Lodgings for Travellers" painted on it.

Redlaw looked about him; from the houses, to the waste piece of ground on which the houses stood, or rather did not altogether tumble down, unfenced, undrained, unlighted, and bordered by a sluggish ditch; from that, to the sloping line of arches, part of some neighbouring viaduct or bridge with which it was surrounded, and which lessened gradually, towards them, until the last but one was a mere kennel for a dog, the last a plundered little heap of bricks; from that, to the child, close to him, cowering and trembling with the cold, and limping on one little foot, while he coiled the other round his leg to warm it, yet staring at all these things with that frightful likeness of expression so apparent in his face, that Redlaw started from him.

"In there!" said the boy, pointing out the house again. "I'll wait."

"Will they let me in?" asked Redlaw.

"Say you're a doctor," he answered with a nod. "There's plenty ill here."

Looking back on his way to the house-door, Redlaw saw him trail himself upon the dust and crawl within the shelter of the smallest arch, as if he were a rat. He had no pity for the thing, but he was afraid of it; and when it looked out of its den at him, he hurried to the house as a retreat.

"Sorrow, wrong, and trouble," said the Chemist, with a painful effort at some more distinct remembrance, "at least haunt this place darkly. He can do no harm, who brings forgetfulness of such things here!"

With these words, he pushed the yielding door, and went in.

There was a woman sitting on the stairs, either asleep or forlorn, whose head was bent down on her hands and knees. As it was not easy to pass without treading on her, and as she was perfectly regardless of his near approach, he stopped, and touched her on the shoulder. Looking up, she showed him quite a young face, but one whose bloom and promise were all swept away, as if the haggard winter should unnaturally kill the spring.

With little or no show of concern on his account, she moved nearer to the wall to leave him a wider passage.

"What are you?" said Redlaw, pausing, with his hand upon the broken stair-rail.

"What do you think I am?" she answered, showing him her face again.

He looked upon the ruined Temple of God, so lately made, so soon disfigured; and something, which was not compassion—for the springs in which a true compassion for such miseries has its rise, were dried up in his breast—but which was nearer to it, for the moment, than any feeling that had lately struggled into the darkening, but not yet wholly darkened, night of his mind—mingled a touch of softness with his next words.

"I am come here to give relief, if I can," he said. "Are you thinking of any wrong?"

She frowned at him, and then laughed; and then her laugh prolonged itself into a shivering sigh, as she dropped her head again, and hid her fingers in her hair.

"Are you thinking of a wrong?" he asked, once more.

"I am thinking of my like," she said, with a momentary look at him.

He had a perception that she was one of many, and that he saw the type of thousands, when he saw her, drooping at his feet.

"What are your parents?" he demanded.

"I had a good home once. My father was a gardener, far away, in the country."

"Is he dead?"

"He's dead to me. All such things are dead to me. You a gentleman, and not know that!" She raised her eyes again, and laughed at him.

"Girl!" said Redlaw, sternly, "before this death, of all such things, was brought about, was there no wrong done to you? In spite of all that you can do, does no remembrance of wrong cleave to you? Are there not times upon times when it is misery to you?"

So little of what was womanly was left in her appearance, that now, when she burst into tears, he stood amazed. But he was more amazed, and much disquieted, to note that in her awakened recollection of this wrong, the first trace of her old humanity and frozen tenderness appeared to show itself.

He drew a little off, and in doing so, observed that her arms were black, her face cut, and her bosom bruised.

"What brutal hand has hurt you so?" he asked.

"My own. I did it myself!" she answered quickly.

"It is impossible."

"I'll swear I did! He didn't touch me. I did it to myself in a passion, and threw myself down here. He wasn't near me. He never laid a hand upon me!"

In the white determination of her face, confronting him with this untruth, he saw enough of the last perversion and distortion of good surviving in that miserable breast, to be stricken with remorse that he had ever come near her.

"Sorrow, wrong, and trouble!" he muttered, turning his fearful gaze away. "All that connects her with the state from which she has fallen, has those roots! In the name of God, let me go by!"

Afraid to look at her again, afraid to touch her, afraid to think of having sundered the last thread by which she held upon the mercy of Heaven, he gathered his cloak about him, and glided swiftly up the stairs.

Opposite to him, on the landing, was a door, which stood partly open, and which, as he ascended, a man with a candle in his hand, came forward from within to shut. But this man, on seeing him, drew back, with much emotion in his manner, and, as if by a sudden impulse, mentioned his name aloud.

In the surprise of such a recognition there, he stopped, endeavouring to recollect the wan and startled face. He had no time to consider it, for, to his yet greater amazement, old Philip came out of the room, and took him by the hand.

"Mr. Redlaw," said the old man, "this is like you, this is like you, sir! you have heard of it, and have come after us to render any help you can. Ah, too late, too late!"

Redlaw, with a bewildered look, submitted to be led into the room. A man lay there, on a truckle-bed, and William Swidger stood at the bedside.

"Too late!" murmured the old man, looking wistfully into the Chemist's face; and the tears stole down his cheeks.

"That's what I say, father," interposed his son in a low voice. "That's where it is, exactly. To keep as quiet as ever we can while he's a-dozing, is the only thing to do. You're right, father!"

Redlaw paused at the bedside, and looked down on the figure that was stretched upon the mattress. It was that of a man, who should have been in the vigour of his life, but on whom it was not likely the sun would ever shine again. The vices of his forty or fifty years' career had so branded him, that, in comparison with their effects upon his face, the heavy hand of time upon the old man's face who watched him had been merciful and beautifying.

"Who is this?" asked the Chemist, looking round.

"My son George, Mr. Redlaw," said the old man, wringing his hands. "My eldest son, George, who was more his mother's pride than all the rest!"

Redlaw's eyes wandered from the old man's grey head, as he laid it down upon the bed, to the person who had recognised him, and who had kept aloof, in the remotest corner of the room. He seemed to be about his own age; and although he knew no such hopeless decay and broken man as he appeared to be, there was something in the turn of his figure, as he stood with his back towards him, and now went out at the door, that made him pass his hand uneasily across his brow.

"William," he said in a gloomy whisper, "who is that man?"

"Why you see, sir," returned Mr. William, "that's what I say, myself. Why should a man ever go and gamble, and the like of that, and let himself down inch by inch till he can't let himself down any lower?"

"Has *he* done so?" asked Redlaw, glancing after him with the same uneasy action as before.

"Just exactly that, sir," returned William Swidger, "as I'm told. He knows a little about medicine, sir, it seems; and having been wayfaring towards London with my unhappy brother that you see here," Mr. William passed his coat-sleeve across his eyes, "and being lodging upstairs for the night—what I say, you see, is that strange companions come together here sometimes—he looked in to attend upon him, and came for us at his request. What a mournful spectacle, sir! But that's where it is. It's enough to kill my father!"

Redlaw looked up, at these words, and, recalling where he was and with whom, and the spell he carried with him—which his surprise had obscured—retired a little, hurriedly, debating with himself whether to shun the house that moment, or remain.

Yielding to a certain sullen doggedness, which it seemed to be a part of his condition to struggle with, he argued for remaining.

"Was it only yesterday," he said, "when I observed the memory of this old man to be a tissue of sorrow and trouble, and shall I be afraid, to-night, to shake it? Are such remembrances as I can drive away, so precious to this dying man that I need fear for *him*? No! I'll stay here."

But he stayed, in fear and trembling none the less for these words; and, shrouded in his black cloak with his face turned from them, stood away from the bedside, listening to what they said, as if he felt himself a demon in the place.

"Father!" murmured the sick man, rallying a little from his stupor.

"My boy! My son George!" said old Philip.

"You spoke, just now, of my being mother's favourite, long ago. It's a dreadful thing to think now, of long ago!"

"No, no, no!" returned the old man. "Think of it. Don't say it's dreadful. It's not dreadful to me, my son."

"It cuts you to the heart, father." For the old man's tears were falling on him.

"Yes, yes," said Philip, "so it does; but it does me good. It's a heavy sorrow to think of that time, but it does me good, George. Oh, think of it too, think of it too, and your heart will be softened more and more! Where's my son William? William, my boy, your mother loved him dearly to the last, and with her latest breath said, 'Tell him I forgave him, blessed him, and prayed for him.' Those were her words to me. I have never forgotten them, and I'm eighty-seven!"

"Father!" said the man upon the bed, "I am dying, I know. I am so far gone, that I can hardly speak, even of what my mind most runs on. Is there any hope for me beyond this bed?"

"There is hope," returned the old man, "for all who are softened and penitent. There is hope for all such. Oh!" he exclaimed, clasping his hands and looking up, "I was thankful, only yesterday, that I could remember this unhappy son when he was an innocent child. But what a comfort it is, now, to think that even God himself has that remembrance of him!"

Redlaw spread his hands upon his face, and shrunk like a murderer.

"Ah!" feebly moaned the man upon the bed. "The waste since then, the waste of life since then!"

"But he was a child once," said the old man. "He played with children. Before he lay down on his bed at night, and fell into his guiltless rest, he said his prayers at his poor mother's knee. I have seen him do it, many a time; and seen her lay his head upon her breast, and kiss him. Sorrowful as it was to her, and to me, to think of this, when he went so wrong, and when our hopes and plans for him were all broken, this gave him still a hold upon us, that nothing else could have given. Oh, Father, so much better than the fathers upon earth! Oh, Father, so much more afflicted by the errors of thy children! take this wanderer back! Not as he is, but as he was then, let him cry to thee, as he has so often seemed to cry to us!"

As the old man lifted up his trembling hands, the son, for whom he made the supplication, laid his sinking head against him for support and comfort, as if he were indeed the child of whom he spoke.

When did man ever tremble, as Redlaw trembled, in the silence that ensued! He knew it must come upon them, knew that it was coming fast.

"My time is very short, my breath is shorter," said the sick man, supporting himself on one arm, and with the other groping in the air, "and I remember there is something on my mind concerning the man who was here just now. Father and William—wait!—is there really anything in black, out there?"

"Yes, yes, it is real," said his aged father.

"Is it a man?"

"What I say myself, George," interposed his brother, bending kindly over him. "It's Mr. Redlaw."

"I thought I had dreamed of him. Ask him to come here."

The Chemist, whiter than the dying man, appeared before him. Obedient to the motion of his hand, he sat upon the bed.

"It has been so ripped up, to-night, sir," said the sick man, laying his hand upon his heart, with a look in which the mute, imploring agony of his condition was concentrated, "by the sight of my poor old father, and the thought of all the trouble I have been the cause of, and all the wrong and sorrow lying at my door, that——"

Was it the extremity to which he had come, or was it the dawning of another change, that made him stop?

"—that what I *can* do right, with my mind running on so much, so fast, I'll try to do. There was another man here. Did you see him?"

Redlaw could not reply by any word; for when he saw that fatal sign he knew so well now, of the wandering hand upon the forehead, his voice died at his lips. But he made some indication of assent.

"He is penniless, hungry, and destitute. He is completely beaten down, and has no resource at all. Look after him! Lose no time! I know he has it in his mind to kill himself."

It was working. It was on his face. His face was changing, hardening, deepening in all its shades, and losing all its sorrow.

"Don't you remember? Don't you know him?" he pursued.

He shut his face out for a moment, with the hand that again wandered over his forehead, and then it lowered on Redlaw, reckless, ruffianly, and callous.

"Why, d—n you!" he said, scowling round, "what have you been doing to me here! I have lived bold, and I mean to die bold. To the Devil with you!"

And so lay down upon his bed, and put his arms up, over his head and ears, as resolute from that time to keep out all access, and to die in his indifference.

If Redlaw had been struck by lightning, it could not have struck him from the bedside with a more tremendous shock. But the old man, who had left the bed while his son was speaking to him, now returning, avoided it quickly likewise, and with abhorrence.

"Where's my boy William?" said the old man hurriedly. "William, come away from here. We'll go home."

"Home, father!" returned William. "Are you going to leave your own son?"

"Where's my own son?" replied the old man.

"Where? why, there!"

"That's no son of mine," said Philip, trembling with resentment. "No such wretch as that, has any claim on me. My children are pleasant to look at, and they wait upon me, and get my meat and drink ready, and are useful to me. I've a right to it! I'm eighty-seven!"

"You're old enough to be no older," muttered William, looking at him grudgingly, with his hands in his pockets. "I don't know what good you are, myself. We could have a deal more pleasure without you."

"*My* son, Mr. Redlaw!" said the old man. "*My* son, too! The boy talking to me of *my* son! Why, what has he ever done to give me any pleasure, I should like to know?"

"I don't know what you have ever done to give *me* any pleasure," said William, sulkily.

"Let me think," said the old man. "For how many Christmas times running, have I sat in my warm place, and never had to come out in the cold night air; and have made good cheer, without being disturbed by any such uncomfortable, wretched sight as him there? Is it twenty, William?"

"Nigher forty, it seems," he muttered. "Why, when I look at my father, sir, and come to think of it," addressing Redlaw, with an impatience and irritation that were quite new, "I'm whipped if I can see anything in him but a calendar of ever so many years of eating and drinking, and making himself comfortable, over and over again."

"I—I'm eighty-seven," said the old man, rambling on, childishly and weakly, "and I don't know as I ever was much put out by anything. I'm not going to begin now, because of what he calls my son. He's not my son. I've had a power of pleasant times. I recollect once—no, I don't—no, it's broken off. It was something about a game of cricket and a friend of mine, but it's somehow broken off. I wonder who he was—I suppose he died? But I don't know. And I don't care, neither; I don't care a bit."

In his drowsy chuckling, and the shaking of his head, he put his hands into his waistcoat-pockets. In one of them he found a bit of holly (left there, probably last night), which he now took out, and looked at.

"Berries, eh?" said the old man. "Ah! It's a pity they're not good to eat. I recollect, when I was a little chap about as high as that, and out a-walking with—let me see—who was I out a-walking with?—no, I don't remember how that was. I don't remember as I ever walked with any one particular, or cared for any one, or any one for me. Berries, eh? There's good cheer when there's berries. Well; I ought to have my share of it, and to be waited on, and kept warm and comfortable; for I'm eighty-seven, and a poor old man. I'm eigh-ty-seven. Eigh-ty-seven!"

The drivelling, pitiable manner in which, as he repeated this, he nibbled at the leaves, and spat the morsels out; the cold, uninterested eye with which his youngest son (so changed) regarded him; the determined apathy with which his eldest son lay hardened in his sin; —impressed themselves no more on Redlaw's observation; for he broke his way from the spot to which his feet seemed to have been fixed, and ran out of the house.

His guide came crawling forth from his place of refuge, and was ready for him before he reached the arches.

"Back to the woman's?" he inquired.

"Back, quickly!" answered Redlaw. "Stop nowhere on the way."

For a short distance the boy went on before; but their return was more like a flight than a walk, and it was as much as his bare feet could do, to keep pace with the Chemist's rapid strides. Shrinking from all who passed, shrouded in his cloak, and keeping it drawn closely about him, as though there were mortal contagion in any fluttering touch of his garments, he made no pause until they reached the door by which they had come out. He unlocked it with his key, went in, accompanied by the boy, and hastened through the dark passages to his own chamber.

The boy watched him as he made the door fast, and withdrew behind the table, when he looked round.

"Come!" he said. "Don't you touch me! You've not brought me here to take my money away."

Redlaw threw some more upon the ground. He flung his body on it immediately, as if to hide it from him, lest the sight of it should tempt him to reclaim it; and not until he saw him seated by his lamp, with his face hidden in his hands, began furtively to pick it up. When he had done so, he crept near the fire, and, sitting down in a great chair before it, took from his breast some broken scraps of food, and fell to munching, and to staring at the blaze, and now and then to glancing at his shillings, which he kept clenched up in a bunch, in one hand.

"And this," said Redlaw, gazing on him with increased repugnance and fear, "is the only companion I have left on earth."

How long it was before he was aroused from his contemplation of this creature, whom he dreaded so—whether half an hour, or half the night—he knew not. But the stillness of the room was broken by the boy (whom he had seen listening) starting up, and running towards the door.

"Here's the woman coming!" he exclaimed.

The Chemist stopped him on his way, at the moment when she knocked.

"Let me go to her, will you?" said the boy.

"Not now," returned the Chemist. "Stay here. Nobody must pass in or out of the room now. Who's that?"

"It's I, sir," cried Milly. "Pray, sir, let me in!"

"No! not for the world!" he said.

"Mr. Redlaw, Mr. Redlaw, pray, sir, let me in."

"What is the matter?" he said, holding the boy.

"The miserable man you saw, is worse, and nothing I can say will wake him from his terrible infatuation. William's father has turned childish in a moment. William himself is changed. The shock has been too sudden for him; I cannot understand him; he is not like himself. Oh, Mr. Redlaw, pray advise me, help me!"

"No! No! No!" he answered.

"Mr. Redlaw! Dear sir! George has been muttering, in his doze, about the man you saw there, who, he fears, will kill himself."

"Better he should do it, than come near me!"

"He says, in his wanderings, that you know him; that he was your friend once, long ago; that he is the ruined father of a student here—my mind misgives me, of the young gentleman who has been ill. What is to be done? How is he to be followed? How is he to be saved? Mr. Redlaw, pray, oh, pray, advise me! Help me!"

All this time he held the boy, who was half-mad to pass him, and let her in.

"Phantoms! Punishers of impious thoughts!" cried Redlaw, gazing round in anguish. "Look upon me! From the darkness of my mind, let the glimmering of contrition that I know is there, shine up, and show my misery! In the material world, as I have long taught, nothing can be spared; no step or atom in the wondrous structure could be lost, without a blank being made in the great universe. I know, now, that it is the same with good and evil, happiness and sorrow, in the memories of men. Pity me! Relieve me!"

There was no response, but her "Help me, help me, let me in!" and the boy's struggling to get to her.

"Shadow of myself! Spirit of my darker hours!" cried Redlaw, in distraction. "Come back, and haunt me day and night, but take this gift away! Or, if it must still rest with me, deprive me of the dreadful power of giving it to others. Undo what I have done. Leave me benighted, but restore the day to those whom I have cursed. As I have spared this woman from the first, and as I never will go forth again, but will die here, with no hand to tend me, save this creature's who is proof against me,—hear me!"

The only reply still was, the boy struggling to get to her, while he held him back; and the cry, increasing in its energy, "Help! let me in.

He was your friend once, how shall he be followed, how shall he be saved? They are all changed, there is no one else to help me, pray, pray, let me in!"

CHAPTER III *The Gift Reversed*

Night was still heavy in the sky. On open plains, from hill-tops, and from the decks of solitary ships at sea, a distant low-lying line, that promised by-and-by to change to light, was visible in the dim horizon; but its promise was remote and doubtful, and the moon was striving with the night-clouds busily.

The shadows upon Redlaw's mind succeeded thick and fast to one another, and obscured its light as the night-clouds hovered between the moon and earth, and kept the latter veiled in darkness. Fitful and uncertain as the shadows which the night-clouds cast, were their concealments from him, and imperfect revelations to him; and, like the night-clouds still, if the clear light broke forth for a moment, it was only that they might sweep over it, and make the darkness deeper than before.

Without, there was a profound and solemn hush upon the ancient pile of buildings, and its buttresses and angles made dark shapes of mystery upon the ground, which now seemed to retire into the smooth white snow and now seemed to come out of it, as the moon's path was more or less beset. Within, the Chemist's room was indistinct and murky, by the light of the expiring lamp; a ghostly silence had succeeded to the knocking and the voice outside; nothing was audible but, now and then, a low sound among the whitened ashes of the fire, as of its yielding up its last breath. Before it on the ground the boy lay fast asleep. In his chair, the Chemist sat, as he had sat there since the calling at his door had ceased—like a man turned to stone.

At such a time, the Christmas music he had heard before, began to play. He listened to it at first, as he had listened in the churchyard; but presently—it playing still, and being borne towards him on the night-air, in a low, sweet, melancholy strain—he rose, and stood stretching his hands about him, as if there were some friend approaching within his reach, on whom his desolate touch might rest, yet do no harm. As he did this, his face became less fixed and wondering; a gentle trembling came upon him; and at last his eyes filled with tears, and he put his hands before them, and bowed down his head.

His memory of sorrow, wrong, and trouble, had not come back to him; he knew that it was not restored; he had no passing belief or hope that it was. But some dumb stir within him made him capable, again, of being moved by what was hidden, afar off, in the music. If it were only that it told him sorrowfully the value of what he had lost, he thanked Heaven for it with a fervent gratitude.

As the last chord died upon his ears, he raised his head to listen to its lingering vibration. Beyond the boy, so that his sleeping figure lay at its feet, the Phantom stood, immovable and silent, with its eyes upon him.

Ghastly it was, as it had ever been, but not so cruel and relentless in its aspect—or he thought or hoped so, as he looked upon it, trembling. It was not alone, but in its shadowy hand it held another hand.

And whose was that? Was the form that stood beside it indeed Milly's, or but her shade and picture? The quiet head was bent a little, as her manner was, and her eyes were looking down, as if in pity, on the sleeping child. A radiant light fell on her face, but did not touch the Phantom; for, though close beside her, it was dark and colourless as ever.

"Spectre!" said the Chemist, newly troubled as he looked, "I have not been stubborn or presumptuous in respect to her. Oh, do not bring her here. Spare me that!"

"This is but a shadow," said the Phantom; "when the morning shines seek out the reality whose image I present before you."

"Is it my inexorable doom to do so?" cried the Chemist.

"It is," replied the Phantom.

"To destroy her peace, her goodness; to make her what I am myself, and what I have made of others!"

"I have said, 'seek her out,'" returned the Phantom. "I have said no more."

"Oh, tell me," exclaimed Redlaw, catching at the hope which he fancied might lie hidden in the words. "Can I undo what I have done?"

"No," returned the Phantom.

"I do not ask for restoration to myself," said Redlaw. "What I abandoned, I abandoned of my own will, and have justly lost. But for those to whom I have transferred the fatal gift; who never sought it; who unknowingly received a curse of which they had no warning, and which they had no power to shun; can I do nothing?"

"Nothing," said the Phantom.

"If I cannot, can any one?"

The Phantom, standing like a statue, kept his gaze upon him for a while; then turned its head suddenly, and looked upon the shadow at its side.

"Ah! Can she?" cried Redlaw, still looking upon the shade.

The Phantom released the hand it had retained till now, and softly raised its own with a gesture of dismissal. Upon that, her shadow, still preserving the same attitude, began to move or melt away.

"Stay," cried Redlaw with an earnestness to which he could not give enough expression. "For a moment! As an act of mercy! I know that some change fell upon me, when those sounds were in the air just now. Tell me, have I lost the power of harming her? May I go near her without dread? Oh, let her give me any sign of hope!"

The Phantom looked upon the shade as he did—not at him—and gave no answer.

"At least, say this—has she, henceforth, the consciousness of any power to set right what I have done?"

"She has not," the Phantom answered.

"Has she the power bestowed on her without the consciousness?"

The Phantom answered: "Seek her out." And her shadow slowly vanished.

They were face to face again, and looking on each other, as intently and awfully as at the time of the bestowal of the gift, across the boy who still lay on the ground between them, at the Phantom's feet.

"Terrible instructor," said the Chemist, sinking on his knee before it, in an attitude of supplication, "by whom I was renounced, but by whom I am revisited (in which, and in whose milder aspect, I would fain believe I have a gleam of hope), I will obey without inquiry, praying that the cry I have sent up in the anguish of my soul has been, or will be, heard, in behalf of those whom I have injured beyond human reparation. But there is one thing—"

"You speak to me of what is lying here," the Phantom interposed, and pointed with its finger to the boy.

"I do," returned the Chemist. "You know what I would ask. Why has this child alone been proof against my influence, and why, why have I detected in its thoughts a terrible companionship with mine?"

"This," said the Phantom, pointing to the boy, "is the last, completest illustration of a human creature, utterly bereft of such remembrances as you have yielded up. No softening memory of sorrow, wrong, or trouble enters here, because this wretched mortal from his birth has been abandoned to a worse condition than the beasts, and has, within his knowledge, no one contrast, no humanising touch, to make a grain of such a memory spring up in his hardened breast. All within this desolate creature is barren wilderness. All within the man bereft of what you have resigned, is the same barren wilderness. Woe to such a man! Woe, tenfold, to the nation that shall count its monsters such as this, lying here, by hundreds, and by thousands!"

Redlaw shrunk, appalled, from what he heard.

"There is not," said the Phantom, "one of these—not one—but shows a harvest that mankind MUST REAP. From every seed of evil in this boy, a field of ruin is grown that shall be gathered in, and garnered up, and sown again in many places in the world, until regions are overspread with wickedness enough to raise the waters of another Deluge. Open and unpunished murder in a city's streets would be less guilty in its daily toleration, than one such spectacle as this."

It seemed to look down upon the boy in his sleep. Redlaw, too, looked down upon him with a new emotion.

"There is not a father," said the Phantom, "by whose side in his daily or his nightly walk, these creatures pass; there is not a mother among all the ranks of loving mothers in this land; there is no one risen from the state of childhood, but shall be responsible in his or her degree for this enormity. There is not a country throughout the earth on which it would not bring a curse. There is no religion upon earth that it would not deny; there is no people upon earth it would not put to shame."

The Chemist clasped his hands, and looked, with trembling fear and pity, from the sleeping boy to the Phantom, standing above him with its finger pointing down.

"Behold, I say," pursued the Spectre, "the perfect type of what it was your choice to be. Your influence is powerless here, because from this child's bosom you can banish nothing. His thoughts have been in "terrible companionship" with yours, because you have gone down to his unnatural level. He is the growth of man's indifference; you are the growth of man's presumption. The beneficent design of Heaven is in each case overthrown, and from the two poles of the immaterial world you come together."

The Chemist stooped upon the ground beside the boy, and, with the same kind of compassion for him that he now felt for himself, covered him as he slept, and no longer shrunk from him with abhorrence or indifference.

Soon, now, the distant line on the horizon brightened, the darkness faded, the sun rose red and glorious, and the chimney stacks and gables of the ancient building gleamed in the clear air, which turned the smoke and vapour of the city into a cloud of gold. The very sundial in his shady corner, where the wind was used to spin with such un-windy constancy, shook off the finer particles of snow that had accumulated on his dull old face in the night, and looked out at the little white wreaths eddying round and round him. Doubtless some blind groping of the morning made its way down into the forgotten crypt so cold and earthy, where the Norman arches were half buried in the ground, and stirred the dull deep sap in the lazy vegetation hanging to the walls, and quickened the slow principle of life within the little world of wonderful and delicate creation which existed there, with some faint knowledge that the sun was up.

The Tetterbys were up, and doing. Mr. Tetterby took down the shutters of the shop, and, strip by strip, revealed the treasures of the window to the eyes, so proof against their seductions, of Jerusalem Buildings. Adolphus had been out so long already, that he was half-way on to Morning Pep-per. Five small Tetterbys, whose ten round eyes were much inflamed by soap and friction, were in the tortures of a cool wash in the back kitchen; Mrs. Tetterby presiding. Johnny, who was pushed and hustled through his toilet with great rapidity when Moloch chanced to be in an exacting frame of mind (which was always the case), staggered up and down with his charge before the shop door, under greater difficulties than usual; the weight of Moloch being much increased by a complication of defences against the cold, composed of knitted worsted-work, and forming a complete suit of chain-armour, with a head-piece and blue gaiters.

It was a peculiarity of this baby to be always cutting teeth. Whether they never came, or whether they came and went away again, is not in evidence; but it had certainly cut enough, on the showing of Mrs. Tetterby, to make a handsome dental provision for the sign of the Bull and Mouth. All sorts of objects were impressed for the rubbing of its gums, notwithstanding that it always carried, dangling at its waist (which was immediately under its chin), a bone ring, large enough to have represented the rosary of a young nun. Knife-handles, umbrella-tops, the heads of walking-sticks selected from the stock, the fingers of the family in general, but especially of Johnny, nutmeg-graters, crusts, the handles of doors, and the cool knobs on the tops of pokers, were among the commonest instruments indiscriminately applied for this baby's relief. The amount of electricity that must have been rubbed out of it in a week, is not to be calculated. Still Mrs. Tetterby always said "it was coming through, and then the child would be herself;" and still it never did come through, and the child continued to be somebody else.

The tempers of the little Tetterbys had sadly changed with a few hours. Mr. and Mrs. Tetterby themselves were not more altered than their offspring. Usually they were an unselfish, good-natured, yielding little race, sharing short-commons when it happened (which was pretty often) contentedly and even generously, and taking a great deal of enjoyment out of a very little meat. But they were fighting now, not only for the soap and water, but even for the breakfast which was yet in perspective. The hand of every little Tetterby was against the other little Tetterbys; and even Johnny's hand—the patient, much-enduring, and devoted Johnny—rose against the baby! Yes, Mrs. Tetterby, going to the door by a mere accident, saw him viciously pick out a weak place in the suit of armour where a slap would tell, and slap that blessed child.

Mrs. Tetterby had him into the parlour by the collar, in that same flash of time, and repaid him the assault with usury thereto.

"You brute, you murdering little boy," said Mrs. Tetterby. "Had you the heart to do it?"

"Why don't her teeth come through, then," retorted Johnny, in a loud rebellious voice, "instead of bothering me? How would you like it yourself?"

"Like it, sir!" said Mrs. Tetterby, relieving him of his dishonoured load.

"Yes, like it," said Johnny. "How would you? Not at all. If you was me, you'd go for a soldier. I will, too. There an't no babies in the army."

Mr. Tetterby, who had arrived upon the scene of action, rubbed his chin thoughtfully, instead of correcting the rebel, and seemed rather struck by this view of a military life.

"I wish I was in the army myself, if the child's in the right," said Mrs. Tetterby, looking at her husband, "for I have no peace of my life here. I'm a slave—a Virginia slave;" some indistinct association with their weak descent on the tobacco trade perhaps suggested this aggravated expression to Mrs. Tetterby. "I never have a holiday, or any pleasure at all, from year's end to year's end! Why, Lord bless and save the child," said Mrs. Tetterby, shaking the baby with an irritability hardly suited to so pious an aspiration, "what's the matter with her now?"

Not being able to discover, and not rendering the subject much clearer by shaking it, Mrs. Tetterby put the baby away in a cradle, and, folding her arms, sat rocking it angrily with her foot.

"How you stand there, 'Dolphus," said Mrs. Tetterby to her husband. "Why don't you do something?"

"Because I don't care about doing anything," Mr. Tetterby replied.

"I am sure I don't," said Mr. Tetterby.

"I'll take my oath I don't," said Mr. Tetterby.

A diversion arose here among Johnny and his five younger brothers, who, in preparing the family breakfast table, had fallen to skirmishing for the temporary possession of the loaf, and were buffeting one another with great heartiness; the smallest boy of all, with precocious discretion, hovering outside the knot of combatants, and harassing their legs. Into the midst of this fray, Mr. and Mrs. Tetterby both precipitated themselves with great ardour, as if such ground were the only ground on which they could not agree; and having, with no visible remains of their late soft-heartedness, laid about them without any lenity, and done much execution, resumed their former relative positions.

"You had better read your paper than do nothing at all," said Mrs. Tetterby.

"What's there to read in a paper?" returned Mr. Tetterby, with excessive discontent.

"What?" said Mrs. Tetterby. "Police!"

"It's nothing to me," said Tetterby. "What do I care what people do, or are done to?"

"Suicides," suggested Mrs. Tetterby.

"No business of mine," replied her husband.

"Births, deaths, and marriages, are those nothing to you?" said Mrs. Tetterby.

"If the births were all over for good and all to-day; and the deaths were all to begin to come off to-morrow; I don't see why it should interest me, till I thought it was a-coming to my turn," grumbled Tetterby. "As to marriages, I've done it myself. I know quite enough about *them*."

To judge from the dissatisfied expression of her face and manner, Mrs. Tetterby appeared to entertain the same opinions as her husband; but she opposed him, nevertheless, for the gratification of quarrelling with him.

"Oh, you're a consistent man," said Mrs. Tetterby, "an't you? You, with the screen of your own making there, made of nothing else but bits of newspaper, which you sit and read to the children by the half-hour together!"

"Say used to, if you please," returned her husband. "You won't find me doing so any more. I'm wiser now."

"Bah! wiser, indeed!" said Mrs. Tetterby. "Are you better?"

The question sounded some discordant note in Mr. Tetterby's breast. He ruminated dejectedly, and passed his hand across and across his forehead.

"Better!" murmured Mr. Tetterby. "I don't know as any of us are better, or happier either. Better, is it?"

He turned to the screen, and traced about it with his finger, until he found a certain paragraph of which he was in quest.

"This used to be one of the family favourites, I recollect," said Tetterby, in a forlorn and stupid way, "and used to draw tears from the children, and make 'em good, if there was any little bickering or discontent among 'em, next to the story of the robin redbreasts in the wood. 'Melancholy case of destitution. Yesterday a small man, with a baby in his arms, and surrounded by half-a-dozen ragged little ones, of various ages between ten and two, the whole of whom were evidently in a famishing condition, appeared before the worthy magistrate, and made the following recital:'—Ha! I don't understand it, I'm sure," said Tetterby; "I don't see what it has got to do with us."

"How old and shabby he looks," said Mrs. Tetterby, watching him.

"I never saw such a change in a man. Ah! dear me, dear me, dear me, it was a sacrifice!"

"What was a sacrifice?" her husband sourly inquired.

Mrs. Tetterby shook her head; and without replying in words, raised a complete sea-storm about the baby, by her violent agitation of the cradle.

"If you mean your marriage was a sacrifice, my good woman—" said her husband.

"I *do* mean it," said his wife.

"Why, then I mean to say," pursued Mr. Tetterby, as sulkily and surlily as she, "that there are two sides to that affair; and that *I* was the sacrifice; and that I wish the sacrifice hadn't been accepted."

"I wish it hadn't, Tetterby, with all my heart and soul I do assure you," said his wife. "You can't wish it more than I do, Tetterby."

"I don't know what I saw in her," muttered the newsman, "I'm sure:—certainly, if I saw anything, it's not there now. I was thinking so, last night, after supper, by the fire. She's fat, she's ageing, she won't bear comparison with most other women."

"He's common-looking, he has no air with him, he's small, he's beginning to stoop, and he's getting bald," muttered Mrs. Tetterby.

"I must have been half out of my mind when I did it," muttered Mr. Tetterby.

"My senses must have forsook me. That's the only way in which I can explain it to myself," said Mrs. Tetterby, with elaboration.

In this mood they sat down to breakfast. The little Tetterbys were not habituated to regard that meal in the light of a sedentary occupation, but discussed it as a dance or trot; rather resembling a savage ceremony, in the occasional shrill whoops, and brandishings of bread and butter, with which it was accompanied, as well as in the intricate filings off into the street and back again, and the hoppings up and down the doorsteps, which were incidental to the performance. In the present instance, the contentions between these Tetterby children for the milk-and-water jug, common to all, which stood upon the table, presented so lamentable an instance of angry passions risen very high indeed, that it was an outrage on the memory of Doctor Watts. It was not until Mr. Tetterby had driven the whole herd out at the front door, that a moment's peace was secured; and even that was broken by the discovery that Johnny had surreptitiously come back, and was at that instant choking in the jug like a ventriloquist, in his indecent and rapacious haste.

"These children will be the death of me at last!" said Mrs. Tetterby, after banishing the culprit. "And the sooner the better, I think."

"Poor people," said Mr. Tetterby, "ought not to have children at all. They give *us* no pleasure."

He was at that moment taking up the cup which Mrs. Tetterby had rudely pushed towards him, and Mrs. Tetterby was lifting her own cup to her lips, when they were both stoppd, as if they were transfixed.

"Here! Mother! Father!" cried Johnny, running into the room. "Here's Mrs. William coming down the street!"

And if ever, since the world began, a young boy took a baby from a cradle with the care of an old nurse, and hushed and soothed it tenderly, and tottered away with it cheerfully, Johnny was that boy, and Moloch was that baby, as they went out together!

Mr. Tetterby put down his cup; Mrs. Tetterby put down her cup. Mr. Tetterby rubbed his forehead; Mrs. Tetterby rubbed hers. Mr. Tetterby's face began to smooth and brighten; Mrs. Tetterby's face began to smooth and brighten.

"Why, Lord forgive me," said Mr. Tetterby to himself, "what evil tempers have I been giving way to? What has been the matter here?"

"How could I ever treat him ill again, after all I said and felt last night?" sobbed Mrs. Tetterby, with her apron to her eyes.

"Am I a brute," said Mr. Tetterby, "or is there any good in me at all? Sophia! My little woman!"

"'Dolphus dear," returned his wife.

"I—I've been in a state of mind," said Mr. Tetterby, "that I can't abear to think of, Sophy."

"Oh! It's nothing to what I've been in, Dolf," cried his wife in a great burst of grief.

"My Sophia," said Mr. Tetterby, "don't take on. I never shall forgive myself. I must have nearly broke your heart, I know."

"No, Dolf, no. It was me! Me!" cried Mrs. Tetterby.

"My little woman," said her husband, "don't. You make me reproach myself dreadful, when you show such a noble spirit. Sophia, my dear, you don't know what I thought. I showed it bad enough, no doubt; but what I thought, my little woman!"—

"Oh, dear Dolf, don't!" cried his wife.

"Sophia," said Mr. Tetterby, "I must reveal it. I couldn't rest in my conscience unless I mentioned it. My little woman—"

"Mrs. William's very nearly here!" screamed Johnny at the door.

"My little woman, I wondered how," gasped Mr. Tetterby, supporting himself by his chair, "I wondered how I had ever admired you— I forgot the precious children you have brought about me, and thought you didn't look as slim as I could wish. I—I never gave a recollection," said Mr. Tetterby, with severe self-accusation, "to the cares you've had as my wife, and along of me and mine, when you might have had hardly any with another man, who got on better and was luckier than me (anybody might have found such a man easily, I am sure); and I quarrelled with you for having aged a little in the rough years you have lightened for me. Can you believe it, my little woman? I hardly can myself."

Mrs. Tetterby, in a whirlwind of laughing and crying, caught his face within her hands, and held it there.

"Oh, Dolf!" she cried. "I am so happy that you thought so; I am so grateful that you thought so! For I thought that you were common-looking, Dolf; and so you are, my dear, and may you be the commonest of all sights in my eyes, till you close them with your own good hands. I thought that you were small; and so you are, and I'll make much of you because you are, and more of you because I love my husband. I thought that you began to stoop; and so you do, and you shall lean on me, and I'll do all I can to keep you up. I thought there was no air about you; but there is, and it's the air of home, and that's the purest and the best there is, and GOD bless home once more, and all belonging to it, Dolf!"

"Hurrah! Here's Mrs. William!" cried Johnny.

So she was, and all the children with her; and as she came in, they kissed her, and kissed one another, and kissed the baby, and kissed their father and mother, and then ran back and flocked and danced about her, trooping on with her in triumph.

Mr. and Mrs. Tetterby were not a bit behind-hand in the warmth of their reception. They were as much attracted to her as the children were; they ran towards her, kissed her hands, pressed round her, could not receive her ardently or enthusiastically enough. She came among them like the spirit of all goodness, affection, gentle consideration, love, and domesticity.

"What! are you all so glad to see me, too, this bright Christmas morning?" said Milly, clapping her hands in a pleasant wonder. "Oh dear, how delightful this is!"

More shouting from the children, more kissing, more trooping round her, more happiness, more love, more joy, more honour, on all sides, than she could bear.

"Oh dear!" said Milly, "what delicious tears you make me shed. How can I ever have deserved this! What have I done to be so loved?"

"Who can help it?" cried Mr. Tetterby.

"Who can help it?" cried Mrs. Tetterby.

"Who can help it?" echoed the children, in a joyful chorus. And they danced and trooped about her again, and clung to her, and laid their rosy faces against her dress, and kissed and fondled it, and could not fondle it, or her, enough.

"I never was so moved," said Milly, drying her eyes, "as I have been this morning. I must tell you, as soon as I can speak.—Mr. Redlaw came to me at sunrise, and with a tenderness in his manner, more as if I had been his darling daughter than myself, implored me to go with him to where William's brother George is lying ill. We went together, and all the way along he was so kind, and so subdued, and seemed to put such trust and hope in me, that I could not help crying with pleasure. When we got to the house, we met a woman at the door (somebody had bruised and hurt her, I am afraid) who caught me by the hand, and blessed me as I passed."

"She was right," said Mr. Tetterby. Mrs. Tetterby said she was right. All the children cried out she was right.

"Ah, but there's more than that," said Milly. "When we got up-stairs, into the room, the sick man who had lain for hours in a state from which no effort could rouse him, rose up in his bed, and, bursting into tears, stretched out his arms to me, and said that he had led a mis-spent life, but that he was truly repentant now, in his sorrow for the past, which was all as plain to him as a great prospect, from which a dense black cloud had cleared away, and that he entreated me to ask his poor old father for his pardon and his blessing, and to say a prayer beside his bed. And when I did so, Mr. Redlaw joined in it so fervently, and then so thanked and thanked me, and thanked Heaven, that my heart quite overflowed, and I could have done nothing but sob and cry, if the sick man had not begged me to sit down by him,—which made me quiet of course. As I sat there, he held my hand in his until he sunk in a doze; and even then, when I withdrew my hand to leave him to come here (which Mr. Redlaw was very earnest indeed in wishing me to do), his hand felt for mine, so that some one else was obliged to take my place and make believe to give him my hand back. Oh dear, oh dear," said Milly, sobbing. "How thankful and how happy I should feel, and do feel, for all this!"

While she was speaking, Redlaw had come in, and, after pausing for a moment to observe the group of which she was the centre, had silently ascended the stairs. Upon those stairs he now appeared again; remaining there, while the young student passed him, and came running down.

"Kind nurse, gentlest, best of creatures," he said, falling on his knee to her, and catching at her hand, "forgive my cruel ingratitude!"

"Oh dear, oh dear!" cried Milly innocently, "here's another of them! Oh dear, here's somebody else who likes me. What shall I ever do!"

The guileless, simple way in which she said it, and in which she put her hands before her eyes and wept for very happiness, was as touching as it was delightful.

"I was not myself," he said. "I don't know what it was—it was some consequence of my disorder perhaps—I was mad. But I am so no longer. Almost as I speak, I am restored. I heard the children crying out your name, and the shade passed from me at the very sound of it. Oh don't weep! Dear Milly, if you could read my heart, and only know with what affection and what grateful homage it is glowing, you would not let me see you weep. It is such deep reproach."

"No, no," said Milly, "it's not that. It's not indeed. It's joy. It's wonder that you should think it necessary to ask me to forgive so little, and yet it's pleasure that you do."

"And will you come again? and will you finish the little curtain?"

"No," said Milly, drying her eyes, and shaking her head. "You won't care for *my* needlework now."

"Is it forgiving me, to say that?"

She beckoned him aside, and whispered in his ear.

"There is news from your home, Mr. Edmund."

"News? How?"

"Either your not writing when you were very ill, or the change in your handwriting when you began to be better, created some suspicion of the truth; however that is——but you're sure you'll not be the worse for any news, if it's not bad news?"

"Sure."

"Then there's some one come!" said Milly.

"My mother?" asked the student, glancing round involuntarily towards Redlaw, who had come down from the stairs.

"Hush! No," said Milly.

"It can be no one else."

"Indeed," said Milly, "are you sure?"

"It is not——" Before he could say more, she put her hand close upon his mouth.

"Yes it is!" said Milly. "The young lady (she is very like the miniature, Mr. Edmund, but she is prettier) was too unhappy to rest without satisfying her doubts, and came up, last night, with a little servant-maid. As you always dated your letters from the college, she came there; and before I saw Mr. Redlaw this morning, I saw her. *She* likes me too!" said Milly. "Oh dear, that's another!"

"This morning! Where is she now?"

"Why, she is now," said Milly, advancing her lips to his ear, "in my little parlour in the Lodge, and waiting to see you."

He pressed her hand, and was darting off, but she detained him.

"Mr. Redlaw is much altered, and has told me this morning that his memory is impaired. Be very considerate to him, Mr. Edmund; he needs that from us all."

The young man assured her, by a look, that her caution was not ill-bestowed; and as he passed the Chemist on his way out, bent respectfully and with an obvious interest before him.

Redlaw returned the salutation courteously and even humbly, and looked after him as he passed on. He drooped his head upon his hand too, as trying to reawaken something he had lost. But it was gone.

The abiding change that had come upon him since the influence of the music, and the Phantom's reappearance, was, that now he truly felt how much he had lost, and could compassionate his own condition, and contrast it, clearly, with the natural state of those who were around him. In this, an interest in those who were around him was revived, and a meek, submissive sense of his calamity was bred, resembling that which sometimes obtains in age, when its mental powers are weakened, without insensibility or sullenness being added to the list of its infirmities.

He was conscious that, as he redeemed, through Milly, more and more of the evil he had done, and as he was more and more with her, this change ripened itself within him. Therefore, and because of the attachment she inspired him with (but without other hope), he felt that he was quite dependent on her, and that she was his staff in his affliction.

So, when she asked him whether they should go home now, to where the old man and her husband were, and he readily replied "yes"—being anxious in that regard—he put his arm through hers, and walked beside her; not as if he were the wise and learned man to whom the wonders of nature were an open book, and hers were the uninstructed mind, but as if their two positions were reversed, and he knew nothing, and she all.

He saw the children throng about her, and caress her, as he and she went away together thus, out of the house; he heard the ringing of their laughter, and their merry voices; he saw their bright faces, clustering around him like flowers; he witnessed the renewed contentment and affection of their parents; he breathed the simple air of their poor home, restored to its tranquillity; he thought of the unwholesome blight he had shed upon it, and might, but for her, have been diffusing then; and perhaps it is no wonder that he walked submissively beside her, and drew her gentle bosom nearer to his own.

When they arrived at the Lodge, the old man was sitting in his chair in the chimney-corner, with his eyes fixed on the ground, and his son was leaning against the opposite side of the fireplace, looking at him. As she came in at the door, both started, and turned round towards her, and a radiant change came upon their faces.

"Oh dear, dear, dear, they are pleased to see me like the rest!" cried Milly, clapping her hands in an ecstasy, and stopping short. "Here are two more!"

Pleased to see her! Pleasure was no word for it. She ran into her husband's arms, thrown wide open to receive her, and he would have been glad to have her there, with her head lying on his shoulder, through the short winter's day. But the old man couldn't spare her. He had arms for her too, and he locked her in them.

"Why, where has my quiet Mouse been all this time?" said the old man. "She has been a long while away. I find that it's impossible for me to get on without Mouse. I—where's my son William?—I fancy I have been dreaming, William."

"That's what I say, myself, father," returned his son. "I have been in an ugly sort of dream, I think. How are you, father? Are you pretty well?"

"Strong and brave, my boy," returned the old man.

It was quite a sight to see Mr. William shaking hands with his father, and patting him on the back, and rubbing him gently down with his hand, as if he could not possibly do enough to show an interest in him.

"What a wonderful man you are, father!—How are you, father? Are you really pretty hearty, though?" said William, shaking hands with him again, and patting him again, and rubbing him gently down again.

"I never was fresher or stouter in my life, my boy."

"What a wonderful man you are, father! But that's exactly where it is," said Mr. William, with enthusiasm. "When I think of all that my father's gone through, and all the chances and changes, and sorrows and troubles, that have happened to him in the course of his long life, and under which his head has grown grey, and years upon years have gathered on it, I feel as if we couldn't do enough to honour the old gentleman, and make his old age easy.—How are you, father? Are you really pretty well, though?"

Mr. William might never have left off repeating this inquiry, and shaking hands with him again, and patting him again, and rubbing him down again, if the old man had not espied the Chemist, whom until now he had not seen.

"I ask your pardon, Mr. Redlaw," said Philip, "but didn't know you were here, sir, or should have made less free. It reminds me, Mr. Redlaw, seeing you here on a Christmas morning, of the time when you was a student yourself, and worked so hard that you was backwards and forwards in our Library even at Christmas-time. Ha! ha! I'm old enough to remember that; and I remember it right well, I do, though I am eighty-seven. It was after you left here that my poor wife died. You remember my poor wife, Mr. Redlaw?"

The Chemist answered yes.

"Yes," said the old man. "She was a dear creetur.—I recollect you come here one Christmas morning with a young lady—I ask your pardon, Mr. Redlaw, but I think it was a sister you was very much attached to?"

The Chemist looked at him, and shook his head. "I had a sister," he said vacantly. He knew no more.

"One Christmas morning," pursued the old man, "that you come here with her—and it began to snow, and my wife invited the young lady to walk in, and sit by the fire that is always a-burning on Christmas Day in what used to be, before our ten poor gentlemen commuted, our great Dinner Hall. I was there; and I recollect, as I was stirring up the blaze for the young lady to warm her pretty feet by, she read the scroll out loud, that is underneath that picter. 'Lord, keep my memory green!' She and my poor wife fell a-talking about it; and it's a strange thing to think of, now, that they both said (both being so unlike to die) that it was a good prayer, and that it was one they would put up very earnestly, if they were called away young, with reference to those who were dearest to them. 'My brother,' says the young lady—'My husband,' says my poor wife.—'Lord, keep his memory of me green, and do not let me be forgotten!'"

Tears more painful, and more bitter than he had ever shed in all his life, coursed down Redlaw's face. Philip, fully occupied in recalling his story, had not observed him until now, nor Milly's anxiety that he should not proceed.

"Philip!" said Redlaw, laying his hand upon his arm, "I am a stricken man, on whom the hand of Providence has fallen heavily, although deservedly. You speak to me, my friend, of what I cannot follow; my memory is gone."

"Merciful Power!" cried the old man.

"I have lost my memory of sorrow, wrong, and trouble," said the Chemist, "and with that I have lost all man would remember!"

To see old Philip's pity for him, to see him wheel his own great chair for him to rest in, and look down upon him with a solemn sense of his bereavement, was to know, in some degree, how precious to old age such recollections are.

The boy came running in, and ran to Milly.

"Here's the man," he said, "in the other room. I don't want *him*."

"What man does he mean?" asked Mr. William.

"Hush!" said Milly.

Obedient to a sign from her, he and his old father softly withdrew. As they went out, unnoticed, Redlaw beckoned to the boy to come to him.

"I like the woman best," he answered, holding to her skirts.

"You are right," said Redlaw, with a faint smile. "But you needn't fear to come to me. I am gentler than I was. Of all the world, to you, poor child!"

The boy still held back at first, but yielding little by little to her urging, he consented to approach, and even to sit down at his feet. As Redlaw laid his hand upon the shoulder of the child, looking on him with compassion and a fellow-feeling, he put out his other hand to Milly. She stooped down on that side of him, so that she could look into his face; and after silence, said:

"Mr. Redlaw, may I speak to you?"

"Yes," he answered, fixing his eyes upon her. "Your voice and music are the same to me."

"May I ask you something?"

"What you will."

"Do you remember what I said, when I knocked at your door last night? About one who was your friend once, and who stood on the verge of destruction?"

"Yes. I remember," he said, with some hesitation.

"Do you understand it?"

He smoothed the boy's hair—looking at her fixedly the while, and shook his head.

"This person," said Milly, in her clear, soft voice, which her mild eyes, looking at him, made clearer and softer, "I found soon afterwards. I went back to the house, and, with Heaven's help, traced him. I was not too soon. A very little and I should have been too late."

He took his hand from the boy, and laying it on the back of that hand of hers, whose timid and yet earnest touch addressed him no less appealingly than her voice and eyes, looked more intently on her.

"He *is* the father of Mr. Edmund, the young gentleman we saw just now. His real name is Longford.—You recollect the name?"

"I recollect the name."

"And the man?"

"No, not the man. Did he ever wrong me?"

"Yes."

"Ah! Then it's hopeless—hopeless."

He shook his head, and softly beat upon the hand he held, as though mutely asking her commiseration.

"I did not go to Mr. Edmund last night," said Milly.—"You will listen to me just the same as if you did remember all?"

"To every syllable you say."

"Both because I did not know, then, that this really was his father, and because I was fearful of the effect of such intelligence upon him, after his illness, if it should be. Since I have known who this person is, I have not gone either; but that is for another reason. He has long been separated from his wife and son—has been a stranger to his home almost from this son's infancy, I learn from him—and has abandoned and deserted what he should have held most dear. In all that time he has been falling from the state of a gentleman, more and more, until—" she rose up, hastily, and going out for a moment, returned, accompanied by the wreck that Redlaw had beheld last night.

"Do you know me?" asked the Chemist.

"I should be glad," returned the other, "and that is an unwonted word for me to use, if I could answer no."

The Chemist looked at the man, standing in self-abasement and degradation before him, and would have looked longer, in an ineffectual struggle for enlightenment, but that Milly resumed her late position by his side, and attracted his attentive gaze to her own face.

"See how low he is sunk, how lost he is!" she whispered, stretching out her arm towards him, without looking from the Chemist's face. "If you could remember all that is connected with him, do you not think it would move your pity to reflect that one you ever loved (do not let us mind how long ago, or in what belief that he has forfeited), should come to this?"

"I hope it would," he answered. "I believe it would."

His eyes wandered to the figure standing near the door, but came back speedily to her, on whom he gazed intently, as if he strove to learn some lesson from every tone of her voice, and every beam of her eyes.

"I have no learning, and you have much," said Milly; "I am not used to think, and you are always thinking. May I tell you why it seems to me a good thing for us to remember wrong that has been done us?"

"Yes."

"That we may forgive it."

"Pardon me, great Heaven!" said Redlaw, lifting up his eyes, "for having thrown away thine own high attribute!"

"And if," said Milly, "if your memory should one day be restored, as we will hope and pray it may be, would it not be a blessing to you to recall at once a wrong and its forgiveness?"

He looked at the figure by the door, and fastened his attentive eyes on her again; a ray of clearer light appeared to him to shine into his mind, from her bright face.

"He cannot go to his abandoned home. He does not seek to go there. He knows that he could only carry shame and trouble to those he had so cruelly neglected; and that the best reparation he can make them now, is to avoid them. A very little money carefully bestowed, would remove him to some distant place, where he might live and do no wrong, and make such atonement as is left within his power for the wrong he has done. To the unfortunate lady who is his wife, and to his son, this would be the best and kindest boon that their best friend could give them—one too that they need never know of; and to him, shattered in reputation, mind, and body, it might be salvation."

He took her head between his hands, and kissed it, and said: "It shall be done. I trust to you to do it for me, now and secretly; and to tell him that I would forgive him, if I were so happy as to know for what."

As she rose, and turned her beaming face towards the fallen man, implying that her mediation had been successful, he advanced a step, and without raising his eyes, addressed himself to Redlaw.

"You are so generous," he said, "—you ever were—that you will try to banish your rising sense of retribution in the spectacle that is before you. I do not try to banish it from myself, Redlaw. If you can, believe me."

The Chemist entreated Milly, by a gesture, to come nearer to him; and, as he listened, looked in her face, as if to find in it the clue to what he heard.

"I am too decayed a wretch to make professions; I recollect my own career too well, to array any such before you. But from the day on which I made my first step downward, in dealing falsely by you, I have gone down with a certain, steady, doomed progression. That, I say."

Redlaw, keeping her close at his side, turned his face towards the speaker, and there was sorrow in it. Something like mournful recognition too.

"I might have been another man, my life might have been another life, if I had avoided that first fatal step. I don't know that it would have been. I claim nothing for the possibility. Your sister is at rest, and better than she could have been with me, if I had continued even what you thought me: even what I once supposed myself to be."

Redlaw made a hasty motion with his hand, as if he would have put that subject on one side.

"I speak," the other went on, "like a man taken from the grave. I should have made my own grave, last night, had it not been for this blessed hand."

"Oh dear, he likes me too!" sobbed Milly, under her breath. "That's another!"

"I could not have put myself in your way, last night, even for bread. But to-day, my recollection of what has been is so strongly stirred, and is presented to me, I don't know how, so vividly, that I have dared to come at her suggestion, and to take your bounty, and to thank you for it, and to beg you, Redlaw, in your dying hour, to be as merciful to me in your thoughts, as you are in your deeds."

He turned towards the door, and stopped a moment on his way forth.

"I hope my son may interest you for his mother's sake. I hope he may deserve to do so. Unless my life should be preserved a long time, and I should know that I have not misused your aid, I shall never look upon him more."

Going out, he raised his eyes to Redlaw for the first time. Redlaw, whose steadfast gaze was fixed upon him, dreamily held out his hand. He returned and touched it—little more—with both his own—and bending down his head, went slowly out.

In the few moments that elapsed, while Milly silently took him to the gate, the Chemist dropped into his chair, and covered his face with his hands. Seeing him thus, when she came back, accompanied by her husband and his father (who were both greatly concerned for him), she avoided disturbing him, or permitting him to be disturbed; and kneeled down near the chair to put some warm clothing on the boy.

"That's exactly where it is. That's what I always say, father!" exclaimed her admiring husband. "There's a motherly feeling in Mrs. William's breast that must and will have went!"

"Ay, ay," said the old man; "you're right. My son William's right!"

"It happens all for the best, Milly dear, no doubt," said Mr. William, tenderly, "that we have no children of our own; and yet I sometimes wish you had one to love and cherish. Our little dead child that you built such hopes upon, and that never breathed the breath of life—it has made you quiet-like, Milly."

"I am very happy in the recollection of it, William dear," she answered. "I think of it every day."

"I was afraid you thought of it a good deal."

"Don't say afraid; it is a comfort to me; it speaks to me in so many ways. The innocent thing that never lived on earth is like an angel to me, William."

"You are like an angel to father and me," said Mr. William, softly. "I know that."

"When I think of all those hopes I built upon it, and the many times I sat and pictured to myself the little smiling face upon my bosom that never lay there, and the sweet eyes turned up to mine that never opened to the light," said Milly, "I can feel a greater tenderness, I think, for all the disappointed hopes in which there is no harm. When I see a beautiful child in its fond mother's arms, I love it all the better, thinking that my child might have been like that, and might have made my heart as proud and happy."

Redlaw raised his head, and looked towards her.

"All through life, it seems by me," she continued, "to tell me something. For poor neglected children, my little child pleads as if it were alive, and had a voice I knew, with which to speak to me. When I hear of youth in suffering or shame, I think that my child might have come to that, perhaps, and that God took it from me in His mercy. Even in age and grey hair, such as father's is at present: saying that it too might have lived to be old, long and long after you and I were gone, and to have needed the respect and love of younger people."

Her quiet voice was quieter than ever, as she took her husband's arm, and laid her head against it.

"Children love me so, that sometimes I half fancy—it's a silly fancy, William—they have some way I don't know of, of feeling for my little child, and me, and understanding why their love is precious to me. If I have been quiet since, I have been more happy, William, in a hundred ways. Not least happy, dear, in this—that even when my little child was born and dead but a few days and I was weak and sorrowful, and could not help grieving a little, the thought arose, that if I tried to lead a good life, I should meet in Heaven a bright creature, who would call me, Mother!"

Redlaw fell upon his knees, with a loud cry.

"O Thou," he said, "who through the teaching of pure love, has graciously restored me to the memory which was the memory of Christ upon the cross, and of all the good who perished in His cause, receive my thanks, and bless her!"

Then, he folded her to his heart; and Milly, sobbing more than ever, cried, as she laughed, "He is come back to himself! He likes me very much indeed, too! Oh dear, dear, dear me, here's another!"

Then, the student entered, leading by the hand a lovely girl, who was afraid to come. And Redlaw so changed towards him, seeing in him and his youthful choice, the softened shadow of that chastening passage in his own life, to which, as to a shady tree, the dove so long imprisoned in his solitary ark might fly for rest and company, fell upon his neck, entreating them to be his children.

Then, as Christmas is a time in which, of all times in the year, the memory of every remediable sorrow, wrong, and trouble in the world around us, should be active with us, not less than our own experiences, for all good, he laid his hand upon the boy, and, silently calling Him to witness who laid His hand on children in old time, rebuking, in the majesty of His prophetic knowledge, those who kept them from Him, vowed to protect him, teach him, and reclaim him.

Then, he gave his right hand cheerily to Philip, and said that they would that day hold a Christmas dinner in what used to be, before the ten poor gentlemen commuted, their great Dinner Hall; and that they would bid to it as many of that Swidger family, who, his son had told him, were so numerous that they might join hands and make a ring round England, as could be brought together on so short a notice.

And it was that day done. There were so many Swidgers there, grown up and children, that an attempt to state them in round numbers might engender doubts, in the distrustful, of the veracity of this history. Therefore the attempt shall not be made. But there they were, by dozens and scores—and there was good news and good hope there, ready for them, of George, who had been visited again by his father and brother, and by Milly, and again left in a quiet sleep. There, present at the dinner, too, were the Tetterbys, including young Adolphus, who arrived in his prismatic comforter, in good time for the beef. Johnny and the baby were too late, of course, and came in all on one side, the one exhausted, the other in a supposed state of double-tooth; but that was customary, and not alarming.

It was sad to see the child who had no name or lineage, watching the other children as they played, not knowing how to talk with them, or sport with them, and more strange to the ways of childhood than a rough dog. It was sad, though in a different way, to see what an instinctive knowledge the youngest children there, had of his being different from all the rest, and how they made timid approaches to him with soft words, and touches, and with little presents, that he might not be unhappy. But he kept by Milly, and began to love her— that was another, as she said!—and, as they all liked her dearly, they were glad of that, and when they saw him peeping at them from behind her chair, they were pleased that he was so close to it.

All this, the Chemist, sitting with the student and his bride that was to be, and Philip, and the rest, saw.

Some people have said since, that he only thought what has been herein set down; others, that he read it in the fire, one winter night about the twilight time; others, that the Ghost was but the representation of his own gloomy thoughts, and Milly the embodiment of his better wisdom. *I* say nothing.

—Except this. That as they were assembled in the old Hall, by no other light than that of a great fire (having dined early), the shadows once more stole out of their hiding-places, and danced about the room, showing the children marvellous shapes and faces on the walls, and gradually changing what was real and familiar there, to what was wild and magical. But that there was one thing in the Hall, to which the eyes of Redlaw, and of Milly and her husband, and of the old man, and of the student, and his bride that was to be, were often turned, which the shadows did not obscure or change. Deepened in its gravity by the firelight, and gazing from the darkness of the panelled wall like life, the sedate face in the portrait, with the beard and ruff, looked down at them from under its verdant wreath of holly, as they looked up at it; and, clear and plain below, as if a voice had uttered them, were the words "Lord, keep my memory green."

—1847

Life and Its Battle

In 1850, Dickens founded his own magazine, *Household Words*, and carried on the editing of it continuously until 1859, when his disagreement with his publishers Bradbury and Evans caused him to withdraw from his partnership with them and to establish his second magazine, *All the Year Round*, which he then edited continuously until his death in June 1870. For these magazines he wrote a great quantity of stories, essays, and editorials; two of his novels were serialized in them—*Hard Times* in 1854 in *Household Words*, and *A Tale of Two Cities* in *All the Year Round* in 1859. He also published the novels, tales, and prose of many writers of the 1850's and '60's, among them Mrs. Gaskell, Samuel Lover, and Wilkie Collins; and he made the two periodicals famous domestic and Dickensian institutions of mid-Victorian England.

After 1850 his Christmas stories appeared in the regular or extra December issues of these two magazines; and the twenty-one tales he wrote between 1850 and 1870 comprise the volume of his collected works entitled *Christmas Stories*. Five of the best of these follow here. "The Holly Tree" was published in the extra Christmas number of *Household Words* in December 1855. (The "extra Christmas numbers" of the two magazines were enlarged holiday issues, usually about twice the size of ordinary issues.) "Somebody's Luggage" came out in the extra number of *All the Year Round* in December 1862; "Mrs. Lirriper's Lodgings" in the extra number of the same magazine in December 1863; "Doctor Marigold" as part of the group of tales entitled "Doctor Marigold's Prescriptions" in the extra number of December 1865; and "Mugby Junction," with its drama of the spectral railway which had already played a role in *Dombey and Son* in 1848, in the extra number of December 1866.

The Holly-Tree THREE BRANCHES

~~~~~~

FIRST BRANCH *Myself*

I have kept one secret in the course of my life. I am a bashful man.
Nobody would suppose it, nobody ever does suppose it, nobody ever
did suppose it, but I am naturally a bashful man. This is the secret
which I have never breathed until now.

I might greatly move the reader by some account of the innumerable places I have not been to, the innumerable people I have not
called upon or received, the innumerable social evasions I have been
guilty of, solely because I am by original constitution and character
a bashful man. But I will leave the reader unmoved, and proceed
with the object before me.

That object is to give a plain account of my travels and discoveries
in the Holly-Tree Inn; in which place of good entertainment for man
and beast I was once snowed up.

It happened in the memorable year when I parted for ever from
Angela Leath, whom I was shortly to have married, on making the
discovery that she preferred my bosom friend. From our school-days
I had freely admitted Edwin, in my own mind, to be far superior to
myself; and, though I was grievously wounded at heart, I felt the
preference to be natural, and tried to forgive them both. It was under
these circumstances that I resolved to go to America—on my way to
the Devil.

Communicating my discovery neither to Angela nor to Edwin, but
resolving to write each of them an affecting letter conveying my blessing and forgiveness, which the steam-tender for shore should carry
to the post when I myself should be bound for the New World, far
beyond recall,—I say, locking up my grief in my own breast, and consoling myself as I could with the prospect of being generous, I quietly
left all I held dear, and started on the desolate journey I have mentioned.

The dead winter-time was in full dreariness when I left my chambers for ever, at five o'clock in the morning. I had shaved by candle-
light, of course, and was miserably cold, and experienced that general

all-pervading sensation of getting up to be hanged which I have usually found inseparable from untimely rising under such circumstances.

How well I remember the forlorn aspect of Fleet-street when I came out of the Temple! The street-lamps flickering in the gusty northeast wind, as if the very gas were contorted with cold; the white-topped houses; the bleak, star-lighted sky; the market people and other early stragglers, trotting to circulate their almost frozen blood; the hospitable light and warmth of the few coffee-shops and public-houses that were open for such customers; the hard, dry, frosty rime with which the air was charged (the wind had already beaten it into every crevice), and which lashed my face like a steel whip.

It wanted nine days to the end of the month, and end of the year. The Post-office packet for the United States was to depart from Liverpool, weather permitting, on the first of the ensuing month, and I had the intervening time on my hands. I had taken this into consideration, and had resolved to make a visit to a certain spot (which I need not name) on the farther borders of Yorkshire. It was endeared to me by my having first seen Angela at a farmhouse in that place, and my melancholy was gratified by the idea of taking a wintry leave of it before my expatriation. I ought to explain, that, to avoid being sought out before my resolution should have been rendered irrevocable by being carried into full effect, I had written to Angela overnight, in my usual manner, lamenting that urgent business, of which she should know all particulars by-and-by—took me unexpectedly away from her for a week or ten days.

There was no Northern Railway at that time, and in its place there were stage-coaches; which I occasionally find myself, in common with some other people, affecting to lament now, but which everybody dreaded as a very serious penance then. I had secured the box-seat on the fastest of these, and my business in Fleet-street was to get into a cab with my portmanteau, so to make the best of my way to the Peacock at Islington, where I was to join this coach. But when one of our Temple watchmen, who carried my portmanteau into Fleet-street for me, told me about the huge blocks of ice that had for some days past been floating in the river, having closed up in the night, and made a walk from the Temple Gardens over to the Surrey shore, I began to ask myself the question, whether the box-seat would not be likely to put a sudden and a frosty end to my unhappiness. I was heart-broken, it is true, and yet I was not quite so far gone as to wish to be frozen to death.

When I got up to the Peacock,—where I found everybody drinking hot purl, in self-preservation,—I asked if there were an inside seat to spare. I then discovered that, inside or out, I was the only passenger. This gave me a still livelier idea of the great inclemency of the weather, since that coach always loaded particularly well. However, I took a little purl (which I found uncommonly good), and got into the coach. When I was seated, they built me up with straw to the waist, and, conscious of making a rather ridiculous appearance, I began my journey.

It was still dark when we left the Peacock. For a little while, pale, uncertain ghosts of houses and trees appeared and vanished, and then it was hard, black, frozen day. People were lighting their fires; smoke was mounting straight up high into the rarefied air; and we were rattling for Highgate Archway over the hardest ground I have ever heard the ring of iron shoes on. As we got into the country, everything seemed to have grown old and gray. The roads, the trees, thatched roofs of cottages and homesteads, the ricks in farmers' yards. Out-door work was abandoned, horse-troughs at roadside inns were frozen hard, no stragglers lounged about, doors were close shut, little turnpike houses had blazing fires inside, and children (even turnpike people have children, and seem to like them) rubbed the frost from the little panes of glass with their chubby arms, that their bright eyes might catch a glimpse of the solitary coach going by. I don't know when the snow began to set in; but I know that we were changing horses somewhere when I heard the guard remark, "That the old lady up in the sky was picking her geese pretty hard to-day." Then, indeed, I found the white down falling fast and thick.

The lonely day wore on, and I dozed it out, as a lonely traveller does. I was warm and valiant after eating and drinking,—particularly after dinner; cold and depressed at all other times. I was always bewildered as to time and place, and always more or less out of my senses. The coach and horses seemed to execute in chorus Auld Lang Syne, without a moment's intermission. They kept the time and tune with the greatest regularity, and rose into the swell at the beginning of the Refrain, with a precision that worried me to death. While we changed horses, the guard and coachman went stumping up and down the road, printing off their shoes in the snow, and poured so much liquid consolation into themselves without being any the worse for it, that I began to confound them, as it darkened again, with two great white casks standing on end. Our horses tumbled down in solitary places, and we got them up,—which was the pleasantest variety I had, for it warmed me. And it snowed and snowed, and still it snowed, and never left off snowing. All night long we went on in this manner. Thus we came round the clock, upon the Great North Road, to the performance of Auld Lang Syne all day again. And it snowed and snowed, and still it snowed, and never left off snowing.

I forget now where we were at noon on the second day, and where we ought to have been; but I know that we were scores of miles behindhand, and that our case was growing worse every hour. The drift was becoming prodigiously deep; landmarks were getting snowed out; the road and the fields were all one; instead of having fences and hedge-rows to guide us, we went crunching on over an unbroken surface of ghastly white that might sink beneath us at any moment and drop us down a whole hillside. Still the coachman and guard—who kept together on the box, always in council, and looking well about them—made out the track with astonishing sagacity.

When we came in sight of a town, it looked, to my fancy, like a large drawing on a slate, with abundance of slate-pencil expended on the churches and houses where the snow lay thickest. When we came within a town, and found the church clocks all stopped, the dial-faces choked with snow, and the inn-signs blotted out, it seemed as if the whole place were overgrown with white moss. As to the coach, it was a mere snowball; similarly, the men and boys who ran along beside us to the town's end, turning our clogged wheels and encouraging our horses, were men and boys of snow; and the bleak wild solitude to which they at last dismissed us was a snowy Sahara. One would have thought this enough: notwithstanding which, I pledge my word that it snowed and snowed, and still it snowed, and never left off snowing.

We performed Auld Lang Syne the whole day; seeing nothing, out of towns and villages, but the track of stoats, hares, and foxes, and sometimes of birds. At nine o'clock at night, on a Yorkshire moor, a cheerful burst from our horn, and a welcome sound of talking, with a glimmering and moving about of lanterns, roused me from my drowsy state. I found that we were going to change.

They helped me out, and I said to a waiter, whose bare head became as white as King Lear's in a single minute, "What Inn is this?"

"The Holly-Tree, Sir," said he.

"'Upon my word, I believe," said I, apologetically, to the guard and coachman, "that I must stop here."

Now the landlord, and the landlady, and the ostler, and the post-boy, and all the stable authorities, had already asked the coachman, to the wide-eyed interest of all the rest of the extablishment, if he meant to go on. The coachman had already replied, "Yes, he'd take her through it,"—meaning by Her the coach,—"if so be as George would stand by him." George was the guard, and he had already sworn that he *would* stand by him. So the helpers were already getting the horses out.

My declaring myself beaten, after this parley, was not an announcement without preparation. Indeed, but for the way to the announcement being smoothed by the parley, I more than doubt whether, as an innately bashful man, I should have had the confidence to make it. As it was, it received the approval even of the guard and coachman. Therefore, with many confirmations of my inclining, and many remarks from one bystander to another, that the gentleman could go for'ard by the mail to-morrow, whereas to-night he would only be froze, and where was the good of a gentleman being froze,—ah, let alone buried alive (which latter clause was added by a humorous helper as a joke at my expense, and was extremely well received), I saw my portmanteau got out stiff, like a frozen body; did the handsome thing by the guard and coachman; wished them good-night and a prosperous journey; and, a little ashamed of myself, after all, for leaving them to fight it out alone, followed the landlord, landlady, and waiter of the Holly-Tree upstairs.

I thought I had never seen such a large room as that into which they showed me. It had five windows, with dark red curtains that would have absorbed the light of a general illumination; and there were complications of drapery at the top of the curtains, that went wandering about the wall in a most extraordinary manner. I asked for a smaller room, and they told me there was no smaller room. They could screen me in, however, the landlord said. They brought a great old japanned screen, with natives (Japanese, I suppose) engaged in a variety of idiotic pursuits all over it; and left me roasting whole before an immense fire.

My bedroom was some quarter of a mile off, up a great staircase at the end of a long gallery; and nobody knows what a misery this is to a bashful man who would rather not meet people on the stairs. It was the grimmest room I have ever had the nightmare in; and all the furniture, from the four posts of the bed to the two old silver candlesticks, was tall, high-shouldered, and spindle-waisted. Below, in my sitting-room, if I looked round my screen, the wind rushed at me like a mad bull; if I stuck to my armchair, the fire scorched me to the colour of a new brick. The chimneypiece was very high, and there was a bad glass—what I may call a wavy glass—above it, which, when I stood up, just showed me my anterior phrenological developments,— and these never look well, in any subject, cut short off at the eyebrow. If I stood with my back to the fire, a gloomy vault of darkness above and beyond the screen insisted on being looked at; and, in its dim remoteness, the drapery of the ten curtains of the five windows went twisting and creeping about, like a nest of gigantic worms.

I suppose that what I observe in myself must be observed by some other men of similar character in *themselves*; therefore I am emboldened to mention, that, when I travel, I never arrive at a place but I immediately want to go away from it. Before I had finished my supper of broiled fowl and mulled port, I had impressed upon the waiter in detail my arrangements for departure in the morning. Breakfast and bill at eight. Fly at nine. Two horses, or, if needful, even four.

Tired though I was, the night appeared about a week long. In oases of nightmare, I thought of Angela, and felt more depressed than ever by the reflection that I was on the shortest road to Gretna Green. What had I to do with Gretna Green? I was not going *that* way to the Devil, but by the American route, I remarked in my bitterness.

In the morning I found that it was snowing still, that it had snowed all night, and that I was snowed up. Nothing could get out of that spot on the moor, or could come at it, until the road had been cut out by labourers from the market-town. When they might cut their way to the Holly-Tree nobody could tell me.

It was now Christmas-eve. I should have had a dismal Christmas-time of it anywhere, and consequently that did not so much matter; still, being snowed up was like dying of frost, a thing I had not bargained for. I felt very lonely. Yet I could no more have proposed to the landlord and landlady to admit me to their society (though I should have liked it very much) than I could have asked them to present me with a piece of plate. Here my great secret, the real bashfulness of my character, is to be observed. Like most bashful men, I judge of other people as if they were bashful too. Besides being far too shamefaced to make the proposal myself, I really had a delicate misgiving that it would be in the last degree disconcerting to them.

Trying to settle down, therefore, in my solitude, I first of all asked what books there were in the house. The waiter brought me a *Book of Roads*, two or three old Newspapers, a little Song-Book, terminating in a collection of Toasts and Sentiments, a little Jest-Book, an odd volume of *Peregrine Pickle*, and the *Sentimental Journey*. I knew every word of the two last already, but I read them through again, then tried to hum all the songs (Auld Lang Syne was among them); went entirely through the jokes,—in which I found a fund of melancholy adapted to my state of mind; proposed all the toasts, enunciated all the sentiments, and mastered the papers. The latter had nothing in them but stock advertisements, a meeting about a county rate, and a highway robbery. As I am a greedy reader, I could not make this supply hold out until night; it was exhausted by tea-time. Being then entirely cast upon my own resources, I got through an hour in considering what to do next. Ultimately, it came into my head (from which I was anxious by any means to exclude Angela and Edwin), that I would endeavour to recall my experience of Inns, and would try how long it lasted me. I stirred the fire, moved my chair a little to one side of the screen,—not daring to go far, for I knew the wind was waiting to make a rush at me, I could hear it growling,—and began.

My first impressions of an Inn dated from the Nursery; consequently I went back to the Nursery for a starting-point, and found myself at the knee of a sallow woman with a fishy eye, an aquiline nose, and a green gown, whose specialty was a dismal narrative of a landlord by the roadside, whose visitors unaccountably disappeared for many years, until it was discovered that the pursuit of his life had been to

convert them into pies. For the better devotion of himself to this
branch of industry, he had constructed a secret door behind the head
of the bed; and when the visitor (oppressed with pie) had fallen asleep,
this wicked landlord would look softly in with a lamp in one hand and
a knife in the other, would cut his throat, and would make him into
pies; for which purpose he had coppers, underneath a trap-door, always
boiling; and rolled out his pastry in the dead of the night. Yet even he
was not insensible to the stings of conscience, for he never went to
sleep without being heard to mutter, "Too much pepper!" which was
eventually the cause of his being brought to justice. I had no sooner
disposed of this criminal than there started up another of the same
period, whose profession was originally housebreaking; in the pursuit
of which art he had had his right ear chopped off one night, as he was
burglariously getting in at a window, by a brave and lovely servant-
maid (whom the aquiline-nosed woman, though not at all answering
the description, always mysteriously implied to be herself). After
several years, this brave and lovely servant-maid was married to the
landlord of a country Inn; which landlord had this remarkable characteristic, that he always wore a silk nightcap, and never would on any
consideration take it off. At last, one night, when he was fast asleep,
the brave and lovely woman lifted up his silk nightcap on the right
side, and found that he had no ear there; upon which she sagaciously
perceived that he was the clipped housebreaker, who had married her
with the intention of putting her to death. She immediately heated the
poker and terminated his career, for which she was taken to King
George upon his throne, and received the compliments of royalty on
her great discretion and valour. This same narrator, who had a Ghoul-
ish pleasure, I have long been persuaded, in terrifying me to the utmost confines of my reason, had another authentic anecdote within
her own experience, founded, I now believe, upon *Raymond and
Agnes, or the Bleeding Nun*. She said it happened to her brother-in-
law, who was immensely rich,—which my father was not; and immensely tall,—which my father was not. It was always a point with
this Ghoul to present my dearest relations and friends to my youthful
mind under circumstances of disparaging contrast. The brother-in-law
was riding once through a forest on a magnificent horse (we had no
magnificent horse at our house), attended by a favourite and valuable
Newfoundland dog (we had no dog), when he found himself benighted, and came to an Inn. A dark woman opened the door, and he
asked her if he could have a bed there. She answered yes, and put his
horse in the stable, and took him into a room where there were two
dark men. While he was at supper, a parrot in the room began to talk,
saying, "Blood, blood! Wipe up the blood!" Upon which one of the
dark men wrung the parrot's neck, and said he was fond of roasted
parrots, and he meant to have this one for breakfast in the morning.

After eating and drinking heartily, the immensely rich, tall brother-in-law went up to bed; but he was rather vexed, because they had shut his dog in the stable, saying that they never allowed dogs in the house. He sat very quiet for more than an hour, thinking and thinking, when, just as his candle was burning out, he heard a scratch at the door. He opened the door, and there was the Newfoundland dog! The dog came softly in, smelt about him, went straight to some straw in the corner which the dark men had said covered apples, tore the straw away, and disclosed two sheets steeped in blood. Just at that moment the candle went out, and the brother-in-law, looking through a chink in the door, saw the two dark men stealing upstairs; one armed with a dagger that long (about five feet); the other carrying a chopper, a sack, and a spade. Having no remembrance of the close of this adventure, I suppose my faculties to have been always so frozen with terror at this stage of it, that the power of listening stagnated within me for some quarter of an hour.

These barbarous stories carried me, sitting there on the Holly-Tree hearth, to the Roadside Inn, renowned in my time in a sixpenny book with a folding plate, representing in a central compartment of oval form the portrait of Jonathan Bradford, and in four corner compartments four incidents of the tragedy with which the name is associated, —coloured with a hand at once so free and economical, that the bloom of Jonathan's complexion passed without any pause into the breeches of the ostler, and, smearing itself off into the next division, became rum in a bottle. Then I remembered how the landlord was found at the murdered traveller's bedside, with his own knife at his feet, and blood upon his hand; how he was hanged for the murder, notwithstanding his protestation that he had indeed come there to kill the traveller for his saddle-bags, but had been stricken motionless on finding him already slain; and how the ostler, years afterwards, owned the deed. By this time I had made myself quite uncomfortable. I stirred the fire, and stood with my back to it as long as I could bear the heat, looking up at the darkness beyond the screen, and at the wormy curtains creeping in and creeping out, like the worms in the ballad of Alonzo the Brave and the Fair Imogene.

There was an Inn in the cathedral town where I went to school, which had pleasanter recollections about it than any of these. I took it next. It was the Inn where friends used to put up, and where we used to go to see parents, and to have salmon and fowls, and be tipped. It had an ecclesiastical sign,—the Mitre,—and a bar that seemed to be the next best thing to a bishopric, it was so snug. I loved the landlord's youngest daughter to distraction,—but let that pass. It was in this Inn that I was cried over by my rosy little sister, because I had acquired a black eye in a fight. And though she had been, that Holly-

Tree night, for many a long year where all tears are dried, the Mitre softened me yet.

"To be continued to-morrow," said I, when I took my candle to go to bed. But my bed took it upon itself to continue the train of thought that night. It carried me away, like the enchanted carpet, to a distant place (though still in England), and there, alighting from a stage-coach at another Inn in the snow, as I had actually done some years before, I repeated in my sleep a curious experience I had really had here. More than a year before I made the journey in the course of which I put up at that Inn, I had lost a very near and dear friend by death. Every night since, at home or away from home, I had dreamed of that friend; sometimes as still living; sometimes as returning from the world of shadows to comfort me; always as being beautiful, placid, and happy, never in association with any approach to fear or distress. It was at a lonely Inn in a wide moorland place, that I halted to pass the night. When I had looked from my bedroom window over the waste of snow on which the moon was shining, I sat down by my fire to write a letter. I had always, until that hour, kept it within my own breast that I dreamed every night of the dear lost one. But in the letter that I wrote I recorded the circumstance, and added that I felt much interested in proving whether the subject of my dream would still be faithful to me, travel-tired, and in that remote place. No. I lost the beloved figure of my vision in parting with the secret. My sleep has never looked upon it since, in sixteen years, but once. I was in Italy, and awoke (or seemed to awake), the well-remembered voice distinctly in my ears, conversing with it. I entreated it, as it rose above my bed and soared up to the vaulted roof of the old room, to answer me a question I had asked touching the Future Life. My hands were still outstretched towards it as it vanished, when I heard a bell ringing by the garden wall, and a voice in the deep stillness of the night calling on all good Christians to pray for the souls of the dead; it being All Souls' Eve.

To return to the Holly-Tree. When I awoke next day, it was freezing hard, and the lowering sky threatened more snow. My breakfast cleared away, I drew my chair into its former place, and, with the fire getting so much the better of the landscape that I sat in twilight, resumed my Inn remembrances.

That was a good Inn down in Wiltshire where I put up once, in the days of the hard Wiltshire ale, and before all beer was bitterness. It was on the skirts of Salisbury Plain, and the midnight wind that rattled my lattice window came moaning at me from Stonehenge. There was a hanger-on at that establishment (a supernaturally preserved Druid I believe him to have been, and to be still), with long white hair, and a flinty blue eye always looking afar off; who claimed to have been a shepherd, and who seemed to be ever watching for the reappearance, on the verge of the horizon, of some ghostly flock of sheep that had been mutton for many ages. He was a man with a weird belief in him that no one could count the stones of Stonehenge twice, and make the same number of them; likewise, that any one who counted them three times nine times, and then stood in the centre and said, "I dare!" would behold a tremendous apparition, and be stricken dead. He pretended to have seen a bustard (I suspect him to have been familiar with the dodo), in manner following: He was out upon the plain at the close of a late autumn day, when he dimly discerned, going on before him at a curious fitfully bounding pace, what he at first supposed to be a gig-umbrella that had been blown from some conveyance, but what he presently believed to be a lean dwarf man upon a little pony. Having followed this object for some distance without gaining on it, and having called to it many times without receiving any answer, he pursued it for miles and miles, when, at length coming up with it, he discovered it to be the last bustard in Great Britain, degenerated into a wingless state, and running along the ground. Resolved to capture him or perish in the attempt, he closed with the bustard; but the bustard, who had formed a counter-resolution that he should do neither, threw him, stunned him, and was last seen making off due west. This weird man, at that stage of metempsychosis, may have been a sleep-walker or an enthusiast or a robber; but I awoke one night to find him in the dark at my bedside, repeating the Athanasian Creed in a terrific voice. I paid my bill next day, and retired from the county with all possible precipitation.

That was not a commonplace story which worked itself out at a little Inn in Switzerland, while I was staying there. It was a very homely place, in a village of one narrow zigzag street, among mountains, and you went in at the main door through the cow-house, and among the mules and the dogs and the fowls, before ascending a great bare staircase to the rooms; which were all of unpainted wood, without plastering or papering,—like rough packing-cases. Outside there was nothing but the straggling street, a little toy church with a copper-coloured steeple, a pine forest, a torrent, mists, and mountain-sides. A young man belonging to this Inn had disappeared eight weeks before (it was winter-time), and was supposed to have had some undiscovered love affair, and to have gone for a soldier. He had got up in the night, and dropped into the village street from the loft in which he slept with another man; and he had done it so quietly, that his companion and fellow-labourer had heard no movement when he was awakened in the morning, and they said, "Louis, where is Henri?" They looked for him high and low, in vain, and gave him up. Now, outside this Inn, there stood, as there stood outside every dwelling in the village, a stack of firewood; but the stack belonging to the Inn was higher than any of the rest, because the Inn was the richest house, and burnt the most fuel. It began to be noticed, while they were looking high and low, that a Bantam cock, part of the live stock of the Inn, put himself wonderfully out of his way to get to the top of this wood-stack; and that he would stay there for hours and hours, crowing, until he appeared in danger of splitting himself. Five weeks went on,—six weeks, —still this terrible Bantam, neglecting his domestic affairs, was always on the top of the wood-stack, crowing the very eyes out of his head. By this time it was perceived that Louis had become inspired with a violent animosity towards the terrible Bantam, and one morning he was seen by a woman, who sat nursing her goître at a little window in a gleam of sun, to catch up a rough billet of wood, with a great oath, hurl it at the terrible Bantam crowing on the wood-stack, and bring him down dead. Hereupon the woman, with a sudden light in her mind, stole round to the back of the wood-stack, and, being a good climber, as all those women are, climbed up, and soon was seen upon the summit, screaming, looking down the hollow within, and crying, "Seize Louis, the murderer! Ring the church bell! Here is the body!" I saw the murderer that day, and I saw him as I sat by my fire at the Holly-Tree Inn, and I see him now, lying shackled with cords on the stable litter, among the mild eyes and the smoking breath of the cows, waiting to be taken away by the police, and stared at by the fearful village. A heavy animal,—the dullest animal in the stables,—with a stupid head, and a lumpish face devoid of any trace of sensibility, who had been, within the knowledge of the murdered youth, an embezzler of certain small moneys belonging to his master, and who had taken this hopeful mode of putting a possible accuser out of his way. All of which he confessed next day, like a sulky wretch who couldn't be troubled any more, now that they had got hold of him, and meant to make an end of him. I saw him once again, on the day of my departure from the Inn. In that Canton the headsman still does his office with a sword; and I came upon this murderer sitting bound to a chair, with his eyes bandaged, on a scaffold in a little market-place. In that instant, a great sword (loaded with quicksilver in the thick part of the blade) swept round him like a gust of wind or fire, and there was no such creature in the world. My wonder was, not that he was so suddenly dispatched, but that any head was left unreaped, within a radius of fifty yards of that tremendous sickle.

That was a good Inn, too, with the kind, cheerful landlady and the honest landlord, where I lived in the shadow of Mont Blanc, and where one of the apartments has a zoological papering on the walls, not so accurately joined but that the elephant occasionally rejoices in a tiger's hind legs and tail, while the lion puts on a trunk and tusks, and the bear, moulting as it were, appears as to portions of himself like a leopard. I made several American friends at that Inn, who all called Mont Blanc Mount Blank,—except one good-humoured gentleman, of a very sociable nature, who became on such intimate terms with it that he spoke of it familiarly as "Blank;" observing, at breakfast, "Blank looks pretty tall this morning;" or considerably doubting in the courtyard in the evening, whether there warn't some go-ahead naters in our country, Sir, that would make out the top of Blank in a couple of hours from first start—now!

Once I passed a fortnight at an Inn in the North of England, where I was haunted by the ghost of a tremendous pie. It was a Yorkshire pie, like a fort,—an abandoned fort with nothing in it; but the waiter had a fixed idea that it was a point of ceremony at every meal to put the pie on the table. After some days I tried to hint, in several delicate ways, that I considered the pie done with; as for example, by emptying fag-ends of glasses of wine into it; putting cheese-plates and spoons into it, as into a basket; putting wine-bottles into it, as into a cooler; but always in vain, the pie being invariably cleaned out again and brought up as before. At last, beginning to be doubtful whether I was not the victim of a spectral illusion, and whether my health and spirits might not sink under the horrors of an imaginary pit, I cut a triangle out of it, fully as large as the musical instrument of that name in a powerful orchestra. Human prevision could not have foreseen the result—but the waiter mended the pie. With some effectual species of cement, he adroitly fitted the triangle in again, and I paid my reckoning and fled.

The Holly-Tree was getting rather dismal. I made an overland expedition beyond the screen, and penetrated as far as the fourth window. Here I was driven back by stress of weather. Arrived at my winter-quarters once more, I made up the fire, and took another Inn.

It was in the remotest part of Cornwall. A great annual Miner's Feast was being holden at the Inn, when I and my travelling companions presented ourselves at night among the wild crowd that were dancing before it by torchlight. We had had a break-down in the dark, on a stony morass some miles away; and I had the honour of leading one of the unharnassed post-horses. If any lady or gentleman, on perusal of the present lines, will take any very tall post-horse with his traces hanging about his legs, and will conduct him by the bearing-rein into the heart of a country dance of a hundred and fifty couples, that lady or gentleman will then, and only then, form an adequate idea of the extent to which that post-horse will tread on his conductor's toes. Over and above which, the post-horse, finding three hundred people whirling about him, will probably rear, and also lash out with his hind legs, in a manner incompatible with dignity or self-respect on his conductor's part. With such little drawbacks on my usually impressive aspect, I appeared at this Cornish Inn, to the unutterable wonder of the Cornish Miners. It was full, and twenty times full, and nobody could be received but the post-horse,—though to get rid of that noble animal was something. While my fellow-travellers and I were discussing how to pass the night and so much of the next day as must intervene before the jovial blacksmith and the jovial wheelwright would be in a condition to go out on the morass and mend the coach, an honest man stepped forth from the crowd and proposed his unlet floor of two rooms, with supper of eggs and bacon, ale and punch. We joyfully accompanied him home to the strangest of clean houses, where we were well entertained to the satisfaction of all parties. But the novel feature of the entertainment was, that our host was a chairmaker, and that the chairs assigned to us were mere frames, altogether without bottoms of any sort; so that we passed the evening on perches. Nor was this the absurdest consequence; for when we unbent at supper, and any one of us gave way to laughter, he forgot the peculiarity of his position, and instantly disappeared. I myself, doubled up into an attitude from which self-extrication was impossible, was taken out of my frame, like a clown in a comic pantomime who has tumbled into a tub, five times by the taper's light during the eggs and bacon.

The Holly-Tree was fast reviving within me a sense of loneliness. I began to feel conscious that my subject would never carry on until I was dug out. I might be a week here,—weeks!

There was a story with a singular idea in it, connected with an Inn I once passed a night at in a picturesque old town on the Welsh border. In a large double-bedded room of this Inn there had been a suicide by poison, in one bed, while a tired traveller slept unconscious in the other. After that time, the suicide bed was never used, but the other constantly was; the disused bedstead remaining in the room empty, though as to all other respects in its old state. The story ran, that whosoever slept in this room, though never so entire a stranger, from never so far off, was invariably observed to come down in the morning with an impression that he smelt Laudanum, and that his mind always turned upon the subject of suicide; to which, whatever kind of man he might be, he was certain to make some reference if he conversed with any one. This went on for years, until it at length induced the landlord to take the disused bedstead down, and bodily burn it,—bed, hangings, and all. The strange influence (this was the story) now changed to a fainter one, but never changed afterwards. The occupant of that room, with occasional but very rare exceptions, would come down in the morning, trying to recall a forgotten dream he had had in the night. The landlord, on his mentioning his perplexity, would suggest various commonplace subjects, not one of which, as he very well knew, was the true subject. But the moment the landlord suggested "Poison," the traveller started, and cried, "Yes!" He never failed to accept that suggestion, and he never recalled any more of the dream.

This reminiscence brought the Welsh Inns in general before me;

with the women in their round hats, and the harpers with their white beards (venerable, but humbugs, I am afraid), playing outside the door while I took my dinner. The transition was natural to the Highland Inns, with the oatmeal bannocks, the honey, the venison steaks, the trout from the loch, the whisky, and perhaps (having the materials so temptingly at hand) the Athol brose. Once was I coming south from the Scottish Highlands in hot haste, hoping to change quickly at the station at the bottom of a certain wild historical glen, when these eyes did with mortification see the landlord come out with a telescope and sweep the whole prospect for the horses; which horses were away picking up their own living, and did not heave in sight under four hours. Having thought of the loch-trout, I was taken by quick association to the Anglers' Inns of England (I have assisted at innumerable feats of angling by lying in the bottom of the boat, whole summer days, doing nothing with the greatest perseverance; which I have generally found to be as effectual towards the taking of fish as the finest tackle and the utmost science), and to the pleasant white, clean, flower-pot-decorated bedrooms of those inns, overlooking the river, and the ferry, and the green ait, and the church-spire, and the country bridge; and to the peerless Emma with the bright eyes and the pretty smile, who waited, bless her! with a natural grace that would have converted Blue-Beard. Casting my eyes upon my Holly-Tree fire, I next discerned among the glowing coals the pictures of a score or more of those wonderful English posting-inns which we are all so sorry to have lost, which were so large and so comfortable, and which were such monuments of British submission to rapacity and extortion. He who would see these houses pining away, let him walk from Basingstoke, or even Windsor, to London, by way of Hounslow, and moralise on their perishing remains; the stables crumbling to dust; unsettled labourers and wanderers bivouacking in the outhouses; grass growing in the yards; the rooms, where erst so many hundred beds of down were made up, let off to Irish lodgers at eighteenpence a week; a little ill-looking beer-shop shrinking in the tap of former days, burning coach-house gates for firewood, having one of its two windows bunged up, as if it had received punishment in a fight with the Railroad; a low, bandy-legged, brick-making bulldog standing in the doorway. What could I next see in my fire so naturally as the new railway-house of these times near the dismal country station; with nothing particular on draught but cold air and damp, nothing worth mentioning in the larder but new mortar, and no business doing beyond a conceited affectation of luggage in the hall? Then I came to the Inns of Paris, with the pretty apartment of four pieces up one hundred and seventy-five waxed stairs, the privilege of ringing the bell all day long without influencing anybody's mind or body but your own, and the not-too-much-for-dinner, considering the price. Next to the provincial Inns of

France, with the great church-tower rising above the courtyard, the
horse-bells jingling merrily up and down the street beyond, and the
clocks of all descriptions in all the rooms, which are never right, unless
taken at the precise minute when, by getting exactly twelve hours too
fast or too slow, they unintentionally become so. Away I went, next,
to the lesser roadside Inns of Italy; where all the dirty clothes in the
house (not in wear) are always lying in your anteroom; where the
mosquitoes make a raisin pudding of your face in summer, and the
cold bites it blue in winter; where you get what you can, and forget
what you can't; where I should again like to be boiling my tea in a
pocket-handkerchief dumpling, for want of a teapot. So to the old
palace Inns and old monastery Inns, in towns and cities of the same
bright country; with their massive quadrangular staircases, whence you
may look from among clustering pillars high into the blue vault of
heaven; with their stately banqueting-rooms, and vast refectories; with
their labyrinths of ghostly bedchambers, and their glimpses into
gorgeous streets that have no appearance of reality or possibility. So to
the close little Inns of the Malaria districts, with their pale attendants,
and their peculiar smell of never letting in the air. So to the immense
fantastic Inns of Venice, with the cry of the gondolier below, as he
skims the corner; the grip of the watery odours on one particular little
bit of the bridge of your nose (which is never released while you stay
there); and the great bell of St. Mark's Cathedral tolling midnight.
Next I put up for a minute at the restless Inns upon the Rhine, where
your going to bed, no matter at what hour, appears to be the tocsin for
everybody else's getting up; and where, in the table-d'hôte room at the
end of the long table (with several Towers of Babel on it at the other
end, all made of white plates), one knot of stoutish men, entirely
dressed in jewels and dirt, and having nothing else upon them, *will* remain all night, clinking glasses, and singing about the river that flows,
and the grape that grows, and Rhine wine that beguiles, and Rhine
woman that smiles and hi drink drink my friend and ho drink drink my
brother, and all the rest of it. I departed thence, as a matter of course,
to other German Inns, where all the eatables are soddened down to
the same flavour, and where the mind is disturbed by the apparition
of hot puddings, and boiled cherries, sweet and slab, at awfully unexpected periods of the repast. After a draught of sparkling beer from
a foaming glass jug, and a glance of recognition through the windows
of the student beer-houses at Heidelberg and elsewhere, I put out to
sea for the Inns of America, with their four hundred beds apiece, and
their eight or nine hundred ladies and gentlemen at dinner every day.
Again I stood in the bar-rooms thereof, taking my evening cobbler,
julep, sling, or cocktail. Again I listened to my friend the General,—
whom I had known for five minutes, in the course of which period he
had made me intimate for life with two Majors, who again had made

me intimate for life with three Colonels, who again had made me
brother to twenty-two civilians,—again, I say, I listened to my friend
the General, leisurely expounding the resources of the establishment,
as to gentlemen's morning-room, Sir; ladies' morning-room, Sir; gentlemen's evening-room, Sir; ladies' evening-room, Sir; ladies' and gentlemen's evening reuniting-room, Sir; music-room, Sir; reading-room, Sir;
over four hundred sleeping-rooms, Sir; and the entire planned and
finished within twelve calendar months from the first clearing off of
the old encumbrances on the plot, at a cost of five hundred thousand
dollars, Sir. Again I found, as to my individual way of thinking, that
the greater, the more gorgeous, and the more dollarous the establishment was, the less desirable it was. Nevertheless, again I drank my
cobbler, julep, sling, or cocktail, in all good-will, to my friend the General, and my friends the Majors, Colonels, and civilians all; full well
knowing that, whatever little motes my beamy eyes may have descried
in theirs, they belong to a kind, generous, large-hearted, and great
people.

I had been going on lately at a quick pace to keep my solitude out
of my mind; but here I broke down for good, and gave up the subject.
What was I to do? What was to become of me? Into what extremity
was I submissively to sink? Supposing that, like Baron Trenck, I
looked out for a mouse or spider, and found one, and beguiled my
imprisonment by training it? Even that might be dangerous with a
view to the future. I might be so far gone when the road did come to
be cut through the snow, that, on my way forth, I might burst into
tears, and beseech, like the prisoner who was released in his old age
from the Bastille, to be taken back again to the five windows, the ten
curtains, and the sinuous drapery.

A desperate idea came into my head. Under any other circumstances I should have rejected it; but, in the strait at which I was, I held
it fast. Could I so far overcome the inherent bashfulness which withheld me from the landlord's table and the company I might find there,
as to call up the Boots, and ask him to take a chair,—and something
in a liquid form,—and talk to me? I could. I would. I did.

SECOND BRANCH   *The Boots*

Where had he been in his time? he repeated, when I asked him the question. Lord, he had been everywhere! And what had he been? Bless you, he had been everything you could mention a'most!

Seen a good deal? Why, of course he had. I should say so, he could assure me, if I only knew about a twentieth part of what had come in *his* way. Why, it would be easier for him, he expected, to tell what he hadn't seen than what he had. Ah! A deal, it would.

What was the curiousest thing he had seen? Well! He didn't know. He couldn't momently name what was the curiousest thing he had seen,—unless it was a Unicorn,—and he see *him* once at a Fair. But supposing a young gentleman not eight year old was to run away with a fine young woman of seven, might I think *that* a queer start? Certainly. Then that was a start as he himself had had his blessed eyes on, and he had cleaned the shoes they run away in—and they was so little that he couldn't get his hand into 'em.

Master Harry Walmers' father, you see, he lived at the Elmses, down away by Shooter's Hill there, six or seven miles from Lunnon. He was a gentleman of spirit, and good-looking, and held his head up when he walked, and had what you may call Fire about him. He wrote poetry, and he rode, and he ran, and he cricketed, and he danced, and he acted, and he done it all equally beautiful. He was uncommon proud of Master Harry as was his only child; but he didn't spoil him neither. He was a gentleman that had a will of his own and a eye of his own, and that would be minded. Consequently, though he made quite a companion of the fine bright boy, and was delighted to see him so fond of reading his fairy books, and was never tired of hearing him say my name is Norval, or hearing him sing his songs about Young May Moons is beaming love, and When he as adores thee has left but the name, and that; still he kept the command over the child, and the child *was* a child, and it's to be wished more of 'em was!

How did Boots happen to know all this? Why, through being under-gardener. Of course he couldn't be under-gardener, and be always about, in the summer-time, near the windows on the lawn, a mowing, and sweeping, and weeding, and pruning, and this and that, without getting acquainted with the ways of the family. Even supposing Master Harry hadn't come to him one morning early, and said, "Cobbs, how should you spell Norah, if you was asked?" and then began cutting it in print all over the fence.

He couldn't say he had taken particular notice of children before that; but really it was pretty to see them two mites a going about the place together, deep in love. And the courage of the boy! Bless your soul, he'd have throwed off his little hat, and tucked up his little sleeves, and gone in at a Lion, he would, if they had happened to meet one, and she had been frightened of him. One day he stops, along with her, where Boots was hoeing weeds in the gravel, and says, speaking up, "Cobbs," he says, "I like *you*." "Do you, Sir? I'm proud to hear it." "Yes, I do, Cobbs. Why do I like you, do you think, Cobbs?" "Don't know, Master Harry, I am sure." "Because Norah likes you, Cobbs." "Indeed, Sir? That's very gratifying." "Gratifying, Cobbs? It's better than millions of the brightest diamonds to be liked by Norah." "Certainly, Sir." "You're going away, ain't you, Cobbs?" "Yes, Sir." "Would you like another situation, Cobbs?" "Well, Sir, I shouldn't object, if it was a good 'un." "Then, Cobbs," says he, "you shall be our Head Gardener when we are married." And he tucks her, in her little sky-blue mantle, under his arm, and walks away.

Boots could assure me that it was better than a picter, and equal to a play, to see them babies, with their long, bright, curling hair, their sparkling eyes, and their beautiful light tread, a rambling about the garden, deep in love. Boots was of opinion that the birds believed they was birds, and kept up with 'em, singing to please 'em. Sometimes they would creep under the Tulip-tree, and would sit there with their arms round one another's necks, and their soft cheeks touching, a reading about the Prince and the Dragon, and the good and bad enchanters, and the king's fair daughter. Sometimes he would hear them planning about having a house in a forest, keeping bees and a cow, and living entirely on milk and honey. Once he came upon them by the pond, and heard Master Harry say, "Adorable Norah, kiss me, and say you love me to distraction, or I'll jump in head-foremost." And Boots made no question he would have done it if she hadn't complied. On the whole, Boots said it had a tendency to make him feel as if he was in love himself—only he didn't exactly know who with.

"Cobbs," said Master Harry, one evening, when Cobbs was watering the flowers, "I am going on a visit, this present Midsummer, to my grandmamma's at York."

"Are you indeed, Sir? I hope you'll have a pleasant time. I am going into Yorkshire, myself, when I leave here."

"Are you going to your grandmamma's, Cobbs?"

"No, Sir. I haven't got such a thing."

"Not as a grandmamma, Cobbs?"

"No, Sir."

The boy looked on at the watering of the flowers for a little while, and then said, "I shall be very glad indeed to go, Cobbs,—Norah's going."

"You'll be all right then, Sir," says Cobbs, "with your beautiful sweetheart by your side."

"Cobbs," returned the boy, flushing, "I never let anybody joke about it, when I can prevent them."

"It wasn't a joke, Sir," says Cobbs, with humility,—"wasn't so meant."

"I am glad of that, Cobbs, because I like you, you know, and you're going to live with us.—Cobbs!"

"Sir."

"What do you think my grandmamma gives me when I go down there?"

"I couldn't so much as make a guess, Sir."

"A Bank of England five-pound note, Cobbs."

"Whew!" says Cobbs, "that's a spanking sum of money, Master Harry."

"A person could do a good deal with such a sum of money as that, —couldn't a person, Cobbs?"

"I believe you, Sir!"

"Cobbs," said the boy, "I'll tell you a secret. At Norah's house, they have been joking her about me, and pretending to laugh at our being engaged,—pretending to make game of it, Cobbs!"

"Such, Sir," says Cobbs, "is the depravity of human natur."

The boy, looking exactly like his father, stood for a few minutes with his glowing face towards the sunset, and then departed with, "Good-night, Cobbs. I'm going in."

If I was to ask Boots how it happened that he was a going to leave that place just at that present time, well, he couldn't rightly answer me. He did suppose he might have stayed there till now if he had been anyways inclined. But, you see, he was younger then, and he wanted change. That's what he wanted,—change. Mr. Walmers, he said to him when he gave him notice of his intentions to leave, "Cobbs," he says, "have you anythink to complain of? I make the inquiry because if I find that any of my people really has anythink to complain of, I wish to make it right if I can." "No, Sir," says Cobbs; "thanking you, Sir, I find myself as well sitiwated here as I could hope to be anywheres. The truth is, Sir, that I'm a-going to seek my fortun'." "O, indeed, Cobbs!" he says; "I hope you may find it." And Boots could assure me—which he did, touching his hair with his bootjack, as a salute in the way of his present calling—that he hadn't found it yet.

Well, Sir! Boots left the Elmses when his time was up, and Master Harry, he went down to the old lady's at York, which old lady would have given that child the teeth out of her head (if she had had any), she was so wrapped up in him. What does that Infant do,—for Infant you may call him and be within the mark,—but cut away from that old lady's with his Norah, on a expedition to go to Gretna Green and be married!

Sir, Boots was at this identical Holly-Tree Inn (having left it several times since to better himself, but always come back through one thing or another), when, one summer afternoon, the coach drives up, and out of the coach gets them two children. The Guard says to our Governor, "I don't quite make out these little passengers, but the young gentleman's words was, that they was to be brought here." The young gentleman gets out; hands his lady out; gives the Guard something for himself; says to our Governor, "We're to stop here to-night, please. Sitting-room and two bedrooms will be required. Chops and cherry-pudding for two!" and tucks her, in her little sky-blue mantle, under his arm, and walks into the house much bolder than Brass.

Boots leaves me to judge what the amazement of that establishment was, when these two tiny creatures all alone by themselves was marched into the Angel,—much more so, when he, who had seen them without their seeing him, give the Gorvernor his views of the expedition they was upon. "Cobbs," says the Governor, "if this is so, I must set off myself to York, and quiet their friends' minds. In which case you must keep your eye upon 'em, and humour 'em, till I come back. But before I take these measures, Cobbs, I should wish you to find from themselves whether your opinion is correct. "Sir, to you," says Cobbs, "that shall be done directly."

So Boots goes upstairs to the Angel, and there he finds Master Harry on a e-normous sofa,—immense at any time, but looking like the Great Bed of Ware, compared with him,—a drying the eyes of Miss Norah with his pocket-hankecher. Their little legs was entirely off the ground, of course, and it really is not possible for Boots to express to me how small them children looked.

"It's Cobbs! It's Cobbs!" cried Master Harry, and comes running to him, and catching hold of his hand. Miss Norah comes running to him on t'other side and catching hold of his t'other hand, and they both jump for joy.

"I see you a getting out, Sir," says Cobbs. "I thought it was you. I thought I couldn't be mistaken in your height and figure. What's the object of your journey, Sir?—Matrimonial?"

"We are going to be married, Cobbs, at Gretna Green," returned the boy. "We have run away on purpose. Norah has been in rather low spirits, Cobbs; but she'll be happy, now we have found you to be our friend."

"Thank you, Sir, and thank you, Miss," says Cobbs, "for your good opinion. Did you bring any luggage with you, Sir?"

If I will believe Boots when he gives me his word and honour upon it, the lady had got a parasol, a smelling-bottle, a round and a half of cold buttered toast, eight peppermint drops, and a hair-brush,

—seemingly a doll's. The gentleman had got about half-a-dozen yards of string, a knife, three or four sheets of writing-paper folded up surprising small, a orange, and a Chaney mug with his name upon it.

"What may be the exact natur of your plans, Sir?" says Cobbs.

"To go on," replied the boy,—which the courage of that boy was something wonderful!—"in the morning, and be married to-morrow."

"Just so, Sir," says Cobbs. "Would it meet your views, Sir, if I was to accompany you?"

When Cobbs said this, they both jumped for joy again, and cried out, "Oh, yes, yes, Cobbs! Yes!"

"Well, Sir," says Cobbs. "If you will excuse my having the freedom to give an opinion, what I should recommend would be this. I'm acquainted with a pony, Sir, which, put in a pheayton that I could borrow, would take you and Mrs. Harry Walmers, Junior, (myself driving, if you approved,) to the end of your journey in a very short space of time. I am not altogether sure, Sir, that this pony will be at liberty to-morrow, but even if you had to wait over to-morrow for him, it might be worth your while. As to the small account here, Sir, in case you was to find yourself running at all short, that don't signify; because I'm a part proprietor of this inn, and it could stand over."

Boots assures me that when they clapped their hands, and jumped for joy again, and called him "Good Cobbs!" and "Dear Cobbs!" and bent across him to kiss one another in the delight of their confiding hearts, he felt himself the meanest rascal for deceiving 'em that ever was born.

"Is there anything you want just at present, Sir?" says Cobbs, mortally ashamed of himself.

"We should like some cakes after dinner," answered Master Harry, folding his arms, putting out one leg, and looking straight at him, "and two apples,—and jam. With dinner we should like to have toast-and-water. But Norah has always been accustomed to half a glass of currant wine at dessert. And so have I."

"It shall be ordered at the bar, Sir," says Cobbs; and away he went.

Boots has the feeling as fresh upon him at this minute of speaking as he had then, that he would far rather have had it out in half-a-dozen rounds with the Governor than have combined with him; and that he wished with all his heart there was any impossible place where those two babies could make an impossible marriage, and live impossibly happy ever afterwards. However, as it couldn't be, he went into the Governor's plans, and the Governor set off for York in half an hour.

The way in which the women of that house—without exception—every one of 'em—married *and* single—took to that boy when they heard the story, Boots considers surprising. It was as much as he could do to keep 'em from dashing into the room and kissing him. They climbed up all sorts of places, at the risk of their lives, to look at him through a pane of glass. They was seven deep at the keyhole. They was out of their minds about him and his bold spirit.

In the evening, Boots went into the room to see how the runaway couple was getting on. The gentleman was on the window-seat, supporting the lady in his arms. She had tears upon her face, and was lying, very tired and half asleep, with her head upon his shoulder.

"Mrs. Harry Walmers, Junior, fatigued, Sir?" says Cobbs.

"Yes, she is tired, Cobbs; but she is not used to be away from home, and she has been in low spirits again. Cobbs, do you think you could bring a biffin, please?"

"I ask your pardon, Sir," says Cobbs. "What was it you——?"

"I think a Norfolk biffin would rouse her, Cobbs. She is very fond of them."

Boots withdrew in search of the required restorative, and, when he brought it in, the gentleman handed it to the lady, and fed her with a spoon, and took a little himself; the lady being heavy with sleep, and rather cross. "What should you think, Sir," says Cobbs, "of a chamber candle-stick?" The gentleman approved; the chambermaid went first, up the great staircase; the lady, in her sky-blue mantle, followed, gallantly escorted by the gentleman; the gentleman embraced her at her door, and retired to his own apartment, where Boots softly locked him up.

Boots couldn't but feel with increased acuteness what a base deceiver he was, when they consulted him at breakfast (they had ordered sweet milk-and-water, and toast and currant jelly, overnight) about the pony. It really was as much as he could do, he don't mind confessing to me, to look them two young things in the face, and think what a wicked old father of lies he had grown up to be. Howsomever, he went on a lying like a Trojan about the pony. He told 'em that it did so unfort'nately happen that the pony was half clipped, you see, and that he couldn't be taken out in that state, for fear it should strike to his inside. But that he'd be finished clipping in the course of the day, and that to-morrow morning at eight o'clock the pheayton would be ready. Boots's view of the whole case, looking back on it in my room, is, that Mrs. Harry Walmers, Junior, was beginning to give in. She hadn't had her hair curled when she went to bed, and she didn't seem quite up to brushing it herself, and its getting in her eyes put her out. But nothing put out Master Harry. He sat behind his breakfast-cup, a tearing away at the jelly, as if he had been his own father.

After breakfast, Boots is inclined to consider that they drawed soldiers,—at least, he knows that many such was found in the fireplace, all on horseback. In the course of the morning, Master Harry rang the bell,—it was surprising how that there boy did carry on,—

and said, in a sprightly way, "Cobbs, is there any good walks in this neighbourhood?"

"Yes, Sir," says Cobbs. "There's Love-lane."

"Get out with you, Cobbs!"—that was that there boy's expression, —"you're joking."

"Begging your pardon, Sir," says Cobbs, "there really is Love-lane. And a pleasant walk it is, and proud shall I be to show it to yourself and Mrs. Harry Walmers, Junior."

"Norah, dear," said Master Harry, "this is curious. We really ought to see Love-lane. Put on your bonnet, my sweetest darling, and we will go there with Cobbs."

Boots leaves me to judge what a Beast he felt himself to be, when that young pair told him, as they all three jogged along together, that they had made up their minds to give him two thousand guineas a year as head-gardener, on accounts of his being so true a friend to 'em. Boots could have wished at the moment that the earth would have opened and swallowed him up, he felt so mean, with their beaming eyes a looking at him, and believing him. Well, Sir, he turned the conversation as well as he could, and he took 'em down Love-lane to the water-meadows, and there Master Harry would have drowned himself in half a moment more, a getting out a water-lily for her,— but nothing daunted that boy. Well, Sir, they was tired out. All being so new and strange to 'em, they was tired as tired could be. And they laid down on a bank of daisies, like the children in the wood, leastways meadows, and fell asleep.

Boots don't know—perhaps I do,—but never mind, it don't signify either way—why it made a man fit to make a fool of himself to see them two pretty babies a lying there in the clear still sunny day, not dreaming half so hard when they was asleep as they done when they was awake. But, Lord! when you come to think of yourself, you know, and what a game you have been up to ever since you was in your own cradle, and what a poor sort of a chap you are, and how it's always either Yesterday with you, or else To-morrow, and never To-day, that's where it is!

Well, Sir, they woke up at last, and then one thing was getting pretty clear to Boots, namely that Mrs. Harry Walmerses, Junior's, temper was on the move. When Master Harry took her round the waist, she said he "teased her so;" and when he says, "Norah, my young May Moon, your Harry tease you?" she tells him, "Yes; and I want to go home!"

A biled fowl, and baked bread-and-butter pudding, brought Mrs. Walmers up a little; but Boots could have wished, he must privately own to me, to have seen her more sensible of the woice of love, and less abandoning of herself to currants. However, Master Harry, he kept up, and his noble heart was as fond as ever. Mrs. Walmers turned very sleepy about dusk, and began to cry. Therefore, Mrs. Walmers went off to bed as per yesterday; and Master Harry ditto repeated.

About eleven or twelve at night comes back the Governor in a chaise, along with Mr. Walmers and a elderly lady. Mr. Walmers looks amused and very serious, both at once, and says to our missis, "We are much indebted to you, ma'am for your kind care of our little children, which we can never sufficiently acknowledge. Pray, ma'am, where is my boy?" Our missis says, "Cobbs has the dear child in charge, Sir. Cobbs, show Forty!" then he says to Cobbs, "Ah, Cobbs, I am glad to see *you!* I understood you was here!" And Cobbs says, "Yes, Sir. Your most obedient, Sir."

I may be surprised to hear Boots say it, perhaps; but Boots assures me that his heart beat like a hammer, going upstairs. "I beg your pardon, Sir," says he, while unlocking the door; "I hope you are not angry with Master Harry. For Master Harry is a fine boy, Sir, and will do you credit and honour." And Boots signifies to me, that, if the fine boy's father had contradicted him in the daring state of mind in which he then was, he thinks he should have "fetched him a crack," and taken the consequences.

But Mr. Walmers only says, "No, Cobbs. No, my good fellow. Thank you!" And, the door being opened, goes in.

Boots goes in too, holding the light, and he sees Mr. Walmers go up to the bedside, bend gently down, and kiss the little sleeping face. Then he stands looking at it for a minute, looking wonderfully like it (they do say he ran away with Mrs. Walmers); and then he gently shakes the little shoulder.

"Harry, my dear boy! Harry!"

Master Harry starts up and looks at him. Looks at Cobbs too. Such is the honour of that mite, that he looks at Cobbs, to see whether he has brought him into trouble.

"I am not angry, my child. I only want you to dress yourself and come home."

"Yes, pa."

Master Harry dresses himself quickly. His breast begins to swell when he has nearly finished, and it swells more and more as he stands, at last, a looking at his father: his father standing a looking at him, the quiet image of him.

"Please may I"—the spirit of that little creatur, and the way he kept his rising tears down!—"please, dear pa—may I—kiss Norah before I go?"

"You may, my child."

So he takes Master Harry in his hand, and Boots leads the way with the candle, and they come to that other bedroom, where the elderly lady is seated by the bed, and poor little Mrs. Harry Walmers, Junior, is fast asleep. There the father lifts the child up to the pillow, and he lays his little face down for an instant by the little warm face of poor unconscious little Mrs. Harry Walmers, Junior, and gently draws it to him,—a sight so touching to the chambermaids who are peeping through the door, that one of them calls out, "It's a shame to part 'em!" But this chambermaid was always, as Boots informs me, a soft-hearted one. Not that there was any harm in that girl. Far from it.

Finally, Boots says, that's all about it. Mr. Walmers drove away in the chaise, having hold of Master Harry's hand. The elderly lady and Mrs. Harry Walmers, Junior, that was never to be (she married a Captain long afterwards, and died in India), went off next day. In conclusion, Boots put it to me whether I hold with him in two opinions: firstly, that there art not many couples on their way to be married who are half as innocent of guile as those two children; secondly, that it would be a jolly good thing for a great many couples on their way to be married, if they could only be stopped in time, and brought back separately.

THIRD BRANCH   *The Bill*

I had been snowed up a whole week. The time had hung so lightly on my hands, that I should have been in great doubt of the fact but for a piece of documentary evidence that lay upon my table.

The road had been dug out of the snow on the previous day, and the document in question was my bill. It testified emphatically to my having eaten and drunk, and warmed myself, and slept among the sheltering branches of the Holly-Tree, seven days and nights.

I had yesterday allowed the road twenty-fours hours to improve itself, finding that I required that additional margin of time for the completion of my task. I had ordered my bill to be upon the table, and a chaise to be at the door, "at eight o'clock to-morrow evening." It was eight o'clock to-morrow evening when I buckled up my travelling writing-desk in its leather case, paid my bill, and got on my warm coats and wrappers. Of course, no time now remained for my travelling on to add a frozen tear to the icicles which were doubtless hanging plentifully about the farmhouse where I had first seen Angela. What I had to do was to get across to Liverpool by the shortest open road, there to meet my heavy baggage and embark. It was quite enough to do, and I had not an hour too much time to do it in.

I had taken leave of all my Holly-Tree friends—almost, for the time being, of my bashfulness too—and was standing for half a minute at the Inn door watching the ostler as he took another turn at the cord which tied my portmanteau on the chaise, when I saw lamps coming down towards the Holly-Tree. The road was so padded with snow that no wheels were audible; but all of us who were standing at the Inn door saw lamps coming on, and at a lively rate too, between the walls of snow that had been heaped up on either side of the track. The chambermaid instantly divined how the case stood, and called to the ostler, "Tom, this is a Gretna job!" The ostler, knowing that her sex instinctively scented a marriage, or anything in that direction, rushed up the yard bawling, "Next four out!" and in a moment the whole establishment was thrown into commotion.

I had a melancholy interest in seeing the happy man who loved and was beloved; and therefore, instead of driving off at once, I remained at the Inn door when the fugitives drove up. A bright-eyed fellow, muffled in a mantle, jumped out so briskly that he almost overthrew me. He turned to apologise, and, by Heaven, it was Edwin!

"Charley!" said he, recoiling. "Gracious powers, what do you do here?"

"Edwin," said I, recoiling, "gracious powers, what do *you* do here?" I struck my forehead as I said it, and an insupportable blaze of light seemed to shoot before my eyes.

He hurried me into the little parlour (always kept with a slow fire in it and no poker), where posting company waited while their horses were putting to, and, shutting the door, said:

"Charley, forgive me!"

"Edwin!" I returned. "Was this well? When I loved her so dearly! When I had garnered up my heart so long!" I could say no more.

He was shocked when he saw how moved I was, and made the cruel observation, that he had not thought I should have taken it so much to heart.

I looked at him. I reproached him no more. But I looked at him.

"My dear, dear Charley," said he, "don't think ill of me, I beseech you! I know you have a right to my utmost confidence, and, believe me, you have ever had it until now. I abhor secrecy. Its meanness is intolerable to me. But I and my dear girl have observed it for your sake."

He and his dear girl! It steeled me.

"You have observed it for my sake, Sir?" said I, wondering how his frank face could face it out so.

"Yes!—and Angela's," said he.

I found the room reeling round in an uncertain way, like a labouring humming-top. "Explain yourself," said I, holding on by one hand to an armchair.

"Dear old darling Charley!" returned Edwin, in his cordial manner, "consider! When you were going on so happily with Angela, why should I compromise you with the old gentleman by making you a party to our engagement, and (after he had declined my proposals) to our secret intention? Surely it was better that you should be able honourably to say, 'He never took counsel with me, never told me, never breathed a word of it.' If Angela suspected it, and showed me all the favour and support she could—God bless her for a precious creature and a priceless wife!—I couldn't help that. Neither I nor Emmeline ever told her, any more than we told you. And for the same good reason, Charley; trust me, for the same good reason, and no other upon earth!"

Emmeline was Angela's cousin. Lived with her. Had been brought up with her. Was her father's ward. Had property.

"Emmeline is in the chaise, my dear Edwin!" said I, embracing him with the greatest affection.

"My good fellow!" said he, "do you suppose I should be going to Gretna Green without her?"

I ran out with Edwin, I opened the chaise door, I took Emmeline in my arms, I folded her to my heart. She was wrapped in soft white fur, like the snowy landscape: but was warm, and young, and lovely. I put their leaders to with my own hands, I gave the boys a five-pound note apiece, I cheered them as they drove away, I drove the other way myself as hard as I could pelt.

I never went to Liverpool, I never went to America, I went straight back to London, and I married Angela. I have never until this time, even to her, disclosed the secret of my character, and the mistrust and the mistaken journey into which it led me. When she, and they, and our eight children and their seven—I mean Edwin's and Emmeline's, whose eldest girl is old enough now to wear white for herself, and to look very like her mother in it—come to read these pages, as of course they will, I shall hardly fail to be found out at last. Never mind! I can bear it. I began at the Holly-Tree, by idle accident, to associate the Christmas-time of year with human interest, and with some inquiry into, and some care for, the lives of those by whom I find myself surrounded. I hope that I am none the worse for it, and that no one near me or afar off is the worst for it. And I say, May the green Holly-Tree flourish, striking its roots deep into our English ground, and having its germinating qualities carried by the birds of Heaven all over the world!

—1855

Somebody's Luggage IN FOUR CHAPTERS

~~~~~~

CHAPTER I *His leaving it till called for*

The writer of these humble lines being a Waiter, and having come of a family of Waiters, and owning at the present time five brothers who are all Waiters, and likewise an only sister who is a Waitress, would wish to offer a few words respecting his calling; first having the pleasure of hereby in a friendly manner offering the Dedication of the same unto JOSEPH, much respected Head Waiter at the Slamjam Coffee-house, London, E.C., than which a individual more eminently deserving of the name of man, or a more amenable honour to his own head and heart, whether considered in the light of a Waiter or regarded as a human being, do not exist.

In case confusion should arise in the public mind (which it is open to confusion on many subjects) respecting what is meant or implied by the term Waiter, the present humble lines would wish to offer an explanation. It may not be generally known that the person as goes out to wait is *not* a Waiter. It may not be generally known that the hand as is called in extra, at the Freemasons' Tavern, or the London, or the Albion, or otherwise, is *not* a Waiter. Such hands may be took on for Public Dinners by the bushel (and you may know them by their breathing with difficulty when in attendance, and taking away the bottle ere yet it is half out); but such are *not* Waiters. For you cannot lay down the tailoring, or the shoemaking, or the brokering, or the green-grocering, or the pictorial-periodicalling, or the second-hand wardrobe, or the small fancy businesses,—you cannot lay down those lines of life at your will and pleasure by the halfday or evening, and take up Waitering. You may suppose you can, but you cannot; or you may go so far as to say you do, but you do not. Nor yet can you lay down the gentleman's-service when stimulated by prolonged incompatibility on the part of Cooks (and here it may be remarked that Cooking and Incompatibility will be mostly found united), and take up Waitering. It has been ascertained that what a gentleman will sit meek under, at home, he will not bear out of doors, at the Slamjam or any similar establishment. Then, what is the inference to be drawn respecting true Waitering? You must be bred to it. You must be born to it.

Would you know how born to it, Fair Reader,—if of the adorable female sex? Then learn from the biographical experience of one that is a Waiter in the sixty-first year of his age.

You were conveyed,—ere yet your dawning powers were otherwise developed than to harbour vacancy in your inside,—you were conveyed, by surreptitious means, into a pantry adjoining the Admiral Nelson, Civic and General Dining-Rooms, there to receive by stealth that healthful sustenance which is the pride and boast of the British female constitution. Your mother was married to your father (himself a distant Waiter) in the profoundest secrecy; for a Waitress known to be married would ruin the best of businesses,—it is the same as on the stage. Hence your being smuggled into the pantry, and that—to add to the infliction—by an unwilling grandmother. Under the combined influence of the smells of roast and boiled, and soup, and gas, and malt liquors, you partook of your earliest nourishment; your unwilling grandmother sitting prepared to catch you when your mother was called and dropped you; your grandmother's shawl ever ready to stifle your natural complainings; your innocent mind surrounded by uncongenial cruets, dirty plates, dish-covers, and cold gravy; your mother calling down the pipe for veals and porks, instead of soothing you with nursery rhymes. Under these untoward circumstances you were early weaned. Your unwilling grandmother, ever growing more unwilling as your food assimilated less, then contracted habits of shaking you till your system curdled, and your food would not assimilate at all. At length she was no longer spared, and could have been thankfully spared much sooner. When your brothers began to appear in succession, your mother retired, left off her smart dressing (she had previously been a smart dresser), and her dark ringlets (which had previously been flowing), and haunted your father late of nights, lying in wait for him, through all weathers, up the shabby court which led to the back door of the Royal Old Dust-Bin (said to have been so named by George the Fourth), where your father was Head. But the Dust-Bin was going down then, and your father took but little,—excepting from a liquid point of view. Your mother's object in those visits was of a housekeeping character, and you was set on to whistle your father out. Sometimes he came out, but generally not. Come or not come, however, all that part of his existence which was unconnected with open Waitering was kept a close secret, and was acknowledged by your mother to be a close secret, and you and your mother flitted about the court, close secrets both of you, and would scarcely have confessed under torture that you knew your father, or that your father had any name than Dick (which wasn't his name, though he was never known by any other), or that he had kith or kin or chick or child. Perhaps the attraction of this mystery, combined with your father's having a damp compartment to himself, behind a leaky cistern, at the Dust-Bin,—a sort of a cellar compartment, with a sink in it, and a smell, and a plate-rack, and a bottle-rack, and three windows that didn't match each other or anything else, and no daylight,—caused your young mind to feel convinced that you must grow up to be a Waiter too; but you did feel convinced of it, and so did all your brothers, down to your sister. Every one of you felt convinced that you was born to the Waitering. At this stage of your career, what was your feelings one day when your father came home to your mother in open broad daylight,—of itself an act of Madness on the part of a Waiter, —and took to his bed (leastwise, your mother and family's bed), with the statement that his eyes were devilled kidneys. Physicians being in vain, your father expired, after repeating at intervals for a day and a night, when gleams of reason and old business fitfully illuminated his being, "Two and two is five. And three is sixpence." Interred in the parochial department of the neighbouring churchyard, and accompanied to the grave by as many Waiters of long standing as could spare the morning time from their soiled glasses (namely, one), your bereaved form was attired in a white neckankecher, and you was took on from motives of benevolence at The George and Gridiron, theatrical and supper. Here, supporting nature on what you found in the plates (which was as it happened, and but too often thoughtlessly, immersed in mustard), and on what you found in the glasses (which rarely went beyond driblets and lemon), by night you dropped asleep standing, till you was cuffed awake, and by day was set to polishing every individual article in the coffee-room. Your couch being sawdust; your counterpane being ashes of cigars. Here, frequently hiding a heavy heart under the smart tie of your white neckankecher (or correctly speaking lower down and more to the left), you picked up the rudiments of knowledge from an extra, by the name of Bishops, and by calling plate-washer, and gradually elevating your mind with chalk on the back of the corner-box partition, until such time as you used the inkstand when it was out of hand, attained to manhood, and to be the Waiter that you find yourself.

I could wish here to offer a few respectful words on behalf of the calling so long the calling of myself and family, and the public interest in which is but too often very limited. We are not generally understood. No, we are not. Allowance enough is not made for us. For, say that we ever show a little drooping listlessness of spirits, or what might be termed indifference or apathy. Put it to yourself what would your own state of mind be, if you was one of an enormous family every member of which except you was always greedy, and in a hurry. Put it to yourself that you was regularly replete with animal food at the slack hours of one in the day and again at nine P.M., and that the repleter you was, the more voracious all your fellow-creatures came in. Put it to yourself that it was your business, when your digestion was well on, to take a personal interest and sympathy in a hundred gentlemen fresh and fresh (say, for the sake of argument, only a hundred), whose imaginations was given up to grease and fat and gravy and melted butter, and abandoned to questioning you about cuts of this, and dishes of that,—each of 'em going on as if him and you and the bill of fare was alone in the world. Then look what you are expected to know. You are never out, but they seem to think you regularly attend everywhere. "What's this, Christopher, that I hear about the smashed Excursion Train?"—"How are they doing at the Italian Opera, Christopher?"—"Christopher, what are the real particulars of this business at the Yorkshire Bank?" Similarly a ministry gives me more trouble than it gives the Queen. As to Lord Palmerston, the constant and wearing connexion into which I have been brought with his lordship during the last few years is deserving of a pension. Then look at the Hypocrites we are made, and the lies (white, I hope) that are forced upon us! Why must a sedentary-pursuited Waiter be considered to be a judge of horseflesh, and to have a most tremenjous interest in horse-training and racing? Yet it would be half our little incomes out of our pockets if we didn't take on to have those sporting tastes. It is the same (inconceivable why!) with Farming. Shooting, equally so. I am sure that so regular as the months of August, September, and October come round, I am ashamed of myself in my own private bosom for the way in which I make believe to care whether or not the grouse is strong on the wing (much their wings, or drumsticks either, signifies to me, uncooked!), and whether the partridges is plentiful among the turnips, and whether the pheasants is shy or bold, or anything else you please to mention. Yet you may see me, or any other Waiter of my standing, holding on by the back of the box, and leaning over a gentleman with his purse out and his bill before him, discussing these points in a confidential tone of voice, as if my happiness in life entirely depended on 'em.

I have mentioned our little incomes. Look at the most unreasonable point of all, and the point on which the greatest injustice is done us! Whether it is owing to our always carrying so much change in our right-hand trousers-pocket, and so many halfpence in our coat-tails, or whether it is human nature (which I were loth to believe), what is meant by the everlasting fable that Head Waiters is rich? How did that fable get into circulation? Who first put it about, and what are the facts to establish the unblushing statement? Come forth, thou slanderer, and refer the public to the Waiter's will in Doctors' Commons supporting thy malignant hiss! Yet this is so commonly dwelt upon—especially by the screws who give Waiters the least—that denial is vain; and we are obliged, for our credit's sake, to carry our heads as if we were going into a business, when of the two we are much more likely to go into a union. There was formerly a screw as frequented the Slamjam ere yet the present writer had quitted that establishment on a question of tea-ing his assistant staff out of his own pocket, which screw carried the taunt to its bitterest height. Never soaring above threepence, and as often as not grovelling on the earth a penny lower, he yet represented the present writer as a large holder of Consols, a lender of money on mortgage, a Capitalist. He has been overheard to dilate to other customers on the allegation that the present writer put out thousands of pounds at interest in Distilleries and Breweries. "Well, Christopher," he would say (having grovelled his lowest on the earth, half a moment before), "looking out for a House to open, eh? Can't find a business to be disposed of on a scale as is up to your resources, humph?" To such a dizzy precipice of falsehood has this misrepresentation taken wing, that the well-known and highly-respected OLD CHARLES, long eminent at the West Country Hotel, and by some considered the Father of the Waitering, found himself under the obligation to fall into it through so many years that his own wife (for he had an unbeknown old lady in that capacity towards himself) believed it! And what was the consequence? When he was borne to his grave on the shoulders of six picked Waiters, with six more for change, six more acting as pall-bearers, all keeping step in a pouring shower without a dry eye visible, and a concourse only inferior to Royalty, his pantry and lodgings was equally ransacked high and low for property, and none was found! How could it be found, when, beyond his last monthly collection of walking-sticks, umbrellas, and pocket-handkerchiefs (which happened to have been not yet disposed of, though he had ever been through life punctual in clearing off his collections by the month), there was no property existing? Such, however, is the force of this universal libel, that the widow of Old Charles, at the present hour an inmate of the Almshouses of the Cork-Cutters' Company, in Blue Anchor-road (identified sitting at the door of one of 'em, in a clean cap and a Windsor arm-chair, only last Monday), expects John's hoarded wealth to be found hourly! Nay, ere yet he had succumbed to the grisly dart, and when his portrait was painted in oils life-size, by subscription of the frequenters of the West Country, to hang over the coffee-room chimneypiece, there were not wanting those who contended that what is termed the accessories of such a portrait ought to be the Bank of England out of window, and a strong-box on the table. And but for better-regulated minds contending for a bottle and screw and the attitude of drawing,—and carrying their point,—it would have been so handed down to posterity.

I am now brought to the title of the present remarks. Having, I hope without offence to any quarter, offered such observations as I felt it my duty to offer, in a free country which has ever dominated the seas, on the general subject, I will now proceed to wait on the particular question.

At a momentous period of my life, when I was off, so far as concerned notice given, with a House that shall be nameless,—for the question on which I took my departing stand was a fixed charge for waiters, and no House as commits itself to that eminently un-English act of more than foolishness and baseness shall be advertised by me, —I repeat, at a momentous crisis, when I was off with a House too mean for mention, and not yet on with that to which I have ever since had the honour of being attached in the capacity of Head[1], I was casting about what to do next. Then it were that proposals were made to me on behalf of my present establishment. Stipulations were necessary on my part, emendations were necessary on my part: in the end, ratifications ensued on both sides, and I entered on a new career.

We are a bed business, and a coffee-room business. We are not a general dining business, nor do we wish it. In consequence, when diners drop in, we know what to give 'em as will keep 'em away another time. We are a Private Room or Family business also; but coffee-room principal. Me and the Directory and the Writing Materials and cetrer occupy a place to ourselves—a place fended off up a step or two at the end of the coffee-room, in what I call the good old-fashioned style. The good old-fashioned style is, that whatever you want, down to a wafer, you must be olely and solely dependent on the Head Waiter for. You must put yourself a new-born Child into his hands. There is no other way in which a business untinged with Continental Vice can be conducted. (It were bootless to add, that if languages is required to be jabbered and English is not good enough, both families and gentlemen had better go somewhere else.)

When I began to settle down in this right-principled and well-conducted House, I noticed, under the bed in No. 24 B (which it is up a angle off the staircase, and usually put off upon the lowly-minded), a heap of things in a corner. I asked our Head Chambermaid in the course of the day,

"What are them things in 24 B?"

To which she answered with a careless air,

"Somebody's Luggage."

Regarding her with a eye not free from severity, I says,

"Whose Luggage?"

Evading my eye, she replied,

"Lor! How should I know!"

—Being, it may be right to mention, a female of some pertness, though acquainted with her business.

A Head Waiter must be either Head or Tail. He must be at one

[1] *Its name and address at length, with other full particulars, all editorially struck out.*

extremity or the other of the social scale. He cannot be at the waist of it, or anywhere else but the extremities. It is for him to decide which of the extremities.

On the eventful occasion under consideration, I give Mrs. Pratchett so distinctly to understand my decision, that I broke her spirit as towards myself, then and there, and for good. Let not inconsistency be suspected on account of my mentioning Mrs. Pratchett as "Mrs.," and having formerly remarked that a waitress must not be married. Readers are respectfully requested to notice that Mrs. Pratchett was not a waitress, but a chambermaid. Now a chambermaid *may* be married; if Head, generally is married,—or says so. It comes to the same thing as expressing what is customary. (N.B. Mr. Pratchett is in Australia, and his address there is "the Bush.")

Having took Mrs. Pratchett down as many pegs as was essential to the future happiness of all parties, I requested her to explain herself.

"For instance," I says, to give her a little encouragement, "who is Somebody?"

"I give you my sacred honour, Mr. Christopher," answers Pratchett, "that I haven't the faintest notion."

But for the manner in which she settled her cap-strings, I should have doubted this; but in respect of positiveness it was hardly to be discriminated from an affidavit.

"Then you never saw him?" I followed her up with.

"Nor yet," said Mrs. Pratchett, shutting her eyes and making as if she had just took a pill of unusual circumference,—which gave a remarkable force to her denial,—"nor yet any servant in this house. All have been changed, Mr. Christopher, within five year, and Somebody left his luggage here before then."

Inquiry of Miss Martin yielded (in the language of the Bard of A. 1.) "confirmation strong." So it had really and truly happened. Miss Martin is the young lady at the bar as makes out our bills; and though higher than I could wish considering her station, is perfectly well-behaved.

Farther investigations led to the disclosure that there was a bill against this Luggage to the amount of two sixteen six. The luggage had been lying under the bedstead of 24 B over six year. The bedstead is a four-poster, with a deal of old hanging and valance, and is, as I once said, probably connected with more than 24 Bs,—which I remember my hearers was pleased to laugh at, at the time.

I don't know why,—when DO we know why?—but this Luggage laid heavy on my mind. I fell a wondering about Somebody, and what he had got and been up to. I couldn't satisfy my thoughts why he should leave so much Luggage against so small a bill. For I had the Luggage out within a day or two and turned it over, and the following were the items:—A black portmanteau, a black bag, a desk, a dressing-case, a brown-paper parcel, a hat-box, and an umbrella strapped to a walking-stick. It was all very dusty and fluey. I had our porter up to get under the bed and fetch it out; and though he habitually wallows in dust,—swims in it from morning to night, and wears a close-fitting waistcoat with black calimanco sleeves for the purpose, —it made him sneeze again, and his throat was that hot with it that it was obliged to be cooled with a drink of Allsopp's draft.

The Luggage so got the better of me, that instead of having it put back when it was well dusted and washed with a wet cloth,—previous to which it was so covered with feathers that you might have thought it was turning into poultry, and would by and by begin to Lay,—I say, instead of having it put back, I had it carried into one of my places downstairs. There from time to time I stared at it and stared at it, till it seemed to grow big and grow little, and come forward at me and retreat again, and go through all manner of performances resembling intoxication. When this had lasted weeks,—I may say months, and not be far out,—I one day thought of asking Miss Martin for the particulars of the Two sixteen six total. She was so obliging as to extract it from the books,—it dating before her time,—and here follows a true copy:

COFFEE-ROOM.

1856.		No. 4.	£	s.	d.
Feb. 2d,	Pen and Paper		0	0	6
	Port Negus		0	2	0
	Ditto		0	2	0
	Pen and Paper		0	0	6
	Tumbler broken		0	2	6
	Brandy		0	2	0
	Pen and paper		0	0	6
	Anchovy toast		0	2	6
	Pen and paper		0	0	6
	Bed		0	3	0
Feb. 3d,	Pen and paper		0	0	6
	Breakfast		0	2	6
	"	Broiled ham	0	2	0
	"	Eggs	0	1	0
	"	Watercresses	0	1	0
	Breakfast—Shrimps		0	1	0
	Pen and paper		0	0	6
	Blotting-paper		0	0	6
	Messenger to Paternoster-row and back		0	1	6
	Again, when No Answer		0	1	6
	Brandy 2s., Devilled Pork chop 2s.		0	4	0
	Pens and paper		0	1	0
	Messenger to Albermarle-street and back		0	1	0

Again (detained), when No Answer	o	1	6
Salt-cellar broken	o	3	6
Large Liqueur-glass Orange Brandy	o	1	6
Dinner, Soup, Fish, Joint, and bird	o	7	6
Bottle old East India Brown	o	8	o
Pen and paper	o	o	6
	£2	**16**	**6**

MEM.: *January 1st, 1857. He went out after dinner, directing Luggage to be ready when he called for it. Never called.*

So far from throwing a light upon the subject, this bill appeared to me, if I may so express my doubts, to involve it in a yet more lurid halo. Speculating it over with the Mistress, she informed me that the luggage had been advertised in the Master's time as being to be sold after such and such a day to pay expenses, but no farther steps had been taken. (I may here remark, that the Mistress is a widow in her fourth year. The Master was possessed of one of those unfortunate constitutions in which Spirits turns to Water, and rises in the ill starred Victim.)

My speculating it over, not then only, but repeatedly, sometimes with the Mistress, sometimes with one, sometimes with another, led up to the Mistress's saying to me,—whether at first in joke or in earnest, or half joke and half earnest, it matters not:

"Christopher, I am going to make you a handsome offer."

(If this should meet her eye—a lovely blue,—may she not take it ill my mentioning that if I had been eight or ten year younger, I would have done as much by her! That is, I would have made her a offer. It is for others than me to denominate it a handsome one.)

"Christopher, I am going to make you a handsome offer."

"Put a name to it, ma'am."

"Look here, Christopher. Run over the articles of Somebody's Luggage. You've got it all by heart, I know."

"A black portmanteau, ma'am, a black bag, a desk, a dressing-case, a brown-paper parcel, a hat-box, and an umbrella strapped to a walking-stick."

"All just as they were left. Nothing opened, nothing tampered with."

"You are right, ma'am. All locked but the brown-paper parcel, and that sealed."

The Mistress was leaning on Miss Martin's desk at the bar-window, and she taps the open book that lays upon the desk,—she has a pretty-made hand to be sure,—and bobs her head over it and laughs.

"Come," says she, "Christopher. Pay me Somebody's bill, and you shall have Somebody's Luggage."

I rather took to the idea from the first moment; but,

"It mayn't be worth the money," I objected, seeming to hold back.

"That's a Lottery," says the Mistress, folding her arms upon the book,—it ain't her hands alone that's pretty made, the observation extends right up her arms. "Won't you venture two pound sixteen shillings and sixpence in the Lottery? Why, there's no blanks!" says the Mistress, laughing and bobbing her head again, "you *must* win. If you lose, you must win! All prizes in this Lottery! Draw a blank, and remember, Gentlemen-Sportsmen, you'll still be entitled to a black portmanteau, a black bag, a desk, a dressing-case, a sheet of brown paper, a hat-box, and an umbrella strapped to a walking-stick!"

To make short of it, Miss Martin come round me, and Mrs. Pratchett come round me, and the Mistress she was completely round me already, and all the women in the house come round me, and if it had been Sixteen two instead of Two sixteen, I should have thought myself well out of it. For what can you do when they do come round you?

So I paid the money—down—and such a laughing as there was among 'em! But I turned the tables on 'em regularly, when I said:

"My family-name is Blue-Beard. I'm going to open Somebody's Luggage all alone in the Secret Chamber, and not a female eye catches sight of the contents!"

Whether I thought proper to have the firmness to keep to this, don't signify, or whether any female eye, and if any, how many, was really present when the opening of the Luggage came off. Somebody's Luggage is the question at present: Nobody's eyes, nor yet noses.

What I still look at most, in connexion with that Luggage, is the extraordinary quantity of writing-paper, and all written on! And not our paper neither,—not the paper charged in the bill, for we know our paper,—so he must have been always at it. And he had crumpled up this writing of his, everywhere, in every part and parcel of his luggage. There was writing in his dressing-case, writing in his boots, writing among his shaving-tackle, writing in his hat-box, writing folded away down among the very whalebones of his umbrella.

His clothes wasn't bad, what there was of 'em. His dressing-case was poor,—not a particle of silver stopper,—bottle apertures with nothing in 'em, like empty little dog-kennels,—and a most searching description of tooth-powder diffusing itself around, as under a deluded mistake that all the chinks in the fittings was divisions in teeth. His clothes I parted with, well enough, to a second-hand dealer not far from St. Clement's Danes, in the Strand,—him as the officers in the Army mostly dispose of their uniforms to, when hard pressed with debts of honour, if I may judge from their coats and epaulets diversifying the window with their backs towards the public. The same party bought in one lot the portmanteau, the bag, the desk, the dressing-case, the hat-box, the umbrella, strap, and walking-stick. On my remarking that I should have thought those articles not quite in his line, he said: "No more ith a man'th grandmother, Mithter Chrithtopher; but if any man will bring hith grandmother here, and offer her at a fair trifle below what the'll feth with good luck when the 'th thcoured and turned—I'll buy her!"

These transactions brought me home, and, indeed, more than home, for they left a goodish profit on the original investment. And now there remained the writings; and the writings I particular wish to bring under the candid attention of the reader.

I wish to do so without postponement, for this reason. This is to say, namely, viz. i.e., as follows, thus:—Before I proceed to recount the mental sufferings of which I became the prey in consequence of the writings, and before following up that harrowing tale with a statement of the wonderful and impressive catastrophe, as thrilling in its nature as unlooked for in any other capacity, which crowned the ole and filled the cup of unexpectedness to overflowing, the writings themselves ought to stand forth to view. Therefore it is that they now come next. One word to introduce them, and I lay down my pen (I hope, my unassuming pen) until I take it up to trace the gloomy sequel of a mind with something on it.

He was a smeary writer, and wrote a dreadful bad hand. Utterly regardless of ink, he lavished it on every undeserving object,—on his clothes, his desk, his hat, the handle of his tooth-brush, his umbrella. Ink was found freely on the coffee-room carpet by No. 4 table, and two blots was on his restless couch. A reference to the document I have given entire will show that on the morning of the third of February, eighteen fifty-six, he procured his no less than fifth pen and paper. To whatever deplorable act of ungovernable composition he immolated those materials obtained from the bar, there is no doubt that the fatal deed was committed in bed, and that it left its evidences but too plainly, long afterwards, upon the pillow-case.

He had put no Heading to any of his writings. Alas! Was he likely to have a Heading without a Head, and where was *his* Head when he took such things into it? In some cases, such as his Boots, he would appear to have hid the writings; thereby involving his style in greater obscurity. But his boots was at least pairs,—and no two of his writings can put in any claim to be so regarded. Here follows (not to give more specimens) what was found in—

CHAPTER II *His boots*

"Eh! well then, Monsieur Mutuel! What do I know, what can I say? I assure you that he calls himself Monsieur The Englishman."

"Pardon. But I think it is impossible," said Monsieur Mutuel,—a spectacled, snuffy, stooping old gentleman in carpet shoes and a cloth cap with a peaked shade, a loose blue frock-coat reaching to his heels, a large limp white shirt-frill, and cravat to correspond,—that is to say, white was the natural colour of his linen on Sundays, but it toned down with the week.

"It is," repeated Monsieur Mutuel, his amiable old walnut-shell countenance very walnut-shelly indeed as he smiled and blinked in the bright morning sunlight,—"it is, my cherished Madame Bouclet, I think, impossible!"

"Hey!" (with a little vexed cry and a great many tosses of her head.) "But it is not impossible that you are a Pig!" retorted Madame Bouclet, a compact little woman of thirty-five or so. "See then, —look there,—read! 'On the second floor Monsieur L'Anglais.' Is it not so?"

"It is so," said Monsieur Mutuel.

"Good. Continue your morning walk. Get out!" Madame Bouclet dismissed him with a lively snap of her fingers.

The morning walk of Monsieur Mutuel was in the brightest patch that the sun made in the Grande Place of a dull old fortified French town. The manner of his morning walk was with his hands crossed behind him; an umbrella, in figure the express image of himself, always in one hand; a snuff-box in the other. Thus, with the shuffling gait of the Elephant (who really does deal with the very worst trousers-maker employed by the Zoological world, and who appeared to have recommended him to Monsieur Mutuel), the old gentleman sunned himself daily when sun was to be had—of course, at the same time sunning a red ribbon at his button-hole; for was he not an ancient Frenchman?

Being told by one of the angelic sex to continue his morning walk and get out, Monsieur Mutuel laughed a walnut-shell laugh, pulled off his cap at arm's length with the hand that contained his snuff-box, kept it off for a considerable period after he had parted from Madame Bouclet, and continued his morning walk and got out, like a man of gallantry as he was.

The documentary evidence to which Madame Bouclet had referred Monsieur Mutuel was the list of her lodgers, sweetly written forth by her own Nephew and Bookkeeper, who held the pen of an Angel, and posted up at the side of her gateway, for the information of the Police: "Au second, M. L'Anglais, Propriétaire." On the second floor, Mr. The Englishman, man of property. So it stood; nothing could be plainer.

Madame Bouclet now traced the line with her forefinger, as it were to confirm and settle herself in her parting snap at Monsieur Mutuel, and so placing her right hand on her hip with a defiant air, as if nothing should ever tempt her to unsnap that snap, strolled out into the Place to glance up at the windows of Mr. The Englishman. That worthy happening to be looking out of window at the moment, Madame Bouclet gave him a graceful salutation with her head, looked to the right and looked to the left to account to him for her being there, considered for a moment, like one who accounted to herself for somebody she had expected not being there, and re-entered her own gateway. Madame Bouclet let all her house giving on the Place in furnished flats or floors, and lived up the yard behind in company with Monsieur Bouclet her husband (great at billiards), an inherited brewing business, several fowls, two carts, a nephew, a little dog in a big kennel, a grape-vine, a counting-house, four horses, a married sister (with a share in the brewing business), the husband and two children of the married sister, a parrot, a drum (performed on by the little boy of the married sister), two billeted soldiers, a quantity of pigeons, a fife (played by the nephew in a ravishing manner), several domestics and supernumeraries, a perpetual flavour of coffee and soup, a terrific range of artificial rocks and wooden precipices at least four feet high, a small fountain, and half-a-dozen large sunflowers.

Now the Englishman, in taking his Appartement,—or, as one might say on our side of the Channel, his set of chambers,—had given his name, correct to the letter, LANGLEY. But as he had a British way of not opening his mouth very wide on foreign soil, except at meals, the Brewery had been able to make nothing of it but L'Anglais. So Mr. The Englishman he had become and he remained.

"Never saw such a people!" muttered Mr. The Englishman, as he now looked out of window. "Never did, in my life!"

This was true enough, for he had never before been out of his own country,—a right little island, a tight little island, a bright little island, a show-fight little island, and full of merit of all sorts; but not the whole round world.

"These chaps," said Mr. The Englishman to himself, as his eye rolled over the Place, sprinkled with military here and there, "are no more like soldiers—" Nothing being sufficiently strong for the end of his sentence, he left it unended.

This again (from the point of view of his experience) was strictly correct; for though there was a great agglomeration of soldiers in the town and neighbouring country, you might have held a grand Review and Field-day of them every one, and looked in vain among them all for a soldier choking behind his foolish stock, or a soldier lamed by his ill-fitting shoes, or a soldier deprived of the use of his limbs by straps and buttons, or a soldier elaborately forced to be self-helpless in all the small affairs of life. A swarm of brisk, bright, active, bustling, handy, odd, skirmishing fellows, able to turn cleverly at anything, from a siege to soup, from great guns to needles and thread, from the broadsword exercise to slicing an onion, from making war to making omelets, was all you would have found.

What a swarm! From the Great Place under the eye of Mr. The Englishman, where a few awkward squads from the last conscription were doing the goose-step—some members of those squads still as to their bodies, in the chrysalis peasant-state of Blouse, and only military butterflies as to their regimentally-clothed legs—from the Great Place, away outside the fortifications, and away for miles along the dusty roads, soldiers swarmed. All day long, upon the grass-grown ramparts of the town, practising soldiers trumpeted and bugled; all day long, down in angles of dry trenches, practising soldiers drummed and drummed. Every forenoon, soldiers burst out of the great barracks into the sandy gymnasium-ground hard by, and flew over the wooden horse, and hung on to flying ropes, and dangled upside-down between parallel bars, and shot themselves off wooden platforms,— splashes, sparks, coruscations, showers of soldiers. At every corner of the town-wall, every guard-house, every gateway, every sentry-box, every drawbridge, every reedy ditch, and rushy dike, soldiers, soldiers, soldiers. And the town being pretty well all wall, guard-house, gateway, sentry-box, drawbridge, reedy ditch, and rushy dike, the town was pretty well all soldiers.

What would the sleepy old town have been without the soldiers, seeing that even with them it had so overslept itself as to have slept its echoes hoarse, its defensive bars and locks and bolts and chains all rusty, and its ditches stagnant! From the days when VAUBAN engineered it to that perplexing extent that to look at it was like being knocked on the head with it, the stranger becoming stunned and stertorous under the shock of its incomprehensibility,—from the days when VAUBAN made it the express incorporation of every substantive and adjective in the art of military engineering, and not only twisted you into it and twisted you out of it, to the right, to the left, opposite, under here, over there, in the dark, in the dirt, by the gateway, archway, covered way, dry way, wet way, fosse, portcullis, drawbridge, sluice, squat tower, pierced wall, and heavy battery, but likewise took a fortifying dive under the neighbouring country, and came to the surface three or four miles off, blowing out incomprehensible mounds and batteries among the quiet crops of chicory and beet-root,—from those days to these the town had been asleep, and dust and rust and must had settled on its drowsy Arsenals and Magazines, and grass had grown up in its silent streets.

On market-days alone, its Great Place suddenly leaped out of bed. On market-days, some friendly enchanter struck his staff upon the stones of the Great Place, and instantly arose the liveliest booths and stalls, and sittings and standings, and a pleasant hum of chaffering and huckstering from many hundreds of tongues, and a pleasant, though peculiar, blending of colours,—white caps, blue blouses, and green vegetables,—and at last the Knight destined for the adventure seemed to have come in earnest, and all the Vaubanois sprang up awake. And now, by long, low-lying avenues of trees, jolting in white-hooded donkey-cart, and on donkey-back, and in tumbril and wagon, and cart and cabriolet, and afoot with barrow and burden,—and along the dikes and ditches and canals, in little peak-prowed country boats —came peasant-men and women in flocks and crowds, bringing articles for sale. And here you had boots and shoes, and sweetmeats and stuffs to wear, and here (in the cool shade of the Town-hall) you had milk and cream and butter and cheese, and here you had fruits and onions and carrots, and all things needful for your soup, and here you had poultry and flowers and protesting pigs, and here new shovels, axes, spades, and bill-hooks for your farming work, and here huge mounds of bread, and here your unground grain in sacks, and here your children's dolls, and here the cake-seller, announcing his wares by beat and roll of drum. And hark! fanfaronade of trumpets, and here into the Great Place, resplendent in an open carriage, with four gorgeously-attired servitors up behind, playing horns, drums, and cymbals, rolled "the Daughter of a Physician" in massive golden chains and earrings, and blue-feathered hat, shaded from the admiring sun by two immense umbrellas of artificial roses, to dispense (from motives of philanthropy) that small and pleasant dose which had cured so many thousands! Toothache, earache, headache, heartache, stomachache, debility, nervousness, fits, fainting, fever, ague, all equally cured by the small and pleasant dose of the great Physician's great daughter! The process was this,—she, the Daughter of a Physician, proprietress of the superb equipage you now admired with its confirmatory blasts of trumpet, drum, and cymbal, told you so: On the first day after taking the small and pleasant dose, you would feel no particular influence beyond a most harmonious sensation of indescribable and irresistible joy; on the second day you would be so astonishingly better that you would think yourself changed into somebody else; on the third day you would be entirely free from your disorder, whatever its nature and however long you had had it, and would seek out the Physician's Daughter to throw yourself at her feet, kiss the hem of her garment, and buy as many more of the small and pleasant doses as by the sale of all your few effects you could obtain; but she would be inaccessible,—gone for herbs to the Pyramids of Egypt,—and you would be (though cured) reduced to despair! Thus would the Physician's Daughter drive her trade (and briskly too), and thus would the buying and selling and mingling of tongues and colours continue, until the changing sunlight, leaving the Physician's Daughter in the shadow of high roofs, admonished her to jolt out westward, with a departing effect of gleam and glitter on the splendid equipage and brazen blast. And now the enchanter struck his staff upon the stones of the Great Place once more, and down went the booths, the sittings and standings, and vanished the merchandise, and with it the barrows, donkeys, donkey-carts, and tumbrils, and all other things on wheels and feet, except the slow scavengers with unwieldy carts and meagre horses clearing up the rubbish, assisted by the sleek town pigeons, better plumped out than on non-market days. While there was yet an hour or two to wane before the autumn sunset, the loiterer outside town-gate and drawbridge, and postern and double-ditch, would see the last white-hooded cart lessening in the avenue of lengthening shadows of trees, or the last country boat, paddled by the last market-woman on her way home, showing black upon the reddening, long, low, narrow dike between him and the mill; and as the paddle-parted scum and weed closed over the boats's track, he might be comfortably sure that its sluggish rest would be troubled no more until next market-day.

As it was not one of the Great Place's days for getting out of bed, when Mr. The Englishman looked down at the young soldiers practising the goose-step there, his mind was left at liberty to take a military turn.

"These fellows are billeted everywhere about," said he; "and to see them lighting the people's fires, boiling the people's pots, minding the people's babies, rocking the people's cradles, washing the people's greens, and making themselves generally useful, in every sort of un-military way, is most ridiculous! Never saw such a set of fellows,—never did in my life!"

All perfectly true again. Was there not Private Valentine in that very house, acting as sole housemaid, valet, cook, steward, and nurse, in the family of his captain, Monsieur le Capitaine de la Cour,—cleaning the floors, making the beds, doing the marketing, dressing the captain, dressing the dinners, dressing the salads, and dressing the baby, all with equal readiness? Or, to put him aside, he being in loyal attendance on his Chief, was there not Private Hyppolite, billeted at the Perfumer's two hundred yards off, who, when not on duty, volunteered to keep shop while the fair Perfumeress stepped out to speak to a neighbour or so, and laughingly sold soap with his war-sword girded on him? Was there not Emile, billeted at the Clockmaker's, perpetually turning to of an evening, with his coat off, winding up the stock? Was there not Eugène, billeted at the Tinman's, cultivating, pipe in mouth, a garden four feet square, for the Tinman, in the little court, behind the shop, and extorting the fruits of the earth from the same, on his knees, with the sweat of his brow? Not to multiply examples, was there not Baptiste, billeted on the poor Water-carrier, at that very instant sitting on the pavement in the sunlight, with his martial legs asunder, and one of the Water-carrier's spare pails between them, which (to the delight and glory of the heart of the Water-carrier coming across the Place from the fountain, yoked and burdened) he was painting bright-green outside and bright-red within? Or, to go no farther than the Barber's at the very next door, was there not Corporal Théophile——

"No," said Mr. The Englishman, glancing down at the Barber's, "he is not there at present. There's the child, though."

A mere mite of a girl stood on the steps of the Barber's shop, looking across the Place. A mere baby, one might call her, dressed in the close white linen cap which small French country children wear (like the children in Dutch pictures), and in a frock of homespun blue, that had no shape except where it was tied round her little fat throat. So that, being naturally short and round all over, she looked, behind, as if she had been cut off at her natural waist, and had had her head neatly fitted on it.

"There's the child, though."

To judge from the way in which the dimpled hand was rubbing the eyes, the eyes had been closed in a nap, and were newly opened. But they seemed to be looking so intently across the Place, that the Englishman looked in the same direction.

"O!" said he presently. "I thought as much. The Corporal's there."

The Corporal, a smart figure of a man of thirty, perhaps a thought under the middle size, but very neatly made,—a sun-burnt Corporal with a brown peaked beard,—faced about at the moment, addressing voluble words of instruction to the squad in hand. Nothing was amiss or awry about the Corporal. A lithe and nimble Corporal, quite complete, from the sparkling dark eyes under his knowing uniform cap to his sparkling white gaiters. The very image and presentment of a Corporal of his country's army, in the line of his shoulders, the line of his waist, the broadest line of his Bloomer trousers, and their narrowest line at the calf of his leg.

Mr. The Englishman looked on, and the child looked on, and the Corporal looked on (but the last-named at his men), until the drill ended a few minutes afterwards, and the military sprinkling dried up directly, and was gone. Then said Mr. The Englishman to himself, "Look here! By George!" And the Corporal, dancing towards the Barber's with his arms wide open, caught up the child, held her over his head in a flying attitude, caught her down again, kissed her, and' made off with her into the Barber's house.

Now Mr. The Englishman had had a quarrel with his erring and disobedient and disowned daughter, and there was a child in that case too. Had not his daughter been a child, and had she not taken angel-flights above his head as this child had flown above the Corporal's? "He's a"—National Participled—"fool!" said the Englishman, and' shut his window.

But the windows of the house of Memory, and the windows of the house of Mercy, are not so easily closed as windows of glass and wood. They fly open unexpectedly; they rattle in the night; they must be nailed up. Mr. The Englishman had tried nailing them, but had not driven the nails quite home. So he passed but a disturbed evening and a worse night.

By nature a good-tempered man? No; very little gentleness, confounding the quality with weakness. Fierce and wrathful when crossed? Very, and stupendously unreasonable. Moody? Exceedingly so. Vindictive? Well; he *had* had scowling thoughts that he would formally curse his daughter, as he had seen it done on the stage. But remembering that the real Heaven is some paces removed from the mock one in the great chandelier of the Theatre, he had given that up.

And he had come abroad to be rid of his repudiated daughter for the rest of his life. And here he was.

At bottom, it was for this reason, more than for any other, that Mr. The Englishman took it extremely ill that Corporal Théophile should be so devoted to little Bebelle, the child at the Barber's shop. In an unlucky moment he had chanced to say to himself, "Why, confound the fellow, he is not her father!" There was a sharp sting in the speech which ran into him suddenly, and put him in a worse mood. So he had National Participled the unconscious Corporal with most hearty emphasis, and had made up his mind to think no more about such a mountebank.

But it came to pass that the Corporal was not to be dismissed. If he had known the most delicate fibres of the Englishman's mind, instead of knowing nothing on earth about him, and if he had been the most obstinate Corporal in the Grand Army of France, instead of being the most obliging, he could not have planted himself with more determined immovability plump in the midst of all the Englishman's thoughts. Not only so, but he seemed to be always in his view. Mr. The Englishman had but to look out of window, to look upon the Corporal with little Bebelle. He had but to go for a walk, and there was the Corporal walking with Bebelle. He had' but to come home again, disgusted, and the Corporal and Bebelle were at home before him. If he looked out at his back windows early in the morning, the Corporal was in the Barber's back yard, washing and dressing and

brushing Bebelle. If he took refuge at his front windows, the Corporal
brought his breakfast out into the Place, and shared it there with
Bebelle. Always Corporal and always Bebelle. Never Corporal without
Bebelle. Never Bebelle without Corporal.

Mr. The Englishman was not particularly strong in the French
language as a means of oral communication, though he read it very
well. It is with languages as with people,—when you only know them
by sight, you are apt to mistake them; you must be on speaking terms
before you can be said to have established an acquaintance.

For this reason, Mr. The Englishman had to gird up his loins
considerably before he could bring himself to the point of exchanging ideas with Madame Bouclet on the subject of this Corporal
and this Bebelle. But Madame Bouclet looking in apologetically one
morning to remark, that, O Heaven! she was in a state of desolation
because the lamp-maker had not sent home that lamp confided to him
to repair, but that truly he was a lamp-maker against whom the whole
world shrieked out, Mr. The Englishman seized the occasion.

"Madame, that baby——"

"Pardon, monsieur. That lamp."

"No, no, that little girl."

"But, pardon!" said Madame Bouclet, angling for a clew, "one
cannot light a little girl, or send her to be repaired?"

"The little girl—at the house of the barber."

"Ah-h-h!" cried Madame Bouclet, suddenly catching the idea with
her delicate little line and rod. "Little Bebelle? Yes, yes, yes! And her
friend the Corporal? Yes, yes, yes, yes! So genteel of him,—is it not?"

"He is not——?"

"Not at all; not at all! He is not one of her relations. Not at all!"

"Why, then, he——"

"Perfectly!" cried Madame Bouclet, "you are right, monsieur. It is
so genteel of him. The less relation, the more genteel. As you say."

"Is she——?"

"The child of the barber?" Madame Bouclet whisked up her skil-
ful little line and rod again. "Not at all, not at all! She is the child of—
in a word, of no one."

"The wife of the barber, then——?"

"Indubitably. As you say. The wife of the barber receives a small
stipend to take care of her. So much by the month. Eh, then! It is
without doubt very little, for we are all poor here."

"You are not poor, madame."

"As to my lodgers," replied Madame Bouclet, with a smiling
and a gracious bend of her head, "no. As to all things else, so-so."

"You flatter me, madame."

"Monsieur, it is you who flatter me in living here."

Certain fishy gasps on Mr. The Englishman's part, denoting that he was about to resume his subject under difficulties, Madame Bouclet observed him closely, and whisked up her delicate line and rod again with triumphant success.

"O no, monsieur, certainly not. The wife of the barber is not cruel to the poor child, but she is careless. Her health is delicate, and she sits all day, looking out at window. Consequently, when the Corporal first came, the poor little Bebelle was much neglected."

"It is a curious——" began Mr. The Englishman.

"Name? That Bebelle? Again you are right, monsieur. But it is a playful name for Gabrielle."

"And so the child is a mere fancy of the Corporal's?" said Mr. The Englishman, in a gruffly disparaging tone of voice.

"Eh, well!" returned Madame Bouclet, with a pleading shrug: "one must love something. Human nature is weak."

("Devilish weak," muttered the Englishman, in his own language.)

"And the Corporal," pursued Madame Bouclet, "being billeted at the barber's,—where he will probably remain a long time, for he is attached to the General,—and finding the poor unowned child in need of being loved, and finding himself in need of loving,—why, there you have it all, you see!"

Mr. The Englishman accepted this interpretation of the matter with an indifferent grace, and observed to himself, in an injured manner, when he was again alone: "I shouldn't mind it so much, if these people were not such a"—National Participled—"sentimental people!"

There was a Cemetery outside the town, and it happened ill for the reputation of the Vaubanois, in this sentimental connexion, that he took a walk there that same afternoon. To be sure there were some wonderful things in it (from the Englishman's point of view), and of a certainty in all Britain you would have found nothing like it. Not to mention the fanciful flourishes of hearts and crosses in wood and iron, that were planted all over the place, making it look very like a Firework-ground, where a most splendid pyrotechnic display might be expected after dark, there were so many wreaths upon the graves, embroidered, as it might be, "To my mother," "To my daughter," "To my father," "To my brother," "To my sister," "To my friend," and those many wreaths were in so many stages of elaboration and decay, from the wreath of yesterday, all fresh colour and bright beads, to the wreath of last year, a poor mouldering wisp of straw! There were so many little gardens and grottoes made upon graves, in so many tastes, with plants and shells and plaster figures and porcelain pitchers, and so many odds and ends! There were so many tributes of remembrance hanging up, not to be discriminated by the closest inspection from little round waiters, whereon were depicted in glowing hues either a lady or a gentleman with a white pocket-handkerchief out of all proportion, leaning, in a state of the most faultless mourning and most profound affliction, on the most architectural and gorgeous urn! There were so many surviving wives who had put their names on the tombs of their deceased husbands, with a blank for the date of their own departure from this weary world; and there were so many surviving husbands who had rendered the same homage to their deceased wives; and out of the number there must have been so many who had long ago married again! In fine, there was so much in the place that would have seemed mere frippery to a stranger, save for the consideration that the lightest paper flower that lay upon the poorest heap of earth was never touched by a rude hand, but perished there, a sacred thing!

"Nothing of the solemnity of Death here," Mr. The Englishman had been going to say, when this last consideration touched him with a mild appeal, and on the whole he walked out without saying it. "But these people are," he insisted, by way of compensation, when he was well outside the gate, "they are so"—Participled—"sentimental!"

His way back lay by the military gymnasium-ground. And there he passed the Corporal glibly instructing young soldiers how to swing themselves over rapid and deep water-courses on their way to Glory, by means of a rope, and himself deftly plunging off a platform, and flying a hundred feet or two, as an encouragement to them to begin. And there he also passed, perched on a crowning eminence (probably by the Corporal's careful hands), the small Bebelle, with her round eyes wide open, surveying the proceeding like a wondering sort of blue and white bird.

"If that child was to die," this was his reflection as he turned his back and went his way,—"and it would almost serve the fellow right for making such a fool of himself,—I suppose we should have *him* sticking up a wreath and a waiter in that fantastic burying-ground."

Nevertheless, after another early morning or two of looking out of window, he strolled down into the Place, when the Corporal and Bebelle were walking there, and touching his hat to the Corporal (an immense achievement), wished him Good-day.

"Good-day, monsieur."

"This is a rather pretty child you have here," said Mr. The Englishman, taking her chin in his hand, and looking down into her astonished blue eyes.

"Monsieur, she is a very pretty child," returned the Corporal, with a stress on his polite correction of the phrase.

"And good?" said the Englishman.

"And very good. Poor little thing!"

"Hah!" The Englishman stooped down and patted her cheek, not without awkwardness, as if he were going too far in his conciliation. "And what is this medal round your neck, my little one?"

Bebelle having no other reply on her lips than her chubby right fist, the Corporal offered his services as interpreter.

"Monsieur demands, what is this, Bebelle?"

"It is the Holy Virgin," said Bebelle.

"And who gave it you?" asked the Englishman.

"Théophile."

"And who is Théophile?"

Bebelle broke into a laugh, laughed merrily and heartily, clapped her chubby hands, and beat her little feet on the stone pavement of the Place.

"He doesn't know Théophile! Why, he doesn't know any one! He doesn't know anything!" Then, sensible of a small solecism in her manners, Bebelle twisted her right hand in a leg of the Corporal's Bloomer trousers, and, laying her cheek against the place, kissed it.

"Monsieur Théophile, I believe?" said the Englishman to the Corporal.

"It is I, monsieur."

"Permit me." Mr. The Englishman shook him heartily by the hand and turned away. But he took it mighty ill that old Monsieur Mutuel in his patch of sunlight, upon whom he came as he turned, should pull off his cap to him with a look of pleased approval. And he muttered, in his own tongue, as he returned the salutation, "Well, walnut-shell! And what business is it of *yours*?"

Mr. The Englishman went on for many weeks passing but disturbed evenings and worse nights, and constantly experiencing that those aforesaid windows in the houses of Memory and Mercy rattled after dark, and that he had very imperfectly nailed them up. Likewise, he went on for many weeks daily improving the acquaintance of the Corporal and Bebelle. That is to say, he took Bebelle by the chin, and the Corporal by the hand, and offered Bebelle sous and the Corporal cigars, and even got the length of changing pipes with the Corporal and kissing Bebelle. But he did it all in a shamefaced way, and always took it extremely ill that Monsieur Mutuel in his patch of sunlight should note what he did. Whenever that seemed to be the case, he always growled in his own tongue, "There you are again, walnut-shell! What business is it of *yours*?"

In a word, it had become the occupation of Mr. The Englishman's life to look after the Corporal and little Bebelle, and to resent old Monsieur Mutuel's looking after *him*. An occupation only varied by a fire in the town one windy night, and much passing of water-buckets from hand to hand (in which the Englishman rendered good service), and much beating of drums,—when all of a sudden the Corporal disappeared.

Next, all of a sudden, Bebelle disappeared.

She had been visible a few days later than the Corporal,—sadly deteriorated as to washing and brushing,—but she had not spoken when addressed by Mr. The Englishman, and had looked scared and had run away. And now it would seem that she had run away for good. And there lay the Great Place under the windows, bare and barren.

In his shamefaced and constrained way, Mr. The Englishman asked no question of any one, but watched from his front windows and watched from his back windows, and lingered about the Place, and peeped in at the Barber's shop, and did all this and much more with a whistling and tune-humming pretence of not missing anything, until one afternoon when Monsieur Mutuel's patch of sunlight was in shadow, and when, according to all rule and precedent, he had no right whatever to bring his red ribbon out of doors, behold here he was, advancing with his cap already in his hand twelve paces off!

Mr. The Englishman had got as far into his usual objurgation as, "What bu—si—" when he checked himself.

"Ah, it is sad, it is sad! Hélas, it is unhappy, it is sad!" Thus old Monsieur Mutuel, shaking his grey head.

"What busin—at least, I would say, what do you mean, Monsieur Mutuel?"

"Our Corporal. Hélas, our dear Corporal!"

"What has happened to him?"

"You have not heard?"

"No."

"At the fire. But he was so brave, so ready. Ah, too brave, too ready!"

"May the Devil carry you away!" the Englishman broke in impatiently; "I beg your pardon,—I mean me,—I am not accustomed to speak French,—go on, will you?"

"And a falling beam——"

"Good God!" exclaimed the Englishman. "It was a private soldier who was killed?"

"No. A Corporal, the same Corporal, our dear Corporal. Beloved by all his comrades. The funeral ceremony was touching,—penetrating. Monsieur The Englishman, your eyes fill with tears."

"What bu—si——"

"Monsieur The Englishman, I honour those emotions. I salute you with profound respect. I will not obtrude myself upon your noble heart."

Monsieur Mutuel,—a gentleman in every thread of his cloudy linen, under whose wrinkled hand every grain in the quarter of an ounce of poor snuff in his poor little tin box became a gentleman's property, —Monsieur Mutuel passed on, with his cap in his hand.

"I little thought," said the Englishman, after walking for several minutes, and more than once blowing his nose, "when I was looking round that cemetery—I'll go there!"

Straight he went there, and when he came within the gate he paused, considering whether he should ask at the lodge for some direction to the grave. But he was less than ever in a mood for asking questions, and he thought, "I shall see something on it to know it by."

In search of the Corporal's grave he went softly on, up this walk and down that, peering in, among the crosses and hearts and columns and obelisks and tombstones, for a recently disturbed spot. It troubled him now to think how many dead there were in the cemetery,—he had not thought them a tenth part so numerous before,—and after he had walked and sought for some time, he said to himself, as he struck down a new vista of tombs, "I might suppose that every one was dead but I."

Not every one. A live child was lying on the ground asleep. Truly he had found something on the Corporal's grave to know it by, and the something was Bebelle.

With such a loving will had the dead soldier's comrades worked at his resting-place, that it was already a neat garden. On the green turf of the garden Bebelle lay sleeping, with her cheek touching it. A plain, unpainted little wooden Cross was planted in the turf, and her short arm embraced this little Cross, as it had many a time embraced the Corporal's neck. They had put a tiny flag (the flag of France) at his head, and a laurel garland.

Mr. The Englishman took off his hat, and stood for a while silent. Then, covering his head again, he bent down on one knee, and softly roused the child.

"Bebelle! My little one!"

Opening her eyes, on which the tears were still wet, Bebelle was at first frightened; but seeing who it was, she suffered him to take her in his arms, looking steadfastly at him.

"You must not lie here, my little one. You must come with me."

"No, no. I can't leave Théophile. I want the good dear Théophile."

"We will go and seek him, Bebelle. We will go and look for him in England. We will go and look for him at my daughter's, Bebelle."

"Shall we find him there?"

"We shall find the best part of him there. Come with me, poor forlorn little one. Heaven is my witness," said the Englishman, in a low voice, as, before he rose, he touched the turf above the gentle Corporal's breast, "that I thankfully accept this trust!"

It was a long way for the child to have come unaided. She was soon asleep again, with her embrace transferred to the Englishman's neck. He looked at her worn shoes, and her galled feet, and her tired face, and believed that she had come there every day.

He was leaving the grave with the slumbering Bebelle in his arms, when he stopped, looked wistfully down at it, and looked wistfully at the other graves around. "It is the innocent custom of the people," said Mr. The Englishman, with hesitation. "I think I should like to do it. No one sees."

Careful not to wake Bebelle as he went, he repaired to the lodge where such little tokens of remembrance were sold, and bought two wreaths. One, blue and white and glistening silver, "To my friend;" one of a soberer red and black and yellow, "To my friend." With these he went back to the grave, and so down on one knee again. Touching the child's lips with the brighter wreath, he guided her hand to hang it on the Cross; then hung his own wreath there. After all, the wreaths were not far out of keeping with the little garden. To my friend. To my friend.

Mr. The Englishman took it very ill when he looked round a street corner into the Great Place, carrying Bebelle in his arms, that old Mutuel should be there airing his red ribbon. He took a world of pains to dodge the worthy Mutuel, and devoted a surprising amount of time and trouble to skulking into his own lodging like a man pursued by Justice. Safely arrived there at last, he made Bebelle's toilet with as accurate a remembrance as he could bring to bear upon that work of the way in which he had often seen the poor Corporal make it, and having given her to eat and drink, laid her down on his own bed. Then he slipped out into the Barber's shop, and after a brief interview with the Barber's wife, and a brief recourse to his purse and card-case, came back again with the whole of Bebelle's personal property in such a very little bundle that it was quite lost under his arm.

As it was irreconcilable with his whole course and character that he should carry Bebelle off in state, or receive any compliments or congratulations on that feat, he devoted the next day to getting his two portmanteaus out of the house by artfulness and stealth, and to comporting himself in every particular as if he were going to run away,—except, indeed, that he paid his few debts in the town, and prepared a letter to leave for Madame Bouclet, enclosing a sufficient sum of money in lieu of notice. A railway train would come through at midnight, and by that train he would take away Bebelle to look for Théophile in England and at his forgiven daughter's.

At midnight, on a moonlight night, Mr. The Englishman came creeping forth like a harmless assassin, with Bebelle on his breast instead of a dagger. Quiet the Great Place, and quiet the never-stirring streets; closed the cafés; huddled together motionless their billiard-balls; drowsy the guard or sentinel on duty here and there; lulled for the time, by sleep, even the insatiate appetite of the Office of Town-dues.

Mr. The Englishman left the Place behind, and left the streets behind, and left the civilian-inhabited town behind, and descended down among the military works of Vauban, hemming all in. As the shadow of the first heavy arch and postern fell upon him and was left behind, as the shadow of the second heavy arch and postern fell upon him and was left behind, as his hollow tramp over the first drawbridge was succeeded by a gentler sound, as his hollow tramp over the second drawbridge was succeeded by a gentler sound, as he overcame the stagnant ditches one by one, and passed out where the flowing waters were and where the moonlight, so the dark shades and the hollow sounds and the unwholesomely locked currents of his soul were vanquished and set free. See to it, Vaubans of your own hearts, who gird them in with triple walls and ditches, and with bolt and chain and bar and lifted bridge,—raze those fortifications, and lay them level with the all-absorbing dust, before the night cometh when no hand can work!

All went prosperously, and he got into an empty carriage in the train, where he could lay Bebelle on the seat over against him, as on a couch, and cover her from head to foot with his mantle. He had just drawn himself up from perfecting this arrangement, and had just leaned back in his own seat contemplating it with great satisfaction, when he became aware of a curious appearance at the open carriage window,—a ghostly little tin box floating up in the moonlight, and hovering there.

He leaned forward, and put out his head. Down among the rails and wheels and ashes, Monsieur Mutuel, red ribbon and all!

"Excuse me, Monsieur The Englishman," said Monsieur Mutuel, holding up his box at arm's length, the carriage being so high and he so low; "but I shall reverence the little box for ever, if your so generous hand will take a pinch from it at parting."

Mr. The Englishman reached out of the window before complying, and—without asking the old fellow what business it was of his—shook hands and said, "Adieu! God bless you!"

"And, Mr. The Englishman, God bless *you!*" cried Madame Bouclet, who was also there among the rails and wheels and ashes. "And God will bless you in the happiness of the protected child now with you. And God will bless you in the happiness of the protected child now with you. And God will bless you in your own child at home. And God will bless you in your own remembrances. And this from me!"

He had barely time to catch a bouquet from her hand, when the train was flying throught the night. Round the paper that enfolded it was bravely written (doubtless by the nephew who held the pen of an Angel), "Homage to the friend of the friendless."

"Not bad people, Bebelle!" said Mr. The Englishman, softly drawing the mantle a little from her sleeping face, that he might kiss it, "though they are so——"

Too "sentimental" himself at the moment to be able to get out that word, he added nothing but a sob, and travelled for some miles, through the moonlight, with his hand before his eyes.

CHAPTER III *His brown-paper parcel*

My works are well known. I am a young man in the Art line. You have seen my works many a time, though it's fifty thousand to one if you have seen me. You say you don't want to see me? You say your interest is in my works, and not in me? Don't be too sure about that. Stop a bit.

Let us have it down in black and white at the first go off, so that there may be no unpleasantness or wrangling afterwards. And this is looked over by a friend of mine, a ticket writer, that is up to literature. I am a young man in the Art line—in the Fine-Art line. You have seen my works over and over again, and you have been curious about me, and you think you have seen me. Now, as a safe rule, you never have seen me, and you never do see me, and you never will see me. I think that's plainly put—and it's what knocks me over.

If there's a blighted public character going, I am the party.

It has been remarked by a certain (or an uncertain) philosopher, that the world knows nothing of its greatest men. He might have put it plainer if he had thrown his eye in my direction. He might have put it, that while the world knows something of them that apparently go in and win, it knows nothing of them that really go in and don't win. There it is again in another form—and that's what knocks me over.

Not that it's only myself that suffers from injustice, but that I am more alive to my own injuries than to any other man's. Being, as I have mentioned, in the Fine-Art line, and not the Philanthropic line, I openly admit it. As to company in injury, I have company enough. Who are you passing every day at your Competitive Excruciations? The fortunate candidates whose heads and livers you have turned upside down for life? Not you. You are really passing the Crammers and Coaches. If your principle is right, why don't you turn out to-morrow morning with the keys of your cities on velvet cushions, your musicians playing, and your flags flying, and read addresses to the Crammers and Coaches on your bended knees, beseeching them to come out and govern you? Then again, as to your public business of all sorts, your Financial statements and your Budgets; the Public knows much, truly, about the real doers of all that! Your Nobles and Right Honourables are first-rate men? Yes, and so is a goose a first-rate bird. But I'll tell you this about the goose;—you'll find his natural flavour disappointing, without stuffing.

Perhaps I am soured by not being popular? But suppose I AM popular. Suppose my works never fail to attract. Suppose that, whether they are exhibited by natural light or by artificial, they inevitably draw the public. Then no doubt they are preserved in some Collection? No, they are not; they are not preserved in any Collection. Copyright? No, nor yet copyright. Anyhow they must be somewhere? Wrong again, for they are often nowhere.

Says you, "At all events, you are in a moody state of mind, my friend." My answer is, I have described myself as a public character with a blight upon him—which fully accounts for the curdling of the milk in *that* cocoa-nut.

Those that are acquainted with London are aware of a locality on the Surrey side of the river Thames, called the Obelisk, or, more generally, the Obstacle. Those that are not acquainted with London will also be aware of it, now that I have named it. My lodging is not far from that locality. I am a young man of that easy disposition, that I lie abed till it's absolutely necessary to get up and earn something, and then I lie abed again till I have spent it.

It was on an occasion when I had had to turn to with a view to victuals, that I found myself walking along the Waterloo Road, one evening after dark, accompanied by an acquaintance and fellow-lodger in the gas-fitting way of life. He is very good company, having worked at the theatres, and, indeed, he has a theatrical turn himself, and wishes to be brought out in the character of Othello; but whether on account of his regular work always blacking his face and hands more or less, I cannot say.

"Tom," he says, "what a mystery hangs over you!"

"Yes, Mr. Click"—the rest of the house generally give him his name, as being first, front, carpeted all over, his own furniture, and if not mahogany, an out-and-out imitation—"yes, Mr. Click, a mystery does hang over me."

"Makes you low, you see, don't it?" says he, eyeing me sideways.

"Why, yes, Mr. Click, there are circumstances connected with it that have," I yielded to a sigh, "a lowering effect."

"Gives you a touch of the misanthrope too, don't it?" says he. "Well, I'll tell you what. If I was you, I'd shake it off."

"If I was you, I would, Mr. Click; but, if you was me, you wouldn't."

"Ah!" says he, "there's something in that."

When we had walked a little further, he took it up again by touching me on the chest.

"You see, Tom, it seems to me as if, in the words of the poet who wrote the domestic drama of The Stranger, you had a silent sorrow there."

"I have, Mr. Click."

"I hope, Tom," lowering his voice in a friendly way, "it isn't coining, or smashing?"

"No, Mr. Click. Don't be uneasy."

"Nor yet forg——" Mr. Click checked himself, and added, "counterfeiting anything, for instance?"

"No, Mr. Click. I am lawfully in the Art line—Fine-Art line—but I can say no more."

"Ah! Under a species of star? A kind of malignant spell? A sort of a gloomy destiny? A cankerworm pegging away at your vitals in secret, as well as I make it out?" said Mr. Click, eyeing me with some admiration.

I told Mr. Click that was about it, if we came to particulars; and I thought he appeared rather proud of me.

Our conversation had brought us to a crowd of people, the greater part struggling for a front place from which to see something on the pavement, which proved to be various designs executed in coloured chalks on the pavement stones, lighted by two candles stuck in mud sconces. The subjects consisted of a fine fresh salmon's head and shoulders, supposed to have been recently sent home from the fishmonger's; a moonlight night at sea (in a circle); dead game; scrollwork; the head of a hoary hermit engaged in devout contemplation; the head of a pointer smoking a pipe; and a cherubim, his flesh creased as in infancy, going on a horizontal errand against the wind. All these subjects appeared to me to be exquisitely done.

On his knees on one side of this gallery, a shabby person of modest appearance who shivered dreadfully (though it wasn't at all cold), was engaged in blowing the chalk-dust off the moon, toning the outline of the back of the hermit's head with a bit of leather, and fattening the down-stroke of a letter or two in the writing. I have forgotten to mention that writing formed a part of the composition, and that it also—as it appeared to me—was exquisitely done. It ran as follows, in fine round characters: "An honest man is the noblest work of God. 1 2 3 4 5 6 7 8 9 0. £ s. d. Employment in an office is humbly requested. Honour the Queen. Hunger is a 0 9 8 7 6 5 4 3 2 1 sharp thorn. Chip chop, cherry chop, fol de rol de ri do. Astronomy and mathematics. I do this to support my family."

Murmurs of admiration at the exceeding beauty of this performance went about among the crowd. The artist, having finished his touching (and having spoilt those places), took his seat on the pavement, with his knees crouched up very nigh his chin; and halfpence began to rattle in.

"A pity to see a man of that talent brought so low; ain't it?" said one of the crowd to me.

"What he might have done in the coach-painting, or house-decorating!" said another man, who took up the first speaker because I did not.

"Why, he writes—alone—like the Lord Chancellor!" said another man.

"Better," said another. "I know *his* writing. *He* couldn't support his family this way."

Then, a woman noticed the natural fluffiness of the hermit's hair, and another woman, her friend, mentioned of the salmon's gills that you could almost see him gasp. Then, an elderly country gentleman stepped forward and asked the modest man how he executed his work? And the modest man took some scraps of brown paper with colours in 'em out of his pockets, and showed them. Then a fair-complexioned donkey, with sandy hair and spectacles, asked if the hermit was a portrait? To which the modest man, casting a sorrowful glance upon it, replied that it was, to a certain extent, a recollection of his father. This caused a boy to yelp out, "Is the Pinter a smoking the pipe your mother?" who was immediately shoved out of view by a sympathetic carpenter with his basket of tools at his back.

At every fresh question or remark the crowd leaned forward more eagerly, and dropped the halfpence more freely, and the modest man gathered them up more meekly. At last, another elderly gentleman came to the front, and gave the artist his card, to come to his office to-morrow, and get some copying to do. The card was accompanied by sixpence, and the artist was profoundly grateful, and, before he put the card in his hat, read it several times by the light of his candles to fix the address well in his mind, in case he should lose it. The crowd was deeply interested by this last incident, and a man in the second row with a gruff voice growled to the artist, "You've got a chance in life now, ain't you?" The artist answered (sniffing in a very low-spirited way, however), "I'm thankful to hope so." Upon which there was a general chorus of "*You* are all right," and the halfpence slackened very decidedly.

I felt myself pulled away by the arm, and Mr. Click and I stood alone at the corner of the next crossing.

"Why, Tom," said Mr. Click, "what a horrid expression of face you've got!"

"Have I?" says I.

"Have you?" says Mr. Click. "Why, you looked as if you would have his blood?"

"Whose blood?"

"The artist's."

"The artist's?" I repeated. And I laughed, frantically, wildly, gloomily, incoherently, disagreeably. I am sensible that I did. I know I did.

Mr. Click stared at me in a scared sort of a way, but said nothing until we had walked a street's length. He then stopped short, and said, with excitement on the part of his forefinger:

"Thomas, I find it necessary to be plain with you. I don't like the envious man. I have identified the cankerworm that's pegging away at *your* vitals, and it's envy, Thomas."

"Is it?" says I.

"Yes, it is," says he. "Thomas, beware of envy. It is the green-eyed monster which never did and never will improve each shining hour, but quite the reverse. I dread the envious man, Thomas. I confess that I am afraid of the envious man, when he is so envious as you are. Whilst you contemplated the works of a gifted rival, and whilst you heard that rival's praises, and especially whilst you met his humble glance as he put that card away, your countenance was so malevolent as to be terrific. Thomas, I have heard of the envy of them that follows the Fine-Art line, but I never believed it could be what yours is. I wish you well, but I take my leave of you. And if you should ever get into trouble through knifeing—or say, garotting—a brother artist, as I believe you will, don't call me to character, Thomas, or I shall be forced to injure your case."

Mr. Click parted from me with those words, and we broke off our acquaintance.

I became enamoured. Her name was Henrietta. Contending with my easy disposition, I frequently got up to go after her. She also dwelt in the neighbourhood of the Obstacle, and I did fondly hope that no other would interpose in the way of our union.

To say that Henrietta was volatile is but to say that she was woman. To say that she was in the bonnet-trimming is feebly to express the taste which reigned predominant in her own.

She consented to walk with me. Let me do her the justice to say that she did so upon trial. "I am not," said Henrietta, "as yet prepared to regard you, Thomas, in any other light than as a friend; but as a friend I am willing to walk with you, on the understanding that softer sentiments may flow."

We walked.

Under the influence of Henrietta's beguilements, I now got out of bed daily. I pursued my calling with an industry before unknown, and it cannot fail to have been observed at that period, by those most familiar with the streets of London, that there was a larger supply. But hold! The time is not yet come!

One evening in October I was walking with Henrietta, enjoying the cool breezes wafted over Vauxhall Bridge. After several slow turns, Henrietta gaped frequently (so inseparable from woman is the love of excitement), and said, "Let's go home by Grosvenor Place, Piccadilly, and Waterloo"—localities, I may state for the information of the stranger and the foreigner, well known in London, and the last a Bridge.

"No. Not by Piccadilly, Henrietta," said I.

"And why not Piccadilly, for goodness' sake?" said Henrietta.

Could I tell her? Could I confess to the gloomy presentiment that overshadowed me? Could I make myself intelligible to her? No.

"I don't like Piccadilly, Henrietta."

"But I do," said she. "It's dark now, and the long rows of lamps in Piccadilly after dark are beautiful. I *will* go to Piccadilly!"

Of course we went. It was a pleasant night, and there were numbers of people in the streets. It was a brisk night, but not too cold, and not damp. Let me darkly observe, it was the best of all nights—FOR THE PURPOSE.

As we passed the garden wall of the Royal Palace, going up Grosvenor Place, Henrietta murmured:

"I wish I was a Queen!"

"Why so, Henrietta?"

"I would make *you* Something," said she, and crossed her two hands on my arm, and turned away her head.

Judging from this that the softer sentiments alluded to above had begun to flow, I adapted my conduct to that belief. Thus happily we passed on into the detested thoroughfare of Piccadilly. On the right of that thoroughfare is a row of trees, the railing of the Green Park, and a fine broad eligible piece of pavement.

"Oh my!" cried Henrietta presently. "There's been an accident!"

I looked to the left, and said, "Where, Henrietta?"

"Not there, stupid!" said she. "Over by the Park railings. Where the crowd is. Oh no, it's not an accident, it's something else to look at! What's them lights?"

She referred to two lights twinkling low amongst the legs of the assemblage: two candles on the pavement.

"Oh, do come along!" cried Henrietta, skipping across the road with me. I hung back, but in vain. "Do let's look!"

Again, designs upon the pavement. Centre compartment, Mount Vesuvius going it (in a circle), supported by four oval compartments, severally representing a ship in heavy weather, a shoulder of mutton attended by two cucumbers, a golden harvest with distant cottage of proprietor, and a knife and fork after nature; above the centre compartment a bunch of grapes, and over the whole a rainbow. The whole, as it appeared to me, exquisitely done.

The person in attendance on these works of art was in all respects, shabbiness excepted, unlike the former personage. His whole appearance and manner denoted briskness. Though threadbare, he expressed to the crowd that poverty had not subdued his spirit, or tinged with any sense of shame this honest effort to turn his talents to some account. The writing which formed part of his composition was conceived in a similarly cheerful tone. It breathed the following sentiments: "The writer is poor, but not despondent. To a British 1 2 3 4 5 6 7 8 9 0 Public he £ s. d. appeals. Honour to our brave Army! And also 0 9 8 7 6 5 4 3 2 1 to our gallant Navy. BRITONS STRIKE the A B C D E F G writer in common chalks would be grateful for any suitable employment HOME! HURRAH!" The whole of this writing appeared to me to be exquisitely done.

But this man, in one respect like the last, though seemingly hard at it with a great show of brown paper and rubbers, was only really fattening the down-stroke of a letter here and there, or blowing the loose chalk off the rainbow, or toning the outside edge of the shoulder of mutton. Though he did this with the greatest confidence, he did it (as it struck me) in so ignorant a manner, and so spoilt everything he touched, that when he began upon the purple smoke from the chimney of the distant cottage of the proprietor of the golden harvest (which smoke was beautifully soft), I found myself saying aloud, without considering of it:

"Let that alone, will you?"

"Halloa!" said the man next to me in the crowd, jerking me roughly from him with his elbow, "why didn't you send a telegram? If we had known you was coming, we'd have provided something better for you. You understand the man's work better than he does himself, don't you? Have you made your will? You're too clever to live long."

"Don't be hard upon the gentleman, Sir," said the person in attendance on the works of art, with a twinkle in his eye as he looked at me; "he may chance to be an artist himself. If so, Sir, he will have a fellow-feeling with me, Sir, when I"—he adapted his action to his words as he went on, and gave a smart slap of his hands between each touch, working himself all the time about and about the composition —"when I lighten the bloom of my grapes—shade off the orange in my rainbow—dot the i of my Britons—throw a yellow light into my cow-cum-*ber*—insinuate another morsel of fat into my shoulder of mutton—dart another zigzag flash of lightning at my ship in distress!"

He seemed to do this so neatly, and was so nimble about it, that the halfpence came flying in.

"Thanks, generous public, thanks!" said the professor. "You will stimulate me to further exertions! My name will be found in the list of British Painters yet. I shall do better than this, with encouragement. I shall indeed."

"You never can do better than that bunch of grapes," said Henrietta. "Oh, Thomas, them grapes!"

"Not better than *that*, lady? I hope for the time when I shall paint anything but your own bright eyes and lips equal to life."

"(Thomas, did you ever?) But it must take a long time, Sir," said Henrietta, blushing, "to paint equal to that."

"I was prenticed to it, Miss," said the young man, smartly touching up the composition—"prenticed to it in the caves of Spain and Portingale, ever so long and two year over."

There was a laugh from the crowd; and a new man who had worked himself in next me, said, "He's a smart chap, too; ain't he?"

"And what a eye!" exclaimed Henrietta softly.

"Ah! He need have a eye," said the man.

"Ah! He just need," was murmured among the crowd.

"He couldn't come that 'ere burning mountain without a eye," said the man. He had got himself accepted as an authority, somehow, and everybody looked at his finger as it pointed out Vesuvius. "To come that effect in a general illumination would require a eye; but to come it with two dips—why, it's enough to blind him!"

That impostor, pretending not to have heard what was said, now winked to any extent with both eyes at once, as if the strain upon his sight was too much, and threw back his long hair—it was very long—as if to cool his fevered brow. I was watching him doing it, when Henrietta suddenly whispered, "Oh, Thomas, how horrid you look!" and pulled me out by the arm.

Remembering Mr. Click's words, I was confused when I retorted, "What do you mean by horrid?"

"Oh gracious! Why, you looked," said Henrietta, "as if you would have his blood."

I was going to answer, "So I would, for twopence——from his nose," when I checked myself and remained silent.

We returned home in silence. Every step of the way, the softer sentiments that had flowed, ebbed twenty mile an hour. Adapting my conduct to the ebbing, as I had done to the flowing, I let my arm drop limp, so as she could scarcely keep hold of it, and I wished her such a cold good night at parting, that I keep within the bounds of truth when I characterise it as a Rasper.

In the course of the next day I received the following document:

"*Henrietta informs Thomas that my eyes are open to you. I must ever wish you well, but walking and us is separated by an unfarmable abyss. One so malignant to superiority—Oh that look at him!—can never never conduct*

"HENRIETTA

"*P.S.—To the altar.*"

Yielding to the easiness of my disposition, I went to bed for a week, after receiving this letter. During the whole of such time, London was bereft of the usual fruits of my labour. When I resumed it, I found that Henrietta was married to the artist of Piccadilly.

Did I say to the artist? What fell words were those, expressive of what a galling hollowness, of what a bitter mockery! I—I—I—am the artist. I was the real artist of Piccadilly, I was the real artist of the Waterloo Road, I am the only artist of all those pavement-subjects which daily and nightly arouse your admiration. I do 'em, and I let 'em out. The man you behold with the papers of chalks and the rubbers, touching up the down-strokes of the writing and shading off the salmon, the man you give the credit to, the man you give the money to, hires—yes! and I live to tell it!—hires those works of art of me, and brings nothing to 'em but the candles.

Such is genius in a commercial country. I am not up to the shivering, I am not up to the liveliness, I am not up to the wanting-employment-in-an-office move; I am only up to originating and executing the work. In consequence of which you never see me; you think you see me when you see somebody else, and that somebody else is a mere Commercial character. The one seen by self and Mr. Click in the Waterloo Road can only write a single word, and that I taught him, and it's MULTIPLICATION—which you may see him execute upside down, because he can't do it the natural way. The one seen by self and Henrietta by the Green Park railings can just smear into existence the two ends of a rainbow, with his cuff and a rubber—if very hard put upon making a show—but he could no more come the arch of the rainbow, to save his life, than he could come the moonlight, fish, volcano, shipwreck, mutton, hermit, or any of my most celebrated effects.

To conclude as I began: if there's a blighted public character going, I am the party. And often as you have seen, do see, and will see, my Works, it's fifty thousand to one if you'll ever see me, unless, when the candles are burnt down and the Commercial character is gone, you should happen to notice a neglected young man perseveringly rubbing out the last traces of the pictures, so that nobody can renew the same. That's me.

CHAPTER IV   *His wonderful end*

It will have been, ere now, perceived that I sold the foregoing writings. From the fact of their being printed in these pages, the inference will, ere now, have been drawn by the reader (may I add, the gentle reader?) that I sold them to One who never yet——[1]

[1] *The remainder of this complimentary sentence editorially struck out.*

Having parted with the writings on most satisfactory terms,—for, in opening negotiations with the present Journal, was I not placing myself in the hands of One of whom it may be said, in the words of Another,[1]—I resumed my usual functions. But I too soon discovered that peace of mind had fled from a brow which, up to that time, Time had merely took the hair off, leaving an unruffled expanse within.

It were superfluous to veil it,—the brow to which I allude is my own.

Yes, over that brow uneasiness gathered like the sable wing of the fabled bird, as—as no doubt will be easily identified by all right-minded individuals. If not, I am unable, on the spur of the moment, to enter into particulars of him. The reflection that the writings must now inevitably get into print, and that He might yet live and meet with them, sat like the Hag of Night upon my jaded form. The elasticity of my spirits departed. Fruitless was the Bottle, whether Wine or Medicine. I had recourse to both, and the effect of both upon my system was witheringly lowering.

In this state of depression, into which I subsided when I first began to revolve what could I ever say if He—the unknown—was to appear in the Coffee-room and demand reparation, I one forenoon in this last November received a turn that appeared to be given me by the finger of Fate and Conscience, hand in hand. I was alone in the Coffee-room, and had just poked the fire into a blaze, and was standing with my back to it, trying whether heat would penetrate with soothing influence to the Voice within, when a young man in a cap, of an intelligent countenance, though requiring his hair cut, stood before me.

"Mr. Christopher, the Head Waiter?"

"The same."

The young man shook his hair out of his vision,—which it impeded, —took a packet from his breast, and handing it over to me, said, with his eye (or did I dream?) fixed with a lambent meaning on me, "THE PROOFS."

Although I smelt my coat-tails singeing at the fire, I had not the power to withdraw them. The young man put the packet in my faltering grasp, and repeated,—let me do him the justice to add, with civility:

"THE PROOFS. A. Y. R."

With those words he departed.

A. Y. R.? And You Remember. Was that his meaning? At Your Risk. Were the letters short for *that* reminder? Anticipate Your Retribution. Did they stand for *that* warning? Our-dacious Youth Repent? But no; for that, a O was happily wanting, and the vowel here was a A.

[1]*The remainder of this complimentary sentence editorially struck out.*

I opened the packet, and found that its contents were the foregoing writings printed just as the reader (may I add the discerning reader?) peruses them. In vain was the reassuring whisper,—A. Y. R., All the Year Round,—it could not cancel the Proofs. Too appropriate name. The Proofs of my having sold the Writings.

My wretchedness daily increased. I had not thought of the risk I ran, and the defying publicity I put my head into, until all was done, and all was in print. Give up the money to be off the bargain and prevent the publication, I could not. My family was down in the world, Christmas was coming on, a brother in the hospital and a sister in the rheumatics could not be entirely neglected. And it was not only ins in the family that had told on the resources of one unaided Waitering; outs were not wanting. A brother out of a situation, and another brother out of money to meet an acceptance, and another brother out of his mind, and another brother out at New York (not the same, though it might appear so), had really and truly brought me to a stand till I could turn myself round. I got worse and worse in my meditations, constantly reflecting "The Proofs," and reflecting that when Christmas drew nearer, and the Proofs were published, there could be no safety from hour to hour but that He might confront me in the Coffee-room, and in the face of day and his country demand his rights.

The impressive and unlooked-for catastrophe towards which I dimly pointed the reader (shall I add, the highly intellectual reader?) in my first remarks now rapidly approaches.

It was November still, but the last echoes of the Guy Foxes had long ceased to reverberate. We was slack,—several joints under our average mark, and wine, of course, proportionate. So slack had we become at last, that Beds Nos. 26, 27, 28, and 31, having took their six o'clock dinners, and dozed over their respective pints, had drove away in their respective Hansoms for their respective Night Mail-trains and left us empty.

I had took the evening paper to No. 6 table,—which is warm and most to be preferred,—and, lost in the all-absorbing topics of the day, had dropped into a slumber. I was recalled to consciousness by the well-known intimation, "Waiter!" and replying, "Sir!" found a gentle-man standing at No. 4 table. The reader (shall I add, the observant reader?) will please to notice the locality of the gentleman,—*at No. 4 table*.

He had one of the new-fangled uncollapsible bags in his hand (which I am against, for I don't see why you shouldn't collapse, while you are about it, as your fathers collapsed before you), and he said:

"I want to dine, waiter. I shall sleep here to-night."

"Very good, Sir. What will you take for dinner, Sir?"

"Soup, bit of codfish, oyster sauce, and the joint."

"Thank you, Sir."

I rang the chambermaid's bell; and Mrs. Pratchett marched in, according to custom, demurely carrying a lighted flat candle before her, as if she was one of a long public procession, all the other members of which was invisible.

In the meanwhile the gentleman had gone up to the mantelpiece, right in front of the fire, and had laid his forehead against the mantelpiece (which it is a low one, and brought him into the attitude of leap-frog), and had heaved a tremenjous sigh. His hair was long and lightish; and when he laid his forehead against the mantelpiece, his hair all fell in a dusty fluff together over his eyes; and when he now turned round and lifted up his head again, it all fell in a dusty fluff together over his ears. This give him a wild appearance, similar to a blasted heath.

"O! The chambermaid. Ah!" He was turning something in his mind. "To be sure. Yes. I won't go upstairs now, if you will take my bag. It will be enough for the present to know my number.—Can you give me 24 B?"

(O Conscience, what a Adder art thou!)

Mrs. Pratchett allotted him the room, and took his bag to it. He then went back before the fire, and fell a biting his nails.

"Waiter!" biting between the words, "give me," bite, "pen and paper; and in five minutes," bite, "let me have, if you please," bite, "a," bite, "Messenger."

Unmindful of his waning soup, he wrote and sent off six notes before he touched his dinner. Three were City; three West-End. The City letters were to Cornhill, Ludgate-hill, and Farringdon-street. The West-End letters were to Great Marlborough-street, New Burlington-street, and Piccadilly. Everybody was systematically denied at every one of the six places, and there was not a vestige of any answer. Our light porter whispered to me, when he came back with that report, "All Booksellers."

But before then he had cleared off his dinner, and his bottle of wine. He now—mark the concurrence with the document formerly given in full!—knocked a plate of biscuits off the table with his agitated elber (but without breakage), and demanded boiling brandy-and-water.

Now fully convinced that it was Himself, I perspired with the utmost freedom. When he become flushed with the heated stimulant referred to, he again demanded pen and paper, and passed the succeeding two hours in producing a manuscript which he put in the fire when completed. He then went up to bed, attended by Mrs. Pratchett. Mrs. Pratchett (who was aware of my emotions) told me, on coming down, that she had noticed his eye rolling into every corner of the passages and staircase, as if in search of his Luggage, and that, looking back as she shut the door of 24 B, she perceived him with his coat already thrown off immersing himself bodily under the bedstead, like a chimley-sweep before the application of machinery.

The next day—I forbear the horrors of that night—was a very foggy day in our part of London, insomuch that it was necessary to light the Coffee-room gas. We was still alone, and no feverish words of mine can do justice to the fitfulness of his appearance as he sat at No. 4 table, increased by there being something wrong with the meter.

Having again ordered his dinner, he went out, and was out for the best part of two hours. Inquiring on his return whether any of the answers had arrived, and receiving an unqualified negative, his instant call was for Mulligatawny, the Cayenne Pepper, and Orange Brandy.

Feeling that the mortal struggle was now at hand, I also felt that I must be equal to him, and with that view resolved that whatever he took I would take. Behind my partition, but keeping my eye on him over the curtain, I therefore operated on Mulligatawny, Cayenne Pepper, and Orange Brandy. And at a later period of the day, when he again said, "Orange Brandy," I said so too, in a lower tone, to George, my Second Lieutenant (my First was absent on leave), who acts between me and the bar.

Throughout that awful day he walked about the Coffee-room continually. Often he came close up to my partition, and then his eye rolled within, too evidently in search of any signs of his Luggage. Half-past six came, and I laid his cloth. He ordered a bottle of Old Brown. I likewise ordered a bottle of Old Brown. I likewise ordered a bottle of Old Brown. He drank his. I drank mine (as nearly as my duties would permit) glass for glass against his. He topped with coffee and a small glass. I topped with coffee and a small glass. He dozed. I dozed. At last "Waiter!"—and he ordered his bill. The moment was now at hand when we two must be locked in the deadly grapple.

Swift as the arrow from the bow, I had formed my resolution; in other words, I had hammered it out between nine and nine. It was, that I would be the first to open up the subject with a full acknowledgment, and would offer any gradual settlement within my power. He paid his bill (doing what was right by attendance) with his eye rolling about him to the last for any tokens of his Luggage. One only time our gaze then met, with the lustrous fixedness (I believe I am correct in imputing that character to it?) of the well-known Basilisk. The decisive moment had arrived.

With a tolerable steady hand, though with humility, I laid The Proofs before him.

"Gracious Heavens!" he cries out, leaping up, and catching hold of his hair. "What's this? Print!"

"Sir," I replied, in a calming voice, and bending forward, "I humbly acknowledge to being the unfortunate cause of it. But I hope, Sir, that when you have heard the circumstances explained, and the innocence of my intentions——"

To my amazement, I was stopped short by his catching me in both his arms, and pressing me to his breast-bone; where I must confess to my face (and particular, nose) having undergone some temporary vexation from his wearing his coat buttoned high up, and his buttons being uncommon hard.

"Ha, ha, ha!" he cries, releasing me with a wild laugh, and grasping my hand. "What is your name, my Benefactor?"

"My name, Sir" (I was crumpled, and puzzled to make him out), "is Christopher; and I hope, Sir, that, as such, when you've heard my ex——"

"In print!" he exclaims again, dashing the proofs over and over as if he was bathing in them. "In print!! O Christopher! Philanthropist! Nothing can recompense you,—but what sum of money would be acceptable to you?"

I had drawn a step back from him, or I should have suffered from his buttons again.

"Sir, I assure you, I have been already well paid, and——"

"No, no, Christopher! Don't talk like that! What sum of money would be acceptable to you, Christopher? Would you find twenty pounds acceptable, Christopher?"

However great my surprise, I naturally found words to say, "Sir, I am not aware that the man was ever yet born without more than the average amount of water on the brain as would *not* find twenty pounds acceptable. But—extremely obliged to you, Sir, I'm sure;" for he had tumbled it out of his purse and crammed it in my hand in two banknotes; "but I could wish to know, Sir, if not intruding, how I have merited this liberality?"

"Know then, my Christopher," he says, "that from boyhood's hour I have unremittingly and unavailingly endeavoured to get into print. Know, Christopher, that all the Booksellers alive—and several dead— have refused to put me into print. Know, Christopher, that I have written unprinted Reams. But they shall be read to you, my friend and brother. You sometimes have a holiday?"

Seeing the great danger I was in, I had the presence of mind to answer, "Never!" To make it more final, I added, "Never! Not from the cradle to the grave."

"Well," says he, thinking no more about that, and chuckling at his proofs again. "But I am in print! The first flight of ambition emanating from my father's lowly cot is realised at length! The golden bow,"—he was getting on,—"struck by the magic hand, has emitted a complete and perfect sound! When did this happen, my Christopher?"

"Which happen, Sir?"

"This," he held it out at arm's length to admire it,—"this Per-rint."

When I had given him my detailed account of it, he grasped me by the hand again, and said:

"Dear Christopher, it should be gratifying to you to know that you are an instrument in the hands of Destiny. Because you *are*."

A passing Something of a melancholy cast put it into my head to shake it, and to say, "Perhaps we all are."

"I don't mean that," he answered; "I don't take that wide range; I confine myself to the special case. Observe me well, my Christopher! Hopeless of getting rid, through any effort of my own, of any of the manuscripts among my Luggage,—all of which, send them where I would, were always coming back to me,—it is now some seven years since I left that Luggage here, on the desperate chance, either that the too, too faithful manuscripts would come back to me no more, or that some one less accursed than I might give them to the world. You follow me, my Christopher?"

"Pretty well, Sir." I followed him so far as to judge that he had a weak head, and that the Orange, the Boiling, and Old Brown combined was beginning to tell. (The Old Brown, being heady, is best adapted to seasoned cases.)

"Years elapsed, and those compositions slumbered in dust. At length, Destiny, choosing her agent from all mankind, sent You here, Christopher, and lo! the Casket was burst asunder, and the Giant was free!"

He made hay of his hair after he said this, and he stood a-tiptoe.

"But," he reminded himself in a state of excitement, "we must sit up all night, my Christopher. I must correct these Proofs for the press. Fill all the inkstands, and bring me several new pens."

He smeared himself and he smeared the Proofs, the night through, to that degree that when Sol gave him warning to depart (in a four-wheeler), few could have said which was them, and which was him, and which was blots. His last instructions was, that I should instantly run and take his corrections to the office of the present Journal. I did so. They most likely will not appear in print, for I noticed a message being brought round from Beauford Printing House, while I was a throwing this concluding statement on paper, that the ole resources of that establishment was unable to make out what they meant. Upon which a certain gentleman in company, as I will not more particularly name,—but of whom it will be sufficient to remark, standing on the broad basis of a wave-girt isle, that whether we regard him in the light of,—[1]laughed, and put the corrections in the fire.

—1862

[1]*The remainder of this complimentary parenthesis editorially struck out.*

NOTE.—*Dickens partly contributed to another of the chapters, entitled "His Umbrella;" but for this the reader is referred to the number as republished in a collected volume—the Nine Christmas numbers of All the Year Round.*

Mrs. Lirriper's Lodgings   IN TWO CHAPTERS

~~~~~~

CHAPTER I   *How Mrs. Lirriper carried on the business*

Whoever would begin to be worried with letting Lodgings that wasn't a lone woman with a living to get is a thing inconceivable to me, my dear; excuse the familiarity, but it comes natural to me in my own little room, when wishing to open my mind to those that I can trust, and I should be truly thankful if they were all mankind, but such is not so, for have but a Furnished bill in the window and your watch on the mantelpiece, and farewell to it if you turn your back for but a second, however gentlemanly the manners; nor is being of your own sex any safeguard, as I have reason, in the form of sugar-tongs to know, for that lady (and a fine woman she was) got me to run for a glass of water, on the plea of going to be confined, which certainly turned out true, but it was in the Station-house.

Number Eighty-one Norfolk Street, Strand—situated midway between the City and St. James's, and within five minutes' walk of the principal places of public amusement—is my address. I have rented this house many years, as the parish rate-books will testify; and I could wish my landlord was as alive to the fact as I am myself; but no, bless you, not a half a pound of paint to save his life, nor so much, my dear, as a tile upon the roof, though on your bended knees.

My dear, you never have found Number Eighty-one Norfolk Street Strand advertised in Bradshaw's *Railway Guide*, and with the blessing of Heaven you never will or shall so find it. Some there are who do not think it lowering themselves to make their names that cheap, and even going the lengths of a portrait of the house not like it with a blot in every window and a coach and four at the door, but what will suit Wozenham's lower down on the other side of the way will not suit me, Miss Wozenham having her opinions and me having mine, though when it comes to systematic underbidding capable of being proved on oath in a court of justice and taking the form of "If Mrs. Lirriper names eighteen shillings a week, I name fifteen and six," it then comes to a settlement between yourself and your conscience, supposing for the sake of argument your name to be Wozenham, which I am well aware it is not or my opinion of you would be greatly lowered, and as to airy bedrooms and a night-porter in constant attendance the less said the better, the bedrooms being stuffy and the porter stuff.

It is forty years ago since me and my poor Lirriper got married at St. Clement's Danes, where I now have a sitting in a very pleasant pew with genteel company and my own hassock, and being partial to evening service not too crowded. My poor Lirriper was a handsome figure of a man, with a beaming eye and a voice as mellow as a musical instrument made of honey and steel, but he had ever been a free liver being in the commercial travelling line and travelling what he called a limekiln road—"a dry road, Emma my dear," my poor Lirriper says to me, "where I have to lay the dust with one drink or another all day long and half the night, and it wears me Emma"— and this led to his running through a good deal and might have run through the turnpike too when that dreadful horse that never would stand still for a single instant set off, but for its being night and the gate shut, and consequently took his wheel, my poor Lirriper and the gig smashed to atoms and never spoke afterwards. He was a handsome figure of a man, and a man with a jovial heart and a sweet temper; but if they had come up then they never could have given you the mellowness of his voice, and indeed I consider photographs wanting in mellowness as a general rule and making you look like a new-ploughed field.

My poor Lirriper being behindhand with the world and being buried at Hatfield church in Hertfordshire, not that it was his native place but that he had a liking for the Salisbury Arms where we went upon our wedding-day and passed as happy a fortnight as ever happy was, I went round to the creditors and I says "Gentlemen I am acquainted with the fact that I am not answerable for my late husband's debts but I wish to pay them for I am his lawful wife and his good name is dear to me. I am going into the Lodgings gentlemen as a business and if I prosper every farthing that my late husband owed shall be paid for the sake of the love I bore him, by this right hand." It took a long time to do but it was done, and the silver cream-jug which is between ourselves and the bed and the mattress in my room upstairs (or it would have found legs so sure as ever the Furnished bill was up) being presented by the gentlemen engraved "To Mrs. Lirriper a mark of grateful respect for her honourable conduct" gave me a turn which was too much for my feelings, till Mr. Betley which at that time had the parlours and loved his joke says "Cheer up Mrs. Lirriper, you should feel as if it was only your christening and they were your godfathers and godmothers which did promise for you." And it brought me round, and I don't mind confessing to you my dear that I then put a sandwich and a drop of sherry in a little basket and went down to Hatfield churchyard outside the coach and kissed my hand and laid it with a kind of proud and swelling love on my husband's grave, though bless you it had taken me so long to clear his name that my wedding-ring was worn quite fine and smooth when I laid it on the green waving grass.

I am an old woman now and my good looks are gone but that's me my dear over the plate-warmer and considered like in the times when you used to pay two guineas on ivory and took your chance pretty much how you came out, which made you very careful how you left it about afterwards because people were turned so red and uncomfortable by mostly guessing it was somebody else quite different, and there was once a certain person that had put his money in a hop business that came in one morning to pay his rent and his respects being the second floor that would have taken it down from its hook and put it in his breast-pocket—you understand my dear—for the L, he says of the original—only there was no mellowness in *his* voice and I wouldn't let him, but his opinion of it you may gather from his saying to it "Speak to me Emma!" which was far from a rational observation no doubt but still a tribute to its being a likeness, and I think myself it *was* like me when I was young and wore that sort of stays.

But it was about the Lodgings that I was intending to hold forth and certainly I ought to know something of the business having been in it so long, for it was early in the second year of my married life that I lost my poor Lirriper and I set up at Islington directly afterwards and afterwards came here, being two houses and eight-and-thirty years and some losses and a deal of experience.

Girls are your first trial after fixtures and they try you even worse than what I call the Wandering Christians, though why *they* should roam the earth looking for bills and then coming in and viewing the apartments and stickling about terms and never at all wanting them or dreaming of taking them being already provided, is a mystery I should be thankful to have explained if by any miracle it could be. It's wonderful they live so long and thrive so on it but I suppose the exercise makes it healthy, knocking so much and going from house to house and up and down stairs all day, and then their pretending to be so particular and punctual is a most astonishing thing, looking at their watches and saying "Could you give me the refusal of the rooms till twenty minutes past eleven the day after to-morrow in the forenoon, and supposing it to be considered essential by my friend from the country could there be a small iron bedstead put in the little room upon the stairs?" Why when I was new to it my dear I used to consider before I promised and to make my mind anxious with calculations and to get quite wearied out with disappointments, but now I says "Certainly by all means" well knowing it's a Wandering Christian and I shall hear no more about it, indeed by this time I know most of the Wandering Christians by sight as well as they know me, it being the habit of each individual revolving round London in that capacity to come back about twice a year, and it's very remarkable that it runs in families and the children grow up to it, but even were it otherwise I should no sooner hear of the friend from the country which is a certain sign than I should nod and say to myself You're a Wandering Christian, though whether they are (as I *have* heard) persons of small property with a taste for regular employment and frequent change of scene I cannot undertake to tell you.

Girls as I was beginning to remark are one of your first and your lasting troubles, being like your teeth which begin with convulsions and never cease tormenting you from the time you cut them till they cut you, and then you don't want to part with them which seems hard but we must all succumb or buy artificial, and even where you get a will nine times out of ten you'll get a dirty face with it and naturally lodgers do not like good society to be shown in with a smear of black across the nose or a smudgy eyebrow. Where they pick the black up is a mystery I cannot solve, as in the case of the willingest girl that ever came into a house half-starved poor thing, a girl so willing that I called her Willing Sophy down upon her knees scrubbing early and late and ever cheerful but always smiling with a black face. And I says to Sophy, "Now Sophy my good girl have a regular day for your stoves and keep the width of the Airy between yourself and the blacking and do not brush your hair with the bottoms of the saucepans and do not meddle with the snuffs of the candles and it stands to reason that it can no longer be" yet there it was and always on her nose, which turning up and being broad at the end seemed to boast of it and caused warning from a steady gentleman and excellent lodger with breakfast by the week but a little irritable and use of a sitting-room when required, his words being "Mrs. Lirriper I have arrived at the point of admitting that the Black is a man and a brother, but only in a natural form and when it can't be got off." Well consequently I put poor Sophy on to other work and forbid her answering the door or answering a bell on any account but she was so unfortunately willing that nothing would stop her flying up the kitchen-stairs whenever a bell was heard to tingle. I put it to her "O Sophy Sophy for goodness' goodness' sake where does it come from?" To which that poor unlucky willing mortal bursting out crying to see me so vexed replied "I took a deal of black into me ma'am when I was a small child being much neglected and I think it must be, that it works out," so it continuing to work out of that poor thing and not having another fault to find with her I says "Sophy what do you seriously think of my helping you away to New South Wales where it might not be noticed?" Nor did I ever repent the money which was well spent, for she married the ship's cook on the voyage (himself a Mulotter) and did well and lived happy, and so far as ever I heard it was *not* noticed in a new state of society to her dying day.

In what way Miss Wozenham lower down on the other side of the way reconciled it to her feelings as a lady (which she is not) to entice Mary Anne Perkinsop from my service is best known to herself, I do not know and I do not wish to know how opinions are formed at Wozenham's on any point. But Mary Anne Perkinsop although I behaved handsomely to her and she behaved unhandsomely to me was worth her weight in gold as overawing lodgers without driving them away, for lodgers would be far more sparing of their bells with Mary Anne than I ever knew them to be with Maid or Mistress, which is a great triumph especially when accompanied with a cast in the eye and a bag of bones, but it was the steadiness of her way with them through her father's having failed in Pork. It was Mary Anne's looking so respectable in her person and being so strict in her spirits that conquered the tea-and-sugarest gentleman (for he weighed them both in a pair of scales every morning) that I have ever had to deal with and no lamb grew meeker, still it afterwards came round to me that Miss Wozenham happening to pass and seeing Mary Anne take in the milk of a milkman that made free in a rosy-faced way (I think no worse of him) with every girl in the street but was quite frozen up like the statue at Charing-cross by her, saw Mary Anne's value in the lodging business and went as high as one pound per quarter more, consequently Mary Anne with not a word betwixt us says "If *you* will provide yourself Mrs. Lirriper in a month from this day I have already done the same," which hurt me and I said so, and she then hurt me more by insinuating that her father having failed in Pork had laid her open to it.

My dear I do assure you it's a harassing thing to know what kind of girls to give the preference to, for if they are lively they get bell'd off their legs and if they are sluggish you suffer from it yourself in complaints and if they are sparkling-eyed they get made love to, and if they are smart in their persons they try on your Lodgers' bonnets and if they are musical I defy you to keep them away from bands and organs, and allowing for any difference you like in their heads their heads will be always out of window just the same. And then what the gentlemen like in girls the ladies don't, which is fruitful hot water for all parties, and then there's temper though such a temper as Caroline Maxey's I hope not often. A good-looking black-eyed girl was Caroline and a comely-made girl to your cost when she did break out and laid about her, as took place first and last through a new-married couple come to see London in the first floor and the lady very high and it *was* supposed not liking the good looks of Caroline having none of her own to spare, but anyhow she did try Caroline though that was no excuse. So one afternoon Caroline comes down into the

kitchen flushed and flashing, and she says to me "Mrs. Lirriper that
woman in the first has aggravated me past bearing," I says "Caroline
keep your temper," Caroline says with a curdling laugh "Keep my
temper? You're right Mrs. Lirriper, so I will. Capital D her!" bursts
out Caroline (you might have struck me into the centre of the earth
with a feather when she said it) "I'll give her a touch of the temper
that I keep!" Caroline downs with her hair my dear, screeches and
rushes upstairs, I following as fast as my trembling legs could bear me,
but before I got into the room the dinner-cloth and pink-and-white
service all dragged off upon the floor with a crash and the new-married
couple on their backs in the firegrate, him with the shovel and tongs
and a dish of cucumber across him and a mercy it was summer-time.
"Caroline" I says "be calm," but she catches off my cap and tears it in
her teeth as she passes me, then pounces on the new-married lady
makes her a bundle of ribbons takes her by the two ears and knocks
the back of her head upon the carpet Murder screaming all the time
Policemen running down the street and Wozenham's windows (judge
of my feelings when I came to know it) thrown up and Miss Wozenham calling out from the balcony with crocodile's tears "It's Mrs.
Lirriper been overcharging somebody to madness—she'll be murdered
—I always thought so—Pleeseman save her!" My dear four of them
and Caroline behind the chiffoniere attacking with the poker and
when disarmed prize-fighting with her double fists, and down and up
and up and down and dreadful! But I couldn't bear to see the poor
young creature roughly handled and her hair torn when they got the
better of her, and I says "Gentlemen Policemen pray remember that
her sex is the sex of your mothers and sisters and your sweethearts,
and God bless them and you!" And there she was sitting down on
the ground handcuffed, taking breath against the skirting-board and
them cool with their coats in strips, and all she says was "Mrs. Lirriper
I'm sorry as ever I touched you, for you're a kind motherly old thing,"
and it made me think that I had often wished I had been a mother
indeed and how would my heart have felt if I had been the mother of
that girl! Well you know it turned out at the Police-office that she had
done it before, and she had her clothes away and was sent to prison,
and when she was to come out I trotted off to the gate in the evening
with just a morsel of jelly in that little basket of mine to give her a
mite of strength to face the world again, and there I met with a
very decent mother waiting for her son through bad company and a
stubborn one he was with his half-boots not laced. So out came Caroline and I says "Caroline come along with me and sit down under
the wall where it's retired and eat a little trifle that I have brought
with me to do you good," and she throws her arms round my neck
and says sobbing "O why were you never a mother when there are
such mothers as there are?" she says, and in half a minute more she

begins to laugh and says "Did I really tear your cap to shreds?" and when I told her "You certainly did so Caroline" she laughed again and said while she patted my face "Then why do you wear such queer old caps you dear old thing? If you hadn't worn such queer old caps I don't think I should have done it even then." Fancy the girl! Nothing could get out of her what she was going to do except O she would do well enough, and we parted she being very thankful and kissing my hands, and I nevermore saw or heard of that girl, except that I shall always believe that a very genteel cap which was brought anonymous to me one Saturday night in an oilskin basket by a most impertinent young sparrow of a monkey whistling with dirty shoes on the clean steps and playing the harp on the Airy railings with a hoop-stick came from Caroline.

What you lay yourself open to my dear in the way of being the object of uncharitable suspicions when you go into the Lodging business I have not the words to tell you, but never was I so dishonourable as to have two keys nor would I willingly think it even of Miss Wozenham lower down on the other side of the way sincerely hoping that it may not be, though doubtless at the same time money cannot come from nowhere and it is not reason to suppose that Bradshaws put it in for love be it blotty as it may. It *is* a hardship hurting to the feelings that Lodgers open their minds so wide to the idea that you are trying to get the better of them and shut their minds so close to the idea that they are trying to get the better of you, but as Major Jackman says to me "I know the ways of this circular world Mrs. Lirriper, and that's one of 'em all round it" and many is the little ruffle in my mind that the Major has smoothed, for he is a clever man who has seen much. Dear dear, thirteen years have passed though it seems but yesterday since I was sitting with my glasses on at the open front parlour window one evening in August (the parlours being then vacant) reading yesterday's paper my eyes for print being poor though still I am thankful to say a long sight at a distance, when I hear a gentleman come posting across the road and up the street in a dreadful rage talking to himself in a fury and d'ing and c'ing somebody. "By George!" says he out loud and clutching his walking-stick, "I'll go to Mrs. Lirriper's. Which is Mrs. Lirriper's?" Then looking round and seeing me he flourishes his hat right off his head as if I had been the queen and he says, "Excuse the intrusion madam, but pray madam can you tell me at what number in this street there resides a well-known and much-respected lady by the name of Lirriper?" A little flustered though I must say gratified I took off my glasses and courtesied and said "Sir, Mrs. Lirriper is your humble servant." "Astonishing!" says he. "A million pardons! Madam, may I ask you to have the kindness to direct one of your domestics to open the door to a gentleman in search of apartments, by the name of Jackman?" I had

LIFE AND ITS BATTLE

never heard the name but a politer gentleman I never hope to see, for says he "Madam I am shocked at your opening the door yourself to no worthier a fellow than Jemmy Jackman. After you madam. I never precede a lady." Then he comes into the parlours and he sniffs, and he says "Hah! These are parlours! Not musty cupboards" he says "but parlours, and no smell of coal-sacks." Now my dear it having been remarked by some inimical to the whole neighbourhood that it always smells of coal-sacks which might prove a drawback to Lodgers if encouraged, I says to the Major gently though firmly that I think he is referring to Arundel or Surrey or Howard but not Norfolk. "Madam" says he "I refer to Wozenham's lower down over the way—madam you can form no notion what Wozenham's is—madam it is a vast coal-sack, and Miss Wozenham has the principles and manners of a female heaver—madam from the manner in which I have heard her mention you I know she has no appreciation of a lady, and from the manner in which she has conducted herself towards me I know she has no appreciation of a gentleman—madam my name is Jackman—should you require any other reference than what I have already said, I name the Bank of England—perhaps you know it!" Such was the beginning of the Major's occupying the parlours and from that hour to this the same and a most obliging Lodger and punctual in all respects except one irregular which I need not particularly specify, but made up for by his being a protection and at all times ready to fill in the papers of the Assessed Taxes and Juries and that, and once collared a young man with the drawing-room clock under his coat, and once on the parapets with his own hands and blankets put out the kitchen chimney and afterwards attending the summons made a most eloquent speech against the Parish before the magistrates and saved the engine, and ever quite the gentleman though passionate. And certainly Miss Wozenham's detaining the trunks and umbrella was not in a liberal spirit though it may have been according to her rights in law or an act I would myself have stooped to, the Major being so much the gentleman that though he is far from tall he seems almost so when he has his shirt-frill out and his frock-coat on and his hat with the curly brims, and in what service he was I cannot truly tell you my dear whether Militia or Foreign, for I never heard him even name himself as Major but always simple "Jemmy Jackman" and once soon after he came when I felt it my duty to let him know that Miss Wozenham had put it about that he was no Major and I took the liberty of adding "which you are Sir" his words were "Madam at any rate I am not a Minor, and sufficient for the day is the evil thereof" which cannot be denied to be the sacred truth, nor yet his military ways of having his boots with only the dirt brushed off taken to him in the front parlour every morning on a clean plate and varnishing them himself with a little sponge and a saucer and a whistle in a whisper so sure as ever his breakfast is ended, and so neat his ways that it never soils his linen which is scrupulous though more in quality than quantity, neither that nor his mustachios which to the best of my belief are done at the same time and which are as black and shining as his boots, his head of hair being a lovely white.

It was the third year nearly up of the Major's being in the parlours that early one morning in the month of February when Parliament was coming on and you may therefore suppose a number of impostors were about ready to take hold of anything they could get, a gentleman and a lady from the country came in to view the Second, and I well remember that I had been looking out of window and had watched them and the heavy sleet driving down the street together looking for bills. I did not quite take to the face of the gentleman though he was good-looking too but the lady was a very pretty young thing and delicate, and it seemed too rough for her to be out at all though she had only come from the Adelphi Hotel which would not have been much above a quarter of a mile if the weather had been less severe. Now it did so happen my dear that I had been forced to put five shillings weekly additional on the Second in consequence of a loss from running away full dressed as if going out to a dinner-party, which was very artful and had made me rather suspicious taking it along with Parliament, so when the gentleman proposed three months certain and the money in advance and leave then reserved to renew on the same terms for six months more, I says I was not quite certain but that I might have engaged myself to another party but would step downstairs and look into it if they would take a seat. They took a seat and I went down to the handle of the Major's door that I had already began to consult finding it a great blessing, and I knew by his whistling in a whisper that he was varnishing his boots which was generally considered private, however he kindly calls out "If it's you, madam, come in," and I went in and told him.

"Well, madam," says the Major rubbing his nose—as I did fear at the moment with the black sponge but it was only his knuckle, he being always neat and dexterous with his fingers—"well, madam, I suppose you would be glad of the money?"

I was delicate of saying "Yes" too out, for a little extra colour rose into the Major's cheeks and there was irregularity which I will not particularly specify in a quarter which I will not name.

"I am of opinion, madam," says the Major "that when money is ready for you—when it is ready for you, Mrs. Lirriper—you ought to take it. What is there against it, madam, in this case upstairs?"

"I really cannot say there is anything against it, Sir, still I thought I would consult you."

"You said a newly-married couple, I think, madam?" says the Major.

I says "Ye-es. Evidently. And indeed the young lady mentioned to me in a casual way that she had not been married many months."

The Major rubbed his nose again and stirred the varnish round and round in its little saucer with his piece of sponge and took to his whistling in a whisper for a few moments. Then he says "You would call it a Good Let, madam?"

"O certainly a Good Let Sir."

"Say they renew for the additional six months. Would it put you about very much madam if—if the worst was to come to the worst?" said the Major.

"Well I hardly know," I says to the Major. "It depends upon circumstances. Would you object Sir for instance?"

"I?" says the Major. "Object? Jemmy Jackman? Mrs. Lirriper close with the proposal."

So I went upstairs and accepted, and they came in next day which was Saturday and the Major was so good as to draw up a Memorandum of an agreement in a beautiful round hand and expressions that sounded to me equally legal and military, and Mr. Edson signed it on the Monday morning and the Major called upon Mr. Edson on the Tuesday and Mr. Edson called upon the Major on the Wednesday and the Second and the parlours were as friendly as could be wished.

The three months paid for had run out and we had got without any fresh overtures as to payment into May my dear, when there came an obligation upon Mr. Edson to go a business expedition right across the Isle of Man, which fell quite unexpected upon that pretty little thing and is not a place that according to my views is particularly in the way to anywhere at any time but that may be a matter of opinion. So short a notice was it that he was to go next day, and dreadfully she cried poor pretty, and I am sure I cried too when I saw her on the cold pavement in the sharp east wind—it being a very backward spring that year—taking a last leave of him with her pretty bright hair blowing this way and that and her arms clinging round his neck and him saying "There there there. Now let me go Peggy." And by that time it was plain that what the Major had been so accommodating as to say he would not object to happening in the house, would happen in it, and I told her as much when he was gone while I comforted her with my arm up the staircase, for I says "You will soon have others to keep up for my pretty and you must think of that."

His letter never came when it ought to have come and what she went through morning after morning when the postman brought none for her the very postman himself compassionated when she ran down to the door, and yet we cannot wonder at its being calculated to blunt the feelings to have all the trouble of other people's letters and none of the pleasure and doing it oftener in the mud and mizzle than not and at a rate of wages more resembling Little Britain than Great. But at last one morning when she was too poorly to come

running downstairs he says to me with a pleased look in his face that
made me next to love the man in his uniform coat though he was
dripping wet "I have taken you first in the street this morning Mrs.
Lirriper, for here's the one for Mrs. Edson." I went up to her bedroom
with it as fast as ever I could go, and she sat up in bed when she
saw it and kissed it and tore it open and then a blank stare came
upon her. "It's very short!" she says lifting her large eyes to my face.
"O Mrs. Lirriper it's very short!" I says "My dear Mrs. Edson no
doubt that's because your husband hadn't time to write more just at
that time." "No doubt, no doubt," says she, and puts her two hands
on her face and turns round in her bed.

I shut her softly in and I crept downstairs and I tapped at the
Major's door, and when the Major having his thin slices of bacon in
his own Dutch oven saw me he came out of his chair and put me down
on the sofa. "Hush!" says he, "I see something's the matter. Don't
speak—take time." I says "O Major I'm afraid there's cruel work up-
stairs." "Yes yes," says he "I had begun to be afraid of it—take time."
And then in opposition to his own words he rages out frightfully, and
says "I shall never forgive myself madam, that I, Jemmy Jackman,
didn't see it all that morning—didn't go straight upstairs when my
boot-sponge was in my hand—didn't force it down his throat—and
choke him dead with it on the spot!"

The Major and me agreed when we came to ourselves that just at
present we could do no more than take on to suspect nothing and
use our best endeavours to keep that poor young creature quiet, and
what I ever should have done without the Major when it got about
among the organ-men that quiet was our object is unknown, for he
made lion and tiger war upon them to that degree that without seeing
it I could not have believed it was in any gentleman to have such a
power of bursting out with fire-irons walking-sticks water-jugs coals
potatoes off his table the very hat off his head, and at the same time
so furious in foreign languages that they would stand with their handles
half-turned fixed like the Sleeping Ugly—for I cannot say Beauty.

Ever to see the postman come near the house now gave me such a
fear that it was a reprieve when he went by, but in about another
ten days or a fortnight he says again, "Here's one for Mrs. Edson.—
Is she pretty well?" "She is pretty well postman, but not well enough
to rise so early as she used" which was so far gospel-truth.

I carried the letter in to the Major at his breakfast and I says
tottering "Major I have not the courage to take it up to her."

"It's an ill-looking villain of a letter," says the Major.

"I have not the courage Major" I says again in a tremble "to take it
up to her."

After seeming lost in consideration for some moments the Major
says, raising his head as if something new and useful had occurred to

his mind "Mrs. Lirriper, I shall never forgive myself that I, Jemmy Jackman, didn't go straight upstairs that morning when my boot-sponge was in my hand—and force it down his throat—and choke him dead with it."

"Major" I says a little hasty "you didn't do it which is a blessing, for it would have done no good and I think your sponge was better employed on your own honourable boots."

So we got to be rational, and planned that I should tap at her bedroom door and lay the letter on the mat outside and wait on the upper landing for what might happen, and never was gunpowder cannon-balls or shells or rockets more dreaded than that dreadful letter was by me as I took it to the second floor.

A terrible loud scream sounded through the house the minute after she had opened it, and I found her on the floor lying as if her life was gone. My dear I never looked at the face of the letter which was lying open by her, for there was no occasion.

Everything I needed to bring her round the Major brought up with his own hands, besides running out to the chemist's for what was not in the house and likewise having the fiercest of all his many skirmishes with a musical instrument representing a ball-room I do not know in what particular country and company waltzing in and out at folding-doors with rolling eyes. When after a long time I saw her coming to, I slipped on the landing till I heard her cry, and then I went in and says cheerily "Mrs. Edson you're not well my dear and it's not to be wondered at," as if I had not been in before. Whether she believed or disbelieved I cannot say and it would signify nothing if I could, but I stayed by her for hours and then she God ever blesses me! and says she will try to rest for her head is bad.

"Major," I whispers, looking in at the parlours, "I beg and pray of you don't go out."

The Major whispers, "Madam, trust me I will do no such a thing. How is she?"

I says "Major the good Lord above us only knows what burns and rages in her poor mind. I left her sitting at her window. I am going to sit at mine."

It came on afternoon and it came on evening. Norfolk is a delightful street to lodge in—provided you don't go lower down—but of a summer evening when the dust and waste paper lie in it and stray children play in it and a kind of a gritty calm and bake settles on it and a peal of churchbells is practising in the neighbourhood it is a trifle dull, and never have I seen it since at such a time and never shall I see it evermore at such a time without seeing the dull June evening when that forlorn young creature sat at her open corner window on the Second and me at my open corner window (the other corner) on the Third. Something merciful, something wiser and better far than my own self, had moved me while it was yet light to sit in my bonnet and shawl, and as the shadows fell and the tide rose I could sometimes —when I put out my head and looked at her window below—see that she leaned out a little looking down the street. It was just settling dark when I saw *her* in the street.

So fearful of losing sight of her that it almost stops my breath while I tell it, I went downstairs faster than I ever moved in all my life and only tapped with my hand at the Major's door in passing it and slipping out. She was gone already. I made the same speed down the street and when I came to the corner of Howard-street I saw that she had turned it and was there plain before me going towards the west. O with what a thankful heart I saw her going along!

She was quite unacquainted with London and had very seldom been out for more than an airing in our own street where she knew two or three little children belonging to neighbours and had sometimes stood among them at the street looking at the water. She must be going at hazard I knew, still she kept the bye-streets quite correctly as long as they would serve her, and then turned up into the Strand. But at every corner I could see her head turned one way, and that way was always the river way.

It may have been only the darkness and quiet of the Adelphi that caused her to strike into it but she struck into it much as readily as if she had set out to go there, which perhaps was the case. She went straight down to the Terrace and along it and looked over the iron rail, and I often woke afterwards in my own bed with the horror of seeing her do it. The desertion of the wharf below and the flowing of the high water there seemed to settle her purpose. She looked about as if to make out the way down, and she struck out the right way or the wrong way—I don't know which, for I don't know the place before or since—and I followed her the way she went.

It was noticeable that all this time she never once looked back. But there was now a great change in the manner of her going, and instead of going at a steady quick walk with her arms folded before her,— among the dark dismal arches she went in a wild way with her arms opened wide, as if they were wings and she was flying to her death.

We were on the wharf and she stopped. I stopped. I saw her hands at her bonnet-strings, and I rushed between her and the brink and took her round the waist with both my arms. She might have drowned me, I felt then, but she could never have got quit of me.

Down to that moment my mind had been all in a maze and not half an idea had I had in it what I should say to her, but the instant I touched her it came to me like magic and I had my natural voice and my senses and even almost my breath.

"Mrs. Edson!" I says "My dear! Take care. How ever did you lose your way and stumble on a dangerous place like this? Why you must have come here by the most perplexing streets in all London. No wonder you are lost, I'm sure. And this place too! Why I thought nobody ever got here, except me to order my coals and the Major in the parlours to smoke his cigar!"—for I saw that blessed man close by, pretending to it.

"Hah—Hah—Hum!" coughs the Major.

"And good gracious me" I says, "why here he is!'

"Halloa! who goes there?" says the Major in a military manner.

"Well!" I says, "if this don't beat everything! Don't you know us Major Jackman?"

"Halloa!" says the Major. "Who calls on Jemmy Jackman?" (and more out of breath he was, and did it less like life than I should have expected.)

"Why here's Mrs. Edson Major" I says, "strolling out to cool her poor head which has been very bad, has missed her way and got lost, and Goodness knows where she might have got to but for me coming here to drop an order into my coal merchant's letter-box and you coming here to smoke your cigar!—And you really are not well enough my dear" I says to her "to be half so far from home without me.—And your arm will be very acceptable I am sure Major" I says to him "and I know she may lean upon it as heavy as she likes." And now we had both got her—thanks be Above!—one on each side.

She was all in a cold shiver and she so continued till I laid her on her own bed, and up to the early morning she held me by the hand and moaned and moaned "O wicked, wicked, wicked!" But when at last I made believe to droop my head and be overpowered with a dead sleep, I heard that poor young creature give such touching and such humble thanks for being preserved from taking her own life in her madness that I thought I should have cried my eyes out on the counterpane and I knew she was safe.

Being well enough to do and able to afford it, me and the Major laid our little plans next day while she was asleep worn out, and so I says to her as soon as I could do it nicely: "Mrs. Edson my dear, when Mr. Edson paid me the rent for these farther six months——"

She gave a start and I felt her large eyes look at me, but I went on with it and with my needlework.

"—I can't say that I am quite sure I dated the receipt right. Could you let me look at it?"

She laid her frozen cold hand upon mine and she looked through me when I was forced to look up from my needlework, but I had taken the precaution of having on my spectacles.

"I have no receipt" says she.

"Ah! Then he has got it" I says in a careless way. "It's of no great consequence. A receipt's a receipt."

From that time she always had hold of my hand when I could

spare it which was generally only when I read to her, for of course she and me had our bits of needlework to plod at and neither of us was very handy at those little things, though I am still rather proud of my share in them too considering. And though she took to all I read to her, I used to fancy that next to what was taught upon the Mount she took most of all to His gentle compassion for us poor women and to His young life and to how His mother was proud of Him and treasured His sayings in her heart. She had a grateful look in her eyes that never never never will be out of mine until they are closed in my last sleep, and when I chanced to look at her without thinking of it I would always meet that look, and she would often offer me her trembling lip to kiss, much more like a little affectionate halfbroken-hearted child than ever I can imagine any grown person.

One time the trembling of this poor lip was so strong and her tears ran down so fast that I thought she was going to tell me all her woe, so I takes her two hands in mine and I says:

"No my dear not now, you had best not try to do it now. Wait for better times when you have got over this and are strong, and then you shall tell me whatever you will. Shall it be agreed?"

With our hands still joined she nodded her head many times, and she lifted my hands and put them to her lips and to her bosom.

"Only one word now my dear" I says. "Is there any one?"

She looked inquiringly "Any one?"

"That I can go to?"

She shook her head.

"No one is wanted by *me* my dear. Now that may be considered past and gone."

Not much more than a week afterwards—for this was far on in the time of our being so together—I was bending over at her bedside with my ear down to her lips, by turns listening for her breath and looking for a sign of life in her face. At last it came in a solemn way —not in a flash but like a kind of pale faint light brought very slow to the face.

She said something to me that had no sound in it, but I saw she asked me:

"Is this death?"

And I says:

"Poor dear poor dear, I think it is."

Knowing somehow that she wanted me to move her weak right hand, I took it and laid it on her breast and then folded her other hand upon it, and she prayed a good good prayer and I joined in it poor me though there were no words spoke. Then I brought the baby in its wrappers from where it lay, and I says:

"My dear this is sent to a childless old woman. This is for me to take care of."

The trembling lip was put up towards my face for the last time, and I dearly kissed it.

"Yes my dear," I says. "Please God! Me and the Major."

I don't know how to tell it right, but I saw her soul brighten and leap up, and get free and fly away in the grateful look.

So this is the why and wherefore of its coming to pass my dear that we called him Jemmy, being after the Major his own godfather with Lirriper for a surname being after myself, and never was a dear child such a brightening thing in a Lodgings or such a playmate to his grandmother as Jemmy to this house and me, and always good and minding what he was told (upon the whole) and soothing for the temper and making everything pleasanter except when he grew old enough to drop his cap down Wozenham's Airy and they wouldn't hand it up to him, and being worked into a state I put on my best bonnet and gloves and parasol with the child in my hand and I says "Miss Wozenham I little thought ever to have entered *your* house but unless my grandson's cap is instantly restored, the laws of this country regulating the property of the Subject shall at length decide betwixt yourself and me, cost what it may." With a sneer upon her face which did strike me I must say as being expressive of two keys but it may have been a mistake and if there is any doubt let Miss Wozenham have the full benefit of it as is but right, she rang the bell and she says "Jane, is there a street-child's old cap down our Airy?" I says "Miss Wozenham before your housemaid answers that question you must allow me to inform you to your face that my grandson is *not* a street-child and is *not* in the habit of wearing old caps. In fact" I says "Miss Wozenham I am far from sure that my grandson's cap may not be newer than your own" which was perfectly savage in me, her lace being the commonest machine-make washed and torn besides, but I had been put into a state to begin with fomented by impertinence. Miss Wozenham says red in the face "Jane you heard my question, is there any child's cap down our Airy?" "Yes ma'am" says Jane "I think I did see some such rubbish a-lying there." "Then" says Miss Wozenham "let these visitors out, and then throw up that worthless article out of my premises." But here the child who had been staring at Miss Wozenham with all his eyes and more, frowns down his little eyebrows purses up his little mouth puts his chubby legs far apart turns his little dimpled fists round and round slowly over one another like a little coffee-mill, and says to her "Oo impdent to mi Gran, me tut oor hi!" "O!" says Miss Wozenham looking down scornfully at the Mite "this is not a street-child is it not? Really!" I bursts out laughing and I says "Miss Wozenham if this ain't a pretty sight to you I don't envy your feelings and I wish you good-day. Jemmy come along with Gran." And I was still in the best of humours though his cap came

flying up into the street as if it had been just turned on out of the
water-plug, and I went home laughing all the way, all owing to that
dear boy.

The miles and miles that me and the Major have travelled with
Jemmy in the dusk between the lights are not to be calculated, Jemmy
driving on the coach-box which is the Major's brass-bound writing
desk on the table, me inside in the easy-chair and the Major Guard
up behind with a brown-paper horn doing it really wonderful. I do
assure you my dear that sometimes when I have taken a few winks in
my place inside the coach and have come half awake by the flashing
light of the fire and have heard that precious pet driving and the
Major blowing up behind to have the change of horses ready when
we got to the Inn, I have half believed we were on the old North
Road that my poor Lirriper knew so well. Then to see that child and
the Major both wrapped up getting down to warm their feet and
going stamping about and having glasses of ale out of the paper
match-boxes on the chimney-piece is to see the Major enjoying it fully
as much as the child I am very sure, and it's equal to any play when
Coachee opens the coach-door to look in at me inside and say "Wery
'past that 'tage.—'Prightened old lady?"

But what my inexpressible feelings were when we lost that child can
only be compared to the Major's which were not a shade better,
through his straying out at five years old and eleven o'clock in the
forenoon and never heard of by word or sign or deed till half-past
nine at night, when the Major had gone to the Editor of the *Times*
newspaper to put in an advertisement, which came out next day four-
and-twenty hours after he was found, and which I mean always carefully to keep in my lavender drawer as the first printed account of
him. The more the day got on, the more I got distracted and the
Major too and both of us made worse by the composed ways of the
police though very civil and obliging and what I must call their ob-
stinacy in not entertaining the idea that he was stolen. "We mostly
find mum" says the sergeant who came round to comfort me, which
he didn't at all and he had been one of the private constables in
Caroline's time to which he referred in his opening words when he
said "Don't give way to uneasiness in your mind mum, it'll all come as
right as my nose did when I got the same barked by that young woman
in your second floor"—says this sergeant "we mostly find mum as
people ain't over-anxious to have what I may call second-hand children. You'll get him back mum." "O but my dear good Sir" I says
clasping my hands and wringing them and clasping them again "he is
such an uncommon child!" "Yes mum" says the sergeant, "we mostly
find that too mum. The question is what his clothes were worth."
"His clothes" I says "were not worth much Sir for he had only got his
playing-dress on, but the dear child!—" "All right mum" says the

sergeant. "You'll get him back mum. And even if he'd had his best clothes on, it wouldn't come to worse than his being found wrapped up in a cabbage-leaf, a shivering in a lane." His words pierced my heart like daggers and daggers, and me and the Major ran in and out like wild things all day long till the Major returning from his interview with the Editor of the *Times* at night rushes into my little room hysterical and squeezes my hand and wipes his eyes and says "Joy joy—officer in plain clothes came up on the steps as I was letting myself in—compose your feelings—Jemmy's found." Consequently I fainted away and when I came to, embraced the legs of the officer in plain clothes who seemed to be taking a kind of a quiet inventory in his mind of the property in my little room with brown whiskers, and I says "Blessings on you Sir where is the Darling?" and he says "In Kennington Station House." I was dropping at his feet Stone at the image of that Innocence in cells with murderers when he adds "He followed the Monkey." I says deeming it slang language "O Sir explain for a loving grandmother what Monkey!" He says "Him in the spangled cap with the strap under the chin, as won't keep on—him as sweeps the crossings on a round table and don't want to draw his sabre more than he can help." Then I understood it all and most thankfully thanked him, and me and the Major and him drove over to Kennington and there we found our boy lying quite comfortable before a blazing fire having sweetly played himself to sleep upon a small accordion nothing like so big as a flat-iron which they had been so kind to lend him for the purpose and which it appeared had been stopped upon a very young person.

My dear the system upon which the Major commenced and as I may say perfected Jemmy's learning when he was so small that if the dear was on the other side of the table you had to look under it instead of over it to see him with his mother's own bright hair in beautiful curls, is a thing that ought to be known to the Throne and Lords and Commons and then might obtain some promotion for the Major which he well deserves and would be none the worse for (speaking between friends) L. S. D.-ically. When the Major first undertook his learning he says to me:

"I'm going madam," he says "to make our child a Calculating Boy."

"Major," I says, "you terrify me and may do the pet a permanent injury you would never forgive yourself."

"Madam," says the Major, "next to my regret that when I had my boot-sponge in my hand, I didn't choke that scoundrel with it—on the spot——"

"There! For Gracious' sake," I interrupts, "let his conscience find him without sponges."

"—I say next to that regret, madam," says the Major "would be the regret with which my breast," which he tapped, "would be surcharged if this fine mind was not early cultivated. But mark me madam," says the Major holding up his forefinger "cultivated on a principle that will make it a delight."

"Major" I says "I will be candid with you and tell you openly that if ever I find the dear child fall off in his appetite I shall know it is his calculations and shall put a stop to them at two minutes' notice. Or if I find them mounting to his head" I says, "or striking anyways cold to his stomach or leading to anything approaching flabbiness in his legs, the result will be the same, but Major you are a clever man and have seen much and you love the child and are his own godfather, and if you feel a confidence in trying try."

"Spoken madam" says the Major "like Emma Lirriper. All I have to ask, madam, is that you will leave my godson and myself to make a week or two's preparations for surprising you, and that you will give me leave to have up and down any small articles not actually in use that I may require from the kitchen."

"From the kitchen Major?" I says half feeling as if he had a mind to cook the child.

"From the kitchen" says the Major, and smiles and swells, and at the same time looks taller.

So I passed my word and the Major and the dear boy were shut up together for half an hour at a time through a certain while, and never could I hear anything going on betwixt them but talking and laughing and Jemmy clapping his hands and screaming out numbers, so I says to myself "it has not harmed him yet" nor could I on examining the dear find any signs of it anywhere about him which was likewise a great relief. At last one day Jemmy brings me a card in joke in the Major's neat writing "The Messrs. Jemmy Jackman" for we had given him the Major's other name too "request the honour of Mrs. Lirriper's company at the Jackman Institution in the front parlour this evening at five, military time, to witness a few slight feats of elementary arithmetic." And if you'll believe me there in the front parlour at five punctual to the moment was the Major behind the Pembroke table with both leaves up and a lot of things from the kitchen tidily set out on old newspapers spread atop of it, and there was the Mite stood up on a chair with his rosy cheeks flushing and his eyes sparkling clusters of diamonds.

"Now Gran" says he, "oo tit down and don't oo touch ler poople" —for he saw with every one of those diamonds of his that I was going to give him a squeeze.

"Very well Sir" I says "I am obedient in this good company I am sure." And I sits down in the easy-chair that was put for me, shaking my sides.

But picture my admiration when the Major going on almost as quick as if he was conjuring sets out all the articles he names, and says "Three saucepans, an Italian iron, a hand-bell, a toasting-fork, a nutmeg-grater, four potlids, a spice-box, two egg-cups, and a chopping-board—how many?" and when that Mite instantly cries "Tifteen, tut down tive and carry ler 'toppin-board" and then claps his hands draws up his legs and dances on his chair.

My dear with the same astonishing ease and correctness him and the Major added up the tables chairs and sofy, the picters fenders and fire-irons their own selves me and the cat and the eyes in Miss Wozenham's head, and whenever the sum was done Young Roses and Diamonds claps his hands and draws up his legs and dances on his chair.

The pride of the Major! ("*Here's* a mind ma'am!" he says to me behind his hand.)

Then he says aloud, "We now come to the next elementary rule,—which is called——"

"Umtraction!" cries Jemmy.

"Right," says the Major. "We have here a toasting-fork, a potato in its natural state, two potlids, one egg-cup, a wooden spoon, and two skewers, from which it is necessary for commercial purposes to subtract, a sprat-gridiron, a small pickle-jar, two lemons, one pepper-castor, a black beetle-trap and a knob of the dresser-drawer—what remains?"

"Toatin-fork!" cries Jemmy.

"In numbers how many?" says the Major.

"One!" cries Jemmy.

("*Here's* a boy, ma'am!" says the Major to me behind his hand.)

Then the Major goes on:

"We now approach the next elementary rule,—which is entitled——"

"Tickleication" cries Jemmy.

"Correct" says the Major.

But my dear to relate to you in detail the way in which they multiplied fourteen sticks of firewood by two bits of ginger and a larding-needle, or divided pretty well everything else there was on the table by the heater of the Italian iron and a chamber candlestick, and got a lemon over, would make my head spin round and round and round as it did at the time. So I says "if you'll excuse my addressing the chair Professor Jackman I think the period of the lecture has now arrived when it becomes necessary that I should take a good hug of this young scholar." Upon which Jemmy calls out from his station on the chair, "Gran oo open oor arms and me'll make a 'pring into 'em." So I opened my arms to him as I had opened my sorrowful heart when his poor young mother lay a dying, and he had his jump and we had a good long hug together and the Major prouder than any peacock says to me behind his hand, "You need not let him know it madam" (which I certainly need not for the Major was quite audible) "but he is a boy!"

In this way Jemmy grew and grew and went to day-school and continued under the Major too, and in summer we were as happy as the days were long, and in winter we were as happy as the days were short and there seemed to rest a Blessing on the Lodgings for they as good as Let themselves and would have done it if there had been twice the accommodation, when sore and hard against my will I one day says to the Major:

"Major you know what I am going to break to you. Our boy must go to boarding-school."

It was a sad sight to see the Major's countenance drop, and I pitied the good soul with all my heart.

"Yes Major" I says, "though he is as popular with the Lodgers as you are yourself and though he is to you and me what only you and me know, still it is in the course of things and Life is made of partings and we must part with our Pet."

Bold as I spoke, I saw two Majors and half-a-dozen fireplaces, and when the poor Major put one of his neat bright-varnished boots upon the fender and his elbow on his knee and his head upon his hand and rocked himself a little to and fro, I was dreadfully cut up.

"But" says I clearing my throat "you have so well prepared him Major—he has had such a Tutor in you—that he will have none of the first drudgery to go through. And he is so clever besides that he'll soon make his way to the front rank."

"He is a boy" says the Major—having sniffed—"that has not his like on the face of the earth."

"True as you say Major, and it is not for us merely for our own sakes to do anything to keep him back from being a credit and an ornament wherever he goes and perhaps even rising to be a great man, is it Major? He will have all my little savings when my work is done (being all the world to me) and we must try to make him a wise man and a good man, mustn't we Major?"

"Madam" says the Major rising "Jemmy Jackman is becoming an older file than I was aware of, and you put him to shame. You are thoroughly right madam. You are simply and undeniably right.—And if you'll excuse me, I'll take a walk."

So the Major being gone out and Jemmy being at home, I got the child into my little room here and I stood him by my chair and I took his mother's own curls in my hand and I spoke to him loving and serious. And when I had reminded the darling how that he was now in his tenth year and when I had said to him about his getting on in life pretty much what I had said to the Major I broke to him how that we must have this same parting, and there I was forced to stop for there I saw of a sudden the well-remembered lip with its tremble, and it so brought back that time! But with the spirit that was in him he controlled it soon and he says gravely nodding through his tears, "I understand Gran—I know it *must* be, Gran,—go on Gran, don't be afraid of *me*." And when I had said all that ever I could think of, he turned his bright steady face to mine and he says just a little broken here and there "You shall see Gran that I can be a man and that I can do anything that is grateful and loving to you—and if I don't grow up to be what you would like to have me— I hope it will be—because I shall die." And with that he sat down by me and I went on to tell him of the school of which I had excellent recommendations and where it was and how many scholars and what games they played as I had heard and what length of holidays, to all of which he listened bright and clear. And so it came that at last he says "And now dear Gran let me kneel down here where I have been used to say my prayers and let me fold my face for just a minute in your gown and let me cry, for you have been more than father—more than mother—more than brothers sisters friends—to me!" And so he did cry and I too and we were both much the better for it.

From that time forth he was true to his word and ever blithe and ready, and even when me and the Major took him down into Lincolnshire he was far the gayest of the party though for sure and certain he might easily have been that, but he really was and put life into us only when it came to the last Good-bye, he says with a wistful look, "You wouldn't have me not really sorry would you Gran?" and when I says "No dear, Lord forbid!" he says "I am glad of that!" and ran in out of sight.

But now that the child was gone out of the Lodgings the Major fell into a regularly moping state. It was taken notice of by all the Lodgers that the Major moped. He hadn't even the same air of being rather tall that he used to have, and if he varnished his boots with a single gleam of interest it was as much as he did.

One evening the Major came into my little room to take a cup of tea and a morsel of buttered toast and to read Jemmy's newest letter which had arrived that afternoon (by the very same postman more than middle-aged upon the Beat now), and the letter raising him up a little I says to the Major:

"Major you mustn't get into a moping way."

The Major shook his head. "Jemmy Jackman madam," he says with a deep sigh, "is an older file than I thought him."

"Moping is not the way to grow younger Major."

"My dear madam," says the Major, "is there *any* way of growing younger?"

Feeling that the Major was getting rather the best of that point I made a diversion to another.

"Thirteen years! Thir-teen years! Many Lodgers have come and gone, in the thirteen years that you have lived in the parlours Major."

"Hah!" says the Major warming. "Many madam, many."

"And I should say you have been familiar with them all?"

"As a rule (with its exceptions like all rules) my dear madam" says the Major, "they have honoured me with their acquaintance, and not unfrequently with their confidence."

Watching the Major as he drooped his white head and stroked his black mustachios and moped again, a thought which I think must have been going about looking for an owner somewhere dropped into my old noodle if you will excuse the expression.

"The walls of my Lodgings" I says in a casual way—for my dear it is of no use going straight at a man who mopes—"might have something to tell if they could tell it."

The Major neither moved nor said anything but I saw he was attending with his shoulders my dear—attending with his shoulders to what I said. In fact I saw that his shoulders were struck by it.

"The dear boy was always fond of story-books" I went on, like as if I was talking to myself. "I am sure this house—his own home—might write a story or two for his reading one day or another."

The Major's shoulders gave a dip and a curve and his head came up in his shirt-collar. The Major's head came up in his shirt-collar as I hadn't seen it come up since Jemmy went to school.

"It is unquestionable that in intervals of cribbage and a friendly rubber, my dear madam," says the Major, "and also over what used to be called in my young times—in the salad days of Jemmy Jackman —the social glass, I have exchanged many a reminiscence with your Lodgers."

My remark was—I confess I made it with the deepest and artfullest of intentions—"I wish our dear boy had heard them!"

"Are you serious madam?" asks the Major starting and turning full round.

"Why not Major?"

"Madam" says the Major, turning up one of his cuffs, "they shall be written for him."

"Ah! Now you speak" I says giving my hands a pleased clap. "Now you are in a way out of moping Major!"

"Between this and my holidays—I mean the dear boy's" says the Major turning up his other cuff, "a good deal may be done towards it."

"Major you are a clever man and you have seen much and not a doubt of it."

"I'll begin," says the Major looking as tall as ever he did, "to-morrow."

My dear the Major was another man in three days and he was himself again in a week and he wrote and wrote and wrote with his pen scratching like rats behind the wainscot, and whether he had many grounds to go upon or whether he did at all romance I cannot tell you, but what he has written is in the left-hand glass closet of the little bookcase close behind you.

CHAPTER II *How the parlours added a few words*

I have the honour of presenting myself by the name of Jackman. I esteem it a proud privilege to go down to posterity through the instrumentality of the most remarkable boy that ever lived,—by the name of JEMMY JACKMAN, LIRRIPER,—and of my worthy and most highly respected friend, Mrs. Emma Lirriper, of Eighty-one, Norfolk Street, Strand, in the County of Middlesex, in the United Kingdom of Great Britain and Ireland.

It is not for me to express the rapture with which we received that dear and eminently remarkable boy, on the occurrence of his first Christmas holidays. Suffice it to observe that when he came flying into the house with two splendid prizes (Arithmetic, and Exemplary Conduct), Mrs. Lirriper and myself embraced with emotion, and instantly took him to the Play, where we were all three admirably entertained.

Nor is it to render homage to the virtues of the best of her good and honoured sex—whom, in deference to her unassuming worth, I will only here designate by the initials E. L.—that I add this record to the bundle of papers with which our, in a most distinguished degree, remarkable boy has expressed himself delighted, before reconsigning the same to the left-hand glass closet of Mrs. Lirriper's little bookcase.

Neither is it to obtrude the name of the old original superannuated obscure Jemmy Jackman, once (to his degradation) of Wozenham's, long (to his elevation) of Lirriper's. If I could be consciously guilty of that piece of bad taste, it would indeed be a work of supererogation, now that the name is borne by JEMMY JACKMAN LIRRIPER.

No, I take up my humble pen to register a little record of our strikingly remarkable boy, which my poor capacity regards as presenting a pleasant little picture of the dear boy's mind. The picture may be interesting to himself when he is a man.

Our first reunited Christmas-day was the most delightful one we have ever passed together. Jemmy was never silent for five minutes, except in church-time. He talked as we sat by the fire, he talked when we were out walking, he talked as we sat by the fire again, he talked incessantly at dinner, though he made a dinner almost as remarkable as himself. It was the spring of happiness in his fresh young heart flowing and flowing, and it fertilised (if I may be allowed so bold a figure) my much-esteemed friend, and J. J. the present writer.

There were only we three. We dined in my esteemed friend's little room, and our entertainment was perfect. But everything in the establishment is, in neatness, order, and comfort, always perfect. After dinner our boy slipped away to his old stool at my esteemed friend's knee, and there, with his hot chestnuts and his glass of brown sherry (really, a most excellent wine!) on a chair for a table, his face outshone the apples in the dish.

We talked of these jottings of mine, which Jemmy had read through and through by that time; and so it came about that my esteemed friend remarked, as she sat smoothing Jemmy's curls:

"And as you belong to the house too, Jemmy,—and so much more than the Lodgers, having been born in it,—why, your story ought to be added to the rest, I think, one of these days."

Jemmy's eyes sparkled at this, and he said, "So I think, Gran."

Then he sat looking at the fire, and then he began to laugh in a sort of confidence with the fire, and then he said, folding his arms across my esteemed friend's lap, and raising his bright face to hers: "Would you like to hear a boy's story, Gran?"

"Of all things," replied my esteemed friend.

"Would you, godfather?"

"Of all things," I too replied.

"Well, then," said Jemmy, "I'll tell you one."

Here our indisputably remarkable boy gave himself a hug, and laughed again, musically, at the idea of his coming out in that new line. Then he once more took the fire into the same sort of confidence as before, and began:

"Once upon a time, When pigs drank wine, And monkeys chewed tobaccer, 'Twas neither in your time nor mine, But that's no macker——"

"Bless the child!" cried my esteemed friend, "what's amiss with his brain?"

"It's poetry, Gran," returned Jemmy, shouting with laughter. "We aways begin stories that way at school."

"Gave me quite a turn, Major," said my esteemed friend, fanning herself with a plate. "Thought he was light-headed!"

"In those remarkable times, Gran and godfather, there was once a boy,—not me, you know."

"No, no," says my respected friend, "not you. Not him, Major, you understand?"

"No, no," says I.

"And he went to school in Rulandshire——"

"Why not Lincolnshire?" says my respected friend.

"Why not, you dear old Gran? Because *I* go to school in Lincolnshire, don't I?"

"Ah, to be sure!" says my respected friend. "And it's not Jemmy, you understand, Major?"

"No, no," says I.

"Well!" our boy proceeded, hugging himself comfortably, and laughing merrily (again in confidence with the fire), before he again looked up in Mrs. Lirriper's face, "and so he was tremendously in love with his schoolmaster's daughter, and she was the most beautiful creature that ever was seen, and she had brown eyes, and she had brown hair all curling beautifully, and she had a delicious voice, and she was delicious altogether, and her name was Seraphina."

"What's the name of *your* schoolmaster's daughter, Jemmy?" asks my respected friend.

"Polly!" replied Jemmy, pointing his forefinger at her. "There now! Caught you! Ha, ha, ha!"

When he and my respected friend had had a laugh and a hug together, our admittedly remarkable boy resumed with a great relish:

"Well! And so he loved her. And so he thought about her, and dreamed about her, and made her presents of oranges and nuts, and would have made her presents of pearls and diamonds if he could have afforded it out of his pocket-money, but he couldn't. And so her father—O, he WAS a Tartar! Keeping the boys up to the mark, holding examinations once a month, lecturing upon all sorts of subjects at all sorts of times, and knowing everything in the world out of book. And so this boy——"

"Had he any name?" asks my respected friend.

"No, he hadn't, Gran. Ha, ha! There now! Caught you again!"

After this, they had another laugh and another hug, and then our boy went on.

"Well! And so this boy, he had a friend about as old as himself at the same school, and his name (for He *had* a name, as it happened) was—let me remember—was Bobbo."

"Not Bob," says my respected friend.

"Of course not," says Jemmy. "What made you think it was, Gran? Well! And so this friend was the cleverest and bravest and best-looking and most generous of all the friends that ever were, and so he was in love with Seraphina's sister, and so Seraphina's sister was in love with him, and so they all grew up."

"Bless us!" says my respected friend. "They were very sudden about it."

"So they all grew up," our boy repeated, laughing heartily, "and Bobbo and this boy went away together on horseback to seek their fortunes, and they partly got their horses by favour, and partly in a bargain; that is to say, they had saved up between them seven and fourpence, and the two horses, being Arabs, were worth more, only the man said he would take that, to favour them. Well! And so they made their fortunes and came prancing back to the school, with their pockets full of gold, enough to last for ever. And so they rang at the parents' and visitors' bell (not the back gate), and when the bell was answered they proclaimed 'The same as if it was scarlet fever! Every boy goes home for an indefinite period!' And then there was great hurrahing, and then they kissed Seraphina and her sister,—each his own love, and not the other's on any account,—and then they ordered the Tartar into instant confinement."

"Poor man!" said my respected friend.

"Into instant confinement, Gran," repeated Jemmy, trying to look severe and roaring with laughter; "and he was to have nothing to eat but the boys' dinners, and was to drink half a cask of their beer every day. And so then the preparations were made for the two weddings, and there were hampers, and potted things, and sweet things, and nuts, and postage-stamps, and all manner of things. And so they were so jolly, that they let the Tartar out, and he was jolly too."

"I am glad they let him out," says my respected friend, "because he had only done his duty."

"O, but hadn't he overdone it, though!" cried Jemmy. "Well! And so then this boy mounted his horse, with his bride in his arms, and cantered away, and cantered on and on till he came to a certain place where he had a certain Gran and a certain godfather,—not you two, you know."

"No, no," we both said.

"And there he was received with great rejoicings, and he filled the cupboard and the bookcase with gold, and he showered it out on his Gran and his godfather because they were the two kindest and dearest people that ever lived in this world. And so while they were sitting up to their knees in gold, a knocking was heard at the street door, and who should it be but Bobbo, also on horseback with his bride in his arms, and what had he come to say but that he would take (at double rent) all the Lodgings for ever, that were not wanted by this boy and this Gran and this godfather, and that they would all live together, and all be happy! And so they were, and so it never ended!"

"And was there no quarrelling?" asked my respected friend, as Jemmy sat upon her lap and hugged her.

"No! Nobody ever quarrelled."

"And did the money never melt away?"

"No! Nobody could ever spend it all."

"And did none of them ever grow older?"

"No! Nobody ever grew older after that."

"And did none of them ever die?"

"Oh, no, no, no, Gran!" exclaimed our dear boy, laying his cheek upon her breast, and drawing her closer to him. "Nobody ever died."

"Ah, Major, Major!" says my respected friend, smiling benignly upon me, "this beats our stories. Let us end with the Boy's story, Major, for the Boy's story is the best that is ever told!"

In submission to which request on the part of the best of women, I have here noted it down as faithfully as my best abilities, coupled with my best intentions, would admit, subscribing it with my name,

J. JACKMAN.

THE PARLOURS.

MRS. LIRRIPER'S LODGINGS.

—1863

Doctor Marigold IN THREE CHAPTERS

CHAPTER I *To be taken immediately*

I am a Cheap Jack, and my own father's name was Willum Marigold. It was in his lifetime supposed by some that his name was William, but my own father always consistently said, No, it was Willum. On which point I content myself with looking at the argument this way: If a man is not allowed to know his own name in a free country, how much is he allowed to know in a land of slavery? As to looking at the argument through the medium of the Register, Willum Marigold come into the world before Registers come up much,—and went out of it too. They wouldn't have been greatly in his line neither, if they had chanced to come up before him.

I was born on the Queen's highway, but it was the King's at that time. A doctor was fetched to my own mother by my own father, when it took place on a common; and in consequence of his being a very kind gentleman, and accepting no fee but a tea-tray, I was named Doctor, out of gratitude and compliment to him. There you have me. Doctor Marigold.

I am at present a middle-aged man of a broadish build, in cords, leggings, and a sleeved waistcoat the strings of which is always gone behind. Repair them how you will, they go like fiddle-strings. You have been to the theatre, and you have seen one of the wiolin-players screw up his wiolin, after listening to it as if it had been whispering the secret to him that it feared it was out of order, and then you have heard it snap. That's as exactly similar to my waistcoat as a waistcoat and a wiolin can be like one another.

I am partial to a white hat, and I like a shawl round my neck wore loose and easy. Sitting down is my favourite posture. If I have a taste in point of personal jewelry, it is mother-of-pearl buttons. There you have me again, as large as life.

The doctor having accepted a tea-tray, you'll guess that my father was a Cheap Jack before me. You are right. He was. It was a pretty tray. It represented a large lady going along a serpentining up-hill gravel-walk, to attend a little church. Two swans had likewise come astray with the same intentions. When I call her a large lady, I don't mean in point of breadth, for there she fell below my views, but she more than made it up in heighth; her heighth and slimness was—in short THE heighth of both.

I often saw that tray, after I was the innocently smiling cause (or more like screeching one) of the doctor's standing it up on a table against the wall in his consulting-room. Whenever my own father and mother were in that part of the country, I used to put my head (I have heard my own mother say it was flaxen curls at that time, though you wouldn't know an old hearth-broom from it now till you come to the handle, and found it wasn't me) in at the doctor's door, and the doctor was always glad to see me, and said, "Aha, my brother practitioner! Come in, little M.D. How are your inclinations as to sixpence?"

You can't go on for ever, you'll find, nor yet could my father nor yet my mother. If you don't go off as a whole when you are about due, you're liable to go off in part, and two to one your head's the part. Gradually my father went off his, and my mother went off hers. It was in a harmless way, but it put out the family where I boarded them. The old couple, though retired, got to be wholly and solely devoted to the Cheap Jack business, and were always selling the family off. Whenever the cloth was laid for dinner, my father began rattling the plates and dishes, as we do in our line when we put up crockery for a bid, only he had lost the trick of it, and mostly let 'em drop and broke 'em. As the old lady had been used to sit in the cart, and hand the articles out one by one to the old gentleman on the footboard to sell, just in the same way she handed him every item of the family's property, and they disposed of it in their own imaginations from morning to night. At last the old gentleman, lying bedridden in the same room with the old lady, cries out in the old patter, fluent, after having been silent for two days and nights: "Now here, my jolly companions every one,—which the Nightingale club in a village was held, At the sign of the Cabbage and Shears, Where the singers no doubt would have greatly excelled, But for want of taste, voices, and ears,—now, here, my jolly companions, every one, is a working model of a used-up old Cheap Jack, without a tooth in his head, and with a pain in every bone: so like life that it would be just as good if it wasn't better, just as bad if it wasn't worse, and just as new if it wasn't worn out. Bid for the working model of the old Cheap Jack, who has drunk more gunpowder-tea with the ladies in his time than would blow the lid off a washerwoman's copper, and carry it as many thousands of miles higher than the moon as naught nix naught, divided by the national debt, carry nothing to the poor-rates, three under, and two over. Now, my hearts of oak and men of straw, what do you say for the lot? Two shillings, a shilling, tenpence, eightpence, sixpence, fourpence. Twopence? Who said twopence? The gentleman in the scarecrow's hat? I am ashamed of the gentleman in the scarecrow's hat. I really am ashamed of him for his want of public spirit. Now I'll tell you what I'll do with you. Come! I'll throw you in a working model of a old woman that was married to the old Cheap Jack so long ago that upon my word and honour it took place in Noah's Ark, before the Unicorn could get in to forbid the banns by blowing a tune upon his horn. There now! Come! What do you say for both? I'll tell you what I'll do with you. I don't bear you malice for being so backward. Here! If you make me a bid that'll only reflect a little credit on your town, I'll throw you in a warming-pan for nothing, and lend you a toasting-fork for life. Now come; what do you say after that splendid offer? Say two pound, say thirty shillings, say a pound, say ten shillings, say five, say two and six? You don't say even two and six? You say two and three? No. You shan't have the lot for two and three. I'd sooner give it to you, if you was good-looking enough. Here! Missis! Chuck the old man and woman into the cart, put the horse to, and drive 'em away and bury 'em!" Such were the last words of Willum Marigold, my own father, and they were carried out, by him and by his wife, my own mother, on one and the same day, as I ought to know, having followed as mourner.

My father had been a lovely one in his time at the Cheap Jack work, as his dying observations went to prove. But I top him. I don't say it because it's myself, but because it has been universally acknowledged by all that has had the means of comparison. I have worked at it. I have measured myself against other public speakers, —Members of Parliament, Platforms, Pulpits, Counsel learned in the law,—and where I have found 'em good, I have took a bit of imagination from 'em, and where I have found 'em bad, I have let 'em alone. Now I'll tell you what. I mean to go down into my grave declaring that of all the callings ill used in Great Britain, the Cheap Jack calling is the worst used. Why ain't we a profession? Why ain't we endowed with privileges? Why are we forced to take out a hawkers's license, when no such thing is expected of the political hawkers? Where's the difference betwixt us? Except that we are Cheap Jacks, and they are Dear Jacks, I don't see any difference but what's in our favour.

For look here! Say it's election time. I am on the footboard of my cart in the market-place, on a Saturday night. I put up a general miscellaneous lot. I say: "Now here, my free and independent woters, I'm a going to give you such a chance as you never had in all your born days, nor yet the days preceding. Now I'll show you what I am a going to do with you. Here's a pair of razors that'll shave you closer than the Board of Guardians; here's a flat-iron worth its weight in gold; here's a frying-pan artificially flavoured with essence of beef-steaks to that degree that you've only got for the rest of your lives to fry bread and dripping in it and there you are replete with animal food; here's a genuine chronometer watch in such a solid silver case that you may knock at the door with it when you come home late from a social meeting, and rouse your wife and family, and save up your knocker for the postman; and here's half-a-dozen dinner plates that you may play the cymbals with to charm the baby when it's fractious. Stop! I'll throw you in another article, and I'll give you that, and it's a rolling-pin; and if the baby can only get it well into its mouth when its teeth is coming and rub the gums once with it, they'll come through double, in a fit of laughter equal to being tickled. Stop again! I'll throw you in another article, because I don't like the looks of you, for you haven't the appearance of buyers unless I lose by you, and because I'd rather lose than not take money to-night, and that's a looking-glass in which you may see how ugly you look when you don't bid. What do you say now? Come! Do you say a pound? Not you, for you haven't got it. Do you say ten shillings? Not you, for you owe more to the tallyman. Well then, I'll tell you what I'll do with you. I'll heap 'em all on the footboard of the cart,—there they are! razors, flat-iron, frying-pan, chronometer watch, dinner plates, rolling-pin, and looking-glass,—take 'em all away for four shillings, and I'll give you sixpence for your trouble!" This is me, the Cheap Jack. But on the Monday morning, in the same market-place, comes the Dear Jack on the hustings—*his* cart—and what does *he* say? "Now my free and independent woters, I am a going to give you such a chance" (he begins just like me) "as you never had in all your born days, and that's the chance of sending Myself to Parliament. Now I'll tell you what I am a going to do for you. Here's the interests of this magnificent town promoted above all the rest of the civilised and uncivilised earth. Here's your railways carried, and your neighbours' railways jockeyed. Here's all your sons in the Post-office. Here's Britannia smiling on you. Here's the eyes of Europe on you. Here's uniwersal prosperity for you, repletion of animal food, golden corn-fields, gladsome homesteads, and rounds of applause from your own hearts, all in one lot, and that's myself. Will you take me as I stand? You won't? Well, then, I'll tell you what I'll do with you. Come now! I'll throw you in anything you ask for. There! Church-rates, abolition of church-rates, more malt tax, no malt tax, uniwersal education to the highest mark, or uniwersal ignorance to the lowest, total abolition of flogging in the army or a dozen for every private once a month all round. Wrongs of Men or Rights of Women—only say which it shall be, take 'em or leave 'em, and I'm of your opinion altogether, and the lot's your own on your own terms. There! You won't take it yet! Well, then, I'll tell you what I'll do with you. Come! You *are* such free and independent woters, and I *am* so proud of you,—you *are* such a noble and enlightened constituency, and I *am* so ambitious of the honour and dignity of being your member, which is by far the highest level to which the wings of the human mind can soar,—that I'll tell you what I'll do with you. I'll throw you in all the public-houses in your magnificent town for nothing. Will that content you? It won't? You won't take the lot yet? Well, then, before I put the horse in and drive away, and make the offer to the next most magnificent town that can be discovered, I'll tell you what I'll do. Take the lot, and I'll drop two thousand pound in the streets of your magnificent town for them to pick up that can. Not enough? Now look here. This is the very furthest that I'm a going to. I'll make it two thousand five hundred. And still you won't? Here, missis! Put the horse— no, stop half a moment, I shouldn't like to turn my back upon you neither for a trifle, I'll make it two thousand seven hundred and fifty pound. There! Take the lot on your own terms, and I'll count out two thousand seven hundred and fifty pound on the footboard of the cart, to be dropped in the streets of your magnificent town for them to pick up that can. What do you say? Come now! You won't do better, and you may do worse. You take it? Hooray! Sold again, and got the seat!"

These Dear Jacks soap the people shameful, but we Cheap Jacks don't. We tell 'em the truth about themselves to their faces, and scorn to court 'em. As to wenturesomeness in the way of puffing up the lots, the Dear Jacks beats us hollow. It is considered in the Cheap Jack calling, that better patter can be made out of a gun than any article we put up from the cart, except a pair of spectacles. I often hold forth about a gun for a quarter of an hour, and feel as if I need never leave off. But when I tell 'em what the gun can do, and what the gun has brought down, I never go half so far as the Dear Jacks do when they make speeches in praise of *their* guns—their great guns that set 'em on to do it. Besides, I'm in business for myself: I ain't sent down into the market-place to order, as they are. Besides, again, my guns don't know what I say in their laudation, and their guns do, and the whole concern of 'em have reason to be sick and ashamed all round. These are some of my arguments for declaring that the Cheap Jack calling is treated ill in Great Britain, and for turning warm when I think of the other Jacks in question setting themselves up to pretend to look down upon it.

I courted my wife from the footboard of the cart. I did indeed. She was a Suffolk young woman, and it was in Ipswich market-place right opposite the corn-chandler's shop. I had noticed her up at a window last Saturday that was, appreciating highly. I had took to her, and I had said to myself, "If not already disposed of, I'll have that lot." Next Saturday that come, I pitched the cart on the same pitch, and I was in very high feather indeed, keeping 'em laughing the whole of the time, and getting off the goods briskly. At last I took out of my waistcoat-pocket a small lot wrapped in soft paper, and I put it this way (looking up at the window where she was). "Now here, my blooming English maidens, is an article, the last article of the present evening's sale, which I offer to only you, the lovely Suffolk Dumplings biling over with beauty, and I won't take a bid of a thousand pounds for from any man alive. Now what is it? Why, I'll tell you what it is. It's made of fine gold, and it's not broke, though there's a hole in the middle of it, and it's stronger than any fetter that ever was forged, though it's smaller than any finger in my set of ten. Why ten? Because, when my parents made over my property to me, I tell you true, there was twelve sheets, twelve towels, twelve table-cloths, twelve knives, twelve forks, twelve tablespoons, and twelve teaspoons, but my set of fingers was two short of a dozen, and could never since be matched. Now what else is it? Come, I'll tell you. It's a hoop of solid gold, wrapped in a silver curl-paper, that I myself took off the shining locks of the ever-beautiful old lady in Threadneedle-street, London city; I wouldn't tell you so if I hadn't the paper to show, or you mightn't believe it even of me. Now what else is it? It's a man-trap and a handcuff, the parish stocks and a leg-lock, all in gold and all in one. Now what else is it? It's a wedding-ring. Now I'll tell you what I'm a going to do with it. I'm not a going to offer this lot for money; but I mean to give it to the next of you beauties that laughs, and I'll pay her a visit to-morrow morning at exactly half after nine o'clock as the chimes go, and I'll take her out for a walk to put up the banns." *She* laughed, and got the ring handed up to her. When I called in the morning, she says, "O dear! It's never you, and you never mean it?" "It's ever me," says I, "and I am ever yours, and I ever mean it." So we got married, after being put up three times—which, by the bye, is quite in the Cheap Jack way again, and shows once more how the Cheap Jack customs pervade society.

She wasn't a bad wife, but she had a temper. If she could have parted with that one article at a sacrifice, I wouldn't have swopped her away in exchange for any other woman in England. Not that I ever did swop her away, for we lived together till she died, and that was thirteen year. Now, my lords and ladies and gentlefolks all, I'll let you into a secret, though you won't believe it. Thirteen year of temper in a Palace would try the worst of you, but thirteen year of temper in a Cart would try the best of you. You are kept so very close to it in a cart, you see. There's thousands of couples among you getting on like sweet ile upon a whetstone in houses five and six pairs of stairs high, that would go to the Divorce Court in a cart. Whether the jolting makes it worse, I don't undertake to decide; but in a cart it does come home to you, and stick to you. Wiolence in a cart is so wiolent, and aggrawation in a cart is so aggrawating.

We might have had such a pleasant life! A roomy cart, with the large goods hung outside, and the bed slung underneath it when on the road, an iron pot and a kettle, a fireplace for the cold weather, a chimney for the smoke, a hanging-shelf and a cupboard, a dog and a horse. What more do you want? You draw off upon a bit of turf in a green lane or by the roadside, you hobble your old horse and turn him grazing, you light your fire upon the ashes of the last visitors, you cook your stew, and you wouldn't call the Emperor of France your father. But have a temper in the cart, flinging language and the hardest goods in stock at you and where are you then? Put a name to your feelings.

My dog knew as well when she was on the turn as I did. Before she broke out, he would give a howl, and bolt. How he knew it, was a mystery to me; but the sure and certain knowledge of it would wake him up out of his soundest sleep, and he would give a howl, and bolt. At such times I wished I was him.

The worst of it was, we had a daughter born to us, and I love children with all my heart. When she was in her furies she beat the child. This got to be so shocking, as the child got to be four or five year old, that I have many a time gone on with my whip over my shoulder, at the old horse's head, sobbing and crying worse than ever little Sophy did. For how could I prevent it? Such a thing is not to be tried with such a temper—in a cart—without coming to a fight. It's in the natural size and formation of a cart to bring it to a fight. And then the poor child got worse terrified than before, as well as worse hurt generally, and her mother made complaints to the next people we lighted on, and the word went round, "Here's a wretch of a Cheap Jack been a beating his wife."

Little Sophy was such a brave child! She grew to be quite devoted to her poor father, though he could do so little to help her. She had a wonderful quantity of shining dark hair, all curling natural about her. It is quite astonishing to me now, that I didn't go tearing mad when I used to see her run from her mother before the cart, and her mother catch her by this hair, and pull her down by it, and beat her.

Such a brave child I said she was! Ah! with reason.

"Don't you mind next time, father dear," she would whisper to me, with her little face still flushed, and her bright eyes still wet; "if I don't cry out, you may know I am not much hurt. And even if I do cry out, it will only be to get mother to let go and leave off." What I have seen the little spirit bear—for me—without crying out!

Yet in other respects her mother took great care of her. Her clothes were always clean and neat, and her mother was never tired of working at 'em. Such is the inconsistency in things. Our being down in the marsh country in unhealthy weather, I consider the cause of Sophy's taking bad low fever; but however she took it, once she got it she turned away from her mother for evermore, and nothing would persuade her to be touched by her mother's hand. She would shiver and say, "No, no, no," when it was offered at, and would hide her face on my shoulder, and hold me tighter round the neck.

The Cheap Jack business had been worse than ever I had known it, what with one thing and what with another (and not least with railroads, which will cut it all to pieces, I expect, at last), and I was run dry of money. For which reason, one night at that period of little Sophy's being so bad, either we must have come to a dead-lock for victuals and drink, or I must have pitched the cart as I did.

I couldn't get the dear child to lie down or leave go of me, and indeed I hadn't the heart to try, so I stepped out on the footboard with her holding round my neck. They all set up a laugh when they see us, and one chuckle-headed Joskin (that I hated for it) made the bidding, "Tuppence for her!"

"Now, you country boobies," says I, feeling as if my heart was a heavy weight at the end of a broken sashline, "I give you notice that I am a going to charm the money out of your pockets, and to give you so much more than your money's worth that you'll only persuade yourselves to draw your Saturday night's wages ever again arterwards by the hopes of meeting me to lay 'em out with, which you never will, and why not? Because I've made my fortune by selling my goods on a large scale for seventy-five per cent. less than I give for 'em, and I am consequently to be elevated to the House of Peers next week, by the title of the Duke of Cheap and Markis Jackaloorul. Now let's know what you want to-night, and you shall have it. But first of all, shall I tell you why I have got this little girl round my neck? You don't want to know? Then you shall. She belongs to the Fairies. She's a fortune-teller. She can tell me all about you in a whisper, and can put me up to whether you're going to buy a lot or leave it. Now do you want a saw? No, she says you don't, because you're too clumsy to use one. Else here's a saw which would be a lifelong blessing to a handy man, at four shillings, at three and six, at three, at two and six, at two, at eighteen-pence. But none of you shall have it at any price, on account of your well-known awkwardness, which would make it man-slaughter. The same objection applies to this set of three planes which I won't let you have neither, so don't bid for 'em. Now I am a going to ask her what you do want." (Then I whispered, "Your head burns so, that I am afraid it hurts you bad, my pet," and she answered, without opening her heavy eyes, "Just a little, father.") "O! This little fortune-teller says it's a memorandum-book you want. Then why didn't you mention it? Here it is. Look at it. Two hundred superfine hot-pressed wire-wove pages—if you don't believe me, count 'em—ready ruled for your expenses, an everlastingly pointed pencil to put 'em down with, a double-bladed pen-knife to scratch 'em out with, a book of printed tables to calculate your income with, and a camp-stool to sit down upon while you give your mind to it! Stop! And an umbrella to keep the moon off when you give your mind to it on a pitch-dark night. Now I won't ask you how much for the lot, but how little? How little are you thinking of? Don't be ashamed to mention it, because my fortune-teller knows already." (Then making believe to whisper, I kissed her, and she kissed me.) "Why, she says you are thinking of as little as three and threepence! I couldn't have believed it, even of you, unless she told me. Three and threepence! And a set of printed tables in the lot that'll calculate your income up to forty thousand a year! With an income of forty thousand a year, you grudge three and sixpence. Well then, I'll tell you my opinion. I so despise the threepence, that I'd sooner take three shillings. There. For three shillings, three shillings, three shillings! Gone. Hand 'em over to the lucky man."

As there had been no bid at all, everybody looked about and grinned at everybody, while I touched little Sophy's face and asked her if she felt faint, or giddy. "Not very, father. It will soon be over." Then turning from the pretty patient eyes, which were opened now, and seeing nothing but grins across my lighted grease-pot, I went on again in my Cheap Jack style. "Where's the butcher?" (My sorrowful eye had just caught sight of a fat young butcher on the outside of the crowd.) "She says the good luck is the butcher's. Where is he?" Everybody handed on the blushing butcher to the front, and there was a roar, and the butcher felt himself obliged to put his hand in his pocket, and take the lot. The party so picked out, in general, does feel obliged to take the lot—good four times out of six. Then we had another lot, the counterpart of that one, and sold it sixpence cheaper, which is always wery much enjoyed. Then we had the spectacles. It ain't a special profitable lot, but I put 'em on, and I see what the Chancellor of the Exchequer is going to take off the taxes, and I see what the sweetheart of the young woman in the shawl is doing at home, and I see what the Bishops has got for dinner, and a deal more that seldom fails to fetch 'em up in their spirits; and the better their spirits, the better their bids. Then we had the ladies' lot,—the teapot, tea-caddy, glass sugar-basin, half-a-dozen spoons, and caudle-cup—and all the time I was making similar excuses to give a look or two and say a word or two to my poor child. It was while the second ladies' lot was holding 'em enchained that I felt her lift herself a little on my shoulder, to look across the dark street. "What troubles you, darling?" "Nothing troubles me, father. I am not at all troubled. But don't I see a pretty churchyard over there?" "Yes, my dear." "Kiss me twice, dear father, and lay me down to rest upon that churchyard grass so soft and green." I staggered back into the cart with her head dropped on my shoulder, and I says to her mother, "Quick. Shut the door! Don't let those laughing people see!" "What's the matter?" she cries. "O woman, woman," I tells her, "you'll never catch my little Sophy by her hair again, for she has flown away from you!"

Maybe those were harder words than I meant 'em; but from that time forth my wife took to brooding, and would sit in the cart or walk beside it, hours at a stretch, with her arms crossed, and her eyes looking on the ground. When her furies took her (which was rather seldomer than before) they took her in a new way, and she banged herself about to that extent that I was forced to hold her. She got none the better for a little drink now and then, and through some years I used to wonder, as I plodded along at the old horse's head, whether there was many carts upon the road that held so much dreariness as mine, for all my being looked up to as the King of the Cheap Jacks. So sad our lives went on till one summer evening, when, as we were coming into Exeter, out of the farther West of England, we saw a woman beating a child in a cruel manner, who screamed, "Don't beat me! O mother, mother, mother!" Then my wife stopped her ears, and ran away like a wild thing, and next day she was found in the river.

Me and my dog were all the company left in the cart now; and the dog learned to give a short bark when they wouldn't bid, and to give another and a nod of his head when I asked him, "Who said half a crown? Are you the gentleman, Sir, that offered half a crown?" He attained to an immense height of popularity, and I shall always believe taught himself entirely out of his own head to growl at any person in the crowd that bid as low as sixpence. But he got to be well on in years, and one night when I was conwulsing York with the spectacles, he took a conwulsion on his own account upon the very footboard by me, and it finished him.

Being naturally of a tender turn, I had dreadful lonely feelings on me arter this. I conquered 'em at selling times, having a reputation to keep (not to mention keeping myself), but they got me down in private, and rolled upon me. That's often the way with us public characters. See us on the footboard, and you'd give pretty well anything you possess to be us. See us off the footboard, and you'd add a trifle to be off your bargain. It was under those circumstances that I come acquainted with a giant. I might have been too high to fall into conversation with him, had it not been for my lonely feelings. For the general rule is, going round the country, to draw the line at dressing up. When a man can't trust his getting a living to his undisguised abilities, you consider him below your sort. And this giant when on view figured as a Roman.

He was a languid young man, which I attribute to the distance betwixt his extremities. He had a little head and less in it, he had weak eyes and weak knees, and altogether you couldn't look at him without feeling that there was greatly too much of him both for his joints and his mind. But he was an amiable though timid young man (his mother let him out, and spent the money), and we come acquainted when he was walking to ease the horse betwixt two fairs. He was called Rinaldo di Velasco, his name being Pickleson.

This giant, otherwise Pickleson, mentioned to me under the seal of confidence that, beyond his being a burden to himself, his life was made a burden to him by the cruelty of his master towards a step-daughter who was deaf and dumb. Her mother was dead, and she had no living soul to take her part, and was used most hard. She travelled with his master's caravan only because there was nowhere to leave her, and this giant, otherwise Pickleson, did go so far as to believe that his master often tried to lose her. He was such a very languid young man, that I don't know how long it didn't take him to get this story out, but it passed through his defective circulation to his top extremity in course of time.

When I heard this account from the giant, otherwise Pickleson, and likewise that the poor girl had beautiful long dark hair, and was often pulled down by it and beaten, I couldn't see the giant through what stood in my eyes. Having wiped 'em, I give him sixpence (for he was kept as short as he was long), and he laid it out in two three-penn'orths of gin-and-water, which so brisked him up, that he sang the Favourite Comic of Shivery Shakey, ain't it cold?—a popular effect which his master had tried every other means to get out of him as a Roman wholly in vain.

His master's name was Mim, a wery hoarse man, and I knew him to speak to. I went to that Fair as a mere civilian, leaving the cart outside the town, and I looked about the back of the Vans while the performing was going on, and at last, sitting dozing against a muddy cart-wheel, I came upon the poor girl who was deaf and dumb. At the first look I might almost have judged that she had escaped from the Wild Beast Show; but at the second I thought better of her, and thought that if she was more cared for and more kindly used she would be like my child. She was just the same age that my own daughter would have been, if her pretty head had not fell down upon my shoulder that unfortunate night.

To cut it short, I spoke confidential to Mim while he was beating the gong outside betwixt two lots of Pickleson's publics, and I put it to him, "She lies heavy on your own hands; what'll you take for her?" Mim was a most ferocious swearer. Suppressing that part of his reply which was much the longest part, his reply was, "A pair of braces." "Now I'll tell you," says I, "what I'm a going to do with you. I'm a going to fetch you half-a-dozen pair of the primest braces in the cart, and then to take her away with me." Says Mim (again ferocious), "I'll believe it when I've got the goods, and no sooner." I made all the haste I could, lest he should think twice of it, and the bargain was completed, which Pickleson he was thereby so relieved in his mind that he come out at his little back door, longways like a serpent, and give us Shivery Shakey in a whisper among the wheels at parting.

It was happy days for both of us when Sophy and me began to travel in the cart. I at once give her the name of Sophy, to put her ever towards me in the attitude of my own daughter. We soon made out to begin to understand one another, through the goodness of the Heavens, when she knowed that I meant true and kind by her. In a very little time she was wonderful fond of me. You have no idea what it is to have anybody wonderful fond of you, unless you have been got down and rolled upon by the lonely feelings that I have mentioned as having once got the better of me.

You'd have laughed—or the rewerse—it's according to your disposition—if you could have seen me trying to teach Sophy. At first I was helped—you'd never guess by what—milestones. I got some large alphabets in a box, all the letters separate on bits of bone, and saying we was going to WINDSOR, I give her those letters in that order, and then at every milestone I showed her those same letters in that same order again, and pointed towards the abode of royalty. Another time I give her CART, and then chalked the same upon the cart. Another time I give her DOCTOR MARIGOLD, and hung a corresponding inscription outside my waistcoat. People that met us might stare a bit and laugh, but what did *I* care, if she caught the idea? She caught it after long patience and trouble, and then we did begin to get on swimmingly, I believe you! At first she was a little given to consider me the cart, and the cart the abode of royalty, but that soon wore off.

We had our signs, too, and they was hundreds in number. Sometimes she would sit looking at me and considering hard how to communicate with me about something fresh,—how to ask me what she wanted explained,—and then she was (or I thought she was; what does it signify?) so like my child with those years added to her, that I half-believed it was herself, trying to tell me where she had been to up in the skies, and what she had seen since that unhappy night when she flied away. She had a pretty face, and now that there was no one to drag at her bright dark hair, and it was all in order, there was a something touching in her looks that made the cart most peaceful and most quiet, though not at all melancholy. [N.B. In the Cheap Jack patter, we generally sound it lemonjolly, and it gets a laugh.]

The way she learnt to understand any look of mine was truly surprising. When I sold of a night, she would sit in the cart unseen by them outside, and would give a eager look into my eyes when I looked in, and would hand me straight the precise article or articles I wanted. And then she would clap her hands, and laugh for joy. And as for me, seeing her so bright, and remembering what she was when I first lighted on her, starved and beaten and ragged, leaning asleep against the muddy cart-wheel, it give me such heart that I gained a greater heighth of reputation than ever, and I put Pickleson down (by the name of Mim's Travelling Giant otherwise Pickleson) for a fypunnote in my will.

This happiness went on in the cart till she was sixteen year old. By which time I began to feel not satisfied that I had done my whole duty by her, and to consider that she ought to have better teaching than I could give her. It drew a many tears on both sides when I commenced explaining my views to her; but what's right is right, and you can't neither by tears nor laughter do away with its character.

So I took her hand in mine, and I went with her one day to the Deaf and Dumb establishment in London, and when the gentleman come to speak to us, I says to him: "Now I'll tell you what I'll do with you, Sir. I am nothing but a Cheap Jack, but of late years I have laid by for a rainy day notwithstanding. This is my only daughter (adopted), and you can't produce a deafer nor a dumber. Teach her the most that can be taught her in the shortest separation that can be named,—state the figure for it,—and I am game to put the money down. I won't bate you a single farthing, Sir, but I'll put down the money here and now, and I'll thankfully throw you in a pound to take it. There!" The gentleman smiled, and then, "Well, well," says he, "I must first know what she has learned already. How do you communicate with her?" Then I showed him, and she wrote in printed writing many names of things and so forth; and we held some sprightly conversation, Sophy and me, about a little story in a book which the gentleman showed her, and which she was able to read. "This is most extraordinary," says the gentleman; "is it possible that you have been her only teacher?" "I have been her only teacher, Sir," I says, "besides herself." "Then," says the gentleman, and more acceptable words was never spoken to me, "you're a clever fellow, and a good fellow." This he makes known to Sophy, who kisses his hands, clasps her own, and laughs and cries upon it.

We saw the gentleman four times in all, and when he took down my name and asked how in the world it ever chanced to be Doctor, it come out that he was own nephew by the sister's side, if you'll believe me, to the very Doctor that I was called after. This made our footing still easier, and he says to me:

"Now, Marigold, tell me what more do you want your adopted daughter to know?"

"I want her, Sir, to be cut off from the world as little as can be, considering her deprivations, and therefore to be able to read whatever is wrote with perfect ease and pleasure."

"My good fellow," urges the gentleman, opening his eyes wide, "why I can't do that myself!"

I took his joke, and gave him a laugh (knowing by experience how flat you fall without it), and I mended my words accordingly.

"What do you mean to do with her afterwards?" asks the gentleman, with a sort of a doubtful eye. "To take her about the country?"

"In the cart, Sir, but only in the cart. She will live a private life, you understand, in the cart. I should never think of bringing her infirmities before the public. I wouldn't make a show of her for any money."

The gentleman nodded, and seemed to approve.

"Well," says he, "can you part with her for two years?"

"To do her that good,—yes, Sir."

"There's another question," says the gentleman, looking towards her,—"can she part with you for two years?"

I don't know that it was a harder matter of itself (for the other was hard enough to me), but it was harder to get over. However, she was pacified to it at last, and the separation betwixt us was settled. How it cut up both of us when it took place, and when I left her at the door in the dark of an evening, I don't tell. But I know this, remembering that night, I shall never pass that same establishment without a heartache and a swelling in the throat; and I couldn't put you up the best of lots in sight of it with my usual spirit,—no, not even the gun, nor the pair of spectacles,—for five hundred pound reward from the Secretary of State for the Home Department, and throw in the honour of putting my legs under his mahogany arterwards.

Still, the loneliness that followed in the cart was not the old loneliness, because there was a term put to it, however long to look forward to; and because I could think, when I was anyways down, that she belonged to me and I belonged to her. Always planning for her coming back, I bought in a few months' time another cart, and what do you think I planned to do with it? I'll tell you. I planned to fit it up with shelves and books for her reading, and to have a seat in it where I could sit and see her read, and think that I had been her first teacher. Not hurrying over the job, I had the fittings knocked together in contriving ways under my own inspection, and here was her bed in a berth with curtains, and there was her reading-table, and here was her writing-desk, and elsewhere was her books in rows upon rows, picters and no picters, bindings and no bindings, gilt-edged and plain, just as I could pick 'em up for her in lots up and down the country, North and South and West and East, Winds liked best and winds liked least, Here and there and gone astray, Over the hills and far away. And when I had got together pretty well as many books as the cart would neatly hold, a new scheme come into my head, which, as it turned out, kept my time and attention a good deal employed, and helped me over the two years' stile.

Without being of an awaricious temper, I like to be the owner of things. I shouldn't wish, for instance, to go partners with yourself in the Cheap Jack cart. It's not that I mistrust you, but that I'd rather know it was mine. Similarly, very likely you'd rather know it was yours. Well! A kind of a jealousy began to creep into my mind when I reflected that all those books would have been read by other people long before they was read by her. It seemed to take away from her being the owner of 'em like. In this way, the question got into my head: Couldn't I have a book new-made express for her, which she should be the first to read?

It pleased me, that thought did; and as I never was a man to let a thought sleep (you must wake up all the whole family of thoughts you've got and burn their nightcaps, or you won't do in the Cheap Jack line), I set to work at it. Considering that I was in the habit of changing so much about the country, and that I should have to find out a literary character here to make a deal with, and another literary character there to make a deal with, as opportunities presented, I hit on the plan that this same book should be a general miscellaneous lot,—like the razors, flat-iron, chronometer watch, dinner plates, rolling-pin, and looking-glass,—and shouldn't be offered as a single indiwidual article, like the spectacles or the gun. When I had come to that conclusion, I come to another, which shall likewise be yours.

Often had I regretted that she never had heard me on the footboard, and that she never could hear me. It ain't that I am vain, but that you don't like to put your own light under a bushel. What's the worth of your reputation, if you can't convey the reason for it to the person you most wish to value it? Now I'll put it to you. Is it worth sixpence, fippence, fourpence, threepence, twopence, a penny, a halfpenny, a farthing? No, it ain't. Not worth a farthing. Very well, then. My conclusion was that I would begin her book with some account of myself. So that, through reading a specimen or two of me on the footboard, she might form an idea of my merits there. I was aware that I couldn't do myself justice. A man can't write his eye (at least I don't know how to), nor yet can a man write his voice, nor the rate of his talk, nor the quickness of his action, nor his general spicy way. But he can write his turns of speech, when he is a public speaker, —and indeed I have heard that he very often does, before he speaks 'em.

Well! Having formed that resolution, then come the question of a name. How did I hammer hot iron into shape? This way. The most difficult explanation I had ever had with her was, how I come to be called Doctor, and yet was no Doctor. After all, I felt that I had failed of getting it correctly into her mind, with my utmost pains. But trusting to her improvement in the two years, I thought that I might trust to her understanding it when she should come to read it as put down by my own hand. Then I thought I would try a joke with her and watch how it took, by which of itself I might fully judge of her understanding it. We had first discovered the mistake we had dropped into, through her having asked me to prescribe for her when she had supposed me to be a Doctor in a medical point of view; so thinks I, "Now, if I give this book the name of my Prescriptions, and if she catches the idea that my only Prescriptions are for her amusement and interest,—to make her laugh in a pleasant way, or to make her cry in a pleasant way,—it will be a delightful proof to both of us that we have got over our difficulty." It fell out to absolute perfection. For when she saw the book, as I had it got up,—the printed and pressed book,—lying on her desk in her cart, and saw the title, DOCTOR MARIGOLD'S PRESCRIPTIONS, she looked at me for a moment with astonishment, then fluttered the leaves, then broke out a laughing in the charmingest way, then felt her pulse and shook her head, then turned the pages pretending to read them most attentive, then kissed the book to me, and put it to her bosom with both her hands. I never was better pleased in all my life!

But let me not anticipate. (I take that expression out of a lot of romances I bought for her. I never opened a single one of 'em—and I have opened many—but I found the romancer saying "let me not anticipate." Which being so, I wonder why he did anticipate, or who asked him to it.) Let me not, I say, anticipate. This same book took up all my spare time. It was no play to get the other articles together in the general miscellaneous lot, but when it come to my own article! There! I couldn't have believed the blotting, nor yet the buckling to at it, nor the patience over it. Which again is like the footboard. The public have no idea.

At last it was done, and the two years' time was gone after all the other time before it, and where it's all gone to, who knows? The new cart was finished,—yellow outside, relieved with wermilion and brass fittings,—the old horse was put in it, a new 'un and a boy being laid on for the Cheap Jack cart, and I cleaned myself up to go and fetch her. Bright cold weather it was, cart-chimneys smoking, carts pitched

private on a piece of waste ground over at Wandsworth, where you
may see 'em from the Sou'western Railway when not upon the road.
(Look out of the right-hand window going down.)

"Marigold," says the gentleman, giving his hand hearty, "I am very
glad to see you."

"Yet I have my doubts, Sir," says I, "if you can be half as glad to
see me as I am to see you."

"The time has appeared so long,—has it, Marigold?"

"I won't say that, Sir, considering its real length; but——"

"What a start, my good fellow!"

Ah! I should think it was! Grown such a woman, so pretty, so
intelligent, so expressive! I knew then that she must be really like my
child, or I could never have known her, standing quiet by the door.

"You are affected," says the gentleman in a kindly manner.

"I feel, Sir," says I, "that I am but a rough chap in a sleeved waistcoat."

"I feel," says the gentleman, "that it was you who raised her from
misery and degradation, and brought her into communication with
her kind. But why do we converse alone together, when we can converse so well with her? Address her in your own way."

"I am such a rough chap in a sleeved waistcoat, Sir," says I, "and she
is such a graceful woman, and she stands so quiet at the door!"

"Try if she moves at the old sign," says the gentleman.

They had got it up together o' purpose to please me! For when I
give her the old sign, she rushed to my feet, and dropped upon her
knees, holding up her hands to me with pouring tears of love and
joy; and when I took her hands and lifted her, she clasped me round
the neck, and lay there; and I don't know what a fool I didn't make
of myself, until we all three settled down into talking without sound,
as if there was a something soft and pleasant spread over the whole
world for us.

A portion is here omitted from the text, having reference to the
sketches contributed by other writers; but the reader will be pleased
to have what follows retained in a note:

"Now I'll tell you what I am a-going to do with you. I am a-going
to offer you the general miscellaneous lot, her own book, never read
by anybody else but me, added to and completed by me after her
first reading of it, eight-and-forty printed pages, six-and-ninety columns, Whiting's own work, Beaufort House to wit, thrown off by the
steam-ingine, best of paper, beautiful green wrapper, folded like clean
linen come home from the clear-starcher's, and so exquisitely stitched
that, regarded as a piece of needlework alone, it's better than the
sampler of a seamstress undergoing a Competitive examination for
Starvation before the Civil Service Commissioners—and I offer the
lot for what? For eight pound? Not so much. For six pound? Less. For

four pound. Why, I hardly expect you to believe me, but that's the sum. Four pound! The stitching alone cost half as much again. Here's forty-eight original pages, ninety-six original columns, for four pound. You want more for the money? Take it. Three whole pages of advertisements of thrilling interest thrown in for nothing. Read 'em and believe 'em. More? My best of wishes for your merry Christmases and your happy New Years, your long lives and your true prosperities. Worth twenty pound good if they are delivered as I send them. Remember! Here's a final prescription added, "To be taken for life," which will tell you how the cart broke down, and where the journey ended. You think Four Pound too much? And still you think so? Come! I'll tell you what then. Say Four Pence, and keep the secret."]

CHAPTER II *To be taken with a grain of salt*

I have always noticed a prevalent want of courage, even among persons of superior intelligence and culture, as to imparting their own psychological experiences when those have been of a strange sort. Almost all men are afraid that what they could relate in such wise would find no parallel or response in a listener's internal life, and might be suspected or laughed at. A truthful traveller, who should have seen some extraordinary creature in the likeness of a sea-serpent, would have no fear of mentioning it; but the same traveller, having had some singular presentiment, impulse, vagary of thought, vision (so called), dream, or other remarkable mental impression, would hesitate considerably before he would own to it. To this reticence I attribute much of the obscurity in which such subjects are involved. We do not habitually communicate our experiences of these subjective things as we do our experiences of objective creation. The consequence is, that the general stock of experience in this regard appears exceptional, and really is so, in respect of being miserably imperfect.

In what I am going to relate, I have no intention of setting up, opposing, or supporting, any theory whatever. I know the history of the Bookseller of Berlin, I have studied the case of the wife of a late Astronomer Royal as related by Sir David Brewster, and I have followed the minutest details of a much more remarkable case of Spectral Illusion occurring within my private circle of friends. It may be necessary to state as to this last, that the sufferer (a lady) was in no degree, however distant, related to me. A mistaken assumption on that head might suggest an explanation of a part of my own case,—but only a part,—which would be wholly without foundation. It cannot be referred to my inheritance of any developed peculiarity, nor had I ever before any at all similar experience, nor have I ever had any at all similar experience since.

It does not signify how many years ago, or how few, a certain murder was committed in England, which attracted great attention. We hear more than enough of murderers as they rise in succession to their atrocious eminence, and I would bury the memory of this particular brute, if I could, as his body was buried, in Newgate Jail. I purposely abstain from giving any direct clew to the criminal's individuality.

When the murder was first discovered, no suspicion fell—or I ought rather to say, for I cannot be too precise in my facts, it was nowhere publicly hinted that any suspicion fell—on the man who was afterwards brought to trial. As no reference was at that time made to him in the newspapers, it is obviously impossible that any description of him can at that time have been given in the newspapers. It is essential that this fact be remembered.

Unfolding at breakfast my morning paper, containing the account of that first discovery, I found it to be deeply interesting, and I read it with close attention. I read it twice, if not three times. The discovery had been made in a bedroom, and, when I laid down the paper, I was aware of a flash—rush—flow—I do not know what to call it,—no word I can find is satisfactorily descriptive,—in which I seemed to see that bedroom passing through my room, like a picture impossibly painted on a running river. Though almost instantaneous in its passing, it was perfectly clear; so clear that I distinctly, and with a sense of relief, observed the absence of the dead body from the bed.

It was in no romantic place that I had this curious sensation, but in chambers in Piccadilly, very near to the corner of St. James's-street. It was entirely new to me. I was in my easy-chair at the moment, and the sensation was accompanied with a peculiar shiver which started the chair from its position. (But it is to be noted that the chair ran easily on castors.) I went to one of the windows (there are two in the room, and the room is on the second floor) to refresh my eyes with the moving objects down in Piccadilly. It was a bright autumn morning, and the street was sparkling and cheerful. The wind was high. As I looked out, it brought down from the Park a quantity of fallen leaves, which a gust took, and whirled into a spiral pillar. As the pillar fell and the leaves dispersed, I saw two men on the opposite side of the way, going from West to East. They were one behind the other. The foremost man often looked back over his shoulder. The second man followed him, at a distance of some thirty paces, with his right hand menacingly raised. First, the singularity and steadiness of this threatening gesture in so public a thoroughfare attracted my attention; and next, the more remarkable circumstance that nobody heeded it. Both men threaded their way among the other passengers with a smoothness hardly consistent even with the action of walking on a pavement; and no single creature, that I could see, gave them place, touched them, or looked after them. In passing before my windows, they both stared up at me. I saw their two faces very distinctly, and I knew that I could recognise them anywhere. Not that I had consciously noticed anything very remarkable in either face, except that the man who went first had an unusually lowering appearance, and that the face of the man who followed him was of the colour of impure wax.

I am a bachelor, and my valet and his wife constitute my whole establishment. My occupation is in a certain Branch Bank, and I wish that my duties as head of a Department were as light as they are popularly supposed to be. They kept me in town that autumn, when I stood in need of change. I was not ill, but I was not well. My reader is to make the most that can be reasonably made of my feeling jaded, having a depressing sense upon me of a monotonous life, and being "slightly dyspeptic." I am assured by my renowned doctor that my real state of health at that time justifies no stronger description, and I quote his own from his written answer to my request for it.

As the circumstances of the murder, gradually unravelling, took stronger and stronger possession of the public mind, I kept them away from mine by knowing as little about them as was possible in the midst of the universal excitement. But I knew that a verdict of Wilful Murder had been found against the suspected murderer, and that he had been committed to Newgate for trial. I also knew that his trial had been postponed over one Sessions of the Central Criminal Court, on the ground of general prejudice and want of time for the preparation of the defence. I may further have known, but I believe I did not, when, or about when, the Sessions to which his trial stood postponed would come on.

My sitting-room, bedroom, and dressing-room, are all on one floor. With the last there is no communication but through the bedroom. True, there is a door in it, once communicating with the staircase; but a part of the fitting of my bath has been—and had then been for some years—fixed across it. At the same period, and as a part of the same arrangement, the door had been nailed up and canvased over.

I was standing in my bedroom late one night, giving some directions to my servant before he went to bed. My face was towards the only available door of communication with the dressing-room, and it was closed. My servant's back was towards that door. While I was speaking to him, I saw it open, and a man look in, who very earnestly and mysteriously beckoned to me. That man was the man who had gone second of the two along Piccadilly, and whose face was the colour of impure wax.

The figure, having beckoned, drew back, and closed the door. With no longer pause than was made by my crossing the bedroom, I opened the dressing-room door, and looked in. I had a lighted candle already in my hand. I felt no inward expectation of seeing the figure in the dressing-room, and I did not see it there.

Conscious that my servant stood amazed, I turned round to him, and said: "Derrick, could you believe that in my cool senses I fancied I saw a——" As I there laid my hand upon his breast, with a sudden start he trembled violently, and said, "O Lord, yes, Sir! A dead man beckoning!"

Now I do not believe that this John Derrick, my trusty and attached servant for more than twenty years, had any impression whatever of having seen any such figure, until I touched him. The change in him was so startling, when I touched him, that I fully believe he derived his impression in some occult manner from me at that instant.

I bade John Derrick bring some brandy, and I gave him a dram, and was glad to take one myself. Of what had preceded that night's phenomenon, I told him not a single word. Reflecting on it, I was absolutely certain that I had never seen that face before, except on the one occasion in Piccadilly. Comparing its expression when beckoning at the door with its expression when it had stared up at me as I stood at my window, I came to the conclusion that on the first occasion it had sought to fasten itself upon my memory, and that on the second occasion it had made sure of being immediately remembered.

I was not very comfortable that night, though I felt a certainty, difficult to explain, that the figure would not return. At daylight I fell into a heavy sleep, from which I was awakened by John Derrick's coming to my bedside with a paper in his hand.

This paper, it appeared, had been the subject of an altercation at the door between its bearer and my servant. It was a summons to me to serve upon a Jury at the forthcoming Sessions of the Central Criminal Court at the Old Bailey. I had never before been summoned on such a Jury, as John Derrick well knew. He believed—I am not certain at this hour whether with reason or otherwise—that that class of Jurors were customarily chosen on a lower qualification than mine, and he had at first refused to accept the summons. The man who served it had taken the matter very coolly. He had said that my attendance or non-attendance was nothing to him; there the summons was; and I should deal with it at my own peril, and not at his.

For a day or two I was undecided whether to respond to this call, or take no notice of it. I was not conscious of the slightest mysterious bias, influence, or attraction, one way or other. Of that I am as strictly sure as of every other statement that I make here. Ultimately I decided, as a break in the monotony of my life, that I would go.

The appointed morning was a raw morning in the month of November. There was a dense brown fog in Piccadilly, and it became positively black and in the last degree oppressive East of Temple Bar. I found the passages and staircases of the Court-House flaringly lighted with gas, and the Court itself similarly illuminated. I *think* that, until I was conducted by officers into the Old Court and saw its crowded state. I did not know that the Murderer was to be tried that day. I *think* that, until I was so helped into the Old Court with considerable difficulty, I did not know into which of the two Courts sitting my summons would take me. But this must not be received as a positive assertion, for I am not completely satisfied in my mind on either point.

I took my seat in the place appropriated to Jurors in waiting, and I looked about the Court as well as I could through the cloud of fog and breath that was heavy in it. I noticed the black vapour hanging like a murky curtain outside the great windows, and I noticed the stifled sound of wheels on the straw or tan that was littered in the street; also, the hum of the people gathered there, which a shrill whistle, or a louder song or hail than the rest, occasionally pierced. Soon afterwards the Judges, two in number, entered, and took their seats. The buzz in the Court was awfully hushed. The direction was given to put the Murderer to the bar. He appeared there. And in that same instant I recognised in him the first of the two men who had gone down Piccadilly.

If my name had been called then, I doubt if I could have answered to it audibly. But it was called about sixth or eighth in the panel, and I was by that time able to say "Here!" Now, observe. As I stepped into the box, the prisoner, who had been looking on attentively, but with no sign of concern, became violently agitated, and beckoned to his attorney. The prisoner's wish to challenge me was so manifest, that it occasioned a pause, during which the attorney, with his hand upon the dock, whispered with his client, and shook his head. I afterwards had it from that gentleman, that the prisoner's first affrighted words to him were, "*At all hazards, challenge that man!*" But that, as he would give no reason for it, and admitted that he had not even known my name until he heard it called and I appeared, it was not done.

Both on the ground already explained, that I wish to avoid reviving the unwholesome memory of that Murderer, and also because a detailed account of his long trial is by no means indispensable to my narrative, I shall confine myself closely to such incidents in the ten days and nights during which we, the Jury, were kept together, as directly bear on my own curious personal experience. It is in that, and not in the Murderer, that I seek to interest my reader. It is to that, and not to a page of the Newgate Calendar, that I beg attention.

I was chosen Foreman of the Jury. On the second morning of the trial, after evidence had been taken for two hours (I heard the church clocks strike), happening to cast my eyes over my brother jurymen,

I found an inexplicable difficulty in counting them. I counted them several times, yet always with the same difficulty. In short, I made them one too many.

I touched the brother juryman whose place was next me, and I whispered to him, "Oblige me by counting us." He looked surprised by the request, but turned his head and counted. "Why," says he, suddenly, "we are Thirt—; but no, it's not possible. No. We are twelve."

According to my counting that day, we were always right in detail, but in the gross we were always one too many. There was no appearance—no figure—to account for it; but I had now an inward foreshadowing of the figure that was surely coming.

The Jury were housed at the London Tavern. We all slept in one large room on separate tables, and we were constantly in the charge and under the eye of the officer sworn to hold us in safe-keeping. I see no reason for suppressing the real name of that officer. He was intelligent, highly polite, and obliging, and (I was glad to hear) much respected in the City. He had an agreeable presence, good eyes, enviable black whiskers, and a fine sonorous voice. His name was Mr. Harker.

When we turned into our twelve beds at night, Mr. Harker's bed was drawn across the door. On the night of the second day, not being disposed to lie down, and seeing Mr. Harker sitting on his bed, I went and sat beside him, and offered him a pinch of snuff. As Mr. Harker's hand touched mine in taking it from my box, a peculiar shiver crossed him, and he said, "Who is this?"

Following Mr. Harker's eyes, and looking along the room, I saw again the figure I expected,—the second of the two men who had gone down Piccadilly. I rose, and advanced a few steps; then stopped, and looked round at Mr. Harker. He was quite unconcerned, laughed, and said in a pleasant way, "I thought for a moment we had a thirteenth juryman, without a bed. But I see it is the moonlight."

Making no revelation to Mr. Harker, but inviting him to take a walk with me to the end of the room, I watched what the figure did. It stood for a few moments by the bedside of each of my eleven brother jurymen, close to the pillow. It always went to the right-hand side of the bed, and always passed out crossing the foot of the next bed. It seemed, from the action of the head, merely to look down pensively at each recumbent figure. It took no notice of me, or of my bed, which was that nearest to Mr. Harker's. It seemed to go out where the moonlight came in, through a high window, as by an aërial flight of stairs.

Next morning at breakfast, it appeared that everybody present had dreamed of the murdered man last night, except myself and Mr. Harker.

I now felt as convinced that the second man who had gone down Piccadilly was the murdered man (so to speak), as if it had been borne into my comprehension by his immediate testimony. But even this took place, and in a manner for which I was not at all prepared.

On the fifth day of the trial, when the case for the prosecution was drawing to a close, a miniature of the murdered man, missing from his bedroom upon the discovery of the deed, and afterwards found in a hiding-place where the Murderer had been seen digging, was put in evidence. Having been identified by the witness under examination, it was handed up to the Bench, and thence handed down to be inspected by the Jury. As an officer in a black gown was making his way with it across to me, the figure of the second man who had gone down Piccadilly impetuously started from the crowd, caught the miniature from the officer, and gave it to me with his own hands, at the same time saying, in a low and hollow tone,— before I saw the miniature, which was in a locket,—"*I was younger then, and my face was not then drained of blood.*" It also came between me and the brother juryman to whom I would have given the miniature, and between him and the brother juryman to whom he would have given it, and so passed it on through the whole of our number, and back into my possession. Not one of them, however, detected this.

At table, and generally when we were shut up together in Mr. Harker's custody, we had from the first naturally discussed the day's proceedings a good deal. On that fifth day, the case for the prosecution being closed, and we having that side of the question in a completed shape before us, our discussion was more animated and serious. Among our number was a vestryman,—the densest idiot I have ever seen at large,—who met the plainest evidence with the most preposterous objections, and who was sided with by two flabby parochial parasites; all the three impanelled from a district so delivered over to Fever that they ought to have been upon their own trial for five hundred Murders. When these mischievous blockheads were at their loudest, which was towards midnight, while some of us were already preparing for bed, I again saw the murdered man. He stood grimly behind them, beckoning to me. On my going towards them, and striking into the conversation, he immediately retired. This was the beginning of a separate series of appearances, confined to that long room in which *we* were confined. Whenever a knot of my brother jurymen laid their heads together, I saw the head of the murdered man among theirs. Whenever their comparison of notes was going against him, he would solemnly and irresistibly beckon to me.

It will be borne in mind that down to the production of the miniature, on the fifth day of the trial, I had never seen the Appearance in Court. Three changes occurred now that we entered on the case for the defence. Two of them I will mention together, first. The figure was now in Court continually, and it never there addressed itself to me, but always to the person who was speaking at the time. For instance: the throat of the murdered man had been cut straight across. In the opening speech for the defence, it was suggested that the deceased might have cut his own throat. At that very moment, the figure, with its throat in the dreadful condition referred to (this it had concealed before), stood at the speaker's elbow, motioning across and across its windpipe, now with the right hand, now with the left, vigorously suggesting to the speaker himself the impossibility of such a wound having been self-inflicted by either hand. For another instance: a witness to character, a woman, deposed to the prisoner's being the most amiable of mankind. The figure at that instant stood on the floor before her, looking her full in the face, and pointing out the prisoner's evil countenance with an extended arm and an outstretched finger.

The third change now to be added impressed me strongly as the most marked and striking of all. I do not theorise upon it; I accurately state it, and there leave it. Although the Appearance was not itself perceived by those whom it addressed, its coming close to such persons was invariably attended by some trepidation or disturbance on their part. It seemed to me as if it were prevented, by laws to which I was not amenable, from fully revealing itself to others, and yet as if it could invisibly, dumbly, and darkly overshadow their minds. When the leading counsel for the defence suggested that hypothesis of suicide, and the figure stood at the learned gentleman's elbow, frightfully sawing at its severed throat, it is undeniable that the counsel faltered in his speech, lost for a few seconds the thread of his ingenious discourse, wiped his forehead with his handkerchief, and turned extremely pale. When the witness to character was confronted by the Appearance, her eyes most certainly did follow the direction of its pointed finger, and rest in great hesitation and trouble upon the prisoner's face. Two additional illustrations will suffice. On the eighth day of the trial, after the pause which was every day made early in the afternoon for a few minutes' rest and refreshment, I came back into court with the rest of the Jury some little time before the return of the Judges. Standing up in the box and looking about me, I thought the figure was not there, until, chancing to raise my eyes to the gallery, I saw it bending forward, and leaning over a very decent woman, as if to assure itself whether the Judges had resumed their seats or not. Immediately afterwards that woman screamed, fainted, and was carried out. So with the venerable, sagacious, and patient Judge who conducted the trial. When the case was over, and he settled himself and his papers to sum up, the murdered man, entering by the Judges' door, advanced to his Lordship's desk, and looked eagerly

over his shoulder at the pages of his notes which he was turning. A
change came over his Lordship's face; his hand stopped; the peculiar
shiver, that I knew so well, passed over him; he faltered, "Excuse me,
gentlemen, for a few moments. I am somewhat oppressed by the
vitiated air;" and did not recover until he had drunk a glass of water.

Through all the monotony of six of those interminable ten days,—
the same Judges and others on the bench, the same Murderer in the
dock, the same lawyers at the table, the same tones of question and
answer rising to the roof of the Court, the same scratching of the
Judge's pen, the same ushers going in and out, the same lights kindled
at the same hour when there had been any natural light of day, the
same foggy curtain outside the great windows when it was foggy, the
same rain pattering and dripping when it was rainy, the same foot-
marks of turnkeys and prisoner day after day on the same sawdust, the
same keys locking and unlocking the same heavy doors,—through all
the wearisome monotony which made me feel as if I had been Foreman of the Jury for a vast period of time, and Piccadilly had flourished
coevally with Babylon, the murdered man never lost one trace of his
distinctness in my eyes, nor was he at any moment less distinct than
anybody else. I must not omit, as a matter of fact, that I never once
saw the Appearance which I call by the name of the murdered man
look at the Murderer. Again and again I wondered, "Why does he
not?" But he never did.

Nor did he look at me, after the production of the miniature, until
the last closing minutes of the trial arrived. We retired to consider, at
seven minutes before ten at night. The idiotic vestryman and his two
parochial parasites gave us so much trouble that we twice returned into
Court to beg to have certain extracts from the Judge's notes re-read.
Nine of us had not the smallest doubt about those passages, neither,
I believe, had any one in the Court; the dunderheaded triumvirate,
however, having no idea but obstruction, disputed them for that very
reason. At length we prevailed, and finally the Jury returned into
Court at ten minutes past twelve.

The murdered man at that time stood directly opposite the Jury-box,
on the other side of the Court. As I took my place, his eyes rested on
me with great attention; he seemed satisfied, and slowly shook a great
grey veil, which he carried on his arm for the first time, over his head
and whole form. As I gave in our verdict, "Guilty," the veil collapsed,
all was gone, and his place was empty.

The Murderer, being asked by the Judge, according to usage,
whether he had anything to say before sentence of Death should be
passed upon him, indistinctly muttered something which was described in the leading newspapers of the following day as "a few
rambling, incoherent, and half-audible words, in which he was understood to complain that he had not had a fair trial, because the Foreman

of the Jury was prepossessed against him." The remarkable declaration that he really made was this: "*My Lord, I knew I was a doomed man, when the Foreman of my Jury came into the box. My Lord, I knew he would never let me off, because, before I was taken, he somehow got to my bedside in the night, woke me, and put a rope round my neck.*"

CHAPTER III   *To be taken for life*

So every item of my plan was crowned with success. Our reunited life was more than all that we had looked forward to. Content and joy went with us as the wheels of the two carts went round, and the same stopped with us when the two carts stopped. I was as pleased and as proud as a Pug-Dog with his muzzle black-leaded for a evening party, and his tail extra curled by machinery.

But I had left something out of my calculations. Now, what had I left out? To help you to guess I'll say, a figure. Come. Make a guess and guess right. Nought? No. Nine? No. Eight? No. Seven? No. Six? No. Five? No. Four? No. Three? No. Two? No. One? No. Now I'll tell you what I'll do with you. I'll say it's another sort of figure altogether. There. Why then, says you, it's a mortal figure. No, nor yet a mortal figure. By such means you get yourself penned into a corner, and you can't help guessing a *im*mortal figure. That's about it. Why didn't you say so sooner?

Yes. It was a immortal figure that I had altogether left out of my calculations. Neither man's, nor woman's, but a child's. Girl's or boy's? Boy's. "I, says the sparrow, with my bow and arrow." Now you have got it.

We were down at Lancaster, and I had done two nights more than fair average business (though I cannot in honour recommend them as a quick audience) in the open square there, near the end of the street where Mr. Sly's King's Arms and Royal Hotel stands. Mim's travelling giant, otherwise Pickleson, happened at the self-same time to be trying it on in the town. The genteel lay was adopted with him. No hint of a van. Green baize alcove leading up to Pickleson in a Auction Room. Printed poster, "Free list suspended, with the exception of that proud boast of an enlightened country, a free press. Schools admitted by private arrangement. Nothing to raise a blush in the cheek of youth or shock the most fastidious." Mim swearing most horrible and terrific, in a pink calico pay-place, at the slackness of the public. Serious handbill in the shops, importing that it was all but impossible to come to a right understanding of the history of David without seeing Pickleson.

I went to the Auction Room in question, and I found it entirely empty of everything but echoes and mouldiness, with the single exception of Pickleson on a piece of red drugget. This suited my purpose, as I wanted a private and confidential word with him, which was: "Pickleson. Owing much happiness to you, I put you in my will for a fypunnote; but, to save trouble, here's fourpunten down, which may equally suit your views, and let us so conclude the transaction." Pickleson, who up to that remark had had the dejected appearance of a long Roman rushlight that couldn't anyhow get lighted, brightened up at his top extremity, and made his acknowledgements in a way which (for him) was parliamentary eloquence. He likewise did add, that, having ceased to draw as a Roman, Mim had made proposals for his going in as a conwerted Indian Giant worked upon by The Dairyman's Daughter. This, Pickleson, having no acquaintance with the tract named after that young woman, and not being willing to couple gag with his serious views, had declined to do, thereby leading to words and the total stoppage of the unfortunate young man's beer. All of which, during the whole of the interview, was confirmed by the ferocious growling of Mim down below in the pay-place, which shook the giant like a leaf.

But what was to the present point in the remarks of the travelling giant, otherwise Pickleson, was this: "Doctor Marigold,"—I give his words without a hope of conweying their feebleness,—"who is the strange young man that hangs about your carts?"—"The strange young *man*?" I gives him back, thinking that he meant her, and his languid circulation had dropped a syllable. "Doctor," he returns, with a pathos calculated to draw a tear from even a manly eye, "I am weak, but not so weak yet as that I don't know my words. I repeat them, Doctor. The strange young man." It then appeared that Pickleson, being forced to stretch his legs (not that they wanted it) only at times when he couldn't be seen for nothing, to wit in the dead of the night and towards daybreak, had twice seen hanging about my carts, in that same town of Lancaster where I had been only two nights, this same unknown young man.

It put me rather out of sorts. What it meant as to particulars I no more foreboded then than you forebode now, but it put me rather out of sorts. Howsoever, I made light of it to Pickleson, and I took leave of Pickleson, advising him to spend his legacy in getting up his stamina, and to continue to stand by his religion. Towards morning I kept a look out for the strange young man, and—what was more— I saw the strange young man. He was well dressed and well looking. He loitered very nigh my carts, watching them like as if he was taking care of them, and soon after daybreak turned and went away. I sent a hail after him, but he never started or looked round, or took the smallest notice.

We left Lancaster within an hour or two, on our way towards Carlisle. Next morning, at daybreak, I looked out again for the strange young man. I did not see him. But next morning I looked out again, and there he was once more. I sent another hail after him, but as before he gave not the slightest sign of being anyways disturbed. This put a thought into my head. Acting on it I watched him in different manners and at different times not necessary to enter into, till I found that this strange young man was deaf and dumb.

The discovery turned me over, because I knew that a part of that establishment where she had been was allotted to young men (some of them well off), and I thought to myself, "If she favours him, where am I? and where is all that I have worked and planned for?" Hoping —I must confess to the selfishness—that she might *not* favour him, I set myself to find out. At last I was by accident present at a meeting between them in the open air, looking on leaning behind a fir-tree without their knowing of it. It was a moving meeting for all the three parties concerned. I knew every syllable that passed between them as well as they did. I listened with my eyes, which had come to be as quick and true with deaf and dumb conversation as my ears with the talk of people that can speak. He was a-going out to China as clerk in a merchant's house, which his father had been before him. He was in circumstances to keep a wife, and he wanted her to marry him and go along with him. She persisted, no. He asked if she didn't love him. Yes, she loved him dearly, dearly; but she could never disappoint her beloved, good, noble, generous, and I don't-know-what-all father (meaning me, the Cheap Jack in the sleeved waistcoat), and she would stay with him, Heaven bless him! though it was to break her heart. Then she cried most bitterly, and that made up my mind.

While my mind had been in an unsettled state about her favouring this young man, I had felt that unreasonable towards Pickleson, that it was well for him he had got his legacy down. For I often thought, "If it hadn't been for this same weak-minded giant, I might never have come to trouble my head and wex my soul about the young man." But, once that I knew she loved him,—once that I had seen her weep for him,—it was a different thing. I made it right in my mind with Pickleson on the spot, and I shook myself together to do what was right by all.

She had left the young man by that time (for it took a few minutes to get me thoroughly well shook together), and the young man was leaning against another of the fir-trees,—of which there was a cluster, —with his face upon his arm. I touched him on the back. Looking up

and seeing me, he says, in our deaf-and-dumb talk, "Do not be angry."
"I am not angry, good boy. I am your friend. Come with me."

I left him at the foot of the steps of the Library Cart, and I went
up alone. She was drying her eyes.

"You have been crying, my dear."

"Yes, father."

"Why?"

"A headache."

"Not a heartache?"

"I said a headache, father."

"Doctor Marigold must prescribe for that headache."

She took up the book of my Prescriptions, and held it up with a
forced smile; but seeing me keep still and look earnest, she softly laid
it down again, and her eyes were very attentive.

"The Prescription is not there, Sophy."

"Where is it?"

"Here, my dear."

I brought her young husband in, and I put her hand in his, and my
only farther words to both of them were these: "Doctor Marigold's
last Prescription. To be taken for life." After which I bolted.

When the wedding came off, I mounted a coat (blue, and bright
buttons), for the first and last time in all my days, and I give Sophy
away with my own hand. There were only us three and the gentleman
who had had charge of her for those two years. I give the wedding
dinner of four in the Library Cart. Pigeon-pie, a leg of pickled pork,
a pair of fowls, and suitable garden stuff. The best of drinks. I give
them a speech, and the gentleman give us a speech, and all our jokes
told, and the whole went off like a sky-rocket. In the course of the
entertainment I explained to Sophy that I should keep the Library
Cart as my living-cart when not upon the road, and that I should keep
all her books for her just as they stood, till she come back to claim
them. So she went to China with her young husband, and it was a
parting sorrowful and heavy, and I got the boy I had another service;
and so as of old, when my child and wife were gone, I went plodding
along alone, with my whip over my shoulder, at the old horse's head.

Sophy wrote me many letters, and I wrote her many letters. About
the end of the first year she sent me one in an unsteady hand: "Dearest
father, not a week ago I had a darling little daughter, but I am so well
that they let me write these words to you. Dearest and best father, I
hope my child may not be deaf and dumb, but I do not yet know."
When I wrote back, I hinted the question; but as Sophy never answered that question, I felt it to be a sad one, and I never repeated it.
For a long time our letters were regular, but then they got irregular,
through Sophy's husband being moved to another station, and through

my being always on the move. But we were in one another's thoughts, I was equally sure, letters or no letters.

Five years, odd months, had gone since Sophy went away. I was still the King of the Cheap Jacks, and at a greater height of popularity than ever. I had had a first-rate autumn of it, and on the twenty-third of December, one thousand eight hundred and sixty-four, I found myself at Uxbridge, Middlesex, clean sold out. So I jogged up to London with the old horse, light and easy, to have my Christmas-eve and Christmas-day alone by the fire in the Library Cart, and then to buy a regular new stock of goods all round, to sell 'em again and get the money.

I am a neat hand at cookery, and I'll tell you what I knocked up for my Christmas-eve dinner in the Library Cart. I knocked up a beefsteak-pudding for one, with two kidneys, a dozen oysters, and a couple of mushrooms thrown in. It's a pudding to put a man in good humour with everything, except the two bottom buttons of his waistcoat. Having relished that pudding and cleared away, I turned the lamp low, and sat down by the light of the fire, watching it as it shone upon the back of Sophy's books.

Sophy's books so brought up Sophy's self, that I saw her touching face quite plainly, before I dropped off dozing by the fire. This may be a reason why Sophy, with her deaf-and-dumb child in her arms, seemed to stand silent by me all through my nap. I was on the road, off the road, in all sorts of places, North and South and West and East, Winds liked best and winds liked least, Here and there and gone astray, Over the hills and far away, and still she stood silent by me, with her silent child in her arms. Even when I woke with a start, she seemed to vanish, as if she had stood by me in that very place only a single instant before.

I had started at a real sound, and the sound was on the steps of the cart. It was the light hurried tread of a child, coming clambering up. That tread of a child had once been so familiar to me, that for half a moment I believed I was a-going to see a little ghost.

But the touch of a real child was laid upon the outer handle of the door, and the handle turned, and the door opened a little way, and a real child peeped in. A bright little comely girl with large dark eyes.

Looking full at me, the tiny creature took off her mite of a straw hat, and a quantity of dark curls fell all about her face. Then she opened her lips, and said in a pretty voice,

"Grandfather!"

"Ah, my God!" I cries out. "She can speak!"

"Yes, dear grandfather. And I am to ask you whether there was ever any one that I remind you of?"

In a moment Sophy was round my neck, as well as the child, and her husband was a-wringing my hand with his face hid, and we all had to shake ourselves together before we could get over it. And when we did begin to get over it, and I saw the pretty child a-talking, pleased and quick and eager and busy, to her mother, in the signs that I had first taught her mother, the happy and yet pitying tears fell rolling down my face.

—1865

Mugby Junction IN FOUR CHAPTERS

~~~~~~

CHAPTER I *Barbox Brothers*

I

"Guard! What place is this?"

"Mugby Junction, Sir."

"A windy place!"

"Yes, it mostly is, Sir."

"And looks comfortless indeed!"

"Yes, it generally does, Sir."

"Is it a rainy night still?"

"Pours, Sir."

"Open the door. I'll get out."

"You'll have, Sir," said the guard, glistening with drops of wet, and looking at the tearful face of his watch by the light of his lantern as the traveller descended, "three minutes here."

"More, I think.—For I am not going on."

"Thought you had a through ticket, Sir?"

"So I have, but I shall sacrifice the rest of it. I want my luggage."

"Please to come to the van and point it out, Sir. Be good enough to look very sharp, Sir. Not a moment to spare."

The guard hurried to the luggage van, and the traveller hurried after him. The guard got into it, and the traveller looked into it.

"Those two large black portmanteaus in the corner where your light shines. Those are mine."

"Name upon 'em, Sir?"

"Barbox Brothers."

"Stand clear, Sir, if you please. One. Two. Right!" Lamp waved. Signal lights ahead already changing. Shriek from engine. Train gone.

"Mugby Junction!" said the traveller, pulling up the woollen

muffler round his throat with both hands. "At past three o'clock of a
tempestuous morning! So!"

He spoke to himself. There was no one else to speak to. Perhaps,
though there had been any one else to speak to, he would have
preferred to speak to himself. Speaking to himself he spoke to a man
within five years of fifty either way, who had turned grey too soon,
like a neglected fire; a man of pondering habit, brooding carriage of
the head, and suppressed internal voice; a man with many indications
on him of having been much alone.

He stood unnoticed on the dreary platform, except by the rain and
by the wind. Those two vigilant assailants made a rush at him. "Very
well," said he, yielding. "It signifies nothing to me to what quarter
I turn my face."

Thus, at Mugby Junction, at past three o'clock of a tempestuous
morning, the traveller went where the weather drove him.

Not but what he could make a stand when he was so minded, for,
coming to the end of the roofed shelter (it is of considerable extent
at Mugby Junction), and looking out upon the dark night, with a
yet darker spirit-wing of storm beating its wild way through it, he
faced about, and held his own as ruggedly in the difficult direction as
he had held it in the easier one. Thus, with a steady step, the traveller
went up and down, up and down, up and down, seeking nothing
and finding it.

A place replete with shadowy shapes, this Mugby Junction in the
black hours of the four-and-twenty. Mysterious goods trains, covered
with palls and gliding on like vast weird funerals, conveying themselves guiltily away from the presence of the few lighted lamps, as if
their freight had come to a secret and unlawful end. Half-miles of
coal pursuing in a Detective manner, following when they lead,
stopping when they stop, backing when they back. Red-hot embers
showering out upon the ground, down this dark avenue, and down
the other, as if torturing fires were being raked clear; concurrently,
shrieks and groans and grinds invading the ear, as if the tortured were
at the height of their suffering. Iron-barred cages full of cattle jangling
by midway, the drooping beasts with horns entangled, eyes frozen
with terror, and mouths too: at least they have long icicles (or what
seem so) hanging from their lips. Unknown languages in the air,
conspiring in red, green, and white characters. An earthquake,
accompanied with thunder and lightning, going up express to London. Now, all quiet, all rusty, wind and rain in possession, lamps
extinguished, Mugby Junction dead and indistinct, with its robe
drawn over its head, like Cæsar.

Now, too, as the belated traveller plodded up and down, a shadowy
train went by him in the gloom which was no other than the train of
a life. From whatsoever intangible deep cutting or dark tunnel it

emerged, here it came, unsummoned and unannounced, stealing upon him, and passing away into obscurity. Here mournfully went by a child who had never had a childhood or known a parent, inseparable from a youth with a bitter sense of his namelessness, coupled to a man the enforced business of whose best years had been distasteful and oppressive, linked to an ungrateful friend, dragging after him a woman once beloved. Attendant, with many a clank and wrench, were lumbering cares, dark meditations, huge dim disappointments, monotonous years, a long jarring line of the discords of a solitary and unhappy existence.

"—Yours, Sir?"

The traveller recalled his eyes from the waste into which they had been staring, and fell back a step or so under the abruptness, and perhaps the chance appropriateness, of the question.

"Oh! My thoughts were not here for the moment. Yes. Yes. Those two portmanteaus are mine. Are you a Porter?"

"On Porter's wages, Sir. But I am Lamps."

The traveller looked a little confused.

"Who did you say you are?"

"Lamps, Sir," showing an oily cloth in his hand, as further explanation.

"Surely, surely. Is there any hotel or tavern here?"

"Not exactly here, Sir. There is a Refreshment Room here, but——" Lamps, with a mighty serious look, gave his head a warning roll that plainly added—"but it's a blessed circumstance for you that it's not open."

"You couldn't recommend it, I see, if it was available?"

"Ask your pardon, Sir. If it was——?"

"Open?"

"It ain't my place, as a paid servant of the company, to give my opinion on any of the company's toepics,"—he pronounced it more like toothpicks,—"beyond lamp-ile and cottons," returned Lamps in a confidential tone; "but, speaking as a man, I wouldn't recommend my father (if he was to come to life again) to go and try how he'd be treated at the Refreshment Room. Not speaking as a man, no, I would *not*."

The traveller nodded conviction. "I suppose I can put up in the town? There is a town here?" For the traveller (though a stay-at-home compared with most travellers) had been, like many others, carried on the steam winds and the iron tides through that Junction before, without having ever, as one might say, gone ashore there.

"Oh yes, there's a town, Sir! Anyways, there's town enough to put up in. But," following the glance of the other at his luggage, "this is a very dead time of the night with us, Sir. The deadest time. I might a'most call it our deadest and buriedest time."

"No porters about?"

"Well, Sir, you see," returned Lamps, confidential again, "they in general goes off with the gas. That's how it is. And they seem to have overlooked you, through your walking to the furder end of the platform. But, in about twelve minutes or so, she may be up."

"Who may be up?"

"The three forty-two, Sir. She goes off in a sidin' till the Up X passes, and then she"—here an air of hopeful vagueness pervaded Lamps—"does all as lays in her power."

"I doubt if I comprehend the arrangement."

"I doubt if anybody do, Sir. She's a Parliamentary, Sir. And, you see, a Parliamentary, or a Skirmishun——"

"Do you mean an Excursion?"

"That's it, Sir.—A Parliamentary or a Skirmishun, she mostly *doos* go off into a sidin'. But, when she *can* get a chance, she's whistled out of it, and she's whistled up into doin' all as,"—Lamps again wore the air of a highly sanguine man who hoped for the best,—"all as lays in her power."

He then explained that porters on duty, being required to be in attendance on the Parliamentary matron in question, would doubtless turn up with the gas. In the meantime, if the gentleman would not very much object to the smell of lamp-oil, and would accept the warmth of his little room—— The gentleman, being by this time very cold, instantly closed with the proposal.

A greasy little cabin it was, suggestive, to the sense of smell, of a cabin in a Whaler, But there was a bright fire burning in its rusty grate, and on the floor there stood a wooden stand of newly trimmed and lighted lamps, ready for carriage service. They made a bright show, and their light, and the warmth, accounted for the popularity of the room, as borne witness to by many impressions of velveteen trousers on a form by the fire, and many rounded smears and smudges of stooping velveteen shoulders on the adjacent wall. Various untidy shelves accommodated a quantity of lamps and oil-cans, and also a fragrant collection of what looked like the pocket-handkerchiefs of the whole lamp family.

As Barbox Brothers (so to call the traveller on the warranty of his luggage) took his seat upon the form, and warmed his now ungloved hands at the fire, he glanced aside at a little deal desk, much blotched with ink, which his elbow touched. Upon it were some scraps of coarse paper, and a superannuated steel pen in very reduced and gritty circumstances.

From glancing at the scraps of paper, he turned involuntarily to his host, and said, with some roughness:

"Why, you are never a poet, man?"

Lamps had certainly not the conventional appearance of one, as he stood modestly rubbing his squab nose with a handkerchief so exceedingly oily, that he might have been in the act of mistaking himself for one of his charges. He was a spare man of about the Barbox Brothers' time of life, with his features whimsically drawn upward as if they were attracted by the roots of his hair. He had a peculiarly shining transparent complexion, probably occasioned by constant oleaginous application; and his attractive hair, being cut short, and being grizzled, and standing straight up on end as if it in its turn were attracted by some invisible magnet above it, the top of his head was not very unlike a lamp-wick.

"But, to be sure, it's no business of mine," said Barbox Brothers. "That was an impertinent observation on my part. Be what you like."

"Some people, Sir," remarked Lamps in a tone of apology, "are sometimes what they don't like."

"Nobody knows that better than I do," sighed the other. "I have been what I don't like, all my life."

"When I first took, Sir," resumed Lamps, "to composing little Comic-Songs-like——"

Barbox Brothers eyed him with great disfavour.

"—To composing little Comic-Songs-like—and what was more hard—to singing 'em afterwards," said Lamps, "it went against the grain at that time, it did indeed."

Something that was not all oil here shining in Lamps's eye, Barbox Brothers withdrew his own a little disconcerted, looked at the fire, and put a foot on the top bar. "Why did you do it, then?" he asked after a short pause; abruptly enough; but in a softer tone. "If you didn't want to do it, why did you do it? Where did you sing them? Public-house?"

To which Mr. Lamps returned the curious reply: "Bedside."

At this moment, while the traveller looked at him for elucidation, Mugby Junction started suddenly, trembled violently, and opened its gas eyes. "She's got up!" Lamps announced, excited. "What lays in her power is sometimes more, and sometimes less; but it's laid in her power to get up to-night, by George!"

The legend "Barbox Brothers," in large white letters on two black surfaces, was very soon afterwards trundling on a truck through a silent street, and, when the owner of the legend had shivered on the pavement half an hour, what time the porter's knocks at the Inn Door knocked up the whole town first, and the Inn last, he groped his way into the close air of a shut-up house, and so groped between the sheets of a shut-up bed that seemed to have been expressly refrigerated for him when last made.

II

"You remember me, Young Jackson?"

"What do I remember if not you? You are my first remembrance. It was you who told me that was my name. It was you who told me that on every twentieth of December my life had a penitential anniversary in it called a birthday. I suppose the last communication was truer than the first!"

"What am I like, Young Jackson?"

"You are like a blight all through the year to me. You hard-lined, thin-lipped, repressive, changeless woman with a wax mask on. You are like the Devil to me; most of all when you teach me religious things, for you make me abhor them."

"You remember me, Mr. Young Jackson?" In another voice from another quarter.

"Most gratefully, Sir. You were the ray of hope and prospering ambition in my life. When I attended your course, I believed that I should come to be a great healer, and I felt almost happy—even though I was still the one boarder in the house with that horrible mask, and ate and drank in silence and constraint with the mask before me, every day. As I had done every, every, every day, through my school-time and from my earliest recollection."

"What am I like, Mr. Young Jackson?"

"You are like a Superior Being to me. You are like Nature beginning to reveal herself to me. I hear you again, as one of the hushed crowd of young men kindling under the power of your presence and knowledge, and you bring into my eyes the only exultant tears that ever stood in them."

"You remember Me, Mr. Young Jackson?" In a grating voice from quite another quarter.

"Too well. You made your ghostly appearance in my life one day, and announced that its course was to be suddenly and wholly changed. You showed me which was my wearisome seat in the Galley of Barbox Brothers. (When *they* were, if they ever were, is unknown to me; there was nothing of them but the name when I bent to the oar.) You told me what I was to do, and what to be paid; you told me afterwards, at intervals of years, when I was to sign for the Firm, when I became a partner, when I became the Firm. I know no more of it, or of myself."

"What am I like, Mr. Young Jackson?"

"You are like my father, I sometimes think. You are hard enough and cold enough so to have brought up an acknowledged son. I see your scanty figure, your close brown suit, and your tight brown wig;

but you, too, wear a wax mask to your death. You never by a chance remove it—it never by a chance falls off—and I know no more of you."

Throughout this dialogue, the traveller spoke to himself at his window in the morning, as he had spoken to himself at the Junction overnight. And as he had then looked in the darkness, a man who had turned grey too soon, like a neglected fire: so he now looked in the sunlight, an ashier grey, like a fire which the brightness of the sun put out.

The firm of Barbox Brothers had been some offshoot or irregular branch of the Public Notary and bill-broking tree. It had gained for itself a griping reputation before the days of Young Jackson, and the reputation had stuck to it and to him. As he had imperceptibly come into possession of the dim den up in the corner of a court off Lombard Street, on whose grimy windows the inscription Barbox Brothers had for many long years daily interposed itself between him and the sky, so he had insensibly found himself a personage held in chronic distrust, whom it was essential to screw tight to every transaction in which he engaged, whose word was never to be taken without his attested bond, whom all dealers with openly set up guards and wards against. This character had come upon him through no act of his own. It was as if the original Barbox had stretched himself down upon the office floor, and had thither caused to be conveyed Young Jackson in his sleep, and had there effected a metempsychosis and exchange of persons with him. The discovery—aided in its turn by the deceit of the only woman he had ever loved, and the deceit of the only friend he had ever made; who eloped from him to be married together—the discovery, so followed up, completed what his earliest rearing had begun. He shrank, abashed, within the form of Barbox, and lifted up his head and heart no more.

But he did at last effect one great release in his condition. He broke the oar he had plied so long, and he scuttled and sank the galley. He prevented the gradual retirement of an old conventional business from him, by taking the initiative and retiring from it. With enough to live on (though, after all, with not too much), he obliterated the firm of Barbox Brothers from the pages of the Post-Office Directory and the face of the earth, leaving nothing of it but its name on two portmanteaus.

"For one must have some name in going about, for people to pick up," he explained to Mugby High Street, through the Inn window, "and that name at least was real once. Whereas, Young Jackson!— Not to mention its being a sadly satirical misnomer for Old Jackson."

He took up his hat and walked out, just in time to see, passing along on the opposite side of the way, a velveteen man, carrying his day's dinner in a small bundle that might have been larger without suspicion of gluttony, and pelting away towards the Junction at a great pace.

"There's Lamps!" said Barbox Brothers. "And by-the-bye——"

Ridiculous, surely, that a man so serious, so self-contained, and not yet three days emancipated from a routine of drudgery, should stand rubbing his chin in the street, in a brown study about Comic Songs.

"Bedside?" said Barbox Brothers testily. "Sings them at the bedside? Why at the bedside, unless he goes to bed drunk? Does, I shouldn't wonder. But it's no business of mine. Let me see. Mugby Junction, Mugby Junction. Where shall I go next? As it came into my head last night when I woke from an uneasy sleep in the carriage and found myself here, I can go anywhere from here. Where shall I go? I'll go and look at the Junction by daylight. There's no hurry, and I may like the look of one Line better than another."

But there were so many Lines. Gazing down upon them from a bridge at the Junction, it was as if the concentrating Companies formed a great Industrial Exhibition of the works of extraordinary ground spiders that spun iron. And then so many of the Lines went such wonderful ways, so crossing and curving among one another, that the eye lost them. And then some of them appeared to start with the fixed intention of going five hundred miles, and all of a sudden gave it up at an insignificant barrier, or turned off into a workshop. And then others, like intoxicated men, went a little way very straight, and surprisingly slued round and came back again. And then others were so chock-full of trucks of coal, others were so blocked with trucks of casks, others were so gorged with trucks of ballast, others were so set apart for wheeled objects like immense iron cotton-reels: while others were so bright and clear, and others were so delivered over to rust and ashes and idle wheelbarrows out of work, with their legs in the air (looking much like their masters on strike), that there was no beginning, middle, or end to the bewilderment.

Barbox Brothers stood puzzled on the bridge, passing his right hand across the lines on his forehead, which multiplied while he looked down, as if the railway Lines were getting themselves photographed on that sensitive plate. Then was heard a distant ringing of bells and blowing of whistles. Then, puppet-looking heads of men popped out of boxes in perspective, and popped in again. Then, prodigious wooden razors, set up on end, began shaving the atmosphere. Then, several locomotive engines in several directions began to scream and be agitated. Then, along one avenue a train came in. Then, along another two trains appeared that didn't come in, but stopped without. Then, bits of trains broke off. Then, a struggling horse became involved with them. Then, the locomotives shared the bits of trains, and ran away with the whole.

"I have not made my next move much clearer by this. No hurry.

No need to make up my mind to-day, or to-morrow, nor yet the day after. I'll take a walk."

It fell out somehow (perhaps he meant it should) that the walk tended to the platform at which he had alighted, and to Lamps's room. But Lamps was not in his room. A pair of velveteen shoulders were adapting themselves to one of the impressions on the wall by Lamps's fireplace, but otherwise the room was void. In passing back to get out of the station again, he learnt the cause of this vacancy, by catching sight of Lamps on the opposite line of railway, skipping along the top of a train, from carriage to carriage, and catching lighted namesakes thrown up to him by a coadjutor.

"He is busy. He has not much time for composing or singing Comic Songs this morning, I take it."

The direction he pursued now was into the country, keeping very near to the side of one great Line of railway, and within easy view of others. "I have half a mind," he said, glancing around, "to settle the question from this point, by saying, 'I'll take this set of rails, or that, or t'other, and stick to it.' They separate themselves from the confusion, out here, and go their ways."

Ascending a gentle hill of some extent, he came to a few cottages. There, looking about him as a very reserved man might who had never looked about him in his life before, he saw some six or eight young children come merrily trooping and whooping from one of the cottages, and disperse. But not until they had all turned at the little garden-gate, and kissed their hands to a face at the upper window: a low window enough, although the upper, for the cottage had but a story of one room above the ground.

Now, that the children should do this was nothing; but that they should do this to a face lying on the sill of the open window, turned towards them in a horizontal position, and apparently only a face, was something noticeable. He looked up at the window again. Could only see a very fragile, though a very bright face, lying on one cheek on the window-sill. The delicate smiling face of a girl or woman. Framed in long bright brown hair, round which was tied a light blue band or fillet, passing under the chin.

He walked on, turned back, passed the window again, shyly glanced up again. No change. He struck off by a winding branch-road at the top of the hill—which he must otherwise have descended—kept the cottages in view, worked his way round at a distance so as to come out once more into the main road, and be obliged to pass the cottages again. The face still lay on the window-sill, but not so much inclined towards him. And now there were a pair of delicate hands too. They had the action of performing on some musical instrument, and yet it produced no sound that reached his ears.

"Mugby Junction must be the maddest place in England," said

Barbox Brothers, pursuing his way down the hill. "The first thing I find here is a Railway Porter who composes comic songs to sing at his bedside. The second thing I find here is a face, and a pair of hands playing a musical instrument that *don't* play!"

The day was a fine bright day in the early beginning of November, the air was clear and inspiriting, and the landscape was rich in beautiful colours. The prevailing colours in the court off Lombard Street, London city, had been few and sombre. Sometimes, when the weather elsewhere was very bright indeed, the dwellers in those tents enjoyed a pepper-and-salt-coloured day or two, but their atmosphere's usual wear was slate or snuff-coloured.

He relished his walk so well that he repeated it next day. He was a little earlier at the cottage than on the day before, and he could hear the children upstairs singing to a regular measure, and clapping out the time with their hands.

"Still, there is no sound of any musical instrument," he said, listening at the corner, "and yet I saw the performing hands again as I came by. What are the children singing? Why, good Lord, they can never be singing the multiplication table?"

They were, though, and with infinite enjoyment. The mysterious face had a voice attached to it, which occasionally led or set the children right. Its musical cheerfulness was delightful. The measure at length stopped, and was succeeded by a murmuring of young voices, and then by a short song which he made out to be about the current month of the year, and about what work it yielded to the labourers in the fields and farmyards. Then there was a stir of little feet, and the children came trooping and whooping out, as on the previous day. And again, as on the previous day, they all turned at the garden-gate, and kissed their hands—evidently to the face on the window-sill, though Barbox Brothers from his retired post of disadvantage at the corner could not see it.

But, as the children dispersed, he cut off one small straggler—a brown-faced boy with flaxen hair—and said to him:

"Come here, little one. Tell me, whose house is that?"

The child, with one swarthy arm held up across his eyes, half in shyness, and half ready for defence said from behind the inside of his elbow:

"Phœbe's."

"And who," said Barbox Brothers, quite as much embarrassed by his part in the dialogue as the child could possibly be by his, "is Phœbe?"

To which the child made answer:"Why, Phœbe, of course."

The small but sharp observer had eyed his questioner closely, and had taken his moral measure. He lowered his guard, and rather assumed a tone with him: as having discovered him to be an unaccustomed person in the art of polite conversation.

"Phœbe," said the child, "can't be anybobby else but Phœbe. Can she?"

"No, I suppose not."

"Well," returned the child, "then why did you ask me?"

Deeming it prudent to shift his ground, Barbox Brothers took up a new position.

"What do you do there? Up there in that room where the open window is. What do you do there?"

"Cool," said the child.

"Eh?"

"Co-o-ol," the child repeated in a louder voice, lengthening out the word with a fixed look and great emphasis, as much as to say: "What's the use of your having grown up, if you're such a donkey as not to understand me?"

"Ah! School, school," said Barbox Brothers. "Yes, yes, yes. And Phœbe teaches you?"

The child nodded.

"Good boy."

"Tound it out, have you?" said the child.

"Yes, I have found it out. What would you do with twopence, if I gave it you?"

"Pend it."

The knock-down promptitude of this reply leaving him not a leg to stand upon, Barbox Brothers produced the twopence with great lameness, and withdrew in a state of humiliation.

But, seeing the face on the window-sill as he passed the cottage, he acknowledged its presence there with a gesture, which was not a nod, not a bow, not a removal of his hat from his head, but was a diffident compromise between or struggle with all three. The eyes in the face seemed amused, or cheered, or both, and the lips modestly said: "Good day to you, Sir."

"I find I must stick for a time to Mugby Junction," said Barbox Brothers with much gravity, after once more stopping on his return road to look at the Lines where they went their several ways so quietly. "I can't make up my mind yet which iron road to take. In fact, I must get a little accustomed to the Junction before I can decide."

So, he announced at the Inn that he was "going to stay on for the present," and improved his acquaintance with the Junction that night, and again next morning, and again next night and morning: going down to the station, mingling with the people there, looking about him down all the avenues of railway, and beginning to take an interest in the incomings and outgoings of the trains. At first, he often put his head into Lamps's little room, but he never found Lamps there. A pair or two of velveteen shoulders he usually found there, stooping over the fire, sometimes in connexion with a clasped knife and a piece of bread and meat; but the answer to his inquiry, "Where's Lamps?" was, either that he was "t'other side the line," or, that it was his off-time, or (in the latter case) his own personal introduction to another Lamps who was not his lamps. However, he was not so desperately set upon seeing Lamps now, but he bore the disappointment. Nor did he so wholly devote himself to his severe application to the study of Mugby Junction as to neglect exercise. On the contrary, he took a walk every day, and always the same walk. But the weather turned cold and wet again, and the window was never open.

III

At length, after a lapse of some days, there came another streak of fine bright hardy autumn weather. It was a Saturday. The window was open, and the children were gone. Not surprising, this, for he had patiently watched and waited at the corner until they *were* gone.

"Good day," he said to the face; absolutely getting his hat clear off his head this time.

"Good day to you, Sir."

"I am glad you have a fine sky again to look at."

"Thank you, Sir. It is kind of you."

"You are an invalid, I fear?"

"No, Sir. I have very good health."

"But are you not always lying down?"

"Oh yes, I am always lying down, because I cannot sit up! But I am not an invalid."

The laughing eyes seemed highly to enjoy his great mistake.

"Would you mind taking the trouble to come in, Sir? There is a beautiful view from this window. And you would see that I am not at all ill—being so good as to care."

It was said to help him, as he stood irresolute, but evidently desiring to enter, with his diffident hand on the latch of the garden-gate. It did help him, and he went in.

The room upstairs was a very clean white room with a low roof. Its only inmate lay on a couch that brought her face to a level with the window. The couch was white too; and her simple dress or wrapper being light blue, like the band around her hair, she had an ethereal look, and a fanciful appearance of lying among clouds. He felt that she instinctively perceived him to be by habit a downcast taciturn man; it was another help to him to have established that understanding so easily, and got it over.

There was an awkward constraint upon him, nevertheless, as he touched her hand, and took a chair at the side of her couch.

"I see now," he began, not at all fluently, "how you occupy your hand. Only seeing you from the path outside, I thought you were playing upon something."

She was engaged in very nimbly and dexterously making lace. A lace-pillow lay upon her breast; and the quick movements and changes of her hands upon it, as she worked, had given them the action he had misinterpreted.

"That is curious," she answered with a bright smile. "For I often fancy, myself, that I play tunes while I am at work."

"Have you any musical knowledge?"

She shook her head.

"I think I could pick out tunes, if I had any instrument, which could be made as handy to me as my lace-pillow. But I dare say I deceive myself. At all events, I shall never know."

"You have a musical voice. Excuse me; I have heard you sing."

"With the children?" she answered, slightly colouring. "Oh yes. I sing with the dear children, if it can be called singing."

"Barbox Brothers glanced at the two small forms in the room, and hazarded the speculation that she was fond of children, and that she was learned in new systems of teaching them?

"Very fond of them," she said, shaking her head again; "but I know nothing of teaching, beyond the interest I have in it, and the pleasure it gives me when they learn. Perhaps your overhearing my little scholars sing some of their lessons has led you so far astray as to think me a grand teacher? Ah! I thought so! No, I have only read and been told about the system. It seemed so pretty and pleasant, and to treat them so like the merry Robins they are, that I took up with it in my little way. You don't need to be told what a very little way mine is, Sir," she added with a glance at the small forms and round the room.

All this time her hands were busy at her lace-pillow. As they still continued so, and as there was a kind of substitute for conversation in the click and play of its pegs, Barbox Brothers took the opportunity of observing her. He guessed her to be thirty. The charm of her transparent face and large bright brown eyes was, not that they were passively resigned, but that they were actively and thoroughly cheerful. Even her busy hands, which of their own thinness alone might have besought compassion, plied their task with a gay courage that made mere compassion an unjustifiable assumption of superiority, and an impertinence.

He saw her eyes in the act of rising towards his, and he directed his towards the prospect, saying: "Beautiful, indeed!"

"Most beautiful, Sir. I have sometimes had a fancy that I would like to sit up, for once, only to try how it looks to an erect head.

But what a foolish fancy that would be to encourage! It cannot look more lovely to any one than it does to me."

Her eyes were turned to it, as she spoke, with most delighted admiration and enjoyment. There was not a trace in it of any sense of deprivation.

"And those threads of railway, with their puffs of smoke and steam changing places so fast, make it so lively for me," she went on. "I think of the number of people who *can* go where they wish, on their business, or their pleasure; I remember that the puffs make signs to me that they are actually going while I look; and that enlivens the prospect with abundance of company, if I want company. There is the great Junction, too. I don't see it under the foot of the hill, but I can very often hear it, and I always know it is there. It seems to join me, in a way, to I don't know how many places and things that I shall never see."

With an abashed kind of idea that it might have already joined himself to something he had never seen, he said constrainedly: "Just so."

"And so you see, Sir," pursued Phœbe, "I am not the invalid you thought me, and I am very well off indeed."

"You have a happy disposition," said Barbox Brothers: perhaps with a slight excusatory touch for his own disposition.

"Ah! But you should know my father," she replied. "His is the happy disposition!—Don't mind, Sir!" For his reserve took the alarm at a step upon the stairs, and he distrusted that he would be set down for a troublesome intruder. "This is my father coming."

The door opened, and the father paused there.

"Why, Lamps!" exclaimed Barbox Brothers, starting from his chair. "How do you DO, Lamps?"

To which Lamps responded: "The gentleman for Nowhere! How do you DO, Sir?"

And they shook hands, to the greatest admiration and surprise of Lamps's daughter.

"I have looked you up half-a-dozen times since that night," said Barbox Brothers, "but have never found you."

"So I've heerd on, Sir, so I've heerd on," returned Lamps. "It's your being noticed so often down at the Junction, without taking any train, that has begun to get you the name among us of the gentleman for Nowhere. No offence in my having called you by it when took by surprise, I hope, Sir?"

"None at all. It's as good a name for me as any other you could call me by. But may I ask you a question in the corner here?"

Lamps suffered himself to be led aside from his daughter's couch by one of the buttons of his velveteen jacket.

"Is this the bedside where you sing your songs?"

Lamps nodded.

The gentleman for Nowhere clapped him on the shoulder, and they faced about again.

"Upon my word, my dear," said Lamps then to his daughter, looking from her to her visitor, "it is such an amaze to me, to find you brought acquainted with this gentleman, that I must (if this gentleman will excuse me) take a rounder."

Mr. Lamps demonstrated in action what this meant, by pulling out his oily handkerchief rolled up in the form of a ball, and giving himself an elaborate smear, from behind the right ear, up the cheek, across the forehead, and down the other cheek to behind his left ear. After this operation he shone exceedingly.

"It's according to my custom when particular warmed up by any agitation, Sir," he offered by way of apology. "And really, I am throwed into that state of amaze by finding you brought acquainted with Phœbe, that I—that I think I will, if you'll excuse me, take another rounder." Which he did, seeming to be greatly restored by it.

They were now both standing by the side of her couch, and she was working at her lace-pillow. "Your daughter tells me," said Barbox Brothers, still in a half-reluctant shamefaced way, "that she never sits up."

"No, Sir, nor never has done. You see, her mother (who died when she was a year and two months old) was subject to very bad fits, and as she had never mentioned to me that she *was* subject to fits, they couldn't be guarded against. Consequently, she dropped the baby when took, and this happened."

"It was very wrong of her," said Barbox Brothers with a knitted brow, "to marry you, making a secret of her infirmity."

"Well, Sir!" pleaded Lamps in behalf of the long-deceased. "You see, Phœbe and me, we have talked that over too. And Lord bless us! Such a number on us has our infirmities, what with fits, and what with misfits, of one sort and another, that if we confessed to 'em all before we got married, most of us might never get married."

"Might not that be for the better?"

"Not in this case, Sir," said Phœbe, giving her hand to her father.

"No, not in this case, Sir," said her father, patting it between his own.

"You correct me," returned Barbox Brothers with a blush; "and I must look so like a Brute, that at all events it would be superfluous in me to confess to *that* infirmity. I wish you would tell me a little more about yourselves. I hardly know how to ask it of you, for I am conscious that I have a bad stiff manner, a dull discouraging way with me, but I wish you would."

"With all our hearts, Sir," returned Lamps gaily for both. "And first of all, that you may know my name——"

"Stay!" interposed the visitor with a slight flush. "What signifies your name? Lamps is name enough for me. I like it. It is bright and expressive. What do I want more?"

"Why, to be sure, Sir," returned Lamps. "I have in general no other name down at the Junction; but I thought, on account of your being here as a first-class single, in a private character, that you might——"

The visitor waved the thought away with his hand, and Lamps acknowledged the mark of confidence by taking another rounder.

"You are hard-worked, I take for granted?" said Barbox Brothers, when the subject of the rounder came out of it much dirtier than he went into it.

Lamps was beginning, "Not particular so"—when his daughter took him up.

"Oh yes, Sir, he is very hard-worked. Fourteen, fifteen, eighteen hours a day. Sometimes twenty-four hours at a time."

"And you," said Barbox Brothers, "what with your school, Phœbe, and what with your lace-making——"

"But my school is a pleasure to me," she interrupted, opening her brown eyes wider, as if surprised to find him so obtuse. "I began it when I was but a child, because it brought me and other children into company, don't you see? *That* was not work. I carry it on still, because it keeps children about me. *That* is not work. I do it as love, not as work. Then my lace-pillow;" her busy hands had stopped, as if her argument required all her cheerful earnestness, but now went on again at the name; "it goes with my thoughts when I think, and it goes with my tunes when I hum any, and *that's* not work. Why, you yourself thought it was music, you know, Sir. And so it is to me."

"Everything is!" cried Lamps radiantly. "Everything is music to her, Sir."

"My father is, at any rate," said Phœbe, exultingly pointing her thin forefinger at him. "There is more music in my father than there is in a brass band."

"I say! My dear! It's very fillyillially done, you know; but you are flattering your father," he protested, sparkling.

"No, I am not, Sir, I assure you. No, I am not. If you could hear my father sing, you would know I am not. But you never will hear him sing, because he never sings to any one but me. However tired he is, he always sings to me when he comes home. When I lay here long ago, quite a poor little broken doll, he used to sing to me. More than that, he used to make songs, bringing in whatever little jokes we had between us. More than that, he often does so to this day. Oh! I'll tell of you, father, as the gentleman has asked about you. He is a poet, Sir."

"I shouldn't wish the gentleman, my dear," observed Lamps, for the moment turning grave, "to carry away that opinion of your father, because it might look as if I was given to asking the stars in a molloncolly manner what they was up to. Which I wouldn't at once waste the time, and take the liberty, my dear."

"My father," resumed Phœbe, amending her text, "is always on the bright side, and the good side. You told me, just now, I had a happy disposition. How can I help it?"

"Well; but, my dear," returned Lamps argumentatively, "how can I help it? Put it to yourself, Sir. Look at her. Always as you see her now. Always working—and after all, Sir, for but a very few shillings a week—always contented, always lively, always interested in others, of all sorts. I said, this moment, she was always as you see her now. So she is, with a difference that comes to much the same. For, when it is my Sunday off and the morning bells have done ringing, I hear the prayers and thanks read in the touchingest way, and I have the hymns sung to me—so soft, Sir, that you couldn't hear 'em out of this room—in notes that seem to me, I am sure, to come from Heaven and go back to it."

It might have been merely through the association of these words with their sacredly quiet time, or it might have been through the larger association of the words with the Redeemer's presence beside the bedridden; but here her dexterous fingers came to a stop on the lace-pillow, and clasped themselves around his neck as he bent down. There was great natural sensibility in both father and daughter, the visitor could easily see; but each made it, for the other's sake, retiring, not demonstrative; and perfect cheerfulness, intuitive or acquired, was either the first or second nature of both. In a very few moments Lamps was taking another rounder with his comical features beaming, while Phœbe's laughing eyes (just a glistening speck or so upon their lashes) were again directed by turns to him, and to her work, and to Barbox Brothers.

"When my father, Sir," she said brightly, "tells you about my being interested in other people, even though they know nothing about me —which, by-the-bye, I told you myself—you ought to know how that comes about. That's my father's doing."

"No, it isn't!" he protested.

"Don't you believe him, Sir; yes, it is. He tells me of everything he sees down at his work. You would be surprised what a quantity he gets together for me every day. He looks into the carriages, and tells me how the ladies are dressed—so that I know all the fashions! He looks into the carriages, and tells me what pairs of lovers he sees, and what new-married couples on their wedding trip—so that I know all about that! He collects chance newspapers and books—so that I have plenty to read! He tells me about the sick people who are travelling to try to get better—so that I know all about them! In short, as I began by saying, he tells me everything he sees and makes out down at his

LIFE AND ITS BATTLE

work, and you can't think what a quantity he does see and make out."

"As to collecting newspapers and books, my dear," said Lamps, "it's clear I can have no merit in that, because they're not my perquisites. You see, Sir, it's this way: A Guard, he'll say to me, 'Hallo, here you are, Lamps. I've saved this paper for your daughter. How is she a-going on?' A Head Porter, he'll say to me, 'Here! Catch hold, Lamps. Here's a couple of wollumes for your daughter. Is she pretty much where she were?' And that's what makes it double welcome, you see. If she had a thousand pound in a box, they wouldn't trouble themselves about her; but being what she is—that is, you understand," Lamps added, somewhat hurriedly, "not having a thousand pound in a box—they take thought for her. And as concerning the young pairs, married and unmarried, it's only natural I should bring home what little I can about *them*, seeing that there's not a Couple of either sort in the neighbourhood that don't come of their own accord to confide in Phœbe."

She raised her eyes triumphantly to Barbox Brothers as she said:

"Indeed, Sir, that is true. If I could have got up and gone to church, I don't know how often I should have been a bridesmaid. But, if I could have done that, some girls in love might have been jealous of me, and, as it is, no girl is jealous of me. And my pillow would not have been half as ready to put the piece of cake under, as I always find it," she added, turning her face on it with a light sigh, and a smile at her father.

The arrival of a little girl, the biggest of the scholars, now led to an understanding on the part of Barbox Brothers, that she was the domestic of the cottage, and had come to take active measures in it, attended by a pail that might have extinguished her, and a broom three times her height. He therefore rose to take his leave, and took it; saying that, if Phœbe had no objection, he would come again.

He had muttered that he would come "in the course of his walks." The course of his walks must have been highly favourable to his return, for he returned after an interval of a single day.

"You thought you would never see me any more, I suppose?" he said to Phœbe as he touched her hand, and sat down by her couch.

"Why should I think so?" was her surprised rejoinder.

"I took it for granted you would mistrust me."

"For granted, Sir? Have you been so much mistrusted?"

"I think I am justified in answering yes. But I may have mistrusted, too, on my part. No matter just now. We were speaking of the Junction last time. I have passed hours there since the day before yesterday."

"Are you now the gentleman for Somewhere?" she asked with a smile.

"Certainly for Somewhere; but I don't yet know Where. You would never guess what I am travelling from. Shall I tell you? I am travelling from my birthday."

Her hands stopped in her work, and she looked at him with incredulous astonishment.

"Yes," said Barbox Brothers, not quite easy in his chair, "from my birthday. I am, to myself, an unintelligible book with the earlier chapters all torn out, and thrown away. My childhood had no grace of childhood, my youth had no charm of youth, and what can be expected from such a lost beginning?" His eyes meeting hers as they were addressed intently to him, something seemed to stir within his breast, whispering: "Was this bed a place for the graces of childhood and the charms of youth to take to kindly? Oh, shame, shame!"

"It is a disease with me," said Barbox Brothers, checking himself, and making as though he had a difficulty in swallowing something, "to go wrong about that. I don't know how I came to speak of that. I hope it is because of an old misplaced confidence in one of your sex involving an old bitter treachery. I don't know. I am all wrong together."

Her hands quietly and slowly resumed their work. Glancing at her, he saw that her eyes were thoughtfully following them.

"I am travelling from my birthday," he resumed, "because it has always been a dreary day to me. My first free birthday coming round some five or six weeks hence, I am travelling to put its predecessors far behind me, and to try to crush the day—or, at all events, put it out of my sight—by heaping new objects on it.

As he paused, she looked at him; but only shook her head as being quite at a loss.

"This is unintelligible to your happy disposition," he pursued, abiding by his former phrase as if there were some lingering virtue of self-defence in it. "I knew it would be, and am glad it is. However, on this travel of mine (in which I mean to pass the rest of my days, having abandoned all thought of a fixed home), I stopped, as you have heard from your father, at the Junction here. The extent of its ramifications quite confused me as to whither I should go, *from* here. I have not yet settled, being still perplexed among so many roads. What do you think I mean to do? How many of the branching roads can you see from your window?"

Looking out, full of interest, she answered, "Seven."

"Seven," said Barbox Brothers, watching her with a grave smile. "Well! I propose to myself at once to reduce the gross number to those very seven, and gradually to fine them down to one—the most promising for me—and to take that."

"But how will you know, Sir, which *is* the most promising?" she asked, with her brightened eyes roving over the view.

"Ah!" said Barbox Brothers with another grave smile, and considerably improving in his ease of speech. "To be sure. In this way. Where your father can pick up so much every day for a good purpose, I may once and again pick up a little for an indifferent purpose. The gentleman for Nowhere must become still better known at the Junction. He shall continue to explore it, until he attaches something that he has seen, heard, or found out, at the head of each of the seven roads, to the road itself. And so his choice of a road shall be determined by his choice among his discoveries."

Her hands still busy, she again glanced at the prospect, as if it comprehended something that had not been in it before, and laughed as if it yielded her new pleasure.

"But I must not forget," said Barbox Brothers, "(having got so far) to ask a favour. I want your help in this expedient of mine. I want to bring you what I pick up at the heads of the seven roads that you lie here looking out at, and to compare notes with you about it. May I? They say two heads are better than one. I should say myself that probably depends upon the heads concerned. But I am quite sure, though we are so newly acquainted, that your head and your father's have found out better things, Phœbe, than ever mine of itself discovered."

She gave him her sympathetic right hand, in perfect rapture with his proposal, and eagerly and gratefully thanked him.

"That's well!" said Barbox Brothers. "Again I must not forget (having got so far) to ask a favour. Will you shut your eyes?"

Laughing playfully at the strange nature of the request, she did so.

"Keep them shut," said Barbox Brothers, going softly to the door, and coming back. "You are on your honour, mind, not to open your eyes until I tell you that you may?"

"Yes! On my honour."

"Good. May I take your lace-pillow from you for a minute?"

Still laughing and wondering, she removed her hands from it, and he put it aside.

"Tell me. Did you see the puffs of smoke and steam made by the morning fast-train yesterday on road number seven from here?"

"Behind the elm-trees and the spire?"

"That's the road," said Barbox Brothers, directing his eyes toward it.

"Yes. I watched them melt away."

"Anything unusual in what they expressed?"

"No!" she answered merrily.

"Not complimentary to me, for I was in that train. I went—don't open your eyes—to fetch you this, from the great ingenious town. It is not half so large as your lace-pillow, and lies easily and lightly in its place. These little keys are like the keys of a miniature piano, and you supply the air required with your left hand. May you pick out delightful music from it, my dear! For the present—you can open your eyes now—good-bye!"

In his embarrassed way, he closed the door upon himself, and only saw, in doing so, that she ecstatically took the present to her bosom and caressed it. The glimpse gladdened his heart, and yet saddened it; for so might she, if her youth had flourished in its natural course, have taken to her breast that day the slumbering music of her own child's voice.

CHAPTER II   *Barbox Brothers and Co.*

With good-will and earnest purpose, the gentleman for Nowhere began, on the very next day, his researches at the heads of the seven roads. The results of his researches, as he and Phœbe afterwards set them down in fair writing, hold their due places in this veracious chronicle. But they occupied a much longer time in the getting together than they ever will in the perusal. And this is probably the case with most reading matter, except when it is of that highly beneficial kind (for Posterity) which is "thrown off in a few moments of leisure" by the superior poetic geniuses who scorn to take prose pains.

It must be admitted, however, that Barbox by no means hurried himself. His heart being in his work of good-nature, he revelled in it. There was the joy, too (it was a true joy to him), of sometimes sitting by, listening to Phœbe as she picked out more and more discourse from her musical instrument, and as her natural taste and ear refined daily upon her first discoveries. Besides being a pleasure, this was an occupation, and in the course of weeks it consumed hours. It resulted that his dreaded birthday was close upon him before he had troubled himself any more about it.

The matter was made more pressing by the unforeseen circumstance that the councils held (at which Mr. Lamps, beaming most brilliantly, on a few rare occasions assisted) respecting the road to be selected were, after all, in nowise assisted by his investigations. For, he had connected this interest with this road, or that interest with the other, but could deduce no reason from it for giving any road the preference. Consequently, when the last council was holden, that part of the business stood, in the end, exactly where it had stood in the beginning.

"But, Sir," remarked Phœbe, "we have only six roads after all. Is the seventh road dumb?"

"The seventh road? Oh!" said Barbox Brothers, rubbing his chin. "That is the road I took, you know, when I went to get your little present. That is *its* story, Phœbe."

"Would you mind taking that road again, Sir?" she asked with hesitation.

"Not in the least; it is a great high-road after all."

"I should like you to take it," returned Phœbe with a persuasive smile, "for the love of that little present which must ever be so dear to me. I should like you to take it, because that road can never be again like any other road to me. I should like you to take it, in remembrance of your having done me so much good: of your having made me so much happier! If you leave me by the road you travelled when you went to do me this great kindness," sounding a faint chord as she spoke, "I shall feel, lying here watching at my window, as if it must conduct you to a prosperous end, and bring you back some day."

"It shall be done, my dear; it shall be done."

So at last the gentleman for Nowhere took a ticket for Somewhere, and his destination was the great ingenious town.

He had loitered so long about the Junction that it was the eighteenth of December when he left it. "High time," he reflected, as he seated himself in the train, "that I started in earnest! Only one clear day remains between me and the day I am running away from. I'll push onward for the hill-country to-morrow. I'll go to Wales."

It was with some pains that he placed before himself the undeniable advantages to be gained in the way of novel occupation for his senses from misty mountains, swollen streams, rain, cold, a wild seashore, and rugged roads. And yet he scarcely made them out as distinctly as he could have wished. Whether the poor girl, in spite of her new resource, her music, would have any feeling of loneliness upon her now—just at first—that she had not had before; whether she saw those very puffs of steam and smoke that he saw, as he sat in the train thinking of her; whether her face would have any pensive shadow on it as they died out of the distant view from her window; whether, in telling him he had done her so much good, she had not unconsciously corrected his old moody bemoaning of his station in life, by setting him thinking that a man might be a great healer, if he would, and yet not be a great doctor; these and other similar meditations got between him and his Welsh picture. There was within him, too, that dull sense of vacuity which follows separation from an object of interest, and cessation of a pleasant pursuit; and this sense, being quite new to him, made him restless. Further, in losing Mugby Junction, he had found himself again; and he was not the more enamoured of himself for having lately passed his time in better company.

But surely here, not far ahead, must be the great ingenious town. This crashing and clashing that the train was undergoing, and this coupling on to it of a multitude of new echoes, could mean nothing less than approach to the great station. It did mean nothing less. After some stormy flashes of town lightning, in the way of swift revelations of red brick blocks of houses, high red brick chimney-shafts, vistas of red brick railway-arches, tongues of fire, blocks of smoke, valleys of canal, and hills of coal, there came the thundering in at the journey's end.

Having seen his portmanteaus safely housed in the hotel he chose, and having appointed his dinner hour, Barbox Brothers went out for a walk in the busy streets. And now it began to be suspected by him that Mugby Junction was a Junction of many branches, invisible as well as visible, and had joined him to an endless number of by-ways. For, whereas he would, but a little while ago, have walked these streets blindly brooding, he now had eyes and thoughts for a new external world. How the many toiling people lived, and loved, and died; how wonderful it was to consider the various trainings of eye and hand, the nice distinctions of sight and touch, that separated them into classes of workers, and even into classes of workers at sub-divisions of one complete whole which combined their many intelligences and forces, though of itself but some cheap object of use or ornament in common life; how good it was to know that such assembling in a multitude on their part, and such contribution of their several dexterities towards a civilising end, did not deteriorate them as it was the fashion of the supercilious Mayflies of humanity to pretend, but engendered among them a self-respect, and yet a modest desire to be much wiser than they were (the first evinced in their well-balanced bearing and manner of speech when he stopped to ask a question; the second, in the announcements of their popular studies and amusements on the public walls); these considerations, and a host of such, made his walk a memorable one. "I too am but a little part of a great whole," he began to think; "and to be serviceable to myself and others, or to be happy, I must cast my interest into, and draw it out of, the common stock."

Although he had arrived at his journey's end for the day by noon, he had since insensibly walked about the town so far and so long that the lamp-lighters were now at their work in the streets, and the shops were sparkling up brilliantly. Thus reminded to turn towards his quarters, he was in the act of doing so, when a very little hand crept into his, and a very little voice said:

"Oh! if you please, I am lost!"

He looked down, and saw a very little fair-haired girl.

"Yes," she said, confirming her words with a serious nod. "I am indeed. I am lost!"

Greatly perplexed, he stopped, looked about him for help, descried none, and said, bending low:

"Where do you live, my child?"

"I don't know where I live," she returned. "I am lost."

"What is your name?"

"Polly."

"What is your other name?"

The reply was prompt, but unintelligible.

Imitating the sound as he caught it, he hazarded the guess, "Trivits."

"Oh no!" said the child, shaking her head. "Nothing like that."

"Say it again, little one."

An unpromising business. For this time it had quite a different sound.

He made the venture, "Paddens?"

"Oh no!" said the child. "Nothing like that."

"Once more. Let us try it again, dear."

A most hopeless business. This time it swelled into four syllables. "It can't be Tappitarver?" said Barbox Brothers, rubbing his head with his hat in discomfiture.

"No! It ain't," the child quietly assented.

On her trying this unfortunate name once more, with extraordinary efforts at distinctness, it swelled into eight syllables at least.

"Ah! I think," said Barbox Brothers with a desperate air of resignation, "that we had better give it up."

"But I am lost," said the child, nestling her little hand more closely in his, "and you'll take care of me, won't you?"

If ever a man were disconcerted by division between compassion on the one hand, and the very imbecility of irresolution on the other, here the man was. "Lost!" he repeated, looking down at the child. "I am sure *I* am. What is to be done?"

"Where do *you* live?" asked the child, looking up at him wistfully.

"Over there," he answered, pointing vaguely in the direction of his hotel.

"Hadn't we better go there?" said the child.

"Really," he replied, "I don't know but what we had."

So they set off, hand-in-hand. He, through comparison of himself against his little companion, with a clumsy feeling on him as if he had just developed into a foolish giant. She, clearly elevated in her own tiny opinion by having got him so neatly out of his embarrassment.

"We are going to have dinner when we get there, I suppose?" said Polly.

"Well," he rejoined, "I—— Yes, I suppose we are."

"Do you like your dinner?" asked the child.

"Why, on the whole," said Barbox Brothers, "yes, I think I do."

"I do mine," said Polly. "Have you any brothers and sisters?"

"No. Have you?"

"Mine are dead."

"Oh!" said Barbox Brothers. With that absurd sense of unwieldiness of mind and body weighing him down, he would have not known how to pursue the conversation beyond this curt rejoinder, but that the child was always ready for him.

"What," she asked, turning her soft hand coaxingly in his, "are you going to do to amuse me after dinner?"

"Upon my soul, Polly," exclaimed Barbox Brothers, very much at a loss, "I have not the slightest idea!"

"Then I tell you what," said Polly. "Have you got any cards at your house?"

"Plenty," said Barbox Brothers in a boastful vein.

"Very well. Then I'll build houses, and you shall look at me. You mustn't blow, you know."

"Oh no," said Barbox Brothers. "No, no, no. No blowing. Blowing's not fair."

He flattered himself that he had said this pretty well for an idiotic monster; but the child, instantly perceiving the awkwardness of his attempt to adapt himself to her level, utterly destroyed his hopeful opinion of himself by saying compassionately: "What a funny man you are!"

Feeling, after this melancholy failure, as if he every minute grew bigger and heavier in person, and weaker in mind, Barbox gave himself up for a bad job. No giant ever submitted more meekly to be led in triumph by all-conquering Jack than he to be bound in slavery to Polly.

"Do you know any stories?" she asked him.

He was reduced to the humiliating confession: "No."

"What a dunce you must be, mustn't you?" said Polly.

He was reduced to the humiliating confession: "Yes."

"Would you like me to teach you a story? But you must remember it, you know, and be able to tell it right to somebody else afterwards."

He professed that it would afford him the highest mental gratification to be taught a story, and that he would humbly endeavour to retain it in his mind. Whereupon Polly, giving her hand a new little turn in his, expressive of settling down for enjoyment, commenced a long romance, of which every relishing clause began with the words: "So this," or, "And so this." As, "So this boy;" or, "So this fairy;" or, "And so this pie was four yards round, and two yards and a quarter deep." The interest of the romance was derived from the intervention of this fairy to punish this boy for having a greedy appetite. To achieve which purpose, this fairy made this pie, and this boy ate and ate and ate, and his cheeks swelled and swelled and swelled. There were many tributary circumstances, but the forcible interest culminated in the total consumption of this pie, and the bursting of this boy. Truly he was a fine sight, Barbox Brothers, with serious attentive face, and ear bent down, much jostled on the pavements of the busy town, but afraid of losing a single incident of the epic, lest he should be examined in it by-and-by, and found deficient.

Thus they arrived at the hotel. And there he had to say at the bar, and said awkwardly enough: "I have found a little girl!"

The whole establishment turned out to look at the little girl. Nobody knew her; nobody could make out her name, as she set it forth— except one chambermaid, who said it was Constantinople—which it wasn't.

"I will dine with my young friend in a private room," said Barbox Brothers to the hotel authorities, "and perhaps you will be so good as to let the police know that the pretty baby is here. I suppose she is sure to be inquired for soon, if she has not been already. Come along, Polly."

Perfectly at ease and peace, Polly came along, but, finding the stairs rather stiff work, was carried up by Barbox Brothers. The dinner was a most transcendent success, and the Barbox sheepishness, under Polly's directions how to mince her meat for her, and how to diffuse gravy over the plate with a liberal and equal hand, was another fine sight.

"And now," said Polly, "while we are at dinner, you be good, and tell me that story I taught you."

With the tremors of a Civil Service examination upon him, and very uncertain indeed, not only as to the epoch at which the pie appeared in history, but also as to the measurements of that indispensable fact, Barbox Brothers made a shaky beginning, but under encouragement did very fairly. There was a want of breadth observable in his rendering of the cheeks, as well as the appetite, of the boy; and there was a certain tameness in his fairy, referable to an undercurrent of desire to account for her. Still, as the first lumbering performance of a good-humoured monster, it passed muster.

"I told you to be good," said Polly, "and you are good, ain't you?"

"I hope so," replied Barbox Brothers.

Such was his deference that Polly, elevated on a platform of sofa cushions in a chair at his right hand, encouraged him with a pat or two on the face from the greasy bowl of her spoon, and even with a gracious kiss. In getting on her feet upon her chair, however, to give him this last reward, she toppled forward among the dishes, and caused him to exclaim, as he effected her rescue: "Gracious Angels! Whew! I thought we were in the fire, Polly!"

"What a coward you are, ain't you?" said Polly when replaced.

"Yes, I am rather nervous," he replied. "Whew! Don't, Polly! Don't flourish your spoon, or you'll go over sideways. Don't tilt up your legs when you laugh, Polly, or you'll go over backwards. Whew! Polly, Polly, Polly," said Barbox Brothers, nearly succumbing to despair, "we are environed with dangers!"

Indeed, he could descry no security from the pitfalls that were yawning for Polly, but in proposing to her, after dinner, to sit upon a low stool. "I will, if you will," said Polly. So, as peace of mind should go before all, he begged the waiter to wheel aside the table, bring a pack of cards, a couple of footstools, and a screen, and close in Polly and himself before the fire, as it were in a snug room within the room. Then, finest sight of all, was Barbox Brothers on his footstool, with a pint decanter on the rug, contemplating Polly as she built successfully, and growing blue in the face with holding his breath, lest he should blow the house down.

"How you stare, don't you?" said Polly in a houseless pause.

Detected in the ignoble fact, he felt obliged to admit, apologetically: "I am afraid I was looking rather hard at you, Polly."

"Why do you stare?" asked Polly.

"I cannot," he murmured to himself, "recall why.—I don't know, Polly."

"You must be a simpleton to do things and not know why, mustn't you?" said Polly.

In spite of which reproof, he looked at the child again intently, as she bent her head over her card structure, her rich curls shading her face. "It is impossible," he thought, "that I can ever have seen this pretty baby before. Can I have dreamed of her? In some sorrowful dream?"

He could make nothing of it. So he went into the building trade as a journeyman under Polly, and they built three stories high, four stories high; even five.

"I say! Who do you think is coming?" asked Polly, rubbing her eyes after tea.

He guessed: "The waiter?"

"No," said Polly, "the dustman. I am getting sleepy."

A new embarrassment for Barbox Brothers!

"I don't think I am going to be fetched to-night," said Polly. "What do you think?"

He thought not, either. After another quarter of an hour, the dustman not merely impending, but actually arriving, recourse was had to the Constantinopolitan chambermaid: who cheerily undertook that the child should sleep in a comfortable and wholesome room, which she herself would share.

"And I know you will be careful, won't you," said Barbox Brothers, as a new fear dawned upon him, "that she don't fall out of bed?"

Polly found this so highly entertaining that she was under the necessity of clutching him round the neck with both arms as he sat on his footstool picking up the cards, and rocking him to and fro, with her dimpled chin on his shoulder.

"Oh, what a coward you are, ain't you?" said Polly. "Do *you* fall out of bed?"

"N—not generally, Polly."

"No more do I."

With that, Polly gave him a reassuring hug or two to keep him going, and then giving that confiding mite of a hand of hers to be swallowed up in the hand of the Constantinopolitan chambermaid, trotted off, chattering, without a vestige of anxiety.

He looked after her, had the screen removed and the table and chairs replaced, and still looked after her. He paced the room for half an hour. "A most engaging little creature, but it's not that. A most winning little voice, but it's not that. That has much to do with it, but there is something more. How can it be that I seem to know this child? What was it she imperfectly recalled to me when I felt her touch in the street, and, looking down at her, saw her looking up at me?"

"Mr. Jackson!"

With a start he turned towards the sound of the subdued voice, and saw his answer standing at the door.

"Oh, Mr. Jackson, do not be severe with me! Speak a word of encouragement to me, I beseech you."

"You are Polly's mother."

"Yes."

Yes. Polly herself might come to this, one day. As you see what the rose was in its faded leaves; as you see what the summer growth of the woods was in their wintry branches; so Polly might be traced, one day, in a careworn woman like this, with her hair turned grey. Before him were the ashes of a dead fire that had once burned bright. This was the woman he had loved. This was the woman he had lost. Such had been the constancy of his imagination to her, so had Time spared her under its withholding, that now, seeing how roughly the inexorable hand had struck her, his soul was filled with pity and amazement.

He led her to a chair, and stood leaning on a corner of the chimney-piece, with his head resting on his hand, and his face half averted.

"Did you see me in the street, and show me to your child?" he asked.

"Yes."

"Is the little creature, then, a party to deceit?"

"I hope there is no deceit. I said to her, 'We have lost our way, and I must try to find mine by myself. Go to that gentleman, and tell him you are lost. You shall be fetched by-and-by.' Perhaps you have not thought how very young she is?"

"She is very self-reliant."

"Perhaps because she is so young."

He asked, after a short pause, "Why did you do this?"

"Oh, Mr. Jackson, do you ask me? In the hope that you might see something in my innocent child to soften your heart towards me. Not only towards me, but towards my husband."

He suddenly turned about, and walked to the opposite end of the room. He came back again with a slower step, and resumed his former attitude, saying:

"I thought you had emigrated to America?"

"We did. But life went ill with us there, and we came back."

"Do you live in this town?"

"Yes. I am a daily teacher of music here. My husband is a book-keeper."

"Are you—forgive my asking—poor?"

"We earn enough for our wants. That is not our distress. My husband is very, very ill of a lingering disorder. He will never recover——"

"You check yourself. If it is for want of the encouraging word you spoke of, take it from me. I cannot forget the old time, Beatrice."

"God bless you!" she replied with a burst of tears, and gave him her trembling hand.

"Compose yourself. I cannot be composed if you are not, for to see you weep distresses me beyond expression. Speak freely to me. Trust me."

She shaded her face with her veil, and after a little while spoke calmly. Her voice had the ring of Polly's.

"It is not that my husband's mind is at all impaired by his bodily suffering, for I assure you that is not the case. But in his weakness, and in his knowledge that he is incurably ill, he cannot overcome the ascendancy of one idea. It preys upon him, embitters every moment of his painful life, and will shorten it."

She stopping, he said again: "Speak freely to me. Trust me."

"We have had five children before this darling, and they all lie in their little graves. He believes that they have withered away under a curse, and that it will blight this child like the rest."

"Under what curse?"

"Both I and he have it on our conscience that we tried you very heavily, and I do not know but that, if I were as ill as he, I might suffer in my mind as he does. This is the constant burden:—'I believe, Beatrice, I was the only friend that Mr. Jackson ever cared to make, though I was so much his junior. The more influence he acquired in the business, the higher he advanced me, and I was alone in his private confidence. I came between him and you, and I took you from him. We were both secret, and the blow fell when he was wholly unprepared. The anguish it caused a man so compressed must have been terrible; the wrath it awakened inappeasable. So, a curse came to be invoked on our poor pretty little flowers, and they fall.'"

"And you, Beatrice," he asked, when she had ceased to speak, and there had been a silence afterwards, "how say you?"

"Until within these few weeks I was afraid of you, and I believed that you would never, never forgive."

"Until within these few weeks," he repeated. "Have you changed your opinion of me within these few weeks?"

"Yes."

"For what reason?"

"I was getting some pieces of music in a shop in this town, when, to my terror, you came in. As I veiled my face and stood in the dark end of the shop, I heard you explain that you wanted a musical instrument for a bedridden girl. Your voice and manner were so softened, you showed such interest in its selection, you took it away yourself with so much tenderness of care and pleasure, that I knew you were a man with a most gentle heart. Oh, Mr. Jackson, Mr. Jackson, if you could have felt the refreshing rain of tears that followed for me!"

Was Phœbe playing at that moment on her distant couch? He seemed to hear her.

"I inquired in the shop where you lived, but could get no information. As I had heard you say that you were going back by the next train (but you did not say where), I resolved to visit the station at about that time of day, as often as I could, between my lessons, on the chance of seeing you again. I have been there very often, but saw you no more until to-day. You were meditating as you walked the street, but the calm expression of your face emboldened me to send my child to you. And when I saw you bend your head to speak tenderly to her, I prayed to God to forgive me for having ever brought a sorrow on it. I now pray to you to forgive me, and to forgive my husband. I was very young, he was young too, and, in the ignorant hardihood of such a time of life, we don't know what we do to those who have undergone more discipline. You generous man! You good man! So to raise me up and make nothing of my crime against you!"— for he would not see her on her knees, and soothed her as a kind father might have soothed an erring daughter—"thank you, bless you, thank you!"

When he next spoke, it was after having drawn aside the window curtain and looked out awhile. Then he only said:

"Is Polly asleep?"

"Yes. As I came in, I met her going away upstairs, and put her to bed myself."

"Leave her with me for to-morrow, Beatrice, and write me your address on this leaf of my pocket-book. In the evening I will bring her home to you—and to her father."

"Hallo!" cried Polly, putting her saucy sunny face in at the door next morning when breakfast was ready: "I thought I was fetched last night?"

"So you were, Polly, but I asked leave to keep you here for the day, and to take you home in the evening."

"Upon my word!" said Polly. "You are very cool, ain't you?"

However, Polly seemed to think it a good idea, and added:

"I suppose I must give you a kiss, though you *are* cool."

The kiss given and taken, they sat down to breakfast in a highly conversational tone.

"Of course, you are going to amuse me?" said Polly.

"Oh, of course!" said Barbox Brothers.

In the pleasurable height of her anticipations, Polly found it indispensable to put down her piece of toast, cross one of her little fat knees over the other, and bring her little fat right hand down into her left hand with a businesslike slap. After this gathering of herself together, Polly by that time a mere heap of dimples, asked in a wheedling manner:

"What are we going to do, you dear old thing?"

"Why, I was thinking," said Barbox Brothers, "—but are you fond of horses, Polly?"

"Ponies, I am," said Polly, "especially when their tails are long. But horses—n—no—too big, you know."

"Well," pursued Barbox Brothers, in a spirit of grave mysterious confidence adapted to the importance of the consultation, "I did see yesterday, Polly, on the walls, pictures of two long-tailed ponies, speckled all over——"

"No, no NO!" cried Polly, in an ecstatic desire to linger on the charming details. "Not speckled all over!"

"Speckled all over. Which ponies jump through hoops——"

"No, no, NO!" cried Polly as before. "They never jump through hoops!"

"Yes, they do. Oh, I assure you they do! And eat pie in pinafores——"

"Ponies eating pie in pinafores!" said Polly. "What a story-teller you are, ain't you?"

"Upon my honour. —And fire off guns."

(Polly hardly seemed to see the force of the ponies resorting to fire-arms.)

"And I was thinking," pursued the exemplary Barbox, "that if you and I were to go to the Circus where these ponies are, it would do our constitutions good."

"Does that mean amuse us?" inquired Polly. "What long words you do use, don't you?"

Apologetic for having wandered out of his depth, he replied:

"That means amuse us. That is exactly what it means. There are many other wonders besides the ponies, and we shall see them all. Ladies and gentlemen in spangled dresses, and elephants and lions and tigers."

Polly became observant of the teapot, with a curled-up nose indicating some uneasiness of mind.

"They never get out, of course," she remarked as a mere truism.

"The elephants and lions and tigers? Oh, dear no!"

"Oh, dear no!" said Polly. "And of course nobody's afraid of the ponies shooting anybody."

"Not the least in the world."

"No, no, not the least in the world," said Polly.

"I was also thinking," proceeded Barbox, "that if we were to look in at the toy-shop, to choose a doll——"

"Not dressed!" cried Polly with a clap of her hands. "No, no, NO, not dressed!"

"Full-dressed. Together with a house, and all things necessary for house-keeping——"

Polly gave a little scream, and seemed in danger of falling into a swoon of bliss.

"What a darling you are!" she languidly exclaimed, leaning back in her chair. "Come and be hugged, or I must come and hug you."

This resplendent programme was carried into execution with the utmost rigour of the law. It being essential to make the purchase of the doll its first feature—or that lady would have lost the ponies—the toy-shop expedition took precedence. Polly in the magic warehouse, with a doll as large as herself under each arm, and a neat assortment of some twenty more on view upon the counter, did indeed present a spectacle of indecision not quite compatible with unalloyed happiness, but the light cloud passed. The lovely specimen oftenest chosen, oftenest rejected, and finally abided by, was of Circassian descent, possessing as much boldness of beauty as was reconcilable with extreme feebleness of mouth, and combining a sky-blue silk pelisse with rose-coloured satin trousers, and a black velvet hat: which this fair stranger to our northern shores would seem to have founded on the portraits of the late duchess of Kent. The name this distinguished foreigner brought with her from beneath the glowing skies of a sunny clime was (on Polly's authority) Miss Melluka, and the costly nature of her outfit as a housekeeper, from the Barbox coffers, may be inferred from the two facts that her silver tea-spoons were as large as her kitchen poker, and that the proportions of her watch exceeded those of her frying-pan. Miss Melluka was graciously pleased to express her entire approbation of the Circus, and so was Polly; for the ponies *were* speckled, and brought down nobody when they fired, and the savagery of the wild beasts appeared to be mere smoke—which article, in fact, they did produce in large quantities from their insides. The Barbox absorption in the general subject throughout the realisation of these delights was again a sight to see, nor was it less worthy to behold at dinner, when he drank to Miss Melluka, tied stiff in a chair opposite to Polly (the fair Circassian possessing an unbendable spine), and even induced the waiter to assist in carrying out with due decorum the prevailing glorious idea. To wind up, there came the agreeable fever of getting Miss Melluka and all her wardrobe and rich possessions into a fly with Polly, to be taken home. But, by that time, Polly had become unable to look upon such accumulated joys with waking eyes, and had withdrawn her consciousness into the wonderful Paradise of a child's sleep. "Sleep, Polly, sleep," said Barbox Brothers, as her head dropped on his shoulder; "you shall not fall out of this bed easily, at any rate!"

What rustling piece of paper he took from his pocket, and carefully folded into the bosom of Polly's frock, shall not be mentioned. He said nothing about it, and nothing shall be said about it. They drove to a modest suburb of the great ingenious town, and stopped at the fore-court of a small house. "Do not wake the child," said Barbox Brothers softly to the driver; "I will carry her in as she is."

Greeting the light at the opened door which was held by Polly's mother, Polly's bearer passed on with mother and child into a ground-floor room. There, stretched on a sofa, lay a sick man, sorely wasted, who covered his eyes with his emaciated hands.

"Tresham," said Barbox in a kindly voice, "I have brought you back your Polly, fast asleep. Give me your hand, and tell me you are better."

The sick man reached forth his right hand, and bowed his head over the hand into which it was taken, and kissed it. "Thank you, thank you! I may say that I am well and happy."

"That's brave," said Barbox. "Tresham, I have a fancy—— Can you make room for me beside you here?"

He sat down on the sofa as he said the words, cherishing the plump peachy cheek that lay uppermost on his shoulder.

"I have a fancy, Treshman (I am getting quite an old fellow now, you know, and old fellows may take fancies into their heads sometimes), to give up Polly, having found her, to no one but you. Will you take her from me?"

As the father held out his arms for the child, each of the two men looked steadily at the other.

"She is very dear to you, Tresham?"

"Unutterably dear."

"God bless her! It is not much, Polly," he continued, turning his eyes upon her peaceful face as he apostrophized her, "it is not much, Polly, for a blind and sinful man to invoke a blessing on something so far better than himself as a little child is; but it would be much—much upon his cruel head, and much upon his guilty soul—if he could be so wicked as to invoke a curse. He had better have a millstone round his neck, and be cast into the deepest sea. Live and thrive, my pretty baby!" Here he kissed her. "Live and prosper, and become in time the mother of other little children, like the Angels who behold The Father's face!"

He kissed her again, gave her up gently to both her parents, and went out.

But he went not to Wales. No, he never went to Wales. He went straightway for another stroll about the town, and he looked in upon the people at their work, and at their play, here, there, everywhere, and where not. For he was Barbox Brothers and Co. now, and had taken thousands of partners into the solitary firm.

He had at length got back to his hotel room, and was standing before his fire refreshing himself with a glass of hot drink which he had stood upon the chimneypiece, when he heard the town clocks striking, and, referring to his watch, found the evening to have so slipped away, that they were striking twelve. As he put up his watch again, his eyes met those of his reflection in the chimney-glass.

"Why, it's your birthday already," he said, smiling. "You are looking very well. I wish you many happy returns of the day."

He had never before bestowed that wish upon himself. "By Jupiter!" he discovered, "it alters the whole case of running away from one's birthday! It's a thing to explain to Phœbe. Besides, here is quite a long story to tell her, that has sprung out of the road with no story. I'll go back, instead of going on. I'll go back by my friend Lamps's Up X presently."

He went back to Mugby Junction, and, in point of fact, he established himself at Mugby Junction. It was the convenient place to live in, for brightening Phœbe's life. It was the convenient place to live in, for having her taught music by Beatrice. It was the convenient place to live in, for occasionally borrowing Polly. It was the convenient place to live in, for being joined at will to all sorts of agreeable places and persons. So, he became settled there, and, his house standing in an elevated situation, it is noteworthy of him in conclusion, as Polly herself might (not irreverently) have put it:

"There was an Old Barbox who lived on a hill,
And if he ain't gone, he lives there still."

HERE FOLLOWS THE SUBSTANCE OF WHAT WAS SEEN, HEARD, OR OTHERWISE PICKED UP, BY THE GENTLEMAN FOR NOWHERE, IN HIS CAREFUL STUDY OF THE JUNCTION.

CHAPTER III *Main line: the boy at Mugby*

I am the boy at Mugby. That's about what *I* am.

You don't know what I mean? What a pity! But I think you do. I think you must. Look here. I am the boy at what is called the Refreshment Room at Mugby Junction, and what's proudest boast is, that it never yet refreshed a mortal being.

Up in a corner of the Down Refreshment Room at Mugby Junction, in the height of twenty-seven cross draughts (I've often counted 'em while they brush the First-Class hair twenty-seven ways), behind the bottles, among the glasses, bounded on the nor'west by the beer, stood pretty far to the right of a metallic object that's at times the tea-urn and at times the soup-tureen, according to the nature of the last twang imparted to its contents which are the same ground-work, fended off from the traveller by a barrier of stale sponge-cakes erected atop of the counter, and lastly exposed sideways to the glare of Our Missis's eye—you ask a Boy so sitiwated, next time you stop in a hurry at Mugby, for anything to drink; you take particular notice that he'll try to seem not to hear you, that he'll appear in a absent manner to survey the Line through a transparent medium composed of your head and body, and that he won't serve you as long as you can possibly bear it. That's me.

What a lark it is! We are the Model Establishment, we are, at Mugby. Other Refreshment Rooms send their imperfect young ladies up to be finished off by Our Missis. For some of the young ladies, when they're new to the business, come into it mild! Ah! Our Missis, she soon takes that out of 'em. Why, I originally come into the business meek myself. But Our Missis, she soon took that out of *me*.

What a delightful lark it is! I look upon us Refreshmenters as ockipying the only proudly independent footing on the Line. There's Papers, for instance,—my honourable friend, if he will allow me to call him so,—him as belongs to Smith's bookstall. Why, he no more dares to be up to your Refreshmenting games than he dares to jump atop of a locomotive with her steam at full pressure, and cut away upon her alone, driving himself, at limited-mail speed. Papers, he'd get his head punched at every compartment, first, second, and third, the whole length of a train, if he was to ventur to imitate my demeanour. It's the same with the porters, the same with the guards, the same with the ticket clerks, the same the whole way up to the secretary, traffic-manager, or very chairman. There ain't a one among 'em on the nobly independent footing we are. Did you ever catch one of *them*, when you wanted anything of him, making a system of surveying the

Line through a transparent medium composed of your head and body?
I should hope not.

You should see our Bandolining Room at Mugby Junction. It's led
to by the door behind the counter, which you'll notice usually stands
ajar, and it's the room where Our Missis and our young ladies Bando-
lines their hair. You should see 'em at it, betwixt trains, Bandolining
away, as if they was anointing themselves for the combat. When you're
telegraphed, you should see their noses all a-going up with scorn, as if
it was a part of the working of the same Cooke and Wheatstone
electrical machinery. You should hear Our Missis give the word, "Here
comes the Beast to be Fed!" and then you should see 'em indignantly
skipping across the Line, from the Up to the Down, or Wicer Warsaw,
and begin to pitch the stale pastry into the plates, and chuck the
sawdust sangwiches under the glass covers, and get out the—ha, ha,
ha!—the sherry,—O my eye, my eye!—for your Refreshment.

It's only in the Isle of the Brave and Land of the Free (by which,
of course, I mean to say Britannia) that Refreshmenting is so effective,
so 'olesome, so constitutional a check upon the public. There was a
Foreigner, which having politely, with his hat off, beseeched our young
ladies and Our Missis for "a leetel gloss hoff prarndee," and having
had the Line surveyed through him by all and no other acknowledgment, was a-proceeding at last to help himself, as seems to be the
custom in his own country, when Our Missis, with her hair almost
a-coming un-Bandolined with rage, and her eyes omitting sparks, flew
at him, cotched the decanter out of his hand, and said, "Put it down!
I won't allow that!" The foreigner turned pale, stepped back with his
arms stretched out in front of him, his hands clasped, and his shoulders
riz, and exclaimed: "Ah! Is it possible, this! That these disdaineous
females and this ferocious old woman are placed here by the ad-
ministration, not only to empoison the voyagers, but to affront them!
Great Heaven! How arrives it? The English people. Or is he then a
slave? Or idiot?" Another time, a merry, wideawake American gent
had tried the sawdust and spit it out, and had tried the Sherry and
spit that out, and had tried in vain to sustain exhausted natur upon
Butter-Scotch, and had been rather extra Bandolined and Line-
surveyed through, when, as the bell was ringing and he paid Our
Missis, he says, very loud and good-tempered: "I tell Yew what 'tis,
ma'arm. I la'af. Theer! I la'af. I Dew. I oughter ha' seen most things,
for I hail from the Onlimited side of the Atlantic Ocean, and I haive
travelled right slick over the Limited, head on through Jeerusalemm
and the East, and likeways France and Italy, Europe Old World, and
am now upon the track to the Chief Europian Village; but such an
Institution as Yew, and Yewer young ladies, and Yewer fixin's solid
and liquid, afore the glorious Tarnal I never did see yet! And if I
hain't found the eighth wonder of monarchical Creation, in finding

Yew, and Yewer young ladies, and Yewer fixin's solid and liquid, all as aforesaid, established in a country where the people air not absolute Loo-naticks, I am Extra Double Darned with a Nip and Frizzle to the innermostest grit! Wheerfur—Theer!—I la'af! I Dew, ma'arm. I la'af!" And so he went, stamping and shaking his sides, along the platform all the way to his own compartment.

I think it was her standing up agin the Foreigner as giv' Our Missis the idea of going over to France, and droring a comparison betwixt Refreshmenting as followed among the frog-eaters, and Refreshment-ing as triumphant in the Isle of the Brave and Land of the Free (by which, of course, I mean to say agin, Britannia). Our young ladies, Miss Whiff, Miss Piff, and Mrs. Sniff, was unanimous opposed to her going; for, as they says to Our Missis one and all, it is well beknown to the hends of the herth as no other nation except Britain has a idea of anythink, but above all of business. Why then should you tire yourself to prove what is already proved? Our Missis, however (being a teazer at all pints) stood out grim obstinate, and got a return pass by Southeastern Tidal, to go right through, if such should be her dispositions, to Marseilles.

Sniff is husband to Mrs. Sniff, and is a regular insignificant cove. He looks arter the sawdust department in a back room, and is some-times, when we are very hard put to it, let behind the counter with a corkscrew; but never when it can be helped, his demeanour towards the public being disgusting servile. How Mrs. Sniff ever come so far to lower herself as to marry him, I don't know; but I suppose *he* does, and I should think he wished he didn't, for he leads a awful life. Mrs. Sniff couldn't be much harder with him if he was public. Simi-larly, Miss Whiff and Miss Piff, taking the tone of Mrs. Sniff, they shoulder Sniff about when he *is* let in with a corkscrew, and they whisk things out of his hands when in his servility he is a-going to let the public have 'em, and they snap him up when in the crawling baseness of his spirit he is a-going to answer a public question, and they drore more tears into his eyes than ever the mustard does which he all day long lays on to the sawdust. (But it ain't strong.) Once, when Sniff had the repulsiveness to reach across to get the milk-pot to hand over for a baby, I see Our Missis in her rage catch him by both his shoulders, and spin him out into the Bandolining Room.

But Mrs. Sniff,—how different! She's the one! She's the one as you'll notice to be always looking another way from you, when you look at her. She's the one with the small waist buckled in tight in front, and with the lace cuffs at her wrists, which she puts on the edge of the counter before her, and stands a-smoothing while the public foams. This smoothing the cuffs and looking another way while the public foams is the last accomplishment taught to the young ladies as come to Mugby to be finished by Our Missis; and it's always taught by Mrs. Sniff.

When Our Missis went away upon her journey, Mrs. Sniff was left in charge. She did hold the public in check most beautiful! In all my time, I never see half so many cups of tea given without milk to people as wanted it with, nor half so many cups of tea with milk given to people as wanted it without. When foaming ensued, Mrs. Sniff would say: "Then you'd better settle it among yourselves, and change with one another." It was a most highly delicious lark. I enjoyed the Refreshmenting business more than ever, and was so glad I had took to it when young.

Our Missis returned. It got circulated among the young ladies, and it as it might be penetrated to me through the crevices of the Bandolining Room, that she had Orrors to reveal, if revelations so contemptible could be dignified with the name. Agitation become awakened. Excitement was up in the stirrups. Expectation stood a-tiptoe. At length it was put forth that on our slacked evening in the week, and at our slackest time of that evening betwixt trains, Our Missis would give her views of foreign Refreshmenting, in the Bandolining Room.

It was arranged tasteful for the purpose. The Bandolining table and glass was hid in a corner, a armchair was elevated on a packing-case for Our Missis's ockypation, a table and a tumbler of water (no sherry in it, thankee) was placed beside it. Two of the pupils, the season being autumn, and hollyhocks and dahlias being in, ornamented the wall with three devices in those flowers. On one might be read, "MAY ALBION NEVER LEARN;" on another, "KEEP THE PUBLIC DOWN;" on another, "OUR REFRESHMENTING CHARTER." The whole had a beautiful appearance, with which the beauty of the sentiments corresponded.

On Our Missis's brow was wrote Severity, as she ascended the fatal platform. (Not that that was anythink new.) Miss Whiff and Miss Piff sat at her feet. Three chairs from the Waiting Room might have been perceived by a average eye, in front of her, on which the pupils was accommodated. Behind them a very close observer might have discerned a Boy. Myself.

"Where," said Our Missis, glancing gloomily around, "is Sniff?"

"I thought it better," answered Mrs. Sniff, "that he should not be let to come in. He is such an Ass."

"No doubt," assented Our Missis. "But for that reason is it not desirable to improve his mind?"

"Oh, nothing will ever improve *him*," said Mrs. Sniff.

"However," pursued Our Missis, "call him in, Ezekiel."

I called him in. The appearance of the low-minded cove was hailed with disapprobation from all sides, on account of his having brought his corkscrew with him. He pleaded "the force of habit."

"The force!" said Mrs. Sniff. "Don't let us have you talking about force, for Gracious' sake. There! Do stand still where you are, with your back against the wall."

He is a smiling piece of vacancy, and he smiled in the mean way in which he will even smile at the public if he gets a chance (language can say no meaner of him), and he stood upright near the door with the back of his head agin the wall, as if he was a-waiting for somebody to come and measure his heighth for the Army.

"I should not enter, ladies," says Our Missis, "on the revolting disclosures I am about to make, if it was not in the hope that they will cause you to be yet more implacable in the exercise of the power you wield in a constitutional country, and yet more devoted to the constitutional motto which I see before me,"—it was behind her, but the words sounded better so,—"'May Albion never learn!'"

Here the pupils as had made the motto admired it, and cried, "Hear! Hear! Hear!" Sniff, showing an inclination to join in chorus, got himself frowned down by every brow.

"The baseness of the French," pursued Our Missis, "as displayed in the fawning nature of their Refreshmenting, equals, if not surpasses, anythink as was ever heard of the baseness of the celebrated Bonaparte."

Miss Whiff, Miss Piff, and me, we drored a heavy breath, equal to saying, "We thought as much!" Miss Whiff and Miss Piff seeming to object to my droring mine along with theirs, I drored another to aggravate 'em.

"Shall I be believed," says Our Missis, with flashing eyes, "when I tell you that no sooner had I set my foot upon that treacherous shore——"

Here Sniff, either bursting out mad, or thinking aloud, says, in a low voice: "Feet. Plural, you know."

The cowering that come upon him when he was spurned by all eyes, added to his being beneath contempt, was sufficient punishment for a cove so grovelling. In the midst of a silence rendered more impressive by the turned-up female noses with which it was pervaded, Our Missis went on:

"Shall I be believed when I tell you, that no sooner had I landed," this word with a killing look at Sniff, "on that treacherous shore, than I was ushered into a Refreshment Room where there were—I do not exaggerate—actually eatable things to eat?"

A groan burst from the ladies. I not only did myself the honour of jining, but also of lengthening it out.

"Where there were," Our Missis added, "not only eatable things to eat, but also drinkable things to drink?"

A murmur, swelling almost into a scream, ariz. Miss Piff, trembling with indignation, called out, "Name!"

"I *will* name," said Our Missis. "There was roast fowls, hot and cold; there was smoking roast veal surrounded with browned potatoes; there was hot soup with (again I ask shall I be credited?) nothing bitter in it, and no flour to choke off the consumer; there was a variety of cold dishes set off with jelly; there was salad; there was—mark me! *fresh* pastry, and that of a light construction; there was a luscious show of fruit; there was bottles and decanters of sound small wine, of every size, and adapted to every pocket; the same odious statement will apply to brandy; and these were set out upon the counter so that all could help themselves."

Our Missis's lips so quivered, that Mrs. Sniff, though scarcely less convulsed than she were, got up and held the tumbler to them.

"This," proceeds Our Missis, "was my first unconstitutional experience. Well would it have been if it had been my last and worst. But no. As I proceeded farther into that enslaved and ignorant land, its aspect became more hideous. I need not explain to this assembly the ingredients and formation of the British Refreshment sangwich?"

Universal laughter,—except from Sniff, who, as sangwich-cutter, shook his head in a state of the utmost dejection as he stood with it agin the wall.

"Well!" said Our Missis, with dilated nostrils. "Take a fresh, crisp, long, crusty penny loaf made of the whitest and best flour. Cut it longwise through the middle. Insert a fair and nicely fitting slice of ham. Tie a smart piece of ribbon round the middle of the whole to bind it together. Add at one end a neat wrapper of clean white paper by which to hold it. And the universal French Refreshment sangwich busts on your disgusted vision."

A cry of "Shame!" from all—except Sniff, which rubbed his stomach with a soothing hand.

"I need not," said Our Missis, "explain to this assembly the usual formation and fitting of the British Refreshment Room?"

No, no, and laughter. Sniff agin shaking his head in low spirits agin the wall.

"Well," said Our Missis, "what would you say to a general decoration of everythink, to hangings (sometimes elegant), to easy velvet furniture, to abundance of little tables, to abundance of little seats, to brisk bright waiters, to great convenience, to a pervading cleanliness and tastefulness positively addressing the public, and making the Beast thinking itself worth the pains?"

Contemptuous fury on the part of all the ladies. Mrs. Sniff looking as if she wanted somebody to hold her, and everybody else looking as if they'd rayther not.

"Three times," said Our Missis, working herself into a truly terri-

menjious state,—"three times did I see these shameful things, only
between the coast and Paris, and not counting either: at Hazebroucke,
at Arras, at Amiens. But worse remains. Tell me, what would you
call a person who should propose in England that there should be
kept, say at our own model Mugby Junction, pretty baskets, each
holding an assorted cold lunch and dessert for one, each at a certain
fixed price, and each within a passenger's power to take away, to
empty in the carriage at perfect leisure, and to return at another
station fifty or a hundred miles farther on?"

There was disagreement what such a person should be called.
Whether revolutionist, atheist, Bright (I said him), or Un-English.
Miss Piff screeched her shrill opinion last, in the words: "A malignant
maniac!"

"I adopt," says Our Missis, "the brand set upon such a person by
the righteous indignation of my friend Miss Piff. A malignant maniac.
Know, then, that that malignant maniac has sprung from the congenial
soil of France, and that his malignant madness was in unchecked
action on this same part of my journey."

I noticed that Sniff was a-rubbing his hands, and that Mrs. Sniff
had got her eye upon him. But I did not take more particular notice,
owing to the excited state in which the young ladies was, and to
feeling myself called upon to keep it up with a howl.

"On my experience south of Paris," said Our Missis, in a deep
tone, "I will not expatiate. Too loathsome were the task! But fancy
this. Fancy a guard coming round, with the train at full speed, to
inquire how many for dinner. Fancy his telegraphing forward the
number of dinners. Fancy every one expected, and the table elegantly
laid for the complete party. Fancy a charming dinner, in a charming
room, and the head-cook, concerned for the honour of every dish,
superintending in his clean white jacket and cap. Fancy the Beast
travelling six hundred miles on end, very fast, and with great punc-
tuality, yet being taught to expect all this to be done for it!"

A spirited chorus of "The Beast!"

I noticed that Sniff was agin a-rubbing his stomach with a soothing
hand, and that he had drored up one leg. But agin I didn't take
particular notice, looking on myself as called upon to stimulate public
feeling. It being a lark besides.

"Putting everything together," said Our Missis, "French Refreshmenting comes to this, and oh, it comes to a nice total! First: eatable
things to eat, and drinkable things to drink."

A groan from the young ladies, kep' up by me.

"Second: convenience, and even elegance."

Another groan from the young ladies, kep' up by me.

"Third: moderate charges."

This time a groan from me, kep' up by the young ladies.

"Fourth:—and here," says Our Missis, "I claim your angriest sympathy,—attention, common civility, nay, even politeness!"

Me and the young ladies regularly raging mad all together.

"And I cannot in conclusion," says Our Missis, with her spitefullest sneer, "give you a completer pictur of that despicable nation (after what I have related), than assuring you that they wouldn't bear our constitutional ways and noble independence at Mugby Junction, for a single month, and that they would turn us to the right-about and put another system in our places, as soon as look at us; perhaps sooner, for I do not believe they have the good taste to care to look at us twice."

The swelling tumult was arrested in its rise. Sniff, bore away by his servile disposition, had drored up his leg with a higher and a higher relish, and was now discovered to be waving his corkscrew over his head. It was at this moment that Mrs. Sniff, who had kep' her eye upon him like the fabled obelisk, descended on her victim. Our Missis followed them both out, and cries was heard in the sawdust department.

You come into the Down Refreshment Room, at the Junction, making believe you don't know me, and I'll pint you out with my right thumb over my shoulder which is Our Missis, and which is Miss Whiff, and which is Miss Piff, and which is Mrs. Sniff. But you won't get a chance to see Sniff, because he disappeared that night. Whether he perished, tore to pieces, I cannot say; but his corkscrew alone remains, to bear witness to the servility of his disposition.

CHAPTER IV *No. I branch line: the signal-man*

"Halloa! Below there!"

When he heard a voice thus calling to him, he was standing at the door of his box, with a flag in his hand, furled round its short pole. One would have thought, considering the nature of the ground, that he could not have doubted from what quarter the voice came; but instead of looking up to where I stood on the top of the steep cutting nearly over his head, he turned himself about, and looked down the Line. There was something remarkable in his manner of doing so, though I could not have said for my life what. But I know it was remarkable enough to attract my notice, even though his figure was foreshortened and shadowed, down in the deep trench, and mine was high above him, so steeped in the glow of an angry sunset, that I had shaded my eyes with my hand before I saw him at all.

"Halloa! Below!"

From looking down the Line, he turned himself about again, and, raising his eyes, saw my figure high above him.

"Is there any path by which I can come down and speak to you?"

He looked up at me without replying, and I looked down at him without pressing him too soon with a repetition of my idle question. Just then there came a vague vibration in the earth and air, quickly changing into a violent pulsation, and an oncoming rush that caused me to start back, as though it had force to draw me down. When such vapour as rose to my height from this rapid train had passed me, and was skimming away over the landscape, I looked down again, and saw him refurling the flag he had shown while the train went by.

I repeated my inquiry. After a pause, during which he seemed to regard me with fixed attention, he motioned with his rolled-up flag towards a point on my level, some two or three hundred yards distant. I called down to him, "All right!" and made for that point. There, by dint of looking closely about me, I found a rough zigzag descending path notched out, which I followed.

The cutting was extremely deep, and unusually precipitate. It was made through a clammy stone, that became oozier and wetter as I went down. For these reasons, I found the way long enough to give me time to recall a singular air of reluctance or compulsion with which he had pointed out the path.

When I came down low enough upon the zigzag descent to see him again, I saw that he was standing between the rails on the way by which the train had lately passed, in an attitude as if he were waiting for me to appear. He had his left hand at his chin, and that left elbow rested on his right hand, crossed over his breast. His attitude was one of such expectation and watchfulness that I stopped a moment, wondering at it.

I resumed my downward way, and stepping out upon the level of the railroad, and drawing nearer to him, saw that he was a dark sallow man, with a dark beard and rather heavy eyebrows. His post was in as solitary and dismal a place as ever I saw. On either side, a dripping-wet wall of jagged stone, excluding all view but a strip of sky; the perspective one way only a crooked prolongation of this great dungeon; the shorter perspective in the other direction terminating in a gloomy red light, and the gloomier entrance to a black tunnel, in whose massive architecture there was a barbarous, depressing, and forbidding air. So little sunlight ever found its way to this spot, that it had an earthy, deadly smell; and so much cold wind rushed through it, that it struck chill to me, as if I had left the natural world.

Before he stirred, I was near enough to him to have touched him. Not even then removing his eyes from mine, he stepped back one step, and lifted his hand.

This was a lonesome post to occupy (I said), and it had riveted my attention when I looked down from up yonder. A visitor was a rarity, I should suppose; not an unwelcome rarity, I hoped? In me, he merely saw a man who had been shut up within narrow limits all his life, and who, being at last set free, had a newly-awakened interest in these great works. To such purpose I spoke to him; but I am far from sure of the terms I used; for, besides that I am not happy in opening any conversation, there was something in the man that daunted me.

He directed a most curious look towards the red light near the tunnel's mouth, and looked all about it, as if something were missing from it, and then looked at me.

That light was part of his charge? Was it not?

He answered in a low voice,—"Don't you know it is?"

The monstrous thought came into my mind, as I perused the fixed eyes and the saturnine face, that this was a spirit, not a man. I have speculated since, whether there may have been infection in his mind.

In my turn, I stepped back. But in making the action, I detected in his eyes some latent fear of me. This put the monstrous thought to flight.

"You look at me," I said, forcing a smile, "as if you had a dread of me."

"I was doubtful," he returned, "whether I had seen you before."

"Where?"

He pointed to the red light he had looked at.

"There?" I said.

Intently watchful of me, he replied (but without sound), "Yes."

"My good fellow, what should I do there? However, be that as it may, I never was there, you may swear."

"I think I may," he rejoined. "Yes; I am sure I may."

His manner cleared, like my own. He replied to my remarks with readiness, and in well-chosen words. Had he much to do there? Yes; that was to say, he had enough responsibility to bear; but exactness and watchfulness were what was required of him, and of actual work—manual labour—he had next to none. To change that signal, to trim those lights, and to turn this iron handle now and then, was all he had to do under that head. Regarding those many long and lonely hours of which I seemed to make so much, he could only say that the routine of his life had shaped itself into that form, and he had grown used to it. He had taught himself a language down here,—if only to know it by sight, and to have formed his own crude ideas of its pronunciation, could be called learning it. He had also worked at fractions and decimals, and tried a little algebra; but he was, and had been as a boy, a poor hand at figures. Was it necessary for him when on duty always to remain in that channel of damp air, and could he never rise into the sunshine from between those high stone walls? Why, that depended upon times and circumstances. Under some conditions there would be less upon the Line than under others, and the same held good as to certain hours of the day and night. In bright weather, he did choose occasions for getting a little above these lower shadows; but, being at all times liable to be called by his electric bell, and at such times listening for it with redoubled anxiety, the relief was less than I would suppose.

He took me into his box, where there was a fire, a desk for an official book in which he had to make certain entries, a telegraphic instrument with its dial, face, and needles, and the little bell of which he had spoken. On my trusting that he would excuse the remark that he had been well educated, and (I hoped I might say without offence), perhaps educated above that station, he observed that instances of slight incongruity in such wise would rarely be found wanting among large bodies of men; that he had heard it was so in workhouses, in the police force, even in that last desperate resource, the army; and that he knew it was so, more or less, in any great railway staff. He had been, when young (if I could believe it, sitting in that hut,—he scarcely could), a student of natural philosophy, and had attended lectures; but he had run wild, misused his opportunities, gone down, and never risen again. He had no complaint to offer about that. He had made his bed, and he lay upon it. It was far too late to make another.

All that I have here condensed he said in a quiet manner, with his grave dark regards divided between me and the fire. He threw in the word, "Sir," from time to time, and especially when he referred to his youth,—as though to request me to understand that he claimed to be nothing but what I found him. He was several times interrupted by the little bell, and had to read off messages, and send replies. Once he had to stand without the door, and display a flag as a train passed, and make some verbal communication to the driver. In the discharge of his duties, I observed him to be remarkably exact and vigilant, breaking off his discourse at a syllable, and remaining silent until what he had to do was done.

In a word, I should have set this man down as one of the safest of men to be employed in that capacity, but for the circumstance that while he was speaking to me he twice broke off with a fallen colour, turned his face towards the little bell when it did NOT ring, opened the door of the hut (which was kept shut to exclude the unhealthy damp), and looked out towards the red light near the mouth of the tunnel. On both of those occasions, he came back to the fire with the inexplicable air upon him which I had remarked, without being able to define, when we were so far asunder.

Said I, when I rose to leave him, "You almost make me think that I have met with a contented man."

(I am afraid I must acknowledge that I said it to lead him on.)

"I believe I used to be so," he rejoined, in the low voice in which he had first spoken; "but I am troubled, Sir, I am troubled."

He would have recalled the words if he could. He had said them, however, and I took them up quickly.

"With what? What is your trouble?"

"It is very difficult to impart, Sir. It is very, very difficult to speak of. If ever you make me another visit, I will try to tell you."

"But I expressly intend to make you another visit. Say, when shall it be?"

"I go off early in the morning, and I shall be on again at ten to-morrow night, Sir."

"I will come at eleven."

He thanked me, and went out at the door with me. "I'll show my white light, Sir," he said, in his peculiar low voice, "till you have found the way up. When you have found it, don't call out! And when you are at the top, don't call out!"

His manner seemed to make the place strike colder to me, but I said no more than, "Very well."

"And when you come down to-morrow night, don't call out! Let me ask you a parting question. What made you cry, 'Halloa! Below there!' to-night?"

"Heaven knows," said I. "I cried something to that effect——"

"Not to that effect, Sir. Those were the very words. I know them well."

"Admit those were the very words. I said them, no doubt, because I saw you below."

"For no other reason?"

"What other reason could I possibly have?"

"You had no feeling that they were conveyed to you in any supernatural way?"

"No."

He wished me good night, and held up his light. I walked by the side of the down Line of rails (with a very disagreeable sensation of a train coming behind me) until I found the path. It was easier to mount than to descend, and I got back to my inn without any adventure.

Punctual to my appointment, I placed my foot on the first notch of the zigzag next night, as the distant clocks were striking eleven. He was waiting for me at the bottom, with his white light on. "I have not called out," I said, when we came close together; "may I speak now?" "By all means, Sir." "Good night, then, and here's my hand." "Good night, Sir, and here's mine." With that we walked side by side to his box, entered it, closed the door, and sat down by the fire.

"I have made up my mind, Sir," he began, bending forward as

soon as we were seated, and speaking in a tone but a little above a whisper, "that you shall not have to ask me twice what troubles me. I took you for some one else yesterday evening. That troubles me."

"That mistake?"

"No. That some one else."

"Who is it?"

"I don't know."

"Like me?"

"I don't know. I never saw the face. The left arm is across the face, and the right arm is waved,—violently waved. This way."

I followed his action with my eyes, and it was the action of an arm gesticulating, with the utmost passion and vehemence, "For God's sake, clear the way!"

"One moonlight night," said the man. "I was sitting here, when I heard a voice cry, 'Halloa! Below there!' I started up, looked from that door, and saw this Some one else standing by the red light near the tunnel, waving as I just now showed you. The voice seemed hoarse with shouting, and it cried, 'Look out! Look out!' And then again, 'Halloa! Below there! Look out!' I caught up my lamp, turned it on red, and ran towards the figure, calling, 'What's wrong? What has happened? Where?' It stood just outside the blackness of the tunnel. I advanced so close upon it that I wondered at its keeping the sleeve across its eyes. I ran right up at it, and had my hand stretched out to pull the sleeve away, when it was gone."

"Into the tunnel?" said I.

"No. I ran on into the tunnel, five hundred yards. I stopped, and held my lamp above my head, and saw the figures of the measured distance, and saw the wet stains stealing down the walls and trickling through the arch. I ran out again faster than I had run in (for I had a mortal abhorrence of the place upon me), and I looked all round the red light with my own red light, and I went up the iron ladder to the gallery atop of it, and I came down again, and ran back here. I telegraphed both ways. 'An alarm has been given. Is anything wrong?' The answer came back, both ways, 'All well.'"

Resisting the slow touch of a frozen finger tracing out my spine, I showed him how that this figure must be a deception of his sense of sight; and how that figures, originating in disease of the delicate nerves that minister to the functions of the eye, were known to have often troubled patients, some of whom had become conscious of the nature of their affliction, and had even proved it by experiments upon themselves. "As to an imaginary cry," said I, "do but listen for a moment to the wind in this unnatural valley while we speak so low, and to the wild harp it makes of the telegraph wires."

That was all very well, he returned, after we had sat listening for a while, and he ought to know something of the wind and the wires, —he who so often passed long winter nights there, alone and watching. But he would beg to remark that he had not finished.

I asked his pardon, and he slowly added these words, touching my arm,—

"Within six hours after the Appearance, the memorable accident on this Line happened, and within ten hours the dead and wounded were brought along through the tunnel over the spot where the figure had stood."

A disagreeable shudder crept over me, but I did my best against it. It was not to be denied, I rejoined, that this was a remarkable coincidence, calculated deeply to impress his mind. But it was unquestionable that remarkable coincidences did continually occur, and they must be taken into account in dealing with such a subject. Though to be sure I must admit, I added (for I thought I saw that he was going to bring the objection to bear upon me), men of common sense did not allow much for coincidences in making the ordinary calculations of life.

He again begged to remark that he had not finished.

I again begged his pardon for being betrayed into interruptions.

"This," he said, again laying his hand upon my arm, and glancing over his shoulder with hollow eyes, "was just a year ago. Six or seven months passed, and I had recovered from the surprise and shock, when one morning, as the day was breaking, I, standing at the door, looked towards the red light, and saw the spectre again." He stopped, with a fixed look at me.

"Did it cry out?"

"No. It was silent."

"Did it wave its arm?"

"No. It leaned against the shaft of the light, with both hands before the face. Like this."

Once more I followed his action with my eyes. It was an action of mourning. I have seen such an attitude in stone figures on tombs.

"Did you go up to it?"

"I came in and sat down, partly to collect my thoughts, partly because it had turned me faint. When I went to the door again, daylight was above me, and the ghost was gone."

"But nothing followed? Nothing came of this?"

He touched me on the arm with his forefinger twice or thrice, giving a ghastly nod each time:—

"That very day, as a train came out of the tunnel, I noticed, at a carriage window on my side, what looked like a confusion of hands and heads, and something waved. I saw it just in time to signal the driver, Stop! He shut off, and put his brake on, but the train drifted past here a hundred and fifty yards or more. I ran after it, and, as I went along, heard terrible screams and cries. A beautiful young lady had died instantaneously in one of the compartments, and was brought in here, and laid down on this floor between us."

Involuntarily I pushed my chair back, as I looked from the boards at which he pointed to himself.

"True, Sir. True. Precisely as it happened, so I tell it you."

I could think of nothing to say, to any purpose, and my mouth was very dry. The wind and the wires took up the story with a long lamenting wail.

He resumed. "Now, Sir, mark this, and judge how my mind is troubled. The spectre came back a week ago. Ever since, it has been there, now and again, by fits and starts."

"At the light?"

"At the Danger-light."

"What does it seem to do?"

He repeated, if possible with increased passion and vehemence, that former gesticulation of, "For God's sake, clear the way!"

Then he went on. "I have no peace or rest for it. It calls to me, for many minutes together, in an agonised manner, 'Below there! Look out! Look out!' It stands waving to me. It rings my little bell——"

I caught at that. "Did it ring your bell yesterday evening when I was here, and you went to the door?"

"Twice."

"Why, see," said I, "how your imagination misleads you. My eyes were on the bell, and my ears were open to the bell, and if I am a living man, it did NOT ring at those times. No, nor at any other time, except when it was rung in the natural course of physical things by the station communicating with you."

He shook his head. "I have never made a mistake as to that yet, Sir. I have never confused the spectre's ring with the man's. The ghost's ring is a strange vibration in the bell that it derives from nothing else, and I have not asserted that the bell stirs to the eye. I don't wonder that you failed to hear it. But I heard it."

"And did the spectre seem to be there, when you looked out?"

"It WAS there."

"Both times?"

He repeated firmly: "Both times."

"Will you come to the door with me, and look for it now?"

He bit his under lip as though he were somewhat unwilling, but arose. I opened the door, and stood on the step, while he stood in the doorway. There was the Danger-light. There was the dismal mouth of the tunnel. There were the high, wet stone walls of the cutting. There were the stars above them.

"Do you see it?" I asked him, taking particular note of his face. His eyes were prominent and strained, but not very much more so, perhaps, than my own had been when I had directed them earnestly towards the same spot.

"No," he answered. "It is not there."

"Agreed," said I.

We went in again, shut the door, and resumed our seats. I was thinking how best to improve this advantage, if it might be called one, when he took up the conversation in such a matter-of-course way, so assuming that there could be no serious question of fact between us, that I felt myself placed in the weakest of positions.

"By this time you will fully understand, Sir," he said, "that what troubles me so dreadfully is the question, What does the spectre mean?"

I was not sure, I told him, that I did fully understand.

"What is its warning against?" he said, ruminating, with his eyes on the fire, and only by times turning them on me. "What is the danger? Where is the danger? There is danger overhanging somewhere on the Line. Some dreadful calamity will happen. It is not to be doubted this third time, after what has gone before. But surely this is a cruel haunting of *me*. What can *I* do?"

He pulled out his handkerchief, and wiped the drops from his heated forehead.

"If I telegraph Danger, on either side of me, or on both, I can give no reason for it," he went on, wiping the palms of his hands. "I should get into trouble, and do no good. They would think I was mad. This is the way it would work,—Message: 'Danger! Take care!' Answer: 'What Danger? Where?' Message: 'Don't know. But, for God's sake take care!' They would displace me. What else could they do?"

His pain of mind was most pitiable to see. It was the mental torture of a conscientious man, oppressed beyond endurance by an unintelligible responsibility involving life.

"When it first stood under the Danger-light," he went on, putting his dark hair back from his head, and drawing his hands outward across and across his temples in an extremity of feverish distress, "why not tell me where that accident was to happen,—if it must happen? Why not tell me how it could be averted,—if it could have been averted? When on its second coming it hid its face, why not tell me, instead, 'She is going to die. Let them keep her at home'? If it came, on those two occasions, only to show me that its warnings were true, and so to prepare me for the third, why not warn me plainly now? And I, Lord help me! A mere poor signal-man on this solitary station!

Why not go to somebody with credit to be believed, and power to act?"

When I saw him in this state, I saw that for the poor man's sake, as well as for the public safety, what I had to do for the time was to compose his mind. Therefore, setting aside all question of reality or unreality between us, I represented to him that whoever thoroughly discharged his duty must do well, and that at least it was his comfort that he understood his duty, though he did not understand these confounding Appearances. In this effort I succeeded far better than in the attempt to reason him out of his conviction. He became calm; the occupations incidental to his post as the night advanced began to make larger demands on his attention: and I left him at two in the morning. I had offered to stay through the night, but he would not hear of it.

That I more than once looked back at the red light as I ascended the pathway, that I did not like the red light, and that I should have slept but poorly if my bed had been under it, I see no reason to conceal. Nor did I like the two sequences of the accident and the dead girl. I see no reason to conceal that either.

But what ran most in my thoughts was the consideration how ought I to act, having become the recipient of this disclosure? I had proved the man to be intelligent, vigilant, painstaking, and exact; but how long might he remain so, in his state of mind? Though in a subordinate position, still he held a most important trust, and would I (for instance) like to stake my own life on the chances of his continuing to execute it with precision?

Unable to overcome a feeling that there would be something treacherous in my communicating what he had told me to his superiors in the Company, without first being plain with himself and proposing a middle course to him, I ultimately resolved to offer to accompany him (otherwise keeping his secret for the present) to the wisest medical practitioner we could hear of in those parts, and to take his opinion. A change in his time of duty would come round next night, he had apprised me, and he would be off an hour or two after sunrise, and on again soon after sunset. I had appointed to return accordingly.

Next evening was a lovely evening, and I walked out early to enjoy it. The sun was not yet quite down when I traversed the field-path near the top of the deep cutting. I would extend my walk for an hour, I said to myself, half an hour on and half an hour back, and it would then be time to go to my signal-man's box.

Before pursuing my stroll, I stepped to the brink, and mechanically looked down, from the point from which I had first seen him. I cannot describe the thrill that seized upon me, when, close at the mouth of the tunnel, I saw the appearance of a man, with his left sleeve across his eyes, passionately waving his right arm.

The nameless horror that oppressed me passed in a moment, for in a moment I saw that this appearance of a man was a man indeed, and that there was a little group of other men, standing at a short distance, to whom he seemed to be rehearsing the gesture he made. The Danger-light was not yet lighted. Against its shaft, a little low hut, entirely new to me, had been made of some wooden supports and tarpaulin. It looked no bigger than a bed.

With an irresistible sense that something was wrong,—with a flashing self-reproachful fear that fatal mischief had come of my leaving the man there, and causing no one to be sent to overlook or correct what he did,—I descended the notched path with all the speed I could make.

"What is the matter?" I asked the men.

"Signal-man killed this morning, Sir."

"Not the man belonging to that box?"

"Yes, Sir."

"Not the man I know?"

"You will recognise him, Sir, if you knew him," said the man who spoke for the others, solemnly uncovering his own head, and raising an end of the tarpaulin, "for his face is quite composed."

"O, how did this happen, how did this happen?" I asked, turning from one to another as the hut closed in again.

"He was cut down by an engine, Sir. No man in England knew his work better. But somehow he was not clear of the outer rail. It was just at broad day. He had struck the light, and had the lamp in his hand. As the engine came out of the tunnel, his back was towards her, and she cut him down. That man drove her, and was showing how it happened. Show the gentleman, Tom."

The man, who wore a rough dark dress, stepped back to his former place at the mouth of the tunnel.

"Coming round the curve in the tunnel, Sir," he said, "I saw him at the end, like as if I saw him down a perspective-glass. There was no time to check speed, and I knew him to be very careful. As he didn't seem to take heed of the whistle, I shut it off when we were running down upon him, and called to him as loud as I could call."

"What did you say?"

"I said, 'Below there! Look out! Look out! For God's sake, clear the way!'"

I started.

"Ah! it was a dreadful time, Sir. I never left off calling to him. I put this arm before my eyes not to see, and I waved this arm to the last; but it was no use."

Without prolonging the narrative to dwell on any one of its curious circumstances more than on any other, I may, in closing it, point out the coincidence that the warning of the Engine-Driver included, not only the words which the unfortunate Signal-man had repeated to me as haunting him, but also the words which I myself—not he—had attached, and that only in my own mind, to the gesticulation he had imitated.

—1866

Tales for the Dusk

Dickens wrote many short tales, stories, and sketches, apart from his Christmas books and stories, throughout his career. Some of them were planned as parts of the two series of tales he projected—*Master Humphrey's Clock* and *The Uncommercial Traveller*; others were written for his own magazines or for other periodicals of the day in England and America. Six of these tales have been selected here to show Dickens touching on themes or contemporary subjects that went into the making of his novels.

"Hunted Down" was written for the New York *Ledger* and appeared in that newspaper in its issues of August 20 and 27, 1859; it was also serialized in Dickens's own London magazine, *All the Year Round*, for August 4 and 11, 1860. It shows Dickens's fascination by the crime and criminals which figure in a good number of his tales and novels. "George Silverman's Explanation" was written for *The Atlantic Monthly* of Boston, where it was serialized in the issues of January, February, and March, 1868; it too was included in *All the Year Round*, in the issues of February 1, 15, and 29, 1868. "The Detective Police," dealing with the phenomenon of the modern police detective, a feature of Sir Robert Peel's London police force, was written under the title "A Detective Police Party" for Dickens's first magazine, *Household Words*, during its first year, issues of July 27 and August 10, 1850. It anticipates the famous character of Inspector Bucket in *Bleak House* in 1852–53. The "Three Detective Anecdotes" were published in *Household Words* of September 14, 1850. "To Be Read at Dusk," which suggests Dickens's absorption by the phenomena of hypnotism and mesmerism, was written for Lady Blessington's *The Keepsake* in 1852 and was published in a small volume in London in the same year. "A Child's Dream of a Star" was first printed in *Household Words* in its issue of April 6, 1850.

Hunted Down

Most of us see some romances in life. In my capacity as Chief Manager of a Life Assurance Office, I think I have within the last thirty years seen more romances than the generality of men, however unpromising the opportunity may, at first sight, seem.

As I have retired, and live at my ease, I possess the means that I used to want, of considering what I have seen, at leisure. My experiences have a more remarkable aspect, so reviewed, than they had when they were in progress. I have come home from the Play now, and can recall the scenes of the Drama upon which the curtain has fallen, free from the glare, bewilderment, and bustle of the Theatre.

Let me recall one of these Romances of the real world.

There is nothing truer than physiognomy, taken in connexion with manner. The art of reading that book of which Eternal Wisdom obliges every human creature to present his or her own page with the individual character written on it, is a difficult one, perhaps, and is little studied. It may require some natural aptitude, and it must require (for everything does) some patience and some pains. That these are not usually given to it,—that numbers of people accept a few stock commonplace expressions of the face as the whole list of characteristics, and neither seek nor know the refinements that are truest,—that You, for instance, give a great deal of time and attention to the reading of music, Greek, Latin, French, Italian, Hebrew, if you please, and do not qualify yourself to read the face of the master or mistress looking over your shoulder teaching it to you,—I assume to be five hundred times more probable than improbable. Perhaps a little self-sufficiency may be at the bottom of this; facial expression requires no study from you, you think; it comes by nature to you to know enough about it, and you are not to be taken in.

I confess, for my part, that I *have* been taken in, over and over again. I have been taken in by acquaintances, and I have been taken in (of course) by friends; far oftener by friends than by any other class of persons. How came I to be so deceived? Had I quite misread their faces?

No. Believe me, my first impression of those people, founded on face and manner alone, was invariably true. My mistake was in suffering them to come nearer to me and explain themselves away.

CHAPTER II

The partition which separated my own office from our general outer office in the City was of thick plate-glass. I could see through it what passed in the outer office, without hearing a word. I had it put up in place of a wall that had been there for years,—ever since the house was built. It is no matter whether I did or did not make the change in order that I might derive my first impression of strangers, who came to us on business, from their faces alone, without being influenced by anything they said. Enough to mention that I turned my glass partition to that account, and that a Life-Assurance Office is at all times exposed to be practised upon by the most crafty and cruel of the human race.

It was through my glass partition that I first saw the gentleman whose story I am going to tell.

He had come in without my observing it, and had put his hat and umbrella on the broad counter, and was bending over it to take some papers from one of the clerks. He was about forty or so, dark, exceedingly well dressed in black,—being in mourning,—and the hand he extended with a polite air, had a particularly well-fitting black kid glove upon it. His hair, which was elaborately brushed and oiled, was parted straight up the middle; and he presented this parting to the clerk, exactly (to my thinking) as if he had said, in so many words: "You must take me, if you please, my friend, just as I show myself. Come straight up here, follow the gravel path, keep off the grass, I allow no trespassing."

I conceived a very great aversion to that man the moment I thus saw him.

He had asked for some of our printed forms, and the clerk was giving them to him and explaining them. An obliged and agreeable smile was on his face, and his eyes met those of the clerk with a sprightly look. (I have known a vast quantity of nonsense talked about bad men not looking you in the face. Don't trust that conventional idea. Dishonesty will stare honesty out of countenance, any day in the week, if there is anything to be got by it.)

I saw, in the corner of his eyelash, that he became aware of my looking at him. Immediately he turned the parting in his hair toward the glass partition, as if he said to me with a sweet smile, "Straight up here, if you please. Off the grass!"

In a few moments he had put on his hat and taken up his umbrella, and was gone.

I beckoned the clerk into my room, and asked, "Who was that?"

He had the gentleman's card in his hand. "Mr. Julius Slinkton, Middle Temple."

"A barrister, Mr. Adams?"

"I think not, Sir."

"I should have thought him a clergyman, but for his having no Reverend here," said I.

"Probably, from his appearance," Mr. Adams replied, "he is reading for orders."

I should mention that he wore a dainty white cravat, and dainty linen altogether.

"What did he want, Mr. Adams?"

"Merely a form of proposal, Sir, and form of reference."

"Recommended here? Did he say?"

"Yes, he said he was recommended here by a friend of yours. He noticed you, but said that as he had not the pleasure of your personal acquaintance he would not trouble you."

"Did he know my name?"

"O yes, Sir! He said, 'There is Mr. Sampson, I see!'"

"A well-spoken gentleman, apparently?"

"Remarkably so, Sir."

"Insinuating manners, apparently?"

"Very much so, indeed, Sir."

"Hah!" said I. "I want nothing at present, Mr. Adams."

Within a fortnight of that day I went to dine with a friend of mine, a merchant, a man of taste, who buys pictures and books, and the first man I saw among the company was Mr. Julius Slinkton. There he was, standing before the fire, with good large eyes and an open expression of face; but still (I thought) requiring everybody to come at him by the prepared way he offered, and by no other.

I noticed him ask my friend to introduce him to Mr. Sampson, and my friend did so. Mr. Slinkton was very happy to see me. Not too happy; there was no over-doing of the matter; happy in a thoroughly well-bred, perfectly unmeaning way.

"I thought you had met," our host observed.

"No," said Mr. Slinkton. "I did look in at Mr. Sampson's office, on your recommendation; but I really did not feel justified in troubling Mr. Sampson himself, on a point in the everyday routine of an ordinary clerk."

I said I should have been glad to show him any attention on our friend's introduction.

"I am sure of that," said he, "and am much obliged. At another time, perhaps, I may be less delicate. Only, however, if I have real business; for I know, Mr. Sampson, how precious business time is, and what a vast number of impertinent people there are in the world."

I acknowledged his consideration with a slight bow. "You were thinking," said I, "of effecting a policy on your life."

"O dear no! I am afraid I am not so prudent as you pay me the compliment of supposing me to be, Mr. Sampson. I merely inquired for a friend. But you know what friends are in such matters. Nothing may ever come of it. I have the greatest reluctance to trouble men of business with inquiries for friends, knowing the probabilities to be a thousand to one that the friends will never follow them up. People are so fickle, so selfish, so inconsiderate. Don't you, in your business, find them so every day, Mr. Sampson?"

I was going to give a qualified answer; but he turned his smooth, white parting on me with its "Straight up here, if you please!" and I answered "Yes."

"I hear, Mr. Sampson," he resumed presently, for our friend had a new cook, and dinner was not so punctual as usual, "that your profession has recently suffered a great loss."

"In money?" said I.

He laughed at my ready association of loss with money, and replied, "No, in talent and vigour."

Not at once following out his allusion, I considered for a moment. "*Has* it sustained a loss of that kind?" said I. "I was not aware of it."

"Understand me, Mr. Sampson. I don't imagine that you have retired. It is not so bad as that. But Mr. Meltham——"

"O, to be sure!" said I. "Yes! Mr. Meltham, the young actuary of the 'Inestimable.'"

"Just so," he returned in a consoling way.

"He is a great loss. He was at once the most profound, the most original, and the most energetic man I have ever known connected with Life Assurance."

I spoke strongly; for I had a high esteem and admiration for Meltham; and my gentleman had indefinitely conveyed to me some suspicion that he wanted to sneer at him. He recalled me to my guard by presenting that trim pathway up his head, with its infernal "Not on the grass, if you please—the gravel."

"You knew him, Mr. Slinkton."

"Only by reputation. To have known him as an acquaintance or as a friend, is an honour I should have sought if he had remained in society, though I might never have had the good fortune to attain it, being a man of far inferior mark. He was scarcely above thirty, I suppose?"

"About thirty."

"Ah!" he sighed in his former consoling way. "What creatures we are! To break up, Mr. Sampson, and become incapable of business at that time of life!—Any reason assigned for the melancholy fact?"

("Humph!" thought I, as I looked at him. "But I won't go up the track, and I will go on the grass.")

"What reason have you heard assigned, Mr. Slinkton?" I asked, point-blank.

"Most likely a false one. You know what Rumour is, Mr. Sampson. I never repeat what I hear; it is the only way of paring the nails and shaving the head of Rumour. But when *you* ask me what reason I have heard assigned for Mr. Meltham's passing away from among men, it is another thing. I am not gratifying idle gossip then. I was told, Mr. Sampson, that Mr. Meltham had relinquished all his avocations and all his prospects, because he was, in fact, broken-hearted. A disappointed attachment I heard,—though it hardly seems probable, in the case of a man so distinguished and so attractive."

"Attractions and distinctions are no armour against death," said I.

"O, she died? Pray pardon me. I did not hear that. That, indeed, makes it very, very sad. Poor Mr. Meltham! She died? Ah, dear me! Lamentable, lamentable!"

I still thought his pity was not quite genuine, and I still suspected an unaccountable sneer under all this, until he said, as we were parted, like the other knots of talkers, by the announcement of dinner:

"Mr. Sampson, you are surprised to see me so moved on behalf of a man whom I have never known. I am not so disinterested as you may suppose. I have suffered, and recently too, from death myself. I have lost one of two charming nieces, who were my constant companions. She died young—barely three-and-twenty; and even her remaining sister is far from strong. The world is a grave!"

He said this with deep feeling, and I felt reproached for the coldness of my manner. Coldness and distrust had been engendered in me, I knew, by my bad experiences; they were not natural to me; and I often thought how much I had lost in life, losing trustfulness, and how little I had gained, gaining hard caution. This state of mind being habitual to me, I troubled myself more about this conversation than I might have troubled myself about a greater matter. I listened to his talk at dinner, and observed how readily other men responded to it, and with what a graceful instinct he adapted his subjects to the knowledge and habits of those he talked with. As, in talking with me, he had easily started the subject I might be supposed to understand best, and to be the most interested in, so, in talking with others, he guided himself by the same rule. The company was of a varied character; but he was not at fault, that I could discover, with any member of it. He knew just as much of each man's pursuit as made him agreeable to that man in reference to it, and just as little as made it natural in him to seek modestly for information when the theme was broached.

As he talked and talked—but really not too much, for the rest of us seemed to force it upon him—I became quite angry with myself. I took his face to pieces in my mind, like a watch, and examined it in detail. I could not say much against any of his features separately; I could say even less against them when they were put together. "Then is it not monstrous," I asked myself, "that because a man happens to part his hair straight up the middle of his head, I should permit myself to suspect, and even to detest him?"

(I may stop to remark that this was no proof of my sense. An observer of men who finds himself steadily repelled by some apparently trifling thing in a stranger is right to give it great weight. It may be the clue to the whole mystery. A hair or two will show where a lion is hidden. A very little key will open a very heavy door.)

I took my part in the conversation with him after a time, and we got on remarkably well. In the drawing-room I asked the host how long he had known Mr. Slinkton. He answered, not many months; he had met him at the house of a celebrated painter then present, who had known him well when he was travelling with his nieces in Italy for their health. His plans in life being broken by the death of one of them, he was reading with the intention of going back to college as a matter of form, taking his degree, and going into orders. I could not but argue with myself that here was the true explanation of his interest in poor Meltham, and that I had been almost brutal in my distrust on that simple head.

CHAPTER III

On the very next day but one I was sitting behind my glass partition, as before, when he came into the outer office, as before. The moment I saw him again without hearing him, I hated him worse than ever.

It was only for a moment that I had this opportunity; for he waved his tight-fitting black glove the instant I looked at him, and came straight in.

"Mr. Sampson, good-day! I presume, you see, upon your kind permission to intrude upon you. I don't keep my word in being justified by business, for my business here—if I may so abuse the word—is of the slightest nature."

I asked, was it anything I could assist him in?

"I thank you, no. I merely called to inquire outside whether my dilatory friend had been so false to himself as to be practical and sensible. But, of course, he has done nothing. I gave him your papers with my own hand, and he was hot upon the intention, but of course he has done nothing. Apart from the general human disinclination to do anything that ought to be done, I dare say there is a specialty about assuring one's life. You find it like will-making. People are so superstitious, and take it for granted they will die soon afterwards."

"Up here, if you please; straight up here, Mr. Sampson. Neither to the right not to the left." I almost fancied I could hear him breathe the words as he sat smiling at me, with that intolerable parting exactly opposite the bridge of my nose.

"There is such a feeling sometimes, no doubt," I replied; "but I don't think it obtains to any great extent."

"Well," said he, with a shrug and a smile, "I wish some good angel would influence my friend in the right direction. I rashly promised his mother and sister in Norfolk to see it done, and he promised them that he would do it. But I suppose he never will."

He spoke for a minute or two on indifferent topics, and went away.

I had scarcely unlocked the drawers of my writing-table next morning, when he reappeared. I noticed that he came straight to the door in the glass partition, and did not pause a single moment outside.

"Can you spare me two minutes, my dear Mr. Sampson?"

"By all means."

"Much obliged," laying his hat and umbrella on the table; "I came early, not to interrupt you. The fact is, I am taken by surprise in reference to this proposal my friend has made."

"Has he made one?" said I.

"Ye-es," he answered, deliberately looking at me; and then a bright idea seemed to strike him—"or he only tells me he has. Perhaps that may be a new way of evading the matter. By Jupiter, I never thought of that!"

Mr. Adams was opening the morning's letters in the outer office. "What is the name, Mr. Slinkton?" I asked.

"Beckwith."

I looked out at the door and requested Mr. Adams, if there were a proposal in that name, to bring it in. He had already laid it out of his hand on the counter. It was easily selected from the rest, and he gave it me. Alfred Beckwith. Proposal to effect a policy with us for two thousand pounds. Dated yesterday.

"From the Middle Temple, I see, Mr. Slinkton."

"Yes. He lives on the same staircase with me; his door is opposite. I never thought he would make me his reference though."

"It seems natural enough that he should."

"Quite so, Mr. Sampson; but I never thought of it. Let me see." He took the printed paper from his pocket. "How am I to answer all these questions?"

"According to the truth, of course," said I.

"O, of course!" he answered, looking up from the paper with a smile; "I meant they were so many. But you do right to be particular. It stands to reason that you must be particular. Will you allow me to use your pen and ink?"

"Certainly."

"And your desk?"

"Certainly."

He had been hovering about between his hat and his umbrella for a place to write on. He now sat down in my chair, at my blotting-paper and inkstand, with the long walk up his head in accurate perspective before me, as I stood with my back to the fire.

Before answering each question he ran over it aloud, and discussed it. How long had he known Mr. Alfred Beckwith? That he had to calculate by years upon his fingers. What were his habits? No difficulty about them; temperate in the last degree, and took a little too much exercise, if anything. All the answers were satisfactory. When he had written them all, he looked them over, and finally signed them in a very pretty hand. He supposed he had now done with the business. I told him he was not likely to be troubled any farther. Should he leave the papers there? If he pleased. Much obliged. Good morning.

I had had one other visitor before him; not at the office, but at my own house. That visitor had come to my bedside when it was not yet daylight, and had been seen by no one else but by my faithful confidential servant.

A second reference paper (for we required always two) was sent down into Norfolk, and was duly received back by post. This, likewise, was satisfactorily answered in every respect. Our forms were all complied with; we accepted the proposal, and the premium for one year was paid.

CHAPTER IV

For six or seven months I saw no more of Mr. Slinkton. He called once at my house, but I was not at home; and he once asked me to dine with him in the Temple, but I was engaged. His friend's assurance was effected in March. Late in September or early in October I was down at Scarborough for a breath of sea-air, where I met him on the beach. It was a hot evening; he came toward me with his hat in his hand; and there was the walk I had felt so strongly disinclined to take in perfect order again, exactly in front of the bridge of my nose.

He was not alone, but had a young lady on his arm.

She was dressed in mourning, and I looked at her with great interest. She had the appearance of being extremely delicate, and her face was remarkably pale and melancholy; but she was very pretty. He introduced her as his niece, Miss Niner.

"Are you strolling, Mr. Sampson? Is it possible you can be idle?"

It *was* possible, and I *was* strolling.

"Shall we stroll together?"

"With pleasure."

The young lady walked between us, and we walked on the cool sea sand, in the direction of Filey.

"There have been wheels here," said Mr. Slinkton. "And now I look again, the wheels of a hand-carriage! Margaret, my love, your shadow without doubt!"

"Miss Niner's shadow?" I repeated, looking down at it on the sand.

"Not that one," Mr. Slinkton returned, laughing. "Margaret, my dear, tell Mr. Sampson."

"Indeed," said the young lady, turning to me, "there is nothing to tell—except that I constantly see the same invalid old gentleman at all times, wherever I go. I have mentioned it to my uncle, and he calls the gentleman my shadow."

"Does he live in Scarborough?" I asked.

"He is staying here."

"Do you live in Scarborough?"

"No, I am staying here. My uncle has placed me with a family here, for my health."

"And your shadow?" said I, smiling.

"My shadow," she answered, smiling too, "is—like myself—not very robust, I fear; for I lose my shadow sometimes, as my shadow loses me at other times. We both seem liable to confinement to the house. I have not seen my shadow for days and days; but it does oddly happen, occasionally, that wherever I go, for many days together, this gentleman goes. We have come together in the most unfrequented nooks on this shore."

"Is this he?" said I, pointing before us.

The wheels had swept down to the water's edge, and described a great loop on the sand in turning. Bringing the loop back towards us, and spinning it out as it came, was a hand-carriage, drawn by a man.

"Yes," said Miss Niner, "this really is my shadow, uncle."

As the carriage approached us and we approached the carriage, I saw within it an old man, whose head was sunk on his breast, and who was enveloped in a variety of wrappers. He was drawn by a very quiet but very keen-looking man, with iron-grey hair, who was slightly lame. They had passed us, when the carriage stopped, and the old gentleman within, putting out his arm, called to me by my name. I went back, and was absent from Mr. Slinkton and his niece for about five minutes.

When I rejoined them, Mr. Slinkton was the first to speak. Indeed, he said to me in a raised voice before I came up with him:

"It is well you have not been longer, or my niece might have died of curiosity to know who her shadow is, Mr. Sampson."

"An old East India Director," said I. "An intimate friend of our friend's, at whose house I first had the pleasure of meeting you. A certain Major Banks. You have heard of him?"

"Never."

"Very rich, Miss Niner; but very old, and very crippled. An amiable man, sensible—much interested in you. He has just been expatiating on the affection that he has observed to exist between you and your uncle."

Mr. Slinkton was holding his hat again, and he passed his hand up the straight walk, as if he himself went up it serenely, after me.

"Mr. Sampson," he said, tenderly pressing his niece's arm in his, "our affection was always a strong one, for we have had but few near ties. We have still fewer now. We have associations to bring us together, that are not of this world, Margaret."

"Dear uncle!" murmured the young lady, and turned her face aside to hide her tears.

"My niece and I have such remembrances and regrets in common, Mr. Sampson," he feelingly pursued, "that it would be strange indeed if the relations between us were cold or indifferent. If I remember a conversation we once had together, you will understand the reference I make. Cheer up, dear Margaret. Don't droop, don't droop. My Margaret! I cannot bear to see you droop!"

The poor young lady was very much affected, but controlled herself. His feelings, too, were very acute. In a word, he found himself under such great need of a restorative, that he presently went away, to take a bath of sea-water, leaving the young lady and me sitting by a point of rock, and probably presuming—but that you will say was a pardonable indulgence in a luxury—that she would praise him with all her heart.

She did, poor thing! With all her confiding heart, she praised him to me, for his care of her dead sister, and for his untiring devotion in her last illness. The sister had wasted away very slowly, and wild and terrible fantasies had come over her toward the end, but he had never been impatient with her, or at a loss; had always been gentle, watchful, and self-possessed. The sister had known him, as she had known him, to be the best of men, the kindest of men, and yet a man of such admirable strength of character, as to be a very tower for the support of their weak natures while their poor lives endured.

"I shall leave him, Mr. Sampson, very soon," said the young lady; "I know my life is drawing to an end; and when I am gone, I hope he will marry and be happy. I am sure he has lived single so long, only for my sake, and for my poor, poor sister's."

The little hand-carriage had made another great loop on the damp sand, and was coming back again, gradually spinning out a slim figure of eight, half a mile long.

"Young lady," said I, looking around, laying my hand upon her arm, and speaking in a low voice, "time presses. You hear the gentle murmur of that sea?"

She looked at me with the utmost wonder and alarm, saying, "Yes!"

"And you know what a voice is in it when the storm comes?"

"Yes!"

"You see how quiet and peaceful it lies before us, and you know what an awful sight of power without pity it might be, this very night!"

"Yes!"

"But if you had never heard or seen it, or heard of it in its cruelty, could you believe that it beats every inanimate thing in its way to pieces, without mercy, and destroys life without remorse?"

"You terrify me, Sir, by these questions!"

"To save you, young lady, to save you! For God's sake, collect your strength and collect your firmness! If you were here alone, and hemmed in by the rising tide on the flow to fifty feet above your head, you could not be in greater danger than the danger you are now to be saved from."

The figure on the sand was spun out, and straggled off into a crooked little jerk that ended at the cliff very near us.

"As I am, before Heaven and the Judge of all mankind, your friend, and your dead sister's friend, I solemnly entreat you, Miss Niner, without one moment's loss of time, to come to this gentleman with me!"

If the little carriage had been less near to us, I doubt if I could have got her away; but it was so near that we were there before she had recovered the hurry of being urged from the rock. I did not remain there with her two minutes. Certainly within five, I had the inexpressible satisfaction of seeing her—from the point we had sat on, and to which I had returned—half supported and half carried up some rude steps notched in the cliff, by the figure of an active man. With that figure beside her, I knew she was safe anywhere.

I sat alone on the rock, awaiting Mr. Slinkton's return. The twilight was deepening and the shadows were heavy, when he came round the point, with his hat hanging at his button-hole, smoothing his wet hair with one of his hands, and picking out the old path with the other and a pocket-comb.

"My niece not here, Mr. Sampson?" he said, looking about.

"Miss Niner seemed to feel a chill in the air after the sun was down, and has gone home."

He looked surprised, as though she were not accustomed to do anything without him; even to originate so slight a proceeding.

"I persuaded Miss Niner," I explained.

"Ah!" said he. "She is easily persuaded—for her good. Thank you, Mr. Sampson; she is better within doors. The bathing-place was farther than I thought, to say the truth."

"Miss Niner is very delicate," I observed.

He shook his head and drew a deep sigh. "Very, very, very. You may recollect my saying so. The time that has since intervened has not strengthened her. The gloomy shadow that fell upon her sister so early in life seems, in my anxious eyes, to gather over her, ever darker, ever darker. Dear Margaret, dear Margaret! But we must hope."

The hand-carriage was spinning away before us at a most in-decorous pace for an invalid vehicle, and was making most irregular curves upon the sand. Mr. Slinkton, noticing it after he had put his handkerchief to his eyes, said:

"If I may judge from appearances, your friend will be upset, Mr. Sampson."

"It looks probable, certainly," said I.

"The servant must be drunk."

"The servants of old gentlemen will get drunk sometimes," said I.

"The major draws very light, Mr. Sampson."

"The major does draw light," said I.

By this time the carriage, much to my relief, was lost in the darkness. We walked on for a little, side by side over the sand, in silence. After a short while he said, in a voice still affected by the emotion that his niece's state of health had awakened in him,

"Do you stay here long, Mr. Sampson?"

"Why, no. I am going away to-night."

"So soon? But business always holds you in request. Men like Mr. Sampson are too important to others, to be spared to their own need of relaxation and enjoyment."

"I don't know about that," said I. "However, I am going back."

"To London?"

"To London."

"I shall be there too, soon after you."

I knew that as well as he did. But I did not tell him so. Any more than I told him what defensive weapon my right hand rested on in my pocket, as I walked by his side. Any more than I told him why I did not walk on the sea side of him with the night closing in.

We left the beach, and our ways diverged. We exchanged good night, and had parted indeed, when he said, returning,

"Mr. Sampson, *may* I ask? Poor Meltham, whom we spoke of,—dead yet?"

"Not when I last heard of him; but too broken a man to live long, and hopelessly lost to his old calling."

"Dear, dear, dear!" said he, with great feeling. "Sad, sad, sad! The world is a grave!" And so went his way.

It was not his fault if the world were not a grave; but I did not call that observation after him, any more than I had mentioned those other things just now enumerated. He went his way, and I went mine with all expedition. This happened, as I have said, either at the end of September or beginning of October. The next time I saw him, and the last time, was late in November.

CHAPTER V

I had a very particular engagement to breakfast in the Temple. It was a bitter north-easterly morning, and the sleet and slush lay inches deep in the streets. I could get no conveyance, and was soon wet to the knees; but I should have been true to that appointment, though I had to wade to it up to my neck in the same impediments.

The appointment took me to some chambers in the Temple. They were at the top of a lonely corner house overlooking the river. The name, Mr. ALFRED BECKWITH, was painted on the outer door. On the door opposite, on the same landing, the name MR. JULIUS SLINKTON. The doors of both sets of chambers stood open, so that anything said aloud in one set could be heard in the other.

I had never been in those chambers before. They were dismal, close, unwholesome, and oppressive; the furniture, originally good, and not yet old was faded and dirty,—the rooms were in great disorder; there was a strong prevailing smell of opium, brandy, and tobacco; the grate and fire-irons were splashed all over with unsightly blotches of rust; and on a sofa by the fire, in the room where breakfast had been prepared, lay the host, Mr. Beckwith, a man with all the appearances of the worst kind of drunkard, very far advanced upon his shameful way to death.

"Slinkton is not come yet," said this creature, staggering up when I went in; "I'll call him. —Halloa! Julius Cæsar! Come and drink!" As he hoarsely roared this out, he beat the poker and tongs together in a mad way, as if that were his usual manner of summoning his associate.

The voice of Mr. Slinkton was heard through the clatter from the opposite side of the staircase, and he came in. He had not expected the pleasure of meeting me. I have seen several artful men brought to a stand, but I never saw a man so aghast as he was when his eyes rested on mine.

"Julius Cæsar," cried Beckwith, staggering between us, "Mist' Sampson! Mist' Sampson, Julius Cæsar! Julius, Mist' Sampson, is the friend of my soul. Julius keeps me plied with liquor, morning, noon, and night. Julius is a real benefactor. Julius threw the tea and coffee out of window when I used to have any. Julius empties all the water-jugs of their contents, and fills 'em with spirits. Julius winds me up and keeps me going. —Boil the brandy, Julius!"

There was a rusty and furred saucepan in the ashes,—the ashes looked like the accumulation of weeks,—and Beckwith, rolling and staggering between us as if he were going to plunge headlong into the fire, got the saucepan out, and tried to force it into Slinkton's hand.

"Boil the brandy, Julius Cæsar! Come! Do your usual office. Boil the brandy!"

He became so fierce in his gesticulations with the saucepan, that I expected to see him lay open Slinkton's head with it. I therefore put out my hand to check him. He reeled back to the sofa, and sat there panting, shaking, and red-eyed, in his rags of dressing-gown, looking at us both. I noticed then that there was nothing to drink on the table but brandy, and nothing to eat but salted herrings, and a hot, sickly, highly-peppered stew.

"At all events, Mr. Sampson," said Slinkton, offering me the smooth gravel path for the last time, "I thank you for interfering between me and this unfortunate man's violence. However you came here, Mr. Sampson, or with whatever motive you came here, at least I thank you for that."

"Boil the brandy," muttered Beckwith.

Without gratifying his desire to know how I came there, I said, quietly, "How is your niece, Mr. Slinkton?"

He looked hard at me, and I looked hard at him.

"I am sorry to say, Mr. Sampson, that my niece has proved treacherous and ungrateful to her best friend. She left me without a word of notice or explanation. She was misled, no doubt, by some designing rascal. Perhaps you may have heard of it."

"I did hear that she was misled by a designing rascal. In fact, I have proof of it."

"Are you sure of that?" said he.

"Quite."

"Boil the brandy," muttered Beckwith. "Company to breakfast, Julius Cæsar. Do your usual office,—provide the usual breakfast, dinner, tea, and supper. Boil the brandy!"

The eyes of Slinkton looked from him to me, and he said, after a moment's consideration,

"Mr. Sampson, you are a man of the world, and so am I. I will be plain with you."

"O no, you won't," said I, shaking my head.

"I tell you, Sir, I will be plain with you."

"And I tell you you will not," said I. "I know all about you. *You* plain with any one? Nonsense, nonsense!"

"I plainly tell you, Mr. Sampson, he went on, with a manner almost composed, "that I understand your object. You want to save your funds, and escape from your liabilities; these are old tricks of trade with you Office-gentlemen. But you will not do it, Sir; you will not succeed. You have not an easy adversary to play against, when you play against me. We shall have to inquire, in due time, when and how Mr. Beckwith fell into his present habits. With that remark, Sir, I put this poor creature, and his incoherent wanderings of speech, aside, and wish you a good morning and a better case next time."

While he was saying this, Beckwith had filled a half-pint glass with brandy. At this moment, he threw the brandy at his face, and threw the glass after it. Slinkton put his hands up, half blinded with the spirit, and cut with glass across the forehead. At the sound of the breakage, a fourth person came into the room, close the door, and stood at it; he was a very quiet but very keen-looking man, with iron-grey hair, and slightly lame.

Slinkton pulled out his handkerchief, assuaged the pain in his smarting eyes, and dabbled the blood on his forehead. He was a long time about it, and I saw that in the doing of it, a tremendous change came over him, occasioned by the change in Beckwith,—who ceased to pant and tremble, sat upright, and never took his eyes off him. I never in my life saw a face in which abhorrence and determination were so forcibly painted as in Beckwith's then.

"Look at me, you villain," said Beckwith, "and see me as I really am. I took these rooms, to make them a trap for you. I came into them as a drunkard, to bait the trap for you. You fell into the trap, and you will never leave it alive. On the morning when you last went to Mr. Sampson's office, I had seen him first. Your plot has been known to both of us, all along, and you have been counter-plotted all along. What? Having been cajoled into putting that prize of two thousand pounds in your power, I was to be done to death with brandy, and, brandy not proving quick enough, with something quicker? Have I never seen you, when you thought my senses gone, pouring from your little bottle into my glass? Why, you Murderer and Forger, alone here with you in the dead of night, as I have so often been, I have had my hand upon the trigger of a pistol, twenty times, to blow your brains out!"

This sudden starting up of the thing that he had supposed to be his imbecile victim into a determined man, with a settled resolution to hunt him down and be the death of him, mercilessly expressed from head to foot, was, in the first shock, too much for him. Without any figure of speech, he staggered under it. But there is no greater mistake than to suppose that a man who is a calculating criminal, is, in any phase of his guilt, otherwise than true to himself, and perfectly consistent with his whole character. Such a man commits murder, and murder is the natural culmination of his course; such a man has to outface murder, and will do it with hardihood and effrontery. It is a sort of fashion to express surprise that any notorious criminal, having such crime upon his conscience, can so brave it out. Do you think that if he had it on his conscience at all, or had a conscience to have it upon, he would ever have committed the crime?

Perfectly consistent with himself, as I believe all such monsters to be, this Slinkton recovered himself, and showed a defiance that was sufficiently cold and quiet. He was white, he was haggard, he was changed; but only as a sharper who had played for a great stake and had been outwitted and had lost the game.

"Listen to me, you villain," said Beckwith, "and let every word you hear me say be a stab in your wicked heart. When I took these rooms, to throw myself in your way and lead you on to the scheme that I knew my appearance and supposed character and habits would suggest to such a devil, how did I know that? Because you were no stranger to me. I knew you well. And I knew you to be the cruel wretch who, for so much money, had killed one innocent girl while she trusted him implicitly, and who by inches killing another."

Slinkton took out a snuff-box, took a pinch of snuff, and laughed.

"But see here," said Beckwith, never looking away, never raising his voice, never relaxing his face, never unclenching his hand. "See what a dull wolf you have been, after all! The infatuated drunkard who never drank a fiftieth part of the liquor you plied him with, but poured it away, here, there, everywhere—almost before your eyes; who bought over the fellow you set to watch him and to ply him, by outbidding you in his bribe, before he had been at his work three days —with whom you have observed no caution, yet who was so bent on ridding the earth of you as a wild beast, that he would have defeated you if you had been ever so prudent—that drunkard whom you have, many a time, left on the floor of this room, and who has even let you go out of it, alive and undeceived, when you have turned him over with your foot—has, almost as often, on the same night, within an hour, within a few minutes, watched you awake, had his hand at your

pillow when you were asleep, turned over your papers, taken samples
from your bottles and packets of powder, changed their contents,
rifled every secret of your life!"

He had had another pinch of snuff in his hand, but had gradually
let it drop from between his fingers to the floor; where he now
smoothed it out with his foot, looking down at it the while.

"That drunkard," said Beckwith, "who had free access to your
rooms at all times, that he might drink the strong drinks that you
left in his way and be the sooner ended, holding no more terms with
you than he would hold with a tiger, has had his master-key for all
your locks, his test for all your poisons, his clue to your cipher-writing.
He can tell you, as well as you can tell him, how long it took to
complete that deed, what doses there were, what intervals, what signs
of gradual decay upon mind and body; what distempered fancies were
produced, what observable changes, what physical pain. He can tell
you, as well as you can tell him, that all this was recorded day by
day, as a lesson of experience for future service. He can tell you,
better than you can tell him, where that journal is at this moment."

Slinkton stopped the action of his foot, and looked at Beckwith.

"No," said the latter, as if answering a question from him. "Not in
the drawer of the writing-desk that opens with a spring; it is not
there, and it never will be there again.

"Then you are a thief!" said Slinkton.

Without any change whatever in the inflexible purpose, which it
was quite terrific even to me to contemplate, and from the power
of which I had always felt convinced it was impossible for this wretch
to escape, Beckwith returned,

"And I am your niece's shadow, too."

With an imprecation Slinkton put his hand to his head, tore out
some hair, and flung it to the ground. It was the end of the smooth
walk; he destroyed it in the action, and it will soon be seen that
his use for it was past.

Beckwith went on: "Whenever you left here, I left here. Although
I understood that you found it necessary to pause in the completion
of that purpose, to avert suspicion, still I watched you close, with the
poor confiding girl. When I had the diary, and could read it word
by word,—it was only about the night before your last visit to Scarborough,—you remember the night? you slept with a small flat vial
tied to your wrist,—I sent to Mr. Sampson, who was kept out of view.
This is Mr. Sampson's trusty servant standing by the door. We three
saved your niece among us."

Slinkton looked at us all, took an uncertain step or two from the
place where he had stood, returned to it, and glanced about him in a
very curious way,—as one of the meaner reptiles might, looking for a
hole to hide in. I noticed at the same time, that a singular change took

place in the figure of the man,—as if it collapsed within his clothes, and they consequently became ill-shapen and ill-fitting.

"You shall know," said Beckwith, "for I hope the knowledge will be bitter and terrible to you, why you have been pursued by one man, and why, when the whole interest that Mr. Sampson represents would have expended any money in hunting you down, you have been tracked to death at a single individual's charge. I hear you have had the name of Meltham on your lips sometimes?"

I saw, in addition to those other changes, a sudden stoppage come upon his breathing.

"When you sent the sweet girl whom you murdered (you know with what artfully made-out surroundings and probabilities you sent her) to Meltham's office, before taking her abroad to originate the transaction that doomed her to the grave, it fell to Meltham's lot to see her and to speak with her. It did not fall to his lot to save her, though I know he would freely give his own life to have done it. He admired her;—I would say he loved her deeply, if I thought it possible that you could understand the word. When she was sacrificed, he was thoroughly assured of your guilt. Having lost her, he had but one object left in life, and that was to avenge her and destroy you."

I saw the villain's nostrils rise and fall convulsively; but I saw no moving at his mouth.

"That man Meltham," Beckwith steadily pursued, "was as absolutely certain that you could never elude him in this world, if he devoted himself to your destruction with his utmost fidelity and earnestness, and if he divided the sacred duty with no other duty in life, as he was certain that in achieving it he would be a poor instrument in the hands of Providence, and would do well before Heaven in striking you out from among living men. I am that man, and I thank God that I have done my work!"

If Slinkton had been running for his life from swift-footed savages, a dozen miles, he could not have shown more emphatic signs of being oppressed at heart and labouring for breath, than he showed now, when he looked at the pursuer who had so relentlessly hunted him down.

"You never saw me under my right name before; you see me under my right name now. You shall see me once again in the body, when you are tried for your life. You shall see me once again in the spirit, when the cord is round your neck, and the crowd are crying against you!"

When Meltham had spoken these last words, the miscreant suddenly turned away his face, and seemed to strike his mouth with his open hand. At the same instant, the room was filled with a new and powerful odour, and, almost at the same instant, he broke into a crooked run, leap, start,—I have no name for the spasm,—and fell, with a dull weight that shook the heavy old doors and windows in their frames.

That was the fitting end of him.

When we saw that he was dead, we drew away from the room, and Meltham, giving me his hand, said, with a weary air,

"I have no more work on earth, my friend. But I shall see her again elsewhere."

It was in vain that I tried to rally him. He might have saved her, he said; he had not saved her, and he reproached himself; he had lost her, and he was broken-hearted.

"The purpose that sustained me is over, Sampson, and there is nothing now to hold me to life. I am not fit for life; I am weak and spiritless; I have no hope and no object; my day is done."

In truth, I could hardly have believed that the broken man who then spoke to me was the man who had so strongly and so differently impressed me when his purpose was before him. I used such entreaties with him, as I could; but he still said, and always said, in a patient, undemonstrative way,—nothing could avail him,—he was broken-hearted.

He died early in the next spring. He was buried by the side of the poor young lady for whom he had cherished those tender and unhappy regrets; and he left all he had to her sister. She lived to be a happy wife and mother; she married my sister's son, who succeeded poor Meltham; she is living now, and her children ride about the garden on my walking-stick when I go to see her.

George Silverman's Explanation

FIRST CHAPTER

It happened in this wise—

But, sitting with my pen in my hand looking at those words again, without descrying any hint in them of the words that should follow, it comes into my mind that they have an abrupt appearance. They may serve, however, if I let them remain, to suggest how very difficult I find it to begin to explain my explanation. An uncouth phrase: and yet I do not see my way to a better.

SECOND CHAPTER

It happened in this wise—

But, looking at those words, and comparing them with my former opening, I find they are the self-same words repeated. This is the more surprising to me, because I employ them in quite a new connexion. For indeed I declare that my intention was to discard the commencement I first had in my thoughts, and to give the preference to another of an entirely different nature, dating my explanation from an anterior period of my life. I will make a third trial, without erasing this second failure, protesting that it is not my design to conceal any of my infirmities, whether they be of head or heart.

THIRD CHAPTER

Not as yet directly aiming at how it came to pass, I will come upon it by degrees. The natural manner, after all, for God knows that is how it came upon me.

My parents were in a miserable condition of life, and my infant home was a cellar in Preston. I recollect the sound of father's Lancashire clogs on the street pavement above, as being different in my young hearing from the sound of all other clogs; and I recollect, that, when mother came down the cellar-steps, I used tremblingly to speculate on her feet having a good or an ill-tempered look,—on her knees, —on her waist,—until finally her face came into view, and settled the question. From this it will be seen that I was timid, and that the cellar-steps were steep, and that the doorway was very low.

Mother had the gripe and clutch of poverty upon her face, upon her figure, and not least of all upon her voice. Her sharp and high-pitched words were squeezed out of her, as by the compression of bony fingers on a leathern bag; and she had a way of rolling her eyes about and about the cellar, as she scolded, that was gaunt and hungry. Father, with his shoulders rounded, would sit quiet on a three-legged stool, looking at the empty grate, until she would pluck the stool from under him, and bid him go bring some money home. Then he would dismally ascend the steps; and I, holding my ragged shirt and trousers together with a hand (my only braces), would feint and dodge from mother's pursuing grasp at my hair.

A worldy little devil was mother's usual name for me. Whether I cried for that I was in the dark, or for that it was cold, or for that I was hungry, or whether I squeezed myself into a warm corner when there was a fire, or ate voraciously when there was food, she would still say, "O you worldly little devil!" And the sting of it was, that I quite well knew myself to be a worldly little devil. Worldly as to wanting to be housed and warmed, worldly as to wanting to be fed, worldly as to the greed with which I inwardly compared how much I got of those good things with how much father and mother got, when, rarely, those good things were going.

Sometimes they both went away seeking work; and then I would be locked up in the cellar for a day or two at a time. I was at my worldliest then. Left alone, I yielded myself up to a worldly yearning for enough of anything (except misery), and for the death of mother's father, who was a machine-maker at Birmingham, and on whose decease, I had heard mother say, she would come into a whole courtful of houses "if she had her rights." Worldly little devil, I would stand about, musingly fitting my cold bare feet into cracked bricks and crevices of the damp cellar-floor,—walking over my grandfather's body, so to speak, into the courtful of houses, and selling them for meat and drink, and clothes to wear.

At last a change came down into our cellar. The universal change came down even as low as that,—so will it mount to any height on which a human creature can perch,—and brought other changes with it.

We had a heap of I don't know what foul litter in the darkest corner, which we called "the bed." For three days mother lay upon it without getting up, and then began at times to laugh. If I had ever heard her laugh before, it had been so seldom that the strange sound frightened me. It frightened father too; and we took it by turns to give her water. Then she began to move her head from side to side, and sing. After that, she getting no better, father fell a-laughing and a-singing; and then there was only I to give them both water, and they both died.

FOURTH CHAPTER

When I was lifted out of the cellar by two men, of whom one came peeping down alone first, and ran away and brought the other, I could hardly bear the light of the street. I was sitting in the road-way, blinking at it, and at a ring of people collected around me, but not close to me, when, true to my character of worldly little devil, I broke silence by saying, "I am hungry and thirsty!"

"Does he know they are dead?" asked one of another.

"Do you know your father and mother are both dead of fever?" asked a third of me severely.

"I don't know what it is to be dead. I supposed it meant that, when the cup rattled against their teeth, and the water spilt over them. I am hungry and thirsty." That was all I had to say about it.

The ring of people widened outward from the inner side as I looked around me; and I smelt vinegar, and what I know to be camphor, thrown in towards where I sat. Presently some one put a great vessel of smoking vinegar on the ground near me; and then they all looked at me in silent horror as I ate and drank of what was brought for me. I knew at the time they had a horror of me, but I couldn't help it.

I was still eating and drinking, and a murmur of discussion had begun to arise respecting what was to be done with me next, when I heard a cracked voice somewhere in the ring say, "My name is Hawkyard, Mr. Verity Hawkyard, of West Bromwich." Then the ring split in one place; and a yellow-faced, peak-nosed gentleman, clad all in iron-grey to his gaiters, pressed forward with a policeman and another official of some sort. He came forward close to the vessel of smoking vinegar; from which he sprinkled himself carefully, and me copiously.

"He had a grandfather at Birmingham, this young boy, who is just dead too," said Mr. Hawkyard.

I turned my eyes upon the speaker, and said in a ravening manner, "Where's his houses?"

"Hah! Horrible worldliness on the edge of the grave," said Mr. Hawkyard, casting more of the vinegar over me, as if to get my devil out of me. "I have undertaken a slight—a ve-ry slight—trust in behalf of this boy; quite a voluntary trust: a matter of mere honour, if not of mere sentiment: still I have taken it upon myself, and it shall be (O, yes, it shall be!) discharged."

The bystanders seemed to form an opinion of this gentleman much more favourable than their opinion of me.

"He shall be taught," said Mr. Hawkyard, "(O, yes, he shall be taught!) but what is to be done with him for the present? He may be infected. He may disseminate infection." The ring widened considerably. "What is to be done with him?"

He held some talk with the two officials. I could distinguish no word save "Farm-house." There was another sound several times repeated, which was wholly meaningless in my ears then, but which I knew afterwards to be "Hoghton Towers."

"Yes," said Mr. Hawkyard. "I think that sounds promising; I think that sounds hopeful. And he can be put by himself in a ward, for a night or two, you say?"

It seemed to be the police-officer who had said so; for it was he who replied, Yes! It was he, too, who finally took me by the arm, and walked me before him through the streets, into a whitewashed room in a bare building, where I had a chair to sit in, a table to sit at, an iron bedstead and good mattress to lie upon, and a rug and blanket to cover me. Where I had enough to eat too, and was shown how to clean the tin porringer in which it was conveyed to me, until it was as good as a looking-glass. Here, likewise, I was put in a bath, and had new clothes brought to me; and my old rags were burnt, and I was camphored and vinegared and disinfected in a variety of ways.

When all this was done,—I don't know in how many days or how few, but it matters not,—Mr. Hawkyard stepped in at the door, remaining close to it, and said, "Go and stand against the opposite wall, George Silverman. As far off as you can. That'll do. How do you feel?"

I told him that I didn't feel cold, and didn't feel hungry, and didn't feel thirsty. That was the whole round of human feelings, as far as I knew, except the pain of being beaten.

"Well," said he, "you are going, George, to a healthy farm-house to be purified. Keep in the air there as much as you can. Live an out-of-door life there, until you are fetched away. You had better not say much—in fact, you had better be very careful not to say anything— about what your parents died of, or they might not like to take you in. Behave well, and I'll put you to school; O, yes! I'll put you to school, though I'm not obliged to do it. I am a servant of the Lord, George; and I have been a good servant to him, I have, these five-and-thirty years. The Lord has had a good servant in me, and he knows it."

What I then supposed him to mean by this, I cannot imagine. As little do I know when I began to comprehend that he was a prominent member of some obscure denomination or congregation, every member of which held forth to the rest when so inclined, and among whom he was called Brother Hawkyard. It was enough for me to know, on that day in the ward, that the farmer's cart was waiting for me at the street corner. I was not slow to get into it; for it was the first ride I ever had in my life.

It made me sleepy, and I slept. First, I stared at Preston streets as long as they lasted; and, meanwhile, I may have had some small dumb wondering within me whereabouts our cellar was; but I doubt it. Such a worldly little devil was I, that I took no thought who would bury father and mother, or where they would be buried, or when. The question whether the eating and drinking by day, and the covering by night, would be as good at the farm-house as at the ward superseded those questions.

The jolting of the cart on a loose stony road awoke me; and I found that we were mounting a steep hill, where the road was a rutty by-road through a field. And so, by fragments of an ancient terrace, and by some rugged outbuildings that had once been fortified, and passing under a ruined gateway we came to the old farm-house in the thick stone wall outside the old quadrangle of Hoghton Towers: which I looked at like a stupid savage, seeing no specialty in, seeing no antiquity in; assuming all farm-houses to resemble it; assigning the decay I noticed to the one potent cause of all ruin that I knew,—poverty; eyeing the pigeons in their flights, the cattle in their stalls, the ducks in the pond, and the fowls pecking about the yard, with a hungry hope that plenty of them might be killed for dinner while I stayed there; wondering whether the scrubbed dairy vessels, drying in the sunlight, could be goodly porringers out of which the master ate his belly-filling food, and which he polished when he had done, according to my ward experience; shrinkingly doubtful whether the shadows, passing over that airy height on the bright spring day, were not something in the nature of frowns,—sordid, afraid, unadmiring,—a small brute to shudder at.

To that time I had never had the faintest impression of duty. I had had no knowledge whatever that there was anything lovely in this life. When I had occasionally slunk up the cellar-steps into the street, and glared in at shop-windows, I had done so with no higher feelings that we may suppose to animate a mangy young dog or wolf-cub. It is equally the fact that I had never been alone, in the sense of holding unselfish converse with myself. I had been solitary often enough, but nothing better.

Such was my condition when I sat down to my dinner that day, in the kitchen of the old farm-house. Such was my condition when I lay on my bed in the old farm-house that night, stretched out opposite the narrow mullioned window, in the cold light of the moon, like a young vampire.

FIFTH CHAPTER

What do I know now of Hoghton Towers? Very little; for I have been gratefully unwilling to disturb my first impressions. A house, centuries old, on high ground a mile or so removed from the road between Preston and Blackburn, where the first James of England, in his hurry to make money by making baronets, perhaps made some of those remunerative dignitaries. A house, centuries old, deserted and falling to pieces, its woods and gardens long since grass-land or ploughed up, the Rivers Ribble and Darwen glancing below it, and a vague haze of smoke, against which not even the supernatural prescience of the first Stuart could foresee a counterblast, hinting at steampower, powerful in two distances.

What did I know then of Hoghton Towers? When I first peeped in at the gate of the lifeless quadrangle, and started from the mouldering statue becoming visible to me like its guardian ghost; when I stole round by the back of the farmhouse, and got in among the ancient rooms, many of them with their floors and ceilings falling, the beams and rafters hanging dangerously down, the plaster dropping as I trod, the oaken panels stripped away, the windows half walled up, half broken; when I discovered a gallery commanding the old kitchen, and looked down between balustrades upon a massive old table and benches, fearing to see I know not what dead-alive creatures come in and seat themselves, and look up with I know not what dreadful eyes, or lack of eyes, at me; when all over the house I was awed by gaps and chinks where the sky stared sorrowfully at me, where the birds passed, and the ivy rustled, and the stains of winter weather blotched the rotten floors; when down at the bottom of dark pits of staircase, into which the stairs had sunk, green leaves trembled, butterflies fluttered, and bees hummed in and out through the broken doorways; when encircling the whole ruin were sweet scents, and sights of fresh green growth, and ever-renewing life, that I had never dreamed of,—I say, when I passed into such clouded perception of these things as my dark soul could compass, what did I know then of Hoghton Towers?

I have written that the sky stared sorrowfully at me. Therein have I anticipated the answer. I knew that all these things looked sorrowfully at me; that they seemed to sigh or whisper, not without pity for me, "Alas! poor worldly little devil!"

There were two or three rats at the bottom of one of the smaller pits of broken staircase when I craned over and looked in. They were scuffling for some prey that was there; and, when they started and hid themselves close together in the dark, I thought of the old life (it had grown old already) in the cellar.

How not to be this worldly little devil? how not to have a repugnance towards myself as I had towards the rats? I hid in a corner of one of the smaller chambers, frightened at myself, and crying (it was the first time I had ever cried for any cause not purely physical), and I tried to think about it. One of the farm-ploughs came into my range of view just then; and it seemed to help me as it went on with its two horses up and down the field so peacefully and quietly.

There was a girl of about my own age in the farm-house family, and she sat opposite to me at the narrow table at meal-times. It had come into my mind, at our first dinner, that she might take the fever from me. The thought had not disquieted me then. I had only speculated how she would look under the altered circumstances, and whether she would die. But it came into my mind now, that I might try to prevent her taking the fever by keeping away from her. I knew I should have but scrambling board if I did; so much the less worldly and less devilish the deed would be, I thought.

From that hour, I withdrew myself at early morning into secret corners of the ruined house, and remained hidden there until she went to bed. At first, when meals were ready, I used to hear them calling me; and then my resolution weakened. But I strengthened it again by going farther off into the ruin, and getting out of hearing. I often watched for her at the dim windows; and, when I saw that she was fresh and rosy, felt much happier.

Out of this holding her in my thoughts, to the humanising of myself, I suppose some childish love arose within me. I felt, in some sort, dignified by the pride of protecting her,—by the pride of making the sacrifice for her. As my heart swelled with that new feeling, it insensibly softened about mother and father. It seemed to have been frozen before, and now to be thawed. The old ruin and all the lovely things that haunted it were not sorrowful for me only, but sorrowful for mother and father as well. Therefore did I cry again, and often too.

The farm-house family conceived me to be of a morose temper, and were very short with me; though they never stinted me in such broken fare as was to be got out of regular hours. One night when I lifted the kitchen latch at my usual time, Sylvia (that was her pretty name) had but just gone out of the room. Seeing her ascending the opposite stairs, I stood still at the door. She had heard the clink of the latch, and looked round.

"George," she called to me in a pleased voice, "to-morrow is my birthday; and we are to have a fiddler, and there's a party of boys and girls coming in a cart, and we shall dance. I invite you. Be sociable for once, George."

"I am very sorry miss," I answered; "but I—but, no; I can't come."

"You are a disagreeable, ill-humoured lad," she returned disdainfully; "and I ought not to have asked you. I shall never speak to you again."

As I stood with my eyes fixed on the fire, after she was gone, I felt that the farmer bent his brows upon me.

"Eh, lad!" said he; "Sylvy's right. You're as moody and broody a lad as never I set eyes on yet."

I tried to assure him that I meant no harm; but he only said coldly, "Maybe not, maybe not! There, get thy supper, get thy supper; and then thou canst sulk to thy heart's content again."

Ah! if they could have seen me next day, in the ruin, watching for the arrival of the cart full of merry young guests; if they could have seen me at night, gliding out from behind the ghostly statue, listening to the music and the fall of dancing feet, and watching the lighted farm-house windows from the quadrangle when all the ruin was dark; if they could have read my heart, as I crept up to bed by the back way, comforting myself with the reflection, "They will take no hurt from me,"—they would not have thought mine a morose or an unsocial nature.

It was in these ways that I began to form a shy disposition; to be of a timidly silent character under misconstruction; to have an inexpressible, perhaps a morbid, dread of every being sordid or worldly. It was in these ways that my nature came to shape itself to such a mould, even before it was affected by the influences of the studious and retired life of a poor scholar.

SIXTH CHAPTER

Brother Hawkyard (as he insisted on my calling him) put me to school, and told me to work my way. "You are all right, George," he said. "I have been the best servant the Lord has had in his service for this five-and-thirty year (O, I have!); and he knows the value of such a servant as I have been to him (O, yes, he does!); and he'll prosper your schooling as a part of my reward. That's what he'll do, George. He'll do it for me."

From the first I could not like this familiar knowledge of the ways of the sublime, inscrutable Almighty, on Brother Hawkyard's part. As I grew a little wiser, and still a little wiser, I liked it less and less. His manner, too, confirming himself in a parenthesis,—as if, knowing himself, he doubted his own word,—I found distasteful. I cannot tell how much these dislikes cost me; for I had a dread that they were worldly.

As time went on, I became a Foundation-boy on a good foundation, and I cost Brother Hawkyard nothing. When I had worked my way so far, I worked yet harder, in the hope of ultimately getting a presentation to college and a fellowship. My health has never been strong (some vapour from the Preston cellar cleaves to me, I think); and what with much work and some weakness, I came again to be regarded—that is, by my fellow-students—as unsocial.

All through my time as a foundation-boy, I was within a few miles of Brother Hawkyard's congregation; and whenever I was what we called a leave-boy on a Sunday, I went over there at his desire. Before the knowledge became forced upon me that outside their place of meeting these brothers and sisters were no better than the rest of the human family, but on the whole were, to put the case mildly, as bad as most, in respect of giving short weight in their shops, and not speaking the truth,—I say, before this knowledge became forced upon me, their prolix addresses, their inordinate conceit, their daring ignorance, their investment of the Supreme Ruler of heaven and earth with their own miserable meannesses and littlenesses, greatly shocked me. Still, as their term for the frame of mind that could not perceive them to be in an exalted state of grace was the "worldly" state, I did for a time suffer tortures under my inquiries of myself whether that young worldly-devilish spirit of mine could secretly be lingering at the bottom of my non-appreciation.

Brother Hawkyard was the popular expounder in this assembly, and generally occupied the platform (there was a little platform with a table on it, in lieu of a pulpit) first, on a Sunday afternoon. He was by trade a drysalter. Brother Gimblet, an elderly man with a crabbed face, a large dog's-eared shirt-collar, and a spotted blue neckerchief reaching up behind to the crown of his head, was also a drysalter and an expounder. Brother Gimblet professed the greatest admiration for Brother Hawkyard but (I had thought more than once) bore him a jealous grudge.

Let whosoever may peruse these lines kindly take the pains here to read twice my solemn pledge, that what I write of the language and customs of the congregation in question I write scrupulously, literally, exactly, from the life and the truth.

On the first Sunday after I had won what I had so long tried for, and when it was certain that I was going up to college, Brother Hawkyard concluded a long exhortation thus:

"Well, my friends and fellow-sinners, now I told you when I began, that I didn't know a word of what I was going to say to you (and no, I did not!), but that it was all one to me, because I knew the Lord would put into my mouth the words I wanted."

("That's it!" from Brother Gimblet.)

"And he did put into my mouth the words I wanted."

("So he did!" from Brother Gimblet.)

"And why?"

("Ah, let's have that!" from Brother Gimblet.)

"Because I have been his faithful servant for five-and-thirty years, and because he knows it. For five-and-thirty years! And he knows it, mind you! I got those words that I wanted on account of my wages. I got 'em from the Lord, my fellow-sinners. Down! I said, 'Here's a heap of wages due; let us have something down, on account.' And I got it down, and I paid it over to you; and you won't wrap it up in a napkin, nor yet in a towel, nor yet pocketankercher, but you'll put it out at good interest. Very well. Now, my brothers and sisters and fellow-sinners, I am going to conclude with a question, and I'll make it so plain (with the help of the Lord, after five-and-thirty years, I should rather hope!) as that the Devil shall not be able to confuse it in your heads,—which he would be overjoyed to do."

("Just his way. Crafty old blackguard!" from Brother Gimblet.)

"And the question is this, Are the angels learned?"

("Not they. Not a bit on it!" from Brother Gimblet, with the greatest confidence.)

"Not they. And where's the proof? sent ready-made by the hand of the Lord. Why, there's one among us here now, that has got all the learning that can be crammed into him. I got him all the learning that could be crammed into him. His grandfather" (this I had never heard before) "was a brother of ours. He was Brother Parksop. That's what he was. Parksop; Brother Parksop. His worldly name was Parksop, and he was a brother of this brotherhood. Then wasn't he Brother Parksop?"

("Must be. Couldn't help hisself!" from Brother Gimblet.)

"Well, he left that one now here present among us to the care of a brother-sinner of his (and that brother-sinner, mind you, was a sinner of a bigger size in his time than any of you; praise the Lord!), Brother Hawkyard. Me. I got him without fee or reward,—without a morsel of myrrh, or frankincense, nor yet amber, letting alone the honeycomb,— all the learning that could be crammed into him. Has it brought him into our temple, in the spirit? No, Have we had any ignorant brothers and sisters that didn't know round O from crooked S, come in among us meanwhile? Many. Then the angels are *not* learned; then they don't so much as know their alphabet. And now, my friends and fellow-sinners, having brought it to that, perhaps some brother present—perhaps you, Brother Gimblet—will pray a bit for us?"

Brother Gimblet undertook the sacred function, after having drawn his sleeve across his mouth, and muttered, "Well! I don't know as I see my way to hitting any of you quite in the right place neither." He said this with a dark smile, and then began to bellow. What we were specially to be preserved from, according to his solicitations, was, despoilment of the orphan, suppression of testamentary intentions on the part of a father or (say) grandfather, appropriation of the orphan's house-property, feigning to give in charity to the wronged one from whom we withheld his due; and that class of sins. He ended with the petition, "Give us peace!" which, speaking for myself, was very much needed after twenty minutes of his bellowing.

Even though I had not seen him when he rose from his knees, steaming with perspiration, glance at Brother Hawkyard, and even though I had not heard Brother Hawkyard's tone of congratulating him on the vigour with which he had roared, I should have detected a malicious application in this prayer. Unformed suspicions to a similar effect had sometimes passed through my mind in my earlier school-days, and had always caused me great distress; for they were worldly in their nature, and wide, very wide, of the spirit that had drawn me from Sylvia. They were sordid suspicions, without a shadow of proof. They were worthy to have originated in the unwholesome cellar. They were not only without proof, but against proof; for was I not myself a living proof of what Brother Hawkyard had done? and without him, how should I ever have seen the sky look sorrowfully down upon that wretched boy at Hoghton Towers?

Although the dread of a relapse into a stage of savage selfishness was less strong upon me as I approached manhood, and could act in an increased degree for myself, yet I was always on my guard against any tendency to such relapse. After getting these suspicions under my feet, I had been troubled by not being able to like Brother Hawkyard's manner, or his professed religion. So it came about, that, as I walked back that Sunday evening, I thought it would be an act of reparation for any such injury my struggling thoughts had unwillingly done him, if I wrote, and placed in his hands, before going to college, a full acknowledgment of his goodness to me, and an ample tribute of thanks. It might serve as an implied vindication of him against any dark scandal from a rival brother and expounder, or from any other quarter.

Accordingly, I wrote the document with much care. I may add with much feeling too; for it affected me as I went on. Having no set studies to pursue, in the brief interval between leaving the Foundation and going to Cambridge, I determined to walk out to his place of business, and give it into his own hands.

It was a winter afternoon, when I tapped at the door of his little counting-house, which was at the farther end of his long, low shop. As I did so (having entered by the back yard, where casks and boxes were taken in, and where there was the inscription, "Private way to the counting-house"), a shopman called to me from the counter that he was engaged.

"Brother Gimblet" (said the shopman, who was one of the brotherhood) "is with him."

I thought this all the better for my purpose, and made bold to tap again. They were talking in a low tone, and money was passing; for I heard it being counted out.

"Who is it?" asked Brother Hawkyard, sharply.

"George Silverman," I answered, holding the door open. "May I come in?"

Both brothers seemed so astounded to see me that I felt shyer than usual. But they looked quite cadaverous in the early gaslight, and perhaps that accidental circumstance exaggerated the expression of their faces.

"What is the matter?" asked Brother Hawkyard.

"Ay! what is the matter?" asked Brother Gimblet.

"Nothing at all," I said, diffidently producing my document: "I am only the bearer of a letter from myself."

"From yourself, George?" cried Brother Hawkyard.

"And to you," said I.

"And to me, George?"

He turned paler, and opened it hurriedly; but looking over it, and seeing generally what it was, became less hurried, recovered his colour, and said, "Praise the Lord!"

"That's it!" cried Brother Gimblet. "Well put! Amen."

Brother Hawkyard then said, in a livelier strain, "You must know, George, that Brother Gimblet and I are going to make our two businesses one. We are going into partnership. We are settling it now. Brother Gimblet is to take one clear half of the profits (O yes! he shall have it; he shall have it to the last farthing)."

"D.V.!" said Brother Gimblet, with his right fist firmly clinched on his right leg.

"There is no objection," pursued Brother Hawkyard, "to my reading this aloud, George?"

As it was what I expressly desired should be done, after yesterday's prayer, I more than readily begged him to read it aloud. He did so; and Brother Gimblet listened with a crabbed smile.

"It was in a good hour that I came here," he said, wrinkling up his eyes. "It was in a good hour, likewise, that I was moved yesterday to depict for the terror of evildoers a character the direct opposite of Brother Hawkyard's. But it was the Lord that done it: I felt him at it while I was perspiring."

After that it was proposed by both of them that I should attend the congregation once more before my final departure. What my shy reserve would undergo, from being expressly preached at and prayed at, I knew beforehand. But I reflected that it would be for the last time, and that it might add to the weight of my letter. It was well known to the brothers and sisters that there was no place taken for me in *their* paradise; and if I showed this last token of deference to Brother Hawkyard, notoriously in despite of my own sinful inclinations, it might go some little way in aid of my statement that he had been good to me, and that I was grateful to him. Merely stipulating, therefore, that no express endeavour should be made for my conversion,— which would involve the rolling of several brothers and sisters on the floor, declaring that they felt all their sins in a heap on their left side, weighing so many pounds avoirdupois, as I knew from what I had seen of those repulsive mysteries,—I promised.

Since the reading of my letter, Brother Gimblet had been at intervals wiping one eye with an end of his spotted blue neckerchief, and grinning to himself. It was, however, a habit that brother had, to grin in an ugly manner even when expounding. I call to mind a delighted snarl with which he used to detail from the platform the torments reserved for the wicked (meaning all human creation except the brotherhood), as being remarkably hideous.

I left the two to settle their articles of partnership, and count money; and I never saw them again but on the following Sunday. Brother

Hawkyard died within two or three years, leaving all he possessed to Brother Gimblet, in virtue of a will dated (as I have been told) that very day.

Now I was so far at rest with myself, when Sunday came, knowing that I had conquered my own mistrust, and righted Brother Hawkyard in the jaundiced vision of a rival, that I went, even to that coarse chapel, in a less sensitive state than usual. How could I foresee that the delicate, perhaps the diseased, corner of my mind, where I winced and shrunk when it was touched, or was even approached, would be handled as the theme of the whole proceedings?

On this occasion it was assigned to Brother Hawkyard to pray, and to Brother Gimblet to preach. The prayer was to open the ceremonies; the discourse was to come next. Brothers Hawkyard and Gimblet were both on the platform; Brother Hawkyard on his knees at the table, unmusically ready to pray; Brother Gimblet sitting against the wall, grinningly ready to preach.

"Let us offer up the sacrifice of prayer, my brothers and sisters and fellow-sinners." Yes; but it was I who was the sacrifice. It was our poor, sinful, worldly-minded brother here present who was wrestled for. The now-opening career of this our unawakened brother might lead to his becoming a minister of what was called "the church." That was what *he* looked to. The church. Not the chapel, Lord. The church. No rectors, no vicars, no archdeacons, no bishops, no archbishops, in the chapel, but, O Lord! many such in the church. Protect our sinful brother from his love of lucre. Cleanse from our unawakened brother's breast his sin of worldly-mindedness. The prayer said infinitely more in words, but nothing more to any intelligible effect.

Then Brother Gimblet came forward, and took (as I knew he would) the text, "My kingdom is not of this world." Ah! but whose was, my fellow-sinners? Whose? Why, our brother's here present was. The only kingdom he had an idea of was of this world. ("That's it!" from several of the congregation.) What did the woman do when she lost the piece of money? Went and looked for it. What should our brother do when he lost his way? ("Go and look for it," from a sister.) Go and look for it, true. But must he look for it in the right direction, or in the wrong? ("In the right," from a brother.) There spake the prophets! He must look for it in the right direction, or he couldn't find it. But he had turned his back upon the right direction, and he wouldn't find it. Now, my fellow-sinners, to show you the difference betwixt worldly-mindedness and unworldly-mindedness, betwixt kingdoms not of this world and kingdoms *of* this world, here was a letter wrote by even our worldly-minded brother unto Brother Hawkyard. Judge, from hearing of it read, whether Brother Hawkyard was the faithful steward that the Lord had in his mind only t'other day, when, in this very place, he drew you the picter of the unfaithful one; for it was him that done it, not me. Don't doubt that!

Brother Gimblet then groaned and bellowed his way through my composition, and subsequently through an hour. The service closed with a hymn, in which the brothers unanimously roared, and the sisters unanimously shrieked at me, That I by wiles of worldly gain was mocked, and they on waters of sweet love were rocked; that I with mammon struggled in the dark, while they were floating in a second ark.

I went out from all this with an aching heart and a weary spirit: not because I was quite so weak as to consider these narrow creatures interpreters of the Divine Majesty and Wisdom, but because I was weak enough to feel as though it were my hard fortune to be misrepresented and misunderstood, when I most tried to subdue any risings of mere worldliness within me, and when I most hoped that, by dint of trying earnestly, I had succeeded.

SEVENTH CHAPTER

My timidity and my obscurity occasioned me to live a secluded life at college, and to be little known. No relative ever came to visit me, for I had no relative. No intimate friends broke in upon my studies, for I made no intimate friends. I supported myself on my scholarship, and read much. My college time was otherwise not so very different from my time at Hoghton Towers.

Knowing myself to be unfit for the noisier stir of social existence, but believing myself qualified to do my duty in a moderate, though earnest way, if I could obtain some small preferment in the Church, I applied my mind to the clerical profession. In due sequence I took orders, was ordained, and began to look about me for employment. I must observe that I had taken a good degree, that I had succeeded in winning a good fellowship, and that my means were ample for my retired way of life. By this time I had read with several young men; and the occupation increased my income, while it was highly interesting to me. I once accidentally overheard our greatest don say, to my boundless joy, "That he heard it reported of Silverman that his gift of quiet explanation, his patience, his amiable temper, and his conscientiousness made him the best of coaches." May my "gift of quiet explanation" come more seasonably and powerfully to my aid in this present explanation than I think it will!

It may be in a certain degree owing to the situation of my collegerooms (in a corner where the daylight was sobered), but it is in a much larger degree referable to the state of my own mind, that I seem to myself, on looking back to this time of my life, to have been always in the peaceful shade. I can see others in the sunlight; I can see our boats' crews and our athletic young men on the glistening water, or speckled with the moving lights of sunlit leaves; but I myself am always in the shadow looking on. Not unsympathetically, —God forbid!—but looking on alone, much as I looked at Sylvia from the shadows of the ruined house, or looked at the red gleam shining through the farmer's windows, and listened to the fall of dancing feet, when all the ruin was dark that night in the quadrangle.

I now come to the reason of my quoting that laudation of myself above given. Without such reason, to repeat it would have been mere boastfulness.

Among those who had read with me was Mr. Fareway, second son of Lady Fareway, widow of Sir Gaston Fareway, baronet. This young gentleman's abilities were much above the average; but he came of a rich family, and was idle and luxurious. He presented himself to me too late, and afterwards came to me too irregularly, to admit of my being of much service to him. In the end, I considered it my duty to dissuade him from going up for an examination which he could never pass; and he left college without a degree. After his departure, Lady Fareway wrote to me, representing the justice of my returning half my fee, as I had been of so little use to her son. Within my knowledge a similar demand had not been made in any other case; and I most freely admit that the justice of it had not occurred to me until it was pointed out. But I at once perceived it, yielded to it, and returned the money.

Mr. Fareway had been gone two years or more, and I had forgotten him, when he one day walked into my rooms as I was sitting at my books.

Said he, after the usual salutations had passed, "Mr. Silverman, my mother is in town here, at the hotel, and wishes me to present you to her."

I was not comfortable with strangers, and I dare say I betrayed that I was a little nervous or unwilling. "For," said he, without my having spoken, "I think the interview may tend to the advancement of your prospects."

It put me to the blush to think that I should be tempted by a worldly reason, and I rose immediately.

Said Mr. Fareway, as we went along, "Are you a good hand at business?"

"I think not," said I.

Said Mr. Fareway then, "My mother is."

"Truly?" said I.

"Yes: my mother is what is usually called a managing woman. Doesn't make a bad thing, for instance, even out of the spendthrift habits of my eldest brother abroad. In short, a managing woman. This is in confidence."

He had never spoken to me in confidence, and I was surprised by his doing so. I said I should respect his confidence, of course, and said no more on the delicate subject. We had but a little way to walk, and I was soon in his mother's company. He presented me, shook hands with me, and left us two (as he said) to business.

I saw in my Lady Fareway a handsome, well-preserved lady of somewhat large stature, with a steady glare in her great round dark eyes that embarrassed me.

Said my lady, "I have heard from my son, Mr. Silverman, that you would be glad of some preferment in the church."

I gave my lady to understand that was so.

"I don't know whether you are aware," my lady proceeded, "that we have a presentation to a living? I say *we* have; but, in point of fact, I have."

I gave my lady to understand that I had not been aware of this.

Said my lady, "So it is: indeed I have two presentations,—one to two hundred a year, one to six. Both livings are in our county,— North Devonshire,—as you probably know. The first is vacant. Would you like it?"

What with my lady's eyes, and what with the suddenness of this proposed gift, I was much confused.

"I am sorry it is not the larger presentation," said my lady, rather coldly; "though I will not, Mr. Silverman, pay you the bad compliment of supposing that *you* are, because that would be mercenary,—and mercenary I am persuaded you are not."

Said I, with my utmost earnestness, "Thank you, Lady Fareway, thank you, thank you! I should be deeply hurt if I thought I bore the character."

"Naturally," said my lady. "Always detestable, but particularly in a clergyman. You have not said whether you will like the living?"

With apologies for my remissness or indistinctness, I assured my lady that I accepted it most readily and gratefully. I added that I hoped she would not estimate my appreciation of the generosity of her choice by any flow of words; for I was not a ready man in that respect when taken by surprise or touched at heart.

"The affair is concluded," said my lady; "concluded. You will find the duties very light, Mr. Silverman. Charming house; charming little garden, orchard, and all that. You will be able to take pupils. By-the-bye! No: I will return to the word afterwards. What was I going to mention, when it put me out?"

My lady stared at me, as if I knew. And I didn't know. And that perplexed me afresh.

Said my lady, after some consideration, "O, of course, how very dull of me! The last incumbent,—least mercenary man I ever saw,—in consideration of the duties being so light and the house so delicious, couldn't rest, he said, unless I permitted him to help me with my correspondence, accounts, and various little things of that kind; nothing in themselves, but which it worries a lady to cope with. Would Mr. Silverman also like to——? Or shall I——?"

I hastened to say that my poor help would be always at her ladyship's service.

"I am absolutely blessed," said my lady, casting up her eyes (and so taking them off me for one moment), "in having to do with gentlemen who cannot endure an approach to the idea of being mercenary!" She shivered at the word. "And now as to the pupil."

"The——?" I was quite at a loss.

"Mr. Silverman, you have no idea what she is. She is," said my lady, laying her touch upon my coat-sleeve, "I do verily believe, the most extraordinary girl in this world. Already knows more Greek and Latin than Lady Jane Grey. And taught herself! Has not yet, remember, derived a moment's advantage from Mr. Silverman's classical acquirements. To say nothing of mathematics, which she is bent upon becoming versed in, and in which (as I hear from my son and others) Mr. Silverman's reputation is so deservedly high!"

Under my lady's eyes I must have lost the clue, I felt persuaded; and yet I did not know where I could have dropped it.

"Adelina," said my lady, "is my only daughter. If I did not feel quite convinced that I am not blinded by a mother's partiality; unless I was absolutely sure that when you know her, Mr. Silverman, you will esteem it a high and unusual privilege to direct her studies,—I should introduce a mercenary element into this conversation, and ask you on what terms——"

I entreated my lady to go no further. My lady saw that I was troubled, and did me the honour to comply with my request.

EIGHTH CHAPTER

Everything in mental acquisition that her brother might have been, if he would, and everything in all gracious charms and admirable qualities that no one but herself could be,—this was Adelina.

I will not expatiate upon her beauty; I will not expatiate upon her intelligence, her quickness of perception, her powers of memory, her sweet consideration, from the first moment, for the slow-paced tutor who ministered to her wonderful gifts. I was thirty then; I am over sixty now: she is ever present to me in these hours as she was in those, bright and beautiful and young, wise and fanciful and good.

When I discovered that I loved her, how can I say? In the first day? in the first week? in the first month? Impossible to trace. If I be (as I am) unable to represent to myself any previous period of my life as quite separable from her attracting power, how can I answer for this one detail?

Whensoever I made the discovery, it laid a heavy burden on me. And yet, comparing it with the far heavier burden that I afterwards took up, it does not seem to me now to have been very hard to bear. In the knowledge that I did love her, and that I should love her while my life lasted, and that I was ever to hide my secret deep in my own breast, and she was never to find it, there was a kind of sustaining joy or pride, or comfort, mingled with my pain.

But later on,—say, a year later on,—when I made another discovery, then indeed my suffering and my struggle were strong. That other discovery was—

These words will never see the light, if ever, until my heart is dust; until her bright spirit has returned to the regions of which, when imprisoned here, it surely retained some unusual glimpse of remembrance; until all the pulses that ever beat around us shall have long been quiet; until all the fruits of all the tiny victories and defeats achieved in our little breasts shall have withered away. That discovery was that she loved me.

She may have enhanced my knowledge, and loved me for that; she may have over-valued my discharge of duty to her, and loved me for that; she may have refined upon a playful compassion which she would sometimes show for what she called my want of wisdom, according to the light of the world's dark lanterns, and loved me for that; she may—she must—have confused the borrowed light of what I had only learned, with its brightness in its pure, original rays; but she loved me at that time, and she made me know it.

Pride of family and pride of wealth put me as far off from her in my lady's eyes as if I had been some domesticated creature of another kind. But they could not put me farther from her than I put myself when I set my merits against hers. More than that. They could not put me, by millions of fathoms, half so low beneath her as I put myself when in imagination I took advantage of her noble trustfulness, took the fortune that I knew she must possess in her own right, and left her to find herself, in the zenith of her beauty and genius, bound to poor rusty, plodding me.

No! Worldliness should not enter here at any cost. If I had tried to keep it out of other ground, how much harder was I bound to try to keep it out from this sacred place!

But there was something daring in her broad, generous character, that demanded at so delicate a crisis to be delicately and patiently addressed. After many and many a bitter night (O, I found I could cry for reasons not purely physical, at this pass of my life!) I took my course.

My lady had, in our first interview, unconsciously overstated the accommodation of my pretty house. There was room in it for only one pupil. He was a young gentleman near coming of age, very well connected, but what is called a poor relation. His parents were dead. The charges of his living and reading with me were defrayed by an uncle; and he and I were to do our utmost together for three years towards qualifying him to make his way. At this time he had entered into his second year with me. He was well-looking, clever, energetic, enthusiastic, bold; in the best sense of the term, a thorough young Anglo-Saxon.

I resolved to bring these two together.

NINTH CHAPTER

Said I, one night, when I had conquered myself, "Mr. Granville,"— Mr. Granville Wharton his name was,—"I doubt if you have ever yet so much as seen Miss Fareway."

"Well, Sir," returned he, laughing, "you see her so much yourself, that you hardly leave another fellow a chance of seeing her."

"I am her tutor, you know," said I.

And there the subject dropped for that time. But I so contrived as that they should come together shortly afterwards. I had previously so contrived as to keep them asunder; for while I loved her,—I mean before I had determined on my sacrifice,—a lurking jealousy of Mr. Granville lay within my unworthy breast.

It was quite an ordinary interview in the Fareway Park; but they talked easily together for some time: like takes to like, and they had many points of resemblance. Said Mr. Granville to me, when he and I sat at our supper that night, "Miss Fareway is remarkably beautiful, Sir, remarkably engaging. Don't you think so?" "I think so," said I. And I stole a glance at him, and saw that he had reddened and was thoughtful. I remember it most vividly, because the mixed feeling of grave pleasure and acute pain that the slight circumstance caused me was the first of a long, long series of such mixed impressions under which my hair turned slowly grey.

I had not much need to feign to be subdued; but I counterfeited to be older than I was in all respects (Heaven knows! my heart being all too young the while), and feigned to be more of a recluse and bookworm than I had really become, and gradually set up more and more of a fatherly manner towards Adelina. Likewise I made my tuition less imaginative than before; separated myself from my poets and philosophers; was careful to present them in their own light, and me, their lowly servant, in my own shade. Moreover, in the matter of apparel I was equally mindful; not that I had ever been dapper that way; but that I was slovenly now.

As I depressed myself with one hand, so did I labour to raise Mr. Granville with the other; directing his attention to such subjects as I too well knew most interested her, and fashioning him (do not deride or misconstrue the expression, unknown reader of this writing; for I have suffered!) into a greater resemblance to myself in my solitary one strong aspect. And gradually, gradually, as I saw him take more and more to these thrown-out lures of mine, then did I come to know better and better that love was drawing him on, and was drawing her from me.

So passed more than another year; every day a year in its number of my mixed impressions of grave pleasure and acute pain; and then these two, being of age and free to act legally for themselves, came before me hand in hand (my hair being now quite white), and entreated me that I would unite them together. "And indeed, dear tutor," said Adelina, "it is but consistent in you that you should do this thing for us, seeing that we should never have spoken together that first time but for you, and that but for you we could never have met so often afterwards." The whole of which was literally true; for I had availed myself of my many business attendances on, and conferences with, my lady, to take Mr. Granville to the house, and leave him in the outer room with Adelina.

I knew that my lady would object to such a marriage for her daughter, or to any marriage that was other than an exchange of her for stipulated lands, goods, and moneys. But looking on the two, and seeing with full eyes that they were both young and beautiful; and knowing that they were alike in the tastes and acquirements that will outlive youth and beauty; and considering that Adelina had a fortune now, in her own keeping; and considering further that Mr. Granville, though for the present poor, was of a good family that had never lived in a cellar in Preston; and believing that their love would endure, neither having any great discrepancy to find out in the other,—I told them of my readiness to do this thing which Adelina asked of her dear tutor, and to send them forth, husband and wife, into the shining world with golden gates that awaited them.

It was on a summer morning that I rose before the sun to compose myself for the crowning of my work with this end; and my dwelling being near to the sea, I walked down to the rocks on the shore, in order that I might behold the sun in his majesty.

The tranquillity upon the deep, and on the firmament, the orderly withdrawal of the stars, the calm promise of coming day, the rosy suffusion of the sky and waters, the ineffable splendour that then burst forth, attuned my mind afresh after the discords of the night. Methought that all I looked on said to me, and that all I heard in the sea and in the air said to me, "Be comforted, mortal, that thy life is so short. Our preparation for what is to follow has endured, and shall endure, for unimaginable ages."

I married them. I knew that my hand was cold when I placed it on their hands clasped together; but the words with which I had to accompany the action I could say without faltering, and I was at peace.

They being well away from my house and from the place after our simple breakfast, the time was come when I must do what I had pledged myself to them that I would do,—break the intelligence to my lady.

I went up to the house, and found my lady in her ordinary business-room. She happened to have an unusual amount of commissions to intrust to me that day; and she had filled my hands with papers before I could originate a word.

"My lady," I then began, as I stood beside her table.

"Why, what's the matter?" she said quickly, looking up.

"Not much, I would fain hope, after you shall have prepared yourself, and considered a little."

"Prepared myself; and considered a little! You appear to have prepared yourself but indifferently, anyhow, Mr. Silverman." This mighty scornfully, as I experienced my usual embarrassment under her stare.

Said I, in self-extenuation once for all, "Lady Fareway, I have but to say for myself that I have tried to do my duty."

"For yourself?" repeated my lady. "Then there are others concerned, I see. Who are they?"

I was about to answer, when she made towards the bell with a dart that stopped me, and said, "Why, where is Adelina?"

"Forbear! be calm, my lady. I married her this morning to Mr. Granville Wharton."

She set her lips, looked more intently at me than ever, raised her right hand, and smote me hard upon the cheek.

"Give me back those papers! give me back those papers!" She tore them out of my hands, and tossed them on her table. Then seating herself defiantly in her great chair, and folding her arms, she stabbed me to the heart with the unlooked-for reproach, "You worldly wretch!"

"Worldly?" I cried. "Worldly?"

"This, if you please,"—she went on with supreme scorn, pointing me out as if there were some one there to see,—"this, if you please, is the disinterested scholar, with not a design beyond his books! This, if you please, is the simple creature whom any one could overreach in a bargain! This, if you please, is Mr. Silverman! Not of this world; not he! He has too much simplicity for this world's cunning. He has too much singleness of purpose to be a match for this world's double-dealing. What did he give you for it?"

"For what? And who?"

"How much," she asked, bending forward in her great chair, and insultingly tapping the fingers of her right hand on the palm of her left,—"how much does Mr. Granville Wharton pay you for getting him Adelina's money? What is the amount of your percentage upon Adelina's fortune? What were the terms of the agreement that you proposed to this boy when you, the Rev. George Silverman, licensed to marry, engaged to put him in possession of this girl? You made good terms for yourself, whatever they were. He would stand a poor chance against your keenness."

Bewildered, horrified, stunned by this cruel perversion, I could not speak. But I trust that I looked innocent, being so.

"Listen to me, shrewd hypocrite," said my lady, whose anger increased as she gave it utterance; "attend to my words, you cunning schemer, who have carried this plot through with such a practised double face that I have never suspected you. I had my projects for my daughter; projects for family connexion; projects for fortune. You have thwarted and overreached me; but I am not one to be thwarted and overreached without retaliation. Do you mean to hold this living another month?"

"Do you deem it possible, Lady Fareway, that I can hold it another hour, under your injurious words?"

"Is it resigned, then?"

"It was mentally resigned, my lady, some minutes ago."

"Don't equivocate, Sir. Is it resigned?"

"Unconditionally and entirely; and I would that I had never, never come near it?"

"A cordial response from me to *that* wish, Mr. Silverman! But take this with you, Sir. If you had not resigned it, I would have had you deprived of it. And though you have resigned it, you will not get quit of me as easily as you think for. I will pursue you with this story. I will make this nefarious conspiracy of yours, for money, known. You have made money by it, but you have at the same time made an enemy by it. You will take good care that the money sticks to you; I will take good care that the enemy sticks to you."

Then said I finally, "Lady Fareway, I think my heart is broken. Until I came into this room just now, the possibility of such mean wickedness as you have imputed to me never dawned upon my thoughts. Your suspicions——"

"Suspicions! Pah!" said she indignantly. "Certainties."

"Your certainties, my lady, as you call them, your suspicions as I call them, are cruel, unjust, wholly devoid of foundation in fact. I can declare no more; except that I have not acted for my own profit or my own pleasure. I have not in this proceeding considered myself. Once again, I think my heart is broken. If I have unwittingly done any wrong with a righteous motive, that is some penalty to pay."

She received this with another and more indignant "Pah!" and I made my way out of her room (I think I felt my way out with my hands, although my eyes were open), almost suspecting that my voice had a repulsive sound, and that I was a repulsive object.

There was a great stir made, the bishop was appealed to, I received a severe reprimand, and narrowly escaped suspension. For years a cloud hung over me, and my name was tarnished. But my heart did not break, if a broken heart involves death; for I lived through it.

They stood by me, Adelina and her husband, through it all. Those who had known me at college, and even most of those who had only known me there by reputation, stood by me too. Little by little, the belief widened that I was not capable of what was laid to my charge. At length I was presented to a college-living in a sequestered place, and there I now pen my explanation. I pen it at my open window in the summer-time, before me, lying in the churchyard, equal resting-place for sound hearts, wounded hearts, and broken hearts. I pen it for the relief of my own mind, not foreseeing whether or no it will ever have a reader.

The Detective Police

~~~~~~

We are not by any means devout believers in the old Bow Street Police. To say the truth, we think there was a vast amount of humbug about those worthies. Apart from many of them being men of very indifferent character, and far too much in the habit of consorting with thieves and the like, they never lost a public occasion of jobbing and trading in mystery and making the most of themselves. Continually puffed besides by incompetent magistrates anxious to conceal their own deficiencies, and hand-in-glove with the penny-a-liners of that time, they became a sort of superstition. Although as a Preventive Police were utterly ineffective, and as a Detective Police were very loose and uncertain in their operations, they remain with some people a superstition to the present day.

On the other hand, the Detective Force organised since the

establishment of the existing Police, is so well chosen and trained, proceeds so systematically and quietly, does its business in such a workmanlike manner, and is always so calmly and steadily engaged in the service of the public, that the public really do not know enough of it, to know a tithe of its usefulness. Impressed with this conviction, and interested in the men themselves, we represented to the authorities at Scotland Yard, that we should be glad, if there were no official objection, to have some talk with the Detectives. A most obliging and ready permission being given, a certain evening was appointed with a certain Inspector for a social conference between ourselves and the Detectives, at The Household Words Office in Wellington Street, Strand, London. In consequence of which appointment the party "came off," which we are about to describe. And we beg to repeat that, avoiding such topics as it might for obvious reasons be injurious to the public, or disagreeable to respectable individuals, to touch upon in print, our description is as exact as we can make it.

The reader will have the goodness to imagine the Sanctum Sanctorum of Household Words. Anything that best suits the reader's fancy, will best represent that magnificent chamber. We merely stipulate for a round table in the middle, with some glasses and cigars arranged upon it; and the editorial sofa elegantly hemmed in between that stately piece of furniture and the wall.

It is a sultry evening at dusk. The stones of Wellington Street are hot and gritty, and the watermen and hackney-coachmen at the Theatre opposite, are much flushed and aggravated. Carriages are constantly setting down the people who have come to Fairy-Land; and there is a mighty shouting and bellowing every now and then, deafening us for the moment, through the open windows.

Just at dusk, Inspectors Wield and Stalker are announced; but we do not undertake to warrant the orthography of any of the names here mentioned. Inspector Wield presents Inspector Stalker. Inspector Wield is a middle-aged man of a portly presence, with a large, moist, knowing eye, a husky voice, and a habit of emphasising his conversation by the aid of a corpulent fore-finger, which is constantly in juxtaposition with his eyes or nose. Inspector Stalker is a shrewd hard-headed Scotchman—in appearance not at all unlike a very acute, thoroughly-trained schoolmaster, from the Normal Establishment at Glasgow. Inspector Wield one might have known, perhaps, for what he is—Inspector Stalker, never.

The ceremonies of reception over, Inspectors Wield and Stalker observe that they have brought some sergeants with them. The sergeants are presented—five in number, Sergeant Dornton, Sergeant Witchem, Sergeant Mith, Sergeant Fendall, and Sergeant Straw. We have the whole Detective Force from Scotland Yard, with one exception. They sit down in a semi-circle (the two Inspectors at the two ends) at a little distance from the round table, facing the editorial sofa. Every man of them, in a glance, immediately takes an inventory of the furniture and an accurate sketch of the editorial presence. The Editor feels that any gentleman in company could take him up, if need should be, without the smallest hesitation, twenty years hence.

The whole party are in plain clothes. Sergeant Dornton about fifty years of age, with a ruddy face and a high sunburnt forehead, has the air of one who has been a Sergeant in the army—he might have sat to Wilkie for the Soldier in the Reading of the Will. He is famous for steadily pursuing the inductive process, and, from small beginnings, working on from clue to clue until he bags his man. Sergeant Witchem, shorter and thicker-set, and marked with the small-pox, has something of a reserved and thoughtful air, as if he were engaged in deep arithmetical calculations. He is renowned for his acquaintance with the swell mob. Sergeant Mith, a smooth-faced man with a fresh bright complexion, and a strange air of simplicity, is a dab at house-breakers. Sergeant Fendall, a light-haired, well-spoken, polite person, is a prodigious hand at pursuing private inquiries of a delicate nature. Straw, a little wiry Sergeant of meek demeanour and strong sense, would knock at a door and ask a series of questions in any mild character you choose to prescribe to him, from a charity-boy upwards, and seem as innocent as an infant. They are, one and all, respectable-looking men; of perfectly good deportment and unusual intelligence; with nothing lounging or slinking in their manners; with an air of keen observation and quick perception when addressed; and generally presenting in their faces, traces more or less marked of habitually leading lives of strong mental excitement. They have all good eyes; and they all can, and they all do, look full at whomsoever they speak to.

We light the cigars, and hand round the glasses (which are very temperately used indeed), and the conversation begins by a modest amateur reference on the Editorial part to the swell mob. Inspector Wield immediately removes his cigar from his lips, waves his right hand, and says, "Regarding the swell mob, sir, I can't do better than call upon Sergeant Witchem. Because the reason why? I'll tell you. Sergeant Witchem is better acquainted with the swell mob than any officer in London."

Our heart leaping up when we beheld this rainbow in the sky, we turn to Sergeant Witchem, who very concisely, and in well-chosen language, goes into the subject forthwith. Meantime, the whole of his brother officers are closely interested in attending to what he says, and observing its effect. Presently they begin to strike in, one or two together, when an opportunity offers, and the conversation becomes general. But these brother officers only come in to the assistance of each other—not to the contradiction—and a more amicable brotherhood there could not be. From the swell mob, we diverge to the kindred topics of cracksmen, fences, public-house dancers, area-sneaks, designing young people who go out "gonophing," and other "schools." It is observable throughout these revelations, that Inspector Stalker, the Scotchman, is always exact and statistical, and that when any question of figures arises, everybody as by one consent pauses, and looks to him.

When we have exhausted the various schools of Art—during which discussion the whole body have remained profoundly attentive, except when some unusual noise at the Theatre over the way has induced some gentleman to glance inquiringly towards the window in that direction, behind his next neighbour's back—we burrow for information on such points as the following. Whether there really are any highway robberies in London, or whether some circumstances not convenient to be mentioned by the aggrieved party, usually precede the robberies complained of, under that head, which quite change their character? Certainly the latter, almost always. Whether in the case of robberies in houses, where servants are necessarily exposed to doubt, innocence under suspicion ever becomes so like guilt in appearance, that a good officer need be cautious how he judges it? Undoubtedly. Nothing is so common or deceptive as such appearances at first. Whether in a place of public amusement, a thief knows an officer, and officer knows a thief—supposing them, before-hand, strangers to each other—because each recognises in the other, under all disguise, an inattention to what is going on, and a purpose that is not the purpose of being entertained? Yes. That's the way exactly. Whether it is reasonable or ridiculous to trust to the alleged experiences of thieves as narrated by themselves, in prisons, or penitentiaries, or anywhere? In general, nothing more absurd. Lying is their habit and their trade; and they would rather lie—even if they hadn't an interest in it, and didn't want to make themselves agreeable—than tell the truth.

From these topics, we glide into a review of the most celebrated and horrible of the great crimes that have been committed within the last fifteen or twenty years. The men engaged in the discovery of almost all of them, and in the pursuit or apprehension of the murderers, are here, down to the very last instance. One of our guests gave chase to and boarded the emigrant ship, in which the murderess last hanged in London was supposed to have embarked. We learn from him that his errand was not announced to the passengers, who may have no idea of it to this hour. That he went below, with the captain, lamp in hand—it being dark, and the whole steerage abed and sea-sick—and engaged the Mrs. Manning who *was* on board, in a conversation about her luggage, until she was, with no small pains, induced to raise her head, and turn her face towards the light. Satisfied that she was not the object of his search, he quietly re-embarked in the Government steamer alongside, and steamed home again with the intelligence.

When we have exhausted these subjects, too, which occupy a considerable time in the discussion, two or three leave their chairs, whisper Sergeant Witchem, and resume their seats. Sergeant Witchem leaning forward a little, and placing a hand on each of his legs, then modestly speaks as follows:

"My brother-officers wish me to relate a little account of my taking Tally-ho Thompson. A man oughtn't to tell what he has done himself; but still, as nobody was with me, and consequently, as nobody but myself can tell it, I'll do it in the best way I can, if it should meet your approval."

We assure Sergeant Witchem that he will oblige us very much, and we all compose ourselves to listen with great interest and attention.

"Tally-ho Thompson," says Sergeant Witchem, after merely wetting his lips with his brandy-and-water, "Tally-ho Thompson was a famous horse-stealer, couper, and magsman. Thompson, in conjunction with a pal that occasionally worked with him, gammoned a countryman out of a good round sum of money, under pretence of getting him a situation—the regular old dodge—and was afterwards in the 'Hue and Cry' for a horse—a horse that he stole, down in Hertfordshire. I had to look after Thompson, and I applied myself, of course, in the first instance, to discovering where he was. Now, Thompson's wife lived, along with a little daughter, at Chelsea. Knowing that Thompson was somewhere in the country, I watched the house—especially at post-time in the morning—thinking Thompson was pretty likely to write to her. Sure enough, one morning the postman comes up, and delivers a letter at Mrs. Thompson's door. Little girl opens the door, and takes it in. We're not always sure of postmen, though the people at the post-offices are always very obliging. A postman may help us, or he may not—just as it happens. However, I go across the road, and I say to the postman, after he has left the letter, 'Good morning! how are you?' 'How are *you*?' says he. 'You've just delivered a letter for Mrs. Thompson.' 'Yes, I have.' 'You didn't happen to remark what the post-mark was, perhaps?' 'No,' says he, 'I didn't.' 'Come,' says I, 'I'll be plain with you. I'm in a small way of business, and I have given Thompson credit, and I can't afford to lose what he owes me. I know he's got money, and I know he's in the country, and if you could tell me what the postmark was, I should be very much obliged to you, and you'd do a service to a tradesman in a small way of business that can't afford a loss.' 'Well,' he said, 'I do assure you that I did not observe what the post-mark was; all I know is that there was money in the letter,—I should say a sovereign.'

This was enough for me, because of course I knew that Thompson having sent his wife money, it was probable she'd write to Thompson, by return of post, to acknowledge the receipt. So I said 'Thankee' to the postman, and I kept on the watch. In the afternoon I saw the little girl come out. Of course I followed her. She went into a stationer's shop, and I needn't say to you that I looked in at the window. She bought some writing-paper and envelopes, and a pen. I think to myself, 'That'll do!'—watch her home again—and don't go away, you may be sure, knowing that Mrs. Thompson was writing her letter to Tally-ho, and that the letter would be posted presently. In about an hour or so, out came the little girl again, with the letter in her hand. I went up, and said something to the child, whatever it might have been; but I couldn't see the direction of the letter, because she held it with the seal upwards. However, I observed that on the back of the letter there was what we call a kiss—a drop of wax by the side of the seal—and again, you understand, that was enough for me. I saw her post the letter, waited till she was gone, then went into the shop, and asked to see the Master. When he came out, I told him, 'Now, I'm an Officer in the Detective Force; there's a letter with a kiss been posted here just now, for a man that I'm in search of; and what I have to ask of you, is, that you will let me look at the direction of that letter.' He was very civil—took a lot of letters from the box in the window—shook 'em out on the counter with faces downwards— and there among 'm was the identical letter with the kiss. It was directed, Mr. Thomas Pigeon, Post Office, B——, to be left 'till called for. Down I went to B—— (a hundred and twenty miles or so) that night. Early next morning I went to the Post Office; saw the gentle- man in charge of that department; told him who I was; and that my object was to see, and track, the party that should come for the letter of Mr. Thomas Pigeon. He was very polite, and said, 'You shall have every assistance we can give you; you can wait inside the office; and we'll take care to let you know when anybody come for the letter.' Well, I waited there three days, and begin to think that nobody ever *would* come. At last the clerk whispered to me, 'Here! Detective! Somebody's come for the letter!' 'Keep him a minute,' said I, and I ran round to the outside of the office. There I saw a young chap with the appearance of an Ostler, holding a horse by the bridle—stretching the bridle across the pavement, while he waited at the Post Office window for the letter. I began to pat the horse, and that; and I said to the boy, 'Why, this is Mr. Jones's Mare!' 'No. It ain't.' 'No?' said I. 'She's very like Mr. Jones's Mare!' 'She an't Mr. Jones's Mare, any- how,' says he. 'It's Mr. So and So's, of the Warwick Arms.' And up he jumped, and off he went—letter and all. I got a cab, followed on the box, and was so quick after him that I came into the stable- yard of the Warwick Arms, by one gate, just as he came in by another.

I went into the bar, where there was a young woman serving, and called for a glass of brandy-and-water. He came in directly, and handed her the letter. She casually looked at it, without saying anything, and stuck it up behind the glass over the chimney-piece. What was to be done next?

"I turned it over in my mind while I drank my brandy-and-water (looking pretty sharp at the letter the while), but I couldn't see my way out of it at all. I tried to get lodgings in the house, but there had been a horse-fair, or something of that sort, and it was full. I was obliged to put up somewhere else, but I came backwards and forwards to the bar for a couple of days, and there was the letter always behind the glass. At last I thought I'd write a letter to Mr. Pigeon myself, and see what that would do. So I wrote one, and posted it, but I purposely addressed it, Mr. John Pigeon, instead of Mr. Thomas Pigeon, to see what *that* would do. In the morning (a very wet morning it was) I watched the postman down the street, and cut into the bar, just before he reached the Warwick Arms. In he came presently with my letter. 'Is there a Mr. John Pigeon staying here?' 'No!—stop a bit though,' says the barmaid; and she took down the letter behind the glass. 'No,' says she, 'it's Thomas, and *he* is not staying here. Would you do me a favour, and post this for me, as it is so wet?' The postman said Yes; she folded it in another envelope, directed it, and gave it him. He put it in his hat, and away he went.

"I had no difficulty in finding out the direction of that letter. It was addressed Mr. Thomas Pigeon, Post Office, R——, Northampton-shire, to be left till called for. Off I started directly for R——; I said the same at the Post Office there, as I had said at B——; and again I waited three days before anybody came. At last another chap on horse-back came. 'Any letters for Mr. Thomas Pigeon?' 'Where do you come from?' 'New Inn, near R——.' He got the letter, and away *he* went at a canter.

"I made my inquiries about the New Inn, near R——, and hearing it was a solitary sort of house, a little in the horse line, about a couple of miles from the station, I thought I'd go and have a look at it. I found it what it had been described, and sauntered in, to look about me. The landlady was in the bar, and I was trying to get into conversation with her; asked her how business was, and spoke about the wet weather, and so on; when I saw, through an open door, three men sitting by the fire in a sort of parlour, or kitchen; and one of those men, according to the description I had of him, was Tally-ho Thompson!

"I went and sat down among 'em, and tried to make things agreeable; but they were very shy—wouldn't talk at all—looked at me, and at one another, in a way quite the reverse of sociable. I reckoned 'em up, and finding that they were all three bigger men than me, and considering that their looks were ugly—that it was a lonely place—railroad station two miles off—and night coming on—thought I couldn't do better than have a drop of brandy-and-water to keep my courage up. So I called for my brandy-and-water; and as I was sitting drinking it by the fire, Thompson got up and went out.

"Now the difficulty of it was, that I wasn't sure it *was* Thompson, because I had never set eyes on him before; and what I had wanted was to be quite certain of him. However, there was nothing for it now, but to follow, and put a bold face upon it. I found him talking, outside in the yard, with the landlady. It turned out afterwards that he was wanted by a Northampton officer for something else, and that, knowing that officer to be pock-marked (as I am myself), he mistook me for him. As I have observed, I found him talking to the landlady, outside. I put my hand upon his shoulder—this way—and said, 'Tally-ho Thompson, it's no use. I know you. I'm an officer from London, and I take you into custody for felony!' 'That be d—d!' says Tally-ho Thompson.

"We went back into the house, and the two friends began to cut up rough, and their looks didn't please me at all, I assure you. 'Let the man go. What are you going to do with him?' 'I'll tell you what I'm going to do with him. I'm going to take him to London to-night, as sure as I'm alive. I'm not alone here, whatever you may think. You mind your own business, and keep yourselves to yourselves. It'll be better for you, for I know you both very well.' I'd never seen or heard of 'em in all my life, but my bouncing cowed 'em a bit, and they kept off, while Thompson was making ready to go. I thought to myself, however, that they might be coming after me on the dark-road, to rescue Thompson; so I said to the landlady, 'What men have you got in the house, Missis?' 'We haven't got no men here,' she says, sulkily. 'You have got an ostler, I suppose?' 'Yes, we've got an ostler.' 'Let me see him.' Presently he came, and a shaggy-headed young fellow he was. 'Now attend to me, young man,' says I; I'm a Detective Officer from London. This man's name is Thompson. I have taken him into custody for felony. I am going to take him to the railroad station. I call upon you in the Queen's name to assist me; and mind you, my friend, you'll get yourself into more trouble than you know of, if you don't!' You never saw a person open his eyes so wide. 'Now, Thompson, come along!' says I. But when I took out the handcuffs, Thompson cries, 'No! None of that! I won't stand *them*! I'll go along with you quiet, but I won't bear none of that!' 'Tally-ho Thompson,' I said, 'I'm willing to behave as a man to you, if you are willing to behave as a man to me. Give me your word that you'll come peaceably along, and I don't want to handcuff you.' 'I will,' says Thompson, 'but I'll have a glass of brandy first.' 'I don't care if I've another,' said I. 'We'll have two more, Missis,' said the friends, 'and con-found you, Constable, you'll give your man a drop, won't you?' I was agreeable to that, so we had it all round, and then my man and I took Tally-ho Thompson safe to the railroad, and I carried him to London that night. He was afterwards acquitted, on account of a defect in the evidence; and I understand he always praises me up to the skies, and says I'm one of the best of men."

This story coming to a termination amidst general applause, Inspector Wield, after a little grave smoking, fixes his eye on his host, and thus delivers himself:

"It wasn't a bad plant that of mine, on Fikey, the man accused of forging the Sou'-Western Railway debentures—it was only t'other day —because the reason why? I'll tell you.

"I had information that Fikey and his brother kept a factory over yonder there,"—indicating any region on the Surrey side of the river —"where he bought second-hand carriages, so after I'd tried in vain to get hold of him by other means, I wrote him a letter in an assumed name, saying that I'd got a horse and shay to dispose of, and would drive down next day that he might view the lot, and make an offer— very reasonable it was, I said—a reg'lar bargain. Straw and me then went off to a friend of mine that's in the livery and job business, and hired a turn-out for the day, a precious smart turn-out it was—quite a slap-up thing! Down we drove, accordingly, with a friend (who's not in the Force himself); and leaving my friend in the shay near a public-house, to take care of the horse, we went to the factory, which was some little way off. In the factory, there was a number of strong fellows at work, and after reckoning 'em up, it was clear to me that it wouldn't do to try it on there. They were too many for us. We must get our man out of doors. 'Mr. Fikey at home?' 'No, he ain't.' 'Expected home soon?' 'Why, no, not soon.' 'Ah! Is his brother here?' 'I'm his brother.' 'Oh! well, this is an ill-conwenience, this is. I wrote him a letter yesterday, saying I'd got a little turn-out to dispose of, and I've took the trouble to bring the turn-out down a' purpose, and now he ain't in the way.' 'No, he ain't in the way. You couldn't make it convenient to call again, could you?' 'Why, no, I couldn't. I want to sell; that's the fact; and I can't put it off. Could you find him anywheres?' At first he said No, he couldn't, and then he wasn't sure about it, and then he'd go and try. So at last he went up-stairs, where there was a sort of loft, and presently down comes my man himself in his shirt-sleeves.

" 'Well,' he says, 'this seems to be rayther a pressing matter of yours.' 'Yes,' I says, 'it is rather a pressing matter, and you'll find it a bargain—dirt cheap.' 'I ain't in partickler want of a bargain just now,' he says, 'but where is it?' 'Why,' I says, 'the turn-out's just outside. Come and look at it.' He hasn't any suspicions, and away we go. And the first thing that happens is, that the horse runs away with my friend (who knows no more of driving than a child) when he takes a little trot along the road to show his paces. You never saw such a game in your life!

"When the bolt is over, and the turn-out has come to a standstill again, Fikey walks round and round it as grave as a judge—me too. 'There, sir!' I says. 'There's a neat thing!' 'It ain't a bad style of thing,' he says. 'I believe you,' says I. 'And there's a horse!'—for I saw him looking at it. 'Rising eight!' I says, rubbing his fore-legs. (Bless you, there ain't a man in the world knows less of horses than I do, but I'd heard my friend at the Livery Stables say he was eight year old, so I says, as knowing as possible, 'Rising eight.') 'Rising eight, is he?' says he. 'Rising eight,' says I. 'Well,' he says, 'what do you want for it?' 'Why, the first and last figure for the whole concern is five-and-twenty pound!' 'That's very cheap!' he says, looking at me. 'Ain't it?' I says. 'I told you it was a bargain! Now, without any higgling and haggling about it, what I want is to sell, and that's my price. Further, I'll make it easy to you, and take half the money down, and you can do a bit of stiff[1] for the balance.' 'Well,' he says again, 'that's very cheap.' 'I believe you,' says I; 'get in and try it, and you'll buy it. Come! take a trial!'

"Ecod, he gets in, and we get in, and we drive along the road, to show him to one of the railway clerks that was hid in the public-house window to identify him. But the clerk was bothered, and didn't know whether it was him, or wasn't—because the reason why? I'll tell you,—on account of his having shaved his whiskers. 'It's a clever little horse,' he says, 'and trots well; and the shay runs light.' 'Not a doubt about it,' I says. 'And now, Mr. Fikey, I may as well make it all right, without wasting any more of your time. The fact is, I'm Inspector Wield, and you're my prisoner.' 'You don't mean that?' he says. 'I do, indeed.' 'Then burn my body,' says Fikey, 'if this ain't too bad!'

"Perhaps you never saw a man so knocked over with surprise. 'I hope you'll let me have my coat?' he says. 'By all means.' 'Well, then, let's drive to the factory.' 'Why, not exactly that, I think,' said I; 'I've been there, once before, to-day. Suppose we send for it.' He saw it was no go, so he sent for it, and put it on, and we drove him up to London, comfortable."

This reminiscence is in the height of its success, when a general proposal is made to the fresh-complexioned, smooth-faced officer, with the strange air of simplicity, to tell the "Butcher's Story."

The fresh-complexioned, smooth-faced officer, with the strange air of simplicity, began with a rustic smile, and in a soft, wheedling tone of voice, to relate the Butcher's Story, thus:

"It's just about six years ago, now, since information was given at

[1] *Give a bill.*

Scotland Yard of there being extensive robberies of lawns and silks going on, at some wholesale houses in the City. Directions were given for the business being looked into; and Straw, and Fendall, and me, we were all in it."

"When you received your instructions," said we, "you went away, and held a sort of Cabinet Council together!"

The smooth-faced officer coaxingly replied, "Ye-es. Just so. We turned it over among ourselves a good deal. It appeared, when we went into it, that the goods were sold by the receivers extraordinarily cheap—much cheaper than they could have been if they had been honestly come by. The receivers were in the trade, and kept capital shops—establishments of the first respectability—one of 'em at the West End, one down in Westminster. After a lot of watching and inquiry, and this and that among ourselves, we found that the job was managed, and the purchases of the stolen goods made, at a little public-house near Smithfield, down by Saint Bartholomew's; where the Warehouse Porters, who were the thieves, took 'em for that purpose, don't you see? and made appointments to meet the people that went between themselves and the receivers. This public-house was principally used by journeymen butchers from the country, out of place, and in want of situations; so, what did we do, but—ha, ha, ha!—we agreed that I should be dressed up like a butcher myself, and go and live there!"

Never, surely, was a faculty of observation better brought to bear upon a purpose, than that which picked out this officer for the part. Nothing in all creation could have suited him better. Even while he spoke, he became a greasy, sleepy, shy, good-natured, chuckle-headed, unsuspicious, and confiding young butcher. His very hair seemed to have suet in it, as he made it smooth upon his head, and his fresh complexion to be lubricated by large quantities of animal food.

"—So I—ha, ha, ha!" (always with the confiding snigger of the foolish young butcher) "so I dressed myself in the regular way, made up a little bundle of clothes, and went to the public-house, and asked if I could have a lodging there? They says, 'yes, you can have a lodging here,' and I got a bedroom, and settled myself down in the tap. There was a number of people about the place, and coming backwards and forwards to the house; and first one says, and then another says, 'Are you from the country, young man?' 'Yes,' I says, 'I am. I'm come out of Northamptonshire, and I'm quite lonely here, for I don't know London at all, and it's such a mighty big town.' 'It *is* a big town,' they says. 'Oh, it's a *very* big town!' I says. 'Really and truly I never was in such a town. It quite confuses of me!'—and all that, you know.

"When some of the Journeymen Butchers that used the house, found that I wanted a place, they says, 'Oh, we'll get you a place!' And they actually took me to a sight of places, in Newgate Market,

Newport Market, Clare, Carnaby—I don't know where all. But the wages was—ha, ha, ha!—was not sufficient, and I never could suit myself, don't you see? Some of the queer frequenters of the house were a little suspicious of me at first, and I was obliged to be very cautious indeed, how I communicated with Straw or Fendall. Sometimes, when I went out, pretending to stop and look into the shop windows, and just casting my eye round, I used to see some of 'em following me; but being perhaps better accustomed than they thought for, to that sort of thing, I used to lead 'em on as far as I thought necessary or convenient—sometimes a long way—and then turn sharp round, and meet 'em, and say, 'Oh, dear, how glad I am to come upon you so fortunate! This London's such a place, I'm blowed if I an't lost again!' And then we'd go back all together, to the public-house, and—ha, ha, ha! and smoke our pipes, don't you see?

"They were very attentive to me, I am sure. It was a common thing, while I was living there, for some of 'em to take me out, and show me London. They showed me the Prisons—showed me Newgate —and when they showed me Newgate, I stops at the place where the Porters pitch their loads, and says, 'Oh dear, is this where they hang the men? Oh Lor!' 'That!' they says, 'what a simple cove he is ! *That* ain't it!' And then, they pointed out which *was* it, and I says, 'Lor!' and they says, 'Now you'll know it agen, won't you?' And I said I thought I should if I tried hard—and I assure you I kept a sharp look out for the City Police when we were out in this way, for if any of 'em had happened to know me, and had spoke to me, it would have been all up in a minute. However, by good luck such a thing never happened, and all went on quiet: though the difficulties I had in communicating with my brother officers were quite extraordinary.

"The stolen goods that were brought to the public-house by the Warehouse Porters, were always disposed of in a back parlour. For a long time, I never could get into this parlour, or see what was done there. As I sat smoking my pipe, like an innocent young chap, by the tap-room fire, I'd hear some of the parties to the robbery, as they came in and out, say softly to the landlord, 'Who's that? What does *he* do here?' 'Bless your soul,' says the landlord, 'he's only a'—ha, ha, ha!—'he's only a green fellow from the country, as is looking for a butcher's sitiwation. Don't mind *him!*' So, in course of time, they were so convinced of my being green, and go to be so accustomed to me, that I was as free of the parlour as any of 'em, and I have seen as much as Seventy Pounds' Worth of fine lawn sold there, in one night, that was stolen from a warehouse in Friday Street. After the sale the buyers always stood treat—hot supper, or dinner, or what not—and they'd say on those occasions, 'Come on, Butcher! Put your best leg foremost, young 'un, and walk into it!' Which I used to do—

and hear, at table, all manner of particulars that it was very important for us Detectives to know.

"This went on for ten weeks. I lived in the public-house all the time, and never was out of the Butcher's dress—except in bed. At last, when I had followed seven of the thieves, and set 'em to rights—that's an expression of ours, don't you see, by which I mean to say that I traced 'em, and found out where the robberies were done, and all about 'em—Straw, and Fendall, and I, gave one another the office, and at a time agreed upon, a descent was made upon the public-house, and the apprehensions effected. One of the first things the officers did, was to collar me—for the parties to the robbery weren't to suppose yet, that I was anything but a Butcher—on which the landlord cries out, 'Don't take *him*,' he says, 'whatever you do! He's only a poor young chap from the country, and butter wouldn't melt in his mouth!' However, they—ha, ha, ha!—they took me, and pretended to search my bedroom, where nothing was found but an old fiddle belonging to the landlord, that had got there somehow or another. But it entirely changed the landlord's opinion, for when it was produced, he says, 'My fiddle! The Butcher's a pur-loiner! I give him into custody for the robbery of a musical instrument!'

"The man that had stolen the goods in Friday Street was not taken yet. He had told me, in confidence, that he had his suspicions there was something wrong (on account of the City Police having captured one of the party), and that he was going to make himself scarce. I asked him, 'Where do you mean to go, Mr. Shepherdson?' 'Why, Butcher,' says he, 'the Setting Moon, in the Commercial Road, is a snug house, and I shall hang out there for a time. I shall call myself Simpson, which appears to me to be a modest sort of a name. Perhaps you'll give us a look in, Butcher?' 'Well,' says I, 'I think I *will* give you a call'—which I fully intended, don't you see, because, of course, he was to be taken! I went over to the Setting Moon next day, with a brother officer, and asked at the bar for Simpson. They pointed out his room, up-stairs. As we were going up, he looks down over the banisters, and calls out, 'Halloa, Butcher! is that you?' 'Yes, it's me. How do you find yourself?' 'Bobbish,' he says; 'but who's that with you?' 'It's only a young man, that's a friend of mine,' I says. 'Come along, then,' says he; 'any friend of the Butcher's is as welcome as the Butcher!' So I made my friend acquainted with him, and we took him into custody.

"You have no idea, sir, what a sight it was, in Court, when they first knew that I wasn't a Butcher, after all! I wasn't produced at the first examination, when there was a remand; but I was at the second. And when I stepped into the box, in full police uniform, and the whole party saw how they had been done, actually a groan of horror and dismay proceeded from 'em in the dock!

"At the Old Bailey, when their trials came on, Mr. Clarkson was engaged for the defence, and he *couldn't* make out how it was, about the Butcher. He thought, all along, it was a real Butcher. When the counsel for the prosecution said, 'I will now call before you, gentlemen, the Police-officer,' meaning myself, Mr. Clarkson says, 'Why Police-officer? Why more Police-officers? I don't want Police. We have had a great deal too much of the Police. I want the Butcher!' However, sir, he had the Butcher and the Police-officer, both in one. Out of seven prisoners committed for trial, five were found guilty, and some of 'em were transported. The respectable firm at the West End got a term of imprisonment; and that's the Butcher's Story!"

The story done, the chuckle-headed Butcher again resolved himself into the smooth-faced Detective. But he was so extremely tickled by their having taken him about, when he was that Dragon in disguise, to show him London, that he could not help reverting to that point in his narrative; and gently repeating with the Butcher snigger, "'Oh, dear,' I says, 'is that where they hang the men? Oh, Lor!' 'That!' says they. 'What a simple cove he is!'"

It being now late, and the party very modest in their fear of being too diffuse, there were some tokens of separation; when Sergeant Dornton, the soldierly-looking man, said, looking round him with a smile:

"Before we break up, sir, perhaps you might have some amusement in hearing of the Adventures of a Carpet Bag. They are very short; and, I think, curious."

We welcomed the Carpet Bag, as cordially as Mr. Shepherdson welcomed the false Butcher at the Setting Moon. Sergeant Dornton proceeded.

"In 1847, I was despatched to Chatham, in search of one Mesheck, a Jew. He had been carrying on, pretty heavily, in the bill-stealing way, getting acceptances from young men of good connexions (in the army chiefly), on pretence of discount, and bolting with the same.

"Mesheck was off, before I got to Chatham. All I could learn about him was, that he had gone, probably to London, and had with him— a Carpet Bag.

"I came back to town, by the last train from Blackwall, and made inquires concerning a Jew passenger with—a Carpet bag.

"The office was shut up, it being the last train. There were only two or three porters left. Looking after a Jew with a Carpet Bag, on the Blackwall Railway, which was then the high road to a great Military Depôt, was worse than looking after a needle in a hayrick. But it happened that one of these porters had carried, for a certain Jew, to a certain public-house, a certain—Carpet Bag.

"I went to the public-house, but the Jew had only left his luggage there for a few hours, and had called for it in a cab, and taken it away.

I put such questions there, and to the porter, as I thought prudent, and got at this description of—the Carpet Bag.

"It was a bag which had, on one side of it, worked in worsted, a green parrot on a stand. A green parrot on a stand was the means by which to identify that—Carpet Bag.

"I traced Mesheck, by means of this green parrot on a stand, to Cheltenham, to Birmingham, to Liverpool, to the Atlantic Ocean. At Liverpool he was too many for me. He had gone to the United States, and I gave up all thoughts of Mesheck, and likewise of his—Carpet Bag.

"Many months afterwards—near a year afterwards—there was a bank in Ireland robbed of seven thousand pounds, by a person of the name of Doctor Dundey, who escaped to America; from which country some of the stolen notes came home. He was supposed to have bought a farm in New Jersey. Under proper management, that estate could be seized and sold, for the benefit of the parties he had defrauded. I was sent off to America for this purpose.

"I landed at Boston. I went on to New York. I found that he had lately changed New York paper-money for New Jersey paper-money, and had banked cash in New Brunswick. To take this Doctor Dundey, it was necessary to entrap him into the State of New York, which required a deal of artifice and trouble. At one time, he couldn't be drawn into an appointment. At another time, he appointed to come to meet me, and a New York officer, on a pretext I made; and then his children had the measles. At last he came, per steamboat, and I took him, and lodged him in a New York prison called the Tombs; which I dare say you know, sir?"

Editorial acknowledgment to that effect.

"I went to the Tombs, on the morning after his capture, to attend the examination before the magistrate. I was passing through the magistrate's private room, when, happening to look round me to take notice of the place, as we generally have a habit of doing, I clapped my eyes, in one corner, on a—Carpet Bag.

"What did I see upon that Carpet Bag, if you'll believe me, but a green parrot on a stand, as large as life!

"'That Carpet Bag, with the representation of a green parrot on a stand,' said I, 'belongs to an English Jew, name Aaron Mesheck, and to no other man, alive or dead!'

"I give you my word the New York Police Officers were doubled up with surprise.

"'How did you ever come to know that?' said they.

"'I think I ought to know that green parrot by this time,' said I; 'for I have had as pretty a dance after that bird, at home, as ever I had, in all my life!'"

"And was it Mesheck's?" we submissively inquired.

"Was it, sir? Of course it was! He was in custody for another offence, in that very identical Tombs, at that very identical time. And, more than that! Some memoranda, relating to the fraud for which I had vainly endeavoured to take him, were found to be, at that moment, lying in that very same individual—Carpet Bag!"

Such are the curious cioncidences and such is the peculiar ability, always sharpening and being improved by practice, and always adapting itself to every variety of circumstances, and opposing itself to every new device that perverted ingenuity can invent, for which this important social branch of the public service is remarkable! For ever on the watch, with their wits stretched to the utmost, these officers have, from day to day and year to year, to set themselves against every novelty of trickery and dexterity that the combined imaginations of all the lawless rascals in England can devise, and to keep pace with every such invention that comes out. In the Courts of Justice, the materials of thousands of such stories as we have narrated—often elevated into the marvellous and romantic, by the circumstances of the case—are dryly compressed into the set phrase, "in consequence of information I received, I did so and so." Suspicion was to be directed, by careful inference and deduction, upon the right person; the right person was to be taken, wherever he had gone, or whatever he was doing to avoid detection: he is taken, there he is at the bar; that is enough. From information I, the officer, received, I did it; and, according to the custom in these cases, I say no more.

These games of chess, played with live pieces, are played before small audiences, and are chronicled nowhere. The interest of the game supports the player. Its results are enough for Justice. To compare great things with small, suppose LEVERRIER or ADAMS informing the public that from information he had received he had discovered a new planet; or COLUMBUS informing the public of his day that from information he had received he had discovered a new continent; so the Detectives inform it that they have discovered a new fraud or an old offender, and the process is unknown.

Thus, at midnight, closed the proceedings of our curious and interesting party. But one other circumstance finally wound up the evening, after our Detective guests had left us. One of the sharpest among them, and the officer best acquainted with the Swell Mob, had his pocket picked, going home!

Three "Detective" Anecdotes

~~~~~~

I. The pair of gloves

"It's a singler story, sir," said Inspector Wield, of the Detective Police, who, in company with Sergeants Dornton and Mith, paid us another twilight visit, one July evening; "and I've been thinking you might like to know it.

"It's concerning the murder of the young woman, Eliza Grimwood, some years ago, over in the Waterloo Road. She was commonly called The Countess, because of her handsome appearance and her proud way of carrying of herself; and when I saw the poor Countess (I had known her well to speak of), lying dead, with her throat cut, on the floor of her bedroom, you'll believe me that a variety of reflections calculated to make a man rather low in his spirits, came into my head.

"That's neither here nor there. I went to the house the morning after the murder, and examined the body, and made a general observation of the bedroom where it was. Turning down the pillow of the bed with my hand, I found, underneath it, a pair of gloves. A pair of gentleman's dress gloves, very dirty; and inside the lining, the letters Tr, and a cross.

"Well, sir, I took them gloves away, and I showed 'em to the magistrate, over at Union Hall, before whom the case was. He says 'Wield,' he says, 'there's no doubt this is a discovery that may lead to something very important; and what you have got to do, Wield, is to find out the owner of these gloves.'

"I was of the same opinion, of course, and I went at it immediately. I looked at the gloves pretty narrowly, and it was my opinion that they had been cleaned. There was a smell of sulphur and rosin about 'em, you know, which cleaned gloves usually have, more or less. I took 'em over to a friend of mine at Kennington, who was in that line, and I put it to him. 'What do you say now? Have these gloves been cleaned?' 'These gloves have been cleaned,' says he. 'Have you any idea who cleaned them?' says I. 'Not at all,' says he; 'I've a very distinct idea who *didn't* clean 'em and that's myself. But I'll tell you what, Wield, there ain't above eight or nine reg'lar glove-cleaners in London,'—there were not, at that time, it seems—'and

I think I can give you their addresses, and you may find out, by that means, who did clean 'em. Accordingly, he gave me the directions, and I went here, and I went there, and I looked up this man, and I looked up that man; but, though they all agreed that the gloves had been cleaned, I couldn't find the man, woman, or child, that had cleaned that aforesaid pair of gloves.

"What with this person not being at home, and that person being expected home in the afternoon, and so forth, the inquiry took me three days. On the evening of the third day, coming over Waterloo Bridge from the Surrey side of the river, quite beat, and very much vexed and disappointed, I thought I'd have a shilling's worth of entertainment at the Lyceum Theatre to freshen myself up. So I went into the Pit, at half-price, and I sat myself down next to a very quiet, modest sort of young man. Seeing I was a stranger (which I thought it just as well to appear to be) he told me the names of the actors on the stage, and we got into conversation. When the play was over, we came out together, and I said, 'We've been very companionable and agreeable, and perhaps you wouldn't object to a drain?' 'Well, you're very good,' says he; 'I *shouldn't* object to a drain.' Accordingly, we went to a public-house, near the Theatre, sat ourselves down in a quiet room up-stairs on the first floor, and called for a pint of half-and-half apiece, and a pipe.

"Well, sir, we put our pipes aboard, and we drank our half-and-half, and sat a-talking, very sociably, when the young man says, 'You must excuse me stopping very long,' he says, 'because I'm forced to go home in good time. I must be at work all night.' 'At work all night?' says I. 'You ain't a baker?' 'No,' he says, laughing, 'I ain't a baker.' 'I thought not,' says I, 'you haven't the looks of a baker.' 'No,' says he, 'I'm a glove-cleaner.'

"I never was more astonished in my life, than when I heard them words come out of his lips. 'You're a glove-cleaner, are you?' says I. 'Yes,' he says, 'I am.' 'Then, perhaps,' says I, taking the gloves out of my pocket, 'you can tell me who cleaned this pair of gloves? It's a rum story,' I says. 'I was dining over at Lambeth, the other day, at a free-and-easy—quite promiscuous—with a public company—when some gentleman, he left these gloves behind him! Another gentleman and me, you see, we laid a wager of a sovereign, that I wouldn't find out who they belonged to. I've spent as much as seven shillings already, in trying to discover; but, if you could help me, I'd stand another seven and welcome. You see there's TR and a cross, inside.' 'I see,' he says. 'Bless you, I know these gloves very well! I've seen dozens of pairs belonging to the same party.' 'No?' says I. 'Yes,' says he. 'Then you know who cleaned 'em?' says I. 'Rather so,' says he. 'My father cleaned 'em.'

" 'Where does your father live?' says I. 'Just round the corner,' says the young man, 'near Exeter Street, here. He'll tell you who they belong to, directly.' 'Would you come round with me now?' says I. 'Certainly,' says he, 'but you needn't tell my father that you found me at the play, you know, because he mightn't like it.' 'All right!' We went round to the place, and there we found an old man in a white apron, with two or three daughters, all rubbing and cleaning away at lots of gloves, in a front parlour. 'Oh, Father!' says the young man, 'here's a person been and made a bet about the owner-ship of a pair of gloves, and I've told him you can settle it.' 'Good evening, sir,' says I to the old gentleman. 'Here's the gloves your son speaks of. Letters Tr, you see, and a cross.' 'Oh yes,' he says, 'I know these gloves very well; I've cleaned dozens of pairs of 'em. They be-long to Mr. Trinkle, the great upholsterer in Cheapside.' 'Did you get 'em from Mr. Trinkle, direct,' says I, 'if you'll excuse my asking the question?' 'No,' says he; 'Mr. Trinkle always sends 'em to Mr. Phibbs's, the haberdasher's, opposite his shop, and the haberdasher sends 'em to me.' 'Perhaps *you* wouldn't object to a drain?' says I. 'Not in the least!' says he. So I took the old gentleman out, and had a little more talk with him and his son, over a glass, and we parted ex-cellent friends.

"This was late on a Saturday night. First thing on the Monday morning, I went to the haberdasher's shop, opposite Mr. Trinkle's, the great upholsterer's in Cheapside. 'Mr. Phibbs in the way?' 'My name is Phibbs.' 'Oh! I believe you sent this pair of gloves to be cleaned?' 'Yes, I did, for young Mr. Trinkle over the way. There he is in the shop!' 'Oh! that's him in the shop, is it? Him in the green coat?' 'The same individual.' 'Well, Mr. Phibbs, this is an unpleasant affair; but the fact is, I am Inspector Wield of the Detective Police, and I found these gloves under the pillow of the young woman that was murdered the other day, over in the Waterloo Road.' 'Good Heaven!' says he. 'He's a most respectable young man, and if his father was to hear of it, it would be the ruin of him!' 'I'm very sorry for it,' says I, 'but I must take him into custody.' 'Good Heaven!' says Mr. Phibbs, again; 'can nothing be done!' 'Nothing,' says I. 'Will you allow me to call him over here,' says he, 'that his father may not see it done?' 'I don't object to that,' says I; 'but unfortunately, Mr. Phibbs, I can't allow of any communication between you. If any was at-tempted, I should have to interfere directly. Perhaps you'll beckon him over here?' Mr. Phibbs went to the door and beckoned, and the young fellow came across the street directly; a smart, brisk young fellow.

"'Good morning, sir,' says I. 'Good morning, sir,' says he. 'Would you allow me to inquire, sir,' says I, 'if you ever had any acquaintance with a party of the name of Grimwood?' 'Grimwood! Grimwood!' says he. 'No!' 'You know the Waterloo Road?' 'Oh! of course I know the Waterloo Road!' 'Happen to have heard of a young woman being murdered there?' 'Yes, I read it in the paper, and very sorry I was to read it.' 'Here's a pair of gloves belonging to you, that I found under her pillow the morning afterwards!'

"He was in a dreadful state, sir; a dreadful state! 'Mr. Wield,' he says, 'upon my solemn oath I never was there. I never so much as saw her, to my knowledge, in my life!' 'I am very sorry,' says I. 'To tell you the truth; I don't think you *are* the murderer, but I must take you to Union Hall in a cab. However, I think it's a case of that sort, that, at present, at all events, the magistrate will hear it in private.'

"A private examination took place, and then it came out that this young man was acquainted with a cousin of the unfortunate Eliza Grimwood, and that, calling to see this cousin a day or two before the murder, he left these gloves upon the table. Who should come in, shortly afterwards, but Eliza Grimwood! 'Whose gloves are these?' she says, taking 'em up. 'Those are Mr. Trinkle's gloves,' says her cousin. 'Oh!' says she, 'they are very dirty, and of no use to him, I am sure. I shall take 'em away for my girl to clean the stoves with.' And she put 'em in her pocket. The girl had used 'em to clean the stoves, and, I have no doubt, had left 'em lying on the bedroom mantelpiece, or on the drawers, or somewhere; and her mistress, looking round to see that the room was tidy, had caught 'em up and put 'em under the pillow where I found 'em.

"That's the story, sir."

II. *The artful touch*

"One of the most *beautiful* things that ever was done, perhaps," said Inspector Wield, emphasising the adjective, as preparing us to expect dexterity or ingenuity rather than strong interest, "was a move of Sergeant Witchem's. It was a lovely idea!

"Witchem and me were down at Epsom one Derby Day, waiting at the station for the Swell Mob. As I mentioned, when we were talking about these things before, we are ready at the station when there's races, or an Agricultural Show, or a Chancellor sworn in for an university, or Jenny Lind, or anything of that sort; and as the Swell Mob come down, we send 'em back again by the next train. But some of the Swell Mob, on the occasion of this Derby that I refer to, so far kidded us as to hire a horse and shay; start away from London by Whitechapel, and miles round; come into Epsom from the opposite direction; and go to work, right and left, on the course, while we were waiting for 'em at the Rail. That, however, ain't the point of what I'm going to tell you.

"While Witchem and me were waiting at the station, there comes up one Mr. Tatt; a gentleman formerly in the public line, quite an amateur Detective in his way, and very much respected. 'Halloa, Charley Wield,' he says. 'What are you doing here? On the look out for some of your old friends?' 'Yes, the old move, Mr. Tatt.' 'Come along,' he says, 'you and Witchem, and have a glass of sherry.' 'We can't stir from the place,' says I, 'till the next train comes in; but after that, we will with pleasure.' Mr. Tatt waits, and the train comes in, and then Witchem and me go off with him to the Hotel. Mr. Tatt he's got up quite regardless of expense, for the occasion; and in his shirt-front there's a beautiful diamond prop, cost him fifteen or twenty pound—a very handsome pin indeed. We drink our sherry at the bar, and have had our three or four glasses, when Witchem cries suddenly, 'Look out, Mr. Wield! stand fast!' and a dash is made into the place by the Swell Mob—four of 'em—that have come down as I tell you, and in a moment Mr. Tatt's prop is gone! Witchem, he cuts 'em off at the door, I lay about me as hard as I can, Mr. Tatt shows fight like a good 'un, and there we are, all down together, heads and heels, knocking about on the floor of the bar—perhaps you never see such a scene of confusion! However, we stick to our men (Mr. Tatt being as good as any officer), and we take 'em all, and carry 'em off to the station. The station's full of people, who have been took on the course; and it's a precious piece of work to get 'em secured. However, we do it at last, and we search 'em; but nothing's found upon 'em, and they're locked up; and a pretty state of heat we are in by that time, I assure you!

"I was very blank over it, myself, to think that the prop had been passed away; and I said to Witchem, when we had set 'em to rights, and were cooling ourselves along with Mr. Tatt, 'we don't take much by *this* move, anyway, for nothing's found upon 'em, and it's only the braggadocia[1], after all.' 'What do you mean, Mr. Wield?' says Witchem. 'Here's the diamond pin!' and in the palm of his hand there it was, safe and sound! 'Why, in the name of wonder,' says me and Mr. Tatt, in astonishment, 'how did you come by that?' 'I'll tell you how I come by it,' says he. 'I saw which of 'em took it; and when we were all down on the floor together, knocking about, I just gave him a little touch on the back of his hand, as I knew his pal would; and he thought it was his pal; and gave it me!' It was beautiful, beau-ti-ful!

"Even that was hardly the best of the case, for that chap was tried at the Quarter Sessions at Guildford. You know what Quarter Sessions are, sir. Well, if you'll believe me, while them slow justices were looking over the Acts of Parliament, to see what they could do to him,

[1]*Three months' imprisonment as reputed thieves.*

I'm blowed if he didn't cut out of the dock before their faces! He cut out of the dock, sir, then and there; swam across a river; and got up into a tree to dry himself. In the tree he was took—an old woman having seen him climb up—and Witchem's artful touch transported him!"

III. *The Sofa*

"What young men will do, sometimes, to ruin themselves and break their friends' hearts," said Sergeant Dornton, "it's surprising! I had a case at Saint Blank's Hospital which was of this sort. A bad case, indeed, with a bad end!"

"The Secretary, and the House-Surgeon, and the Treasurer, of Saint Blank's Hospital, came to Scotland Yard to give information of numerous robberies having been committed on the students. The students could leave nothing in the pockets of their great-coats, while the great-coats were hanging at the hospital, but it was almost certain to be stolen. Property of various descriptions was constantly being lost; and the gentlemen were naturally uneasy about it, and anxious, for the credit of the institution, that the thief or thieves should be discovered. The case was entrusted to me, and I went to the hospital.

"'Now, gentlemen,' said I, after we had talked it over; 'I understand this property is usually lost from one room.'

"Yes, they said. It was.

"'I should wish, if you please,' said I, 'to see the room.'

"It was a good-sized bare room down-stairs, with a few tables and forms in it, and a row of pegs, all round, for hats and coats.

"'Next, gentlemen,' said I, 'do you suspect anybody?'

"Yes, they said. They did suspect somebody. They were sorry to say, they suspected one of the porters.

"'I should like,' said I, 'to have that man pointed out to me, and to have a little time to look after him.'

"He was pointed out, and I looked after him, and then I went back to the hospital, and said, 'Now, gentlemen, it's not the porter. He's, unfortunately for himself, a little too fond of drink, but he's nothing worse. My suspicion is, that these robberies are committed by one of the students; and if you'll put me a sofa into that room where the pegs are—as there's no closet—I think I shall be able to detect the thief. I wish the sofa, if you please, to be covered with chintz, or something of that sort, so that I may lie on my chest, underneath it, without being seen.'

"The sofa was provided, and next day at eleven o'clock, before any of the students came, I went there, with those gentlemen, to get underneath it. It turned out to be one of those old-fashioned sofas with a great cross-beam at the bottom, that would have broken my back in no time if I could ever have got below it. We had quite a job to break all this away in the time; however, I fell to work, and they fell to work, and we broke it out, and made a clear place for me. I got under the sofa, lay down on my chest, took out my knife, and made a convenient hole in the chintz to look through. It was then settled between me and the gentlemen that when the students were all up in the wards, one of the gentlemen should come in, and hang up a great-coat on one of the pegs. And that that great-coat should have, in one of the pockets, a pocket-book containing marked money.

"After I had been there some time, the students began to drop into the room, by ones, and twos, and threes, and to talk about all sorts of things, little thinking there was anybody under the sofa—and then to go up-stairs. At last there came in one who remained until he was alone in the room by himself. A tallish, good-looking young man of one or two and twenty, with a light whisker. He went to a particular hat-peg, took off a good hat that was hanging there, tried it on, hung his own hat in its place, and hung that hat on another peg, nearly opposite to me. I then felt quite certain that he was the thief, and would come back by-and-by.

"When they were all up-stairs, the gentleman came in with the great-coat. I showed him where to hang it, so that I might have a good view of it; and he went away; and I lay under the sofa on my chest, for a couple of hours or so, waiting.

"At last, the same young man came down. He walked across the room, whistling—stopped and listened—took another walk and whistled—stopped again, and listened—then began to go regularly round the pegs, feeling in the pockets of all the coats. When he came to THE great-coat, and felt the pocket-book, he was so eager and so hurried that he broke the strap in tearing it open. As he began to put the money in his pocket, I crawled out from under the sofa, and his eyes met mine.

"My face, as you may perceive, is brown now, but it was pale at that time, my health not being good; and looked as long as a horse's. Besides which, there was a great draught of air from the door, underneath the sofa, and I had tied a handkerchief round my head; so what I looked like, altogether, I don't know. He turned blue—literally blue—when he saw me crawling out, and I couldn't feel surprised at it.

"'I am an officer of the Detective Police,' said I, 'and have been lying here, since you first came in this morning. I regret, for the sake of yourself and your friends, that you should have done what you have; but this case is complete. You have the pocket-book in your hand and the money upon you; and I must take you into custody!'

"It was impossible to make out any case in his behalf, and on his trial he pleaded guilty. How or when he got the means I don't know; but while he was awaiting his sentence, he poisoned himself in Newgate."

We inquired of this officer, on the conclusion of the fore-going anecdote, whether the time appeared long, or short, when he lay in that constrained position under the sofa?

"Why, you see, sir," he replied, "if he hadn't come in, the first time, and I had not been quite sure he was the thief, and would return, the time would have seemed long. But, as it was, I being dead certain of my man, the time seemed pretty short."

To be Read at Dusk

One, two, three, four, five. There were five of them.

Five couriers, sitting on a bench outside the convent on the summit of the Great St. Bernard in Switzerland, looking at the remote heights, stained by the setting sun, as if a mighty quantity of red wine had been broached upon the mountain top, and had not yet had time to sink into the snow.

This is not my simile. It was made for the occasion by the stoutest courier, who was a German. None of the others took any more notice of it than they took of me, sitting on another bench on the other side of the convent door, smoking my cigar, like them, and—also like them—looking at the reddened snow, and at the lonely shed hard by, where the bodies of belated travellers, dug out of it, slowly wither away, knowing no corruption in that cold region.

The wine upon the mountain top soaked in as we looked; the mountain became white; the sky, a very dark blue; the wind rose; and the air turned piercing cold. The five couriers buttoned their rough coats. There being no safer man to imitate in all such proceedings than a courier, I buttoned mine.

The mountain in the sunset had stopped the five couriers in a conversation. It is a sublime sight, likely to stop conversation. The mountain being now out of the sunset, they resumed. Not that I had heard any part of their previous discourse; for indeed, I had not then broken away from the American gentleman, in the travellers' parlour of the convent, who, sitting with his face to the fire, had undertaken to realise to me the whole progress of events which had led to the accumulation by the Honourable Ananias Dodger of one of the largest acquisitions of dollars ever made in our country.

"My God!" said the Swiss courier, speaking in French, which I do not hold (as some authors appear to do) to be such an all-sufficient excuse for a naughty word, that I have only to write it in that language to make it innocent; "if you talk of ghosts——"

"But I *don't* talk of ghosts," said the German.

"Of what then?" asked the Swiss.

"If I knew of what then," said the German, "I should probably know a great deal more."

It was a good answer, I thought, and it made me curious. So I moved my position to that corner of my bench which was nearest to them, and leaning my back against the convent wall, heard perfectly, without appearing to attend.

"Thunder and lightning!" said the German, warming, "when a certain man is coming to see you, unexpectedly; and, without his own knowledge, sends some invisible messenger, to put the idea of him into your head all day, what do you call that? When you walk along a crowded street—at Frankfort, Milan, London, Paris—and think that a passing stranger is like your friend Heinrich, and then that another passing stranger is like your friend Heinrich, and so begin to have a strange foreknowledge that presently you'll meet your friend Heinrich—which you do, though you believed him at Trieste—what do you call *that?*"

"It's not uncommon, either," murmured the Swiss and the other three.

"Uncommon!" said the German. "It's as common as cherries in the Black Forest. It's as common as maccaroni at Naples. And Naples reminds me! When the old Marchesa Senzanima shrieks at a card-party on the Chiaja—as I heard and saw her, for it happened in a Bavarian family of mine, and I was overlooking the service that evening—I say, when the old Marchesa starts up at the card-table, white through her rouge, and cries, 'My sister in Spain is dead! I felt her cold touch on my back!'—and when that sister *is* dead at the moment—what do you call that?"

"Or when the blood of San Gennaro liquefies at the request of the clergy—as all the world knows that it does regularly once a year, in my native city," said the Neapolitan courier after a pause, with a comical look, "what do you call that?"

"*That!*" cried the German. "Well, I think I know a name for that."

"Miracle?" said the Neapolitan, with the same sly face.

The German merely smoked and laughed; and they all smoked and laughed.

"Bah!" said the German, presently. "I speak of things that really do happen. When I want to see the conjurer, I pay to see a professed one, and have my money's worth. Very strange things do happen without ghosts. Ghosts! Giovanni Baptista, tell your story of the English bride. There's no ghost in that, but something full as strange. Will any man tell me what?"

As there was a silence among them, I glanced around. He whom I took to be Baptista was lighting a fresh cigar. He presently went on to speak. He was a Genoese, as I judged.

"The story of the English bride?" said he. "Basta! one ought not to call so slight a thing a story. Well, it's all one. But it's true. Observe me well, gentlemen, it's true. That which glitters is not always gold: but what I am going to tell, is true."

He repeated this more than once.

Ten years ago, I took my credentials to an English gentleman at Long's Hotel, in Bond Street, London, who was about to travel—it might be for one year, it might be for two. He approved of them; likewise of me. He was pleased to make inquiry. The testimony that he received was favourable. He engaged me by the six months, and my entertainment was generous.

He was young, handsome, very happy. He was enamoured of a fair young English lady, with a sufficient fortune, and they were going to be married. It was the wedding-trip, in short, that we were going to take. For three months' rest in the hot weather (it was early summer then) he had hired an old place on the Riviera, at an easy distance from my city, Genoa, on the road to Nice. Did I know that place? Yes; I told him I knew it well. It was an old palace with great gardens. It was a little bare, and it was a little dark and gloomy, being close surrounded by trees; but it was spacious, ancient, grand, and on the seashore. He said it had been so described to him exactly, and he was well pleased that I knew it. For its being a little bare of furniture, all such places were. For its being a little gloomy, he had hired it principally for the gardens, and he and my mistress would pass the summer weather in their shade.

"So all goes well, Baptista?" said he.

"Indubitably, signore; very well."

We had a travelling chariot for our journey, newly built for us, and in all respects complete. All we had was complete; we wanted for nothing. The marriage took place. They were happy. I was happy, seeing all so bright, being so well situated, going to my own city, teaching my language in the rumble to the maid, la bella Carolina, whose heart was gay with laughter: who was young and rosy.

The time flew. But I observed—listen to this, I pray! (and here the courier dropped his voice)—I observed my mistress sometimes brooding in a manner very strange; in a frightened manner; in an unhappy manner; with a cloudy, uncertain alarm upon her. I think that I began to notice this when I was walking up hills by the carriage side, and master had gone on in front. At any rate, I remember that it impressed itself upon my mind one evening in the South of France, when she called to me to call master back; and when he came back, and walked for a long way, talking encouragingly and affectionately to her, with his hand upon the open window, and hers in it. Now and then, he laughed in a merry way, as if he were bantering her out of something. By-and-by, she laughed, and then all went well again.

It was curious. I asked la bella Carolina, the pretty little one, Was mistress unwell?—No.—Out of spirits?—No.—Fearful of bad roads, or brigands?—No. And what made it more mysterious was, the pretty little one would not look at me in giving answer, but *would* look at the view.

But one day she told me the secret.

"If you must know," said Carolina, "I find, from what I have overheard, that mistress is haunted."

"How haunted?"

"By a dream."

"What dream?"

"By a dream of a face. For three nights before her marriage, she saw a face in a dream—always the same face, and only One."

"A terrible face?"

"No. The face of a dark, remarkable-looking man, in black, with black hair and a grey moustache—a handsome man except for a reserved and secret air. Not a face she ever saw, or at all like a face she ever saw. Doing nothing in the dream but looking at her fixedly, out of darkness."

"Does the dream come back?"

"Never. The recollection of it, is all her trouble."

"And why does it trouble her?"

Carolina shook her head.

"That's master's question," said la bella. "She don't know. She wonders why, herself. But I heard her tell him, only last night, that if she was to find a picture of that face in our Italian house (which she is afraid she will) she did not know how she could ever bear it."

Upon my word, I was fearful after this (said the Genoese courier) of our coming to the old palazzo, lest some such ill-starred picture should happen to be there. I knew there were many there; and, as we got nearer and nearer to the place, I wished the whole gallery in the crater of Vesuvius. To mend the matter, it was a stormy dismal evening when we, at last, approached that part of the Riviera. It

thundered; and the thunder of my city and its environs, rolling among
the high hills, is very loud. The lizards ran in and out of the chinks
in the broken stone wall of the garden, as if they were frightened; the
frogs bubbled and croaked their loudest; the sea-wind moaned, and
the wet trees dripped; and the lightning—body of San Lorenzo, how
it lightened!

We all know what an old palace in or near Genoa is—how time
and the sea air have blotted it—how the drapery painted on the outer
walls has peeled off in great flakes of plaster—how the lower windows
are darkened with rusty bars of iron—how the courtyard is overgrown
with grass—how the outer buildings are dilapidated—how the whole
pile seems devoted to ruin. Our palazzo was one of the true kind. It
had been shut up close for months. Months?—years!—it had an earthy
smell, like a tomb. The scent of the orange trees on the broad back
terrace, and of the lemons ripening on the wall, and of some shrubs
that grew around a broken fountain, had got into the house somehow,
and had never been able to get out again. There was, in every room,
an aged smell, grown faint with confinement. It pined in all the
cupboards and drawers. In the little rooms of communication between
great rooms, it was stifling. If you turned a picture—to come back to
the pictures—there it still was, clinging to the wall behind the frame,
like a sort of bat.

The lattice-blinds were close shut, all over the house. There were two
ugly grey old women in the house, to take care of it; one of them
with a spindle, who stood winding and mumbling in the doorway,
and who would as soon have let in the devil as the air. Master,
mistress, la bella Carolina, and I, went all through the palazzo.
I went first, though I have named myself last, opening the windows
and the lattice-blinds, and shaking down on myself splashes of rain,
and scraps of mortar, and now and then a dozing mosquito, or a
monstrous, fat, blotchy, Genoese spider.

When I had let the evening light into a room, master, mistress, and
la bella Carolina, entered. Then we looked round at all the pictures,
and I went forward again into another room. Mistress secretly had
great fear of meeting with the likeness of that face—we all had; but
there was no such thing. The Madonna and Bambino, San Francisco,
San Sebastiano, Venus, Santa Caterina, Angels, Brigands, Friars,
Temples at Sunset, Battles, White Horses, Forests, Apostles, Doges,
all my old acquaintances many times repeated?—yes. Dark handsome
man in black, reserved and secret, with black hair and grey moustache,
looking fixedly at mistress out of darkness?—no.

At last we got through all the rooms and all the pictures, and came
out into the gardens. They were pretty well kept, being rented by a
gardener, and were large and shady. In one place there was a rustic
theatre, open to the sky; the stage a green slope; the coulisses, three

entrances upon a side, sweet-smelling leafy screens. Mistress moved
her bright eye, even there, as if she looked to see the face come in
upon the scene; but all was well.

"Now, Clara," master said, in a low voice, "you see that it is nothing?
You are happy."

Mistress was much encouraged. She soon accustomed herself to that
grim palazzo, and would sing, and play the harp, and copy the old
pictures, and stroll with master under the green trees and vines all
day. She was beautiful. He was happy. He would laugh and say to me,
mounting his horse for his morning ride before the heat:

"All goes well, Baptista!"

"Yes, signore, thank God, very well."

We kept no company. I took la bella to the Duomo and Annunciata,
to the Café, to the Opera, to the village Festa, to the Public Garden,
to the Day Theatre, to the Marionetti. The pretty little one was
charmed with all she saw. She learnt Italian—heavens! miraculously!
Was mistress quite forgetful of that dream? I asked Carolina sometimes. Nearly, said la bella—almost. It was wearing out.

One day master received a letter, and called me.

"Baptista!"

"Signore!"

"A gentleman who is presented to me will dine here to-day. He is
called the Signor Dellombra. Let me dine like a prince."

It was an odd name. I did not know that name. But there had been
many noblemen and gentlemen pursued by Austria on political suspicions, lately, and some names had changed. Perhaps this was one.
Altro! Dellombra was as good a name to me as another.

When the Signor Dellombra came to dinner (said the Genoese
courier in the low voice, into which he had subsided once before), I
showed him into the reception-room, the great sala of the old palazzo.
Master received him with cordiality, and presented him to mistress.
As she rose, her face changed, she gave a cry, and fell upon the
marble floor.

Then I turned my head to the Signor Dellombra, and saw that he
was dressed in black, and had a reserved and secret air, and was a
dark remarkable-looking man, with black hair and a grey moustache.

Master raised mistress in his arms, and carried her to her own room,
where I sent la bella Carolina straight. La bella told me afterwards
that mistress was nearly terrified to death, and that she wandered in
her mind about her dream, all night.

Master was vexed and anxious—almost angry, and yet full of solicitude. The Signor Dellombra was a courtly gentleman, and spoke with
great respect and sympathy of mistress's being so ill. The African
wind had been blowing for some days (they had told him at his
hotel of the Maltese Cross), and he knew that it was often hurtful.

He hoped the beautiful lady would recover soon. He begged permission to retire, and to renew his visit when he should have the happiness of hearing that she was better. Master would not allow of this, and they dined alone.

He withdrew early. Next day he called at the gate, on horseback, to inquire for mistress. He did so two or three times in that week.

What I observed myself, and what la bella Carolina told me, united to explain to me that master had now set his mind on curing mistress of her fanciful terror. He was all kindness, but he was sensible and firm. He reasoned with her, that to encourage such fancies was to invite melancholy, if not madness. That it rested with herself to be herself. That if she once resisted her strange weakness, so successfully as to receive the Signor Dellombra as an English lady would receive any other guest, it was for ever conquered. To make an end, the signore came again, and mistress received him without marked distress (though with constraint and apprehension still), and the evening passed serenely. Master was so delighted with this change, and so anxious to confirm it, that the Signor Dellombra became a constant guest. He was accomplished in pictures, books, and music; and his society, in any grim palazzo, would have been welcome.

I used to notice, many times, that mistress was not quite recovered. She would cast down her eyes and droop her head, before the Signor Dellombra, or would look at him with a terrified and fascinated glance, as if his presence had some evil influence or power upon her. Turning from her to him, I used to see him in the shaded gardens, or the large half-lighted sala, looking, as I might say, "fixedly upon her out of darkness." But, truly, I had not forgotten la bella Carolina's words describing the face in the dream.

After his second visit I heard master say:

"Now, see, my dear Clara, it's over! Dellombra has come and gone, and your apprehension is broken like glass."

"Will he—will he ever come again?" asked mistress.

"Again? Why, surely, over and over again! Are you cold?" (she shivered).

"No, dear—but—he terrifies me: are you sure that he need come again?"

"The surer for the question, Clara!" replied master, cheerfully.

But he was very hopeful of her complete recovery now, and grew more and more so every day. She was beautiful. He was happy.

"All goes well, Baptista?" he would say to me again.

"Yes, signore, thank God; very well."

We were all (said the Genoese courier, constraining himself to speak a little louder), we were all at Rome for the Carnival. I had been out, all day, with a Sicilian, a friend of mine, and a courier, who was there with an English family. As I returned at night to our hotel,

I met the little Carolina, who never stirred from home alone, running distractedly along the Corso.

"Carolina! What's the matter?"

"O Baptista! O, for the Lord's sake! where is my mistress?"

"Mistress, Carolina?"

"Gone since morning—told me, when master went out on his day's journey, not to call her, for she was tired with not resting in the night (having been in pain), and would lie in bed until the evening; then get up refreshed. She is gone!—she is gone! Master has come back, broken down the door, and she is gone! My beautiful, my good, my innocent mistress!"

The pretty little one so cried, and raved, and tore herself that I could not have held her, but for her swooning on my arm as if she had been shot. Master came up—in manner, face, or voice, no more the master that I knew, than I was he. He took me (I laid the little one upon her bed in the hotel, and left her with the chamber-women), in a carriage, furiously through the darkness, across the desolate Campagna. When it was day, and we stopped at a miserable post-house, all the horses had been hired twelve hours ago, and sent away in different directions. Mark me! by the Signor Dellombra, who had passed there in a carriage, with a frightened English lady crouching in one corner.

I never heard (said the Genoese courier, drawing a long breath) that she was ever traced beyond that spot. All I know is, that she vanished into infamous oblivion, with the dreaded face beside her that she had seen in her dream.

"What do you call *that*?" said the German courier, triumphantly. "Ghosts! There are no ghosts *there!* What do you call this, that I am going to tell you? Ghosts! There are no ghosts *here!*"

I took an engagement once (pursued the German courier) with an English gentleman, elderly and a bachelor, to travel through my country, my Fatherland. He was a merchant who traded with my country and knew the language, but who had never been there since he was a boy—as I judge, some sixty years before.

His name was James, and he had a twin-brother John, also a bachelor. Between these brothers there was a great affection. They were in business together, at Goodman's Fields, but they did not live together. Mr. James dwelt in Poland Street, turning out of Oxford Street, London; Mr. John resided by Epping Forest.

Mr. James and I were to start for Germany in about a week. The exact day depended on business. Mr. John came to Poland Street (where I was staying in the house), to pass that week with Mr. James. But he said to his brother on the second day, "I don't feel very well, James. There's not much the matter with me; but I think I am a little gouty. I'll go home and put myself under the care of my old house-keeper, who understands my ways. If I get quite better, I'll come back and see you before you go. If I don't feel well enough to resume my visit where I leave it off, why *you* will come and see *me* before you go." Mr. James, of course, said he would, and they shook hands—both hands, as they always did—and Mr. John ordered out his old-fashioned chariot and rumbled home.

It was on the second night after that—that is to say, the fourth in the week—when I was awoke out of my sound sleep by Mr. James coming into my bedroom in his flannel-gown, with a lighted candle. He sat upon the side of my bed, and looking at me, said:

"Wilhelm, I have reason to think I have got some strange illness upon me."

I then perceived that there was a very unusual expression in his face.

"Wilhelm," said he, "I am not afraid or ashamed to tell you what I might be afraid or ashamed to tell another man. You come from a sensible country, where mysterious things are inquired into and are not settled to have been weighed and measured—or to have been unweighable and unmeasurable—or in either case to have been completely disposed of, for all time—ever so many years ago. I have just now seen the phantom of my brother."

I confess (said the German courier) that it gave me a little tingling of the blood to hear it.

"I have just now seen," Mr. James repeated, looking full at me, that I might see how collected he was, "the phantom of my brother John. I was sitting up in bed, unable to sleep, when it came into my room, in a white dress, and regarding me earnestly, passed up to the end of the room, glanced at some papers on my writing-desk, turned, and, still looking earnestly at me as it passed the bed, went out at the door. Now, I am not in the least mad, and am not in the least disposed to invest that phantom with any external existence out of myself. I think it is a warning to me that I am ill; and I think I had better be bled."

I got out of bed directly (said the German courier) and began to get on my clothes, begging him not to be alarmed, and telling him that I would go myself to the doctor. I was just ready, when we heard a loud knocking and ringing at the street door. My room being an attic at the back, and Mr. James's being the second-floor room in the front, we went down to his room, and put up the window, to see what was the matter.

"Is that Mr. James?" said a man below, falling back to the opposite side of the way to look up.

"It is," said Mr. James, "and you are my brother's man, Robert."

"Yes, Sir. I am sorry to say, Sir, that Mr. John is ill. He is very bad, Sir. It is even feared that he may be lying at the point of death. He wants to see you, Sir. I have a chaise here. Pray come to him. Pray lose no time."

Mr. James and I looked at one another. "Wilhelm," said he, "this is strange. I wish you to come with me!" I helped him to dress, partly there and partly in the chaise; and no grass grew under the horses' iron shoes between Poland Street and the Forest.

Now, mind! (said the German courier) I went with Mr. James into his brother's room, and I saw and heard myself what follows.

His brother lay upon his bed, at the upper end of a long bed-chamber. His old housekeeper was there, and others were there: I think three others were there, if not four, and they had been with him since early in the afternoon. He was in white, like the figure—necessarily so, because he had his night-dress on. He looked like the figure—necessarily so, because he looked earnestly at his brother when he saw him come into the room.

But, when his brother reached the bed-side, he slowly raised himself in bed, and looking full upon him, said these words:

"JAMES, YOU HAVE SEEN ME BEFORE, TO-NIGHT—AND YOU KNOW IT!" And so died!

I waited, when the German courier ceased, to hear something said of this strange story. The silence was unbroken. I looked round, and the five couriers were gone: so noiselessly that the ghostly mountain might have absorbed them into its eternal snows. By this time, I was by no means in a mood to sit alone in that awful scene, with the chill air coming solemnly upon me—or, if I may tell the truth, to sit alone anywhere. So I went back into the convent-parlour, and, finding the American gentleman still disposed to relate the biography of the Honourable Ananias Dodger, heard it all out.

A Child's Dream of a Star

There was once a child, and he strolled about a good deal, and thought of a number of things. He had a sister, who was a child too, and his constant companion. These two used to wonder all day long. They wondered at the beauty of the flowers; they wondered at the height and blueness of the sky; they wondered at the depth of the bright water; they wondered at the goodness and the power of GOD who made the lovely world.

They used to say to one another, sometimes, Supposing all the children upon earth were to die, would the flowers, and the water, and the sky be sorry? They believed they would be sorry. For, said they, the buds are the children of the flowers, and the little playful streams that gambol down the hill-sides are the children of the water; and the smallest bright specks playing at hide and seek in the sky all night, must surely be the children of the stars; and they would all be grieved to see their playmates, the children of men, no more.

There was one clear shining star that used to come out in the sky before the rest, near the church spire, above the graves. It was larger and beautiful, they thought, than all the others, and every night they watched for it, standing hand in hand at a window. Whoever saw it first cried out, "I see the star!" And often they cried out both together, knowing so well when it would rise, and where. So they grew to be such friends with it, that, before lying down in their beds, they always looked out once again, to bid it good night; and when they were turning round to sleep, they used to say, "God bless the star!"

But while she was still very young, oh very very young, the sister drooped, and came to be so weak that she could no longer stand in the window at night; and then the child looked sadly out by himself, and when he saw the star turned round and said to the patient pale face on the bed, "I see the star!" and then a smile would come upon the face, and a little weak voice used to say, "God bless my brother and the star!"

And so the time came all too soon! when the child looked out alone, and when there was no face on the bed; and when there was a little grave among the graves, not there before; and when the star made long rays down towards him, as he saw it through his tears.

Now, these rays were so bright, and they seemed to make such a shining way from earth to Heaven, that when the child went to his solitary bed, he dreamed about the star; and dreamed that, lying where he was, he saw a train of people taken up that sparkling road by angels. And the star, opening, showed him a great world of light, where many more such angels waited to receive them.

All these angels, who were waiting, turned their beaming eyes upon the people who were carried up into the star; and some came out from the long rows in which they stood, and fell upon the people's necks, and kissed them tenderly, and went away with them down avenues of light, and were so happy in their company, that lying in his bed he wept for joy.

But there were many angels who did not go with them, and among them one he knew. The patient face that once had lain upon the bed was glorified and radiant, but his heart found out his sister among all the host.

His sister's angel lingered near the entrance of the star, and said to the leader among those who had brought the people thither:

"Is my brother come?"

And he said "No."

She was turning hopefully away, when the child stretched out his arms, and cried, "O, sister, I am here! Take me!" and then she turned her beaming eyes upon him, and it was night; and the star was shining into the room, making long rays down towards him as he saw it through his tears.

From that hour forth, the child looked out upon the star as on the home he was to go to, when his time should come; and he thought that he did not belong to the earth alone, but to the star too, because of his sister's angel gone before.

There was a baby born to be a brother to the child; and while he was so little that he never yet had spoken word, he stretched his tiny form out on his bed, and died.

Again the child dreamed of the open star, and of the company of angels, and the train of people, and the rows of angels with their beaming eyes all turned upon those people's faces.

Said his sister's angel to the leader:

"Is my brother come?"

And he said, "Not that one, but another."

As the child beheld his brother's angel in her arms, he cried, "O, sister, I am here! Take me!" And she turned and smiled upon him, and the star was shining.

He grew to be a young man, and was busy at his books when an old servant came to him and said:

"Thy mother is no more. I bring her blessing on her darling son!"

Again at night he saw the star, and all that former company. Said his sister's angel to the leader:

"Is my brother come?"

And he said, "Thy mother!"

A mighty cry of joy went forth through all the star, because the mother was re-united to her two children. And he stretched out his arms and cried, "O, mother, sister, and brother, I am here! Take me!" And they answered him, "Not yet," and the star was shining.

He grew to be a man, whose hair was turning grey, and he was sitting in his chair by the fireside, heavy with grief, and with his face bedewed with tears, when the star opened once again.

Said his sister's angel to the leader: "Is my brother come?"

And he said, "Nay, but his maiden daughter."

And the man who had been the child saw his daughter, newly lost to him, a celestial creature among those three, and he said, "My daughter's head is on my sister's bosom, and her arm is around my mother's neck, and at her feet there is the baby of old time, and I can bear the parting from her, GOD be praised!"

And the star was shining.

Thus the child came to be an old man, and his once smooth face was wrinkled, and his steps were slow and feeble, and his back was bent. And one night as he lay upon his bed, his children standing round, he cried, as he had cried so long ago:

"I see the star!"

They whispered one another, "He is dying."

And he said, "I am. My age is falling from me like a garment, and I move towards the star as a child. And O, my Father, now I thank thee that it has so often opened, to receive those dear ones who await me!"

And the star was shining; and it shines upon his grave.